LETHAL LADIES
A Mystery Guild Lost Classics Omnibus

LETHAL LADIES

THE LADY VANISHES by Ethel Lina White

LAURA by Vera Caspary

REBECCA by Daphne Du Maurier

Mystery Guild
Garden City, New York

CONTENTS

THE
LADY
VANISHES

CHAPTER ONE
WITHOUT REGRETS

The day before the disaster, Iris Carr had her first premonition of danger. She was used to the protection of a crowd, whom—with unconscious flattery—she called "her friends." An attractive orphan of independent means, she had been surrounded always with clumps of people. They thought for her—or rather, she accepted their opinions, and they shouted for her—since her voice was rather too low in register, for mass social intercourse.

Their constant presence tended to create the illusion that she moved in a large circle, in spite of the fact that the same faces recurred with seasonal regularity. They also made her pleasantly aware of popularity. Her photograph appeared in the pictorial papers through the medium of a photographer's offer of publicity, after the Press announcement of her engagement to one of the crowd.

This was Fame.

Then, shortly afterwards, her engagement was broken, by mutual consent—which was a lawful occasion for the reproduction of another portrait. More Fame. And her mother, who died at her birth, might have wept or smiled at these pitiful flickers of human vanity, arising, like bubbles of marsh-gas, on the darkness below.

When she experienced her first threat of insecurity, Iris was feeling especially well and happy after an unconventional health-holiday. With the triumph of near-pioneers, the crowd had swooped down on a beautiful village of picturesque squalor, tucked away in a remote corner of Europe, and taken possession of it by the act of scrawling their names in the visitors' book.

For nearly a month they had invaded the only hotel, to the delighted demoralisation of the innkeeper and his staff. They scrambled up mountains, swam in the lake, and sunbathed on every available slope. When they were indoors, they filled the bar, shouted against the wireless, and tipped for each trifling service. The proprietor beamed at them over his choked cash-register, and the smiling waiters gave them preferential treatment, to the legitimate annoyance of the other English guests.

To these six persons, Iris appeared just one of her crowd, and a typical semi-Society girl—vain, selfish, and useless. Naturally, they had no knowledge of redeeming points—a generosity which made her accept the bill, as a matter of course, when she lunched with her "friends," and a real compassion for such cases of hardship which were clamped down under her eyes.

But while she was only vaguely conscious of fugitive moments of discontent and self-contempt, she was aware of a fastidious streak, which kept her aloof from any tendency to saturnalia. On this holiday she heard Pan's pipes, but had no experience of the kick of his hairy hind quarters.

Soon the slack convention of the crowd had been relaxed. They grew brown, they drank and were merry, while matrimonial boundaries became pleasantly blurred. Surrounded by a mixed bag of vague married couples, it was a sharp shock to Iris when one of the women—Olga—suddenly developed a belated sense of property, and accused her of stealing a husband.

Besides the unpleasantness of the scene, her sense of justice was outraged. She had merely tolerated a neglected male, who seemed a spare part in the dislocated domestic machine. It was not her fault that he had lost his head.

To make matters worse, at this crisis, she failed to notice any signs of real loyalty among her friends, who had plainly enjoyed the excitement. Therefore, to ease the tension, she decided not to travel back to England with the party, but to stay on for two days longer, alone.

She was still feeling sore, on the following day, when she accompanied the crowd to the little primitive railway station. They had already reacted to the prospect of a return to civilisation. They wore fashionable clothes again, and were roughly sorted into legitimate couples, as a natural sequence to the identification of suitcases and reservations.

The train was going to Trieste, which was definitely on the map. It was packed with tourists, who were also going back to pavements and lamp-posts. Forgetful of hillside and starlight, the crowd responded to the general noise and bustle. It seemed to recapture its old loyalty as it clustered round Iris.

"Sure you won't be bored, darling?"

"Change your mind and hop on."

"You've simply *got* to come."

As the whistle was blown, they tried to pull her into their carriage—just as she was, in shorts and nailed boots, and with a brown glaze of sunburn on her unpowdered face. She fought like a boxing-kangaroo to break free, and only succeeded in jumping down as the platform was beginning to slide past the window.

Laughing and panting from the struggle, she stood and waved after the receding train, until it disappeared round the bend of the gorge.

She felt almost guilty as she realised her relief at parting from her friends. But, although the holiday had been a success, she had drawn her pleasure chiefly from primeval sources—sun, water, and mountain-breeze. Steeped in Nature, she had vaguely resented the human intrusion.

They had all been together too closely and too intimately. At times, she had been conscious of jarring notes—a woman's high thin laugh—the tubby outline of a man's body, poised to dive—a continual flippant appeal to "My God."

It was true that while she had grown critical of her friends she had floated with the current. Like the others, she had raved of marvellous scenery, while she accepted it as a matter of course. It was a natural sequence that, when one travelled off the map, the landscape improved automatically as the standard of sanitation lapsed.

At last she was alone with the mountains and the silence. Below her lay a grass-green lake, sparkling with diamond reflections of the sun. The snowy peaks of distant ranges were silhouetted against a cornflower-blue sky. On a hill rose the dark pile of an ancient castle, with its five turrets pointing upwards, like the outspread fingers of a sinister hand.

Everywhere was a riot of colour. The station garden foamed with exotic flowers—flame and yellow—rising from spiked foliage. Higher up the slope, the small wooden hotel was painted ochre and crimson lake. Against the green wall of the gorge rose the last coil of smoke, like floating white feathers.

When it had faded away, Iris felt that the last link had been severed between her and the crowd. Blowing a derisive kiss, she turned away and clattered down the steep stony path. When she reached the glacier-fed river, she lingered on the bridge, to feel the iced air which arose from the greenish-white boil.

As she thought of yesterday's scene, she vowed that she never wanted to see the crowd again. They were connected with an episode which violated her idea of friendship. She had been a little fond of the woman, Olga, who had repaid her loyalty by a crude exhibition of jealousy.

She shrugged away the memory. Here, under the limitless blue, people seemed so small—their passions so paltry. They were merely incidental to the passage from the cradle to the grave. One met them and parted from them, without regrets.

Every minute the gap between her and them was widening. They were steaming away, out of her life. At the thought, she thrilled with a sense of new freedom, as though her spirit were liberated by the silence and solitude.

Yet, before many hours had passed, she would have bartered all the glories of Nature to have called them back again.

CHAPTER TWO
THE THREAT

Some four hours later Iris lay spread-eagled on a slope of the mountain, high above the valley. Ever since she had left the chill twilight of the gorge, at a shrine which marked a union of paths, she had been climbing steadily upwards, by a steep zigzag track.

After she had emerged from the belt of shadow, the sun had beat fiercely through her, but she did not slacken her pace. The fury of her thoughts drove her on, for she could not dislodge Olga from her mind.

The name was like a burr on her brain. *Olga.* Olga had eaten her bread, in the form of toast—for the sake of her figure—and had refused her salt, owing to a dietetic fad. This had made trouble in the kitchen. Olga had used her telephone, and mis-used her car. Olga had borrowed her fur coat, and had lent her a superfluous husband.

At the memory of Olga's Oscar, Iris put on a sprint.

"As if I'd skid for a man who looks like Mickey Mouse," she raged.

She was out of breath when, at last, she threw herself down on the turf and decided to call it a day. The mountain which had challenged her kept withdrawing as she advanced, so she had to give up her intention to reach the top.

As she lay with her eyes almost closed, listening to the ping of the breeze, her serenity returned. A clump of harebells, standing out against the skyline, seemed hardened and magnified to a metallic belfry, while she, herself, was dwarfed and welded into the earth—part of it, like the pebbles and the roots. In imagination she could almost hear the pumping of a giant heart underneath her head.

The moment passed, for she began to think of Olga again. This time, however, she viewed her from a different standpoint, for the altitude had produced the usual illusion of superiority. She reminded herself that the valley was four thousand feet above sea-level, while she had mounted about five thousand feet.

On the basis of this calculation she could afford to be generous, since she was nine thousand feet taller than her former friend—assuming, of course, that Olga was obliging enough as to remain at sea-level.

She decided to wash out the memory as unworthy of further anger.

"But never again," she said. "After this, I'll never help any one again."

Her voice had the passionate fervour of one who dedicates herself to some service. With the virtuous feeling of having profited by a lesson, for which heavy fees had been paid, she smoked a cigarette before the return journey. The air was so clear that mountains she had never seen before quivered out of invisibility and floated in the sky, in mauve transparencies. Far below she could see an arm of the lake—no longer green, but dimmed by distance to a misted blue.

Reluctantly she rose to her feet. It was time to go.

The descent proved not only monotonous, but painful, for the continual backward jolt of her weight threw a strain on unexercised muscles. Her calves began to ache and her toes were stubbed on the stony path.

Growing impatient, she decided to desert the zigzag, in favour of a direct short-cut down the face of the mountain. With the lake as a guide to direction, she hurled herself down the slope.

It was a bold venture, but almost immediately she found that the gradient was too steep. As she was going too quickly to stop, her only course was to drop down to a sitting posture and glissade over the slippery turf—trusting to luck.

From that moment things happened quickly. Her pace increased every second, in spite of her efforts to brake with her feet. Patches of blue and green sped past her, as the valley rushed up to meet her, and smashed into the sky. Bumping over the rough ground, she steered towards a belt of trees at the bottom, in the hope that they might save her from a complete spill.

Unfortunately they proved to be rotten from age, and she crashed through them, to land with a bump in the middle of the stony pass.

Her fall had been partially broken, but she felt very sore and shaken as she scrambled to her feet. In spite of her injuries, she did not forget to give the forced laugh which had been drilled into her, at school, as the accompaniment to any game's casualty.

"Rather amusing," she murmured, picking splinters out of her legs.

But she was pleased to notice the shrine, a few yards farther up the track, for this was a definite tribute to her steering. As she was not far from the hotel, she clattered down the gully, thinking of the comforts which awaited her. A long cold drink, a hot bath, dinner in bed. When she caught sight of a gleam of water, at the bend of the gorge, in her eagerness she broke into a limping run.

She rounded the corner and then stopped, staring before her in utter bewilderment. All the familiar landmarks had disappeared, as though some interfering person had passed an india-rubber over the landscape. There were no little wooden houses, no railway station, no pier, no hotel.

With a pang of dismay she realised that she had steered by a faulty compass. This was not their familiar green lake, in which she and her friends had bathed daily. Instead of being deep and ovoid in shape, it was a winding pale-blue mere, with shallow rushy margins.

In the circumstances, there was but one thing to do—retrace her steps back to the shrine and follow the other gully.

It was definitely amusing and she achieved quite a creditable laugh before she began to plod slowly upwards again.

Her mood was too bleak for her to appreciate the savage grandeur of the scenery. It was a scene of stark desolation, riven by landslips and piled high with shattered rocks. There was no crop of vegetation amid the boulders—no chirp of bird. The only sounds were the rattle of loose stones, dislodged by her feet, and the splash of a shrunken torrent, which foamed over its half-dried course, like a tangled white thread.

Used to perpetual company, Iris began to long for faces and voices. In her loneliness, she was even reduced to the flabbiness of self-pity. She reminded herself that, when she returned to England, she would not go home, like others. She would merely go back.

At present she was living at an hotel, for she had sublet her small luxury flat. Although her mode of living was her own choice, at such a time and such a place she felt that she paid a high price for freedom.

Her mood did not last, for, at the top of the pass, she was faced with a call upon her fortitude. Casting about, to pick up her bearings, she made the discovery that the shrine was different from the original landmark where she had struck the mountain zigzag.

This time she did not laugh, for she felt that humour could be carried too far. Instead she was furious with herself. She believed that she knew these mountains, because, with the others, she had clattered up and down the gorges, like a pack of wild goats.

But she had merely followed—while others led. Among the crowd was the inevitable leader—the youth with the map.

Thrown on her own resources, she had not the least idea of her direction. All she could do was to follow the gorge up to its next ramification and trust to luck.

"If I keep on walking, I must get somewhere," she argued. "Besides, no one can get lost who has a tongue."

She had need of her stoicism, for she had grown desperately weary, in addition to the handicap of a sore heel. When, at last, she reached a branch which gave her a choice of roads, she was too distrustful of her own judgement to experiment. Sitting down on a boulder, she waited on the chance of hailing some passer-by.

It was her zero-hour, when her independence appeared only the faculty to sign cheques drawn on money made by others—and her popularity, but a dividend of the same cheques.

"I've been carried all my life," she thought. "And even if some one comes, I'm the world's worst linguist."

The description flattered her, for she had not the slightest claim to the title of linguist. Her ignorance of foreign languages was the result of being finished at Paris and Dresden. During the time she was at school, she mixed exclusively with other English girls, while the natives who taught her acquired excellent English accents.

This was her rendering of the line in the National Anthem—"Send us victorious."

Patriotism did not help her now, for she felt slightly doubtful when a thick-set swarthy man, wearing leather shorts and dirty coloured braces, swung up the pass.

Among Iris' crowd was a youth who was clever at languages. From his knowledge of common roots, he had managed to use German as a kind of liaison language; but he had to draw on his imagination in order to interpret and be understood.

Iris had a vivid recollection of how the crowd used to hoot with derision at his failures, when she called out to the man in English and asked him to direct her to the village.

He stared at her, shrugged, and shook his head.

Her second attempt—in a louder key—met with no better success. The peasant, who seemed in a hurry, was passing on, when Iris barred his way.

She was acutely aware of her own impotence, as though she were some maimed creature, whose tongue had been torn out. But she had to hold his attention, to compel him to understand. Feeling that she had lapsed from the dignity of a rational being, she was forced to make pantomimic gestures, pointing to the alternative routes in turn, while she kept repeating the name of the village.

"He must get that, unless he's an idiot," she thought.

The man seemed to grasp her drift, for he nodded several times. But, instead of indicating any direction, he broke into an unfamiliar jargon.

As Iris listened to the torrent of guttural sounds, her nerve snapped suddenly. She felt cut off from all human intercourse, as though a boundary-line had been wiped out, and—instead of being in Europe—she were stranded in a corner of Asia.

Without money and without a common language, she could wander indefinitely. At that moment she might be headed away from the village and into the wilds. The gorge had many tributary branches, like the windings of an inland sea.

As she grew afraid, the peasant's face began to waver, like the illusion of some bad dream. She noticed that his skin glistened and that he had a slight goitre; but she was definitely conscious of his steamy goatish smell, for he was sweating from his climb.

"I can't understand you," she cried hysterically. "I can't understand one word. Stop. Oh, *stop*. You'll drive me mad."

In his turn the man heard only a string of gibberish. He saw a girl, dressed like a man, who was unattractively skinny—according to the local standard of beauty—with cut dirty knees. She was a foreigner, although he did not know her nationality. Further, she was worked up to a pitch of excitement, and was exceptionally stupid.

She did not seem to grasp that she was telling him less than half the name of the village, whereas three different hamlets had the same prefix. He had explained this to her, and asked for the full word.

Iris could not have supplied it even if she had understood the man. The name of the village was such a tongue-twister that she had never tried to disentangle it, but, like the rest, had called it by its first three syllables.

The position was stalemate. With a final grimace and shrug, the peasant went on his way, leaving Iris alone with the mountains.

They overhung her like a concrete threat. She had bought picture postcards of them and broadcast them with the stereotyped comment—"Marvellous scenery." Once she had even scrawled "This is my room," and marked a peak with a derisive cross.

Now—the mountains were having their revenge. As she cowered under the projecting cliffs, she felt they had but to shake those towering brows, to crush her to powder beneath an avalanche of boulders. They dwarfed her to insignificance. They blotted out her individuality. They extinguished her spirit.

The spell was broken by the sound of English voices. Round the bend of the pass came the honeymoon couple, from the hotel.

This pair of lovers was respected even by the crowd, for the completeness of their reserve and the splendour of their appearance. The man was tall, handsome, and of commanding carriage. His voice was authoritative, and he held his head at an angle which suggested excessive pride. Waiters scampered at his nod, and the innkeeper—probably on the strength of his private sitting-room—called him "Milord."

His wife was almost as tall, with a perfect figure and a flawless face. She wore beautiful clothes which were entirely unsuitable for the wilds; but it was obvious that she dressed thus as a matter of course, and to please only her husband.

They set their own standard and appeared unconscious of the other visitors, who accepted them as belonging to a higher social sphere. It was suspected that the name "Todhunter," under which they had registered, was a fiction to preserve their anonymity.

They passed Iris almost without notice. The man raised his hat vaguely, but his glance held no recognition. His wife never removed her violet eyes from the stony track, for her heels were perilously high.

She was speaking in a low voice, which was vehement in spite of its muffled tone.

"No darling. Not another day. Not even for *you*. We've stayed too—"

Iris lost the rest of the sentence. She prepared to follow them at a discreet distance, for she had become acutely aware of her own wrecked appearance.

The arrival of the honeymoon pair had restored her sense of values. Their presence was proof that the hotel was not far away, for they never walked any distance. At the knowledge, the mountains shrank back to camera-subjects, while she was reconstructed, from a lost entity, to a London girl who was critical about the cut of her shorts.

Very soon she recognised the original shrine, whence she had deserted the pass. Limping painfully down the track, presently she caught the gleam of the darkening lake and the lights of the hotel, shining through the green gloom.

She began to think again of a hot bath and dinner as she remembered that she was both tired and hungry.

But although apparently only the physical traces of her adventure remained, actually, her sense of security had been assailed—as if the experience were a threat from the future, to reveal the horror of helplessness, far away from all that was familiar.

CHAPTER THREE
CONVERSATION PIECE

When the honeymoon pair returned to the hotel the four remaining guests were sitting outside on the gravelled square, before the veranda. They were enjoying the restful interlude of "between the lights." It was too dark to write letters, or read—too early to dress for dinner. Empty cups and cakecrumbs on one of the tables showed that they had taken afternoon tea in the open and had not moved since.

It was typical of two of them, the Misses Flood-Porter, to settle. They were not the kind that flitted, being in the fifties and definitely set in their figures and their habits. Both had immaculately waved grey hair, which retained sufficient samples of the original tint to give them the courtesy-title of blondes. They had also, in common, excellent natural complexions and rather fierce expressions.

The delicate skin of the elder—Miss Evelyn—was slightly shrivelled, for she was nearly sixty, while Miss Rose was only just out of the forties. The younger sister was taller and stouter; her voice was louder, her colour deeper. In an otherwise excellent character, was a streak of amiable bully, which made her inclined to scold her partner at contract.

During their visit, they had formed a quartette with the Reverend Kenneth Barnes and his wife. They had travelled out on the same train, and they planned to return to England together. The vicar and his wife had the gift of pleasant companionship, which the Misses Flood-Porter—who were without it—attributed to mutual tastes and prejudices.

The courtyard was furnished with iron chairs and tables, enamelled in brilliant colours, and was decorated with tubs of dusty evergreen shrubs. As Miss Flood-Porter looked round her, she thought of her own delightful home in a Cathedral city.

According to the papers, there had been rain in England, so the garden should look its best, with vivid green grass and lush borders of asters and dahlias.

"I'm looking forward to seeing my garden again," she said.

"Ours," corrected her sister, who was John Blunt.

"And I'm looking forward to a comfortable chair," laughed the vicar. "Ha. Here comes the bridal pair."

In spite of a sympathetic interest in his fellows he did not call out a genial greeting. He had learned from his first—and final—rebuff that they had resented any intrusion on their privacy. So he leaned back, puffing at his pipe, while he watched them mount the steps of the veranda.

"Handsome pair," he said in an approving voice.

"I wonder who they *really* are," remarked Miss Flood-Porter. "The man's face is familiar to me. I know I've seen him somewhere."

"On the pictures, perhaps," suggested her sister.

"Oh, do you go?" broke in Mrs. Barnes eagerly, hoping to claim another taste in common, for she concealed a guilty passion for the cinema.

"Only to see George Arliss and Diana Wynyard," explained Miss Flood-Porter.

"That settles it," said the vicar. "He's certainly not George Arliss, and neither is she Diana."

"All the same, I feel certain there is some mystery about them," persisted Miss Flood-Porter.

"So do I," agreed Mrs. Barnes. "I—I wonder if they are really married."

"Are *you?*" asked her husband quickly.

He laughed gently when his wife flushed to her eyes.

"Sorry to startle you, my dear," he said, "but isn't it simpler to believe that we are all of us what we assume to be? Even parsons and their wives." He knocked the ashes out of his pipe, and rose from his chair. "I think I'll stroll down to the village for a chat with my friends."

"How can he talk to them when he doesn't know their language?" demanded Miss Rose bluntly, when the vicar had gone from the garden.

"Oh, he *makes* them understand," explained his wife proudly. "Sympathy, you know, and common humanity. He'd rub noses with a savage."

"I'm afraid we drove him away by talking scandal," said Miss Flood-Porter.

"It was my fault," declared Mrs. Barnes. "I know people think I'm curious. But, really, I have to force myself to show an interest in my neighbour's affairs. It's my protest against our terrible national shyness."

"But we're proud of that," broke in Miss Rose. "England does not need to advertise."

"Of course not. . . . But we only pass this way once. I have to remind myself that the stranger sitting beside me may be in some trouble and that I might be able to help."

The sisters looked at her with approval. She was a slender woman in the mid-forties, with a pale oval face, dark hair, and a sweet expression. Her large brown eyes were both kind and frank—her manner sincere.

It was impossible to connect her with anything but rigid honesty. They knew that she floundered into awkward explanations, rather than run the risk of giving a false impression.

In her turn, she liked the sisters. They were of solid worth and sound respectability. One felt that they would serve on juries with distinction, and do their duty to their God and their neighbour—while permitting no direction as to its nature.

They were also leisured people, with a charming house and garden, well-trained maids and frozen assets in the bank. Mrs. Barnes knew this, so, being human, it gave her a feeling of superiority to reflect that the one man in their party was her husband.

She could appreciate the sense of ownership, because, up to her fortieth birthday, she had gone on her yearly holiday in the company of a huddle of other spinsters. Since she had left school, she had earned her living by teaching, until the miracle happened which gave her—not only a husband—but a son.

Both she and her husband were so wrapped up in the child that the vicar sometimes feared that their devotion was tempting Fate. The night before they set out on their holiday he proposed a pact.

"Yes," he agreed, looking down at the sleeping boy in his cot. "He *is* beautiful. But . . . It is my privilege to read the Commandments to others. Sometimes, I wonder——"

"I know what you mean," interrupted his wife. "Idolatry."

He nodded.

"I am as guilty as you," he admitted. "So I mean to discipline myself. In our position, we have special opportunities to influence others. We must not grow lop-sided, but develop every part of our nature. If this holiday is to do us real good, it *must* be a complete mental change. . . . My dear, suppose we agree not to talk exclusively of Gabriel, while we are away?"

Mrs. Barnes agreed. But her promise did not prevent her from thinking of him continually. Although they had left him in the care of a competent grandmother, she was foolishly apprehensive about his health.

While she was counting the remaining hours before her return to her son, and Miss Flood-Porter smiled in anticipation of seeing her garden, Miss Rose was pursuing her original train of thought. She always ploughed a straight furrow, right to its end.

"I can't understand how any one can tell a lie," she declared. "Unless, perhaps, some poor devil who's afraid of being sacked. But—people like *us*. We know a wealthy woman who boasts of making false declarations at the Customs. Sheer dishonesty."

As she spoke, Iris appeared at the gate of the hotel garden. She did her best to skirt the group at the table, but she could not avoid hearing what was said.

"Perhaps I should not judge others," remarked Mrs. Barnes in the clear carrying voice of a form-mistress. "I've never felt the slightest temptation to tell a lie."

"Liar," thought Iris automatically.

She was in a state of utter fatigue, which bordered on collapse. It was only by the exercise of every atom of willpower that she forced herself to reach the hotel. The ordeal had strained her nerves almost to breaking-point. Although she longed for the quiet of her room, she knew she could not mount the stairs without a short rest. Every muscle felt wrenched as she dropped down on an iron chair and closed her eyes.

"If any one speaks to me, I'll scream," she thought.

The Misses Flood-Porter exchanged glances and turned down the corners of their mouths. Even gentle Mrs. Barnes' soft brown eyes held no welcome, for she had been a special victim of the crowd's bad manners and selfishness.

They behaved as though they had bought the hotel and the other guests were interlopers, exacting preferential treatment—and getting it—by bribery. This infringement of fair-dealing annoyed the other tourists, as they adhered to the terms of their payment to a travelling agency, which included service.

The crowd monopolised the billiard-table and secured the best chairs. They were always served first at meals; courses gave out, and bath-water ran luke-warm.

Even the vicar found that his charity was strained. He did his best to make allowance for the animal spirits of youth, although he was aware that several among the party could not be termed juvenile.

Unfortunately, Iris' so-called friends included two persons who were no testimonial for the English nation; and since it was difficult to distinguish one girl in a bathing-brief from another, Mrs. Barnes was of the opinion that they were all doing the same thing—getting drunk and making love.

Her standard of decency was offended by the sunbathing—her nights disturbed by noise. Therefore she was specially grateful for the prospect of two peaceful days, spent amid glorious scenery and in congenial company.

But, apparently, there was not a complete clearance of the crowd; there was a hangover, in this girl—and there might be others. Mrs. Barnes had vaguely remarked Iris, because she was pretty, and had been pursued by a bathing-gentleman with a matronly figure.

As the man was married, his selection was not to her credit. But she seemed to be so exhausted that Mrs. Barnes' kindly heart soon reproached her for lack of sympathy.

"Are you left all alone?" she called, in her brightest tones.

Iris shuddered at the unexpected overture. At that moment the last thing in the world she wanted was mature interest, which, in her experience, masked curiosity.

"Yes," she replied.

"Oh, dear, what a shame. Aren't you lonely?"

"No."

"But you're rather young to be travelling without friends. Couldn't any of your people come with you?"

"I have none."

"No family at all?"

"No, and no relatives. Aren't I lucky?"

Iris was not near enough to hear the horrified gasp of the Misses Flood-Porter; but Mrs. Barnes' silence told her that her snub had not miscarried. To avoid a further inquisition, she made a supreme effort to rise, for she was stiffening in every joint, and managed to drag herself into the hotel and upstairs to her room.

Mrs. Barnes tried to carry off the incident with a laugh.

"I'm afraid I've blundered again," she said. "She plainly resented me. But it seemed hardly human for us to sit like dummies, and show no interest in her."

"Is she interested in *you?*" demanded Miss Rose. "Or in us? That sort of girl is utterly selfish. She wouldn't raise a finger, or go an inch out of her way, to help any one."

There was only one answer to the question, which Mrs. Barnes was too kind to make. So she remained silent, since she could not tell a lie.

Neither she—nor any one else—could foretell the course of the next twenty-four hours, when this girl—standing alone against a cloud of witnesses—would endure such anguish of spirit as threatened her sanity, on behalf of a stranger for whom she had no personal feeling.

Or rather—if there was actually such a person as Miss Froy.

CHAPTER FOUR
ENGLAND CALLING

Because she had a square on her palm, which, according to a fortune-teller, signified safety, Iris believed that she lived in a protected area. Although she laughed at the time, she was impressed secretly, because hers was a specially sheltered life.

At this crisis, the stars, as usual, seemed to be fighting for her. The mountains had sent out a preliminary warning. During the evening, too, she received overtures of companionship, which might have delivered her from mental isolation.

Yet she deliberately cut every strand which linked her with safety, out of mistaken loyalty to her friends.

She missed them directly she entered the lounge, which was silent and deserted. As she walked along the corridor, she passed empty bedrooms, with stripped beds and littered floors. Mattresses hung from every window and the small verandas were heaped with pillows.

It was not only company which was lacking, but moral support. The crowd never troubled to change for the evening, unless comfort suggested flannel trousers. On one occasion, it had achieved the triumph of a complaint, when a lady appeared at dinner dressed in her bathing-slip.

The plaintiffs had been the Misses Flood-Porter, who always wore expensive but sober dinner-gowns. Iris remembered the incident, when she had finished her bath. Although slightly ashamed of her deference to public opinion, she fished from a suitcase an unpacked afternoon frock of crinkled crêpe.

The hot soak and rest had refreshed her, but she felt lonely, as she leaned over the balustrade. Her pensive pose and the graceful lines of her dress arrested the attention of the bridegroom—Todhunter, according to the register—as he strolled out of his bedroom.

He had not the least knowledge of her identity, or that he had acted as a sort of guiding-star to her, in the gorge. He and his wife took their meals in their private sitting-room and never mingled with the crowd. He concluded, therefore, that she was an odd guest whom he had missed in the general scramble.

Approving her with an experienced eye, he stopped.

"Quiet, to-night," he remarked. "Refreshing change after the din of that horrible rabble."

To his surprise, the girl looked coldly at him.

"It *is* quiet," she said. "But I happen to miss my friends."

As she walked downstairs she felt defiantly glad that she had made him realise his blunder. Championship of her friends mattered more than the absence of social sense. But, in spite of her triumph, the incident was vaguely unpleasant.

The crowd had gloried in its unpopularity, which seemed to it a sign of superiority. It frequently remarked in complacent voices, "We're not popular with these people," or "They don't really like us." Under the influence of its mass-hypnotism, Iris wanted no other label. But now that she was alone, it was not quite so amusing to realise that the other guests, who were presumably decent and well-bred, considered her an outsider.

Her mood was bleakly defiant when she entered the restaurant. It was a big bare room, hung with stiff deep-blue wallpaper, patterned with conventional gilt stars. The electric lights were set in clumsy wrought-iron chandeliers, which suggested a Hollywood set for a medieval castle. Scarcely any of the tables were laid, and only one waiter drooped at the door.

In a few days, the hotel would be shut up for the winter. With the departure of the big English party, most of the holiday staff had become superfluous and had already gone back to their homes in the district.

The remaining guests appeared to be unaffected by the air of neglect and desolation inseparable from the end of the season. The Misses Flood-Porter shared a table with the vicar and his wife. They were all in excellent spirits and gave the impression of having come into their own, as they capped each other's jokes, culled from Punch.

Iris pointedly chose a small table in a far corner. She smoked a cigarette while she waited to be served. The others were advanced in their meal and it was a novel sensation for one of the crowd to be in arrears.

Mrs. Barnes, who was too generous to nurse resentment for her snub, looked at her with admiring eyes.

"How pretty that girl looks in a frock," she said.

"*Afternoon frock*," qualified Miss Flood-Porter. "We always make a point of wearing evening dress for dinner, when we're on the Continent."

"If we didn't dress, we should feel we were letting England down," explained the younger sister.

Although Iris spun out her meal to its limit, she was driven back ultimately to the lounge. She was too tired to stroll and it was early for bed. As she looked round her, she could hardly believe that, only the night before, it had been a scene of continental glitter and gaiety—although the latter quality had been imported from England. Now that it was no longer filled with friends, she was shocked to notice its tawdry theatrical finery. The gilt cane chairs were tarnished, the crimson plush upholstery shabby.

A clutter of cigarette stubs and spent matches in the palm pots brought a lump to her throat. They were all that remained of the crowd.

As she sat apart, the vicar—pipe in mouth—watched her with a thoughtful frown. His clear-cut face was both strong and sensitive, and an almost perfect blend of flesh and spirit. He played rough football with the youths of his parish, and, afterwards, took their souls by assault; but he had also a real understanding of the problems of his women-parishioners.

When his wife told him of Iris' wish for solitude, he could enter into her feeling, because, sometimes, he yearned to escape from people and even from his wife. His own inclination was to leave her to the boredom of her own company; yet he was touched by the dark lines under her eyes and her mournful lips.

In the end, he resolved to ease his conscience at the cost of a rebuff. He knew it was coming, because, as he crossed the lounge, she looked up quickly, as though on guard.

"Another," she thought.

From a distance she had admired the spirituality of his expression; but, to-night, he was numbered among her hostile critics.

"Horrible rabble." The words floated into her memory, as he spoke to her.

"If you are travelling back to England alone, would you care to join our party?"

"When are you going?" she asked.

"Day after to-morrow, before they take off the last through train of the season."

"But I'm going to-morrow. Thanks so much."

"Then I'll wish you a pleasant journey."

The vicar smiled faintly at her lightning decision as he crossed to a table and began to address luggage-labels.

His absence was his wife's opportunity. In her wish not to break her promise, she had gone to the other extreme and had not mentioned her baby to her new friends, save for one casual allusion to "our little boy." But, now that the holiday was nearly over, she could not resist the temptation of showing his photograph, which had won a prize in a local baby competition.

With a guilty glance at her husband's back she drew out of her bag a limp leather case.

"This is my large son," she said, trying to hide her pride.

The Misses Flood-Porter were exclusive animal-lovers and not particularly fond of children. But they said all the correct things with such well-bred conviction that Mrs. Barnes' heart swelled with triumph.

Miss Rose, however, switched off to another subject directly the vicar returned from the writing-table.

"Do you believe in warning dreams, Mr. Barnes?" she asked. "Because, last night, I dreamed of a railway smash."

The question caught Iris' attention and she strained to hear the vicar's reply.

"I'll answer your question," he said, "if you'll first answer mine. What *is* a dream? Is it stifled apprehension— "

"I wonder," said a bright voice in Iris' ear, "I wonder if you would like to see the photograph of my little son, Gabriel?"

Iris realised dimly that Mrs. Barnes—who was keeping up England in limp brown lace—had seated herself beside her and was showing her the photograph of a naked baby.

She made a pretence of looking at it while she tried to listen to the vicar.

"Gabriel," she repeated vaguely.

"Yes, after the Archangel. We named him after him."

"How sweet. Did he send a mug?"

Mrs. Barnes stared incredulously, while her sensitive face grew scarlet. She believed that the girl had been intentionally profane and had insulted her precious little son, to avenge her boredom. Pressing her trembling lips together she rejoined her friends.

Iris was grateful when the humming in her ears ceased. She was unaware of her slip, because she had only caught a fragment of Mrs. Barnes' explanation. Her interest was still held by the talk of presentiments.

"Say what you like," declared Miss Rose, sweeping away the vicar's argument, "I've common sense on my side. They usually try to pack too many passengers into the last good train of the season. I know I'll be precious glad when I'm safely back in England."

A spirit of apprehension quivered in the air at her words.

"But you aren't really afraid of an accident?" cried Mrs. Barnes, clutching Gabriel's photograph tightly.

"Of course not." Miss Flood-Porter answered for her sister. "Only, perhaps we feel we're rather off the beaten track here, and so very far from home. Our trouble is we don't know a word of the language."

"She means," cut in Miss Rose, "we're all right over reservations and coupons, so long as we stick to hotels and trains. But if some accident happened to make us break our journey, or lose a connection, and we were stranded in some small place, we should feel *lost*. Besides it would be awkward about money. We didn't bring any travellers' cheques."

The elder sister appealed to the vicar.

"Do you advise us to take my sister's dream as a warning and travel back to-morrow?"

"No, *don't*," murmured Iris under her breath.

She waited for the vicar's answer with painful interest, for she was not eager to travel on the same train as these uncongenial people, who might feel it their duty to befriend her.

"You must follow your own inclinations," said the vicar. "But if you do leave prematurely, you will not only give a victory to superstition, but you will deprive yourself of another day in these glorious surroundings."

"And our reservations are for the day after to-morrow," remarked Miss Rose. "We'd better not risk any muddles. . . .

And now, I'm going up to pack for my journey back to dear old England."

To the surprise of every one her domineering voice suddenly blurred with emotion. Miss Flood-Porter waited until she had gone out of the lounge, before she explained.

"Nerves. We had a very trying experience, just before we came away. The doctor ordered a complete change so we came here, instead of Switzerland."

Then the innkeeper came in, and, as a compliment to his guests, fiddled with his radio, until he managed to get London on the long wave. Amid a machine-gun rattle of atmospherics, a familiar mellow voice informed them, "You have just been listening to . . ."

But they had heard nothing.

Miss Flood-Porter saw her garden, silvered by the harvest moon. She wondered whether the chrysanthemum buds, three to a pot, were swelling, and if the blue salvias had escaped the slugs.

Miss Rose, briskly stacking shoes in the bottom of a suitcase, quivered at a recollection. Again she saw a gaping hole in a garden-bed, where overnight had stood a cherished clump of white delphiniums.... It was not only the loss of their treasure, but the nerve-racking ignorance of where the enemy would strike next...

The Vicar and his wife thought of their baby, asleep in his cot. They must decide whether they should merely peep at him, or risk waking him with a kiss.

Iris remembered her friends in the roaring express, and was suddenly smitten with a wave of home-sickness.

England was calling.

CHAPTER FIVE
THE NIGHT EXPRESS

Iris was awakened that night, as usual, by the express screaming through the darkness. Jumping out of bed, she reached the window in time to see it outline the curve of the lake with a fiery wire. As it rattled below the hotel, the golden streak expanded to a string of lighted windows, which, when it passed, snapped together again like the links of a bracelet.

After it had disappeared round the gorge, she followed its course by its pall of quivering red smoke. In imagination, she saw it shooting through Europe, as though it were an explosive shuttle ripping through the scorched fabric of the map. It caught up cities and threaded them on a gleaming whistling string. Illuminated names flashed before her eyes and were gone—Bucharest, Zagreb, Trieste, Milan, Basle, Calais.

Once again she was flooded with home-hunger, even though her future address were an hotel. Mixed with it was a gust of foreboding—which was a legacy from the mountains.

"Suppose—something—happened, and I never came back."

At that moment she felt that any evil could block the way to her return. A railway crash, illness, or crime were possibilities, which were actually scheduled in other lives. They were happening all round her and at any time a line might give way in the protective square in her palm.

As she lay and tossed, she consoled herself with the reminder that this was the last time she would lie under the lumpy feather bed. Throughout the next two nights she, too, would be rushing through dark landscape, jerked out of every brief spell of sleep by the flash of lights, whenever the express roared through a station.

The thought was with her when she woke, the next morning, to see the silhouette of mountain-peaks iced against the flush of sunrise.

"I'm going home to-day," she told herself exultantly.

The air was raw when she looked out of her window. Mist was rising from the lake which gleamed greenly through yellowed fans of chestnut trees. But in spite of the blue and gold glory of autumn she felt indifferent to its beauty.

She was also detached from the drawbacks of her room, which usually offended her critical taste. Its wooden walls were stained a crude shade of raw sienna, and instead of running water there was a battered washstand which bore a tin can, covered with a thin towel.

In spirit, Iris had already left the hotel. Her journey was begun before she started. When she went down to the restaurant she was barely conscious of the other guests, who, only a few hours before, had inspired her with antipathy.

The Misses Flood-Porter, who were dressed for writing letters in the open, were breakfasting at a table by the window. They did not speak to her, although they would have bowed as a matter of courtesy, had they caught her eye.

Iris did not notice the omission, because they had gone completely out of her life. She drank her coffee in a silence which was broken by occasional remarks from the sisters, who wondered whether the English weather were kind for a local military wedding.

Her luck held, for she was spared contact with the other guests, who were engrossed by their own affairs. As she passed the bureau, Mrs. Barnes was calling a waiter's attention to a letter in one of the pigeon-holes. Her grey jersey-suit, as well as her packet of sandwiches, advertised an excursion.

The vicar, who was filling his pipe on the veranda, was also in unconventional kit—shorts, sweater, nailed boots, and the local felt hat—adorned with a tiny blue feather—which he had bought as a souvenir of his holiday.

His smile was so happy that Iris thought he looked both festive and good, as though a saint had deserted his shrine, knocking his halo a trifle askew in the process, in order to put a coat of sunburn over his pallid plaster.

Her tolerance faded as she listened to a dialogue which was destined to affect her own future.

"Is that a letter from home?" called the vicar.

"Yes," replied his wife, after a pause.

"I thought Grandma told us to expect no more letters. . . . What's she writing about?"

"She wants me to do a little shopping for her, on our way through London. Some Margaret Rose silk. The little Princess, you know."

"But you'll be tired. It's not very considerate."

"No." Mrs. Barnes' voice was exceptionally sharp. "It's not. Why didn't she *think?*"

Iris condoned her own ungracious conduct of the preceding night, as she left them to their discussion. She told herself that he was justified in protecting herself from the boredom of domestic trifles.

As she strolled past the front of the hotel, she had to draw back to avoid trespassing on the privacy of the honeymoon pair, whose sitting-room opened on to the veranda. They were breakfasting in the open air, off rolls and fruit. The man was resplendent in a Chinese dressing-gown, while his wife wore an elaborate wrapper over satin pyjamas.

The Todhunters annoyed Iris, because they affected her with vague discontent. She was conscious of the same unacknowledged blank when she watched a love-scene played by two film stars. Theirs was passion—perfectly dressed, discreetly censored and with the better profile presented to the camera.

She felt a responsive thrill when the man looked into his bride's eyes with intense personal interest.

"Has it been perfect?" he asked.

Mrs. Todhunter knew exactly how long to pause before her reply. "Yes."

It was faultless timing for he understood what she did not say.

"Not perfect, then," he remarked. "But, darling, is anything——"

Iris passed out of earshot, while she was still slightly envious. Her own experience of love had been merely a succession of episodes which led up to the photographic farce of her engagement.

The morning seemed endless, but at length it wore away. She had little to pack, because—following tradition—her friends had taken the bulk of her luggage with them, to save her trouble. An hour or two were killed, or rather drowned, in the lake, but she was too impatient to lie in the sun.

After she had changed for her journey, she went down to the restaurant. The dish of the day was attractively jellied and garnished with sprigs of tarragon, chervil, and chopped eggs; but she suspected that it was composed of poached eels. Turning away, with a shudder, she took possession of a small buttercup-painted table in the gravelled garden, where she lunched on potato soup and tiny grapes.

The sun flickered through the dense roof of chestnuts, but the iron chair was too hard and cold for comfort. Although the express was not due for more than an hour, she decided to wait for it at the railway station, where she could enjoy a view.

She had worked herself up to a fever, so that the act of leaving the hotel seemed to bring her a step nearer to her journey. It gave her acute pleasure to pay her bill and tip the stragglers of the staff. Although she saw none of her fellow-guests, she hurried through the garden like a truant from school, as though she feared she might be detained, at the last minute.

It was strange to wear a sophisticated travelling-suit and high heels again, as she jolted down the rough path, followed by a porter with her baggage. The sensation was not too comfortable after weeks of liberty, but she welcomed it as part of her return to civilisation. When she was seated on the platform, her suitcase at her feet, and the shimmer of the lake below, she was conscious of having reached a peak of enjoyment.

The air was water-clear and held the sting of altitude. As the sun blazed down on her, she felt steeped in warmth and drenched in light. She took off her hat and gazed at the signal post, anticipating the thrill of its drop, followed by the first glimpse of a foreshortened engine at the end of the rails.

There were other people on the platform, for the arrival of the express was the main event of the day. It was too early for the genuine travellers, but groups of loiterers, both visitors and natives, hung round the fruit- and paper-stalls. They were a cheerful company and noisy in many languages. Iris heard no English until two men came down the road from the village.

They leaned over the palings behind her, to continue an argument. She did not feel sufficient interest, at first, to turn and see their faces, but their voices were so distinctive that, presently, she could visualise them.

The one whom she judged the younger had an eager untidy voice. She felt sure that he possessed an active brain, with a rush of ideas. He spoke too quickly and often stumbled for a word, probably not because his terms were limited, but because he had a choice of too many.

Gradually he won her sympathy, partly because his mind seemed in tune—or rather, in discord—with hers and partly because she disliked the other speaker instinctively. His accent was pedantic and consciously cultured. He spoke deliberately, with an irritating authority, which betrayed his inflexible mind. "Oh, no, my dear Hare." Iris felt it should have been "Watson." "You're abysmally wrong. It has been proved conclusively that there can be no fairer or better system of justice than trial by jury."

"Trial by fatheads," spluttered the younger voice. "You talk of ordinary citizens. No one is ordinary, but a bag of his special prejudices. One woman's got a spite against her sex—one man's cranky on morality. They all damn the prisoner on different issues. And they've all businesses or homes which they want to get back to. They watch the clock and grasp the obvious."

"They are directed by the judge."

"And how much of his direction do they remember? You know how your own mind slips when you're listening to a string of words. Besides, after he's dotted all the i's and crossed the t's for them, they stampede and bring him in the wrong verdict."

"Why should you assume it is wrong? They have formed their own conclusion on the testimony of the witnesses."

"Witnesses." In his heat the young man thumped the railing. "The witness is the most damnable part of the outfit. He may be so stupid as to be putty in the hands of some wily lawyer, or he may be smart and lie away some wretched man's life, just to read about his own wonderful memory and powers of observation and see his photograph in the papers. They're all out for publicity."

The elder man laughed in a superior manner which irritated his companion to the personal touch.

"When I'm accused of bumping you off, professor, I'd rather be tried by a team of judges who'd bring trained legal minds and impartial justice to bear on the facts."

"You're biassed," said the Professor, ". . . Let me try to convince you. The Jury is intelligent in bulk, and can judge character. Certain witnesses are reliable, while others must be viewed with suspicion. For instance, how would you describe that dark woman with the artificial lashes?"

"Attractive."

"Hum. I should call her meretricious and so would any average man of the world. Now, we'll assume that she and that English lady in the Burberry are giving contrary evidence. One of the two must be telling a lie."

"I don't agree. It may depend on the point of view. The man in the street, with his own back garden, is ready to swear to lilac when he sees it; but when he goes to a botanical garden he finds it's labelled syringa."

"The generic name——"

"I know, I know. But if one honest John Citizen swears syringa is white, while another swears it's mauve, you'll grant that there is an opportunity for confusion. Evidence may be like that."

"Haven't you wandered from my point?" asked the conventional voice. "Put those two women, separately, into the witness-box. Now *which* are you going to believe?"

In her turn, Iris compared the hypothetical witnesses. One was a characteristic type of county Englishwoman, with an athletic figure and a pleasant intelligent face. If she strode across the station as though she possessed the right of way, she used it merely as a short cut to her legitimate goal.

On the other hand, the pretty dark woman was an obvious loiterer. Her skin-tight skirt and embroidered peasant blouse might have been the holiday attire of any continental lady; but, in spite of her attractive red lips and expressive eyes, Iris could not help thinking of a gipsy who had just stolen a chicken for the pot.

Against her will, she had to agree with the professor. Yet she felt almost vexed with the younger man when he ceased to argue, because she had backed the losing side.

"I see your point," he said. "The British waterproof wins every time. But Congo rubber was a bloody business and too wholesale a belief in rubber-proofing may lead to a bloody mix-up. . . . Come and have a drink."

"Thank you, if you will allow me to order it. I wish to avail myself of every opportunity of speaking the language."

"Wish I could forget it. It's a disgusting one—all spitting and sneezing. You lecture on Modern Languages, don't you? Many girl students in your classes?"

"Yes. . . . Unfortunately."

Iris was sorry when they moved away, for she had been idly interested in their argument. The crowd on the platform had increased, although the express was not due for another twenty-five minutes, even if it ran to time. She had now to share her bench with others, while a child squatted on her suitcase.

Although spoiled by circumstances she did not resent the intrusion. The confusion could not touch her because she was held by the moment. The glow of sunshine, the green flicker of trees, the gleam of the lake, all combined to hypnotise her to a condition of stationary bliss.

There was nothing to warn her of the attack. When she least expected it, the blow fell.

Suddenly she felt a violent pain at the back of her neck. Almost before she realised it, the white-capped mountains rocked, the blue sky turned black, and she dropped down into darkness.

CHAPTER SIX
THE WAITING-ROOM

When Iris became conscious, her sight returned, at first, in patches. She saw sections of faces floating in the air. It seemed the same face—sallow-skinned, with black eyes and bad teeth.

Gradually she realised that she was lying on a bench in a dark kind of shed while a ring of women surrounded her. They were of peasant type, with a racial resemblance, accentuated by inter-marriage.

They stared down at her with indifferent apathy, as though she were some street spectacle—a dying animal or a man in a fit. There was no trace of compassion in their blank faces, no glint of curiosity in their dull gaze. In their complete detachment they seemed devoid of the instincts of human humanity.

"Where am I?" she asked wildly.

A woman in a black overall suddenly broke into guttural speech, which conveyed no iota of meaning to Iris. She listened with the same helpless panic which had shaken her yesterday in the gorge. Actually the woman's face was so close that she could see the pits in her skin and the hairs sprouting inside her nostrils; yet their fundamental cleavage was so complete that they might have been standing on different planets.

She wanted some one to lighten her darkness—to raise the veil which baffled her and blinded her. *Something* had happened to her of which she had no knowledge.

Her need was beyond the scope of crude pantomime. Only some lucid explanation could clear the confusion of her senses. In that moment she thought of the people at the hotel, from whom she had practically ran away. Now she felt she would give years of her life to see the strong saintly face of the clergyman looking down at her, or meet the kind eyes of his wife.

In an effort to grip reality she looked round her. The place was vaguely familiar, with dark wooden walls and a sanded floor, which served as a communal spittoon. A bar of dusty sunlight, slanting through a narrow window, glinted on thick glasses stacked upon a shelf and on a sheaf of fluttering handbills.

She raised her head higher and felt a throb of dull pain, followed by a rush of dizziness. For a moment she thought she was going to be sick; but the next second nausea was overpowered by a shock of memory.

This was the waiting-room at the station. She had lingered here only yesterday, with the crowd, as it gulped down a final drink. Like jolting trucks banging through her brain her thoughts were linked together by the connecting sequence of the railway. She remembered sitting on the platform, in the sunshine, while she waited for a train.

Her heart began to knock violently. She was on her way back to England. Yet she had not the least idea as to what had happened after her black-out, or how long ago it had occurred. The express might have come—and gone—leaving her behind.

In her overwrought state the idea seemed the ultimate catastrophe. Her head swam again and she had to wait for a mist to clear from her eyes before she could read the figures on her tiny wrist watch.

To her joy she discovered that she had still twenty-five minutes in which to pull herself together before her journey. "What happened to me?" she wondered. "What made me pass out? Was I attacked."

Closing her eyes, she tried desperately to clear her brain. But her last conscious moment held only a memory of blue sky and grass-green lake, viewed as though through a crystal.

Suddenly she remembered her bag and groped to find it. To her dismay it was not beside her, nor could she see it anywhere on the bench. Her suitcase lay on the floor, and her hat had been placed on top of it, as though to prove the limit of her possessions.

"My bag," she screamed, wild-eyed with panic. "Where's my bag?"

It held not only her money and tickets, but her passport. Without it, it was impossible for her to continue her journey. Even if she boarded the train, penniless, she would be turned back at the first frontier.

The thought drove her frantic. She felt sure that these ring

women had combined to rob her when she was helpless and at their
mercy. When she sprang from the bench they pulled her down again.

The blood rushed to her head and she resisted them fiercely. As
she struggled she was conscious of a whirl of confusion—of throbbing
pain, rising voices, and lights flashing before her eyes. There were
breathless panting noises, as an undercurrent to a strange rushing
sound, as though an imprisoned fountain had suddenly burst through
the ground.

In spite of her efforts, the woman in the black pinafore dragged
her down again, while a fat girl, in a bursting bodice, held a glass to
her lips. When she refused to swallow they treated her like a child,
tilting her chin and pouring the spirit down her throat.

It made her cough and gasp, until her head seemed to be swelling
with pain. Terrified by this threat of another attack, she relaxed in
helpless misery. Her instinct warned her that, if she grew excited, at
any moment, the walls might rock—like the snow-mountains—as a
prelude to total extinction.

Next time she might not wake up. Besides, she dared not risk being ill in the village, alone, and so far away from her friends. If she
returned to the hotel she could enlist the financial help of the English
visitors, while, doubtless, another passport could be procured; but it
meant delay.

In addition, these people were all strangers to her, whose holiday
was nearly ended. In another day they would be gone, while she
might be stranded there, indefinitely, exposed to indifference, and
even neglect. The hotel, too, was closing down almost immediately.

"I mustn't be ill," thought Iris. "I must get away at once, while
there is still time."

She felt sure that, if she could board the train, the mere knowledge that she was rolling, mile by mile, back to civilisation, would
brace her to hold out until she reached some familiar place. She
thought of Basle on the milky-jade Rhine, with its excellent hotels
where English was spoken and where she could be ill, intelligibly, and
with dignity.

Everything hung upon the catching of this train. The issue at
stake made her suddenly desperate to find her bag. She was struggling to rise again, when she became conscious that some one was
trying to establish contact with her.

It was an old man in a dirty blouse, with a gnarled elfin face—
brown and lined as the scar on a tree-trunk, from which a branch had
been lopped. He kept taking off his greasy hat and pointing, first upwards, and then to her head.

All at once she grasped his meaning. He was telling her that while she sat on the platform she had been attacked with sunstroke.

The explanation was a great relief, because she was both frightened and baffled by the mystery of her illness. She rarely ailed and had never fainted before. Besides, it had given her proof, that in spite of her own misgiving, the channels were not entirely blocked, provided the issues were not too involved.

Although she still felt sick with anxiety about her train, she managed to smile faintly at the porter. As though he had been waiting for some sign of encouragement, he thrust his hand into the neck of his dirty blouse and drew out her bag.

With a cry, she snatched it from him. Remembering the crowd on the platform, she had no hope of finding her money; but there was a faint chance that her passport had not been stolen.

She tore at the zipp-fastener with shaking fingers, to find, to her utter amazement, that the contents were intact. Tickets, money, passport—even her receipted hotel-bill, were still there.

She had grossly maligned the native honesty, and she hastened to make amends. Here, at last, was a situation she understood. As usual, some one had come to her rescue, true to the tradition of the protective square in her palm. Her part, which was merely to overpay for services rendered, was easy.

The women received their share of the windfall with stolid faces. Apparently they were too stunned with astonishment to show excitement or gratitude. The old porter, on the other hand, beamed triumphantly and gripped Iris' suitcase, to show that he, too, had grasped the situation.

In spite of her resistance to it, the raw spirit, together with her change of circumstance, had revived Iris considerably. She felt practically restored again and mistress of herself as she showed her ticket to the porter.

The effect on him was electric. He yammered with excitement, as he grabbed her arm and rushed with her to the door. Directly they had passed through it, Iris understood the origin of the curious pervading noise which had helped to complicate her nightmare.

It was the gush of steam escaping from an engine. While she had let the precious minutes slip by, the express had entered the station.

Now it was on the point of departure.

The platform was a scene of wild confusion. Doors were being slammed. People were shouting farewells and crowding before the carriages. An official waved a flag and the whistle shrilled.

They were one minute too late. Iris realised the fact that she was beaten, just as the porter—metaphorically—snatched at the psychological moment, and was swung away with it on its flight. He took advantage of the brief interval between the first jerk of the engine and the revolution of the wheels to charge the crowd, like an aged tiger. There was still strength and agility in his sinewy old frame to enable him to reach the nearest carriage and wrench open the door.

His entrance was disputed by a majestic lady in black. She was a personage to whom—as a peasant—his bones instinctively cringed. On the other hand, his patron had paid him a sum far in excess of what he earned in tips during the whole of a brief season.

Therefore, his patron must have her place. Ducking under the august lady's arm, he hurled Iris' suitcase into the compartment and dragged her inside after it.

The carriage was moving when he scrambled out, to fall in a heap on the platform. He was unhurt, however, for when she looked back to wave her thanks, he grinned at her like a toothless gnome.

Already he was yards behind. The station slid by, and the lake began to lap against the piles of the rough landing-stage. It rippled past the window in a sheet of emerald, ruffled by the breeze and burnished by the sun. As the train swung round the curve of the rails to the cutting in the rocks, Iris looked back for a last view of the village—a fantastic huddle of coloured toy-buildings, perched on the green shelf of the valley.

CHAPTER SEVEN
PASSENGERS

As the train rattled out of the cliff tunnel and emerged in a green tree-choked gorge, Iris glanced at her watch. According to the evidence of its hands, the Trieste express was not yet due at the village station.

"It must have stopped when I crashed," she decided. "Sweet luck. It might have lost me my train."

The reminder made her feel profoundly grateful to be actually on her way back to England. During the past twenty four hours she had experienced more conflicting emotion than in a lifetime of easy circumstance and arrangement. She had known the terrifying helplessness of being friendless, sick and penniless—with every wire cut. And then, at the worst, her luck had turned, as it always did.

From force of contrast the everyday business of transport was turned into a temporary rapture. Railway travel was no longer an infliction, only to be endured by the aid of such palliatives as reservations, flowers, fruit, chocolates, light literature, and a group of friends to shriek encouragement.

As she sat, jammed in an uncomfortable carriage, in train which was not too clean, with little prospect of securing a wagon-lit at Trieste, she felt the thrill of a first journey.

The scenery preserved its barbarous character in rugged magnificence. The train threaded its way past piled-up chunks of disrupted landscape, like a Doré steel-engraving of Dante's Inferno. Waterfalls slashed the walls of granite precipices with silver-veining. Sometimes they passed arid patches, where dark pools, fringed with black-feathered rushes, lay in desolate hollows.

Iris gazed at it through the screen of the window—glad of the protective pane of glass. This grandeur was the wreckage of a world shattered by elemental-force, and reminded her that she had just been bruised by her first contact with reality.

She still shrank from the memory of first facts, even though the nightmare railway station was the thick of the mountain away. Now that it was slipping farther behind the coils of the rails with every passing minute, she could dare to estimate the narrow margin by which she had escaped disaster.

Amid the crowd at the station there must have been a percentage of dishonest characters, ready to take advantage of the providential combination of an unconscious foreigner—who did not count—and an expensive handbag which promised a rich loot. Yet the little gnome-like porter chanced to be the man on the spot.

"Things always do turn out for me," she thought. "But—it must be appalling for some of the others."

It was the first time she had realised the fate of those unfortunates who had no squares in their palms. If there were a railway accident, she knew that she would be in the un-wrecked middle portion of the train, just as inevitably as certain other passengers were doomed to be in the telescoped coaches.

As she shuddered at the thought, she glanced idly at the woman who sat opposite to her. She was a negative type in every respect—middle-aged, with a huddle of small indefinite features, and vague colouring. Some one drew a face and then rubbed it nearly out again. Her curly hair was faded and her skin was bleached to oatmeal.

She was not sufficiently a caricature to suggest a stage spinster. Even her tweed suit and matching hat were not too dowdy, although lacking any distinctive note.

In ordinary circumstances, Iris would not have spared her second glance or thought. To-day, however, she gazed at her with compassion.

"If *she* were in a jam, no one would help her out," she thought.

It was discomforting to reflect that the population of the globe must include a percentage of persons without friends, money, or influence; nonentities who would never be missed, and who would sink without leaving a bubble.

To distract her thoughts, Iris tried to look at the scenery again. But the window was now blocked by passengers, who were unable to find seats, so stood in the corridor. For the first time, therefore, she made a deliberate survey of the other occupants of her compartment.

They were six in number—the proper quota—which she had in-

creased to an illegal seven. Her side was occupied by a family party—
two large parents and one small daughter of about twelve.

The father had a shaven head, a little waxed moustache, and several chins. His horn-rimmed glasses and comfortable air gave him the
appearance of a prosperous citizen. His wife had an oiled straight
black fringe, and bushy eyebrows which looked as though they had
been corked. The child wore babyish socks, which did not match her
adult expression. Her hair had apparently been set, after a permanent
wave, for it was still secured with clips.

They all wore new and fashionable suits, which might have been
inspired by a shorthand manual. The father wore stripe—the mother,
spots—and the daughter, checks. Iris reflected idly that if they were
broken up, and reassembled, in the general scramble, they might convey a message to the world in shorthand.

On the evidence, it would be a motto for the home, for they displayed a united spirit, as they shared a newspaper. The mother
scanned the fashions; the little girl read the children's page; and from
the closely-printed columns Iris guessed that the head of the family
studied finance.

She looked away from them to the opposite side of the carriage.
Sitting beside the tweed spinster was a fair pretty girl, who appeared
to have modelled herself from the photograph of any blonde film actress. There were the same sleek waves of hair, the large blue eyes—
with supplemented lashes, and the butterfly brows. Her cheeks were
tinted and her lips painted to geranium bows.

In spite of the delicacy of her features, her beauty was lifeless and
standardised. She wore a tight white suit, with high black satin
blouse, while her cap, gauntlet-gloves and bag were also black. She
sat erect and motionless, holding a rigid pose, as though she were being photographed for a "still."

Although her figure was reduced almost to starvation-point, she
encroached on the tweed spinster's corner, in order to leave a respectful gap between herself and the personage had opposed Iris' entrance.

There was no doubt that this majestic lady belonged to the ruling
classes. Her bagged eyes were fierce with pride, and her nose was an
arrogant beak. Dressed and semi-veiled in heavy black, her enormous
bulk occupied nearly half the seat.

To Iris' astonishment, she was regarding her with a fixed stare of
hostility. It made her feel both guilty and self-conscious.

"I know I crashed the carriage," she thought. "But *she's got*
plenty of room. Wish I could explain, for my own satisfaction."

Leaning forward, she spoke impulsively to the personage.

"Do you speak English?"

Apparently the question was an insult, for the lady closed heavy lids with studied insolence, as though she could not endure a plebeian spectacle.

Iris bit her lip as she glanced at the other passengers. The family party kept their eyes fixed on their paper—the tweed spinster smoothed her skirt, the blonde beauty stared into space. Somehow, Iris received an impression that this well-bred unconsciousness was a tribute of respect to the personage.

"Is she the local equivalent to the sacred black bull?" she wondered angrily. "Can't any one speak until she does? ... Well, to *me*, she's nothing but a fat woman with horrible kid gloves."

She tried to hold on to her critical attitude, but in vain. An overpowering atmosphere of authority seemed to filtrate from the towering black figure.

Now that her excitement was wearing off, she began to feel the after-effects of her slight sunstroke. Her head ached and back of her neck felt as stiff as though it had been reinforced by an iron rod. The symptoms warned her to be careful. With the threat of illness still hanging over her, she knew she should store up every scrap of nervous force, and not waste her reserves in fanciful dislikes.

Her resolution did not save her from increasing discomfort. The carriage seemed not only stuffy, but oppressive with black widow's personality. Iris felt positive that she was a clotted mass of prejudices—an obstruction in the healthy life-stream of the community. Her type was always a clog on progress.

As her face grew damp, she looked toward the closed windows of the compartment. The corridor-end, where she sat, was too crowded to admit any of the outer air, so she struggled to her feet and caught the other strap.

"Do you mind?" she asked with stressed courtesy, hoping, from her intonation, that the other passengers would grasp the fact that she was asking their permission before letting down the glass.

As she expected, the man of the family party rose and took the strap from her. Instead of finishing the job, however, he glanced respectfully at the personage, as though she were sacrosanct, and then frowned at Iris, shaking his head the while.

Feeling furious at the opposition, Iris returned to her corner.

"I've got to take it," she thought. "Take it on the chin. I'm the outsider here."

It was another novel sensation for the most popular member of the crowd, to be in a minority. Besides having to endure the lack of ventilation, the inability to explain her actions, or express a wish, gave her the stunted sense of being deprived of two faculties—speech and hearing.

Presently the door was opened and a tall man squeezed into the carriage. Although she realised that her feelings had grown super-sensitive, Iris thought she had never seen a more repulsive face. He was pallid as potter's clay, with dead dark eyes, and a black spade beard.

He bowed to the personage and began to talk to her, standing the while. His story was evidently interesting, for Iris noticed that the other passengers, including the child, were all listening with close interest.

As he was speaking, his glasses flashed round the compartment, and finally rested on her. His glance was penetrating, yet impersonal, as though she were a specimen on a microscope-slide. Yet, somehow, she received the impression that she was not a welcome specimen, nor one that he had expected to see.

Stooping so that his lips were on a level with the personage's ear, he asked a low-toned question. She replied in a whisper, so that Iris was reminded of two blowflies buzzing in a bottle.

"Am I imagining things, or do these people really dislike me?" she wondered.

She knew that she was growing obsessed by this impression of a general and secret hostility. It was manifestly absurd, especially as the man with the black spade beard had not seen her before. She had merely inconvenienced some strangers, from whom she was divided by the barrier of language.

Shutting her eyes, she tried to forget the people in the carriage. Yet the presence of the man continued to affect her with discomfort. His white face seemed to break through her closed lids, and float in the air before her.

It was a great relief when the buzzing ceased and she heard him go out of the compartment. Directly he had left, she grew normal again, and was chiefly conscious of a very bad headache. The most important things in life were tea and cigarettes; yet she dared not smoke because of the threat of sickness, while tea seemed a feature of a lost civilisation. The train was now rushing through a deserted country of rock and pine. The nearest reminder of habitation was an occasional castle of great antiquity, and usually in ruins. As she was gazing out at the fantastic scenery, an official poked his head in at the door and shouted something which sounded like blasphemy.

The other passengers listened in apathy, but Iris began to open her bag, in case tickets or passport were required. As she did so, she was amazed to hear a crisp English voice.

The tweed spinster had risen from her seat and was asking her a question.

"Are you coming to the restaurant-car to get tea?"

CHAPTER EIGHT
TEA-INTERVAL

Iris was too stunned with surprise to reply. She looked incredulously at the sandy, spiny stretches, flowing past the window, as though expecting to see them turn to Swiss chalets, or blue Italian lakes.

"Oh," she gasped, "you're English."

"Of course. I thought I looked typical.... Are you coming to tea?"

"Oh, *yes.*"

As Iris followed her guide out of the carriage, she was rather disconcerted to find that their compartment was at the end of the corridor. It looked as though her protective square had not insured her against railway smashes, after all.

"Are we next to the engine?" she asked.

"Oh, no," the tweed lady assured her. "There are ordinary coaches in between. It's an extra long train, because of the end of the season rush. They had to pack them in with a shoe-horn."

Apparently she was the type that collected information, for she began to broadcast almost immediately.

"Just glance at the next carriage to ours as you go by—and I'll tell you something."

Although Iris felt no curiosity, she obeyed. Afterwards she was sorry, because she could not forget what she saw.

A rigid figure, covered with rugs, lay stretched on the length of one seat. It was impossible to tell whether it were a man or a woman, for head, eyes and forehead were bandaged, and the features concealed by a criss-cross of plaster strips. Apparently the face had been gashed to mutilation-point.

Iris recoiled in horror, which was increased when she realised that the pallid man with the spade beard was in charge of the invalid. Beside him was a nun, whose expression was so callous that it was difficult to connect her with any act of mercy.

While they chatted together, the patient feebly raised one hand. Although they saw the movement, they ignored it. They might have been porters, responsible for the transport of a bit of lumber, instead of a suffering human being.

The fluttering fingers affected Iris with a rush of acute sympathy. She shrank from the thought that—had the cards fallen otherwise—she, too, might be lying, neglected by some indifferent stranger.

"That nun looks a criminal," she whispered.

"She's not a nun," the tweed lady informed her, "she's a nursing-sister."

"Then I pity her patient. Ghastly to be ill on a journey. And she's not a spectacle. Why can't they pull down the blind?"

"It would be dull for them."

"Poor devil. I suppose it's a man?"

Iris was so foolishly anxious to break the parallel between the motionless figure and herself, that she was disappointed when her companion shook her head.

"No, a woman. They got in at our station, higher up. The doctor was telling the baroness about it. She's just been terribly injured in a motor smash, and there's risk of serious brain injury. So the doctor's rushing her to Trieste, for tricky operation. It's a desperate chance to save her reason and her life."

"Is that man with the black beard a doctor?" asked Iris.

"Yes. Very clever, too."

"Is he? I'd rather have a vet."

The tweed lady, who was leading, did not hear her muttered protest. They had to force their way through the blocked corridors, and had covered about half the distance, when the spinster collided with a tall dark lady in grey, who was standing at the door of a crowded carriage.

"Oh, I'm so sorry," she apologised. "I was just looking out to see if our tea was coming. I gave the order to an attendant."

Iris recognised Mrs. Barnes' voice, and shrank back, for she was not anxious to meet the vicar and his wife.

But her companion gave a cry of delight.

"Oh, you're English, too," she said. "This is my lucky day."

As Mrs. Barnes' soft brown eyes seemed to invite confidence, she added, "I've been in exile for a year."

"Are you on your way home?" asked Mrs. Barnes, with ready sympathy.

"Yes, but I can't believe it. It's far too good to be true. Shall I send a waiter with your tea?"

"That would be really kind. My husband is such a wretched traveller. Like so many big strong men."

Iris listened impatiently, for her temples were beginning to throb savagely. Now that Mrs. Barnes had managed to introduce her husband's name into the conversation, she knew that her own tea might be held up indefinitely.

"Aren't we blocking the way?" she asked.

Mrs. Barnes recognised her with rather a forced smile, for the Gabriel episode still rankled.

"Surprised to see us?" she asked. "We decided, after all, not to wait for the last through train. And our friends—Miss Flood-Porters, came with us. In fact, we're a full muster, for the honeymooners are here, too."

Iris had struggled a little farther down the surging corridor, when the tweed lady spoke to her over her shoulder.

"What a sweet face your friend has. Like a suffering madonna."

"Oh, no, she's very bright," Iris assured her. "And she's definitely not a friend."

They crossed the last dangerously clanking connecting-way, and entered the restaurant-car, which seemed full already. The Misses Flood-Porter—both wearing well-cut white linen travelling-coats—had secured a table and were drinking tea.

Their formal bow, when Iris squeezed by them, was conditional recognition before the final fade-out.

"We'll speak to you during the journey," it seemed to say, "but at Victoria we become strangers."

As Iris showed no inclination to join them, Miss Rose could not resist the temptation to manage a situation.

"Your friend is trying to attract your attention," she called out.

Iris turned and saw that her companion had discovered the last spare corner—a table wedged against the wall—and was reserving a place for herself. When she joined her, the little lady was looking round her with shining eyes.

"I ordered the tea for your nice friends," she said. "Oh, isn't all this *fun?*"

Her pleasure was so spontaneous and genuine that Iris could not condemn it as gush. She stared doubtfully at the faded old-gold plush

window-curtains, the smutty tablecloth, the glass dish of cherry jam—
and then she glanced at her companion.

She received a vague impression of a little puckered face; but
there was a sparkle in the faded blue eyes, and an eager note in the
voice, which suggested a girl.

Afterwards, when she was trying to collect evidence of what she
believed must be an extraordinary conspiracy, it was this discrepancy
between a youthful voice and a middle-aged spinster, which made her
doubt her own senses. In any case, her recollection was far from clear,
for she did not remember looking consciously at her companion
again.

The sun was blazing in through the window, so that she shaded
her eyes with one hand most of the time she was having tea. But as
she listened to the flow of excited chatter, she had the feeling that she
was being entertained by some one much younger than herself.

"Why do you like it?" she asked.

"Because it's travel. We're moving. Everything's moving."

Iris also had the impression that the whole scene was flickering
like an early motion-picture. The waiters swung down the rocking
carriage, balancing trays. Scraps of country flew past the window.
Smuts rained down on the flakes of butter and the sticky cakes. Dusty
motes quivered in the rays of the sun, and the china shook with every
jerk of the engine.

As she tried to drink some tea before it was all shaken over the
rim of her cup, she learned that her companion was an English governess—Miss Winifred Froy—and was on her way home for a holiday.
It came as a shock of surprise to know that this adult lady actually
possessed living parents.

"Pater and Mater say they can talk of nothing else but my return," declared Miss Froy. "They're as excited as children. And so is
Sock."

"Sock?" repeated Iris.

"Yes, short for Socrates. The Pater's name for him. He is our dog.
He's an Old English sheep-dog—not pure—but *so* appealing. And he's
really devoted to me. Mater says he understands that I'm coming
home, but not *when*. *So* the old duffer meets every train. And then
the darling comes back, with his tail down, the picture of depression.
Pater and Mater are looking forward to seeing his frantic joy the
night I *do* come."

"I'd love to see him," murmured Iris.

The old parents' happiness left her unmoved, but she was specially fond of dogs. She got a clear picture of Sock—a shaggy mon-

grel—absurdly clownish and overgrown, with amber eyes beaming under his wisps, and gambolling like a puppy in the joy of reunion.

Suddenly, Miss Froy broke off, at a recollection.

"Before I forget I want to explain why I did not back you up about the window. No wonder you thought I could not be English. It was stuffy—but I didn't like to interfere, because of the baroness."

"D'you mean the appalling black person?"

"Yes, the baroness. I'm under an obligation to her. There was a muddle about my place in the train. I'd booked second-class, but there wasn't a seat left. So the baroness most kindly paid the difference, so that I could travel first-class, in her carriage."

"Yet she doesn't look kind," murmured Iris.

"Perhaps she is rather overwhelming. But she's a member of the family to which I had the honour of being governess. . . . It's not wise to mention names in public, but I was governess to the very highest in the place. These remote districts are still feudal, and centuries behind us. You can have no idea of the *power* of the—of my late employer. What he says *goes*. And he hasn't got to speak. A nod is enough."

"Degrading," muttered Iris, who resented authority.

"It is," agreed Miss Froy. "But it's in the atmosphere, and after a time one absorbs it and one grows spineless. And that's not English. . . . I feel so reinforced, now I've met you. We must stick together."

Iris made no promise. Her fright had not changed her fundamentally, only weakened her nerve. She had the modern prejudice in favour of youth, and had no intention of being tied to a middle-aged spinster for the rest of the journey.

"Are you going back again?" she asked distantly.

"Yes, but not to the castle. It's rather awkward, but I wanted another twelve months to perfect my accent, so I engaged to teach the children of the—Well, we'll call him the leader of the opposition."

She lowered her voice to a whisper.

"The truth is, there is a small but growing Communist element, which is very opposed to my late employer. In fact, they've accused him of corruption and all sorts of horrors. I don't ask myself if it's true, for it's not my business. I only know he's a marvellous man, with wonderful charm and personality. Blood tells. . . . Shall I tell you something rather indiscreet?"

Iris nodded wearily. She was beginning to feel dazed by the heat and incessant clatter. Her tea had not refreshed her, for most of it had splashed into her saucer. The engine plunged and jolted over the met-

als with drunken jerks, belching out wreaths of acrid smoke which
streamed past the windows.

Miss Froy continued her serial, while Iris listened in bored resig-
nation.

"I was terribly anxious to say 'Good-bye' to the—to my employer,
so that I could assure him that my going over to the enemy—so to
speak—was not treachery. His valet and secretary both told me that he
was away at his hunting-lodge. But somehow I felt that they were
putting me off. Anyway, I lay awake until early morning, before it
was light, when I heard water splashing in the bathroom.... Only
one, my dear, for the castle arrangements were primitive, although
my bedroom was like a stage royal apartment, all gilding and pea-
cock-blue velvet, with a huge circular mirror let into the ceiling....
Well, I crept out, like a mouse, and met him in the corridor. There we
were, plain man and woman—I in my dressing-gown, and he in his
bath-robe, and with his hair all wet and rough.... But he was charming. He actually shook my hand and thanked me for my services."

Miss Froy stopped to butter the last scrap of roll. As she was wiping her sticky fingers, she heaved a sigh of happiness.

"I cannot tell you," she said, "what a relief it was to leave under
such pleasant circumstances. I always try to be on good terms with
every one. Of course, I'm insignificant, but I can say truthfully that I
have not got an enemy in the world."

CHAPTER NINE
COMPATRIOTS

A nd now," said Miss Froy, "I supposed we had better go back to our carriage, and make room for others."

The waiter, who was both a judge of character and an opportunist, presented the bill to Iris. Unable to decipher the sprawling numerals, she laid down a note and rose from her seat.

"Aren't you waiting for your change?" asked Miss Froy.

When Iris explained that she was leaving it for a tip, she gasped.

"But it's absurd. Besides, they've already charged their percentage on the bill. . . . As I'm more familiar with the currency, hadn't I better settle up for everything? I'll keep an account, and we can get straight at our journey's end."

The incident was fresh evidence of the smooth working of the protective-square system. Although Iris was travelling alone, a competent courier had presented herself, to rid her of all responsibilities and worries.

"She's decent, although she's a crashing bore," she decided, as she followed Miss Froy down the swaying restaurant-car.

She noticed that the Misses Flood-Porter, who had not finished their leisurely tea, took no notice of herself, but looked exclusively at her companion.

Miss Froy returned Miss Rose's stare with frank interest.

"Those people are English," she whispered to Iris, not knowing that they had met before. "They're part of an England that is passing away. Well-bred privileged people, who live in big houses, and don't spend their income. I'm rather sorry they're dying out."

"Why?" asked Iris.

"Because, although I'm a worker myself, I feel that nice leisured people stand for much that is good. Tradition, charity, national prestige. They may not think you're their equal, but their sense of justice sees that you get equal rights."

Iris said nothing, although she admitted to herself that, while they were at the hotel, the Misses Flood-Porter were more considerate of person and property than her own friends.

When they made their long and shaky pilgrimage through the train, she was amazed by Miss Froy's youthful spirits.

Her laugh rang out whenever she was bumped against other passengers, or was forced, by a lurch of the engine, to clutch a rail.

After they had pushed their way to a clearer passage, she lingered to peep through the windows of the reserved compartments. One of these specially arrested her attention and she invited Iris to share her view.

"Do have a peek," she urged. "There's a glorious couple, just like film stars come to life."

Iris was feeling too jaded to be interested in anything but a railway collision; but as she squeezed her way past Miss Froy, she glanced mechanically through the glass and recognised the bridal pair from the hotel.

Even within the limits of the narrow coupé, the Todhunters had managed to suggest their special atmosphere of opulence and exclusion. The bride wore the kind of elaborate travelling-costume which is worn only on journeys inside a film studio, and had assembled a drift of luxurious possessions.

"Fancy," thrilled Miss Froy, "they've got hot-house fruit with their tea. Grapes and nectarines. . . . He's looking at her with his soul in his eyes, but I can only see her profile. It's just like a beautiful statue. Oh, lady, please turn your head."

Her wish was granted, for, at that comment, Mrs. Todhunter chanced to glance towards the window. She frowned when she saw Miss Froy and spoke to her husband, who rose instantly and pulled down the blind.

Although she was not implicated, Iris felt ashamed of the incident; but Miss Froy only bubbled with amusement.

"He'll know me again," she said. "He looked at me as if he'd like to annihilate me. Quite natural. I was the World—and he wants to forget the World, because he's in paradise. It must be wonderful to be exclusively in love."

"They may not be married," remarked Iris. "Any one can buy a wedding-ring."

"You mean—guilty love? Oh, no, they're too glorious. What name did they register under?"

"Todhunter."

"Then they *are* married. I'm so glad. If it was an irregular affair, they would have signed 'Brown,' or 'Smith.' It's always done."

As she listened to the gush of words behind her, Iris was again perplexed by the discrepancy between Miss Froy's personality and her appearance. It was as though a dryad were imprisoned within the tree-trunk of a withered spinster.

When they reached the end of the corridor, a morbid impulse made her glance towards the carriage which held the invalid. She caught a glimpse of a rigid form and a face hidden by its mass of adhesions, before she looked quickly away, to avoid the eyes of the doctor.

They frightened her, because of their suggestion of baleful hypnotic force. She knew that they would be powerless to affect her in ordinary circumstances; but she was beginning to feel heady and unreal, as though she were in a dream, where every emotion is intensified.

In all probability this condition was a consequent symptom *of* her sunstroke, and was due, partly, to her struggle to hold out, until she could collapse safely at her journey's end. She was directing her will-power towards one aim only, and therefore draining herself of energy.

As a result she was susceptible to imaginary antagonism. When she caught sight of a blur of faces inside the gloom of her carriage, she shrank back, unwilling to enter.

She received unexpected support from Miss Froy, who seemed to divine her reluctance.

"Don't let's sit mum like charity-children any longer," she whispered. "Even if I am under an obligation to the baroness, I am going to remember that these people are only foreigners. They shan't impress me. We're English."

Although the reminder was patriotism reduced to its lowest term of Jingoism, it braced Iris to enter the compartment with a touch of her old abandon. Precaution forgotten, she lit a cigarette without a glance at the other passengers.

"Have you travelled much?" she asked Miss Froy.

"Only in Europe," was the regretful reply. "Mater doesn't really like me going so far from home, but she holds the theory that the younger generation must not be denied their freedom. Still, I've promised to stick to Europe, although, whenever I'm near a boundary, I just ache to hop over the line to Asia."

"Is your mother very old?"

"No, she's eighty years young. A real sport, with the spirit of the modern girl. Pater is seventy-seven. He never let her know he was younger than she, but it leaked out when he had to retire at sixty-five. Poor Mater was terribly upset. She said, 'You have made me feel a cradle-snatcher.'. . . Oh, I can't believe I'm really going to see them again soon.'"

As she listened, Iris watched the smoke curling up from her cigarette. Occasionally she saw a vague little puckered face swaying amid the haze, like an unsuccessful attempt at television. Out of gratitude for services rendered—and still to come—she tried to appreciate the old parents, but she grew very bored by the family saga.

She learned that Pater was tall and thin, and looked classical, while Mater was short and stout, but dignified. Apparently Pater had unquenchable ardour and energy, for at the age of seventy he began to learn Hebrew.

"He's made a detailed time-table for every month of his life, up to ninety," explained Miss Froy. "That's what comes of being a schoolmaster. Now, Mater is passionately fond of novels. Love ones, you know. She makes a long bus journey every week to change her library book. But she says she can't imagine them properly unless she makes me the heroine."

"I'm sure you had a marvellous time," said Iris.

Miss Froy resented the attempt to be tactful.

"Have, and had," she declared. "Pater was a parson before he kept a school, and his curates always proposed to me. I expect it is because I have fair curly hair. . . . And I still have the excitement and hope of the eternal quest. I never forget that a little boy is born for every little girl. And even if we haven't met yet, we are both growing old together, and if we're fated to meet, we *shall.*"

Iris thought sceptically of the mature men who refuse to adhere to the calendar, as she listened with rising resentment. She wanted quiet—but Miss Froy's voice went on and on, like the unreeling of an endless talking-picture.

Presently, however, Miss Froy recaptured her interest, for she began to talk of languages.

"I speak ten, including English," she said. "At first, when you're in a strange country, you can't understand one word, and you feel like a puppy thrown into a pond. You flounder and struggle, so unless you want to drown you've simply got to pick it up. By the end of a year you're as fluent as a native. But I always insist on staying a second year, for the sake of idiomatic polish."

"I expect foreigners to speak English," declared Iris.

"When you're off the map they may not, and then you might find yourself in a terrible fix. Shall I tell you a true story?"

Without waiting for encouragement, Miss Froy spun a yarn which was not calculated to cool Iris' inflamed nerves. It was all very vague and anonymous, but the actual horror was stark.

A certain woman had been certified as insane, but owing to a blunder the ambulance went to the wrong house and forcibly took away an Englishwoman, who did not understand a word of the language, or of her destination. In her indignation and horror at finding herself in a private asylum, she became so vehement and violent that she was kept, at first, under the influence of drugs.

When the mistake was found out, the doctor—who was a most unscrupulous character, was afraid to admit it. At the time he was in financial difficulties, and he feared it might ruin his reputation. So he planned to detain the Englishwoman until he could release her as officially cured.

"But she couldn't know she wasn't in for life," explained Miss Froy, working up the agony. "The horror of it would probably have driven her really insane, only a nurse exposed the doctor's plot, out of revenge. . . . But can you imagine the awful position of that poor Englishwoman? Trapped, with no one to make inquiries about her, or even to know she had disappeared, for she was merely a friendless foreigner, staying a night here and a night there, at some Pension. She didn't understand a word—she couldn't explain—"

"Please *stop*," broke in Iris. "I can imagine it all. Vividly. But would you mind if we stopped talking?"

"Oh, certainly. Aren't you well? It's difficult to be sure, with your sunburn, but I thought you looked green, once or twice."

"I'm very fit, thanks. But my head aches a bit. I've just had a touch of sunstroke."

"Sunstroke? When?"

Knowing that Miss Froy's curiosity had to be appeased, Iris gave a brief account of her attack. As she did so, she glanced round the carriage. It was evident, from the blank faces, that—with one exception—the passengers did not understand English.

Iris could not be certain about the baroness. She had the slightly stupid expression of an autocrat who has acquired power through birth, and not enterprise; yet there was a gleam of intelligence in her eyes that betrayed secret interest in the story.

"Oh, you poor soul," cried Miss Froy, who overflowed with sympathy. "Why didn't you stop me chattering before? I'll give you some aspirin."

Although she hated any fuss, it was a relief to Iris when she was able to sit back in her corner, while Miss Froy hunted the contents of her bag.

"I don't think you had better have dinner in the restaurant-car," she decided. "I'll bring you something here, later. Now, swallow these tablets, and then try to get a little nap."

After Iris had closed her eyes, she could still hear Miss Froy fluttering about her, like a fussy little bird, on guard.

It gave her a curious sense of protection, while the carriage was so warm that she soon became pleasantly drowsy.

As the drug began to take effect, her thoughts grew jumbled, while her head kept jerking forward. Presently she lost consciousness of place, as she felt herself moving onwards with the motion of the train, as though she were riding. Sometimes she took a fence, when the seat seemed to leap under her, leaving her suspended in the air.

Clankety-clankety-clank. On and on. She kept moving steadily upwards. Clankety-clankety-clank. Then the rhythm of the train changed, and she seemed to be sliding backwards down a long slope. Click-click-click-click. The wheels rattled over the rails, with a sound of castanets.

She was sinking deeper and deeper, while the carriage vibrated like the throbbing of an airplane. It was bearing her away—sweeping her outside the carriage—to the edge of a drop. . . .

With a violent start she opened her eyes. Her heart was leaping, as though she had actually fallen from a height. At first she wondered where she was; then as she gradually recognised her surroundings, she found that she was staring at the baroness.

In slight confusion she looked away quickly to the opposite seat.

To her surprise, Miss Froy's place was empty.

CHAPTER TEN
THE VACANT SEAT

Iris was ungratefully glad of Miss Froy's absence. Her doze had confused rather than refreshed her, and she felt she could not endure another long installment of family history She wanted peace; and while it was impossible to have quiet amid the roar and rush of the train, she considered herself entitled, at least, to personal privacy.

As regarded the other passengers, she was free from any risk of contact. Not one of them took the slightest notice of her. The baroness slept in her corner—the others sat motionless and silent. Inside the carriage, the atmosphere was warm and airless as a conservatory.

It soothed Iris to a tranquil torpidity. She felt numbed to thought and feeling, as though she were in a semi-trance and incapable of raising a finger, or framing two consecutive words. Patches of green scenery fluttered past the window, like a flock of emerald birds. The baroness' heavy breathing rose and fell with the regularity of a tide.

Iris vaguely dreaded Miss Froy's return, which must destroy the narcotic spell. At any moment, now, she might hear the brisk step in the corridor. Presumably Miss Froy had gone to wash, and had been obliged to wait her turn, owing to the crowd.

Hoping for the best, Iris closed her eyes again. At first she was apprehensive whenever any one passed by the window, but each false alarm increased her sense of security. Miss Froy ceased to be a menace and shrank to a mere name. The octogenarian parents went back to their rightful place inside some old photograph-album. Even Sock—that shaggy absurd mongrel, whom Iris had grown to like—was blurred to an appealing memory.

Clankety-clankety-clank. The sound of breathing swelled to the surge of a heavy sea, sucking at the rocks. Muted by the thunder of the train, it boomed in unison with the throb of the engine. Clankety-clankety-clank.

Suddenly the baroness' snores arose to an elephantine trumpet which jerked Iris awake. She started up in her seat—tense with apprehension and with every faculty keyed up. The shock had vibrated some seventh sense which made her expectant of disaster, as she glanced swiftly at Miss Froy's place.

It was still empty.

She was surprised by her pang of disappointment. Not long ago she had been praying for Miss Froy's return to be delayed; but now she felt lonely and eager to welcome her.

"I expect I'll soon be cursing her again," she admitted to herself. "But, anyway, she is human."

She glanced at the blonde beauty, who was beginning to remind her of a wax model in a shop window. Not a flat wave of her honey-gold hair was out of place. Even her eyes had the transparency of blue wax.

Chilled by the contrast to the vital little spinster, Iris looked at her watch. The late hour, which told her that she had slept longer than she had suspected, also made her feel rather worried about Miss Froy's prolonged absence.

"She's had enough time to take a bath," she thought. "I—I hope nothing's wrong."

The idea was so disturbing that she exerted all her common sense to dislodge it.

"Absurd," she told herself. "What *could* happen to her? It's not night, when she might open the wrong door by mistake, and step out of the train in the dark. Besides, she's an experienced traveller—not a helpless fool like myself. And she knows about a hundred languages."

A smile flickered over her lips as she remembered one of the little spinster's confidences.

"Languages give me a sense of power. If an international crisis arose in a railway carriage, and there were no interpreters, I could step into the breach and, perhaps, alter the destinies of the world."

The recollection suggested an explanation for Miss Froy's untenanted seat. Probably she was indulging her social instincts by talking to congenial strangers. She was not divided from them by any barrier of language. Moreover, she was in holiday mood and wanted to tell every one that she was going home.

"I'll give her another half-hour," decided Iris. "She must be back by then."

As she looked out of the window, the clouded sky of late afternoon filled her with melancholy. The train had been gradually descending from the heights, and was now steaming through a lush green valley. Mauve crocuses cropped up amid thick pastures, which were darkened by moisture. The scene was definitely autumnal and made her realise that summer was over.

The time slipped away too quickly, because she dreaded reaching the limit which she had appointed. If Miss Froy did not return she would have to make a decision, and she did not know what to do. Of course, as she reminded herself, it was not really her business at all; but her uneasiness grew with the passing of each five minutes of grace.

Presently there was a stir among the other passengers. The little girl began to whine fretfully, while the father appeared to reason with her. Iris guessed that she had complained of sleepiness, and had been persuaded to take a nap, when she saw the mother's preparations to keep her daughter's trim appearance intact.

After the black patent belt and the organdie collar had been removed, she drew out a net and arranged it carefully over the little girl's permanent wave. The blonde beauty showed her first signs of animation as she watched the process, but her interest died when the matron pulled off her child's buckled shoes and replaced them with a pair of shabby bedroom-slippers.

Finally she pointed to Miss Froy's vacant place.

Iris felt a rush of disproportionate resentment when she saw the little girl sitting in the spinster's seat. She wished she could protest by signs, but was too self-conscious to risk making an exhibition of herself.

"When she comes back, Miss Froy will soon turn her out," she thought.

Upon reflection, however, she was not so sure of direct action. When she remembered the friendly spirit Miss Froy displayed towards every one, she felt certain that she had already established a pleasant understanding with her fellow passengers.

The little girl was so heavy with sleep that she closed her eyes directly she curled up in her corner. The parents looked at each other and smiled. They caught the blonde beauty's attention, and she, too, nodded with polite appreciation. Only Iris remained outside the circle.

She knew that she was unjustly prejudiced, since she was the real interloper, yet she hated this calm appropriation of Miss Froy's place. It was as though the other passengers were taking unfair advantage of her absence—since she could not turn out a sleeping child.

Or even as though they were acting on some secret intelligence.

They were behaving as though they knew she was not coming back. In a panic, Iris looked at her watch, to find, to her dismay, that the half-hour had slipped away.

The lapse of time was registered outside the window. The overcast sky had grown darker and the first mists were beginning to collect in the corners of the green saturated fields. Instead of crocuses, she saw the pallid fungoid growths of toadstools or mushrooms.

As the sadness of twilight stole over her, Iris began to hunger for company. She wanted cheerful voices, lights, laughter; but although she thought wistfully of the crowd, she was even more anxious to see a little lined face and hear the high rushing voice.

Now that she was gone, she seemed indefinite as a dream. Iris could not reconstruct any clear picture of her, or understand why she should leave such a blank.

"What was she *like?*" she wondered.

At that moment she chanced to look up at the rack. To her surprise, Miss Froy's suitcase was no longer there.

In spite of logic, her nerves began to flutter at this new development. While she told herself that it was obvious that Miss Froy had moved to another compartment, the circumstances did not fit in. To begin with, the train was so overcrowded that it would be difficult to find an empty unreserved place.

On the other hand, Miss Froy had mentioned some muddle about her seat. It was barely possible that it had proved available, after all.

"No," decided Iris, "the baroness had already paid the difference for her to travel first. And I'm sure she wouldn't leave me without a word of explanation. She talked of bringing me dinner. Besides, I owe her for my tea. I'm simply bound to find her."

She looked at the other passengers, who might hold the key to the mystery. Too distracted now to care about appearances, she made an effort to communicate with them. Feeling that "English" was the word which should have lightened their darkness, she started in German.

"Wo ist die dame *English?*"

They shook their heads and shrugged, to show that they did not understand. So she made a second attempt.

"Où est la dame *English?*"

As no sign of intelligence dawned on their faces, she spoke to them in her own language.

"Where is the English lady?"

The effort was hopeless. She could not reach them, and they

showed no wish to touch her. As they stared at her, she was chilled by
their indifference, as though she were outside the pale of civilised obligations.

Feeling suddenly desperate, she pointed to Miss Froy's seat, and
then arched her brows in exaggerated inquiry. This time she succeeded in arousing an emotion, for the man and his wife exchange
amused glances, while the blonde's lip curled with disdain. Then, as
though she scented entertainment, the little girl opened her black
eyes and broke into a snigger, which she suppressed instantly at a
warning glance from her father.

Stung by their ridicule, Iris glared at them, as she crossed to the
baroness and shook her arm.

"Wake up, please," she entreated.

She heard a smothered gasp from the other passengers, as though
she had committed some act of sacrilege. But she was too overwrought to remember to apologise, when the baroness raised her lids
and stared at her with outraged majesty.

"Where is Miss Froy?" asked Iris.

"Miss Froy?" repeated the baroness. "I do not know any one who
has that name."

Iris pointed to the seat which was occupied by the little girl.

"She sat *there*," she said.

The baroness shook her head.

"You make a mistake," she declared. "No English lady has sat
there ever."

Iris' head began to reel.

"But she *did*," she insisted. "I talked to her. And we went and had
tea together. You must remember."

"There is nothing to remember." The baroness spoke with slow
emphasis. "I do not understand what you mean at all. I tell you
this. . . . There has been no English lady, here, in this carriage, never,
at any time, except you. You are the only English lady here."

CHAPTER ELEVEN
NEEDLE IN A HAYSTACK

Iris opened her lips only to close them again. She had the helpless feeling of being shouted down by some terrific blast of sound. The baroness had made a statement which was an outrage on the evidence of her senses; but it was backed up by the force of an overpowering authority.

As she held the girl's eye, challenging her denial, Iris looked at the leaden eyelids, the deep lines graven from nose to chin—the heavy obstinate chin. The lips were drawn down in a grimace which reminded her of a mask of the Muse of Tragedy.

She realised that further protest was useless. The baroness would flatten down any attempt at opposition with relentless pressure. The most she could do was to acknowledge defeat with a shrug which disdained further argument.

Her composure was only bluff for she felt utterly bewildered as she sank back in her seat. She was scarcely conscious of slides of twilight scenery streaming past the window, or of the other passengers. A village shot out of the shadows and vanished again in the dimness. She caught the flash of a huddle of dark roofs and the white streak of a little river, which boiled under a hooded bridge.

The next second the church tower and wooden houses were left behind as the express rocked on its way back to England. It lurched and shrieked as though in unison with the tangle of Iris' thoughts.

"No Miss Froy? Absurd. The woman must be mad. Does she take me for a fool? . . . But why does she say it? *Why?*"

It was this lack of motive which worried her most. Miss Froy was such a harmless little soul that there could be no reason for her suppression. She was on friendly terms with every one.

Yet the fact remained that she had disappeared, for Iris was positive now that she would not come back to the carriage. In a sudden fit of nerves she sprang to her feet.

"She must be somewhere on the train," she argued. "I'll find her."

She would not admit it, but her own confidence was flawed by the difficulty of finding a reason for Miss Froy's absence. She had taken Iris under her wing, so that it was entirely out of line with her character as a kindly little busybody for her to withdraw in such an abrupt and final manner.

"Does she think I might be sickening from some infectious disease?" she wondered. "After all, she's so terribly keen to get back to her old parents and the dog, that she wouldn't dare run risks of being held up. Naturally she would sacrifice me."

Her progress down the train was a most unpleasant experience. It had been difficult when Miss Froy acted the part of a fussy little tug and had cleared a passage for her. Now that more passengers had grown tired of sitting in cramped compartments and had emerged to stretch, or smoke, the corridor was as closely packed with tourists as a melon with seeds.

Iris did not know how to ask them to step aside and she did not like to push. Moreover, the fact that she was attractive did not escape the notice of some of the men. Each time a swerve of the express caused her to lurch against some susceptible stranger, he usually believed that she was making overtures.

Although she grew hot with annoyance her chief emotion was one of futility. She had no hope of finding Miss Froy in such confusion. Whenever she passed each fresh compartment to peer inside she always saw the same blur of faces.

Because she was beginning to run a temperature, these faces appeared as bleared and distorted as creations of a nightmare. It was a relief when she worked her way down the train, in an unavailing search, to see the vicar and his wife in one of the crowded carriages.

They were sitting opposite each other. Mr. Barnes had closed his eyes and his face was set. In spite of his sunburn it was plain that he was far from well and was exerting his will-power to subdue his symptoms.

His wife watched him with strained attention. She looked wan and miserable, as though—in imagination—she was sharing his every pang of train-sickness.

She did not smile when Iris struggled inside and spoke to her.

"Sorry to bother you but I'm looking for my friend."

"Oh, yes?"

There was the familiar forced brightness in Mrs. Barnes' voice but her eyes were tragic.

"You remember her?" prompted Iris. "She sent the waiter with your tea."

The vicar came to life.

"It was kind indeed," he said. "Will you give her my special thanks?"

"When I find her," promised Iris. "She went out of the carriage some time ago—and she hasn't come back."

"I haven't noticed her pass the window," said Mrs. Barnes. "Perhaps she went to wash. Anyway, she couldn't possibly be lost."

Iris could see that she was concentrating on her husband and had no interest in some unknown woman.

"Can I find her for you?" offered the vicar manfully, struggling to his feet.

"Certainly not." His wife's voice was sharp. "Don't be absurd, Kenneth. You don't know what she looks like."

"That's true. I should be more hindrance than help."

The vicar sank back gratefully and looked up at Iris with a forced smile.

"Isn't it humiliating to be such a wretched traveller?" he asked

"I wouldn't talk," advised his wife.

Iris took the hint and went out of the compartment. She, too, considered the vicar's weakness was a major misfortune. He was not only a man of high principle but she was sure that he possessed imagination and sympathy; yet she was unable to appeal to him for help because nature had laid him low.

Because she was beginning to fear that she faced failure she grew more frantic with determination to find Miss Froy. If she failed she was loaded with a heavy responsibility.

Of all the people in the train she—alone—seemed conscious of the disappearance of a missing passenger.

She shrank from the prospect of trying to arouse these callous strangers from their apathy. As she clung to rails and was buffeted by the impacts of other tourists pushing their way past her, she hated them all. In her strung-up condition she could not realise that these people might experience her own sensations were they suddenly placed in a crowded London Tube or New York Subway and jostled by seemingly hostile and indifferent strangers.

When she reached the reserved portion of the train, the blind was still pulled down over the Todhunters' window, but she recognised the Misses Flood-Porter in one of the reserved coupés. They sat on different sides of the tiny compartment—each with her feet stretched out on the seat. The elder lady wore horn-rimmed glasses and was reading a Tauchnitz, while Miss Rose smoked a cigarette.

They looked very content with life and although kind-hearted, the sight of others standing in the corridors subtly enhanced their appreciation of their own comfort.

"Smug," thought Iris bitterly.

They made her realise her own position. She reminded herself that her place, too, was in a reserved compartment, instead of fighting her way into the privacy of strange people.

"Why am I taking it?" she wondered as she met the unfriendly glance of the ladies. Miss Rose's was perceptibly more frigid as though she were practising gradations, in preparation for the cut direct, at Victoria Station.

At last she had combed the train with the exception of the restaurant-car. Now that tea was finished it was invaded by men who wanted to drink and smoke in comfort.

As she lingered at the entrance to make sure that Miss Froy was not inside seeking her soul-mate of whom she had spoken, a hopeful young man touched Iris' arm. He said something unintelligible which she translated as an invitation to refreshment, and leered into her face.

Furious at the liberty she shook him off and was on the point of turning away, when, amid the rumble of masculine voices, she distinguished the distinctive vowels of an Oxford accent.

She was trying to locate it when she caught sight of the spade-bearded doctor. His bald, domed head, seen through the murk of smoke, reminded her of a moon rising through the mist. His face was blanched and bony—his dead eyes were magnified by his thick glasses.

As they picked her out with an impersonal gaze, she felt as though she had been pinned down and classified as a type.

Suddenly—for no reason at all—she thought of the doctor in Miss Froy's tale of horror.

CHAPTER TWELVE

WITNESSES

Although she was conscious of the interest she aroused, Iris was too overwrought to care. Raising her voice she made a general appeal.

"Please. Is there any one English here?"

The spectacle of a pretty girl in distress made a young man leap to his feet. He was of rather untidy appearance with a pleasant ordinary face and audacious hazel eyes.

"Can I be of use?" he asked quickly.

The voice was familiar to Iris. She had heard it at the railway station, just before her sunstroke. This was the young man who had been opposed to trial by jury. He looked exactly as she had pictured him; he had even a rebellious tuft of hair, of the kind that lies down under treatment, as meekly as a trained hound, but which springs up again, immediately the brush is put away.

In other circumstances she would have been attracted to him instinctively; but in this crisis he seemed to lack ballast.

"Gets fresh with barmaids and cheeks traffic-cops," she reflected swiftly.

"Well?" prompted the young man.

To her dismay Iris found it difficult to control her voice or collect her thoughts when she tried to explain the situation.

"It's all rather complicated," she said shakily. "I'm in a jam. At least, it's nothing to do with me. But I'm sure there's some horrible mistake and I can't speak a word of this miserable language."

"That's all right," said the young man encouragingly. "I speak the lingo. Just put me wise to the trouble."

While Iris still hesitated, doubtful of her choice of champion, a tall, thin man rose reluctantly from his seat, as though chivalry were a painful duty. In this case his academic appearance was not misleading, for directly he spoke Iris recognised the characteristic voice of the professor of modern languages.

"May I offer my services as an interpreter?" he asked formally.

"He's no good," broke in the young man. "He only knows grammar. But I can swear in the vernacular and we may need a spot of profanity."

Iris checked her laugh for she realised that she was on the verge of hysteria.

"An Englishwoman has disappeared from the train," she told the professor. "She's a *real* person, but the baroness says — "

Her voice suddenly failed as she noticed that the doctor was looking at her with fixed attention. The professor's glacial eye also reminded her that she was making an exhibition of herself.

"Could you pull yourself together to make a coherent statement?" he asked.

The chill in his voice was tonic for it braced her to compress the actual situation into a few words. This time she was careful to make no allusion to the baroness but confined herself to Miss Froy's non-return to the carriage.

To her relief the professor appeared to be impressed for he rubbed his long chin gravely.

"You said—an *English* lady?" he asked.

"Yes," replied Iris eagerly. "Miss Froy. She's a governess."

"Ah, yes. . . . Now, are you absolutely certain that she is nowhere on the train?"

"Positive. I've looked everywhere."

"H'm. She would not be likely to leave her reserved seat for an inadequate reason. At what time precisely did she leave the compartment?"

"I don't know. I was asleep. When I woke up she wasn't there."

"Then the first step is to interview the other passengers. If the lady does not return by that time, I may consider calling the guard and asking for an official examination of the train."

The young man winked at Iris, to direct her attention to the fact that the professor was in his element.

"Gaudy chance for you to rub up the lingo, professor," he said.

The remark reminded Iris that while the professor's acquaintance with the language would be academic, the young man probably possessed a more colloquial knowledge. This was important, since she was beginning to think that the confusion over Miss Froy sprang from the baroness' imperfect command of English. Her accent was good, but if she could not understand all that was said she would never admit ignorance.

Determined to leave nothing to chance, Iris appealed to the frivolous youth.

"Will you come, too, and swear for us?" she asked.

"Like a bird," he replied. "A parrot, I mean, of course. Lead on, professor."

Iris' spirits rose as they made their way back through the train. Although she was still worried about Miss Froy, her companion infused her with a sense of comradeship.

"My name's 'Hare,' " he told her. "Much too long for you to remember. Better call me Maximilian—or, if you prefer it, Max. What's yours?"

"Iris Carr."

"Mrs.?"

"Miss."

"Good. I'm an engineer, out here. I'm building a dam up in some mountains."

"What fun. I'm nothing."

Full of confidence in the support of her compatriots, Iris felt exultant as they neared her carriage. Tourists—seated on their suitcases—blocked the way and children chased each other, regardless of adult toes. As a pioneer Hare was better than Miss Froy. While she hooted to warn others of their approach, he rammed a clear passage, like an ice-plough.

The professor stood aside to allow Iris to enter the compartment first. She noticed immediately that the spade-bearded doctor was seated beside the baroness and was talking to her in low rapid tones. He must have left the restaurant-car in a hurry.

The fact made her feel slightly uneasy.

"He's one jump ahead of me," she thought.

The family party shared a bag of nectarines and took no notice of her, while the blonde was absorbed in rebuilding the curves of her geranium lips. The baroness sat unmoved as a huge black granite statue.

There was a glint in Iris' eyes when she made her announcement.

"Two English gentlemen have come to make some inquiries about Miss Froy."

The baroness reared up her head and glared at her, but made no comment. It was impossible to tell whether the announcement were a shock.

"Will you kindly allow me to enter?" asked the professor.

In order to make more room for the investigation, Iris went out into the corridor. From where she stood she could see the invalid's carriage and the nursing-sister who sat at the window. In spite of her preoccupation, she noticed that the woman's face was not repulsive but merely stolid.

"Am I exaggerating everything?" she wondered nervously. "Perhaps, after all, I'm not reliable."

In spite of her pity for the wretched patient it was a real relief when the original nurse, with the callous expression, appeared at the door. The fog of mystery, together with the throb of her temples, combined to make her feel uncertain of herself.

She smiled when Hare spoke to her.

"I'm going to listen-in," he told her. "The professor's bound to be a don at theory, but he might slip up in practice, so I'll check up for you."

Iris looked over his shoulder as she tried to follow the proceedings. The professor seemed to carry out his investigation with thoroughness, patience and personal dignity. Although he bowed to the baroness with respect, before he explained the situation, he conveyed an impression of his own importance.

The personage inclined her head and then appeared to address a general question to her fellow passengers. Iris noticed how her proud gaze swept each face and that her voice had a ring of authority.

Following her lead the professor interrogated every person in turn—only to receive the inevitable shake of the head which appeared the language of the country. Remembering her own experience Iris whispered to Hare.

"Can't they understand him?"

He replied by a nod which told her that he was listening closely and did not wish to be disturbed. Thrown on her own resources she made her own notes and was amused to remark that—in spite of being accustomed to teach mixed classes—the professor was scared of the ladies, including the little girl.

Very soon he confined his questions to the business man who answered with slow deliberation. He was obviously trying to be helpful to a foreigner, who might have difficulty in understanding him. In the end he produced his card and gave it to the professor, who read it, and then returned it with a bow of thanks.

In spite of the general atmosphere of politeness Iris grew impatient and tugged Hare's arm.

"Is he finding out anything about Miss Froy?" she asked.

She was unpleasantly surprised by his grave face.

"Oh, it's rather involved," he told her. "All about where is the pen of the aunt of my gardener?"

Her confidence began to cloud as she grew conscious of an unfriendly atmosphere. The baroness did not remove her eyes from her face during her short speech, to which the professor listened with marked respect. At its end she made a sign to the doctor, as though ordering him to support her statement.

Hitherto he had been a silent witness of the scene. His white impassive face and dead eyes made him resemble one newly-returned from the grave, to attend a repeat performance of the revue of life—to its eternal damnation.

But as he began to talk at his patron's bidding he grew vital and even vehement, for he used his hands to emphasise his words.

When he had finished speaking the professor turned to Iris.

"You appear to have made an extraordinary mistake," he said. "No one in this carriage knows anything about the lady you *say is* missing."

Iris stared at him incredulously.

"Are you telling me I invented her?" she asked angrily.

"I hardly know what to think."

"Then I'll tell you. All these people are telling lies."

Even as she spoke Iris realised the absurdity of her charge. It was altogether too wholesale. No rational person could believe that the passengers would unite to bear false witness. The family party in particular looked solid and respectable, while the father was probably the equivalent to her own lawyer.

The professor was of the same opinion, for his manner grew stiffer.

"The people whom you accuse of being liars are citizens of good standing," he said, "and are known personally to the baroness, who vouches for their integrity. The gentleman is not only a well-known banker in the district, but is also the baroness' banker. The young lady"—he glanced warily at the blonde—"is the daughter of her agent."

"I can't help that," protested Iris. "All I know is that I'm owing Miss Froy for my tea. She paid for me."

"We can check up on that," interrupted Hare. "If she paid, you'll be so much to the good. Just count up your loose cash."

Iris shook her head.

"I don't know how much I had," she confessed. "I'm hopeless about money. I'm always getting R.D. cheques."

Although the professor's mouth turned down at the admission, he intervened in proof of his sense of fair play.

"If you had tea together," he said, "the waiter should remember your companion. I'll interview him next, if you will give me a description of the lady."

Iris had been dreading this moment because of her clouded recollection of Miss Froy. She knew that she had barely glanced at her the whole time they were together. During tea she had been half-blinded by the sun, and when they returned to the carriage she had kept her eyes closed on account of her headache. On their way to and from the restaurant-car, she had always been either in front or behind her companion.

"I can't tell you much," she faltered. "You see, there's nothing much about her to catch hold of. She's middle-aged, and ordinary—and rather colourless."

"Tall or short? Fat or thin? Fair or dark?" prompted Hare.

"Medium. But she said she had fair curly hair."

" 'Said'?" repeated the professor. "Didn't you notice it for yourself?"

"No. But I think it looked faded. I remember she had blue eyes, though."

"Not very enlightening, I'm afraid," remarked the professor.

"What did she wear?" asked Hare suddenly.

"Tweed. Oatmeal, flecked with brown. Swagger coat, finger-length, with patch pockets and stitched cuffs and scarf. The ends of the scarf were fastened with small blue-bone buttons and she wore a natural tussore shirt-blouse, stitched with blue—a different shade—with a small blue handkerchief in the breast-pocket. I'm afraid I didn't notice details much. Her hat was made of the same material, with a stitched brim and a Récamier crown, with a funny bright-blue feather stuck through the band."

"Stop," commanded Hare. "Now that you've remembered the hat, can't you make another effort and put a face under it?"

He was so delighted with the result of his experiment that his dejection was ludicrous when Iris shook her head in the old provoking manner.

"No, I can't remember any face. You see, I had such a frantic headache."

"Exactly," commented the professor dryly. "Cause and effect, I'm afraid. The doctor has been telling us that you had a slight sunstroke."

As though awaiting his cue the doctor—who had been listening intently—spoke to Iris.

"That blow of the sun explains all," he said, speaking in English, with slow emphasis. "It has given you a delirium. You saw some one who is not there. Afterwards, you went to sleep, and you dream. Then, presently, you awake and you are much better. So you saw Miss Froy no more. . . . She is nothing but a delirium—a dream."

CHAPTER THIRTEEN

A DREAM WITHIN
A DREAM

At first Iris was too surprised to protest. She had the bewildered sensation of being the one sane person in a mad world. Her astonishment turned to indignation when the professor caught Hare's eye and gave a nod of mutual understanding.

Then he spoke to Iris in a formal voice.

"I think we may accept that as final. If I had known the circumstances I should not have intervened. I hope you will soon feel better."

"We'd better clear and let Miss Carr get some quiet," suggested Hare, with a doubtful grin.

Iris felt as though she were being smothered with featherbed opposition. Controlling her anger she forced herself to speak calmly.

"I'm afraid it's not so simple as that. As far as I'm concerned the matter's by no means ended. Why should you imagine I'm telling a lie?"

"I do not," the professor assured her. "I am convinced it is your mistake. But, since you've raised the point of fairness, you must admit that the weight of evidence is against you. I have to be fair. . . . Can you explain why six persons should lie?"

Iris had a sudden flash of intuition.

"I can't," she said, "unless one person started the lie, and the others are backing her up. In that case it's only her word against mine. And as I'm English and you're English and this concerns an Englishwoman, it's your duty to believe me."

As she spoke Iris challenged the baroness in an accusing stare. Although the personage heard the charge with complete composure, the professor coughed in protest.

"You mustn't confuse patriotism with prejudice," he said. "Besides your insinuation is absurd. What motive would the baroness have for telling a lie?"

Iris' brain began to swim.

"I don't know," she said weakly. "It's all such a mystery. No one could want to injure Miss Froy. She's too insignificant. Besides, she was proud of having no enemies. And she told me herself that the baroness had geen kind."

"What have I done?" asked the baroness blandly.

"She said that there was a muddle about her place and you paid the excess-fare for her to travel in here."

"That was charming of me. I'm gratified to hear of my generosity. Unfortunately I know nothing of it. But the ticket-collector should be able to refresh my memory."

The professor turned to Iris dutifully.

"What am I to do?" he asked. "You are making things rather difficult by persisting in this attitude. But, if you insist, I will question the man."

"I'll dig him out," offered Hare.

Iris knew that he wanted a chance to escape. She felt that his sympathies were with her while he withheld his faith.

After he had gone the professor began to talk to the baroness and the doctor, presumably for the sake of further practice. Suspicious of every glance and inflection, Iris believed that he was explaining the delicacy of his position and stressing the absurdity of the charge, for the baroness looked almost as benevolent as a sated tigress that kills just for the sport.

She was glad when Hare—his rebellious tuft sticking out like a feather—battled his way down the corridor, followed by the ticket-collector. He was a sturdy young man, in a very tight uniform and he reminded Iris of a toy soldier, with two blobs of crimson-colour on his broad cheeks and a tiny black waxed moustache.

As he entered the baroness spoke to him sharply and then waved to the professor to continue.

By this time Iris' nerve was shattered; she was so sure that the ticket-collector would prove another victim to mass-hypnotism that she was prepared when Hare made a grimace.

"He's telling the old, old story," he said.

"Of course he is." Iris tried to laugh. "I expect he was one of her peasants. He looks bucolic. She seems to own the lot—including you and the professor."

"Now, don't get het up," he urged. "I know just what you are feeling, because I've been through this myself. I'll tell you about it, if I can dislodge this young lady."

The little girl, who had been making precocious eyes at Hare, responded to his invitation to move with shrugs and pouts of protest. All the same she reluctantly went back to her original place, while he squeezed into the corner originally occupied by the elusive spinster.

"Cheer up," he said. "Unless your Miss Froy was invisible, other people in the train must have seen her."

"I know," nodded Iris. "But I can't think. My brain's too sticky."

The professor, who was just leaving the compartment, caught the drift of Hare's argument, for he turned back to speak to Iris.

"If you can produce some definite proof of this lady's existence, I'm still open to conviction. But I sincerely hope that you will not expose us and yourself to further ridicule."

Iris felt too limp for defiance.

"Thank you," she said meekly. "Where shall I find you?"

"In the reserved portion."

"We're sharing a bunny-hutch," supplemented Hare. "Didn't you know we're rich? We started a prosperity chain."

"I hate that man," burst out Iris when the professor had gone.

"Oh, no," protested Hare, "he's not a bad old fossil. You've got him scared stiff because you're young and attractive."

Then the grin faded from his lips.

"I want to bore you with a true story," he said. "Some years ago, I was playing in an international at Twickenham. Just before the match both teams were presented to the Prince of Wales and he shook hands with all of us. Well, after I'd scored the winning try—I had to slip that in—I got kicked on the head in a scrum and passed out. Later on, when I was fairly comfortable in a private ward at the hospital, the nurse came in, all of a flutter, and said there was a special visitor to see me."

"The Prince?" asked Iris, trying to force an intelligent interest.

"The same. Of course, he didn't stay more than a minute. Just smiled at me and said he hoped I'd soon be all right and he was sorry about my accident. I was so steamed up I thought I wouldn't sleep a wink, but I dropped off the instant he had gone. Next morning the nurses said, 'Weren't you pleased to see your captain?' "

"Captain?"

"Yes, the captain of the team. It was definitely not the Prince. . . . And yet I saw him as plainly as I see you. He shook hands with me and said something nice about my try. He was *real*. And that's what a spot of head trouble can do to the best of us."

Iris set her lips obstinately.

"I thought you believed in me," she said. "But you're like the rest. Please go away."

"I will, because I'm sure you ought to keep quiet. Try and get some sleep."

"No. I've got to think this out. If I let myself believe all of you, I should be afraid I was getting mental. And I'm not. I'm *not.*"

"Now take it easy."

"What a soothing nurse you'd make. You only want a silly cap. Listen." Iris dropped her voice. "I'm extra in the dark, because I couldn't understand these questions. Do you really know the language?"

"Better than English now. And it was so elementary that even the professor couldn't slip up. Sorry—but there are no holes anywhere. . . . But you look all in. Let me get you a life-saver."

"No. Miss Froy promised she'd get me something and I prefer to wait for her."

Her defiant eyes told Hare that she was nailing her colours to the mast. Since he regarded Miss Froy as a kind of ghost, he did not think that Iris would derive benefit from anything she might bring, so he resolved to renew his offer later. Meanwhile he could serve her best by leaving her alone.

Just as he was going he remembered something and beckoned Iris into the corridor.

"There was just one bit I didn't tumble to," he confessed. "The baroness spoke to the ticket chap in a dialect which was Chinese to me."

"Then that proves they came from the same district," cried Iris triumphantly.

"Hum. But as we don't know what she said it's not too helpful. Salaams. See you later."

After Hare had gone Iris crouched in her corner, rocking with the vibration of the train. It was clattering through a succession of short tunnels and the air was full of sound, as though a giant roller were flattening out the sky. The noise worried her acutely. She had scarcely eaten all day and was beginning to feel exhausted. But although she was unused to being ill, and was consequently frightened, she was far more alarmed by the jangling of her brain.

She started violently when a nursing-sister appeared in the doorway and beckoned to the doctor. She hardly noticed the relief of his absence, because her thoughts raced in a confused circle round the central incident of the black-out.

"I was on the platform, one second—and the next second I went out. Where did I go? Was the waking up in the waiting-room, and all those women, and the funny little old porter—*real?* Of course they were, or I should not be on the train. . . .

"But I met Miss Froy *afterwards.* They say she's only my dream. So, if she's a dream, it means that I've dreamed the waiting-room and the train and that I'm not on the train at all. I'm not awake yet. . . . If it was true, it would be enough to drive any one mad."

She resolutely fought back the rising tide of hysteria.

"But it's absurd. I am awake and I'm here in this train. *So I did* meet Miss Froy. . . . Only I'm up against some mystery and I have to fight a pack of lies. All right, then, *I will.* "

At this stage her concern was for herself, rather than for Miss Froy. She had been spoiled since her birth, so it was natural for her to be selfish; and because that self was a gay and charming entity, the world had united to keep her fixed at her special angle.

But now her ego was getting involved with the fate of an obscure and unattractive spinster. Once again she began to review the incidents of their meeting. And then, suddenly, her clouded brain cleared and a sealed cell in her memory became unblocked.

The baroness looked at her as she sprang from her seat.

"Is madame worse?" she asked.

"Better, thanks," replied Iris. "And I'm going to test some English memories, just for a change. I'm going to talk to some English visitors from my hotel who saw me with Miss Froy."

CHAPTER FOURTEEN
FRESH EVIDENCE

Now that she was about to establish Miss Froy's existence, Iris began to wonder what had become of her. When she remembered her exhaustive search of the train it seemed positive that she could not be there. But it was also impossible for her to be anywhere else.

The corridors and carriages were thronged with tourists, so that she could not open a door or window to jump out, without attracting immediate attention. It was equally certain that no one could make a parcel of her and dump her on the permanent way, without becoming an object of general interest.

There was no place for her to hide—nor could Iris conceive any motive for such a course. In short, she was protected from any form of injury—accidental or intentional—by the presence of a cloud of witnesses.

In despair Iris shelved the problem.

"She can't be proved missing until it's proved that she was there in the first place," she argued. "That's my job. After that, the others must carry on."

As she remembered the professor's standard for reliable evidence she felt she could understand a showman's pride in his exhibits. Her witnesses must satisfy the most exacting taste—being British to the core.

The baroness looked at her when she opened her bag and drew out her pocket-mirror and lipstick. Although her detachment was complete and her face void of expression, she somehow conveyed an impression of secret activity, as though she were spinning mental threads.

"She's pitting her brain against mine," thought Iris, in a sudden flurry. "I must get in first."

Directly she began to hurry she went to pieces again. Her hands shook so that she painted her mouth with a streak of vivid red—more suggestive of crushed fruit than the crimson blossom after which the tint was named. Unable to find her comb she gave up the attempt and dashed out into the corridor.

Men stared at her and women muttered complaints as she pushed them aside without apology. As a matter of fact she was hardly conscious of them, except as so many obstacles in her way. After so much delay, every wasted moment was a personal reproach. In her excitement she could only see—a long way off—the blurred figure of a little spinster.

She must hurry to reach it. But faces kept coming in between her and her goal—faces that grinned or scowled—the faces of strangers. They melted away like a mist, only to give place to other faces. There was a flash of eyes and teeth—a jam of bodies. She thrust and struggled, while her cheeks burned and a wave of hair fell across her cheeks.

When at last she won through to the clearer stretch of corridor, the sight of the professor—smoking, while he looked through the window—reminded her of the conventions. She felt ashamed of her haste and she spoke breathlessly.

"Do I look like a jigsaw? It was that devastating crowd. They wouldn't let me through."

The professor did not smile, for in spite of a picturesque attraction, her wild hair and brilliant colour produced a wanton effect which did not appeal to him. Neither did Mr. Todhunter approve her, as he criticised her through the open door of his coupé.

Although he claimed to be a judge of feminine charm, he was of the type that prefers a lily-pond to a waterfall. He never lingered before an unframed picture, for he exacted the correct setting for beauty. Abandon was only permissible in a negligée and definitely bad form on a train journey. Although he had often seen Iris, when she looked like a member of an undress beauty chorus, he had never noticed her until the evening when she wore a becoming frock.

"Who's the girl?" asked the bride as she flicked over the pages of a pictorial paper.

He lowered his voice.

"One of the mob from the hotel."

"Help."

In the next coupé Miss Rose Flood-Porter raised her head from the soft leather cushion without which she never travelled. Her movement roused her sister from her doze, and she, too, strained to listen.

Unconscious of her audience Iris spoke to the professor in a high excited voice.

"Your marvellous witnesses have let you down. They were all telling lies. The six of them."

He looked at her burning cheeks with cold concern.

"Is your head worse?" he asked.

"Thanks, I'm perfectly fit. . . . And I can prove Miss Froy was with me, because the English visitors from my hotel saw her, too. We'll get in touch with the English Consul when we reach Trieste and he'll hold up the train for a thorough examination. Oh, you'll see."

Iris thrilled at the prospect of her triumph. At that moment she seemed to see the Union Jack fluttering overhead and hear the strains of the National Anthem.

The professor smiled with dreary patience.

"I'm waiting to be convinced," he reminded her.

"Then you shall be." Iris swung round to find herself facing Mr. Todhunter. "You'll help me find Miss Froy, won't you?" she asked confidently.

He smiled down indulgently at her but he did not reply at once. It was the pause of deliberation and was characteristic of his profession.

"I shall be delighted to co-operate with you," he told her. "But— who is Miss Froy?"

"An English governess who is missing from the train. You must remember her. She peeped in at your window and you jumped up and drew down the blind."

"That is exactly what I should have done in the circumstances. Only, in this case, the special circumstances did not arise. No lady did me the honour to linger by my window."

His words were so unexpected that Iris caught her breath, as though she were falling through space.

"Didn't you *see* her?" she gasped.

"No."

"But your wife called your attention to her. You were both annoyed."

The beautiful Mrs. Todhunter, who had been listening, broke in with none of her habitual languor.

"We are not a peep-show and no one looked in. . . . Do you mind if we shut the door? I want to rest before dinner."

The professor turned to Iris with forced kindness.

"You're tired," he said. "Let me take you back to your carriage."

"No." Iris shook off his hand. "I won't let the matter rest. There are others. These ladies — "

Dashing into the next coupé where the Misses Flood-Porter now sat upright in dignity, she appealed to them.

"You'll help me find Miss Froy, won't you? She's *English.*"

"May I explain?" interposed the professor as the ladies looked to him for enlightenment.

Iris could hardly control her impatience as she listened to the cultured drawl. Her eyes were fixed on the solid fresh faces of the sisters. Then Miss Rose spoke.

"I have no recollection of your companion. Some one may have been with you, but I was not wearing my glasses."

"Neither was I," remarked Miss Flood-Porter. "So you can understand that we shall not be able to help you. It would be against our principles to identify some one of whom we were not sure."

"Most unfair," commented Miss Rose. "So, please, don't refer to us. If you do, we must refuse to interfere."

Iris could hardly believe her ears.

"But isn't it against your principles not to raise a finger to help an Englishwoman who may be in danger?" she asked hotly.

"Danger?" echoed Miss Rose derisively. "What could happen to her on a crowded train? Besides, there are plenty of other people who are probably more observant than ourselves. After all, there is no reason why we should be penalised because we are English."

Iris was too bewildered by the unexpected collapse of her hopes, to speak. She felt she had been betrayed by her compatriots. They might boast of wearing evening dress for the honour of their country, but they had let down England. The Union Jack lay shredded in tatters and the triumphant strains of the National Anthem died down to the screech of a tin whistle.

She hated them all so fiercely that when the vicar's wife put her head round the door she could only glare at her.

Mrs. Barnes gave a general smile as she explained her presence.

"My husband is sleeping now, so I thought I'd run in for a chat. When we travel, I'm first in command, which is a new experience for me and only comes once a year."

She spoke eagerly as though to justify her husband's weakness. Then she turned to Iris, who was following the professor from the coupé.

"Don't let me drive you away."

"Nothing could keep me." Iris spoke with bitter hopelessness. "Of course, you didn't see Miss Froy?"

"Was that the little lady in tweed, with a blue feather in her hat?" asked Mrs. Barnes. "Why, *of course,* I remember her, and her kindness. We were so grateful for the tea."

CHAPTER FIFTEEN

TRANSFORMATION SCENE

H er relief was so overwhelming that Iris felt on the verge of tears as she turned to the professor.

"Are you convinced now?" she asked shakily.

The professor glanced at the vicar's wife with almost an apologetic air, for the lady was a familiar type which he admired and approved, when it was safely married to some one else.

"The question is unnecessary," he said. "It was simply a matter of getting corroborative evidence. I'm sorry to have doubted your word in the first place. It was due to the unfortunate circumstances of your sunstroke."

"Well, what are you going to do?" insisted Iris.

Having made one blunder, the professor was not inclined to be precipitate.

"I think I had better consult Hare," he said. "He is an expert linguist and has quite a fair brain, although he may appear irresponsible at times."

"Let's find him at once," urged Iris.

In spite of her haste she stopped to speak impulsively to the vicar's wife.

"Thank you so very much. You don't know what this means to me."

"I'm glad—but why are you thanking me?" asked Mrs. Barnes, in surprise.

Leaving Miss Rose to explain Iris followed the professor. Hare was frankly incredulous when they ran him to earth in the restaurant car.

"Bless my soul," he explained, "Miss Froy popping up again?

There's something about that good woman that keeps me guessing. I don't mind admitting that I never really believed in the old dear. But what's happened to her?"

The professor took off his glasses to polish them. Without them his eyes appeared weak, rather than cold, while the painful red ridges on either side of his nose aroused Iris' compassion. She felt quite friendly towards him, now that they were united in a common cause—the restitution of Miss Froy.

"The Misses Flood-Porter didn't want to be drawn in," she declared. "That was clear. But why did those six foreigners all tell lies about her?"

"It must be some misunderstanding," said the professor nervously. "Perhaps I——"

"No, you didn't," cut in Hare. "You were a clinking interpreter, professor. You didn't slip up on a thing."

Iris liked him for the ready good nature which prompted him to reassure the professor because she was sure that he considered him privately a pompous bore.

"We'll have to play the good old game of 'Spot the lady,' " went on Hare. "My own idea is, she's disguised as the doctor. That black beard is so obvious that she's making it too easy.... Or she may be pulling the train, dressed up as a ladylike engine. I'd put nothing past Miss Froy."

Iris did not laugh.

"You're not amusing," she said, "because you seem to forget that, besides being a real person, she is still missing. We must *do* something."

"Admittedly," agreed the professor. "But it's a perplexing problem, and I do not care to act without careful consideration."

"He means he wants to smoke," explained Hare. "All right, professor. I'll take care of Miss Carr, while you squeeze out some brain-juice."

He grinned across the ash-dusted table at Iris, when the professor had gone.

"Have I got it right?" he asked. "Is this Miss Froy a complete stranger to you?"

"Of course."

"Yet you're nearly going crackers over her. You must be the most unselfish person alive. Really, it's almost unnatural."

"But I'm not," admitted Iris truthfully. "It's rather the other way round. That's the amusing part. I can't understand myself a bit."

"Well, how did it start?"

"In the usual way. She was very kind to me—helpful, and all that, so that at first, I missed her because she wasn't at the back of me any more. And then, when every one declared I dreamed her, it all turned to a horrible nightmare. It was like trying to explain that every one was out of step but myself."

"Hopeless. But why had you to prove that she was there?"

"Oh, can't you understand? If I didn't, I could never feel that anything, or any one, was *real* again?"

"I shouldn't fly off the handle," remarked Hare stolidly. "I should know it was a post-symptom of brain injury, and therefore perfectly logical."

"But you can't compare your own experience with mine," protested Iris. "You saw a real person and mistook him for the Prince. But I was supposed to have talked to the thin air, while the thin air answered back. . . . I can't tell you what a *relief* it was when Mrs. Barnes remembered her."

She smiled with happiness as she looked out of the window. Now that she was safely anchored to a rational world again, after spinning amid mists of fantasy, the gloomy surroundings had no power to depress her. The afternoon had drawn in early, so that the period of twilight was protracted and it added the final touch of melancholy to the small town through which the express was slowly steaming.

Whenever they crossed a street, Iris could see mean shops, with pitifully shrunken wares—cobbled roads—and glimpses of a soupy swollen river through the gaps between the buildings. The houses—clinging to the rocky hillside, like tufts of lichen on a roof—seemed semi-obliterated by time and weather. Long ago, wood and plaster had been painted grey, but the rain had washed and the sun had peeled some of the walls to a dirty white. Every aspect betrayed poverty and desolation.

"What a horrible place," shuddered Iris, as they passed tall rusty iron gates which enclosed a dock-grown garden. "I wonder who can live here, besides suicides."

"Miss Froy," suggested Hare.

He expected an outburst, but Iris was not listening to him.

"When do we reach Trieste?" she asked.

"Twenty-two-ten."

"And it's five to six now. We mustn't waste any more time. *We must* find her. . . . It sounds exactly like some sloppy picture, but her people are expecting her home. They're old and rather pathetic. And the fool of a dog meets every train."

She stopped—aghast at the sound of her choked voice. To her surprise she found that she was actually affected by the thought of the parents' suspense. As emotion was treason to the tradition of the crowd, she felt ashamed of her weakness.

"I'll have that drink, after all," she declared, blinking the moisture from her eyes. "I feel all mushy—and that's absurd. Old people aren't nearly as pathetic as young ones. They're nearly through—and we've got it all to come."

"You do want a drink," agreed Hare. "I'll dig out a waiter."

As he was rising Iris pulled him back.

"Don't go now," she whispered. "There's that horrible doctor."

The spade-bearded gentleman seemed to be searching for some one; and directly his glasses flashed over the young couple his quest was finished. He crossed directly to their table and bowed to Iris.

"Your friend has returned to the carriage," he said.

"Miss Froy?" Iris forgot her repulsion in her excitement. "How marvellous. Where was she?"

He spread his hands and shrugged.

"All the time she was so near. In the next carriage, talking with my nurses."

"Yes," declared Iris, laughing, "that's just where she would be. The first place I ought to have looked in, and didn't."

"Hum." Hare rubbed his chin doubtfully. "It's all very rum. Sure it's the right one?"

"She is the lady who accompanied madame to the restaurant-car," replied the doctor. "A little short lady—not young, but not very old, with a blue feather in her hat."

"That's Miss Froy," cried Iris.

"But why was there all the mystery?" persisted Hare. "No one knowing a thing about her—and all that."

"Ah, that was because we did not understand madame."

The doctor shrugged deprecatingly. "She talked so fast and she talked of an English lady. Now the lady is German, may be, or Austrian—I do not know—but she is not English."

Iris nodded to Hare.

"I made the same mistake, myself, at first," she told him. "She looks anything and she speaks every language. Come on and you shall check up on her."

The journey along the train was growing so familiar that Iris felt she could make it blindfolded. As she passed by the Barnes' compartment she peeped inside. The vicar looked grimly heroic, with folded arms and knotted brow, while his wife showed visible signs of strain. Her eyes were sunken in black circles, but she smiled bravely at Iris.

"Still looking for your friend?" she asked.

"No," called Iris. "She's found."

"Oh, thank God."

"I didn't like that holy woman," Iris confided to Hare as they struggled on again, "but her stock has simply soared with me. She's really kind."

When they reached the reserved coupés, Iris insisted on collecting the professor, to whom she told her news.

"I want you to come, too, and meet my Miss Froy," she said. "She'll be thrilled when she hears of the sensation she's made."

"A desire to attract attention seems a feminine characteristic," observed the professor acidly.

Iris only laughed with excitement as her heart gave a sudden bound.

"There she is," she cried. "There she is, at the end of the corridor."

Once again she was overwhelmed by the derided human element as she saw the familiar flat figure in the light tweed suit.

"Miss Froy," she cried huskily.

The lady turned so that Iris saw her face. At the sight she recoiled with a cry of horror.

"That's not Miss Froy," she said.

CHAPTER SIXTEEN
THE STAR WITNESS

As Iris stared at the face of a stranger, she was plunged back into the inky darkness of the tunnel. She believed that she had emerged into the daylight and her heart was still singing for the joy of deliverance. But she had been deceived by a ray of sunshine striking through a shaft in the roof.

The horror persisted. Blackness was behind her and before—deadening her faculties and confusing her senses. She felt that she was trapped in a nightmare which would go on for ever, unless she could struggle free.

Miss Froy. She must hold on to Miss Froy. At that moment she suddenly remembered her elusive face distinctly in its strange mixture of maturity and arrested youth, with blue saucer eyes and small features all scratched and faded faintly by time.

An impostor stood before her, wearing Miss Froy's oatmeal tweed suit. The face under the familiar hat was sallow—the black eyes expressionless. It looked wooden, as though it could not weep, and had never smiled.

Breaking out of her nightmare, Iris challenged her.

"You are not Miss Froy."

"No," replied the woman in English, "I have not heard that name ever before. I am Frau Kummer, as I told you, when we had our tea together."

"That's a lie. I never had tea with you. You're a complete stranger to me."

"A stranger, certainly, such as one meets on a journey. But we talked together. Only a little because your poor head ached."

"Ah!"

The significance of the doctor's exclamation was deliberately stressed. It made Iris quiver with apprehension, even while it put her on her guard.

"I mustn't let them get me down," she thought. Then she turned desperately to the professor.

"This is not Miss Froy," she said vehemently.

"The lady has told us that herself," remarked the professor impatiently. "In fact, with the exception of yourself, no one appears to have heard the somewhat uncommon name of 'Froy.' "

It was obvious that he believed that Miss Froy lived at the sign of The Unicorn, in the congenial company of Mrs. Harris and the Spanish prisoner.

"But she's wearing her clothes," persisted Iris, trying to keep her voice from quivering. "Why? *Why?* What's become of Miss Froy? It's some conspiracy—and I'm afraid. . . . She says we had tea together, but we didn't. The waiter knows. Send for him."

To her dismay Hare did not bound off on his mission like a Hermes in nailed boots. Instead, he twisted his lip and looked sheepish.

"Why not call it a day and get some rest?" he suggested in the soothing tone which infuriated Iris.

No one believed her—and the combined force of their incredulity made her doubt herself. The darkness seemed to be closing round her again when she remembered her supporting witness—the vicar's wife.

"Mrs. Barnes," she said faintly.

"I'll fetch her," offered the professor, who was anxious to put an end to the scene.

Although he was kind-hearted and eminently just—when he knew his bearings—he was prejudiced against Iris, because of an unfortunate incident which marred the close of his last term. One of his most brilliant pupils—a plain, sedate young person, about whose progress he had been almost enthusiastic—had suddenly gone back on him and involved him in a very unpleasant emotional scene.

When she came to his study to wish him good-bye, she had broken down completely, assuring him that she had worked solely to please him, and that she could not face the thought of their parting.

As he had insisted on keeping the door open, from motives of prudence, a version of the affair had been put into circulation, to his intense annoyance. Therefore he cursed his luck in being involved with another hysterical girl, as he passed the coupé occupied by the Misses Flood-Porter.

Through the glass he could see Mrs. Barnes, who had returned to finish her interrupted chat, so he entered.

"More trouble for you, I'm afraid," he warned her. "That very emotional young lady now wants you to identify some one. I wonder if you would mind coming with me to her compartment?"

"Certainly," said Edna Barnes. "Is it the kind little lady in parchment tweed, speckled with brown and a blue feather in her hat?"

"Presumably. I seem to recollect the feather." The professor looked down at her strained brown eyes and added kindly. "You look very pale. Not ill, I hope?"

"Oh, no." Mrs. Barnes' voice was extra cheerful. "It's my husband who is ill. But I'm bearing his pain for him, so that he can sleep."

"Absent treatment?"

"Something of the kind, perhaps. When you're married—if there is a real bond—you share more than an income."

"Well, I call it silly," broke in Miss Rose. "He's far stronger than you are."

The professor, however, looked at her sweet face with additional respect.

"I don't like to worry you with this matter," he said. "In my opinion, the girl is hysterical and wants to be in the limelight. She says now that the lady is not the original one, who, according to her—is still missing."

"We'll hope she is the right one, for your sake," remarked Miss Flood-Porter placidly. "If not, she'll keep you hanging about at Trieste, and you'll miss your connection to Milan."

Mrs. Barnes pressed her hand over her eyes.

"Oh, I hope not," she cried. "My husband wants to get this wretched journey over. Still, one has to do one's duty—whatever the cost."

"But it's so futile," declared Miss Rose. "From your description, this missing governess is no chicken and an experienced traveller. She's either lying low and has given the girl the slip for some good reason of her own, or else it's all moonshine."

"Indubitably the latter," remarked the professor, as he accompanied Mrs. Barnes out into the corridor.

Here they met the vicar who had come in search of his wife.

"This *is* my husband," cried Mrs. Barnes, her face lighting up. "Did you think I'd deserted you, Ken?"

While they lingered to chat, Iris sat awaiting the return of Hare with the waiter. She had no real hope of the issue, since she had begun to regard all the officials as being tools of the baroness. A mysterious power was operating on a wholesale scale, to her own confusion. In proof of this, opposite to her was the horrible changeling who wore Miss Froy's clothing. Yet the incident was inexplicable, since she could find no motive for such a clumsy subterfuge.

Every detail of the woman's figure corresponded so exactly with her recollection of Miss Froy, as she stared at the familiar blue bone buttons, that the first real doubt began to sap her confidence. She asked herself whether she were, in reality, the victim of some hallucination. Hare's story about the prince proved that it was no uncommon experience.

She was feeling so limp that it seemed almost the easiest way out of her troubles. After all, she would have her work cut out to fight the constant threat of overhanging illness, without the additional worry of a problematical Miss Froy.

"I shall soon know," she thought, as Hare returned with a waiter in tow.

"You said the chap with the fair hair," he said to Iris. "I've bagged the only blond in the whole collection. By the way, he is proud of speaking English."

Iris remembered the youth directly she saw the straw-coloured plastered hair and slanting forehead. He wore glasses, and looked more like a student or clerk.

"Do you really understand English?" she asked.

"Certainly, madame," he replied eagerly. "I have my certificates, both for grammar and the conversational test."

"Well, do you remember waiting on me at tea? Have you a reliable memory for faces?"

"Yes, madame."

"Then I want you to look at this lady—" Iris pointed to Kummer and added, "Don't look at her clothes, but look at her face. Now tell me—is that the lady who was having tea with me?"

The waiter hesitated slightly, while his pale eyes grew momentarily blank. Then he nodded with decision.

"Yes, madame."

"You're *sure?*"

"Yes, madame, I am positive sure."

As Iris made no comment, Hare tipped the youth and sent him away. Although the interview had corresponded with his own forecast, he felt acutely uncomfortable. He glanced uneasily at the baroness and the doctor, but their faces only registered enforced patience, as they waited for the end of the infliction.

Suddenly a muffled cry rang out from the next carriage. Instantly, the doctor sprang up from his seat and hurried back to his patient.

The sound was so unhuman and inarticulate, with its dulled yet frantic reiteration of "M-m-m-m," that Iris was reminded of some maimed animal, protesting against suffering it could not understand. She had forgotten about the poor broken body—trussed and helpless in the next carriage—lying in complete dependence on two callous women.

The recollection caused all her latent distrust of the doctor to flare up again. She asked herself what awaited the patient at her journey's end? Did she guess that she was being hurried to some operation—doomed to failure, yet recommended solely as an experiment, to satisfy scientific curiosity?

Iris had still sufficient sense to know that she was indulging in neurotic and morbid speculation, so she hurriedly smashed up the sequence of her thoughts. As a characteristic voice told her of the approach of the professor, she tilted her chin defiantly.

"Mrs. Barnes remembered Miss Froy when all the rest pretended to forget her," she said to Hare. "I know she couldn't tell a lie. So I don't care two hoots for all the rest. I'm banking on *her.*"

Edna Barnes advanced, her arm linked within that of her husband, as though for support. As a matter of fact, he was really leaning on her, for the shaking of the train made him feel rather giddy. Although still resolute, his face showed something of the strain of a knight approaching the end of his vigil.

"I understand you want us to identify a friend of yours," he said to Iris, taking command of the situation as a matter of course.

Then he looked down at his wife.

"Edna, my dear," he asked, "is this the lady?"

Unlike the waiter, Mrs. Barnes did not hesitate. Her recognition was instantaneous.

"Yes," she said.

The vicar came forward with outstretched hand.

"I am glad of this opportunity to thank you for your kindness," he said.

Miss Kummer stolidly accepted the tribute paid to Miss Froy. Or—was she really Miss Froy? Iris felt a frantic beating, as though of wings inside her head, as she slipped down into a roaring darkness.

CHAPTER SEVENTEEN
THERE WAS NO MISS FROY

The immediate effect of Iris' faint was to steady her nerves. When she recovered consciousness, to find someone forcing her head down below the level of her knees, she felt thoroughly ashamed of her weakness. There was not a trace of hysteria in her voice as she apologised.

"Sorry to be such a crashing bore. I'm quite all right now."

"Don't you think you had better lie down?" asked Mr. Barnes. "I'm sure the Miss Flood-Porters would be only too glad to lend you their reserved compartment."

Iris was by no means so sure that the ladies measured up to the vicar's own standard of charity; yet she felt a great need of some quiet place, where she could straighten out the tangle in her brain.

"I want to talk to you," she said to Hare, leaving him to do the rest.

As she anticipated, he jumped at the opportunity.

"Sorry to eject you, professor," he said, "but our bunny-hutch is booked for the next half-hour."

"Delighted," murmured the professor grimly.

After swallowing some brandy from the vicar's flask, Iris staggered up from her seat. Her knees felt shaky and her temples were still cold; but the brief period of unconsciousness had relieved the pressure on her heart, so that she was actually better.

As she and Hare—linked together, to the general inconvenience—lurched down the corridor, she noticed that the lights were now turned on. This arbitrary change from day to night, seemed to mark a distinct stage in the journey. Time was speeding up with the train. The rushing landscape was dark as a blurred charcoal-drawing, while a sprinkle of lights showed that they had reached a civilised zone, of which the wretched little town was the first outpost.

Now that the outside world was shut out, the express seemed hotter and smokier. At first the confined space of the coupé affected Iris with a sense of claustrophobia.

"Open the window wide," she gasped.

"There's plenty of air coming in through the top," grumbled Hare, as he obeyed. "You'll be so smothered in smuts that your own mother wouldn't know you."

"I haven't one," said Iris, suddenly feeling very sorry for herself. "But I'm not here to be pathetic. There's something too real and serious at stake. . . . I want to remind you of something you said this morning at the railway station. You were having an argument with the professor, and I overheard it. You said trial by jury was unfair, because it depended on the evidence of witnesses."

"I did," said Hare. "And I stick to every word."

"And then," went on Iris, "the professor talked about reliable evidence, and he compared two women. One was English and country—the sort that collect fir-cones and things when she goes for a walk. The other had bought her eyelashes and was dark."

"I remember *her*. Pretty woman, like a juicy black cherry."

"But the professor damned her. . . . And that's exactly what has happened now. I'm damned as a tainted witness, while he is prejudiced in favour of all those British matrons and Sunday school teachers."

"That's only because they're plain Janes, while you've quite a different face—and thank heaven for it."

Hare's attempt to soothe Iris was a failure, for she flared up.

"I hate my face. It's silly and it means nothing. Besides, why should I be judged on face value if it goes against me? It's not fair. You said it wasn't fair. You told the professor it would lead to a bloody mix-up. . . . You can't blow hot and cold. Unless you're a weather-cock, you've simply got to stand by me."

"All right, I'll stand by. What do you want me to do?"

Iris laid her hot palms on the sticky old-gold plush seat and leaned forward, so that her eyes looked into his.

"I say there *is* a Miss Froy," she told him. "You've got to believe me. But my head feels like a three-ring circus, and I've grown confused. Will you go over it with me, so that I can get it clear?"

"I'd like to hear your version," Hare told her.

He smoked thoughtfully as she went over the story of her meeting with the alleged Miss Froy, up to the time of her disappearance.

"Well, you've got one definite fact," he told her. "What the—the lady told you about the big boss is right. I can make an accurate guess as to her employer. At this moment a certain noble Johnny is in the local limelight over charges of bribery, tampering with contracts, and funny little things like that. The latest is he's accused of bumping off the editor of the revolutionary rag which brought the charges."

He picked up a flimsy yellow sheet of badly printed newspaper.

"It's in the stop press," he explained, "but as he was at his hunting-lodge at the time, the final sensation's squashed. However, nobody will bother. It's quite true about the feudal system being in force in these remote districts."

"But it proves me right," cried Iris in great excitement. "How could I know all about her employer, unless Miss Froy told me? And there's something else. When I told Miss Froy about my sunstroke the baroness was listening. She couldn't know about it in any other way. So Miss Froy was there in the carriage with me."

She looked so radiant that Hare hated to crush her confidence.

"I'm afraid," he said, "that it only proves that Miss Kummer was there. She told you about her employer, and perhaps a spot of family history when you were having tea with her. Later on, you mentioned your sunstroke to her. . . . If you remember, when you came on the train, directly after your sunstroke, you were under the impression that all the other passengers were foreigners. Then you dozed and woke up all confused, and suddenly, Miss Froy, an Englishwoman, comes to life."

"But she had blue eyes and giggled like a schoolgirl," protested Iris. "Besides, there were her old parents and the dog. I couldn't have made them up."

"Why not? Don't you ever dream?"

Dejectedly, Iris conceded the point.

"I suppose so. Yes, you must be right."

"I must remind you," continued Hare, "that Kummer was positively identified by the parson as the lady who sent them their tea. Now, I'm the last person to be biased, because all my uncles and fathers are parsons, and I've met them at breakfast—but the church does imply a definite standard. We insist on parsons having a higher moral code than our own and we try them pretty hard; but you must admit they don't often let us down."

"No," murmured Iris.

"Besides that parson has such a clinking face. Like God's good man."

"But he never saw Miss Froy," Iris reminded him. "He was speaking for his wife."

Hare burst out laughing.

"You have me there," he said. "Well, that shows how we can slip up. He took the stage so naturally, that he got us all thinking he was the witness."

"If you're wrong over one thing, you can be wrong over another," suggested Iris hopefully.

"True. Let's go into it again. You suggest that the baroness got rid of Miss Froy—never mind how—and that the other passengers, being local people and in awe of the family, would back her up. So far, you are right. They would."

"Only it seems such a clumsy plot," said Iris. "Dressing up some one quite different and passing her off as Miss Froy."

"But that bit was an eleventh hour twist," explained Hare. "Remember, you upset their apple-cart, barging in at the last minute. When you made a fuss about Miss Froy, they denied her existence, at first. You were just a despised foreigner, so they thought they could get away with it. But when you said that other English people had seen her, they had to produce some one—and trust to luck that your friends had never heard of Pelman."

He was talking of Miss Froy as though he took her existence for granted. It was such a novelty, that, in her relief, Iris' thoughts slipped off in another direction.

"Can't you get that bit of hair to lie down?" she asked.

"No," he replied, "neither by kindness nor threats. It's my secret sorrow. Thank you. That's the first bit of interest you've shown in me."

"Miss Froy is bringing us together, isn't she? You see, you believe in her too."

"Well, I wouldn't go quite so far. But I promised to believe in you—false lashes and all—against the Flood-Porter Burberry. In that case, we must accept a plot, inspired by the all-highest, and carried out by his relative, the baroness—in connection with the doctor, to bump off Miss Froy. . . . So, naturally, that wipes out all the native evidence—train-staff and all."

"You are really rather marvellous," Iris told him.

"Wait before you hand out bouquets. We pass on to that English crowd. The Misses Flood-Porter seem typical John Bulls. What are they like?"

"They've been to the right school and know the best people."

"Are they decent?"

"Yes."

"Then they'd do the decent thing. I'm afraid that is one up against Miss Froy. . . . Now we'll pass the honeymoon couple—who are presumably not normal—and come to the vicar's wife. What about her?"

"I don't know."

"Remember, you're on oath, and I'm believing you."

"Well,"—Iris hesitated—"I don't think she could tell a lie."

"And I'm positive she wouldn't. I mix with publicans and sinners and know very little about saints. But, to me, she looks like a real good woman. Besides, she supported you the first time. That shows she has no axe to grind. She said Miss Kummer was the lady who accompanied you to tea. Don't you think we must believe her?"

"I suppose so. . . . Yes."

"Well, then, the weight of evidence is against Miss Froy. But since I've declared my distrust of evidence—however convincing it may sound—I'm going to wash out the lot. To my mind, the whole point is—motive."

Iris saw Miss Froy fading away as Hare went on with his inquisition.

"I understand Miss Froy was quite small beer. Would she be mixed up in any plot?"

"No," replied Iris. "She was against the Red element."

"And neither young nor pretty? So she wasn't kidnapped by the order of the high hat?"

"Don't be absurd."

"Any enemies?"

"No, she boasted of being friends with every one."

"Hum. It's hardly a motive for murder, but was the family annoyed because she was going to teach in the opposition camp?"

"No. She told me how her employer shook hands with her when he said 'Good-bye,' and thanked her for her services."

"Well—is it clear to you now? Unless you can show me a real motive for a high life conspiracy against a poor but honest governess, I'm afraid there's an end of Miss Froy. Do you agree?"

There was a long pause while Iris tried to battle against the current that was sweeping Miss Froy away. She told herself that so many people, with diverse interests, could not combine to lie. Besides, as Hare had said, what was the motive?

It was useless to struggle any longer and she let herself be swung out with the tide.

"You must be right," she said. "One can't go against *facts*. . . . Yet, she was so real. And her old parents and the dog were real, too."

She had the feeling that she had just slain something fresh and joyous—that fluttered and fought for life—as she added, "You've won. There is no Miss Froy."

CHAPTER EIGHTEEN
THE SURPRISE

M rs. Froy would have been furious had she known that any one doubted her reality.

While Iris was sighing for the passing of a pleasant ghost, she was at home in the depths of the country, and entertaining friends in her drawing-room.

It was a small room with diamond-paned windows—hung with creepers—which made it rather dark; but in spite of the shabby carpet, it was a gracious place, where odd period chairs fraternised with homely wickerwork, and a beautiful red lacquer cabinet lent the colour which the faded chintz could not supply.

Pots of fine golden chrysanthemums, grown by Mr. Froy, screened the empty iron grate. The guests might have preferred a fire, for there was that slight chill—often associated with old country houses—suggestive of stone flags. Yet the sun could be seen, through the curtain of greenery, shining on the flower-beds outside; for, although the electric lamps were gleaming in the express, the daylight still lingered farther north.

Mrs. Froy was short and stout, with grey hair and great dignity. In addition to having a dominant personality, to-day she felt extra full of vitality. It was born of her excitement at the thought that her daughter was actually on her way home.

The postcard was on the marble mantelshelf, propped up against the massive presentation clock. On its back was printed a crudely coloured picture of mountains, with grass-green bases and white tops, posed against a brilliant blue sky. Scribbled across the heavens, in a round unformed handwriting, was the message.

"Home Friday night. Isn't it topping?"

Mrs. Froy showed it to her guests.

"Everything is 'topping' to my daughter," she explained with proud indulgence. "I'm afraid at one time it used to be 'ripping.' "

A visitor looked at the string of consonants printed at the base of the picture—shied at them—and compromised.

"Is she *there?*" she asked, pointing to the line.

"Yes." Mrs. Froy reeled off the name rapidly and aggressively. She did it to impress, for it was only the home-interpretation of Winnie's address. But, on her return, their daughter would give them the correct pronunciation, and put them through their paces while they tried to imitate her own ferocious gargling.

Then the room would know more of the laughter on which it had thriven and grown gracious.

"My daughter is a great traveller," went on Mrs. Froy. "Here is her latest photograph. Taken at Budapest."

The portrait was not very revealing since it was expensive. It hinted at the lower half of a small vague face, and a hat which photographed very well.

"She looks quite cosmopolitan with her eyes covered by her hat," remarked Mrs. Froy. "Now, this is the Russian one. . . . This one was taken at Madrid, on her birthday. . . . Here she is in Athens."

The collection was chiefly a geographical trophy, for while Mrs. Froy was proud of the printing on the mounts, she secretly resented the middle-aged stranger, who—according to her—was not in the least like her daughter.

She ended the parade by stretching to reach a faded portrait in a silver frame, which stood on a shelf. It was taken at Ilfracombe, and showed a young girl with a slim neck and a smiling face, framed by a mass of curling fair hair.

"This is my favourite," she declared. "Now, this really is Winnie."

It was the girl who had taught in Sunday school, giggled at churchwardens, and refused her father's curates, before she spread adventurous wings and fluttered away.

But she always returned to the nest.

Mrs. Froy looked again at the clock. She tried to picture Winnie in a grand continental express, which stamped proudly all over the map of Europe. The poor girl would have to endure two nights in the train, but she always vowed she loved the experience. Besides, she knew all the little dodges of an experienced traveller, to secure comfort.

Although a gregarious soul, Mrs. Froy began to wonder when her guests would go. There had been a hospitable big tea round the dining-room table, with blackberry pie, and a guest had made a stain on the best tablecloth. Although she had guiltily pushed her plate over it, Mrs. Froy had seen it. And since every minute's delay in rubbing salt into the mark would make its removal more difficult, she had found it difficult to maintain the myopia of a hostess.

Besides she wanted to watch the clock alone, and gloat over the fact that every minute was bringing Winnie's return nearer.

Although her fingers were itching to remove the tablecloth, after she had escorted her visitors to the gate, she did not return immediately to the house. In front of her was the field where she gathered mushrooms every morning. It was vividly green, and the black shadows of the elms were growing longer as the sun dipped lower.

It was rather melancholy and lonely, so that she thought of her husband.

"I wish Theodore would come home."

Apparently he heard her wish for he appeared suddenly at the far end of the meadow—his tall thin black figure striding over the grass, as though he were in competition with the elm-shadows.

Around him capered a dog which had some connection with the breed of Old English sheepdog; but his original line had slipped and he was suppressed in the family tree. During a recent hot spell, his shaggy coat had been clipped, transforming him to a Walt Disney creation.

Sock was the herald and toastmaster of the family. Directly he espied the little dumpy grey lady at the garden gate, he made a bee-line towards her and circled round her, barking excitedly to tell her that the master was coming home.

Having done his duty at her end of the field, he tore back to Mr. Froy with the glad news that the mistress of the house was waiting for him. As he gradually drew them together, both his owners were laughing at his elephantine gambols.

"It must be a great relief to the poor fellow, getting rid of that thatch," said Mr. Froy. "He evidently feels very cool and light now."

"He probably imagines he is a fairy," remarked his wife. "Look at him floating through the air like a puff of thistledown."

"The dear old fool. . . . Won't Winsome laugh?"

"Won't she?"

In imagination, both heard the joyous girlish peal.

"And won't she be thrilled with her room?" went on Mrs. Froy. "Theo, I've a confession. The carpet came when you were out. . . . And I am only human."

Mr. Froy hid his disappointment.

"You mean, you've unpacked it?" he asked. "Well, my dear, I deserved it for running away with Sock, instead of staying and helping you to entertain your visitors."

"Come upstairs and see it. It looks like moss."

They had bought a new carpet for Winifred's bedroom, as a surprise for her return. It represented stringent personal economy, since with a rigid income, any extra purchase meant taking a bite out of the weekly budget.

So he had cut down his allowance of tobacco, and she had given up her rare visits to the cinema. But now that the forty days were over, these good things would have been nothing but ashes and counterfoils.

The carpet remained—a green art-square.

When they reached the bedroom, Mr. Froy looked round him with proud satisfied eyes. It was a typical schoolgirl's bedroom, with primrose washed walls and sepia photogravures of Greuze's beauties—limpid-eyed and framed in dark stained oak. The modern note was there also in photographs of Conrad Veidt and Robert Montgomery, together with school groups and Winnie's hockey-stick.

The faded yellow-rosebud cretonne curtains and bedspread were freshly washed and ironed; a cake of green soap was displayed on the washstand; and two green candles—never to be lit—were stuck into the glass candlesticks before the mirror of the toilet-table.

"We've made it look very nice," said Mr. Froy.

"Yes, but it's not finished yet."

Mrs. Froy pointed to the narrow oak bed, where two lumps at the top and the bottom told of hot water bottles.

"It won't be finished until there's something inside that bed," she said. "I can't believe that in two nights' time I shall be slipping in to kiss her 'Good-night.' "

"Only the first night," advised Mr. Froy. "Remember our daughter is the modern girl. Her generation avoids sentiment."

"Yes, for all her heart, Winnie is modern," agreed his wife. "That is why she gets on so well with every one—high and low. You may depend on it, that even on her journey, by now she has made some useful friends who may be helpful at a pinch. I expect she knows all the best people on the train. And by 'best' I mean it in every sense of the word. . . . I wonder where she is at this moment."

Well for Mrs. Froy that she did not know.

CHAPTER NINETEEN
THE HIDDEN HAND

In the professor's opinion, the Misses Flood-Porter were representative of the best people. At home he had the reputation of being unsociable and self-sufficient; but directly he travelled he developed a distrust of unfamiliar contacts, and a timidity which sought instinctively the security of his own class.

He wanted to hear his own accent reproduced by some one—however uncongenial—who had been to his college, or lunched at his club, or who knew a cousin of one of his acquaintances.

As he smoked in the corridor after his banishment, he glanced rather wistfully at the compartment where the sisters sat. Miss Rose—although his senior—was sufficiently near his age to be a potential danger. But her face dispelled any fears of dormant hysteria. It was slightly underhung and the firm outline of her protruding lip and chin was reassuring.

Although he recoiled automatically when the elder lady caught his eye and invited him to come in with a smiling gesture, he entered and sat down rather stiffly beside Miss Rose.

"Are you being kept out of your reserved carriage by that girl?" asked Miss Rose bluntly.

When the professor explained the situation both sisters were indignant.

"Fainted?" Miss Rose's tone was incredulous. "She was laughing when she passed, arm in arm with that youth. It's all too mysterious for me. Only I sincerely hope she won't stir up a fuss and get us all hung up at Trieste, for nothing."

"It's her dog," explained the elder sister in an aside.

Miss Rose caught her lower lip between her teeth.

"Yes, it's Scottie," she said defiantly. "I'll own up I'm not quite normal over him. But he's so devoted to me—and he pines. The only other person I can trust him to is the butler."

"Strange," remarked the professor. "My own dog has a marked aversion to butlers. Particularly, to my uncle's."

The social temperature rose several degrees, and Miss Rose grew confidential.

"It's like this. Coles—our butler—is due to go on a cruise, directly I come back. It's a new experience for him and he is thrilled. If I'm overdue he will probably stay at home with Scottie, and, of course, I don't want him to lose his holiday. . . . On the other hand, if he went, poor little Scottie would be frantic. He would feel he had lost every friend."

"We have an excellent staff," supplemented Miss Flood-Porter, "but, unfortunately, none of them likes animals."

The professor's long face wrinkled up in a smile which made him resemble a benevolent horse.

"I can enter into your feelings," he told them. "I confess that my own dog makes me lose my sense of proportion. I rarely go abroad, because I cannot take her with me owing to quarantine regulations. But this year a complete change seemed indicated."

The sisters exchanged glances.

"Isn't that strange?" declared Miss Flood-Porter. "That is exactly our own position."

Miss Rose flinched and changed the subject quickly.

"What's your dog?" she asked.

"Sealyham. White."

The professor was sitting bolt upright no longer. Introduced by butlers, and their friendship cemented by the common ownership of dogs, he felt he was in congenial company. So he relaxed to gossip.

"A position of responsibility towards the extraordinary young lady seems to have been thrust upon me," he said. "She appears bent on making things very awkward for every one. I understand she was staying at the same hotel as you. . . . What opinion did you form of her?"

"Don't ask me," said Miss Rose bluntly. "I'm prejudiced. So, perhaps, I shouldn't be fair."

Her sister made the explanation.

"We know nothing about *her,* but she was with a party of near-nudists, who drank all day and night, and were a complete nuisance. The noise was worse than a pneumatic road-drill. And we came so far especially to get perfect rest and quiet."

The professor clicked.

"I quite understand your feelings," he said. "The point is—did she strike you as hysterical?"

"I only know there was a disgraceful scene on the lake yesterday. Two women screaming about a man. She was one."

"I'm not surprised," commented the professor. "At present she is either telling a pack of lies to get into the limelight, or she is suffering from slight delirium as a result of sunstroke. The latter is the charitable view. But it involves responsibility. After all, we are her compatriots."

Miss Rose began to fidget. When she opened her case and drew out a cigarette, her fingers were not quite steady.

"Suppose—she is telling the truth?" she asked. "It's not fair for us to leave the girl behind us at Trieste without any backing. . . . I'm worried stiff not knowing *what* to do."

Had Mrs. Froy been listening, she would have clapped her gouty old hands. At last Miss Rose's attitude was coming into line with her expectations. The best people would be looking after Winnie. So no harm could possibly come to her. . . . But all the same, "Keep her safe—and bring her home to us."

Unfortunately the professor was proof against the power of prayer. He wrinkled up his face in a sceptical grimace.

"Her story is too unfounded for me to credit it," he said. "But even if the vanished governess were not a myth, I cannot conceive any cause for anxiety on her behalf. Her disappearance must be voluntary, because if she had come to any harm, or met with an accident, it would have been notified at once by an eye-witness."

"Exactly," agreed Miss Flood-Porter. "The train is so crowded that if she knew the ropes, she could play 'hide and seek' indefinitely with the ticket-collector."

"Therefore," summed up the professor, "if she *is* hiding, she must have some strong personal reason for such a course. My own feeling is never to interfere with private issues. It would be extremely tactless and inconsiderate of us to start a general search for her."

Miss Rose drew deeply at her cigarette.

"Then you don't think me definitely feeble to put Scottie's interests first?" she asked.

"I should consider that you were letting your dog down if you sacrificed him to such an absolutely preposterous issue," replied the professor.

"That goes for me. Thank you, professor." Miss Rose examined her firm pink hands. "I'm smutty. I'd better wash."

When she had lurched out into the corridor, Miss Flood-Porter spoke to the professor confidentially.

"I couldn't mention it before my sister—she is so sensitive on the subject—but we've just been through a nerve-shattering experience. And I don't see that we did a pennorth of good. . . . Am I boring you?"

"Not in the least."

Miss Flood-Porter began her story of those events which played their part in shaping the conduct of the sisters, and so—indirectly—affected the destiny of a stranger.

"We live in a very quiet neighbourhood, close to the cathedral. It was ruined for every one when a terrible person came to live there. A War profiteer—at least, I call them all that. One day, when he was scorching in his car—drunk, as usual—he knocked down a woman. We saw the accident, and our evidence got him six months' imprisonment, as it was a bad case."

"I congratulate you on your public spirit."

"I'm afraid we, too, were quite pleased with ourselves, until he came out. After that we were marked people. This man—aided by his two boys—persecuted us in every kind of way. Windows were smashed—flower beds raided—horrible things thrown over the garden walls—obscene messages chalked on the gates. We could never catch them in the act, although we appealed to the police and they had a special watch kept on the premises. . . . After a time it got on our nerves. It did not matter where we were, or what we were doing, we were always listening for another crash. It affected my sister most, as she was terrified lest one of her pet animals might be the next victim. Luckily, before it came to that, the man left the town."

Miss Flood-Porter stopped, overcome by the memories she had raised.

It began on the morning when she went out into the garden, to find that her unique white delphiniums had been uprooted during the night.

After that there was the ever-increasing tension—the constant annoyance—the cumulative pecuniary loss—the futility of repairs, when panes of glass were replaced, only to be smashed again. It was like standing at a cross-roads in windy weather and being buffeted by an invisible weather-cock, which whirled round again after it had struck its blow. There were flutters of apprehension whenever the fiendish boys scorched by them on their bicycles, grinning with impudent triumph. And the time came when their nerve was worn down, so that their imaginations raced away with them and they grew fearful of worse evils in store.

It ended on the evening when Miss Flood-Porter found her sister Rose in tears. If the Rock of Gibraltar had suddenly shaken like a jelly, she could not have been more aghast.

She looked up to meet the professor's sympathetic eye.

"Can you blame us," she asked, "when I tell you that, after that, we made a vow never to interfere in anything again—unless it was a case of cruelty to animals or children?"

As Iris passed the window, in token that he was free to return to his own compartment, the professor rose.

"Tell your sister," he advised, "not to worry any more, but to get back to her dog as quickly as possible. No one is going to suffer in any way. In case of any further complications, you can trust me to take charge."

A few minutes later, when Miss Flood-Porter repeated the message, Miss Rose was greatly relieved.

"Now I can go home to Scottie with a *clear* conscience," she said. "Any one must have complete confidence in the professor."

She forgot one important point. The professor was working on the basis that Miss Froy was a fiction of hysteria—while both the sisters had seen her in the flesh.

CHAPTER TWENTY
STRANGERS INTERVENE

After Miss Froy had shrivelled to a never-never, Iris was thrown back on herself again. When her first relief at shelving the riddle had passed, she grew worried by her own sensations. Her knees were shaky, while her head felt light and empty as a blown egg-shell.

Miss Froy would have known that, in addition to the after effects of sunstroke, the girl was exhausted for lack of light nourishment. At this juncture she was a dead loss to Iris, for Hare—with the best intentions—could only offer stimulants.

As she clung to the shaking rail, fighting off recurrent spells of giddiness, Iris told herself that she must forcibly hang out until she reached Basle.

"It would be fatal if I collapsed," she thought fearfully. "Max is too young to be any good. Some busybody would push me out at the first station, and pack me off to the local hospital."

And anything might happen to her there, as in Miss Froy's terrible story. Or did Miss Kummer tell it to her?

It was an ordeal to stand, but although she had insisted on leaving Hare—when she found that both talking and listening had become a strain—she shrank from the thought of return to her own compartment. It was too near the doctor and too remote from her compatriots. At the far end of the corridor she felt bottled up in enemy territory.

Besides—it was haunted by the ghost of a little tweed spinster, of whom it was not wise to think too long.

The high-pitched conversation of the Misses Flood-Porter—audible through the open door—was a distraction.

"I've written to Captain Parker, to meet us with his car at Victoria, to push us through the customs," said Miss Flood-Porter.

"Hope he'll be there," fussed Miss Rose. "If he fails us, we may lose our connection. And I've written to cook that dinner is to be ready at seven-thirty to the dot."

"What did you order?"

"Not chicken. Definitely. It will be some time before I can endure one again. I said a nice cutlet of salmon and a small leg of lamb. Peas, if possible. If it is too late for them, French beans and marrow. I left the sweet to cook."

"That sounds very good. I'm longing to eat a plain English dinner again."

"So am I."

There was a short pause before Miss Rose began to worry anew.

"I do hope there'll be no muddle over our wagon-lits at Trieste."

"Oh, my dear," cried her sister, "don't suggest such a thing. I couldn't face the idea of sitting bolt upright all night. Didn't you hear the manager telephone for them?"

"I stood by him while he was doing it. Of course, I could not understand anything. But he assured me positively that they were being reserved for us."

"Well, we must hope for the best. . . . I've been looking through my engagement-book. It's the bishop's last garden party, the day after we get back."

"Oh, we *couldn't* miss that."

Iris' half-smile was bitter as she listened to the characteristic chatter of two inexperienced women-travellers, who felt very far from their beaten track.

"And I expected *them* to risk losing their reservations and spoiling their dinner," she thought. "What a hope."

Once again she flattened herself against the window, as the flaxen-haired waiter came down the corridor. Miss Rose saw him pass for she bounded out after him.

"Stop," she cried in her most imperious tone. "You speak English?"

"Yes, madame."

"Then get me some matches, please. Matches."

"Oh, yes, madame."

"I wonder if he really understood her," thought Iris, who had grown sceptical of every one.

Her doubts were unfounded, for after a brief interval the waiter returned with a box of matches. He used one to light Miss Rose's cigarette and handed her the remainder with a bow.

"The engine-driver is fulfilling his obligations and the express will reach Trieste within the scheduled time," he informed Miss Rose, who remarked, "Oh, definitely good."

He seemed anxious to oblige every one. When Iris in her turn called out to him, he wheeled round smartly as though eager for service.

As he recognised her, however, a change came over his face. His smile faded, his eyes shifted, and he appeared to conquer an impulse to bolt.

All the same he listened obediently as she gave her order.

"I'm not going to the dining-car for dinner." she told him. "I want you to bring me something to my carriage—right at the end of the corridor. A cup of soup or Bovril, or Ovaltine. Nothing solid. You understand?"

"Oh, yes, madame."

He bowed himself away. But he never brought the soup. . . .

Iris forgot her order directly she had given it. A stream of passengers had begun to file steadily past her, crushing her against the side of the corridor. Since every one was heading in the same direction, she glanced at her watch.

The time told her that the first dinner was about to be served.

"Only three hours now to Trieste," she thought gladly—goaded no longer by the thought of wasted minutes.

Where she stood she was very much in the way of the procession, and—since the majority was hungry—she was resented as an obstacle. She met with ruthless treatment, but it was useless to fight her way out against the human current. When she made the attempt she was nearly knocked down, as some of the rougher element began to push.

No one appeared to notice her plight as she tried to get out of the jam. The train was racing at top speed, and she was shaken and bruised as she gripped the rail. Terrified of being crushed, her palms were sticky and her heart leaped with panic.

At last the pressure was relaxed and she breathed more freely, as she waited for the better-behaved passengers to pass. Presently a combination of strokes, dots and dashes, in black and white, told her that the family party—linked together—was on its way to dinner. Free from the restraining presence of the baroness, they talked and laughed, evidently in high spirits at the prospect of their meal.

Although the parents were sufficiently big to inflict some merciless massage as they squeezed past her, Iris was glad to see them, for she argued that they must be in the tail of the procession. Then the blonde slipped by—cool as a dripping icicle—with unshatterable composure and without one ruffled hair.

Although the corridor was practically clear, Iris still lingered, unable to face the prospect of being alone in the carriage with the baroness. To her relief, however, the personage herself came in sight, accompanied by the doctor. Sure of getting a seat in the dining-car—however late her entrance—she had waited for the mob to disperse.

As her vast black figure surged past Iris, a simile floated into the girl's mind. An insect and a relentless foot.

The doctor threw her a keen professional glance which noted each symptom of distress. With a formal bow he passed on his way, and she was able to bump and sway along the corridors, back to the empty carriage.

She had barely seated herself, after an involuntary glance at Miss Froy's empty corner, when Hare hurried in.

"Coming to first dinner?" he asked. "I warn you, the second one will be only the scrapings."

"No," she told him, "the waiter's bringing me some soup here. I've been in a rough-house and I simply couldn't stand the heat."

He looked at her as she wiped her damp brow.

"Gosh, you look all in. Let me get you a spot. No? . . . Well, then, I've just had an intriguing experience. On my way here, a woman's trembling hand was laid on my sleeve and a woman's piteous voice whispered, 'Could you do something for me?' I turned and looked into the beautiful eyes of the vicar's wife. Needless to say, I pledged myself to the service of the distressed lady."

"Did she want a hot water bottle for her husband?" asked Iris.

"No, she wanted me to send a telegram for her directly we reached Trieste. But now comes the interesting bit. I'm not to let her husband know or suspect anything. After that, I can't hint at the message."

"Who wants to know it?" asked Iris dully.

"Sorry. I see you really are flat. I won't worry you any more. Chin-chin."

Hare left the compartment, only to pop his head again round the corner of the door.

"There's the ugliest ministering angel I've ever seen in the next carriage," he told her. "But what I really came back for was this. Do you know who 'Gabriel' is?"

"An archangel."

"I see. You're definitely *not* in the know."

As the time passed and no waiter appeared with her soup, Iris came to the conclusion that he was too rushed to remember her order. But she felt too limp to care. All that mattered was the crawling hands of her watch, which drew her imperceptibly nearer to Trieste.

As a matter of fact, the fair waiter possessed a heart of gold, together with a palm which twitched as instinctively as a divining-twig in the direction of a tip. He would have found time to rush in that cup of soup, whatever the demand on his resource. The only drawback was he knew nothing about the order.

Like most of his fellow-countrymen, he had been made a good linguist by the method of interchange between families of different nationalities. As he was ambitious, he felt that one extra language might turn the scale in his favour, when he applied for a job. Accordingly, he learned English from his teacher, who had taught himself the language from a book of phonetic pronunciation.

The waiter, who was an apt pupil, passed his school examination and was able to rattle off strings of English phrases. But the first time he heard the language spoken by a Briton, he was unable to understand it.

Fortunately English tourists were rare and most of their conversation was limited to the needs of their meals. While his ear was growing accustomed, therefore, he managed to keep his job by bluff and by being a good guesser.

Miss Rose's unlighted cigarette gave him the clue that she wanted matches. Moreover her voice was loud and she was brief.

But in Iris, he met his Waterloo. Her low husky voice and unfamiliar words beat him completely. After his first nerve-racking experience, he could only fall back on the mechanical, "Yes, madame," and rush to take cover.

Before the other passengers returned to the carriage, Iris had another visitor—the professor. He took off his glasses to polish them nervously, while he explained the nature of his mission.

"Hare has been talking to me, and—frankly—he is worried about you. I don't want to alarm you. Of course, you are not ill—that is, not definitely ill—but we are wondering if you are fit to continue the journey alone."

"Of course I am," cried Iris in a panic. "I'm perfectly fit. And I don't want any one to worry on my account."

"Yet, if you should collapse later, it would be decidedly awkward for you and every one. I was discussing it with the doctor, just now, and he came to the rescue with an admirable suggestion."

As he paused, Iris' heart began to flutter with apprehension, for she knew by instinct what the proposal would be.

"The doctor," went on the professor, "is taking a patient to a hospital at Trieste, and he offers to see you safely placed in a recommended nursing-home for the night."

CHAPTER TWENTY-ONE

LIES

As the professor made his proposal, Iris saw the opening of the trap. But he had forgotten the bait: She was a free agent—and nothing could induce her to walk inside.

"I will not go anywhere with that doctor," she said.

"But—"

"I refuse to discuss it."

The professor seemed about to argue, so she decided that it was no time for politeness.

"I can't pretend to be grateful for your interest," she told him. "I consider it interference."

The professor stiffened at the last word.

"I have not the slightest wish to be intrusive," he said. "But Hare was genuinely concerned about you, and he asked me to use my influence."

"No one can influence me to go with that horrible doctor."

"In that case there is no more to be said."

The professor was only too thankful to be rid of his responsibility. Since the girl was bent on antagonising those who held out a helping hand, there would be time for a smoke, while he waited for the second dinner.

Iris did not like the professor's face, but his Harris-tweed back was British and reassuring. She realised with a pang that she was sending it away.

Acting on impulse she called him back.

"I won't go with that doctor," she said. "He's like death, but—supposing I *should* flop—which is absurd—I'd go with you."

She thought she was making a concession, but at that there were two frightened people in the carriage.

"That is impossible," said the professor sharply, to hide his nervousness. "The circumstances put it out of court. The doctor has made you a kind and helpful offer—which comes best from a medical man."

He opened the door of the trap again, but she shook her head. She would never go inside. Unless—of course—she were tricked.

It was a disquieting reflection, for she was beginning to think that she could trust no one. Even Hare had let her down. While he was, in reality, concerned about her condition, he had been facetious about Mrs. Barnes. According to him, she had asked him to send a telegram to some man called "Gabriel," while her husband was to be kept in the dark.

Since it was impossible to connect the vicar's wife with a clandestine affair, Iris concluded that Hare had been trying to pull the wool over her eyes.

She resented the feebleness of the effort, especially as Mrs. Barnes was connected with a poignant memory. It was she who had driven away Miss Froy and sent her groping back into Limbo.

Iris could not forgive her for that, for she was missing badly the support which only the little governess could give. At this juncture, she knew she would be safe in those experienced hands. She felt terrified, sick, friendless—for she had burned her bridges.

Besides, whenever she thought about the mystery, she felt near the border-line of that world which was filled with shifting shadows—where phantasy usurped reality, and she existed merely in the Red King's dream. Unless she kept a firm grip on herself, her sanity might hang—or crash—on the fact of Miss Froy's existence.

There were others in that trainful of holiday folk who were in a worse plight than herself. One was the invalid in the next carriage. Although she was chiefly unconscious, the flash of every lucid second held the horror of the shock which had stunned her into darkness. And if the moment lasted a fraction too long, there was time for a cloud of awful doubts to arise.

"Where am I? What is going to happen to me? Where are they taking me?"

Luckily, before these questions could be answered, the flare always died down again. So, therefore, she was in better case than Edna Barnes, who was in full possession of her faculties while she endured a protracted martyrdom of mental suffering.

She had been completely happy in anticipation of their last mountain ramble when she saw the letter in the pigeonhole of the bureau. Her mother-in-law's handwriting gave her a warning pang which broke slightly the shock of the contents of the note.

"I've been wondering what to do for the best," wrote the excellent lady. "I don't want to make you anxious during your long journey, yet, on the other hand, I feel I ought to prepare you for a disappointment. I had hoped to have Gabriel in perfect health for your return, and up to now he's been splendid. But now he has developed a cold in his chest. He is quite comfortable and the doctor says he is going on as well as can be expected. So there is no need for you to worry."

Edna Barnes skimmed the letter in a flash which read between the lines. If her mother-in-law had composed it with a view to alarm her, she could not have succeeded better. All the familiar soothing phrases were there. "No need to worry." "As well as can be expected." "Comfortable"—the hospitable formula for a hopeless case.

A cold on the chest could camouflage bronchitis or even pneumonia; and she had heard that a big strong baby, stricken by these complaints, was sometimes snuffed out after a few hours' illness. Her heart nearly burst as she wondered whether, at that moment, he were already dead.

Then her husband called out to inquire the contents of the letter. The answer had been "Margaret Rose silk."

She had lied with a fierce protective instinct to save him from her own agony. There was no need for two to suffer, if she could bear his pain for him. Screening her torment with her habitual smile, she racked her brains desperately for some reason to leave for England that same day.

Just as the vicar took the packet of sandwiches from her, preparatory to their start, she snatched at the excuse of Miss Rose Flood-Porter's warning dream.

Although he was disappointed, the vicar gave way to her in the matter. The sisters, too, decided to take no chances, when they heard that the vicar's wife had changed her plans owing to superstitious presentiments. As the honeymoon couple had previously decided to go, the exodus from the hotel was complete.

For the first time Edna Barnes was glad that her husband suffered from train-sickness. While he sat with closed eyes and gritted teeth, she had some respite from acting. Her only consolation was knowing that she was on her way home. Therefore, when she was threatened with the prospect of an enforced delay at Trieste, she felt desperate.

She was faced with the first real test of her principles—and her conscience won. Deception to save her husband from unnecessary suffering was a form of the lie magnificent. But now she told herself that the cause of humanity must come before family ties, because it was selfless.

She was prepared to do her duty—whatever the cost—by Miss Froy. But when she was assured by those whose judgement she could trust, that the peril was negligible, her resolution slipped.

The cause was too inadequate to exact such a sacrifice. On the evidence, it was nothing but the trumped-up invention of a hysterical girl to attract notice. But Gabriel was ill. He needed her, and he won.

It was after she had identified Miss Kummer as Miss Froy that she suddenly realised the advantage of a willing young man who could send off a telegram to her mother-in-law. As she doubted whether she could receive the reply without her husband's knowledge—since her name might be bawled out by some official—she asked for the latest bulletin to await her at Calais. The sea-crossing would revive the vicar, while it would not be kind to keep him in the dark until he reached home.

Although her eyes were tragic, she smiled faintly at the thought of his unconsciousness. Like a big baby he was sorry for his aches and pains, but he knew nothing of what he was spared.

"Only a mother knows," she thought.

This was exactly Mrs. Froy's own conviction as she sat in the twilight and hungered for her child's return.

CHAPTER TWENTY-TWO
KILLING TIME

As a rule Mrs. Froy lived on the sunny side of the street. This evening, however, the long black shadows of the elms seemed to have stretched out to reach her mind, for she was unaccountably depressed.

The sun no longer shone greenly through the creepers which muffled the windows, but she was accustomed to gloom. For reasons of economy, the lamp was never lit until the last possible moment. Neither was she influenced by the melancholy of the view from her bedroom, which overlooked a corner of the churchyard.

Having dwelt in rectories for so long, it was second-habit for the Froys to live close to the church. Whenever she looked out at the slanting tombstones of forgotten dead, she had trained herself to picture a spectacular resurrection, when the graves suddenly burst open and their glorified contents shot up into the air like a glittering shower of rockets.

This evening, when the green had all turned grey, she had her first misgivings.

"I wonder if it's healthy for us to sleep so near all those mouldering corpses."

In ordinary circumstances she would have scoffed at her idea; but she could not dislodge the black monkey that sat on her shoulder. Vague misgivings and presentiments kept shaking through her mind.

She told herself that she would be profoundly grateful when Winnie was safely home. Travel must be risky—otherwise railway companies would not issue insurance policies. Suppose Winnie were taken ill on the journey and had to be dumped in some foreign waiting-room.

Anything might happen to her—a smash, or even worse. One read of terrible things which happened to girls travelling alone. Not that Winnie was actually a girl—thank goodness—but she was so young for her age.

At this point Mrs. Froy took herself in charge.

"Only two nights more," she reminded herself. "You ought to be happy as a queen, instead of carrying on like a weeping-willow with a stomach ache. Now, you find out what's at the bottom of all this."

Before long she believed she had worked back to the original cause of her depression. It was the blackberry stain on the best table-cloth, which had not yielded entirely to salt.

"Goose," she said. "It'll boil out in the wash."

Making a face at the tombstones, she stumped out of the room and down the stairs in search of her husband.

Contrary to custom she found him in the parlour sitting in the dark.

"Lazybones, why haven't you lit the lamp?" she asked.

"In a minute." Mr. Froy's voice was unusually lifeless. "I've been brooding. Bad habit. . . . It's an extraordinary thing that Winsome has been away so often, yet this is the first time I've ever felt apprehensive about her safety. These continental trains—I suppose I'm growing old. The ground is pulling me."

Mrs. Froy's heart gave a sudden leap as she listened. So he, too, had caught the warning whisper.

Without speaking, she struck a match, turned up the wick of the lamp, lit it, and fitted on the chimney. As she waited for the glass to warm through, she looked at her husband's face, visible in the weak glow.

It appeared white, bloodless and bony—the face of a man who should be going to bed in a damp corner under the window, instead of sharing her spring-mattress.

At the sight she exploded with the righteous wrath of a woman who is rough on shadows.

"Never let me hear you talk like that again," she scolded. "You're as bad as Miss Parsons. She's only sixty-six, yet the last time we came back from town together, she grumbled because the bus was full and she had to stand. I said, 'My dear, don't let every one know that you are not accustomed to court circles.' And then I said, 'Take my seat. I'm young.' "

"Did the people in the bus laugh?" asked Mr. Froy appreciatively. In the circle of mellow lamplight his face had lost its pallor. Before she replied, his wife pounced on the window-cords and rattled the green window-curtains together, shutting out the bogie-twilight.

"Yes," she said, "they simply roared. Then some one started to clap. But when I thought the joke had gone far enough, I stopped it. . . . I *looked* at them."

Although Mrs. Froy was proud of her gifts as a comedian, her sense of dignity was stronger. Her head was held high, as though she were still quelling her audience, as she inquired, "Where is Sock?"

"My dear, I'm afraid he is waiting outside until it is time to meet the train. I do wish I could make the poor fellow understand it's Friday."

"I'll make him," announced Mrs. Froy. "Sock."

The big dog shambled in immediately, for although normally too spoiled to be obedient, he always respected a certain rasp in his mistress's voice.

Mrs. Froy took three biscuits from the tin and laid them in a row on the fender-stool.

"Look, darling," she said. "Mother's got three biscuits for you. This is to-night, but Winnie's not coming to-night. This is to-morrow, but Winnie's not coming to-morrow. *This* is Friday, and Winnie's coming Friday and you shall go and meet the train. . . . Remember— *this* one."

Sock looked up at her as though he were straining to understand—his amber eyes beaming with intelligence under his wisps of hair, for his head had not been shorn.

"He understands," declared Mrs. Froy. "I can always talk to animals. Perhaps our vibrations are the same. I know what's in his mind and I can always make him know what is in mine."

She turned back to the fender-stool and picked up the first biscuit.

"This is to-night," she explained. "Well, to-night's over. So you can eat to-night."

Sock entered into the spirit of the game. While he was making a mess of crumbs on the mat, Mrs. Froy spoke to her husband.

"That's an end of to-night for us, too," she said. "And good riddance. I wish you would remember that it's bad form to go half-way to meet troubles which are not coming to your house, and which have no intention of calling on you. . . . What are you grinning at?"

Shaking with laughter, Mr. Froy pointed to Sock, who was in the act of crunching the last biscuit.

" 'He understands,' " he quoted with gentle mockery.

The sight of his face made Mrs. Froy forget her momentary discomfiture. It looked years younger. There was no question now of where he ought to sleep that night.

She patted Sock, kissed his nose and flicked the biscuit crumbs from his coat.

"Yes," she said tartly, "he understands—and better than you do. Don't you see that he is trying to make the time pass quicker?"

CHAPTER TWENTY-THREE
STAKE YOUR COUNTER

A t that moment others besides Mrs. Froy were anxious to speed up the march of time. Some were on the express which was being stoked up for its final spurt, to reach Trieste on time.

One of these—Mrs. Todhunter—hid her impatience under a pose of nonchalance. Wherever she went, she attracted notice and she also excited feminine envy by her special atmosphere of romance. Apparently she had everything that a woman could want—beauty, poise, exquisite clothes, and a wealthy, distinguished bridegroom.

In reality she was feverishly eager to get back to her husband.

He was a stout middle-aged building-contractor, named Cecil Parmiter. When at home Mrs. Laura Parmiter lived in a super-fine new house, with all those modern improvements which her husband introduced into the blocks of flats he built for others—and with none of their short-comings. She had a comfortable income, a generous allowance, competent servants, leisure, a trusting affectionate husband and two large children.

She had the additional detail of respectability.

Although she was the social queen of her set, she was secretly ambitious and discontented. During the rehearsals of a local pageant, when class-distinctions were levelled, she met a certain rising barrister—a visitor to the district, who had been roped into taking a part. He was a king and she was a queen—and the royal atmosphere lent a glamour to their meetings.

He was infatuated—temporarily—by her statuesque beauty and the facility with which she could quote passages from Swinburne and Browning, culled from her Oxford Book of Verse. After a few meetings in London, under the seal of the apple, he swept her away with him on a passionate adventure.

Although she lost her footing, Mrs. Laura's brain still functioned. She had a definite ulterior motive for her surrender. During a session of Browning lectures, she had read "The Statue and the Bust" and had imbibed its spirit. She determined, therefore, to risk her counter on a bold fling—the chance of a double divorce.

After the preliminary patch of mud was crossed, she would take her rightful place in Society as the beautiful wife of a distinguished barrister. The world soon forgets—while she was confident that she could compel her husband to admit her moral claim to the children.

She lost. . . . And Browning could have been proud of the spirit in which she took her toss.

The barrister was married to a sour elderly wife; but she possessed both a title and wealth. When Mrs. Laura discovered that he had not the slightest intention of making their adventure a prelude to matrimony, her pride forbade her to show any disappointment.

Perhaps her nonchalance was easier to assume by reason of her own disillusionment. The passionate adventure had not matured according to its promise. It taught her that a professional man did not differ so greatly from a tradesman in essentials and that they looked much the same before shaving and without their collars.

Moreover, the barrister had a handicap from which the builder was immune. He was a hard snorer.

To make matters worse, while he was careless of his own failings, his standard for women was so fastidious that she found it a strain to live up to it. She could never relax, or be natural, without being conscious of his criticism or impatience.

Being practical, she determined to cut short the holiday and get back to her husband while the going was good. Fortunately, she had not burned any bridges. Her husband had bought her return ticket to Turin, and she had told him to expect no mail, since he was going on a sea trip to the Shetlands.

Her plan was to leave the barrister at Turin, where he had joined her on the outward journey, and to stay there, for a night, so that her luggage could display the hotel labels.

The end of it all would be a happy domestic reunion and a better understanding, for—by contrast—she had learnt to appreciate her husband's solidity. Thus one more matrimonial shipwreck had been averted by a trial-venture and a smashed code of morality.

As the Todhunters sat in their coupé, waiting for the second dinner to be served, they were a spectacle which attracted the interest of the tourists who straggled past the window. They must still be known by the name in which they had registered, since the barrister was too cautious to sign his own name.

It was "Brown."

However, his parents had done their best for him, and his title of "Sir Peveril Brown" was sufficiently well-known to be dangerous—in addition to a striking profile which had been reproduced often in the pictorial press.

True to her character of Browning's good loser, Mrs. Laura continued to play her part. Although her acquired drawl was replaced sometimes by her natural accent she still looked choice and aloof as a beautiful princess—remote from the rabble. But her fingers kept tapping the greasy old-gold plush seat, while she glanced continuously at her watch.

"Still hours and hours," she said impatiently. "It seems as though we'd never make Trieste—let alone Turin."

"Anxious to drop me?" asked Todhunter incredulously.

"I'm not thinking of you. . . . But children get measles—and deserted husbands prove unfaithful. The world is full of pretty typists."

"In that case, he'd have nothing on you, if it came to a show-up."

She started at the word.

"Show-up? Don't give me the jitters," she cried sharply. "There's no chance of it, is there?"

He stroked his lip.

"I should say we are reasonably secure," he told her. "Still . . . I've handled some queer cases in my career. One never knows what will break. It was unfortunate that there were any English visitors at the hotel. And you are entirely too beautiful to remain anonymous."

Mrs. Laura shook off his hand. She wanted reassurance, not compliments.

"You told me there was no risk," she said. Forgetting that her original scheme had been to force her husband to take action, she added bitterly, "What a fool I've been."

"Why are you suddenly so anxious to get back to your husband?" asked Todhunter.

"Well, to be brutally frank, we are all of us out for what we can get. And he can give me more than you can."

"Haven't I given you a memory you'll never forget?"

Mrs. Laura's eyes flashed angrily, and Todhunter laughed. He had grown rather bored by the languid beauty and her synthetic culture; but now that she had suddenly become alive, he was aware of the fact that she was slipping from him.

"I was only teasing you," he said. "Of course, no one will ever know about us. I could risk nothing like that. . . . But we might have been in a jam if I had not thought a jump ahead when that girl asked me about the peeping woman."

"Why," asked Laura, who had only grasped the fact that Todhunter would never go an inch out of his way to champion an unattractive middle-aged woman.

"Why? Because she's disappeared. If I had not repudiated her, I should have to make a statement at Trieste," Todhunter laughed. "Can't you see the headlines? 'Englishwoman lost on Continental express.' Photograph of Mr. Todhunter who was on his honeymoon, when. . . . And thus and thus. It wouldn't be long before the English press got on to my identity. One of the penalties of fame—however limited."

Mrs. Laura did not look as impressed as he wished, for his words had raised a new issue.

Perhaps, after all, the game was not lost, because it was not yet ended. Although Todhunter had no intention of risking a scandal when he lured her away on this trip, she saw a chance to engineer one and so force his hand.

If she went to the professor and assured him of Miss Froy's existence the result was bound to be future complications. There could be no doubt of the professor's probity and public spirit, which would enforce an investigation—whatever the cost to his personal convenience.

Her violet eyes suddenly glittered. As the beautiful bride of the alleged Todhunter, she was an important detail in the picture, and one that reporters would not overlook or suppress. She always made such an appealing photograph.

Afterwards there would be a sensational divorce case, and Sir Peveril—in honour bound—would be obliged to make her the second Lady Brown.

At the thought she drew a deep breath, for the wheel was still spinning.

Her counter was not yet lost.

CHAPTER TWENTY-FOUR
THE WHEEL SPINS

Mrs. Laura sat and looked at the window which held the reflection of the lighted carriage, thrown on panels of rushing darkness. She smiled at her dimly-mirrored face—smoky-dark, with shadowed eyes and triumphant lips. The wheel was still spinning for her.

And since their fates were interlinked it was spinning also for Miss Froy. The little spinster was in a perilous plight, but she was an obstinate optimist. She clung to the hope that everything would come right in the end, and that at long last she would reach home.

Miss Froy loved her home with that intense perverted passion which causes ardent patriots to desert their native lands and makes men faithless to their wives. Like them, she left what she loved most—for the joy of the return.

This special absence had been a thrilling experience. During the first six months of exile, she had been excited by the novelty of living in semi-royal surroundings. Everything was so exaggerated and unreal that she had a confused sense of having strayed into some fairy tale. She wandered and lost herself amid a maze of pillared halls and gilded apartments. There seemed to be endless marble stairs—countless galleries—all duplicated in enormous mirrors, so that at least one-half of the castle was illusion.

The scenery, in its breathless beauty, held the same bewildering quality of unreality. In her letters to her family she gave up the attempt to describe blue and purple mountains, whose white crests smashed through the sky—boiling jade rivers—lush green valleys—towering precipices.

"There aren't enough adjectives," she wrote. "But it's all simply topping."

True to schedule, however, when she cracked her seventh month of absence, her rapture suffered its first eclipse and she began to realise the drawbacks of living in a castle. To begin with she got lost no longer, and there were not so many marble staircases, since she had located the mirrors.

There were other unpleasant details, including fleas in the thick carpets and rich upholstery, for the hounds were many and the servants few.

Her vast bedroom, which was like a stage royal apartment, was comfortless and cold, since the enormous coloured porcelain stove—resembling a cathedral altar-piece—was insufficiently stoked.

There were ten courses for dinner—but only one knife and fork, which the diner cleaned with bread.

All the men were handsome and respectful, but none seemed to realise that she was a curly-headed girl whose pet sport was refusing curates.

Before her last five months were up she became so homesick that her longing for a small stone house—backed by an apple orchard, and overlooking a country churchyard—grew to a passion. Sick of the theatrical scenery, she would have exchanged all the mountains and rivers for one corner *of* an English meadow with a clump of elms and a duck-pond.

The night before her return her excitement was so great that she could not sleep, in anticipation of her journey. She could not believe in it, although her luggage was packed and labelled. One suitcase held soiled linen, destined for a real good boil. She did her personal washing in the bathroom, by stealth, since she had seen too many pails emptied into the beautiful green river which was the communal laundry.

As she lay and tossed she heard the faint scream of an engine, muted by distance to an amplified mosquito-ping. It was the night express, which—when farther down the valley—woke up the homesick sleepers in the hotel and whistled their thoughts after it, as though it were a monstrous metallic Pied Piper.

Just as, later, it called to Iris, it now drew the little spinster from her bed. She ran to the window and was in time to see it shoot past the end of the gorge, like a golden rod of light slipping into grooves of darkness.

"To-morrow night I shall be in an express, too," she gloated.

It was a rapture to anticipate her long journey, stage by stage and frontier by frontier, until she reached a small dingy station which was merely a halt built amid empty fields. No one would meet her there, because her father was afraid that blundering Sock, in his ecstasy, might leap at the engine and try to lick its face too.

But they would be waiting for her farther down the lane—and her eyes grew misty at the thought of that meeting. Yet even then she would not reach her journey's end until she ran through a dim white gate and a starlit garden, to see the light streaming through an open door.

"Mater," said Miss Froy, with a lump in her throat.

Then a sudden fear touched her heart.

"I've never been so homesick before," she thought. "Is it a warning? Suppose—suppose something happened—to keep me from getting home."

Something happened—something so monstrous and unexpected that she could not really believe in it. It was an adventure which could only be credited in connection with any one else.

At first she was certain that some one would soon come to her aid. She told herself it was a fortunate circumstance that she had met the charming English girl. They were compatriots, and she could rely on her with utmost confidence, because—were the situation reversed—she knew she would tear the train apart, wheel by wheel, in order to find her.

But as the time crawled on and nothing happened, doubts began to flock into her mind. She remembered that the girl had a touch of sunstroke and was far from well. She might be worse, or even seriously ill. Besides it would be difficult to try to explain the circumstances when one was ignorant of the language.

There was an even worse possibility. Iris might have tried to intervene and been snatched up, too, in the great machine which had caught her up in one of its revolutions. At the thought, Miss Froy's lip grew beaded from desperation and fear.

Then, suddenly, she felt the braking of the train. Its clatter and roar died down to a grinding slither, and with a mighty jerk the engine stopped.

"They've missed me," she thought triumphantly. "Now they are going to search the train."

And once again she saw the lights of home streaming through the open door.

As she waited in happy expectation she would have been surprised and gratified to know that the beautiful bride—who looked like a film star—was thinking of her.

Although she was only a pawn, she was the central figure in a plot to restore her liberty. At that moment the professor was standing in the corridor just outside Mrs. Laura's coupé. She had only to call to him and Miss Froy's ultimate release would be put in train.

As there was plenty of time before Trieste was reached, she delayed in order to be quite certain of the wisdom of her decision. Once she had applied the match she could not stop the blaze of publicity.

In reality, however, her mind was made up. Although she had discovered the barrister's drawbacks he was the original prize for which she had played. When she was Lady Brown, Sir Peveril would be merely a husband and she knew how to deal with this useful domestic animal. Hitherto she had been humiliated by the knowledge that his programme did not include marriage, and in her anxiety to impress him favourably, she had developed an inferiority complex.

Royal smashing tactics suited her better. Her voice was arrogant as she spoke to the barrister.

"What are we stopping for?" she asked, looking out at a squalid platform, dimly visible in a few flickering lights.

"Frontier," explained the barrister.

"Help. Have we got to get out and go through the Customs?"

"No, we take on the officials here. . . . What's that shockheaded lunatic up to?"

The barrister frowned as Hare raced into the telegraph office, shouting back the while to the guard who was yelling to him. It was evidently a first-class slanging match, but unintelligible to the English passengers who were deprived of its finer points.

As a matter of fact it had struck the bright young man that he could save his own valuable time at Trieste if he took advantage of the halt to send off Mrs. Barnes' telegram to Bath, England. The idea, however, did not make him popular with his compatriots.

"Fool's holding us up," growled the barrister, looking at his watch.

To his surprise Laura was perfectly calm at the menace to their time-table.

"Does it matter?" she drawled. "We shall get there."

"We might lose our connection. We've cut it pretty fine. That reminds me of something. I was wondering whether, in your interests, we had better part before we get into Italy. We might run up against some one we know."

"Personally I should not compare Italy with Piccadilly Circus. Still, it's on the map. What do you want to do?"

"I could take the Trieste-Paris express. Could you manage by yourself at Milan?"

"Perfectly. I shall find some one. Or some one will find me. In any case, I can look after myself."

There was a confident note in her voice—associated with the dismissal of cooks—for the professor had just gone back to his compartment. She rose from her seat, prepared to follow him, when the Customs officials appeared at the end of the corridor.

That check was of vital importance to Miss Froy. As Laura did not wish to be interrupted, she wanted for the professor's luggage to be examined. In the interval the barrister had sensed a situation which prompted a few leading questions.

"What makes you look so serious?" he asked.

"You forget, this may be serious for me."

"In what way? We're not parting for ever, are we? I can meet you in London."

"How nice."

Now that her pride was no longer a buffer between the natural woman and self-expression, Laura felt mistress of the situation. She held the winning card.

"I'm wondering," she said, "if I can endure the name of 'Brown,' after being Mrs. Parmiter."

"Will the occasion arise?"

"Well, if there's a divorce, you could hardly let me down. It's not done, is it, darling?"

"But, my sweet, there will be no divorce."

"I'm not so sure. I know you made it very plain to me that you would not give your wife the evidence to divorce you. But she'll read about us in the papers—and no woman could stand for that."

"You seem very sure of your publicity. Perhaps you have a better knowledge of the possibilities than I have?"

The barrister glowered at her as though she were a hostile witness, for he had realised the threat which underlay her smiles.

She meant to try to rush a situation.

"I can reassure you on one point," he said coldly. "If your husband brings an action, you may lose your own charming name. But you will not be called upon to make the greater sacrifice. There is already one Lady Brown. . . . My wife will never divorce me."

Laura stared at him incredulously.

"You mean, she'd take it lying down?" she asked.

"Does the posture matter? The point is that we have a complete understanding. It would be against our mutual interests ever to part company. . . . But I think here is no real risk of publicity. Do you?"

He knew he had won and she knew it too. His cool level voice stirred up Laura's smouldering passion.

"If there was," she said, "it seems as if I was the only one that stood to lose. You boast that your wife won't divorce you. Well, my husband would. And I thank God for it. At least I am married to a real man with decent natural feelings."

The barrister screwed his monocle in his eye in an instinctive effort to preserve his dignity.

"I'm afraid I've disappointed you," he said. "I had no idea that I had led you to hope for anything beyond a pleasant and unconventional holiday."

Before Laura could speak, the Customs officer entered their compartment and was very courteous and obliging over the luggage and passport of the distinguished Englishman and his beautiful bride.

After he had gone the professor appeared again in the corridor—still puffing at his pipe.

Laura shivered at the sight of him because he reminded her of what she had nearly lost by a premature disclosure. Her fine house, her social position, her respectability, and perhaps even her children would all have been swept away for a man who would not marry her.

"Thanks be I sounded him first," she told herself.

Her gain was Miss Froy's loss. The express carried a ghost-passenger, whose passport—although in order—was never examined. An experienced traveller, she realised what had actually happened when the train began to move slowly for the second time.

"Frontier," she thought.

But in the interval between picking up the Customs officials and dropping them again, she swept through a cycle of emotions, as she shot up from midnight to sunshine, and then—through the gradual twilight of suspense, deferred hope and anxiety—sank back again into darkness.

The train rushed on.

CHAPTER TWENTY-FIVE
"STRANGE DISAPPEARANCE"

After the Professor had left her Iris slumped down in her seat and listened to the choppy current of the train's frantic rhythm. The grimed glass was beginning to grow steamy, so that it was difficult to see anything outside the window, except an occasional line of lights when the express flashed through some small station.

Since Miss Froy had been proved non-existent by the laws of logic she felt too flat to be interested in her surroundings. She had not even sufficient spirit to remain angry with the professor for his interference.

"All travellers are selfish," she reflected. "It was those Miss Flood-Porters. They were afraid they might be saddled with me, so they got at the professor. I expect he consulted the doctor about what could be done."

She straightened herself in an effort to relieve the aching of her back. The continual shaking of the train had worn her out, while her neck felt as though it were made of plaster of Paris and would crack in two if she jerked it. At that moment she longed for a comfortable bed where she could rest, far from the incessant rattle and din.

It was the doctor's suggestion—a good night's rest. Yet, although she began to doubt her own wisdom in trying to swim against the current, she remained set in her determination to oppose advice.

Presently Hare entered and sat opposite to her in Miss Kummer's seat.

"Well?" he asked hopefully. "Going to stop off at Trieste?"

"No," replied Iris stiffly.

"But are you sure you're fit to go on?"

"Does it matter to you?"

"No. But, all the same, I'm worried stiff about you."

"Why?"

"Hanged if I know. It's not a habit of mine."

Against her will Iris smiled faintly. She could not forget Miss Froy. The memory of her was a grumbling undercurrent, like the aching of a stopped tooth. Yet whenever Hare was present he acted in the same manner as a local application that deadened the pain. In spite of her misery there was a queer thrill in being alone with him on the same nightmare journey.

"Cheer up," he said. "You'll soon be home. Back with your colony of friends."

The prospect seemed suddenly distasteful to Iris.

"I don't want to see one of them," she declared petulantly. "I don't want to get back. I've no home. And nothing seems worth while."

"What do you do with yourself?"

"Nothing. . . . Oh, play about."

"With other chaps?"

"Yes. We all do the same things. Silly things. There's not one real person among the lot of us. . . . Sometimes I get terrified. I'm wasting my youth. What's at the end of it all?"

Hare made no attempt to console her or answer her question. He stared out at the darkness with a half-smile playing round his mouth. When he began to talk, it was about himself.

"My life's very different from yours. I never know where I'm going next. But it's always rough. And things happen. Not always pleasant things. . . . Still, if I could take you with me on my next job, you'd get a complete change. You'd go without every comfort a refined home should have—but I'd lay you odds you'd never feel bored again."

"Sounds lovely. . . . Are you proposing to me?"

"No. Just waiting to dodge when you start to throw custard pies at me."

"But lots of men propose to me. And I'd like to go to a rough place."

"Fine. Now I can go into it seriously. Got any money?"

"Some. Just chicken feed."

"Suits me. I've none."

They were scarcely conscious of what they said as they talked at random in the only language they knew—their light words utterly at variance with the yearning in their eyes.

"You know," said Hare, breaking a pause, "all this is rot. I'm only doing it to take your mind off things."

"You mean—Miss Froy?"

"Yes, confound the woman."

To his surprise Iris changed the subject.

"What sort of brain have you?" she asked.

"Fair to middling, when it's lubricated. It works best on beer."

"Could you write a detective thriller?"

"No. Can't spell."

"But could you solve one?"

"Every time."

"Then suppose you give me a demonstration. You've been very clever in proving Miss Froy could not exist. But—if she did—could you find out what might have happened to her? Or is it too difficult?"

Hare burst out laughing.

"I used to think," he said, "that if ever I liked a girl, I'd be cut out by some beautiful band conductor with waved hair. I'm hanged if I thought I'd have to play second fiddle to an ancient governess. Time's revenge, I suppose. Long ago, I bit one. And she was a good governess. . . . Well, here goes."

He lit his pipe and furrowed his brow while Iris watched him with intense interest. His face—no longer slack and careless—was hardened into lines of concentration, so that he looked almost a different man. Sometimes he ran his fingers through his hair, when his rebellious tuft flared up rampant and sometimes he chuckled.

Presently he gave a crow of triumph.

"I've got it to fit. Bit of jiggery-pokery in parts, but it hangs together. Now would you like to hear an original story called 'The Strange Disappearance of Miss Froy'?"

Iris winced at the light tone.

"I'd love to," she told him.

"Then you're for it. But, first of all, when you boarded the train, was there one nun next door to you, or two?"

"I only noticed one as we passed the carriage. She had a horrible face."

"Hum. My story demands a second one, later on."

"That's convenient, because there is another one. I met her in the corridor."

"Seen her since?"

"No, but I shouldn't notice one way or another. There's such a jam."

"Good. That proves that no one would be likely to notice whether there was one nun, or two, connected with the invalid outfit. Especially as it's corked up at the end of the corridor. You see, I've got to play about with these blessed nuns, so they're very important."

"Yes. Go on."

"I haven't started yet. The nun part was preamble. Here really goes. . . . Miss Froy is a spy who's got some information which she's sneaking out of the country. So she's got to be bumped off. And what better way than on a railway journey?"

"You mean—they've thrown her on the rails going through a tunnel?" asked Iris faintly.

"Don't be absurd. And don't look so wan. If they chucked her on the line her body would be found and awkward questions asked. No, she's got to *disappear*. And what I was getting at was this. On a journey, a lot of valuable time will be wasted before it can be proved even that she is missing. At first her people will think she's lost a connection or stopped at Paris for a day or two, to shop. So, by the time they get busy, the trail will be stone cold."

"But they wouldn't know what to do. They're old and helpless."

"Tough luck. You're making my tale positively pathetic. But even if they are influential and know the ropes, when they begin to make inquiries they'd find themselves up against a conspiracy of silence."

"Why, is the whole train in the plot?"

"No, just the baroness, the doctor and the nuns. Of course, there'd be a passive conspiracy of silence, as I mentioned before. None of the passengers, who are local folk, would dare to contradict any statement of the baroness."

"But, don't forget the baroness said something to the ticket collector which you couldn't understand."

"Is this my yarn or yours? But—perhaps you're right. There may be a railway official or two in it. In fact, there must have been some dirty work at the cross-roads over her reserved seat. They had to be sure that she would be in the baroness' compartment, and at the end of the train."

"Next door to the doctor, too. . . . But what's *happened to her?*"

In spite of her resolution to keep cool, Iris clenched her fingers in suspense as she waited.

"Aha," gloated Hare. "That's where my brain comes in. . . . Miss Froy is lying in the next compartment to this, covered with rugs, and disguised with bandages and trimmings. Her own mother wouldn't know her now."

"How? When?"

"It happened when you obligingly dropped off to sleep. Enter the doctor. He asks Miss Froy if she could render some slight service to his patient. I'm sure I don't know why he should rope her in as he's got a nurse on tap. But she'll go."

"I know she would."

"Well, directly she enters the compartment she gets the surprise of her life. To begin with all the blinds are drawn down and the place is in darkness. She smells a rat, but before she can squeal the three of them set on her."

"The three?"

"Ja, the patient is one of the gang. One of them pinions her, the other throttles her so she can't shout, and the doctor is busy giving her an injection, to make her unconscious."

Iris felt her heart hammer as she pictured the scene.

"It *could* happen," she said.

Hare gave her a delighted beam.

"Wish I had you to listen to my golf-stories. You've got the right reaction to lies. Artistic ones, of course. . . . By the way, one of the nuns is a man. The one with the ugly face."

"I believe she is."

"Don't be so prejudiced. All men aren't ugly. Well, Miss Froy is now down and out, so they're able to bandage her up roughly, and stick a lot of plaster over her face, to disguise her. Then they tie her up, gag her, and lay her out, in the place of the false patient, who was already dressed in uniform, only she was covered with rugs. So she's only to pull off her plaster and stick a veil over her bandaged head, to look the perfect nun. Number two."

"I saw a second one in the corridor," nodded Iris.

"But, by now, you've unearthed some English people who will remember Miss Froy, and you've roped in the parson's wife. As I think I explained before, the conspirators have to produce some one, and trust to bluff. So, down comes the blind again, while the second nun—the one who posed as the original patient, dresses herself in Miss Froy's clothes."

As Iris remained silent Hare looked rather depressed.

"Admittedly feeble," he said, "but the best I can do."

Iris scarcely heard him, for she was nerving herself to ask a question.

"What will happen to her when they reach Trieste?"

"Oh, this is the part my readers will adore," explained Hare. "She'll be put in an ambulance and taken to some lonely house, overlooking deep deserted water—a creek, or arm of the river, or something. You know the sort of thing—black oily water lapping a derelict quay. Then she'll be weighted, and all that, and neatly dumped among the mud and ooze. But I'm not altogether ruthless. I'll let them keep her drugged to the bitter end. So the old dear'll know nothing about it. . . . Here. What's up?"

Iris had sprung to her feet and was tugging at the door.

"Everything you say may be true," she panted. "We mustn't waste time. We must do something."

Hare forced her back to her seat.

"Here—you," he said. Already she meant everything to him but he'd completely forgotten her name. "This is simply a yarn I made up for you."

"But I must get to that patient," cried Iris. "It's Miss Froy. I must see for myself."

"Don't be a fool. The patient next door is *real*, and she's been smashed up. If we forced our way into that carriage and started to make any fuss the doctor would order us out. And quite right too."

"Then you won't help me?" asked Iris despairingly.

"Definitely no. I'm sorry to keep harping on it, but I can't forget your sunstroke. And when I remember my own experience and how I mistook my own footer captain—"

"For the Prince of Wales. I know, I know."

"I'm frightfully sorry I led you on. I only told you how things *might* be worked. But I'm just like the old lady who saw a giraffe for the first time. Honestly, 'I *don't believe it.*' "

CHAPTER TWENTY-SIX

SIGNATURE

O f course," agreed Iris dully, "you were just making it up. What a fool I am."

As she tried to stifle her disappointment some one—farther down the corridor—began to speak in an unnaturally loud voice. The words were unintelligible to her and sounded like an incantation for rain; but Hare's face lit up.

"Some one's got a wireless set," he said springing up. "It's the news. Back in two shakes."

When he returned he told Iris what he had heard.

"Another good murder sensation gone west. The medical evidence on the editor states he was shot about midnight—while the High Hat had left for his hunting lodge directly after dinner. So they can't hang it on him. Pity."

As he spoke something floated across Iris' memory, like one of those spirals of cobweb which are wafted on the air on still autumn mornings. She started up as Hare looked at his watch.

"Nearly time for the second dinner," he told her. "Coming?"

"No. But the others will be coming back."

"What's the odds? Are you frightened of them?"

"Don't be absurd. But they make a little clump, all together, this end. And I—I don't like being so near that doctor."

"Not frightened then. Well, our compartment will be empty while the professor and I are having dinner. I am willing to sub-let it, at a nominal rent, to a good tenant."

After he had gone Iris felt the old limpness stealing over her. A long-drawn howl, as though some damned soul were lamenting, fol-

lowed by the rattle of machine-gun fire, told her that they were passing through a tunnel. It suggested a gruesome possibility.

Suppose—at that minute—a dead body were being thrown out of
the train.

She reminded herself that Hare's story was fiction and managed
to drive it from her mind. But another tale—which she had read in a
magazine and which was supposed to be authentic—slipped in to take
its place.

It was about two ladies who arrived by night at a continental
hotel, on their way back from an oriental tour. The daughter carefully noted the number of her mother's room before she went to her
own. When she returned some time later, she found no trace of her
mother, while the room itself had different furniture and a new wallpaper.

When she made inquiries, the entire staff, from the manager
downwards, assured her that she had come to the hotel alone. The
mother's name was not in the register. The cab-driver and the
porters at the railway terminus all supported the conspiracy.

The mother had been blown out like a match.

Of course there was an explanation. In the daughter's absence
the mother had died of plague, contracted in the East. The mere rumour would have kept away millions of visitors from the exhibition
about to be held in the city. With such important interests at stake a
unit had to be sacrificed.

Iris' hands began to grow clammy as she wondered whether Miss
Froy's disappearance might not be a parallel on a very small scale. In
her case it would not involve a vast and complicated organisation, or
a fantastic conspiracy—merely the collusion of a few interested persons.

And Hare had shown her how it *could* be worked.

She began to try to fit the facts to the theory. To begin with, although the baroness was wealthy, she was sharing a compartment
with the proletariat. Why? Because she had decided to take her journey at the last minute and was unable to make a reservation? In that
case, the Flood-Porters and the Todhunters could not have secured
coupés.

Then was it meanness? Or was it because she wanted a special
compartment at the end of the corridor, next to the doctor's carriage,
where they would not be seen nor disturbed?

Further—was it chance that the rest of the seats were occupied by
local people whose destinies she swayed to a great extent?

The questions hung in the air while a cloud of fresh suspicions quivered into Iris' mind. It was an extraordinary fact that the blinds remained undrawn in the invalid's compartment. She was left on show—so to speak—to declare the goods. Was that to prepare the way for a version of the old strategy—to hide an object in some place where it was visible to every one?

Only—what had poor little Miss Froy done? Hare was right when he declared that he was influenced mainly by the question of motive. As far as Iris could tell she had discharged her duties so faithfully that her august employer had personally thanked for her services rendered.

Suddenly Iris caught her breath with excitement.

"That was why," she whispered.

The personage was supposed to be in his hunting-lodge at the time of the murder. Yet Miss Froy, by tactlessly lying awake, had surprised him coming from the one and only bathroom, where presumably he had been washing before he flitted.

She had destroyed his alibi.

Her knowledge would be a positive danger in view of the fact that she was returning to teach the children of the Red leader. Every one knew that she was a confirmed gossip and rattle. She would be proud of the personage's confidence and advertise it. And, as a British subject—with no axe to grind—her testimony would have weight against a mass of interested evidence.

When the personage shook hands so graciously with her, he was sealing her doom.

Iris pictured the hurried family conference at dawn—the hasty summons to the necessary confederates. Telephones would be humming with secret messages. In view of the urgency, it followed of necessity that Miss Froy's suppression could not be the perfect crime.

She tried to control the gallop of her imagination.

"Maximilian-Max"—she had not forgotten his name, since "Hare was too long"—"spun me a yarn. He was stretching the facts to make them fit in. Perhaps I'm doing the same. It's futile to palpitate about some one who may not exist. After all, as they say, she may be only a delusion. . . . I do wish I could be sure."

Her wish was granted in a dramatic manner. The carriage had grown hot and the steam on the window was turning gradually to beads of moisture, which was beginning to trickle downwards.

Iris followed the slow slide of one of these drops from the top to a grimy corner of uncleaned pane.

Suddenly she gave a start as she noticed a tiny name which had been written on the smoked glass.

Leaning over she was able to decipher the signature.

It was "Winifred Froy."

CHAPTER TWENTY-SEVEN
THE ACID TEST

I ris stared at the name, hardly able to believe that her eyes were not playing her a trick. The tiny neat handwriting was round and unformed as that of a schoolgirl, and suggested the character of the little governess—half-prim adult, and half-arrested youth.

It was proof positive that Miss Froy had sat recently in the corner seat. Iris vaguely remembered that she was knitting when she first entered the carriage. When she scrawled her name on the grimy glass with the point of one of her pins, she was working off some of the gush of her holiday mood.

"*I* was right, after all," thought Iris exultantly.

It was an overwhelming relief to emerge from the fog of her nightmare. But her exhilaration was blotted out almost immediately by a sense of impending crisis.

She was no longer fighting shadows—but facing actual danger.

A terrible fate awaited Miss Froy. She was the only person on the train who realised the peril. And time was slipping remorselessly away. A glance at her watch showed that it was ten minutes past nine. In less than an hour they would arrive at Trieste.

Trieste now assumed a terrible significance. It was the place of execution.

The train was rushing at tremendous speed, in a drive to make up lost time. It rattled and shrieked as it swung round the curves—shaking the carriages as though it recked nothing of its human load. Iris felt that they were in the grip of an insensate maddened force, which, itself, was a victim to a relentless system.

The driver would be fined for every minute over the scheduled time of arrival.

The sense of urgency made Iris spring up from her seat, only to stagger back again at a sudden wave of faintness. She felt a knocking inside her head and stabbing pains behind her eyeballs, as the result of her unguarded movement. With a vague hope that it might act as an opiate she lit a cigarette.

A babel of voices in the corridor told her that the passengers were returning from dinner. The family party, with the blonde, came first. They were all in excellent spirits after their meal and took no notice of Iris, who glowered at them from her corner. She resented their passive conspiracy, even though they were ignorant of any threat to Miss Froy, and were pleased only to be of some slight service to the baroness.

They were followed by the woman who wore Miss Froy's tweed suit and feathered hat. At the sight of the impostor, Iris' temperature rushed up again as she asked herself whether this were actually the second nursing-sister whom she had met in the corridor.

Both had dull black eyes, a sallow skin, and bad teeth; but the peasants in the railway waiting-room had looked much the same. As it was impossible to reach any conclusion, Iris rose and dashed out into the corridor.

She was strung up to action and intended to storm the next carriage. But blocking her way and almost filling the narrow space was the gigantic black figure of the baroness. As she towered above her, Iris realised that she was bottled up in the danger-zone of the train—away from every one she knew.

She felt suddenly helpless and afraid as she looked away from the grim face to the shrieking darkness rushing past the window. The maniac shrieks of the engine and the frantic shaking of the train increased her sense of nightmare. Once again her knees began to shake and she had a terrible fear that she was going to faint.

Her horror of becoming insensible and so being at their mercy made her fight the dizziness with every ounce of her strength. Licking her dry lips, she managed to speak to the baroness.

"Let me pass, please."

Instead of giving way, the baroness looked at her twitching face.

"You are in pain," she said. "That is not good, for you are young and you travel without friends. I will ask the nurse here for a tablet to relieve your head."

"No, thank you," said Iris firmly. "Please, will you stand on one side?"

The baroness took no notice of her request, or of her refusal. Instead, she shouted some imperative command which brought the callous-faced nurse to the doorway of the invalid's carriage. Iris noticed sub-consciously that the baroness' words did not conform to a conventional request, but were a peremptory order for prompt action.

The glass of the patient's window was also growing steamy from heat, but Iris tried to look inside. The still form laid out on the seat appeared to have no face—only a white blur.

As she asked herself what lay underneath the bandages, the nurse noticed her interest. She pounced forward and gripped the girl's arm, as though to pull her inside.

Iris looked up at the brutal mouth, the dark shading round the lips and the muscular fingers, which were covered with short black hairs.

"It is a man," she thought.

Terror urged her to an elemental action of self-defence. She was scarcely conscious of what she did as she pressed the end of her smouldering cigarette against the back of the woman's hand. Taken by surprise, she relaxed her grip with what sounded like an oath.

In that instant Iris pushed past the baroness and dashed down the corridor, fighting her way against the stream of returning diners. Although they opposed her advance, she was glad of their presence, because they formed a barrier between her and the baroness.

As her terror waned, she began to realise that every one in the train seemed to be laughing at her. The guard openly sneered as he twisted his little black spiked moustache. There was a white flash of teeth and hoots of smothered laughter. The passengers evidently considered her slightly mad and were amused by a funny spectacle.

Their derision made Iris aware of the situation. She felt self-conscious and ashamed as though she were in an unclothed kind of dream.

"Heavens, what have I done?" she asked herself. "That nurse only offered me some aspirin, or something. And I burned her wrist. If they're really on the level, they will think me mad."

Then her terror flared up again at the thought of Miss Froy.

"They won't listen to me. But I must make them understand about her. . . . This train seems a mile long. I'll never get there. . . . Faces. Grinning faces. . . . Miss Froy. I must be in time."

She seemed imprisoned in some horrible nightmare, where her limbs were weighted with lead and refused to obey her will. The passengers blocked her way, so that she appeared to recede two steps where she advanced one. To her distorted imagination, the faces of these strangers were caricatures of humanity—blank, insensible and heartless. While Miss Froy was going to be murdered, no one cared for anything but dinner.

After an age-long struggle through several sections of the train—when the connecting-passages turned to clanking iron concertinas, which tried to catch her and press her to death—she reached the restaurant-car. As she heard the clink of china and the hum of voices, her brain-storm passed and she lingered in the entrance—her returning sense of convention at war with elemental fear and horror.

Soup was being served, and the diners were spooning it up vigorously, for they had been waiting a long time for their meal. In her lucid interval, Iris realised the hopeless prospect of trying to convince hungry men who had only just begun their dinner.

Once again she ran the gauntlet of faces as she reeled down the gangway. Two waiters, whispering to one another, tittered, and she felt sure that they were sneering at her.

The professor, who shared a table with Hare, saw her first, and an expression of apprehension flitted across his long face. He was chatting to the doctor, who had lingered over his coffee and liqueur, since the places for the second dinner were not all filled.

Iris felt chilled by her reception when they all stared at her in silence. Even Hare's eyes held no welcome, as he watched her with a worried frown.

In desperation she appealed to the professor.

"For heaven's sake go on with your soup. Don't stop—but please listen. This is of deadly importance. I know there is a Miss Froy. I know there's a conspiracy against her. And I know why."

The professor gave a resigned shrug as he continued drinking his soup. As Iris poured out her incoherent story, she was herself appalled by the weakness of her arguments. Before she finished she despaired of convincing him. He listened in stony silence, and was obviously absorbed by the exact proportion of salt to add to his soup.

At the end of the tale he raised his brows interrogatively as he glanced at the doctor, who broke into some rapid explanation. Watching their faces with anxious eyes, Iris could tell that Hare was disturbed by what was said, for he cut into the conversation.

"That's not her yarn. It's mine. I spun it for a lark, and the poor kid sucked it in. So, if any one's loopy, it's——"

He broke off, suddenly aware of what he had revealed. But Iris was too distraught to notice implications.

"Won't you come now?" she entreated the professor.

He looked at his empty plate which the waiter had placed in readiness for the fish course.

"Can't it wait until after dinner?" he asked wearily.

"Wait? Won't you understand. It's deadly, terribly urgent. When we reach Trieste it will be too late."

Again the professor mutely consulted the doctor, who stared fixedly at Iris as though he were trying to hypnotise her. When at last he spoke, it was in English for her benefit.

"Perhaps we had better come at once to see my patient. I'm sorry that your dinner should be spoiled, professor. But the young lady is in a very highly-strung condition. It may be—safer—to try and reassure her."

Wearing the expression of a martyr to his sense of justice, the professor unfolded himself from his seat. Once again the little procession staggered in single file down the corridors of the reeling train. As they neared the end, Hare turned and spoke to Iris in a fierce whisper.

"Don't be a blasted fool and start anything."

Her heart sank as she realised that his advice was too late. The nursing-sister was already displaying her hand for the benefit of the doctor and the professor. Iris noticed vaguely that she had wound a handkerchief around her wrist as though she wished to conceal it from too close a scrutiny.

Then the doctor turned to her and spoke in soothing-syrupy accents.

"My dear young lady, wasn't it rather—impetuous—to burn my poor nurse? And all because she offered you a harmless tablet to relieve the pain of your head. . . . See, professor, how her face twitches."

Iris shrank as he touched her forehead with a cold forefinger to illustrate his meaning.

Suddenly she remembered that when one is losing a defensive game, the only hope is to attack. Plucking up her courage, she managed to steady her voice.

"I cannot be sorry enough about the burn. It's no excuse to say I was hysterical. But there was some excuse for my being so. There is so much that I cannot understand."

The doctor accepted her challenge.

"Such as—?" he asked.

"Well, the professor tells me you offered to take me to a nursing home at Trieste."

"The offer is still open."

"Yet you are supposed to be rushing a patient to hospital for a dangerous operation. How could you possible bother yourself with a complete stranger? . . . It makes one wonder exactly how serious her injuries are. Or if she has any at all."

The doctor stroked his beard.

"My offer was made merely to relieve the professor of an unwelcome responsibility, which is in my line and not in his. But I am afraid that you exaggerate your own importance. My intention was to give you a seat in the ambulance which took us to the hospital. After we had gone inside with our patient, the driver would follow his instructions and drive you to some recommended nursing home. It was not for professional service—but merely to give you a good night's rest, so that you could continue your journey on the following day."

The proposal sounded so reasonable that Iris could only fall back on her second question.

"Where is the other nurse?"

The doctor paused perceptibly before his reply.

"There is only one nurse."

As she looked at his impassive face, further screened by his black spade-beard, Iris knew instinctively that it was useless to protest. The result would be the same—denials on every side. No one but herself would have seen that second nurse. Just as no one would accept Miss Froy's signature as genuine—supposing that it had not been already destroyed by condensation.

The doctor spoke to the professor.

"I am sorry to detain you further," he said, "but here is a young lady who believes very terrible things. We must try to convince her of her *delusions.*"

He crossed to the shrouded form of his patient and pulled up a corner of one of the rugs, displaying a neat pair of legs.

"Can you identify these stockings or these boots?" he asked.

Iris shook her head as she looked at the thick silk stockings and regulation brown calf single-strap shoes.

"You know I can't," she said. "But you might have better luck if you would raise just one bandage and let me see her face."

The doctor grimaced with horror.

"Ah," he said, "I see you do not understand. I must tell you something that is not pretty. Listen." He touched the swathed forehead with a butterfly flick of his fingertips. "There is no face here at all. *No face.* Only lumps of raw flesh. Perhaps we shall make quite another face, if we are lucky. We shall see."

His fingers moved on and hovered for a second over the bandage which covered the eyes of the figure.

"We await the oculist's verdict on these," he said. "Till then, we dare not expose them to a flicker of light. It may be total blindness, for one eye is but pulp. But science can work marvels."

He smiled at Iris and continued.

"But most terrible of all is the injury to the brain. I will not describe it, for already you look sick. First of all we must attend to that. Afterwards—the rest, if the patient still lives."

"I don't believe you," Iris told him. "It's all lies."

"In that case," said the doctor smoothly, "you can convince yourself. You have only to tear one little strip of plaster from the face, to see.... But if you do, I warn you that bleeding will start again and the patient will die instantly from shock.... You will be charged with murder and you will be hanged.... But since you are so sure of the face which is under these bandages, you will not hesitate.... *Will* you tear off this strip?"

Iris felt Hare's fingers closing over her arm, as she hesitated. Her instinct told her that the doctor was putting up a bluff, and that she ought to grasp at even the hundredth chance to save Miss Froy's life.

Yet the doctor had done his work too well. The thought of that mutilated face spouting fountains of blood made her shrink back. Afterwards? The rope—or Broadmoor for life. It was too horrible a prospect to contemplate.

"I—I can't," she whispered.

"Ah," sneered the doctor, "you talk, but you are not so brave."

For the first time it struck Iris that he had never intended to risk his patient. Had he done so, he would have committed professional suicide. Both he and the nurse were on guard, to anticipate her movements.

All the same, he had some ulterior object in view, for he seemed disappointed.

At the time Iris was too sick at heart over her own cowardice to question further. She realised that she had two enemies in the carriage.

The doctor—and herself.

CHAPTER TWENTY-EIGHT
RAISE YOUR HAND

I ris started from her daze to realise that the professor was talking of dinner.

"If you would hurry back to the dining-car, Hare," he said hopefully, "you might explain to the waiter that we've missed the fish course."

"He'd only say it was 'off,'" Hare told him. "They've got to rush the second dinner through before we make Trieste."

"Tut, tut." The professor clicked. "In that case, we had better return at once. Perhaps you would go on ahead and order extra portions of meat, since we've gone without our fish."

"Not their fault. We walked out on the fish. But I'll see what can be done about it."

Hare checked himself and turned to Iris rather doubtfully.

"Do you mind?" he asked.

She gave an hysterical laugh, for it had just struck her that although the professor was confident of his ability to conduct her investigation, he could not risk his linguistic talent where vital interests were concerned.

"Go back, for pity's sake," she said. "Nothing matters but dinner, does it?"

The professor, whose lean face had brightened at the prospect of food, resented her reproach. Although famished, he felt he must defend his own reputation for meticulous justice.

"Are you being quite fair?" he asked. "We've paid a stiff price for a meal, so we are entitled to claim—at least—a portion of it. And you must admit we have not spared time or convenience in trying to convince you of your mistake."

She shook her head, but she was oppressed by a weight of hopelessness. There seemed nothing more to be done to help Miss Froy. Any attempt at interference would only expose her to the risk of reprisal.

It was not cowardice alone that made her fear the power of the doctor, but common sense. Since she was the sole person on the train who believed in Miss Froy's existence, it stood to reason that she could be of use to her only if she were a free agent.

Her one chance lay in convincing the professor that there was a real need of further investigation. Although she disliked him, he possessed those qualities which counted in such a crisis. He was pigheaded, coolly humane, and rigidly just. If he were morally certain that he was right, nothing could shake him, and he would plug away at his objective in face of all opposition.

It was bad luck that—at the moment—he was concentrating on his dinner.

Her curdled brain cleared just as he was about to leave the carriage.

"Professor," she said, "if I'm right, when you get back to England you'll read about a missing Englishwoman—Miss Froy. When you do, it will be too late to save her. Won't it haunt you for the rest of your life, that you wouldn't listen to me now?"

"I might regret it," admitted the professor, "only the occasion is not likely to arise."

"But if you'll only do something—a very little thing—later you won't have to be sorry at all. And you won't have to cut short your dinner."

"What is it that you want me to do?"

"Go with the doctor to the Trieste hospital and watch while a bandage or strip of plaster is removed. Just enough to show you that there is genuine injury."

Although the professor was staggered by the suggestion, he considered it slowly with habitual conscientiousness. It encouraged Iris to follow up her advantage with a fresh argument.

"You must admit, I can do nothing. I'm not a lunatic and it might mean manslaughter. Besides, the doctor wouldn't let me. So it boils down to this. His precious test means nothing at all."

At her words, the first distrust of the doctor entered the professor's mind. It was visible in his puckered face and drumming fingers. He always counted the cost before he entertained any project, although it was typical of his high sense of duty that it could not deter him.

In this case the drawbacks were numerous, the chief of which was finance. Although he was no spendthrift, his standard of living at Cambridge was only covered by his salary, and he had to encroach on his capital for holidays. To get a complete mental change he went away at least three times a year, so he had to practise economy.

As the most expensive part of this special trip was the long railway journey, he had booked through one of the cheaper tourist agencies which specialised in cut-prices. Therefore, his ticket would not admit his breaking the journey anywhere.

To make matters more difficult he was short of cash, since his dislike of communal travel had made him yield to the temptation of sharing a coupé with Hare on the return journey.

There was another and more urgent reason why he should not stop at Trieste for the night. Delay involved the sacrifice of a cherished engagement. He had been invited to spend the following week-end with an elderly peer—an intellectual recluse—who lived in a remote corner of Wales. If he reached England on Saturday, instead of Friday, it would be too late.

The doctor watched him closely as he frowned and tapped his cheek-bones.

"Is it not convenient for you to stop at Trieste?" he asked.

"Definitely inconvenient."

"I am sorry. Because, in my own interest, I must beg of you to do what this young lady asks."

"Why?" asked the professor, incensed by this double assault on his week-end.

"Because I am growing convinced that there must be some reason for this poor young lady's distress. It is always 'Miss Froy.' Is that a common name in England, like 'Smith'?"

"It is not familiar to me."

"But she had heard it before—and in connection with some terrible experience. I do not know what has happened. But l think that there really is a lady called 'Miss Froy,' and that some harm has happened to her. I think, too, that this poor young lady knew, but the shock has driven away all memory."

"Absurd," interrupted Iris. "I won't——"

"Shut up," whispered Hare fiercely.

He had listened with close attention, for he was beginning to wonder whether the doctor had not found the true explanation of Iris' delusion. She had been unconscious until just before she managed to catch the train. Although the explanation was sunstroke, it might have been supplied through the agency of some interested person, who wanted to confuse her recollection.

"You will understand," went on the doctor, "that I do not wish to be under any suspicion, if—later—a lady might be declared missing."

"It's a preposterous idea," said the professor. "Besides, the hospital authorities would back you up."

"But how am I to prove that it is this patient I bring to them, and not some substitute? But if you, professor, would accompany me to the hospital and wait for the surgeon's initial examination, there can be no further question. It is your high reputation that I crave for my protection."

The professor smiled bleakly, for he was very hungry. Although he was an excellent bridge player, he had no knowledge of poker. Consequently the doctor's offer seemed to him proof positive that there was not even the flimsiest foundation for Iris' fantastic theory.

"I think you are carrying professional caution too far," he said. "Miss Carr"—unlike Hare, he was used to memorising names—"has declared that she went to the dining-car with one lady whom she called 'Miss Froy'—and that lady has since been identified as a Miss Kummer. . . . She is not well, which accounts for her mistake. . . . In the circumstances, there is no shred of evidence that the real Miss Froy— if there is such a person—is on the train at all."

"Then, in case of future trouble, may I apply to you to support any statement I might make?" asked the doctor.

"Certainly. I will give you my card."

The professor wheeled round and turned dinnerwards.

Hare divined that Iris was on the verge of an explosion.

Hitherto he had managed to restrain her by the warning pressure of his hand on her arm, but she was at the end of her patience.

"Don't throw a scene," he implored. "It's no good. Come back to the coop."

Instead of obeying she raised her voice.

"Miss Froy. Can you hear me? Hold up your hand if you can."

CHAPTER TWENTY-NINE
TRIESTE

Miss Froy heard her. She held up her hand.

Although she was blinded by her bandage, she had recognised Iris' voice among a murmur of other sounds. In a confused fashion she realised that people were talking; but their tones were blurred and broken, as though they were far away—giving the impression of an imperfect long-distance call.

She tried to speak to them, but could not because of her gag. Once before she had contrived to move it partially, with frenzied pressure—remembering the while how her father used to tease her about the power of her tongue. She put every ounce of strength into that cry for help, but it was an uncouth incoherent sound, like an animal in pain.

No one heard her—and her captors had wedged the gag tighter, increasing her discomfort. Her arms were bound to her body above the elbows, and her legs were tied together at the ankles by a surgical bandage. The doctor made no attempt to hide it when he exposed her shoes and stockings for identification. He knew that among such a profusion of strappings, one more or less would never be remarked.

However, her hands were free from the wrists, because the supply of bindings had given out, and—in any case—they were powerless to do more than wave feebly. Miss Froy's heart fluttered with joy as she told herself that her clever girl knew that an instantaneous response to her appeal, however slight, would show that the patient recognised her name and was giving proof of identity.

So she spread out her fingers—fan-wise—and flapped them in the air in a pathetic S.O.S.

Then once again her mind, which she was unable to control, slid away. It was cobwebbed and smeared from drugs, but every now and again a corner would clear, like the transparent red stains of juice that veins the scum of boiling jam. In these lucid moments a whirl of memories returned, but in the end her mind always went back to that first moment of shock.

It was incredible—monstrous. She had been sitting in her compartment when the doctor had entered and asked if any one would help him raise his patient. He explained that the nurse had gone away for a few minutes and the poor creature in his charge had grown restless, as though she were uncomfortable.

It was second-nature to Miss Froy to respond. She was not only always ready to be of service, but she was also anxious to see the crash casualty at closed quarters, besides learning perhaps more about the accident. It would be something with which to thrill the family when she related her adventures on Friday night.

When they entered the patient's compartment the doctor asked her to raise the head while he lifted the body. It was with specially deep sympathy that she bent over the prostrate form, because she was reminded of the contrast between them.

"She's smashed," she thought, "and I'm well and happy. I'm going home."

Suddenly a long pair of white linen-clad arms shot out and clutched her throat.

The helpless patient was gripping her windpipe in a merciless grip. In that appalling moment she remembered a Grand Guignol horror, when an electrified corpse had strangled the man who had galvanised it to synthetic life. Then the pressure tightened, lights flashed under her eyelids, and she knew no more.

For some time the eclipse had been total. Then, gradually there were infinitesimal rifts in the darkness of her senses. She became conscious that she was trussed, gagged and blinded, while muffled voices discussed her fate.

It was not a cheerful prospect. Although she was ignorant of her crime, she had an inkling of her sentence. It was connected with an ambulance which would meet them at Trieste. But it would take her to no hospital.

Yet in spite of cramp and thirst, of bodily anguish and mental torment, she never gave up hope.

It was said in the family that she followed Aunt Jane. In her lifetime, this Victorian lady had wanted a talking-doll, a tricycle, an operatic career, a husband, a legacy. She got none of these things, but she never discarded a single wish, nor doubted that each would be granted—in the end.

When the end came, she was seventy-seven and a pensioner on family charity; yet she closed her eyes with as lively a faith in the talking-doll as in the legacy which would grant her a leisured life and a dignified death.

Aunt Jane helps to explain why Miss Froy remained tolerably calm in the face of each fresh disappointment. Mercifully, however, her clear moments were of brief duration. Most of the time she was in a drugged dream, when she was for ever trying to get home.

She always managed to reach the gate and saw the lighted garden path with its exaggerated hollows—when a displaced pebble revealed a pit. The turf borders and the pink and purple Chinese asters were unnaturally vivid in the lamplight, while the pungent scent of early chrysanthemums hung on the frosty air.

But although she was so near that she could see the cracked red tile in the passage, she knew that something was wrong, and that she would never reach the door. . . . It was when she was struggling out of one of these tantalising visions, that she heard Iris calling her name and telling her to hold up her hand.

Unfortunately she did not know that there was a bad block in her system of communication. None of the channels were clear, so that her brain did not register the message from her ears until after the doctor—in a state of indignant horror—had literally swept his visitors out into the corridor. Even after that, some time elapsed before her nerve-centres were linked up with the intelligence department, and by then it was too late.

The blinds had all been drawn down, so there was no one besides the nurse to witness the futile signal of her fluttering fingers.

Outside the door the doctor wiped his face in his agitation.

"That was a terrible thing to do," he said, his voice vibrating with passion. "I was wrong to let you in at all. But I never dreamed you would be so imbecile as to try and injure my poor patient."

As Iris shrank involuntarily before his rage, he appealed to the professor.

"You can understand, professor, that absolute quiet is essential for my patient. The grave injury to the head——"

"How can she get quiet on a railway journey?" broke in Iris, as the engine plunged into a tunnel with an ear-splitting yell.

"That is something quite different," explained the doctor. "One can sleep through traffic. It is the slight unaccustomed sound which wakens one from sleep. If she had heard you she might have been

called back, while I am doing my utmost—in mercy—to keep her unconscious."

"I quite understand," the professor assured him. "And I regret this
has happened." His voice was glacial as he spoke to Iris. "You had
better get back to your carriage, Miss Carr."

"Yes, come on," urged Hare.

Iris felt that they were all against her. In sudden defiance she
launched a lone offensive.

"Directly we reach Trieste I am going to the British Embassy," she
told them.

They were brave words, but her head was swimming and her
knees shook so violently that she felt incapable of carrying out her
threat. All the same, her intentions filled her with an illusion of
power. Then Hare tackled her in his old international form and carried her along the corridors with the impetus of a tidal-bore, while
the professor plodded in the rear.

"My only hope is we shall get some sort of a dinner," was his
parting remark to the doctor.

Iris was too bewildered by what had happened to resist Hare's
high-handed treatment. She could not understand why there had
been no response to her cry. It shook her confidence and made her
feel that her moral cowardice in failing to expose the mystery patient
was justified.

Yet even if she were a genuine accident case, the danger which
threatened Miss Froy was not dormant. When she was back in the
coupé she presented Hare with an ultimatum.

"Are you with me or against me? Are you stopping at Trieste?"

"No," replied Hare firmly. "Neither are you."

"I see. Then you didn't mean what you said about liking me—and
all that."

"I certainly meant—all that."

"Well, if you don't come with me to the Embassy, I'm through
with you."

Hare tugged at his collar miserably.

"Can't you realise I'm your only friend?" he asked.

"If you were a friend you'd prove it."

"Wish I could, only I haven't the spunk. As your best friend, I
ought to knock you out, so that you'd stay put for the next twenty-
four hours, and rest your poor old head."

"Oh, I hate you," stormed Iris. "For heaven's sake, go away."

In the next compartment the Misses Flood-Porter overheard
scraps of the dialogue.

"That girl certainly contrives to get some excitement out of a railway journey," remarked the elder sister astringently.

While the young people were quarrelling about her, Miss Froy was lying rigid, with still hands. It had gradually dawned upon her that she had no audience, so her demonstration was wasted. However, she had one crumb of comfort when Iris mentioned appealing to the British Consul. She had heard that cry of defiance through the closed door.

Presently she realised that the hint had not been wasted. There was a low rumbling conference inside the carriage.

"Trieste," remarked a masculine voice. It belonged to the doctor's chauffeur, who was wearing the incongruous uniform of a nursing-sister. "What now?"

"We must waste no time at Trieste," replied the doctor. "We shall have to drive all night, like hell, to get back to protection."

"But—where will you dump the body now?"

The doctor mentioned a place.

"It is on our road," he explained. "The wharf is deserted—and the eels swarm."

"Good. They will be hungry. Very soon there will be no face to tell tales, if it should be found later. . . . Will you dump the clothes and baggage there too?"

"Fool. They would be a certain mark of identification there. No, we take them with us in the car. You will incinerate them without delay directly we get back."

Although her brain was so misty, some vibration of her senses made Miss Froy aware that they were talking about her. She shuddered instinctively at the thought of black stagnant water, thick with mud and scummed with refuse. She had such a violent dislike to corruption.

But she missed the real implication.

The chauffeur went on to anticipate difficulties.

"What if any one makes inquiries at the Trieste hospitals?"

"We shall explain that the patient died in transit."

"But if they demand to see the corpse?"

"They will see it. There will be no difficulty about that, once we are back. The mortuary will provide me with a female corpse which I will mutilate."

"Hum. I wish I was safely at home. There is still that girl."

"Yes," remarked the doctor, "it is extraordinary how the English will regard themselves as the policemen of the world. Even a girl has the habit. But it is a mistake to think them a stupid nation. That professor has a good brain, and he is no fool. . . . But luckily, he is honourable, and believes that all the world must be honourable, too. He will support all I say."

"Still, I wish I was back," harped the chauffeur.

"The risk is great," his employer reminded him. "So, also, is the reward."

The drone of masculine voices which drummed against Miss Froy's semi-sealed ears—like the hum of a spinning wheel—ceased. The chauffeur thought of the garage he would buy, while the doctor planned to retire from practice.

He did not relish his present commission, but the ruling family claimed his loyalty and self-interest forbade disobedience. Directly the baroness had sent for him, privately, by night, he had evolved the best scheme he could devise on the spur of the moment, to clear an obstacle in the illustrious pathway.

He knew why he had been chosen, for he, himself, would not use a delicate surgical instrument to cut a tarry string. His reputation was smutted because of recent mishaps at the local hospital. His scientific curiosity was keener than his wish to exterminate disease, and he was under suspicion of having prolonged operations unduly, and at the expense of life.

From the beginning the venture had been unlucky, because of the interference of the English girl. But for her, the little plan would have worked perfectly, by reason of its simplicity, and the small number of confederates. He knew that he and his chauffeur would take their lives in their hands when they scorched homewards through dangerous passes, rounding dizzy precipices on one wheel, in their effort to race the express back to their native territory.

But once they were back, every emergency would be forestalled. An adequate explanation would be forthcoming to any inquiry. No one would have any awkward knowledge to disclose and every wire that connected the dead patient with Miss Froy would be cut.

"Will you dump the English girl in the sewer, too?" asked the chauffeur suddenly.

"No," replied the doctor. "Further complication would be dangerous. But when we reach Trieste she will not be in a position to make further trouble for us."

Miss Froy heard his words and, for the first time, her optimism failed her. With a wave of agonised longing she thought of the family at home, for she had sent them her timetable, and she guessed they would be tracing it on the map.

True to her forecast, at that moment they were thinking of her.

They had done their best to fight their unusual depression, for they had lighted a fire—composed principally of fir-cones—and had been guilty of an extravagant supper—scrambled eggs.

Sock lay on the rug watching the flames. In spite of the welcome warmth, he was still subdued after his disappointment, for he had rushed off against orders to meet the train, with a hope new-born.

Mr. Froy looked at his wife and noticed that the underlip of her small firm mouth was pendulous and that she sagged in her chair. For the first time he realised that she was his senior, and that he, too, had grown old.

Then he glanced at the clock.

"Winsome's nearly come to the end of her first stage home-wards," he told his wife. "She'll soon reach Trieste."

Mrs. Froy passed the information on to the dog.

"Sock, the little mistress is really on her way home now. Every minute she is coming nearer—nearer—nearer. In another half-hour she'll be at Trieste."

Trieste.

CHAPTER THIRTY
RECANTATION

The waiter managed to salvage some dinner for the professor and Hare, who ate through the courses in silence. As they were finishing their cheese and biscuits, the doctor entered the dining-car and seated himself at their table.

"I am sorry to disturb you," he said, "but I want a little conference about the young English lady."

The professor stifled an exclamation, for he feared that Iris had broken out in some fresh indiscretion.

"Coffee, please," he said to the waiter. "Black. . . . Well—what is the trouble *now?*"

"As a medical man I find myself faced with a responsibility," explained the doctor. "The lady is in a dangerous mental state."

"What grounds have you for your conclusion?" asked the professor, who never accepted a statement without data.

The doctor shrugged.

"Surely it is obvious to the meanest intelligence that she is suffering from a delusion. She invents some one who is not here. But there are other signs. She is highly excitable—suspicious of every one—inclined to be violent——"

As he noticed Hare's involuntary grimace, he broke off and turned to the younger man.

"Pardon. Is the young lady your affianced?"

"No," grunted Hare.

"But perhaps a lover—or a dear friend? Yet it would not surprise me to hear that she has been very angry recently with you. Has she?"

"I'm not really popular at present," admitted Hare.

"Thank you for the confidence, for it confirms my diagnosis. It is always a sign of mental malady when they turn upon those they love best."

He could tell he had captured Hare's sympathy as he continued.

"There is no real danger if we can take a precaution. It is essential at this stage that her brain should be rested. If she could have a long sleep, I am confident she will wake up quite well again. But if we let her persist in working herself up into a fever, the mental mischief may be—irreparable."

"I think there is something in that, professor," agreed Hare. "It's exactly what I've been thinking myself."

"What do you propose?" asked the professor cautiously.

"I should suggest," replied the doctor, "that you persuade her to swallow a harmless sedative which I can give you."

"She will object."

"Then it should be given by force."

"Impossible. We cannot control her wishes."

"Then, perhaps, you could trick her into taking it?"

As the professor remained mulishly silent, the doctor half rose from the table.

"I can assure you," he said, "that I have more than enough responsibility of my own to shoulder, with my patient. I only felt it my duty to warn you. We doctors are pledged to the service of humanity—whether we receive fees or no. But now that I have explained the position, I can leave the decision to you. My own conscience is clear."

The doctor was on the point of departing with dignity, when Hare called him back.

"Don't go, doctor. I feel the same as you about this. I've had personal experience of delusions, with concussion." He turned eagerly to the professor. "Can't we wangle it somehow?"

The professor's long upper lip seemed to lengthen in his disapproval.

"I could not be a party to such a course," he said. "It would be gross interference with Miss Carr's personal liberty. She is a free agent."

"Then—you'd prefer to remain 'good form' and see her go bughouse?" asked Hare indignantly.

The professor smiled acidly.

"My own impression is," he told them, "that there is not the slightest danger of that. I have had experience of such cases.

"My work brings me into contact with neurotic young women. To my mind, Miss Carr is merely hysterical."

"Then—what do you propose?" asked Hare.

"I think a salutary shock will probably bring her to her senses."

Reinforced by his meal, the professor felt master of the situation. He finished his coffee and liqueur, flicked a crumb from his waistcoat, and rose in a leisurely manner.

"I will reason with Miss Carr," he said.

He strolled out of the dining-car and lurched along the corridors. As he passed the coupé occupied by the Misses Flood-Porter, he was tempted to resign his mission and join them in a little chat. The ladies looked so composed and immaculate—for they were well in advance of their preparations for arrival at Trieste—that he was hopeful that further conversation would reveal some mutual friend.

Resolute in his self-imposed duty, he entered his carriage and seated himself opposite to Iris. His first glance told him that she had been lighting cigarette after cigarette, only to throw them away, barely smoked. Although her action was merely a sign of nervous tension, he looked with distaste at the litter of spent matches on the floor and seats.

"Will you take some advice offered in a friendly spirit?" he asked, speaking to her as though she were a fractious child.

"No," replied Iris mutinously. "I want to hear the truth, for a change."

"The truth may be a bit of a shock. But you've asked for it, so you shall have it. . . . The doctor has just told me that, as a result of your sunstroke, you are—very slightly, and only temporarily—deranged."

The professor honestly believed that he was dealing with a neurotic girl who was telling lies from a love of sensation, so he watched her reaction with complacent confidence. When he saw the horror in her eyes, he felt his experiment was justified.

"Do you mean—mad?" she asked in a whisper.

"Oh, dear, no. Nothing to be frightened of. But he is not happy about your safety as you are travelling alone. He may be forced to take steps to ensure it, unless you can manage to keep perfectly quiet."

"What steps?" asked Iris. "Do you mean that nursing home? I should resist. No one can do anything to me against my will."

"In the circumstances, violence would be most unwise. It would only confirm the doctor's fears. But I want to make the position quite clear to you. Listen."

The professor sawed the air with his forefinger and spoke impressively.

"You have only to keep calm and everything will be all right. No one will interfere with you in any way, unless you remind them of your existence. To be brutally frank, you've made yourself a public nuisance. It's got to stop."

The professor was not so unhuman as he seemed. His own unpleasant experience with his infatuated student had prejudiced him against emotion, but he thought he was acting in Iris' interests.

Therefore he could have no idea of the hell of fear into which he plunged her. She was white to her lips as she shrank into the corner of the carriage. She was afraid of him—afraid of every one in the train. Even Hare seemed to have entered into the conspiracy against her. The whole world appeared roped into a league that threatened her sanity.

Lighting yet one more cigarette with shaking fingers, she tried to realise the position. It seemed clear that she had blundered into important issues and that, consequently, she had to be suppressed. The professor had been sent to bribe her with immunity in return for her silence.

Even while she rejected compromise angrily, she had to face the cold truth. She had not a ghost of a chance to fight these influential people. If she persisted in her hopeless quest to find Miss Froy, the doctor would merely pull wires and whisk her away to some nursing home in Trieste.

She remembered Miss Froy's tale of the woman who had been held in a private mental asylum. The same might happen to her. Any opposition on her part would be used as evidence against her sanity. They could keep her imprisoned and under the influence of drugs, until she really crashed under the strain.

It would be some appreciable time before any one missed her. She was not expected in England, for she had not troubled to engage rooms at an hotel. Her friends would believe that she was still abroad. When at last her lawyers or the bank made inquiries, it would be too late. They would trace her to the nursing home, and arrive to find a lunatic.

In her distraught state, she plunged herself into a morass of distorted fears and exaggerated perils. But although her reason was nearly submerged by a tidal wave of panic, one corner of her brain still functioned on common-sense lines.

It convinced her that Miss Froy's rescue was an utterly hopeless proposition.

"Well?" asked the professor patiently, as she tossed away her unsmoked cigarette.

Suddenly Iris thought of the familiar Calais-Dover express—the white cliffs—Victoria Station—with almost frantic longing. She felt homesick for England and the cheery casual crowd of her friends. Before her eyes, in letters of fire, flashed the familiar slogan—"SAFETY FIRST."

"Well?" repeated the professor. "Have you come to your senses?"

Utterly worn out and paralysed with fear, Iris slipped into the trough of lost hopes. She reminded herself that Miss Froy was merely a stranger whom she had tried to help. To persist merely meant a double—and useless—sacrifice.

"Yes," she replied dully.

"You'll make no more scenes?" went on the professor.

"No."

"Good. . . . Now, will you admit to me that you invented Miss Froy?"

Iris felt plunged in the hell of Judas Iscariot and all traitors as she made her denial.

"Yes. I invented her. There's no Miss Froy."

CHAPTER THIRTY-ONE
A CUP OF SOUP

The doctor looked after the professor as he went from the dining-car.

"That is a very clever man," he said dryly. "He would cure illness by a scolding. Yet he may be right. Indeed, for the first time in my career, I hope I shall be proved wrong."

He watched Hare's frowning face closely and asked, "What is your opinion?"

"I know he's making a damnable blunder," growled the young man.

" 'He that knows, and knows that he knows,' " quoted the doctor, " 'he is wise.' . . . Well—what then?"

"Hanged if I know."

"Ah, you feel, perhaps, that the professor is cleverer than you?"

"I feel nothing of the kind. Our lines are different."

"Then probably you are not used to exert authority?"

"Oh, no. I've only got to control hundreds of toughs—and some of them ready on the draw."

"Then, frankly, I do not understand your hesitation. Unless, of course, you fear the young lady's anger when she discovers she has been tricked. She has what you call 'spirit,' and what I call 'temper,' since I have a very sweet wife myself. . . . Well, it is for you to decide whether you prefer the angry words of a sane woman to the gentle smile of an imbecile."

"Don't rub it in," muttered Hare. "I've got to *think.*"

"There is not much time left," the doctor reminded him.

"I know. But—it's the hell of a risk."

"Not at all. Here is my card. I will write a declaration on it that the drug is harmless, under penalty of heavy damages, should the lady be ill afterwards as a direct result. . . . I will do more. You shall have a sample to take back to England, so that you may have it analysed."

Hare pulled at his lip. He knew that the doctor's offer was fair, yet he could not shake off his distrust of the unknown.

The doctor seemed to read his thoughts.

"Perhaps," he said, "you hesitate because I am not Dr. Smith, of London, England. Yet, if you were in a strange city and had a raging toothache, you would seek relief from the first dentist. Remember, a man's name on a brass plate, with certain letters after it, is a profession's guarantee of good faith to the public."

He let the argument sink in while Hare continued to maltreat his face and hair. Presently he glanced at his watch, and then thrust his wrist before the young man's eyes.

"See the time. I must go back to my patient."

Hare sprang up as though galvanised.

"One minute, doctor. How could we give the stuff?"

The doctor knew that the bridge had been crossed as he hastened to explain.

"That poor young lady has had no dinner," he said reproachfully. "Surely you will bring her a small cup of soup, since there will be no opportunities on the Italian train, until they couple the breakfast-car."

"Chump," exclaimed Hare, hitting his head. "I never thought that she'd be hungry. . . . But if she is asleep, how will I manage changing trains at Trieste?"

"Ah, my dear sir, you must not expect miracles. You are too impatient. The drug will not take full effect until she is in the Italian train. Then, she will sleep and sleep. But at Trieste she will merely be very dull, very heavy, very docile. And"—the doctor's eyes narrowed—"she will be far too torpid to worry about any phantom lady."

"Suits me all right. . . . I'll take a chance."

The doctor accompanied him to the kitchen-car and fought a battle with the protesting chef. In the end medical authority won the day. Not long afterwards, Hare, with anxious eyes and tightly compressed lips, began his fateful journey along the corridors, holding a half-filled bowl.

But he carried so much more than soup. Within the narrow circle of the cup lay the destiny of a woman.

As he staggered on his way—by a coincidence due to the time, in a small stone house in England, Mrs. Froy's thoughts turned to nour-ishment.

"I do hope Winnie will eat something before she gets to Trieste," she said to Mr. Froy. "Her dinner won't stand by her all through the night. Besides she is always too excited to eat on a journey. She merely pecks her first supper at home."

Her husband gave a guilty smile, for he knew the reason for Win-nie's lack of appetite.

Meanwhile, Hare was still scared by the responsibility of his step. While he assured himself that he was actually carrying a gift of san-ity to Iris, he could not rid himself of apprehension. Tormented by in-decision, he proposed a foolish test for himself.

"If I don't spill any it's going to be O.K. But if I do, I'll cry off."

He crabbed slowly along, with utmost care and caution while the train seemed to put on an extra spurt of speed. The soup splashed fu-riously against the rim of the cup—for ever on the point of brimming over. Yet, in some extraordinary manner, it always whirled within its confines.

Hare was reminded of a simple circus trick he used to practise—as a boy—with a hoop and a glass of water. Apparently the same princi-ple operated now, and the soup could not be spilt from sheer velocity of motion.

But just before he reached the reserved portion of the train he came to grief completely. As he was crossing the connecting passage, a small boy—rushing from the pursuit of a smaller girl—charged into him and received a baptism of soup, together with an undesirable name.

Hare broke off in his malediction to wipe his fingers.

"That's torn it," he muttered. "Well, it's out of my hands now."

Meanwhile Iris was actually in the grip of a brainstorm. When the professor left her she was numb with fear. Some vital mainspring in her brain seemed to have snapped, reducing her mind to a limp tan-gle. Miss Froy was a lost cause—so she denied her. But nothing was left but a void, without aim or hope or self-respect.

"I was her only chance," she told herself. "And now I've crashed too."

The knowledge was torture which she tried vainly to forget. But vivid little thumbnail pictures persisted in flashing before her closed eyes. Two bent old people, huddled in a lighted doorway—waiting. Sock—a woolly blunderbuss—rushing off to meet a mistress who would never come home.

She was most affected by the thought of the dog, for she assumed the senility of the aged parents. She told herself that the shock would probably kill them both, since they would be too devoted—or too used to each other—to survive singly. And then—what would become of the dog, stranded and hungry in a country cottage?

She worked herself into a positive fever about him. As her temperature rose, her head began to ache so furiously that it seemed to bang in a series of small explosions which kept time with the frantic revolutions of the wheels.

"You're get-ting near. You're get-ting near."

And then the rhythm changed and began to chop out a devil's tattoo. "Nearer—nearer—nearer—*nearer*—NEARER."

Nearer to Trieste. The express was in the relentless grip of the schedule. The pulsations of the engine throbbed through Iris like the shaking arteries of an overdriven heart. It rocked and roared over the rails—a metal monster racing an invisible rival.

It had to beat Time.

When Hare came into her carriage she hardly raised her eyes, and did not speak to him.

"Still hating me?" he asked.

"I only hate myself," she said dully.

He looked furtively at her twitching face and burning cheeks, which, to his mind, confirmed the doctor's diagnosis of dangerously overstrung nerves, while he assured himself that—since he could not give her that essential sock on the jaw—he was rendering her a real service.

"I've brought you some soup," he said guiltily.

She shrank from it even while she thanked him.

"Sweet of you—but I couldn't touch it."

"Try. It'll make a new man of you."

"All right, then. Leave it, will you?"

"No, that's too old a dodge. The instant I go you'll chuck it out of the window. Well—I'm not going."

Iris clutched her head.

"I feel so sick," she pleaded.

"Lack of nourishment. Listen, my child, there's a history of the try-try-again kind connected with that simple bowl of soup. I slaughtered the chef to get it in the first place. Then, on my way here, some wretched kid bowled the whole lot over. . . . I said, 'Kismet.' And then I said, 'She's had nothing all day and she'll have nothing until to-morrow's breakfast.'

"And I went all the way back and slaughtered another chef, all to bring you a second cup."

"Oh, well—" sighed Iris helplessly. "But have I got to be grateful?"

She swallowed the first spoonful with reluctance, grimacing as though it were a nauseous draught; then she paused, while Hare waited in acute suspense.

"What is it?" she asked. "It's got a horribly druggy taste."

"It's the same soup I wolfed down at dinner. That's all I know," lied Hare.

"Well, I'd better get it over."

Raising the cup to her lips, she gulped it down with a shudder.

"You'll feel better soon," Hare assured her as he took the empty bowl from her nerveless hands.

For some time they sat in silence, while he watched her stealthily, hoping to detect the first sign of drowsiness. He knew that drugs affect people differently, and that it was difficult to gauge the right dose for Iris, because of her abnormal condition.

"If anything goes wrong," he thought desperately, "I'll have to take the rap."

At intervals he heard the whine of the professor's voice, as he strained it in an effort to be audible above the uproar of the train. He was in the next compartment, improving an acquaintance with the Misses Flood-Porter, which he hoped to authorise with the discovery of a third-party link.

"You live in Somersetshire," he remarked. "It is a county where I have stayed often. I wonder if we know any mutual friends."

"I hate every single person living there," said Miss Rose vehemently, sweeping away any claimants to friendship.

"Stag-hunting," supplemented Miss Flood-Porter.

Relieved by the explanation the professor began gently and skilfully to extricate a few worthy persons from under the wholesale ban. He was rewarded when the ladies recognised a name.

"Oh, yes. Charming people. Great friends of ours."

The contact was complete and they all shouted against each other.

Iris recognised the voices for, after a time, she spoke to Hare.

"That's the professor, isn't it? I wish you'd tell him I want to sleep, but can't, because he's making too much noise. And slip in something about him being a public nuisance, will you? He'd appreciate it. Because that's what he called me."

The speech was so unexpectedly jaunty, that Hare stared her in surprise. He did not know whether he were imagining changes, but her eyes were less strained, while her face seemed to have lost the glazed flush of fever.

"That doctor's sold me a pup," he thought wrathfully. "She is not settling down. She's gingering up. At this rate she'll be fighting-mad at Trieste."

As a matter of fact their little conspiracy was hampered by their ignorance of working conditions. On the rare occasions when Iris was unwell, her response to treatment was almost immediate. In her abnormal state she was now beating her own speed record. Although its effects were bound to be short-lived, she was feeling miraculously restored by the nourishment, while the drug was beginning imperceptibly to soothe her brain-storm, like the first film of oil spreading over a rough sea.

She was conscious of a glow of spurious strength, followed by a rush of confidence, as she climbed out of the traitor's hell into which she had hurled herself.

"Lost causes are the only causes worth fighting for," she told herself.

In her relief at her own restoration, she smiled at Hare, who grinned back at her.

"Didn't I tell you you'd feel better after that nice strong good nourishing soup?" he asked.

"It tasted as though it was made from a mummy—but it has picked me up," she admitted. "My head's clearer. I realise now that the professor was right. I've made an awful fool of myself."

Hare chalked up a good mark to the properties of the drug.

"You mean—you've chucked Miss Froy off the train?" he asked incredulously.

"Please, don't bring her up again. Of course, there's no such person. I told the professor so."

Iris felt a momentary pang as she looked into his guileless eyes.

"It's a shame to trick him," she thought.

She had resolved on a policy of stratagem. She would sham docility, to avert suspicion. When Trieste was reached, she would contrive to give them the slip and hire a taxi, in which to follow the ambulance. They would not suspect any outside interest in their movements, since she was definitely out of the running.

Having warned the taxi-driver in advance to memorise the address to which Miss Froy was taken, he would drive furiously back to the British Embassy. She had always found Italians gallant and susceptible, so she was sure of enlisting their sympathies and getting immediate action.

Her jammed brain was now clicking on with amazing speed. She told herself that the success of her plan depended on whether she could fool them all. She must return to her own carriage, which was full of the doctor's spies, and sham the requisite limp submission.

"I mustn't overdo it," she thought. "They might want to fuss over me if they thought I was ill."

She counted on the confusion when the passengers, with their luggage, changed trains at the terminus. Hare must be sent off on some errand, since he was her only obstacle. The rest of the travellers would remain true to type and look after their own interests.

She raised her eyes and met Hare's earnest gaze. He was thinking of the nice long sleep which awaited her in the Italian train.

"It's a shame to trick her," he thought.

CHAPTER THIRTY-TWO
THE DREAM

Although it was still some distance from Trieste, the train was already astir with the projected bustle of its arrival. Passengers were beginning to lock opened suitcases and to pull on their coats and hats. Infected by the unrest, the leisurely professor left the Misses Flood-Porter and entered his own coupé.

"I don't want to disturb you," he hinted to Iris. "But we shall soon reach Trieste."

Iris showed none of her former morbid reluctance to return to her own carriage.

"I must get my suitcase," she said, eager to impress the professor with her obedience.

He rewarded her with an approving smile. For the last time she made the shaky journey along the train. Nobody laughed at her or took any notice of her, for every one was too pre-occupied with affairs. Suitcases and bags had already been lifted down from racks and stacked outside the carriages, increasing the congestion. Mothers screamed to collect those children who were still chasing each other in the corridors.

They washed their chocolate-grimed mouths with corners of moistened handkerchiefs. Banana skins were thrown out of the windows—newspapers bundled under the seats.

The heat and the jam were so oppressive that Iris was actually glad to reach her own compartment. But before she could enter, she shrank back as the doctor came out of the invalid's carriage. His face looked dry and white as the pith of willow above the black blotch of his spade-beard, and his eyes—magnified by his glasses—were dark turgid pools.

As he looked at her, she felt that it was useless to try to deceive him. Like an expert chess player he would have forseen any possible move of her own and would be prepared with a counter stroke.

"Is madame better?" he asked.

"Oh, yes. I'm merely slack. Everything seems an effort. And once I sit down I shan't want to move again."

Iris was encouraged by the success of her strategy when the two men exchanged a glance of understanding. She went inside her compartment, but no one appeared to take any interest in her return. The mother and child were reassembling the contents of the family suitcases, while the blonde made an elaborate toilet. The father had taken charge of the baroness' dressing-bag and was evidently prepared to act as temporary courier.

Iris sat and watched them until the spectacle of noses being powdered and waves reset reminded her of her own need to repair. It was essential to make a good impression at the Embassy. She opened her bag languidly and drew out her flapjack, yawning the while with sudden drowsiness. Blinking her eyes violently, she began to apply powder and lipstick.

But before she could finish, her lids were drooping so continuously that she could not see properly. To her dismay, she realised that she was being overwhelmed with waves of sleep.

They were too powerful to resist, although she struggled vainly to keep awake. One after another they swept over her, piling up in a ceaseless procession.

The other passengers began to waver like shadows. Outside, Trieste was visible as a quivering red glow on the night sky. The engine thundered and panted in a last stupendous effort to breast that invisible tape stretched in front of the buffers. Almost abreast, skimmed the vast shadow, with beating wings and swinging scythe.

There was exultation in the stokehold and driver's car, for they were actually ahead of the schedule. Time was beaten, so they relaxed their efforts and slackened speed gradually in readiness for their arrival at Trieste.

Iris' head had fallen forward and her eyes were closed. Then a dog barked in the distance, jerking her awake. As she stared out of the window with clouded gaze, a few scattered lights speckling the darkness told her that they were reaching the outskirts of Trieste.

In that moment she thought of Miss Froy.

"Trieste," she agonised. "I must keep awake."

Then, once again, everything grew blurred and she sank back in her corner.

When Hare returned to the carriage his jaw dropped at the sight of her huddled figure. He called to the doctor, who merely rubbed his bony hands with satisfaction.

"Excellent," he said. "She has responded with most extraordinary rapidity."

"But how will I get her out at Trieste?" demanded Hare.

"You will have no trouble. You can wake her at a touch. This is merely preliminary—what you call a cat's-sleep. She will be merely somewhat dazed."

The doctor turned away, but paused to give a word of advice.

"Better leave her alone until you have secured porters. If you wake her too soon she may sleep again. Each time it will be for longer."

Hare took the hint and stood in the corridor, staring out of the window. The reflection of the lighted train flowing over the masonry of roofs and walls transformed them to the semblance of quivering landscape and water. In every carriage luggage was being lowered. Voices shouted for service. The fleeting friendships of a railway journey were being at once sealed and broken in handshakes and farewells.

Iris slept. . . .

In the coupé of the bridal pair, the barrister—Todhunter, for a few minutes longer—was doing his utmost to reconcile a gesture of renunciation with a strategic retreat.

"Shall we say 'Good-bye' now?" he suggested. "Before we are surrounded with a cloud of witnesses."

Mrs. Laura ignored his overture.

" 'Good-bye,' " she said, carefully curling her lashes upwards. "Thanks for your hospitality. It's been a cheap holiday for me. Cheap in every sense."

In the next coupé the Misses Flood-Porter were facing a major tragedy. It was Miss Flood-Porter who threw the bombshell.

"Rose, did you see the brown suitcase put in the van?"

"No."

"Then I believe it's been left behind. It was pushed under the bed, if you remember."

Their faces were rigid with horror, for their purchases had been packed together for conscientious declaration.

"I was counting on Captain Parker to get them through the Customs for us," lamented Miss Rose. "But it may be in the van."

"It may. We can do nothing but hope for the best."

Iris slept on. . . .

When she was a child she suffered from an unsuspected inferiority complex, due to the difference between her lot and that of other children. Although pampered by adults she was exposed to the secret hostility of some of her companions. She was not equal to reprisals, but, at night, her inhibitions found expression in dreams of power, when she sacked the toy-stores and sweet-shops of London with glorious immunity.

Time brought its revenge and Iris got on top of her own little world. But now the professor's hostility, the antagonism of the doctor and baroness, together with the derision of the other passengers had combined with her sunstroke to make the old inferiority complex flare up again.

The result was that she passed from unconsciousness into one of her childish dreams of power.

She thought she was still on the express and on her way to rescue Miss Froy. The corridors were hundreds of miles long, so that it took her centuries to complete what passed within the limit of a minute. The doctor and a crowd of passengers kept trying to oppose her passages, but she had only to push back their faces, when they dissolved like smoke.

She was mowing them down in swathes when she was aroused by the scream of the engine. Shouts and sudden flashes of light told her that they were rushing into Trieste. Instantly she staggered to her feet—half-awake and half in a dream—and walked directly into the next compartment.

Her action took every one by surprise. No one expected it as it was believed that she was asleep. The doctor and the disguised chauffeur were looking out of the window, watching for the arrival of the ambulance. But Hare—who was chatting to the guard—saw her enter, and he made a frantic effort to stop her.

He was too late. Still under the influence of her dream of power and secure in her knowledge of immunity which raised her high above the fear of consequences—Iris rushed towards the invalid and tore the plaster from her face.

The doctor had made the final mistake of an unlucky venture when he gave her the sleeping-draught. Had she carried out her threat to go to the Embassy, she might have encountered incredulity and delay. But the drug had given her the courage to do the impossible thing.

As the criss-cross of strips peeled off and dangled in her fingers like a star-fish, Hare held his breath with horror. Then the guard behind him gave a whistle of astonishment as, instead of spurting blood and raw mutilated flesh, the sound though reddened skin of a middle-aged woman was revealed. Iris gave a low cry of recognition. *"Miss Froy."*

CHAPTER THIRTY-THREE
THE HERALD

Two days later Iris stood on the platform of Victoria Station, watching the dispersal of the passengers. Among the first to leave were the Misses Flood-Porter. Confident in their right to preferential treatment, they stood aloof with pleased expressions, while an influential gentleman, with an authoritative voice and an infallible method with officials, shouted and shepherded their luggage through the Customs.

Once, by mistake, they looked at Iris, but they were too preoccupied to bow. This was England, where she went out of their lives.

They were very gracious, however, to Mrs. Barnes, when she came to wish them "Good-bye." Her face was radiant with happiness born of a telegram which she had received at Calais.

"Gabriel's cold quite gone very well again."

In spite of her impatience to get home to him she lingered to listen to the last snatch of gossip from the sisters.

"Wasn't it *peculiar* about the honeymoon couple?" asked the elder Miss Flood-Porter. "I know he wasn't on the Venice train, because I looked. And she got off at Milan—alone."

"Yes," nodded Mrs. Barnes. "I know my husband wouldn't like me to say it—but it makes you wonder if they were really married."

"Of course they weren't," scoffed Miss Rose. "I'm precious glad we had nothing to do with them. If there had been a divorce action later on, *we* might have been subpœnaed as witnesses."

"Exactly," agreed her sister. "It just shows how careful one should be when one is abroad. We always keep to our rule *never* to get mixed up in other people's business."

Iris smiled rather bitterly at the conscious virtue in their voices. It reminded her of what she had suffered as a result of their policy of superb isolation. With a shrug she turned her back on the affectionate leave-taking to watch instead the long thin white beams—as of a myriad searchlights—thrown by the sun through the smoky glass roof.

Although she was still shaky she felt quick with fresh life—glad to be back—glad to be alive. While Hare was scouting round the piles of luggage, her thoughts slipped back journey. Her memories were dim, with many blanks.

There was a black-out at Trieste, when she crashed completely, and she did not realise her surroundings until she was rushing through the darkness in the Italian train. Some one with lustrous black eyes looked after her, while Hare came and went. She slept most of the time, but whenever she woke she was conscious of happiness.

The carriage was crowded with other passengers, all shouting, smoking and gesticulating. She could not understand a word, but she felt in perfect tune and sympathy with all of them. There was so much happiness in the world with the prospect of joyous reunions. The barriers of language were down, so that they were not alien nationalities but fellow-citizens of the world, united by the common touch.

In the morning she discovered another passenger in the carriage—a little drab, middle-aged woman, with a small lined face and vivid blue eyes.

Iris gave a cry of rapture as she hugged her.

"Miss Froy. You horrible little brute to give me all that trouble. . . . Oh, darling, darling."

In spite of the joy of reunion Miss Froy proved a bad exchange for the Italian stranger. Her fussy attentions, her high tinkling laugh, her incessant chatter, became such a strain that Hare had to scheme for intervals of release.

For all the drawbacks, however, there was a sense of great adventure and high hope about the journey. The wind seemed to blow them along when they travelled across the flat stretches of France. Everything moved with them—streaming smoke and fluttering clouds. The wide fields and white sky swam in light, so that they felt that they were sailing through a magic country.

Although she was better Hare refused to answer any of Iris' questions.

"Tell you in London," he always said.

She reminded him of his promise when he returned with her suitcase, duly chalked.

"I can't wait another minute," she told him.

"Righto," he agreed. "Take a pew."

Squatting together on a luggage truck and smoking cigarettes, she listened to his story.

"It was all very tame. No rough-house—no nothing. The guard was a hero. He knew just what to do, and the doctor and the two nurses went like lambs. You see, they'll probably only be charged with attempted abduction."

"What happened to the baroness?" asked Iris.

"Oh, she just sailed out, twice her natural size. No connection at all with the next carriage. . . . But she'll pull wires and wangle their discharge. Wheels within wheels, you know."

Iris felt indifferent to their fate.

"What did the others say when they heard about Miss Froy?" she inquired eagerly. "After all, I was right—and every one was out of step but me."

"To be quite candid," said Hare, "it all went in one ear and out at the other. We had a close shave at Venice and some of the Miss Flood-Porters' luggage was missing. They were in such a panic about it that they were prostrate afterwards. And the parson's wife was very worried about her husband."

"But the professor?"

"Well, he's the sort that doesn't like to be proved wrong. When he saw Miss Froy running about like a two-year-old, he thought it was all exaggerated. I overheard him saying to Miss Flood-Porter, 'People generally get what they invite. I cannot imagine anything of the kind happening to Miss Rose.' "

"Neither can I. . . . Every one seems to be saying 'Good-bye.' Here's my Miss Froy."

Hare hurriedly made his escape just in time to avoid the little woman. She looked wonderfully fit and seemed actually rejuvenated by her terrible experience.

Although she had grown so irritated by the touch of those hard, dry hands, Iris felt a pang of regret now that the parting was near.

"I'm stopping in London for a few hours," confided Miss Froy. "Selfridge's, my dear. Just wandering. Topping."

She looked after Hare as he chased a taxi, and lowered her voice.

"I'm just making up my story to tell them at home. Mater will be *thrilled.*"

"But do you think it wise to tell her?" objected Iris. "At her age it might prove a shock."

"Oh, you mean about me." Miss Froy shook her head and gave

Iris the conspiratorial wink of one schoolgirl to another. "I'm going to keep mum about *that*. She'd throw a fit and she wouldn't let me go back."

"Are you?" gasped Iris.

"Of course. I shall have to give evidence at the trial, very likely. Besides, all the exciting things seem to happen abroad."

"You're a marvel. . . . But what is the story you're making up?"

Miss Froy grew suddenly young.

"It's about you—and your romance. Is it true?"

Iris did not know herself until that minute.

"Yes," she replied. "I'm going with him on his next trip."

"Then I'm first to congratulate you. And, one day, perhaps you'll congratulate me. . . . And now I must fly to send off my wire."

Not long afterwards, a telegram was received at the little grey stone house. Mr. and Mrs. Froy read it together, and later each read it, privately, to Sock.

"Home 8.10 too topping Winnie."

That evening Mrs. Froy stood at the window of Winnie's bedroom. Although she could not see the railway station, she got a glimpse of one amber signal lamp through a gap in the trees.

Everything was ready for her daughter's return. The table was laid in the dining-room and decorated with vases of white dahlias and claret-tinted carrot-tops. The hot-water bottles had been removed from the bed. The rarely-used lamp had been lit in the hall, and the front door thrown open in readiness, so that a strip of light carpeted the mossy garden path.

The supper was keeping hot in the oven. Mrs. Froy always cooked sausages and mashed potatoes for the first meal, under the mistaken impression that it was Winnie's favourite dish. It had been, some thirty years ago—but Winnie never had the heart to undeceive her.

Outside the window was darkness and silence. The stars were frosty and the keen air held the odour of autumnal bonfires. Then, suddenly, the stillness was torn by the scream of the distant train.

Mrs. Froy could trace its approach by the red cloud, quivering about the belt of elms which hid the station. She knew when it stopped, because the engine panted and blew off some steam.

It rattled on again, leaving her guessing. She wondered whether it had brought Winnie. Perhaps she had lost her connection in London. She could see nothing—hear nothing—for she was growing deaf and her eyes were beginning to fail.

The surrounding darkness baffled her and cheated her with unredeemed promises. Figures advanced through the gloom, but—just as her heart leaped in welcome—they always changed back to trees. She strained vainly to catch the first sound of voices—her husband's deep tones and a girl's high-pitched treble.

As she held her breath in suspense, somewhere in the distance a dog barked. Again and again, in frantic excitement Then through the open gate and up the lighted path charged the clumsy shape of a big shaven dog—capering like an overgrown puppy—whirling round in circles—leaping at his shadow—falling over himself in his blundering haste.

It was the herald who had rushed on ahead, to tell her that the young mistress had come home.

THE END

LAURA

PART ONE

CHAPTER ONE

The city that Sunday morning was quiet. Those millions of New Yorkers who, by need or preference, remain in town over a summer week-end had been crushed spiritless by humidity. Over the island hung a fog that smelled and felt like water in which too many soda-water glasses have been washed. Sitting at my desk, pen in hand, I treasured the sense that, among those millions, only I, Waldo Lydecker, was up and doing. The day just past, devoted to shock and misery, had stripped me of sorrow. Now I had gathered strength for the writing of Laura's epitaph. My grief at her sudden and violent death found consolation in the thought that my friend, had she lived to a ripe old age, would have passed into oblivion, whereas the violence of her passing and the genius of her admirer gave her a fair chance at immortality.

My doorbell rang. Its electric vibrations had barely ceased when Roberto, my Filipino manservant, came to tell me that Mr. McPherson had asked to see me.

"Mark McPherson!" I exclaimed, and then, assuming the air of one who might meet Mussolini without trepidation, I bade Roberto ask Mr. McPherson to wait. Mahomet had not rushed out to meet the mountain.

This visit of a not unimportant member of the Police Department—although I am still uncertain of his title or office—conferred a certain honor. Lesser folk are unceremoniously questioned at Headquarters. But what had young McPherson to do with the murder? His triumphs were concerned with political rather than civil crime. In the case of The People of New York *vs.* Associated Dairymen his findings had been responsible—or so the editorial writers said—for bringing down the price of milk a penny a quart. A senatorial committee had borrowed him for an investigation of labor rackets, and only recently his name had been offered by a group of progressives as leader of a national inquiry into defense profits.

Screened by the half-open door of my study, I watched him move restlessly about my drawing-room. He was the sort of man, I saw at once, who affects to scorn affectation; a veritable Cassius who emphasized the lean and hungry look by clothing himself darkly in blue, double-breasted worsted, unadorned white shirt and dull tie. His hands were long and tense, his face slender, his eyes watchful, his nose a direct inheritance from those dour ancestors who had sniffed sin with such constancy that their very nostrils had become aggressive. He carried his shoulders high and walked with a taut erectness as if he were careful of being watched. My drawing-room irritated him; to a man of his fiercely virile temperament, the delicate perfection must be cloying. It was audacious, I admit, to expect appreciation. Was it not slightly optimistic of me to imagine that good taste was responsible for the concentration with which he studied my not unworthy collection of British and American glassware?

I noted that his scowl was fixed upon a shining object, one of my peculiar treasures. Habit, then, had made him alert to detail. On the mantel of Laura's living-room he had, no doubt, observed the partner to my globe-and-pedestal vase of mercury glass. He stretched his hand toward the shelf.

I leaped like a mother leopard.

"Careful, young man. That stuff's priceless."

He turned so sharply that the small rug slid along the polished floor. As he steadied himself against the cabinet, porcelain and glass danced upon the shelves.

"A bull in a china shop," I remarked. The pun restored my humor. I extended my hand.

He smiled mechanically. "I'm here to talk about the Laura Hunt case, Mr. Lydecker."

"Naturally. Have a seat."

He settled his long frame carefully upon a frail chair. I offered cigarettes from a Haviland casket, but he pulled out a pipe.

"You're supposed to be quite an authority on crime yourself, Mr. Lydecker. What do you think about this business?"

I warmed. No writer, however popular, disdains a reader, however humble. "I am honored to know that you read *And More Anon*."

"Only when my paper happens to open to the page."

The affront was not displeasing. In the world I frequent, where personality is generously exposed and friendship offered without reticence, his aloofness struck an uncommon note. I offered my charm. "You may not be a Lydecker fan, Mr. McPherson, but I confess that I've followed your career with breathless excitement."

"You ought to know enough not to believe everything you read in the papers," he said dryly.

I was not to be discouraged. "Isn't criminal investigation a bit out of your line? A trifle unimportant for a man of your achievements?"

"I've been assigned to the case."

"Office politics?"

Except for the purp-purp of his pipe, the room was silent.

"The month is August," I mused. "The Commissioner is off on his holiday, the Deputy Commissioner has always been resentful of your success, and since retail murder is somewhat out of fashion these days and usually, after the first sensation, relegated to Page Two or worse, he has found a convenient way of diminishing your importance."

"The plain truth, if you want to know it"—he was obviously annoyed with himself for bothering to give an excuse—"is that he knew I wanted to see the Dodgers play Boston yesterday afternoon."

I was enchanted. "From trifling enmities do great adventures grow."

"Great adventures! A two-timing dame gets murdered in her flat. So what? A man did it. Find the man. Believe me, Mr. Lydecker, I'm seeing the game this afternoon. The killer himself couldn't stop me."

Pained by his vulgar estimate of my beloved Laura, I spoke mockingly. "Baseball, eh? No wonder your profession has fallen upon evil days. The Great Detectives neither rested nor relaxed until they had relentlessly tracked down their quarry."

"I'm a workingman, I've got hours like everyone else. And if you expect me to work overtime on this third-class mystery, you're thinking of a couple of other fellows."

"Crime doesn't stop because it's Sunday."

"From what I've seen of your late girl friend, Mr. Lydecker, I'd bet my bottom dollar that whoever did that job takes his Sunday off like the rest of us. Probably sleeping until noon and waking himself up with three brandies. Besides, I've got a couple of men working on detail."

"To a man of your achievement, Mr. McPherson, the investigation of a simple murder is probably as interesting as a column of figures to a public accountant who started as a bookkeeper."

This time he laughed. The shell of toughness was wearing thin. He shifted in his chair.

"The sofa," I urged gently, "might be easier on that leg."

He scowled. "Observant, aren't you?"

"You walk carefully, McPherson. Most members of your profession tread like elephants. But since you're sensitive, let me assure you that it's not conspicuous. Extreme astigmatism gives me greater power in the observation of other people's handicaps."

"It's no handicap," he retorted.

"Souvenir of service?" I inquired.

He nodded. "Babylon."

I bounced out of my chair. "The Siege of Babylon, Long Island! Have you read my piece? Wait a minute . . . don't tell me you're the one with the silver fibula."

"Tibia."

"How magnificently exciting! Mattie Grayson! There was a man. Killers aren't what they used to be."

"That's okay with me."

"How many detectives did he get?"

"Three of us with the machine-gun at his mother-in-law's house. Then a couple of us went after him down the alley. Three died and another guy—he got it in the lungs—is still up in Saranac."

"Honorable wounds. You shouldn't be sensitive. How brave it was of you to go back!"

"I was lucky to get back. There was a time, Mr. Lydecker, when I saw a great future as a night watchman. Bravery's got nothing to do with it. A job's a job. Hell, I'm as gun-shy as a traveling salesman that's known too many farmers' daughters."

I laughed aloud. "For a few minutes there, McPherson, I was afraid you had all the Scotch virtues except humor and a taste for good whiskey. How about the whiskey, man?"

"Don't care if I do."

I poured him a stiff one. He took it like the pure waters of Loch Lomond and returned the empty glass for another.

"I hope you don't mind the crack I made about your column, Mr. Lydecker. To tell the truth, I do read it once in a while."

"Why don't you like it?"

Without hesitancy he answered, "You're smooth all right, but you've got nothing to say."

"McPherson, you're a snob. And what's worse, a Scotch snob, than which—as no less an authority than Thackeray has remarked—the world contains no more offensive creature."

He poured his own whiskey this time.

"What is your idea of good literature, Mr. McPherson?"

When he laughed he looked like a Scotch boy who has just learned to accept pleasure without fear of sin. "Yesterday morning, after the body was discovered and we learned that Laura Hunt had stood you up for dinner on Friday night, Sergeant Schultz was sent up here to question you. So he asks you what you did all evening ..."

"And I told him," I interrupted, "that I had eaten a lonely dinner, reviling the woman for her desertion, and read Gibbon in a tepid tub."

"Yeh, and you know what Schultz says? He says this writer guy, Gibbon, must be pretty hot for you to have to read him in a cold bath." After a brief pause, he continued, "I've read Gibbon myself, the whole set, and Prescott and Motley and Josephus' *History of the Jews*." There was exuberance in the fession.

"At college or *pour le sport?*" I asked.

"When does a dick get a chance to go to college? But being laid up in the hospital fourteen months, what can you do but read books?"

"That, I take it, is when you became interested in the social backgrounds of crime."

"Up to that time I was a cluck," he confessed modestly.

"Mattie Grayson's machine-gun wasn't such a tragedy, then. You'd probably still be a cluck on the Homicide Squad."

"You like a man better if he's not hundred per cent, don't you, Mr. Lydecker?"

"I've always doubted the sensibilities of Apollo Belvedere."

Roberto announced breakfast. With his natural good manners, he had set a second place at the table. Mark protested at my invitation since he had come here, not as a guest, but in the pursuit of duty which must be as onerous to me as to himself.

I laughed away his embarrassment. "This is in the line of duty. We haven't even started talking about the murder and I don't propose to starve while we do."

Twenty-four hours earlier a cynical but not unkindly police officer had come into my dining-room with the news that Laura's body had been discovered in her apartment. No morsel of food had passed my lips since that moment when Sergeant Schultz had interrupted a peaceful breakfast with the news that Laura Hunt, after failing to keep her dinner engagement with me, had been shot and killed. Now, in the attempt to restore my failing appetite, Roberto had stewed kidneys and mushrooms in claret. While we ate, Mark described the scene at the morgue where Laura's body had been identified by Bessie, her maid, and her aunt, Susan Treadwell.

In spite of deep suffering, I could not but enjoy the contrast between the young man's appreciation of the meal and the morbid quality of his talk. "When they were shown the body"—he paused to lift a morsel on his fork—"both women collapsed. It was hard to take even if you didn't know her. A lot of blood"—he soaked a bit of toast in the sauce. "With BB shot . . . You can imagine . . ."

I closed my eyes as if she lay there on the Aubusson rug, as Bessie had discovered her, naked except for a blue silk taffeta robe and a pair of silver slippers.

"Fired at close range"—he spooned relish on his plate. "Mrs. Treadwell passed out, but the servant took it like a veteran. She's a queer duck, that Bessie."

"She's been more than maid to Laura. Guide, philosopher, and worst enemy of all of Laura's best friends. Cooks like an angel, but serves bitter herbs with the choicest roasts. No man that entered the apartment was, in Bessie's opinion, good enough for Laura."

"She was cool as a cucumber when the boys got there. Opened the door and pointed to the body so calmly you'd have thought it was an everyday thing for her to find her boss murdered."

"That's Bessie," I commented. "But wait till you get her roused."

Roberto brought in the coffee. Eighteen stories below a motorist blew his siren. Through open windows we heard the rhythms of a Sunday morning radio concert.

"No! No! No!" I cried as Roberto handed Mark my Napoleon cup. I reached across the table and took it myself, leaving the Empress Josephine for my guest.

He drank his coffee in silent disapproval, watching as I unscrewed the carnelian cap of the silver box in which I keep my saccharine tablets. Although I spread butter lavishly on my brioches, I cling religiously to the belief that the substitution of saccharine for sugar in coffee will make me slender and fascinating. His scorn robbed my attitudes of character.

"I must say you go about your work in a leisurely way," I remarked petulantly. "Why don't you go out and take some fingerprints?"

"There are times in the investigation of a crime when it's more important to look at faces."

I turned to the mirror. "How singularly innocent I seem this morning! Tell me, McPherson, have you ever seen such candid eyes?" I took off my glasses and presented my face, round and pink as a cherub's. "But speaking of faces, McPherson, have you met the bride-groom?"

"Shelby Carpenter. I'm seeing him at twelve. He's staying with Mrs. Treadwell."

I seized the fact avidly. "Shelby staying there! Wouldn't he just?"

"He finds the Hotel Framingham too public. Crowds wait in the lobby to see the fellow who was going to marry a murder victim."

"What do you think of Shelby's alibi?"

"What do I think of yours?" he retorted.

"But you've agreed that it's quite normal for a man to spend an evening at home with Gibbon."

"What's wrong about a man going to a Stadium concert?" Puritan nostrils quivered. "Among a lot of music-lovers and art collectors, that seems a pretty natural way to spend an evening."

"If you knew the bridegroom, you'd not think a twenty-five-cent seat normal. But he finds it a convenient way of not having been seen by any of his friends."

"I'm always grateful for information, Mr. Lydecker, but I prefer forming my own opinions."

"Neat, McPherson. Very neat."

"How long had you known her, Mr. Lydecker?"

"Seven, eight—yes, it was eight years," I told him. "We met in '34. Shall I tell you about it?"

Mark puffed at his pipe, the room was filled with its rancid sweet odor. Roberto entered noiselessly to refill the coffee-cups. The radio orchestra played a rhumba.

"She rang my doorbell, McPherson, much as you rang it this morning. I was working at my desk, writing, as I remember, a birth-day piece about a certain eminent American, the Father of Our Country. I should never have committed such a cliché, but, as my editor had asked for it and as we were in the midst of some rather delicate financial rearrangements, I had decided that I could not but gain by appeasement. Just as I was about to throw away a substantial in-crease in earning power as indulgence for my boredom, this lovely child entered my life."

I should have been an actor. Had I been physically better suited to the narcissistic profession, I should probably have been among the greatest of my time. Now, as Mark let the second cup of coffee grow cold, he saw me as I had been eight years before, wrapped in the same style of Persian dressing-gown, padding on loose Japanese clogs to answer the doorbell.

"Carlo, who was Roberto's predecessor, had gone out to do the daily marketing. I think she was surprised to see that I answered my own doorbell. She was a slender thing, timid as a fawn and fawn-like, too, in her young uncertain grace. She had a tiny head, delicate for even that thin body, and the tilt of it along with the bright shyness of her slightly oblique dark eyes further contributed to the sense that Bambi—or Bambi's doe—had escaped from the forest and galloped up the eighteen flights to this apartment.

"When I asked why she had come, she gave a little clucking sound. Fear had taken her voice. I was certain that she had walked around and around the building before daring to enter, and that she had stood in the corridor hearing her own heart pound before she dared touch a frightened finger to my doorbell.

" 'Well, out with it!' Unwilling to acknowledge that I had been touched by her pretty shyness, I spoke harshly. My temper was more choleric in those days, Mr. McPherson.

"She spoke softly and very rapidly. I remember it as all one sentence, beginning with a plea that I forgive her for disturbing me and then promising that I should receive huge publicity for reward if I would endorse a fountain pen her employers were advertising. It was called the Byron.

"I exploded. 'Give *me* publicity, my good girl! Your reasoning is sadly distorted. It's my name that will give distinction to your cheap fountain pen. And how dared you take the sacred name of Byron? Who gave you the right? I've a good mind to write the manufacturers a stiff letter.'

"I tried not to notice the brightness of her eyes, McPherson. I was not aware at this time that she had named the fountain pen herself and that she was proud of its literary sound. She persisted bravely, telling me about a fifty-thousand-dollar advertising campaign which could not fail to glorify my name.

"I felt it my duty to become apoplectic. 'Do you know how many dollars' worth of white space my syndicated columns now occupy? And do you realize that manufacturers of typewriters, toothpaste, and razors with fifty-thousand-dollar checks in their pockets are turned away from this door daily? You talk of giving me publicity!'

"Her embarrassment was painful. I asked if she would stay and have a glass of sherry. Doubtless she would have preferred flight, but she was too shy to refuse. While we drank the sherry, I made her tell me about herself. This was her first job and it represented the apex of her ambitions at the time. She had visited sixty-eight advertising agencies before she got the job. Buried beneath that air of timidity was a magnificent will. Laura knew she was clever, and she was willing to suffer endless rebuffs in order to prove her talents. When she had finished, I said, 'I suppose you think I'm moved by your story and that I'm going to break down and give you that endorsement.' "

"Did you?" Mark inquired.

"McPherson, I am the most mercenary man in America. I never take any action without computing the profit."

"You gave her the endorsement."

I bowed my head in shame. "For seven years Waldo Lydecker has enthusiastically acclaimed the Byron Pen. Without it, I am sure that my collected essays would never sell one hundred thousand copies."

"She must have been a terrific kid," he remarked.

"Only mildly terrific at that period. I recognized her possibilities, however. The next week I entertained her at dinner. That was the beginning. Under my tutelage she developed from a gauche child to a gracious New Yorker. After a year no one would have suspected that she came from Colorado Springs. And she remained loyal and appreciative, McPherson. Of all my friends she is the only one with whom I was willing to share my prestige. She became as well known at opening nights as Waldo Lydecker's graying Van Dyke or his gold-banded stick."

My guest offered no comment. The saturnine mood had returned. Scotch piety and Brooklyn poverty had developed his resistance to chic women. "Was she ever in love with you?"

I recoiled. My answer came in a thick voice. "Laura was always fond of me. She rejected suitor after suitor during those eight years of loyalty."

The contradiction was named Shelby Carpenter. But explanation would come later. Mark knew the value of silence in dealing with such a voluble creature as myself.

"My *love* for Laura," I explained, "was not merely the desire of a mature man for a pretty young thing. There was a deeper basis of affection. Laura had made me a generous man. It's quite fallacious to believe that we grow fond of those whom we've hurt. Remorse cannot compensate. It's more human to shun those whose presence reminds us of a shoddy past. Generosity, not evil, flourishes like the green bay tree. Laura considered me the kindest man in the universe, hence I had to grow to that stature. For her I was always Jovian, in humanity as well as intelligence."

I suspected doubt behind his swift glance of appraisal. He rose. "It's getting late. I've got a date with Carpenter."

"Behold, the bridegroom waits!" As we walked to the door, I added, "I wonder how you're going to like Shelby."

"It's not my business to like or dislike anyone. I'm only interested in her friends . . ."

"As suspects?" I teased.

"For information. I shall probably call on you again, Mr. Lydecker."

"Whenever you like. I do indeed hope to aid, if I can, in the apprehension of the vile being—we can't call him human, can we?—who could have performed such a villainous and uselessly tragic deed. But in the meantime I shall be curious to know your opinion of Shelby."

"You don't think much of him yourself, do you?"

"Shelby was Laura's other life." I stood with my hand on the doorknob. "To my prejudiced way of thinking, the more commonplace and less distinguished side of her existence. But judge for yourself, young man."

We shook hands.

"To solve the puzzle of her death, you must first resolve the mystery of Laura's life. This is no simple task. She had no secret fortune, no hidden rubies. But, I warn you, McPherson, the activities of crooks and racketeers will seem simple in comparison with the motives of a modern woman."

He showed impatience.

"A complicated, cultivated modern woman. 'Concealment, like a worm i' the bud, fed on her damask cheek.' I shall be at your command whenever you call, McPherson. Au revoir."

I stood at the door until he had got into the elevator.

CHAPTER TWO

While a not inconsiderable share of my work has been devoted to the study of murder, I have never stooped to the narration of a mystery story. At the risk of seeming somewhat less than modest, I shall quote from my own works. The sentence, so often reprinted, that opens my essay "Of Sound and Fury,"[1] is pertinent here:

"When, during the 1936 campaign, I learned that the President was a devotee of mystery stories, I voted a straight Republican ticket."

My prejudices have not been shed. I still consider the conventional mystery story an excess of sound and fury, signifying, far worse than nothing, a barbaric need for violence and revenge in that timid horde known as the reading public. The literature of murder investigation bores me as profoundly as its practice irritated Mark McPherson. Yet I am bound to tell this story, just as he was obliged to continue his searches, out of a deep emotional involvement in the case of Laura Hunt. I offer the narrative, not so much as a detective yarn as a love story.

I wish I were its hero. I fancy myself a pensive figure drawn, without conscious will, into a love that was born of violence and destined for tragedy. I am given to thinking of myself in the third person. Many a time, when I have suffered some clumsy misadventure, I am saved from remorse by the substitution for unsavory memory of another captivating installment in *The Life and Times of Waldo Lydecker*. Rare are the nights when I fail to lull myself to sleep without

[1] In the volume *Time, You Thief,* by Waldo Lydecker, 1938.

the sedative of some such heroic statement as "Waldo Lydecker stood, untroubled, at the edge of a cliff beneath which ten thousand angry lions roared."

I make this confession at the risk of exhibiting absurdity. My proportions are, if anything, too heroic. While I measure three inches above six feet, the magnificence of my skeleton is hidden by the weight of my flesh. My dreams dwindle in contrast. Yet I dare say that if the dreams of any so-called normal man were exposed, like Dali drawings, to the vulgar eyes of the masses, there would be no more gravity and dignity left for mankind. At certain times in history, flesh was considered a sign of good disposition, but we live in a tiresome era wherein exercise is held sacred and heroes are always slender. I have more than once endured the ordeal of reducing, but I always give it up when I reflect that no philosophy or fantasy dare enter a mind as usurious as Shylock's over each pound of flesh. So I have learned, at the age of fifty-two, to accept this burden with the same philosophical calm with which I endure such indecencies as hot weather and war news.

But it will not be possible to write of myself heroically in those chapters wherein Mark McPherson moves the story. I have long learned to uphold my ego in a world that also contains Shelby Carpenter, but the young detective is a more potent man. There is no wax in Mark; he is hard coin metal who impresses his own definite stamp upon those who seek to mould him.

He is definite but not simple. His complexities trouble him. Contemptuous of luxury, he is also charmed by it. He resents my collection of glass and porcelain, my Biedermeier and my library, but envies the culture which has developed appreciation of surface lustres. His remarking upon my preference for men who are less than hundred per cent exposed his own sensitivity. Reared in a world that honors only hundred per cents, he has learned in maturity what I knew as a miserable, obese adolescent, that the lame, the halt, and the blind have more malice in their souls, therefore more acumen. Cherishing secret hurt, they probe for the pains and weaknesses of others. And probing is the secret of finding. Through telescopic lenses I discerned in Mark the weakness that normal eyesight might never discover.

The hard coin metal of his character fails to arouse my envy. I am jealous of severed bone, of tortured muscle, of scars whose existence demands such firmness of footstep, such stern, military erectness. My own failings, obesity, astigmatism, the softness of pale flesh, can find no such heroic apology. But a silver shinbone, the legacy of a dying desperado! There is romance in the very anatomy of the man.

For an hour after he had gone, I sat upon the sofa, listless, toying with my envy. That hour exhausted me. I turned for solace to Laura's epitaph. Rhythms failed, words eluded me. Mark had observed that I wrote smoothly but said nothing. I have sometimes suspected this flaw in my talent, but have never faced myself with the admission of failure. Upon that Sunday noon I saw myself as a fat, fussy, and useless male of middle age and doubtful charm. By all that is logical I should have despised Mark McPherson. I could not. For all of his rough edges, he was the man I should have been, the hero of the story.

The hero, but not the interpreter. That is my omniscient rôle. As narrator and interpreter, I shall describe scenes which I never saw and record dialogues which I did not hear. For this impudence I offer no excuse. I am an artist, and it is my business to recreate movement precisely as I create mood. I know these people, their voices ring in my ears, and I need only close my eyes and see characteristic gestures. My written dialogue will have more clarity, compactness, and essence of character than their spoken lines, for I am able to edit while I write, whereas they carried on their conversations in a loose and pointless fashion with no sense of form or crisis in the building of their scenes. And when I write of myself as a character in the story, I shall endeavor to record my flaws with the same objectivity as if I were no more important than any other figure in this macabre romance.

CHAPTER THREE

Laura's Aunt Susan once sang in musical comedy. Then she became a widow. The period between—the hyphen of marriage—is
best forgotten. Never in the years I have known her have I heard
her lament the late Horace Q. Treadwell. The news of Laura's death
had brought her hastily from her summer place on Long Island to the
mausoleum on upper Fifth Avenue. One servant, a grim Finn, had accompanied her. It was Helga who opened the door for Mark and led
him through a maze of dark canals into a vast uncarpeted chamber in
which every piece of furniture, every picture and ornament, wore a
shroud of pale, striped linen.

This was Mark's first visit to a private home on Fifth Avenue. As
he waited, he paced the long room, accosting and retreating from his
lean, dark-clad image in a full-length gold-framed mirror. His
thoughts dwelt upon the meeting with the bereaved bridegroom.
Laura was to have married Shelby Carpenter on the following Thursday. They had passed their blood tests and answered the questions on
the application for a marriage license.

Mark knew these facts thoroughly. Shelby had been disarmingly
frank with the police sergeant who asked the first questions. Folded
in Mark's coat-pocket was a carbon record of the lovers' last meeting.
The facts were commonplace but not conventional.

Laura had been infected with the week-end sickness. From the
first of May until the last of September, she joined the fanatic mob in
week-end pilgrimages to Connecticut. The mouldy house described in
"The Fermenting of New England,"[1] was Laura's converted barn. Her

[1] In the volume *Time, You Thief,* by Waldo Lydecker, 1938.

garden suffered pernicious anaemia and the sums she spent to fertil-
ize that rocky soil would have provided a purple orchid every day of
the year with a corsage of *Odontoglossum grande* for Sundays. But
she persisted in the belief that she saved a vast fortune because, for
five months of the year, she had only to buy flowers once a week.

After my first visit, no amount of persuasion could induce me to
step foot upon the Wilton train. Shelby, however, was a not unwilling
victim. And sometimes she took the maid, Bessie, and thus relieved
herself of household duties which she pretended to enjoy. On this Friday, she had decided to leave them both in town. She needed four or
five days of loneliness, she told Shelby, to bridge the gap between a
Lady Lilith Face Cream campaign and her honeymoon. It would never
do to start as a nervous bride. This reasoning satisfied Shelby. It never
occurred to him that she might have other plans. Nor did he question
her farewell dinner with me. She had arranged, or so she told Shelby,
to leave my house in time to catch the ten-twenty train.

She and Shelby had worked for the same advertising agency. At
five o'clock on Friday afternoon, he went into her office. She gave
her secretary a few final instructions, powdered her nose, reddened
her lips, and rode down in the elevator with him. They stopped for
Martinis at the Tropicale, a bar frequented by advertising and radio
writers. Laura spoke of her plans for the week. She was not certain as
to the hour of her return, but she did not expect Shelby to meet her
train. The trip to and from Wilton was no more to her than a subway
ride. She set Wednesday as the day of her return and promised to
telephone him immediately upon her arrival.

As Mark pondered these facts, his eyes on the checkerboard of light
and dark woods set into Mrs. Treadwell's floor, he became aware that
his restlessness was the subject of nervous scrutiny. The long mirror
framed his first impression of Shelby Carpenter. Against the shrouded
furniture, Shelby was like a brightly lithographed figure on the gaudy
motion-picture poster decorating the sombre granite of an ancient
opera house. The dark suit chosen for this day of mourning could not
dull his vivid grandeur. Male energy shone in his tanned skin, gleamed
from his clear gray eyes, swelled powerful biceps. Later, as Mark told
me of the meeting, he confessed that he was puzzled by an almost overwhelming sense of familiarity. Shelby spoke with the voice of a
stranger but with lips whose considered smile seemed as familiar as
Mark's own reflection. All through the interview and in several later
meetings, Mark sought vainly to recall some earlier association. The
enigma enraged him. Failure seemed to indicate a softening process
within himself. Encounters with Shelby diminished his self-confidence.

They chose chairs at opposite ends of the long room. Shelby had offered, Mark accepted, a Turkish cigarette. Oppressed by Fifth Avenue magnificence, he had barely the courage to ask for an ashtray. And this a man who had faced machine-guns.

Shelby had borne up bravely during the ordeal at Headquarters. As his gentle Southern voice repeated the details of that tragic farewell, he showed clearly that he wished to spare his visitor the effort of sympathy.

"So I put her in the taxi and gave the driver Waldo Lydecker's address. Laura said, 'Good-bye until Wednesday,' and leaned out to kiss me. The next morning the police came to tell me that Bessie had found her body in the apartment. I wouldn't believe it. Laura was in the country. That's what she'd told me, and Laura had not lied to me before."

"We found the taxi-driver and checked with him," Mark informed him. "As soon as they'd turned the corner, she said that he was not to go to Mr. Lydecker's address, but to take her to Grand Central. She'd telephoned Mr. Lydecker earlier in the afternoon to break the dinner date. Have you any idea why she should have lied to you?"

Cigarette smoke curled in flawless circles from Shelby's flawless lips. "I don't like to believe she lied to me. Why should she tell me she was dining with Waldo if she wasn't?"

"She lied twice, first in regard to dining with Mr. Lydecker, and second about leaving town that night."

"I can't believe it. We were always so honest with each other."

Mark accepted the statement without comment. "We've interviewed the porters on duty Friday night at Grand Central and a couple remember her face."

"She always took the Friday night train."

"That's the catch. The only porter who swears to a definite recollection of Laura on this particular night also asked if he'd have his picture in the newspapers. So we strike a dead-end there. She might have taken another taxi from the Forty-Second or Lexington Avenue exits."

"Why?" Shelby sighed. "Why should she have done such a ridiculous thing?"

"If we knew, we might have a reasonable clue. Now as to your alibi, Mr. Carpenter . . ."

Shelby groaned.

"I won't make you go through it again. I've got the details. You had dinner at the Myrtle Cafeteria on Forty-Second Street, you walked to Fifth Avenue, took a bus to a Hundred and Forty-Sixth Street, bought a twenty-five-cent seat for the concert..."

Shelby pouted like a hurt child. "I've had some bad times, you know. When I'm alone I try to save money. I'm just getting on my feet again."

"There's no shame in saving money," Mark reminded him. "That's the only reasonable explanation anyone's given for anything so far. You walked home after the concert, eh? Quite a distance."

"The poor man's exercise." Shelby grinned feebly.

Mark dropped the alibi, and with one of those characteristic swift thrusts, asked: "Why didn't you get married before this? Why did the engagement last so long?"

Shelby cleared his throat.

"Money, wasn't it?"

A schoolboy flush ripened Shelby's skin. He spoke bitterly. "When I went to work for Rose, Rowe and Sanders, I made thirty-five dollars a week. She was getting a hundred and seventy-five." He hesitated, the color of his cheeks brightened to the tones of an overripe peach. "Not that I resented her success. She was so clever that I was awed and respectful. And I wanted her to make as much as she could; believe that, Mr. McPherson. But it's hard on a man's pride. I was brought up to think of women... differently."

"And what made you decide to marry?"

Shelby brightened. "I've had a little success myself."

"But she was still holding a better job. What made you change your mind?"

"There wasn't so much discrepancy. My salary, if not munificent, was respectable. And I felt that I was advancing. Besides, I'd been catching up with my debts. A man doesn't like to get married, you know, while he owes money."

"Except to the woman he's marrying," a shrill voice added.

In the mirror's gilt frame Mark saw the reflection of an advancing figure. She was small, robed in deepest mourning and carrying under her right arm a Pomeranian whose auburn coat matched her own bright hair. As she paused in the door with the marble statues and bronze figurines behind her, the gold frame giving margins to the portrait, she was like a picture done by one of Sargent's imitators who had failed to carry over to the twentieth century the dignity of the nineteenth. Mark had seen her briefly at the inquest and had thought her young to be Laura's aunt. Now he saw that she was well over fifty. The rigid perfection of her face was almost artificial, as if flesh-pink velvet were drawn over an iron frame.

Shelby leaped. "Darling! You remarkable creature! How you've recovered! How can you be so beautiful, darling, when you've gone through such intolerable agonies?" He led her to the room's most important chair.

"I hope you find the fiend"—she addressed Mark but gave attention to her chiffon. "I hope you find him and scrouge his eyes out and drive hot nails through his body and boil him in oil." Her vehemence spent, she tossed Mark her most enchanting smile.

"Comfortable, darling?" Shelby inquired. "How about your fan? Would you like a cool drink?"

Had the dog's affection begun to bore her, she might have dismissed it with the same pretty indifference. To Mark she said: "Has Shelby told you the story of his romantic courtship? I hope he's not left out any of the thrilling episodes."

"Now, darling, what would Laura have said if she could hear you?"

"She'd say I was a jealous bitch. And she'd be right. Except that I'm not jealous. I wouldn't have you on a gold platter, darling."

"You mustn't mind Auntie Sue, Mr. McPherson. She's prejudiced because I'm poor."

"Isn't he cute?" cooed Auntie Sue, petting the dog.

"I never asked Laura for money"—Shelby might have been taking an oath at an altar. "If she were here, she'd swear it, too. I never asked. She knew I was having a hard time and insisted, simply insisted upon lending it to me. She always made money so easily, she said."

"She worked like a dog!" cried Laura's aunt.

The Pomeranian sniffed. Aunt Sue pressed its small nose to her cheek, then settled it upon her lap. Having achieved this enviable position, the Pomeranian looked upon the men smugly.

"Do you know, Mrs. Treadwell, if your niece had any—" Mark produced the word uneasily "—enemies?"

"Enemies!" the good lady shrieked. "Everyone adored her. Didn't everyone adore her, Shelby? She had more friends than money."

"That," Shelby added gravely, "was one of the finest things about her."

"Anyone who had troubles came to her," Aunt Sue declaimed, quite in the manner of the immortal Bernhardt. "I warned her more than once. It's when you put yourself out for people that you find yourself in trouble. Don't you think that's true, Mr. McPherson?"

"I don't know. I've probably not put myself out for enough people." The posturing offended him; he had become curt.

His annoyance failed to check the lady's histrionic aspirations. " 'The evil that men do lives after them; the good is oft buried with their bones,' " she misquoted, and giggling lightly, added, "although her poor bones aren't buried yet. But we must be truthful, even about the dead. It wasn't money principally with Laura, it was people, if you know what I mean. She was always running around, doing favors, wasting her time and strength on people she scarcely knew. Remember that model, Shelby, the girl with the fancy name? Laura got me to give her my leopard coat. It wasn't half worn out either. I could have got another winter out of it and spared my mink. Don't you remember, Shelby?"

Shelby had become infatuated with a bronze Diana who had been threatening for years to leap, with dog and stag, from her pedestal.

Auntie Sue continued naughtily: "And Shelby's job! Do you know how he got it, Mr. McPherson? He'd been selling washing machines—or was it casings for frankfurters, darling? Or was that the time when you earned thirty dollars a week writing letters for a school that taught people to be successful business executives?"

Shelby turned defiantly from Diana. "What's that to be ashamed of? When I met Laura, Mr. McPherson, I happened to be working as correspondent for the University of the Science of Finance. Laura saw some of my copy, realized that I was wasting a certain gift or flair, and with her usual generosity . . ."

"Generosity wasn't the half of it," Auntie Sue interrupted.

"She spoke to Mr. Rowe about me and a few months later, when there was a vacancy, he called me in. You can't say I've been ungrateful"—he forgave Mrs. Treadwell with his gentle smile. "It was she, not I, who suggested that you forget it."

"There were a number of other things, darling, that Laura asked me to forget."

"Mustn't be vicious, dear. You'll be giving Mr. McPherson a lot of misleading ideas." With the tenderness of a nurse Shelby rearranged Auntie Sue's cushions, smiling and treating her malice like some secret malady.

The scene took on a theatric quality. Mark saw Shelby through the woman's eyes, clothed in the charm he had donned, like a bright domino, for the woman's pleasure. The ripe color, the chiseled features, the clear, long-lashed eyes had been created, his manner said, for her particular enjoyment. Through it all Mark felt that this was not a new exhibition. He had seen it somewhere before. So irritated by faltering memory that he had to strain harshness from his voice, he told them he was through with them for the day, and rose to go.

Shelby rose, too. "I'll go out for a bit of air. If you think you can get along without me for a while."

"Of course, darling. It's been wicked of me to take up so much of your time." Shelby's feeble sarcasm had softened the lady. White, faded, ruby-tipped hands rested on his dark sleeve. "I'll never forget how kind you've been."

Shelby forgave magnanimously. He put himself at her disposal as if he were already Laura's husband, the man of the family whose duty it was to serve a sorrowing woman in this hour of grief.

Like a penitent mistress returning to her lover, she cooed at Shelby. "With all your faults, you've got manners, darling. That's more than most men have nowadays. I'm sorry I've been so bad-tempered."

He kissed her forehead.

As they left the house, Shelby turned to Mark. "Don't take Mrs. Treadwell too seriously. Her bark is worse than her bite. It's only that she'd disapproved of my marrying her niece, and now she's got to stand by her opinions."

"What she disapproved of," Mark observed, "was Laura's marrying you."

Shelby smiled ruefully. "We ought all to be a little more decent now, oughtn't we? After all! Probably Auntie Sue is sorry she hurt poor Laura by constantly criticizing me, and now she's too proud to say so. That's why she had to take it out on me this morning."

They stood in the burning sunlight. Both were anxious to get away, yet both hesitated. The scene was unfinished. Mark had not learned enough, Shelby had not told all he wanted Mark to know.

When, after a brief pause devoted to a final struggle with his limping memory, Mark cleared his throat, Shelby started as if he had been roused from the remoteness of a dream. Both smiled mechanically.

"Tell me," Mark commanded, "where have I seen you before?"

Shelby couldn't imagine. "But I've been around. Parties and all that. One sees people at bars and restaurants. Sometimes a stranger's face is more familiar than your best friend's."

Mark shook his head. "Cocktail bars aren't in my line."

"You'll remember when you're thinking of something else. That's how it always is." Then, without changing his tone, Shelby added, "You know, Mr. McPherson, that I was beneficiary of Laura's insurance, don't you?"

Mark nodded.

"I wanted to tell you myself. Otherwise you might think . . .

well . . . it's only natural in your work to—" Shelby chose the word tactfully "—suspect every motive. Laura carried an annuity, you know, and there was a twenty-five-thousand-dollar death benefit. She'd had it in her sister's name, but after we decided to get married she insisted upon making it out to me."

"I'll remember that you told me," Mark promised.

Shelby offered his hand. Mark took it. They hesitated while the sun smote their uncovered heads.

"I hope you don't think I'm completely a heel, Mr. McPherson," Shelby said ruefully. "I never liked borrowing from a woman."

CHAPTER FOUR

When, at precisely twelve minutes past four by the ormolu clock on my mantel, the telephone interrupted, I was deep in the Sunday papers. Laura had become a Manhattan legend. Scarlet-minded headline artists had named her tragedy THE BACHELOR GIRL MURDER and one example of Sunday edition belles-lettres was tantalizingly titled SEEK ROMEO IN EAST SIDE LOVE-KILLING. By the necromancy of modern journalism, a gracious young woman had been transformed into a dangerous siren who practiced her wiles in that fascinating neighborhood where Park Avenue meets Bohemia. Her generous way of life had become an uninterrupted orgy of drunkenness, lust, and deceit, as titivating to the masses as it was profitable to the publishers. At this very hour, I reflected as I lumbered to the telephone, men were bandying her name in pool parlors and women shouting her secrets from tenement windows.

I heard Mark McPherson's voice on the wire. "Mr. Lydecker, I was just wondering if you could help me. There are several questions I'd like to ask you."

"And what of the baseball game?" I inquired.

Self-conscious laughter vibrated the diaphragm and tickled my ear. "It was too late. I'd have missed the first couple of innings. Can you come over?"

"Where?"

"The apartment. Miss Hunt's place."

"I don't want to come up there. It's cruel of you to ask me."

"Sorry," he said after a moment of cold silence. "Perhaps Shelby Carpenter can help me. I'll try to get in touch with him."

"Never mind. I'll come."

Ten minutes later I stood beside him in the bay window of Laura's living-room. East Sixty-Second Street had yielded to the spirit of carnival. Popcorn vendors and pushcart peddlers, sensing the profit in disaster, offered ice-cream sandwiches, pickles, and nickel franks to buzzards who battened on excitement. Sunday's sweethearts had deserted the green pastures of Central Park to stroll arm-in-arm past her house, gaping at daisies which had been watered by the hands of a murder victim. Fathers pushed perambulators and mothers scolded the brats who tortured the cops who guarded the door of a house in which a bachelor girl had been slain.

"Coney Island moved to the Platinum Belt," I observed.

Mark nodded. "Murder is the city's best free entertainment. I hope it doesn't bother you, Mr. Lydecker."

"Quite the contrary. It's the odor of tuberoses and the timbre of organ music that depress me. Public festivity gives death a classic importance. No one would have enjoyed the spectacle more than Laura."

He sighed.

"If she were here now, she'd open the windows, pluck daisies out of her window-boxes and strew the sidewalks. Then she'd send me down the stairs for a penny pickle."

Mark plucked a daisy and tore off the petals.

"Laura loved dancing in the streets. She gave dollar bills to organ-grinders."

He shook his head. "You'd never think it, judging from the neighborhood."

"She also had a taste for privacy."

The house was one of a row of converted mansions, preserved in such fashion that Victorian architecture sacrificed none of its substantial elegance to twentieth-century chic. High stoops had given way to lacquered doors three steps down; scrofulous daisies and rachitic geraniums bloomed in extraordinarily bright blue and green window-boxes; rents were exorbitant. Laura had lived here, she told me, because she enjoyed snubbing Park Avenue's pretentious foyers. After a trying day in the office, she could neither face a superman in gilt braid nor discuss the weather with politely indifferent elevator boys. She had enjoyed opening the street door with a key and climbing the stairs to her remodeled third floor. It was this taste for privacy that led to her death, for there had been no one to ask at the door if Miss Hunt expected a visitor on the night the murderer came.

"The doorbell rang," Mark announced suddenly.

"What?"

"That's how it must have happened. The doorbell rang. She was in the bedroom without clothes on. By the time she'd put on that silk thing and her slippers, he'd probably rung a second time. She went to the door and as she opened it, the shot was fired!"

"How do you know all this?" I demanded.

"She fell backward. The body lay there."

We both stared at the bare, polished floor. He had seen the body, the pale blue garment blood-stained and the blood running in rivulets to the edge of the green carpet.

"The door downstairs had evidently been left unlocked. It was unlocked when Bessie came to work yesterday morning. Before she came upstairs, Bessie looked for the superintendent to bawl him out for his carelessness, but he'd taken his family down to Manhattan Beach for the week-end. The tenants of the first and second floors are away for the summer and there was no one else in the house. The houses on both sides are empty, too, at this time of year."

"Probably the murderer thought of that," I observed.

"The door might have been left open for him. She might have been expecting a caller."

"Do you think so?"

"You knew her, Mr. Lydecker. Tell me, what kind of a dame was she anyway?"

"She was not the sort of woman you call a dame," I retorted.

"Okay. But what was she like?"

"Look at this room. Does it reveal nothing of the person who planned and decorated it? Does it contain, for your eyes, the vulgar memories of a bachelor girl? Does it seem to you the home of a young woman who would lie to her fiancé, deceive her oldest friend, and sneak off to a rendezvous with a murderer?"

I awaited his answer like a touchy Jehovah. If he failed to appreciate the quality of the woman who had adorned this room, I should know that his interest in literature was but the priggish aspiration of a seeker after self-improvement, his sensitivity no more than proletarian prudery. For me the room still shone with Laura's lustre. Perhaps it was in the crowding memories of firelit conversations, of laughing dinners at the candle-bright refectory table, of midnight confidences fattened by spicy snacks and endless cups of steaming coffee. But even as it stood for him, mysterious and bare of memory, it must have represented, in the deepest sense of the words, a *living room*.

For answer he chose the long green chair, stretched his legs on the ottoman, and pulled out his pipe. His eyes traveled from the black marble fireplace in which the logs were piled, ready for the first cool evening, to softly faded chintz whose deep folds shut out the glare of the hot twilight.

After a time he burst out: "I wish to Christ my sister could see this place. Since she married and went to live in Kew Gardens, she won't have kitchen matches in the parlor. This place has—" he hesitated "—it's very comfortable."

I think the word in his mind had been *class*, but he kept it from me, knowing that intellectual snobbism is nourished by such trivial crudities. His attention wandered to the bookshelves.

"She had a lot of books. Did she ever read them?"

"What do you think?"

He shrugged. "You never know about women."

"Don't tell me you're a misogynist."

He clamped his teeth hard upon his pipestem and glanced at me with an air of urchin defiance.

"Come, now, what of the girl friend?" I pleaded.

He answered dryly: "I've had plenty in my life. I'm no angel."

"Ever loved one?"

"A doll in Washington Heights got a fox fur out of me. And I'm a Scotchman, Mr. Lydecker. So make what you want of it."

"Ever know one who wasn't a doll? Or a dame?"

He went to the bookshelves. While he talked, his hands and eyes were concerned with a certain small volume bound in red morocco. "Sometimes I used to take my sisters' girl friends out. They never talked about anything except going steady and getting married. Always wanted to take you past furniture stores to show you the parlor suites. One of them almost hooked me."

"And what saved you?"

"Mattie Grayson's machine-gun. You were right. It was no tragedy."

"Didn't she wait?"

"Hell, yes. The day they discharged me, there she was at the hospital door. Full of love and plans; her old man had plenty of dough, owned a fish store, and was ready to furnish the flat, first payment down. I was still using crutches so I told her I wouldn't let her sacrifice herself." He laughed aloud. "After the months I'd put in reading and thinking, I couldn't go for a parlor suite. She's married now, got a couple of kids, lives in Jersey."

"Never read any books, eh?"

"Oh, she's probably bought a couple of sets for the bookcase. Keeps them dusted and never reads them."

He snapped the cover on the red morocco volume. The shrill blast of the popcorn whistle insulted our ears and the voices of children rose to remind us of the carnival of death in the street below. Bessie Clary, Laura's maid, had told the police that her first glimpse of the body had been a distorted reflection in the mercury-glass globe on Laura's mantel. That tarnished bubble caught and held our eyes, and we saw in it fleetingly, as in a crystal ball, a vision of the inert body in the blue robe, dark blood matted in the dark hair.

"What did you want to ask me, McPherson? Why did you bring me up here?"

His face had the watchfulness that comes after generations to a conquered people. The Avenger, when he comes, will wear that proud, guarded look. For a moment I glimpsed enmity. My fingers beat a tattoo on the arm of my chair. Strangely, the padded rhythms seemed to reach him, for he turned, staring as if my face were a memory from some fugitive reverie. Another thirty seconds had passed, I dare say, before he took from her desk a spherical object covered in soiled leather.

"What's this, Mr. Lydecker?"

"Surely a man of your sporting tastes is familiar with that ecstatic toy, McPherson."

"But why did *she* keep a baseball on her desk?" He emphasized the pronoun. *She* had begun to live. Then, examining the tattered leather and loosened bindings, he asked, "Has she had it since '38?"

"I'm sure I didn't notice the precise date when this *objet d'art* was introduced into the household."

"It's autographed by Cookie Lavagetto. That was his big year. Was she *a* Dodgers fan?"

"There were many facets to her character."

"Was Shelby a fan, too?"

"Will the answer to that question help you solve the murder, my dear fellow?"

He set the baseball down so that it should lie precisely where Laura had left it. "I just wanted to know. If it bothers you to answer the question, Mr. Lydecker . . ."

"There's no reason to get sullen about it," I snapped. "As a matter of fact, Shelby wasn't a fan. He preferred . . . why do I speak of him in the past tense? He prefers the more aristocratic sports, tennis, riding, hunting, you know."

"Yep," he said.

Near the door, a few feet from the spot where the body had fallen, hung Stuart Jacoby's portrait of Laura. Jacoby, one of the imitators of Eugene Speicher, had produced a flattened version of a face that was anything but flat. The best feature of the painting, as they had been her best feature, were the eyes. The oblique tendency, emphasized by the sharp tilt of dark brows, gave her face that shy, fawn-like quality which had so enchanted me the day I opened the door to a slender child who had asked me to endorse a fountain pen. Jacoby had caught the fluid sense of restlessness in the position of her body, perched on the arm of a chair, a pair of yellow gloves in one hand, a green hunter's hat in the other. The portrait was a trifle unreal, however, a trifle studied, too much Jacoby and not enough Laura.

"She wasn't a bad-looking da—" He hesitated, smiled ruefully, "—girl, was she, Mr. Lydecker?"

"That's a sentimental portrait. Jacoby was in love with her at the time."

"She had a lot of men in love with her, didn't she?"

"She was a very kind woman. Kind and generous."

"That's not what men fall for."

"She had delicacy. If she was aware of a man's shortcomings, she never showed it."

"Full of bull?"

"No, extremely honest. Her flattery was never shallow. She found the real qualities and made them important. Surface faults and affectations fell away like false friends at the approach of adversity."

He studied the portrait. "Why didn't she get married, then? Earlier, I mean?"

"She was disappointed when she was very young."

"Most people are disappointed when they're young. That doesn't keep them from finding someone else. Particularly women."

"She wasn't like your erstwhile fiancé, McPherson. Laura had no need for a parlor suite. Marriage wasn't her career. She had her career, she made plenty of money, and there were always men to squire and admire her. Marriage could give her only one sort of completion, and she was keeping herself for that."

"Keeping herself busy," he added dryly.

"Would you have prescribed a nunnery for a woman of her temperament? She had a man's job and a man's worries. Knitting wasn't one of her talents. Who are you to judge her?"

"Keep your shirt on," Mark said. "I didn't make any comments."

I had gone to the bookshelves and removed the volume to which he had given such careful scrutiny. He gave no sign that he had noticed, but fixed his fury upon an enlarged snapshot of Shelby looking uncommonly handsome in tennis flannels.

Dusk had descended. I switched on the lamp. In that swift transition from dusk to illumination, I caught a glimpse of darker, more impenetrable mystery. Here was no simple Police Department investigation. In such inconsistent trifles as an ancient baseball, a worn *Gulliver*, a treasured snapshot, he sought clues, not to the passing riddle of a murder, but to the eternally enigmatic nature of woman. This was a search no man could make with his eyes alone; the heart must also be engaged. He, stern fellow, would have been the first to deny such implication, but I, through these prognostic lenses, perceived the true cause of his resentment against Shelby. His private enigma, so much deeper than the professional solution of the crime, concerned the answer to a question which has ever baffled the lover, "What did she see in that other fellow?" As he glowered at the snapshot I knew that he was pondering on the quality of Laura's affection for Shelby, wondering whether a woman of her sensitivity and intelligence could be satisfied merely with the perfect mould of a man.

"Too late, my friend," I said jocosely. "The final suitor has rung her doorbell."

With a gesture whose fierceness betrayed the zeal with which his heart was guarded, he snatched up some odds and ends piled on Laura's desk, her address and engagement book, letters and bills bound by a rubber band, unopened bank statements, checkbooks, an old diary, and a photograph album.

"Come on," he snapped. "I'm hungry. Let's get out of this dump."

CHAPTER FIVE

W e've discovered certain clues, but we are not ready to make a statement."

The reporters found McPherson dignified, formal, and somewhat aloof that Monday morning. He felt a new importance in himself as if his life had taken on new meaning. The pursuit of individual crime had ceased to be trivial. A girl reporter, using female tricks to win information denied her trousered competitors, exclaimed, "I shouldn't mind being murdered half so much, Mr. McPherson, if you were the detective seeking clues to my private life."

His mouth twisted. The flattery was not delicate.

Her address and engagement books, bank statements, bills, check stubs, and correspondence filled his desk and his mind. Through them he had discovered the richness of her life, but also the profligacy. Too many guests and too many dinners, too many letters assuring her of undying devotion, too much of herself spent on the casual and petty, the transitory, the undeserving. Thus his Presbyterian virtue rejected the danger of covetousness. He had discovered the best of life in a gray-walled hospital room and had spent the years that followed asking himself timorously whether loneliness must be the inevitable companion of appreciation. This summing-up of Laura's life answered his question, but the answer failed to satisfy the demands of his stern upbringing. He learned, as he read her letters, balanced her unbalanced accounts, added the sums of unpaid bills, that while the connoisseur of living is not lonely, the price is high. To support the richness of life she had worked until she was too tired to approach her wedding day with joy or freedom.

The snapshot album was filled with portraits of Shelby Carpenter. In a single summer, Laura had fallen victim to his charms and the candid camera. She had caught him full face and profile, closeup and bust, on the tennis court, at the wheel of her roadster, in swimming trunks, in overalls, in hip boots with a basket slung over his shoulder, a fishing reel in his hand. Mark paused at the portrait of Shelby, the hunter, surrounded by dead ducks.

Surely the reader must, by this time, be questioning the impertinence of a reporter who records unseen actions as nonchalantly as if he had been hiding in Mark's office behind a framed photograph of the New York Police Department Baseball Team, 1912. But I would take oath, and in that very room where they keep the sphygmomanometer, that a good third of this was told me and a richer two-thirds intimated on that very Monday afternoon when, returning from a short journey to the barber's, I found Mark waiting in my apartment. And I would further swear, although I am sure the sensitive hand of the lie-detector would record an Alpine sweep at the satement, that he had yielded to the charm of old porcelain. For the second time I discovered him in my drawing-room, his hands stretched toward my favorite shelf. I cleared my throat before entering. He turned with a rueful smile.

"Don't look so sheepish," I admonished. "I'll never tell them at the Police Department that you're acquiring taste."

His eyes shot red sparks. "Do you know what Doctor Sigmund Freud said about collectors?"

"I know what Doctor Waldo Lydecker thinks of people who quote Freud." We sat down. "To what kind whim of Fate do I owe this unexpected visit?"

"I happened to be passing by."

My spirits rose. This casual visit was not without a certain warm note of flattery. Yesterday's disapproval had melted like an ice-cube surprised by a shower of hot coffee. But even as I hastened to fetch whiskey for my guest, I cautioned myself against an injudicious display of enthusiasm. Whereas a detective may be a unique and even trustworthy friend, one must always remember that he has made a profession of curiosity.

"I've been with Shelby Carpenter," he announced as we drank a small toast to the solution of the mystery.

"Indeed," said I, assuming the air of a cool but not ungracious citizen who cherishes a modicum of privacy.

"Does he know anything about music?"

"He talks a music-lover's patter, but his information is shallow.

You'll probably find him raising ecstatic eyes to heaven at the name of Beethoven and shuddering piously if someone should be so indiscreet as to mention Ethelbert Nevin."

"Would he know the difference—" Mark consulted his notebook "—between 'Finlandia' by Si-bee-lee-us and 'Toccata and Fugue' by Johann Sebastian Bach?"

"Anyone who can't distinguish between Sibelius and Bach, my dear fellow, is fit for treason, stratagem, and spoils."

"I'm a cluck when it comes to music. Duke Ellington's my soup." He offered a sheet from his notebook. "This is what Carpenter told me they were playing on Friday night. He didn't bother to check on the program. This is what they played."

I drew a sharp breath.

"It shoots his alibi as full of holes as a mosquito net. But it still doesn't prove he murdered her," Mark reminded me with righteous sharpness.

I poured him another drink. "Come, now, you haven't told me what you think of Shelby Carpenter."

"It's a shame he isn't a cop."

I cast discretion to the wind. Clapping him on the shoulder, I cried zestfully: "My dear lad, you are precious! A cop! The flower of old Kentucky! Mah deah suh, the ghosts of a legion of Confederate Colonels rise up to haunt you. Old Missy is whirling in her grave. Come, another drink on that, my astute young Hawkshaw. Properly we should be drinking mint juleps, but unfortunately Uncle Tom of Manila has lost the secret." And I went off into roars of unrestrained appreciation.

He regarded my mirth with some skepticism. "He's got all the physical requirements. And you wouldn't have to teach him to be polite."

"And fancy him in a uniform," I added, my imagination rollicking. "I can see him on the corner of Fifth Avenue where Art meets Bergdorf-Goodman. What a tangle of traffic at the hour when the cars roll in from Westchester to meet the husbands! There would be no less rioting in Wall Street, I can tell you, than on a certain historic day in '29."

"There are a lot of people who haven't got the brains for their college educations." The comment, while uttered honestly, was tinged faintly with the verdigris of envy. "The trouble is that they've been brought up with ideas of class and education so they can't relax and work in common jobs. There are plenty of fellows in these fancy offices who'd be a lot happier working in filling stations."

"I've seen many of them break under the strain of intelligence," I agreed. "Hundreds have been committed for life to the cocktail bars of Madison Avenue. There ought to be a special department in Washington to handle the problem of old Princeton men. I dare say Shelby looks down with no little condescension upon your profession."

A curt nod rewarded my astuteness. Mr. McPherson did not fancy Mr. Carpenter, but, as he had sternly reminded me on a former occasion, it was his business to observe rather than to judge the people encountered in professional adventure.

"The only thing that worries me, Mr. Lydecker, is that I can't place the guy. I've seen that face before. But where and when? Usually I'm a fool for faces. I can give you names and dates and the places I've seen them." His jaw shot forward and his lips pressed themselves into the tight mould of determination.

I laughed with secret tolerance as he gave me what he considered an objective picture of his visit to the offices of Rose, Rowe and Sanders, Advertising Counsellors. In that hot-air-conditioned atmosphere he must have seemed as alien as a share-cropper in a night club. He tried hard not to show disapproval, but opinion was as natural to him as appetite. There was fine juicy prejudice in his portrait of three advertising executives pretending to be dismayed by the notoriety of a front-page murder. While they mourned her death, Laura's bosses were not unaware of the publicity value of a crime which cast no shadow upon their own respectability.

"I bet they had a conference and decided that a high-class murder wouldn't lose any business."

"And considered the titillating confidences they could whisper to prospective clients at lunch," I added.

Mark's malice was impudent. Bosses aroused no respect in his savage breast. His proletarian prejudices were as rigid as any you will find in the upper reaches of so-called Society. It pleased him more to discover sincere praise and mourning among her fellow-workers than to hear her employers' high estimate of Laura's character and talents. Anyone who was smart, he opined, could please the boss, but it took the real stuff for a girl in a high-class job to be popular with her fellow-employees.

"So you think Laura had the real stuff?"

He affected deafness. I studied his face, but caught no shadow of conflict. It was not until several hours later that I reviewed the conversation and reflected upon the fact that he was shaping Laura's character to fit his attitudes as a young man might when enamored of a living woman. My mind was clear and penetrating at the time, for it was midnight, the hour at which I am most brave and most free. Since I learned some years ago that the terrors of insomnia could be overcome by a half-hour's brisk walk, I have not once allowed lassitude, weather, nor the sorry events of a disappointing day to interfere with this nocturnal practice. By habit I chose a street which had become important to me since Laura moved into that apartment.

Naturally I was shocked to see a light burning in the house of the dead; but after a moment's reflection, I knew that a young man who had once scorned overtime had given his heart to a job.

CHAPTER SIX

Two rituals on Tuesday marked the passing of Laura Hunt. The first, a command performance in the coroner's office, gathered together that small and none too congenial group who had been concerned in the activities of her last day of life. Because she had failed me in that final moment, I was honored with an invitation. I shall not attempt to report the unimaginative proceedings which went to hideous lengths to prove a fact that everyone had known from the start—that Laura Hunt was dead; the cause, murder by the hand of an unknown assailant.

The second ritual, her funeral, took place that afternoon in the chapel of W. W. Heatherstone and Son. Old Heatherstone, long experienced in the interment of movie stars, ward leaders, and successful gangsters, supervised the arrangements so that there might be a semblance of order among the morbid who started their clamor at his doors at eight o'clock in the morning.

Mark had asked me to meet him on the balcony that overlooked the chapel.

"But I don't attend funerals."

"She was your friend."

"Laura was far too considerate to demand that anyone venture out at such a barbaric hour and to exhibit emotions which, if earnest, are far too personal for scrutiny."

"But I wanted you to help me identify some of the people whose names are in her address book."

"Do you think the murderer will be there?"

"It's possible."

"How'd we know him? Do you think he might swoon at the bier?"

"Will you come?"

"No," I said firmly, and added, "Let Shelby help you this time."

"He's chief mourner. You must come. No one will see you. Use the side entrance and tell them you're meeting me. I'll be on the balcony."

Her friends had loved Laura and been desolate at her passing, but they would not have been human if they had failed to enjoy the excitement. Like Mark, they hoped for some crisis of discovery. Eyes that should have been downcast in grief and piety were sliding this way and that in the hope of perceiving the flushed countenance, the guilty gesture that would enable lips, later, to boast, "I knew it the moment I saw that sly face and noted the way he rubbed his hands together during the Twenty-Third Psalm."

She lay in a coffin covered in white silk. Pale ringless hands had been folded against the lavender-tinted white moiré of her favorite evening gown. An arrangement of gardenias, draped like a confirmation veil, covered the ruined face. The only mourners deserving seats in the section reserved for deepest suffering were Auntie Sue and Shelby Carpenter. Her sister, brother-in-law, and some far-western cousins had been unwilling or unable to make the long journey for the sake of this hour in the mortuary. After the service was read, the organ pealed and Heatherstone attendants wheeled the casket into a private chamber from which it was later transferred to the crematorium.

It is from the lush sentimentality of the newspaper versions that I prune this brief account of the obsequies. I did not attend. Mark waited in vain.

As he descended from the balcony and joined the slowly moving mass, he noted a hand, gloved in black, signalling him. Bessie Clary pushed her way through the crowd.

"I got something to tell you, Mr. McPherson."

He took her arm. "Shall we go upstairs where it's quiet or does this place depress you?"

"If you wouldn't mind, we could go back to the flat," Bessie suggested. "It's up there, what I got to show you."

Mark had his car. Bessie sat beside him primly, black gloved hands folded in the lap of her black silk dress.

"It's hot enough to kill a cat," she said by way of making conversation.

"What have you got to tell me?"

"You needn't to yell at me. I ain't afraid of cops, or dicks either." She drew out her best handkerchief and blew such a clarion note that her nose seemed an instrument fashioned for the purpose of sounding defiance. "I was brought up to spit whenever I saw one."

"I was brought up to hate the Irish," Mark observed, "but I'm a grown man now. I haven't asked for love, Miss Clary. What is it you want to tell me?"

"You won't get on my good side by that Miss Clary stuff either. Bessie's my name, I'm domestic and I got nothing to be ashamed of."

They drove across the Park in silence. When they passed the policeman who stood guard at the door of Laura's house, Bessie smiled down upon him with virtuous hauteur. Once in the apartment, she assumed the airs of ownership, raised windows, adjusted curtains, emptied trays filled with ashes from Mark's pipe.

"Cops, brought up in barns," she sniffed as she drew hatpins from out of the structure that rode high on her head. "Don't know how to act when they get in a decent house." When she had drawn off black gloves, folded them and stored them in her bag, settled herself on the straightest chair, and fixed a glassy stare upon his face, she asked, "What do they do to people that hide something from the cops?"

The question, so humble in contrast with her belligerence, provided him with a weapon. "So you've been trying to shield the murderer? That's dangerous, Bessie!"

Her knotted hands unfolded. "What makes you think I know the murderer?"

"By hiding evidence, you have become an accessory after the fact. What is the evidence, and what was your purpose in concealing it?"

Bessie turned her eyes ceilingward as though she expected help from heaven. "If I'd hold out on you, you'd never know nothing about it. And if they hadn't played that music at the funeral, I'd never've told you. Church music makes me soft."

"Whom were you shielding, Bessie?"

"Her."

"Miss Hunt?"

Bessie nodded grimly.

"Why, Bessie? She's dead."

"Her reputation ain't," Bessie observed righteously and went to the corner cabinet, in which Laura had always kept a small stock of liquor. "Just look at this."

Mark leaped. "Hey, be careful. There may be fingerprints."

Bessie laughed. "Maybe there was a lot of fingerprints around here! But the cops never seen them."

"You wiped them off, Bessie? For God's sakes!"

"That ain't all I wiped off," Bessie chuckled. "I cleaned off the bed and table in there and the bathroom before the cops come."

Mark seized bony wrists. "I've a good mind to take you into custody."

She pulled her hands away. "I don't believe in fingerprints anyway. All Saturday afternoon the cops was sprinkling white powder around my clean flat. Didn't do them no good because I polished all the furniture on Friday after she'd went to the office. If they found any fingerprints, they was mine."

"If you don't believe in fingerprints, why were you so anxious to get rid of those in the bedroom?"

"Cops got dirty minds. I don't want the whole world thinking she was the kind that got drunk with a fellow in her bedroom, God rest her soul."

"Drunk in her bedroom? Bessie, what does this mean?"

"So help me," Bessie swore, "there was two glasses."

He seized her wrists again. "Why are you making up this story, Bessie? What have you to gain by it?"

Hers was the hauteur of an enraged duchess. "What right you got to yell at me? You don't believe me, huh? Say, I was the one that cared about her reputation. You never even knew her. What are you getting so mad about?"

Mark retreated, the sudden display of temper puzzling and shaming him. His fury had grown out of all proportions to its cause.

Bessie drew out a bottle. "Where do you think I found this? Right there." She pointed through the open door to the bedroom. "On the table by the bed. With two dirty glasses."

Laura's bedroom was as chaste and peaceful as the chamber of a young girl whose experience of love has been confined to sonnets, dreams, and a diary. The white Swiss spread lay smooth and starched, the pillow rounded neatly at the polished pine headboard, a white-and-blue knitted afghan folded at the foot.

"I cleaned up the room and washed the glasses before the first cop got here. Lucky I come to my senses in time," Bessie sniffed. "The bottle I put in the cabinet so's no one would notice. It wasn't her kind of liquor. I can tell you this much, Mr. McPherson, this here bottle was brought in after I left on Friday."

Mark examined the bottle. It was Three Horses Bourbon, a brand favored by frugal tipplers. "Are you sure, Bessie? How do you know? You must keep close watch on the liquor that's used in this place."

Bessie's iron jaw shot forward; cords stiffened in her bony neck. "If you don't believe me, ask Mr. Mosconi, the liquor fellow over on

Third Avenue. We always got ours from Mosconi, better stuff than this, I'm telling you. She always left me the list and I ordered on the phone. This here's the brand we use." She swung the doors wider and revealed, among the neatly arranged bottles, four unopened fifths of J and D Blue Grass Bourbon, the brand which I had taught her to buy.

Such unexpected evidence, throwing unmistakable light on the last moments of the murdered, should have gladdened the detective heart. Contrarily, Mark found himself loath to accept the facts. This was not because he had reason to disbelieve Bessie's story, but because the sordid character of her revelations had disarranged the pattern of his thinking. Last night, alone in the apartment, he had made unscientific investigation of Laura's closets, chests of drawers, dressing-table, and bathroom. He knew Laura, not only with his intelligence, but with his senses. His fingers had touched fabrics that had known her body, his ears had heard the rustle of her silks, his nostrils sniffed at the varied, heady fragrances of her perfumes. Never before had the stern young Scot known a woman in this fashion. Just as her library had revealed the quality of her mind, the boudoir had yielded the secrets of feminine personality.

He did not like to think of her drinking with a man in her bedroom like a cutie in a hotel.

In his coldest, most official voice he said, "If there was someone in the bedroom with her, we have a completely new picture of the crime."

"You mean it wasn't like you said in the paper, that it must have happened when the doorbell rang and she went to open it?"

"I accepted that as the most probable explanation, considering the body's position." He crossed from the bedroom slowly, his eyes upon the arrangement of carpets on the polished floor. "If a man had been in the bedroom with her, he might have been on the point of leaving. She went to the door with him, perhaps." He stood rigid at the spot where the river of dark blood had been dammed by the thick pile of the carpet. "Perhaps they were quarreling and, just as he reached the door, he turned and shot her."

"Gosh," said Bessie, blowing her nose weakly, "it gives you the creeps, don't it?"

From the wall Stuart Jacoby's portrait smiled down.

CHAPTER SEVEN

On Wednesday afternoon, twenty-four hours after the funeral, Lancaster Corey came to see me. I found him contemplating my porcelains lustfully.

"Corey, my good fellow, to what do I owe this dispensation?"

We wrung each other's hands like long-lost brothers.

"I'll not mince words, Waldo. I've come on business."

"I smelled sulphur and brimstone. Have a drink before you reveal your diabolical schemes."

He twisted the end of his white, crisp mustache. "I've got a great opportunity for you, my good friend. You know Jacoby's work. Getting more valuable every day."

I made a sound with my lips.

"It's not that I'm trying to sell you a picture. As a matter of fact, I've already got a buyer. You know Jacoby's portrait of Laura Hunt . . . several of the papers carried reproductions after the murder. Tragic, wasn't it? Since you were so attached to the lady, I thought you'd want to bid before . . ."

"I knew there was something divine about your visit, Corey. Now I see that it's your insolence."

He shrugged off the insult. "Merely a courtesy."

"How dare you?" I shouted. "How dare you come to my house and coolly offer me that worthless canvas? In the first place, I consider it a bad imitation of Speicher. In the second place, I deplore Speicher. And in the third, I loathe portraits in oil."

"Very well. I shall feel free to sell it to my other buyer." He snatched up his Fedora.

"Wait a minute," I commanded. "How can you offer what you

don't own? That picture is hanging on the wall of her apartment now. She died without a will, the lawyers will have to fight it out."

"I believe that Mrs. Treadwell, her aunt, is assuming responsibility for the family. You might communicate with her or with Salsbury, Haskins, Warder, and Bone, her attorneys. The landlord, I heard this morning, had released the estate from its obligation to fulfill the lease on condition that the apartment is vacated by the first of the month. They're going to make a special effort to hurry the proceedings . . ."

His knowledge infuriated me. "The vultures gather!" I shouted, smacking my forehead with an anguished palm. And a moment later cried out in alarm: "Do you know what arrangements have been made for her other things? Whether there's to be a sale?"

"This bid came through a private channel. Someone who had seen the portrait in her apartment, no doubt, made inquiries of several dealers. He hadn't known that we were Jacoby's agents . . ."

"His taste makes it clear that he knows very little about painting."

Corey made a purse of his lips. "Everyone is not as prejudiced as you are, Waldo. I prophesy the day when Jacoby will be worth real money."

"Comfort yourself, my sweet buzzard. Both you and I shall be dead by that time. But tell me," I continued mockingly, "is your prospective sucker some connoisseur who saw the picture in the Sunday tabloids and wants to own the portrait of a murder victim?"

"I do not believe that it would be strictly ethical to give my customer's name."

"Your pardon, Corey. My question must have shocked your delicate sensibilities of a business man. Unfortunately I shall have to write the story without using names."

Lancaster Corey responded like a hunting dog to the smell of rabbit. "What story?"

"You have just given me material for a magnificent piece!" I cried, simulating creative excitement. "An ironic small story about the struggling young painter whose genius goes unrecognized until one of his sitters is violently murdered. And suddenly he, because he had done her portrait, becomes the painter of the year. His name is not only on the lips of collectors, but the public, the public, Corey, know him as they know Mickey Rooney. His prices skyrocket, fashionable women beg to sit for him, he is reproduced in *Life, Vogue, Town and Country* . . ."

My fantasy so titivated his greed that he could no longer show pride. "You've got to mention Jacoby's name. The story would be meaningless without it."

"And a footnote, no doubt, explaining that his works are on view in the galleries of Lancaster Corey."

"That wouldn't hurt."

I spoke bitterly. "Your point of view is painfully commercial. Such considerations never enter my mind. Art, Corey, endures. All else passes. My piece would be as vivid and original as a Jacoby portrait."

"Just include his name. One mention of it," Corey pleaded.

"That inclusion would remove my story from the realms of literature and place it in the category of journalism. In that case, I'd have to know the facts, even if I did not include all of them. To protect my reputation for veracity, you understand."

"You've won," Corey admitted and whispered the art-lover's name.

I sank upon the Biedermeier, laughing as I had not laughed since Laura had been here to share such merry secrets of human frailty.

Along with this genial and amusing tidbit, Corey had, however, brought some distressing information. As soon as I had got rid of him, I changed my clothes, seized hat and stick, and bade Roberto summon a taxi.

Hence to Laura's apartment, where I found not only Mrs. Treadwell, whom I had expected to find there, but Shelby and the Pomeranian. Laura's aunt was musing on the value of the few genuinely antique pieces, Shelby taking inventory, and the dog sniffing chair legs.

"To what do we owe this unexpected pleasure?" cried Mrs. Treadwell, who, in spite of expressing open disapproval of my friendship with her niece, had always fluttered before my fame.

"To cupidity, dear lady. I have come to share the booty."

"This is a painful task." She sank back into an upholstered chair watching, through heavily blackened lashes, my every movement and glance. "But my lawyer simply insists."

"How generous of you!" I chattered. "You spare yourself no pains. In spite of grief and sentiment, you carry on bravely. I dare say you'll account for every button in poor Laura's wardrobe."

A key turned in the lock. We assumed postures of piety as Mark entered.

"Your men let us in, Mr. McPherson," explained Mrs. Treadwell. "I called your office, but you weren't in. I hope there's nothing wrong about our . . . our attempt to bring order. Poor Laura was so careless, she never knew what she owned."

"I gave orders to let you in if you came," Mark told her. "I hope you've found everything as it should be."

"Someone has been in the closet. One of the dresses has fallen off the hook and perfume was spilled."

"The police are heavy-handed," was my innocent observation.

Mark, I thought, took extra pains to appear nonchalant.

"There's nothing of great value," Mrs. Treadwell remarked. "Laura would never put her money into things that lasted. But there are certain trinkets, souvenirs that people might appropriate for sentimental reasons." She smiled so sweetly in my direction that I knew she suspected the reason for my presence.

I took direct action. "Perhaps you know, Mrs. Treadwell, that this vase did not belong to Laura." I nodded toward the mercury glass globe upon the mantel. "I'd merely lent it to her."

"Now, Waldo, don't be naughty. I saw you bring that vase on Christmas, all tied up in red ribbons. You must remember, Shelby."

Shelby looked up as if he had not heard the argument. The rôle of innocence, he knew by experience, would protect him equally from my wit and her revenge. "Sorry, darling, I didn't hear what you were saying." He returned to his inventories.

"Not ribbons, dear lady. There was a string tied to my Christmas package. Laura wasn't to give it away. You know that Spanish prodigality of hers, handing things to anyone who admired them. This vase is part of my collection and I intend to take it now. That's quite in order, don't you think, McPherson?"

"You'd better leave it. You might find yourself in trouble," Mark said.

"How petty-official of you! You're acting like a detective."

He shrugged as if my good opinion were of no importance. I laughed and turned the talk to inquiry about the progress of his work. Had he found any clues that might lead to the murderer's house?

"Plenty," he taunted.

"Oh, do tell us," Mrs. Treadwell begged, sliding forward in her chair and clasping her hands together in a gesture of rapturous attention. Shelby had climbed upon a chair so that he might record the titles of volumes on the topmost bookshelf. From this vantage-point, he glanced down at Mark with fearless curiosity. The Pomeranian sniffed at the detective's trousers. All awaited revelation. All Mark said was, "I hope you don't mind," and took out his pipe. The snub was meant to arouse fear and bid us mind the majesty of the law.

I seized the moment for my own. "It might interest you to know that I've got a clue." My eyes were fixed on Mrs. Treadwell, but beyond her floating veil the mirror showed me Mark's guarded countenance.

"Do you know there's an art-lover connected with this case? As probable heir, Mrs. Treadwell, you might be pleased to know that this little museum piece—" I directed her attention to the Jacoby portrait "—has already been bid for."

"Really! How much?"

"I'd keep the price up if I were you. The portrait may have a sentimental value for the buyer."

"Who is it?" asked Shelby.

"Someone with money? Could we ask a thousand?" demanded Mrs. Treadwell.

Mark used the pipe as a shield for self-consciousness. Behind his cupped hand, I noted rising color. A man girding himself for the torture chamber could not have shown greater dignity.

"Someone we know?"

"Do you think there might be a clue in it?" I asked mischievously. "If this is a *crime passionnel*, the killer might be a man of sentiment. Don't you think the lead's worth following, McPherson?"

His answer was something between a grunt and a sigh.

"It's terribly exciting," said Mrs. Treadwell. "You've got to tell me, Waldo, you've just got to."

I was never a child to torture butterflies. The death agonies of small fish have never been a sight that I witnessed with pleasure. I remember blanching with terror and scurrying across the lane when, during an ill-advised visit to a farm, I was forced to watch a decapitated chicken running around and around its astonished head. Even on the stage I prefer death to follow a swift, clean stroke of a sharp blade. To spare Mark's blushes I spoke hastily and with the air of gravity: "I cannot betray the confidence of Lancaster Corey. An art dealer is, after all, somewhat in the position of a doctor or lawyer. In matters of taste, discretion is the better part of profit."

I sought his eyes, but Mark turned away. His next move, I thought, was meant to divert conversation, but I learned later that he had had a definite purpose in meeting Shelby here this afternoon.

"I've been working and could use a drink," he announced. "As chief trustee, Mrs. Treadwell, would you mind if I took some of Miss Hunt's liquor?"

"How stingy you make me sound! Shelby, darling, be useful. I wonder if the icebox is turned on."

Shelby leaped from his perch and went into the kitchen. Mark opened the corner cabinet.

"He certainly knows his way about this apartment," I observed.

He paid no attention. "What do you drink, Mrs. Treadwell? Yours is Scotch, isn't it, Lydecker?"

He waited until Shelby returned before he brought out the Bourbon. "I think I'll drink this today. What's yours, Carpenter?"

Shelby glanced at the bottle, decorated with the profiles of three noble steeds. His hands tensed, but he could not hold them steady enough to keep the glasses from rattling on the tray.

"None—for—me—thanks."

The softness had fled his voice. He was as harsh as metal, and his chiseled features, robbed of color, had the marble virtue of a statue erected to the honor of a dead Victorian.

CHAPTER EIGHT

Mark asked me to dine with him that night.

"But I thought you were displeased with me."

"Why?"

"I failed you at the funeral."

"I know how you felt." His hand lay for a moment upon my coat-sleeve.

"Then why didn't you help me get my vase away from that she-vulture?"

"I was being petty-official," he teased. "I'd like to take you to dinner, Mr. Lydecker. Will you come?"

He carried a book in his coat-pocket. I saw only the top inch of the binding, but unless I was mistaken, it was the work of a not unfamiliar author.

"I am flattered," I remarked with a jocular nod toward the bulging pocket.

He fingered the book, with some affection, I fancied.

"Have you read it yet, McPherson?" He nodded. "And do you still consider me smooth but trivial?"

"Sometimes you're not bad," he conceded.

"Your flattery overwhelms me," I retorted. "And where shall we dine?"

His car was open and he drove so wildly that I clung with one hand to the door, with the other to my black Homburg. I wondered why he chose the narrowest streets in the slums until I saw the red neon above Montagnino's door. Montagnino himself met us and to my surprise greeted Mark as an honored customer. I saw then that it would take little effort to guide him along the road of good taste. We passed through a corridor steamy with the odors of tomato paste, peppers, and oregano to the garden, which was, on this incredible night, only a few degrees cooler than the kitchen; with the air of a Caesar conferring honor upon pet commoners, Montagnino led us to a table beside a trellis twined with artificial lilac. Through the dusty wooden lattice and weary cotton vines we witnessed a battle between the hordes of angry clouds and a fierce copper moon. The leaves of the one living tree in the neighborhood, a skinny catalpa, hung like the black bones of skeleton hands, as dead as the cotton lilac. With the flavors of Montagnino's kitchen and the slum smells was mingled the sulphurous odor of the rising storm.

We dined on mussels cooked with mustard greens in Chianti and a chicken, fried in olive oil, laid upon a bed of yellow taglierini and garlanded with mushrooms and red peppers. At my suggestion we drank that pale still wine with the magic name, *Lacrymae Christi*. Mark had never tasted it, but once his tongue had tested and approved the golden flavor, he tossed it off like Scotch whiskey. He came of a race of drinkers who look contemptuously upon an alcoholic content of twelve per cent, unaware that the fermented grape works its enchantments more subtly than the distilled spirits of grain. I do not imply that he was drunk; let us say, rather, that the Tears of Christ opened his heart. He became less Scottish and more boyish; less the professional detective and more the youth in need of a confidant.

I remarked that I had dined here with Laura. We had eaten the same food at this very table. The same weary cotton leaves had hung above her head. The place had been one of her favorites. Had he guessed it when he planned the dinner?

He shrugged. A mechanical contrivance filled the restaurant with music and sent faint melody into the garden. Noel Coward wrote an unforgettable line (whose precise wording I have forgotten) upon the ineluctable charm of old popular songs. That is why, I venture to say, a nation sways to George Gershwin while the good works of Calvin Coolidge have become arid words in unread volumes. Old tunes had been as much a part of Laura as her laughter. Her mind had been a fulsome catalogue of musical trivia. A hearty and unashamed lowbrow, she had listened to Brahms but had heard Kern. Her one Great had been Bach, whom she learned to cherish, believe it or not, by listening to a Benny Goodman record.

When I mentioned this to Mark, he nodded gravely and said, "Yep, I know."

"What do you know and how do you know so much?" I demanded, suddenly outraged by his superior airs. "You act as though you'd been Laura's friend for years."

"I looked at her records," he said. "I even played some of them. Make what you want of that, Mr. Lydecker."

I poured him another glass of wine. His belligerency dwindled and it was not long afterward that he poured forth the revelations recorded in foregoing chapters: the scene with Bessie; his annoyance at the clumsy flattery of the girl reporter; the sudden interest in painting which had caused him to discover Lancaster Corey and ask the price of the Jacoby portrait; and finally, with the second bottle of wine, of Shelby Carpenter.

I confess that I was not without guilt in plying him with liquor and provocative questions. We discussed the insurance policy, the false alibi, and, at my subtle instigation, Shelby's familiarity with firearms.

"He's quite the sporting type, you know. Hunting, shooting, and all that. Once had a collection of guns, I believe."

Mark nodded knowingly.

"Have you checked on them? How do you go about getting all these items of information? Or did Shelby confess that, too?"

"I'm a detective. What do you think I do with my time? It was a simple matter of two and two on the guns. Photographs in her album and storage receipts in his room at the Framingham. He went up to the warehouse with me himself on Monday and we looked over the arsenal. His father used to hunt foxes in a red coat, he told me."

"Well?" I awaited revelation.

"According to the records in the warehouse, nothing had been touched for over a year. Most of the stuff showed rust and the dust was an inch thick."

"Of course a man might have guns that he didn't put into a warehouse for safekeeping."

"He's not the type to use a sawed-off shotgun."

"A sawed-off shotgun!" I exclaimed. "Do you know positively?"

"We know nothing *positively*." He underscored the adverb brusquely. "But where do you use BB shot?"

"I'm no sportsman," I confessed.

"Imagine anyone trying to carry a shotgun around the streets of this town. How could he get away with it?"

"Sawed-off shotguns are carried by gangsters," I observed. "At least according to the education I've received at that fount of popular learning, the movies."

"Did Laura know any gangsters?"

"In a way, McPherson, we're all gangsters. We all have our confederates and our sworn foes, our loyalties and our enmities. We have our pasts to shed and our futures to protect."

"In the advertising business they use different weapons," he observed.

"If a man were desperate, might he not sacrifice sportsmanship for the nonce and step out of his class? And tell me, McPherson, just how does one saw off a sawed-off shotgun?"

My plea for practical information was disregarded. Mark became guarded again. I spoke of the insurance policy.

"Shelby's eagerness to tell you about it was undoubtedly a device for disarming you with his charming frankness."

"I've thought of that."

The music changed. My hand, holding a wineglass, was stayed on its journey to my lips. My face was drained of color. In the bewildered countenance of my companion I caught a reflection of my pallor.

Yellow hands slid coffee-cups across the table. At the next table a woman laughed. The moon had lost its battle with the clouds and retreated, leaving no trace of copper brilliance in the ominous sky. The air had grown heavier. In the window of a tenement a slim girl stood, her angular dark silhouette sharpened by a naked electric bulb.

At the table on our left a woman was singing:

> So I smile and say,
> When a lovely flame dies,
> Smoke gets in your eyes.

Fixing offended eyes upon her face, I spoke in my courtliest tones. "Madame, if you would spare the eardrums of one who heard Tamara introduce that enchanting song, you will restrain your clumsy efforts at imitation."

She made a remark and gesture which, lest my readers be squeamish, I shall not describe. Mark's eyes were fixed on my face with the squinting attentiveness of a scientist at a microscope.

I laughed and said hastily: "That melody is significant. Common as it has become, it has never lost a peculiarly individual flavor. Jerry Kern has never surpassed it, you know."

"The first time you heard it you were with Laura," Mark said.

"How astute of you!"

"I'm getting used to your ways, Mr. Lydecker."

"You shall be rewarded," I promised, "by the story of that night."

"Go on."

"It was in the fall '33, you know, that Max Gordon put on the show, *Roberta*, book by Hammerstein Junior after a novel by Alice Duer Miller. Trivia, of course, but, as we know, there is no lack of sustenance in whipped cream. It was Laura's first opening night. She was no end excited, her eyes burning like a child's, her voice rising in adolescent squeaks as I pointed out this and that human creature who had been, until that night, magic names to the little girl from Colorado Springs. She wore a gown of champagne-colored chiffon and jade-colored slippers. Extraordinarily effective with her eyes and hair.

" 'Laura, my precious babe,' I said to her, 'we shall drink to your frock in champagne.' It was her first taste of it, McPherson. Her pleasure gave me the sensation that God must know when He transforms the blasts of March into the melting winds of April.

"Add to this mood a show which is all glitter and chic, and top it with the bittersweet froth of song, throatily sung by a Russian girl with a guitar. I felt a small warmth upon my hand, and then, as the song continued, a pressure that filled me with swelling ecstasy. Do you think this a shameful confession? A man of my sort has many easy emotions—I have been known to shout with equal fervor over the Beethoven Ninth or a penny lollypop—but few great moments. But I swear to you, McPherson, in this simple sharing of melody we had attained something which few achieve in the more conventional attitudes of affection.

"Her eyes were swimming. Later she told me that she had recently been rejected in love—imagine anyone rejecting Laura. The fellow, I take it, was rather insensitive. She had, alas, a low taste in love. Through the confession I clung to her hand tightly, that small, tender hand which held such extraordinary firmness that she used to say it was slightly masculine. But the elements are so mixed in us, McPherson, that Nature must blush to quote Shakespeare when she stands and says to all the world, 'This was a man!' "

The music flowed between the white dusty boards of the trellis, through vines of artificial lilac. I had never before spoken aloud nor written of the reverie which had filled me since that night with Laura at the theatre, yet I felt certain security in entrusting it to a man whose nostalgia was concerned with a woman whose face he had never seen.

At long last the song ceased. Freed from pensive memories, I drained my glass and returned to the less oppressive topic of murder. I had by this time sufficient command of myself to speak of the scene we had witnessed in Laura's room and of Shelby's pallor at the sight of the Bourbon bottle. Mark said that the evidence gathered thus far was too circumstantial and frail to give substance to a case against the bridegroom.

"Do tell me this, McPherson. In your opinion is he guilty?"

I had given myself freely. In return I expected frankness. He answered with an insolent smile.

I set to work on his emotions. "Poor Laura," I sighed. "How ironic for her if it actually was Shelby! After having loved so generously, to discover treachery. Those last hideous moments before she died!"

"Death was almost instantaneous. Within a few seconds she was unconscious."

"You're pleased, Mark, aren't you? You're glad to know she had no time to regret the love she had given?"

He said icily, "I've expressed no such opinion."

"Don't be ashamed. Your heart's no softer than any other Scot's. Sir Walter and Sir James would have been delighted with you. A nature rocky as the hills, a tombstone and a wee bit o' heather."

"You rockbound Americans, you're sentimental like worms." Bony hands gripped the table. "Let's have another drink."

I suggested Courvoisier.

"You order. I can't pronounce it."

After a short pause, he said: "Listen, Mr. Lydecker, there's one thing I want to know. Why did she keep putting off the wedding? She was crazy about him, she had pictures of him all over the place, and still she kept postponing it. Why?"

"The familiar curse of gold."

He shook his head. "Carpenter and I have gone into that. The guy's fairly decent about it, if a man can be decent and take money from a woman. But this is what gets me. They're going together for a hell of a long time and at last they decide to break down and get married. So she plans a vacation and a honeymoon, and then has to have a week by herself before she goes through with it. What was holding her back?"

"She was tired. She wanted to rest."

"When everyone says the same thing and it's the easiest answer, you know damn well it's baloney."

"Are you suggesting that Laura might have been seeking excuses for postponing the wedding? That she wasn't awaiting the great day with the tremulous expectancy of a happy bride?"

"Could be."

"Strange," I sighed. "Incredibly strange and tragic for us to be sitting here, at this very table, under these same weary lilacs, listening to her favorite tunes and stewing over our jealousy. She's dead, man, dead!"

Nervous hands toyed with the stem of the brandy snifter. Then, with his dark eyes piercing the gossamer of my defenses, he asked, "If you were so crazy about her, why didn't you do something about Shelby?"

I met this scrutiny contemptuously.

"Why?"

"Laura was a grown woman. Her freedom was dear to her and jealously guarded. She knew her own heart. Or thought she did."

"If I had known her ..." he began in a voice of masculine omnipotence, but paused, leaving the rest unsaid.

"What a contradictory person you are, McPherson!"

"Contradictory!" He tossed the word into the very centre of the garden. Several diners stared at us. "I'm contradictory. Well, what about the rest of you? And what about her? Wherever you turn, a contradiction."

"It's the contradictions that make her seem alive to you. Life itself is contradictory. Only death is consistent."

With a great sigh he unburdened himself of another weighty question. "Did she ever talk to you about *Gulliver*?"

My mind leaped nimbly in pursuit. "It's one of your favorites, too, I take it."

"How do you know that?" he challenged.

"Your boasted powers of observation are failing sadly, my dear fellow, if you failed to notice that I took care to see what volume it was that you examined so scrupulously in her apartment on Sunday afternoon. I knew that book well. It was an old copy and I had it rebound for her in red morocco."

He smiled shyly. "I knew you were spying on me."

"You said nothing, because you wished to let me think it was a murder clue you sought among the Lilliputians. If it gives you pleasure, young man, I'll confirm the hope that she shared your literary enthusiasms."

His gratitude was charming. I counted the days that had passed since he had spoken of Laura as a two-timing dame. Had I reminded him tonight, I dare say he would have punched my face.

The genial combination of good food, wine, music, brandy, and sympathy had corrupted his defenses. He spoke with touching frankness. "We lived within half a mile of each other for over three years. Must have taken the same bus, the same subway, passed each other on the street hundreds of times. She went to Schwartz's for her drugs, too."

"Remarkable coincidence," I said.

The irony was lost. He had surrendered.

"We must have passed each other on the street often."

It was a slender morsel of consolation he had found among all the grim facts. I resolved then and there to write about this frustrated romance, so fragile and so typical of New York. It was the perfect O. Henry story. I can hear old Sydney Porter coughing himself into a fever over it.

"Wonderful ankles," he muttered, half-aloud. "The first thing I look at is the ankles. Wonderful."

They had turned off the music and most of the diners had left the garden. A couple passed our table. The girl, I noted, had remarkable ankles. Mark did not turn his head. He dwelt, for that brief moment, in the fancy of a meeting at Schwartz's drugstore. He had been buying pipe tobacco and she had put a dime into the postage-stamp machine. She might have dropped her purse. Or perhaps there had been a cinder in her eye. She had uttered but a single word, "Thanks," but for him sweet bells jangled and the harps of heaven were joined in mighty paean. A glance at her ankles, a meeting of their eyes, and it was as simple as with Charles Boyer and Margaret Sullavan.

"Have you ever read my story of Conrad?"[1] I inquired.

My question interrupted the schoolboy reverie. He regarded me with a desolate glance.

"It is a legend told over port and cigars at Philadelphia dining-tables some seventy-five years ago, and whispered in softer tones over tapestry frames and macramé work. The story has of late been attributed to me, but I take no credit. What I am telling is a tale whose only basis of truth lies in its power over stolid folk celebrated for their honesty and lack of imagination. I refer to the Amish of Pennsylvania.

"Conrad was one of these. A stalwart, earthy lad more given to the cultivation of rutabagas than to flights of superstitious fancy. One day as he worked in the field, he heard a great crash upon the road. Running, hoe in hand, he came upon the confusion attendant upon an accident. A vegetable cart had collided with a smart carriage. To his great surprise Conrad found a woman in his arms in the place of his hoe.

"Among the Amish, who boasted that they were known as *plain*,

---

[1]"Conrad of Lebanon," in the volume, *February, Which Alone*, by Waldo Lydecker, 1936.

buttons were considered ungodly ornament. To this moment in his life Conrad had seen only girls in faded ginghams hooked tight across their chests and with hair stretched from their temples into wiry pigtails. He wore a blue work shirt fastened severely to the throat and upon his chin a fringe, like monkey fur, of thin whiskers affected by his people as a mark of piety.

"The injury to the lady's carriage was repaired sooner than the damage to Conrad's heart. Never could he close his eyes without beholding a vision of this creature with her powdered skin, her wanton lips, and mischievous eyes, as black as the ebony stick of her lilac-silk parasol. From that day on, Conrad was no longer content with his pig-tailed neighbors and his rutabagas. He must find Troy and seek Helen. He sold his farm, walked dusty roads to Philadelphia, and being canny as the pious always are, invested his small capital in a lucrative business whose proprietor was willing to teach him the trade.

"Without money, without access to the society frequented by the elegant creature, Conrad was actually no closer to her than he had been at Lebanon. Yet his faith never flagged. He believed, as he believed in evil and sin, that he would again hold her in his arms.

"And the miracle occurred. Before so many years had passed that he was too old to know the joy of fulfillment, he held her close to his breast, his heart pounding with such a savage beat that its vigor gave life to every inanimate thing around him. And once again, as on the hot noon when he first beheld her, the lids lifted like curtains over those dark eyes ..."

"How did he make it?" Mark inquired. "How did he get to know her?"

I waved aside the interruption. "She had never seemed so lovely as now, and though he had heard her name whispered in the city and knew her reputation to be unsavory, he felt that his eyes had never met such purity as he saw in that marble brow, nor such chastity as was encased in those immobile lips. Let us forgive Conrad his confusion. At such moments a man's mind does not achieve its highest point of logic. Remember, the lady was clothed all in white from the tips of her satin slippers to the crown of blossoms in her dark hair. And the shadows, lilac-tinted, in the shroud ..."

At the word Mark recoiled.

I fixed my eyes upon him innocently. "Shroud. In those days it was still the custom."

"Was she," he asked, biting down slowly as if each word were poisoned fruit, "dead?"

"Perhaps I neglected to mention that he had become apprenticed to an undertaker. And while the surgeon had declared her dead before Conrad was called to the dwelling, he afterward . . ."

Mark's eyes were dark holes burning through the white fabric of a mask. His lips puckered as if the poisoned fruit were bitter.

"I cannot tell if the story is true," I said, sensing his unrest and hastening the moral, "but since Conrad came of a people who never encouraged fantasy, one cannot help but pay him the respect of credence. He returned to Lebanon, but the folk around reported that women were forevermore destroyed for him. Had he known and lost a living love, he would never have been so marked as by this short excursion into necrophilia."

Thunder rumbled closer. The sky had become sulphurous. As we left the garden, I touched his arm gently.

"Tell me, McPherson, how much were you prepared to pay for the portrait?"

He turned on me a look of dark malevolence. "Tell me, Lydecker, did you walk past Laura's apartment every night before she was killed, or is it a habit you've developed since her death?"

Thunder crashed above us. The storm was coming closer.

PART TWO

CHAPTER ONE

When Waldo Lydecker learned what happened after our dinner at Montagnino's on Wednesday night, he could write no more about the Laura Hunt case. The prose style was knocked right out of him.

He had written the foregoing between ten o'clock on Wednesday night and four on Thursday afternoon with only five hours' sleep, a quart of black coffee, and three hearty meals to keep up his strength. I suppose he had intended to fit the story to one of those typical Lydecker last paragraphs where a brave smile always shows through the tears.

I am going on with the story. My writing won't have the smooth professional touch which, as he would say, distinguishes Waldo Lydecker's prose. God help any of us if we'd tried to write our reports with style. But for once in my life, since this is unofficial anyway, I am going to forget Detective Bureau shorthand and express a few personal opinions. This is my first experience with citizens who get their pictures into that part of the funny papers called the Society Section. Even professionally I've never been inside a night club with leopard-skin covers on the chairs. When these people want to insult each other, they say *darling,* and when they get affectionate they throw around words that a Jefferson Market bailiff wouldn't use to a pimp. Poor people brought up to hear their neighbors screaming filth every Saturday night are more careful of their language than well-bred smart-alecks. I know as many four-letter words as anybody in the business and use them when I feel like it. But not with ladies. Nor in writing. It takes a college education to teach a man that he can put on paper what he used to write on a fence.

I'm starting the story where Waldo ended . . . In Montagnino's back yard after the third brandy.

As we stepped out of the restaurant, the heat hit us like a blast from a furnace. The air was dead. Not a shirt-tail moved on the wash-lines of McDougal Street. The town smelled like rotten eggs. A thunderstorm was rolling in.

"Can I drive you home?"

"No, thanks; I feel like walking."

"I'm not drunk. I can drive," I said.

"Have I implied that you're drunk? It's my whim to walk. I'm working tonight." He started off, pounding his stick against the pavement. "Thanks for the feast," he called as I drove off.

I took it slowly because my head was still heavy. I drove past the corner where I should have turned for the Athletic Club, and then I knew that I didn't want to go home. I didn't feel like bowling or pool, my mind wasn't sharp enough for poker, and I've never sat in the lounge in the two years I've lived there. The steel furniture in my bedroom reminded me of a dentist's office. There wasn't a comfortable chair in the room, and if you lay on the couch the cover wrinkled under you. These are all the excuses I can find for going to Laura's apartment that night. Maybe I was just drunk.

Before I went upstairs, I stopped to raise the top of my car and shut the windows. Later, when the thing that happened caused me to question my sanity, I remembered that I had performed the acts of a sober man. I had the key in my pocket and I let myself in as coolly as if I'd been entering my own place. As I opened the door I saw the first streaks of lightning through the blinds. Thunder crashed. It was followed by the stillness that precedes heavy rain. I was sweating and my head ached. I got myself a drink of water from the kitchen, took off my coat, opened my collar, and stretched in the long chair. The light hurt my eyes and I turned it off. I fell asleep before the storm broke.

Thunder sounded like a squadron of bombers above the roof. Lightning did not flash away immediately. After a few seconds I saw that it was not lightning at all, but the lamp with the green shade. I had not turned it on. I had not moved from the long chair.

Thunder crashed again. Then I saw her. She held a rain-streaked hat in one hand and a pair of light gloves in the other. Her rain-spattered silk dress was moulded tight to her body. She was five-foot seven, weighed about one-thirty, dark eyes slightly slanted, dark hair, and tanned skin. Nothing wrong about her ankles either.

"What are you doing here?" she said.

I couldn't answer.

"What are you doing here?"

I remembered the wine and looked around to see if she'd brought any pink elephants.

"If you don't get out this moment," she said, and her voice trembled, "I'll call the police."

"I am the police," I said.

My voice told me that I was alive. I jerked myself out of the chair. The girl backed away. The picture of Laura Hunt was just behind her.

I had a voice. I spoke with authority. "You're dead."

My wild stare and the strange accusation convinced her that she was facing a dangerous lunatic. She edged toward the door.

"Are you . . ." But I couldn't say the name. She had spoken, she was wet with rain, she had been frightened and had tried to escape. Were these real evidences of life just another set of contradictions?

I don't know how long we stood, facing each other and awaiting revelation. For a crazy half-second I remembered what my grandmother used to tell me about meeting in heaven those whom we had lost on earth. Peal after peal of thunder shook the house. Lightning flashed past the window. The ground seemed to be trembling below us and the skies splitting overhead. This was Laura Hunt's apartment; I felt in my pocket for my pipe.

I had bought a paper. As I unfolded it, I said: "Have you seen any newspapers lately? Don't you know what's happened?" The questions made me feel sane again.

She shrank away, clinging with both hands to the table.

I said: "Please don't be frightened; there must be an explanation. If you haven't seen the papers . . ."

"I haven't. I've been in the country. My radio's broken." And then slowly, as if she were fitting the pieces together, she said: "Why? Do the papers say I'm . . ."

I nodded. She took the paper. There was nothing on Page One. A new battle on the Eastern Front and a speech by Churchill had pushed her off the front pages. I turned to Page Four. There was her picture.

Wind howled through the narrow court between the houses. Rain spattered the window-panes. The only sound inside the house was the rhythm of her breathing. Then she looked over the paper into my face and her eyes were filled with tears.

"The poor thing," she said. "The poor, poor kid."

"Who?"

"Diane Redfern. A girl I knew. I'd lent her the apartment."

CHAPTER TWO

Weeat on the couch while I told her about the discovery of the body, the destruction of the face by BB shot, and the identification at the morgue by her aunt and Bessie Clary.

She said: "Yes, of course. We were about the same size and she had my robe on. We wore the same size; I'd given her a few of my dresses. Her hair was a little lighter, but if there was a lot of blood . . ."

She groped for her purse. I gave her my handkerchief.

After she had dried her eyes, she read the rest of the story in the paper. "Are you Mark McPherson?"

I nodded.

"You haven't found the murderer?"

"Nope."

"Did he want to murder her or me?"

"I don't know."

"What are you going to do now that I'm alive?"

"Find out who murdered the other girl."

She sighed and sank back against the cushions. "You'd better have a drink," I said, and went to the corner cabinet. "Scotch, gin, or Bourbon?"

There was the bottle of Three Horses. I should have asked her about it then, before she had time to think. But I was thinking less about the job than the girl, and still so dazed that I wasn't even sure that I was alive, awake and in my right mind.

"How do you know my house so well, Mr. McPherson?"

"There isn't much about you I don't know."

"Gosh," she said; and after a little while, she laughed and asked:

"Do you realize that you're the only person in New York who knows I'm alive? The only one of six million people?"

Thunder and lightning had ceased, but rain beat on the windows. It made us feel separate from everyone else in the city, and important because we shared a secret.

She held up her glass. "To life!"

"To resurrection," I said.

We laughed.

"Go and change your dress," I said. "You'll catch cold."

"Oh," she said. "You're giving me orders."

"Change it. You'll catch cold."

"How masterful, Mr. McPherson!"

She went. I was too nervous to sit down. I was like a kid in a dark house on Hallowe'en; everything seemed mystic and supernatural, and I listened at the door so I should hear her moving about the bedroom, and know that she had not vanished again. My mind was filled with a miracle, life and resurrection, and I had to battle my way through clouds before I could think like a human being. Finally I managed to anchor myself to a chair and light my pipe.

There was, of course, no more Laura Hunt case. But what about the other girl? The body had been cremated. You've got to have a *corpus delicti* to prove murder.

This did not mean that my job was finished. Neither the Department nor the D.A.'s office would let a case slip through their hands so smoothly. Our job was to establish circumstantial evidence of the girl's disappearance, to discover where she had last been seen and by whom. Unless we had cogent evidence that the crime had been committed, the murderer might confess and still escape conviction.

"What do you know about this girl?" I called in to Laura. "What did you say her name was? Were you close friends?"

The bedroom door opened and there was Laura in a long, loose sort of gold-colored robe that made her look like a saint on the window of the Catholic Church. She carried the magazine that had been on the bed-table. On the back cover there was a photograph of a girl in evening clothes smiling at a fellow as he lit her cigarette. The advertisement said:

COMPANIONABLE!
THERE'S NOTHING AS COMPANIONABLE AS A LANCASTER

"Oh, she was a model?"

"Wasn't she lovely?" Laura asked.

"She looks like a model," I said.

"She was beautiful," Laura insisted.

"What else?"

"What else what?"

"What was she like? How well did you know her? Where did she live? How much did she earn? Married, single, divorced? How old? Did she have a family? Who were her friends?"

"Please, Mr. McPherson. One question at a time. What was Diane like?" She hesitated. "I don't think a woman can answer that question quite honestly. You ought to ask a man."

"Your opinion would probably be safer."

"I might be prejudiced. Women with faces like mine can't be too objective about girls like Diane."

"I see nothing wrong with your face, Miss Hunt."

"Skip it. I've never tried to get by on my beauty. And if I should tell you that I considered Diane rather unintelligent and awfully shallow and quite a negative person, you might think I was jealous."

"If you felt that way about her, why did you let her have your apartment?"

"She lived in a hot little room in a boarding-house. And since nobody would have been using this place for a few days, I gave her the key."

"Why did you keep it so secret? Even Bessie didn't know."

"There was nothing secret about it. I had lunch with Diane on Friday. She told me how beastly hot it was in her room and I said she might come up here and live in comparative comfort. If I'd have come home on Friday afternoon or seen Bessie, I'd have mentioned it, but Bessie would have found it out anyway when she came to work on Saturday."

"Have you ever lent your apartment before?"

"Of course. Why not?"

"They said you were generous. Impulsive, too, aren't you?"

She laughed again. "My Aunt Susie says I'm a sucker for a hard-luck story, but I always tell her the sucker wins in the end. You don't get neuroses worrying over people's motives and wondering whether they're trying to use you."

"Sometimes you get shot by mistake," I said. "You happened to be lucky this time."

"Go on," she laughed. "You're not so hardboiled, McPherson. How many shirts have you given away in your life?"

"I'm a Scotchman," I said stiffly; I did not want to show too much pleasure at the way she had read my character.

She laughed again. "Scotch thrift is vastly overrated. My granny Kirkland was the most liberal and open-handed woman in the world."

"You had a Scotch grandmother?"

"From a place called Pitlochry."

"Pitlochry! I've heard of Pitlochry. My father's people came from Blair-Atholl."

We shook hands.

"Were your people very religious?" Laura asked.

"Not my father. But original sin started in my mother's family."

"Ah-hah!" she said. "Dissension in the home. Don't tell me that your father read Darwin."

"Robert Ingersoll."

She clapped her hand to her head. "What a childhood you must have had!"

"Only when my old man took a drop too much. Otherwise Robert Ingersoll never even got to the Apostles' forty-yard line."

"But the name had a sort of magic and you read him secretly as you grew older."

"How did you know?"

"And you decided to learn everything in the world so people couldn't push you around."

That started the life story. It must have sounded like a combination of Frank Merriwell and Superman in ninety-nine volumes, each worth a nickel. McPherson *vs.* Associated Dairymen. McPherson in Washington. McPherson's Big Night with the Hopheads. Down Among the Bucket Shops with Mark McPherson. Labor Spy Rackets as Seen by McPherson. Killers I Have Known. From there somehow we got back to Mark McPherson's Childhood Days. From Rags to Riches, or Barefoot Boy in Brooklyn. I guess I described every game I'd pitched for the Long Island Mohawks. And told her about the time I knocked out Rocco, the Wop Terror, and how Sparks Lampini, who had bet his paper route on Rocco, knocked me out for revenge. And about my folks, my mother, and my sister who had made up her mind to marry the boss, and what a heel she had turned out to be. I even told her about the time we all had diphtheria and Davey, the kid brother, died. It must have been ten years since I had mentioned Davey.

She sat with her hands folded against the gold-colored cloth of her dress and a look on her face as if she were hearing the Commandments read by Moses himself. That's probably what Waldo meant by delicate flattery.

She said, "You don't seem at all like a detective."

"Have you ever known any detectives?"

"In detective stories there are two kinds, the hardboiled ones who are always drunk and talk out of the corners of their mouths and do it all by instinct; and the cold, dry, scientific kind who split hairs under a microscope."

"Which do you prefer?"

"Neither," she said. "I don't like people who make their livings out of spying and poking into people's lives. Detectives aren't heroes to me, they're detestable."

"Thanks," I said.

She smiled a little. "But you're different. The people you've gone after ought to be exposed. Your work is important. I hope you've got a million more stories to tell me."

"Sure," I said, swelling like a balloon. "I'm the Arabian Nights. Spend a thousand and one evenings with me and you won't hear the half of my daring exploits."

"You don't talk like a detective, either."

"Neither hardboiled nor scientific?"

We laughed. A girl had died. Her body had lain on the floor of this room. That is how Laura and I met. And we couldn't stop laughing. We were like old friends, and later, at half-past three, when she said she was hungry, we went into the kitchen and opened some cans. We drank strong tea at the kitchen table like home-folks. Everything was just the way I had felt it would be with her there, alive and warm and interested in a fellow.

CHAPTER THREE

L isten!" she said.

We heard the sound of rain and the crackling of wood in the fireplace and foghorns on the East River. "We're in the midst of Manhattan and this is our private world," she said.

I liked it. I didn't want the rain to stop or the sun to rise. For once in my life I had quit being restless.

She said, "I wonder what people are going to say when they hear I'm not dead."

I thought of the people whose names were in her address book and the stuffed shirts at her office. I thought of Shelby, but what I said was, "One thing I don't want to miss is Waldo when he finds out." I laughed.

She said: "Poor darling Waldo! Did he take it hard?"

"What do you think?"

"He loves me," she said.

I put another log on the fire. My back was turned so that I could not see her face when she asked about Shelby. This was Thursday, the twenty-eighth of August; it was to have been their wedding day.

I answered without turning around. "Shelby has been okay. He's been frank and cooperative, and kind to your aunt."

"Shelby has great self-control. You liked him, didn't you?"

I kept poking at the fire until I almost succeeded in smothering it. There had been the phoney alibi and the bottle of Three Horses Bourbon, the insurance money and the collection of unused shotguns. But now I had run into a new set of contradictions. Two and two no longer added up to four. The twenty-five-thousand-dollar insurance motive was definitely out.

It was hard for me to start asking her questions. She seemed tired. And Shelby was to have been today's bridegroom. I asked only one question:

"Did Shelby know this girl?"

She answered instantly. "Why, yes, of course. She modeled for several of the accounts in our office. All of us knew Diane." She yawned.

"You're tired, aren't you?"

"Would you mind very much if I tried to get some sleep? In the morning—later, I mean—I'll answer all the questions you want to ask."

I phoned the office and told them to send a man to watch her front door.

"Is that necessary?" she said.

"Someone tried to murder you before. I'm not going to take any chances."

"How thoughtful of you! Detectives are all right, I suppose, when they're on your side."

"Look here, Miss Hunt, will you promise me something?"

"You know me much too well to call me Miss Hunt, Mark."

My heart beat like the drum in a Harlem dance band.

"Laura," I said; she smiled at me. "You'll promise, Laura, not to leave this house until I give you permission. Or answer the phone."

"Who'd ring if everybody thinks I'm dead?"

"Promise me, just in case."

She sighed. "All right. I won't answer. And can't I phone anyone either?"

"No," I said.

"But people would be glad to know I'm alive. There are people I ought to tell right away."

"Look here, you're the one living person who can help solve this crime. Laura Hunt must find the person who tried to murder Laura Hunt. Are you game?"

She offered her hand.

The sucker took it and believed her.

CHAPTER FOUR

I t was almost six when I checked in at the club. I decided that I'd need a clear head for the day's work and left a call for eight. I dreamed for two hours about Laura Hunt. The dream had five or six variations, but the meaning was always the same. She was just beyond my reach. As soon as I came close, she floated off into space. Or ran away. Or locked a door. Each time I came to, I cursed myself for letting a dream hold me in such horror. As time passed and I struggled from dream to dream, the real incidents of the night became less real than my nightmares. Each time I woke, cold and sweating, I believed more firmly that I had dreamed of finding her in the apartment and that Laura was still dead.

When the desk clerk called, I jumped as if a bomb had gone off under my bed. Exhausted, my head aching, I swore never to drink Italian wine again. The return of Laura Hunt seemed so unreal that I wondered if I had ever actually considered reporting it to the Department. I stared hard at real things, the steel tubes of the chairs and writing desk, the brown curtains at the windows, the chimneys across the street. Then I saw, on the bureau with my wallet and keys, a spot of red. This brought me out of bed with a leap. It was the stain of lip rouge on my handkerchief which she had used. So I knew she was alive.

As I reached for the telephone, I remembered that I had told her not to answer it. She was probably sleeping anyway, and wouldn't have been pleased if a thoughtless mug called her at that hour.

I went down to the office, wrote out my report on the typewriter, sealed and filed all copies. Then I went in to see Deputy Commissioner Preble.

Every morning I had gone into his office to report on the Laura Hunt case and every day he had said the same thing.

"Stick to the case a little longer, my boy, and maybe you'll find that murder's big enough for your talents."

His cheeks were like purple plums. I wanted to squash them with my fists. We represented opposing interests, I being one of the Commissioner's inside men, and more active than anyone in the Department on the progressive angle. Deputy Commissioner Preble was his party's front. Now that they were out of power, his was strictly an appeasement job.

As I walked into his office, he gave me the usual razzberry. Before I could say a word he started: "Do you know what this case is costing the Department? I've had a memo sent to your office. You'd better step on it or I'll have to assign someone to the case who knows how to handle homicide."

"You might have thought of that in the beginning," I said, because I wasn't going to let him know that I hadn't been on to his tactics. He had been waiting all along to show me up by letting me work until I'd hit a dead end and then handing the case to one of his favorites.

"What have you to say? Another of those minute-and-a-half reports, huh?"

"You needn't worry about our not getting Laura Hunt's murderer," I said. "That part of the case is completed."

"What do you mean? You've got him?" He looked disappointed.

"Laura Hunt isn't dead."

His eyes popped like golf balls. "She's in her apartment now. I had Ryan on guard until eight this morning, then Behrens came on. No one knows of this yet."

He pointed at his head. "Perhaps I ought to get in touch with Bellevue, McPherson. Psychopathic Ward."

I told him briefly what had happened. Although the heat wave was over and there was a chill in the air, he fanned himself with both hands.

"Who murdered the other girl?"

"I don't know yet."

"What does Miss Hunt say about it?"

"I've reported everything that she told me."

"Do you think she knows anything she hasn't told you?"

I said: "Miss Hunt was suffering from shock after she heard that her friend had been killed. She wasn't able to talk a lot."

He snorted. "Is she pretty, McPherson?"

I said: "I'm going to question her this morning. I also intend to surprise several people who think she is dead. It would be better if this were kept out of the newspapers until I've had time to work out my plans."

It was strictly Front Page even for the *Times*, and a coast-to-coast hook-up on the news broadcasts. I could tell by his face that he was working out an angle that would immortalize the name of Preble.

He said: "This changes the case, you know. There is no *corpus delicti*. We'll have to investigate the death of the other girl. I'm wondering, McPherson . . ."

"I wondered, too," I said. "You'll find it all in my report. A sealed copy has been sent to the Commissioner's office and you'll find yours on your secretary's desk. And I don't want to be relieved. You assigned me to the case in the beginning and I'm sticking until it's finished." I shouted and pounded on the desk, knowing that a man is most easily intimidated by his own methods. "And if one word of this gets into the papers before I've given the green light, there'll be hell to pay around here on Monday when the Commissioner gets back."

I told only one other person about Laura's return. That was Jake Mooney. Jake is a tall, sad-faced Yankee from Providence, known among the boys as the Rhode Island Clam. Once a reporter wrote, "Mooney maintained a clam-like silence," and it got Jake so angry that he's lived up to the name ever since. By the time I came out of Preble's office, Jake had got a list of the photographers for whom Diane Redfern posed.

"Go and see these fellows," I said. "Get what you can on her. Look over her room. Don't tell anyone she's dead."

He nodded.

"I want all the papers and letters you find in her room. And be sure to ask the landlady what kind of men she knew. She might have picked up some boy friends who played with sawed-off shotguns."

The telephone rang. It was Mrs. Treadwell. She wanted me to come to her house right away.

"There's something I ought to tell you, Mr. McPherson. I'd intended going back to the country today; there was nothing more I could do for poor Laura, was there? My lawyers are going to take care of her things. But now something has happened . . ."

"All right, I'll be there, Mrs. Treadwell."

As I drove up Park Avenue, I decided to keep Mrs. Treadwell waiting while I saw Laura. She had promised to stay in the apartment and keep away from the telephone, and I knew there was no fresh food in the house. I drove around to Third Avenue, bought milk, cream, butter, eggs, and bread.

Behrens was on guard at the door. His eyes bulged at the sight of the groceries, but he evidently thought I'd set up housekeeping.

I had the key in my pocket. But before I entered, I called a warning.

She came out of the kitchen. "I'm glad you didn't ring the bell," she said. "Since you told me about the murder—" she shuddered and looked at the spot where the body had fallen "—I'm afraid of every stray sound."

"I'm sure you're the only detective in the world who'd think of *that*," she said when I gave her the groceries. "Have you eaten breakfast?"

"Now that you've reminded me, no."

It seemed natural for me to be carrying in the groceries and lounging in the kitchen while she cooked. I had thought of that kind of girl, with all those swell clothes and a servant to wait on her, as holding herself above housework. But not Laura.

"Should we be elegant and carry it to the other room or folksy and eat in the kitchen?"

"Until I was a grown man, I never ate in anything but a kitchen."

"Then it's the kitchen," she said. "There's no place like home."

While we were eating, I told her that I had informed the Deputy Commissioner of her return.

"Was he startled?"

"He threatened to commit me to the Psychopathic Ward. And then—" I looked straight into her eyes "—he asked if I thought you knew anything about that other girl's death."

"And what did you say?"

"Listen," I said, "there are going to be a lot of questions asked and you'll probably have to tell a lot more than you'd like about your private life. The more honest you are, the easier it will be for you in the end. I hope you don't mind my telling you this."

"Don't you trust me?"

I said, "It's my job to suspect everyone."

She looked at me over her coffee-cup. "And just what do you suspect me of?"

I tried to be impersonal. "Why did you lie to Shelby about going to Waldo Lydecker's for dinner on Friday night?"

"So that's what's bothering you?"

"You lied, Miss Hunt."

"Oh, I'm Miss Hunt to you now, Mister McPherson."

"Quit sparring," I said. "Why did you lie?"

"I'm afraid if I told you the truth, you might not understand."

"Okay," I said. "I'm dumb. I'm a detective. I don't speak English."

"I'm sorry if I've hurt your feelings, but—" she drew the knife along the checks in the red-and-white tablecloth "—it's hardly the sort of thing that one finds on a police blotter. Blotter, isn't that what you call it?"

"Go on," I said.

"You see," she said, "I've been a single woman for such a long time."

"It's as clear as mud," I said.

"Men have bachelor dinners," she said. "They get drunk. They go out for a last binge with chorus girls. That, I guess, is what freedom means to them. So they've got to make a splurge before they get married."

I laughed. "Poor Waldo! I bet he wouldn't care very much to be compared with a chorus girl."

She shook her head. "Freedom meant something quite different to me, Mark. Maybe you'll understand. It meant owning myself, possessing all my silly and useless routines, being the sole mistress of my habits. Do I make sense?"

"Is that why you kept putting off the wedding?"

She said: "Get me a cigarette, will you? They're in the living room."

I got her the cigarettes and lit my pipe.

She went on talking. "Freedom meant my privacy. It's not that I want to lead any sort of double life, it's simply that I resent intrusion. Perhaps because Mama always used to ask where I was going and what time I'd be home and always made me feel guilty if I changed my mind. I love doing things impulsively, and I resent it to a point where my spine stiffens and I get gooseflesh if people ask where and what and why." She was like a child, crying to be understood.

"On Friday I had a date with Waldo for a sort of bachelor dinner before I left for Wilton. It was to be my last night in town before my wedding . . ."

"Didn't Shelby resent it?"

"Naturally. Wouldn't you?" She laughed and showed the tip of her tongue between her lips. "Waldo resented Shelby. But I couldn't help it. I never flirted or urged them on. And I'm fond of Waldo; he's a fussy old maid, but he's been kind to me, very kind. Besides, we've been friends for years. Shelby just had to make the best of it. We're civilized people, we don't try to change each other."

"And Shelby, I suppose, had habits that weren't hundred per cent with you?"

She ignored the question. "On Friday I fully intended to dine with Waldo and take the ten-twenty train. But in the afternoon I changed my mind."

"Why?"

"Why?" she mocked. "That's precisely why I didn't tell him. Because he'd ask why."

I got angry. "You can have your prejudices if you like, and God knows I don't care if you want to make your habits sacred, but this is a murder case. Murder! There must have been some reason why you changed your mind."

"I'm like that."

"Are you?" I asked. "They told me you were a kind woman who thought more of an old friend than to stand him up for the sake of a selfish whim. You're supposed to be generous and considerate. It sounds like a lot of bull to me!"

"Why, Mr. McPherson, you are a vehement person."

"Please tell me exactly why you changed your mind about having dinner at Waldo's."

"I had a headache."

"I know. That's what you told him."

"Don't you believe me?"

"Women always have headaches when they don't want to do something. Why did you come back from lunch with such a headache that you phoned Waldo before you took your hat off?"

"My secretary told you that, I suppose. How important trifles become when something violent happens!"

She walked over to the couch and sat down. I followed. Suddenly she touched my arm with her hand and looked up into my eyes so sweetly that I smiled. We both laughed and the trifles became less important.

She said: "So help me, Mark, I've told you the truth. I felt so wretched after lunch on Friday, I just couldn't face Waldo's chatter, and I couldn't sit through dinner with Shelby either because he'd have been too pleased at my breaking the date with Waldo. I just had to get away from everybody."

"Why?"

"What a persistent man you are!"

She shivered. The day was cold. Rain beat against the window. The sky was the color of lead.

"Should I make you a fire?"

"Don't bother." Her voice was cold, too.

I got logs out of the cabinet under the bookshelves and built her a fire. She sat at the end of the couch, her knees tucked up, her arms hugging her body. She seemed defenseless.

"There," I said. "You'll be warm soon."

"Please, please, Mark, believe me. There was no more to it than that. You're not just a detective who sees nothing but surface actions. You're a sensitive man, you react to nuances. So please try to understand, please."

The attack was well-aimed. A man is no stronger than his vanity. If I doubted her, I'd show myself to be nothing more than a crude detective.

"All right," I said, "we'll skip it now. Maybe you saw a ghost at lunch. Maybe your girl friend said something that reminded you of something else. Hell, everybody gets temperamental once in a while."

She slipped off the couch and ran toward me, her hands extended. "You're a darling, really. I knew last night that I'd never have to be afraid of you."

I took her hands. They were soft to touch, but strong underneath. Sucker, I said to myself, and decided to do something about it then and there. My self-respect was involved. I was a detective, a servant of the people, a representative of law and order.

I went to the liquor cabinet. "Ever seen this before?"

It was the bottle with the Three Horses on the label.

She answered without the slightest hesitation, "Of course; it's been in the house for weeks."

"This isn't the brand you usually buy, is it? Did you get this from Mosconi's, too?"

She answered in one long unpunctuated sentence. "No no I picked it up one night we were out of Bourbon I had company for dinner and stopped on the way home from the office it was on Lexington or maybe Third Avenue I don't remember."

She lied like a goon. I had checked with Mosconi and discovered that on Friday night, between seven and eight, Shelby Carpenter had stopped at the store, bought the bottle of Three Horses, and, instead of charging it to Miss Hunt's account, had paid cash.

CHAPTER FIVE

W hat took you so long, Mr. McPherson? You should have come earlier. Maybe it's too late now, maybe he's gone forever."

In a pink bed, wearing a pink jacket with fur on the sleeves, lay Mrs. Susan Treadwell. I sat like the doctor on a straight chair.

"Shelby?"

She nodded. Her pink massaged skin looked dry and old, her eyes were swollen and the black stuff had matted under her lashes. The Pomeranian lay on the pink silk comfort, whimpering.

"Do make Wolf stop that sniffling," begged the lady. She dried her eyes with a paper handkerchief that she took from a silk box. "My nerves are completely gone. I can't bear it."

The dog went on whimpering. She sat up and spanked it feebly.

"He's gone?" I asked. "Where?"

"How do I know?" She looked at a diamond wristwatch. "He's been gone since six-thirty this morning."

I was not upset. One of our men had been following Shelby since I'd checked with Mosconi on the Bourbon bottle.

"You were awake when he left? You heard him go? Did he sneak out?"

"I lent him my car," she sniffled.

"Do you think he was trying to escape the law, Mrs. Treadwell?"

She blew her nose and dabbed at her eyes again. "Oh, I knew it was weak of me, Mr. McPherson. But you know Shelby, he has a way with him. He asks you for something and you can't resist him; and then you hate yourself for giving in. He said it was a matter of life and death, and if I ever discovered the reason, I'd always be grateful."

I let her cry for a few minutes before I asked, "Do you believe that he committed the murder . . . the murder of your niece, Mrs. Treadwell?"

"No! No! I don't, Mr. McPherson. He just hasn't got the stomach. Criminals go after what they want, but Shelby's just a big kid. He's always being sorry for something. My poor, poor Laura!"

I said nothing about Laura's return.

"You don't like Shelby very much, do you, Mrs. Treadwell?"

"He's a darling boy," she said, "but not for Laura. Laura couldn't afford him."

"Oh," I said.

She was afraid I had got the wrong impression and added quickly: "Not that he's a gigolo. Shelby comes from a wonderful family. But in some ways a gigolo's cheaper. You know where you are. With a man like Shelby you can't slip the money under the table."

I decided that it was lucky that most of my cases had not involved women. Their logic confused me.

"She was always doing the most absurd things about his pride. Like the cigarette case. That was typical. And then he had to go and lose it."

By this time I'd lost the scent.

"She couldn't afford it, of course; she had to charge it on my account and pay me back by the month. A solid gold cigarette case, he had to have it, she said, so he'd feel equal to the men he lunched with at the club and the clients in their business. Does it make sense to you, Mr. McPherson?"

"No," I said honestly, "it doesn't."

"But it's just like Laura."

I could have agreed to that, too, but I controlled myself.

"And he lost it?" I asked, leading her back to the trail.

"Um-hum. In April, before she'd even finished paying for it. Can you imagine?" Suddenly, for no reason that I could understand, she took an atomizer from the bed-table and sprayed herself with perfume. Then she made up her lips and combed her hair. "I thought of the cigarette case as soon as he'd gone off with the keys to my car. Did I feel like a sucker!"

"I understand that," I said.

Her smile was a clue to the business with the perfume and lipstick. I was a man, she had to get around me.

"You're not going to blame me for giving him the car? Really, I didn't think of it at the time. He has a way with him, you know."

"You shouldn't have given it to him if you felt that way," said the stern detective.

She fell for it.

"It was weak, Mr. McPherson, I know how weak I was to have done it. I should have been more suspicious, I know I should, especially after that phone call."

"What phone call, Mrs. Treadwell?"

It was only by careful questioning that I got the story straight. If I told it her way, there would be no end to this chapter. The phone had wakened her at half-past five that morning. She lifted the receiver in time to hear Shelby, on the upstairs extension, talking to the night clerk at the Hotel Framingham. The clerk apologized for disturbing him at this hour, but said that someone wanted to get in touch with him on a life-and-death matter. That person was waiting on another wire. Should the clerk give that party Mr. Carpenter's number?

"I'll call back in ten minutes," Shelby had said. "Tell them to call you again."

He had dressed and tiptoed down the stairs.

"He was going out to phone," Mrs. Treadwell said. "He was afraid I'd listen on the extension."

At twenty minutes past six she had heard him coming up the stairs. He had knocked at her bedroom door, apologized for waking her, and asked for the use of the car.

"Does that make me an accessory or something, Mr. McPherson?" Tears rolled down her cheeks.

I phoned the office and asked if there had been any reports from the man who had been following Shelby Carpenter. Nothing had been heard since he went on duty at midnight, and the man who was to have relieved him at eight in the morning was still waiting.

As I put down the phone, the dog began to bark. Shelby walked in.

"Good morning." He went straight to the bed. "I'm glad you rested, darling. It was cruel of me to disturb you at that mad hour. But you don't show it at all. You're divine this morning." He kissed her forehead and then turned to welcome me.

"Where've you been?" she asked.

"Can't you guess, darling?"

He petted the dog. I sat back and watched. There was something familiar and unreal about Shelby. I was always uncomfortable when he was in the room, and always struggling to remember where I had seen him. The memory was like a dream, unsubstantial and baffling.

"I can't imagine where anyone would go at that wild hour, darling. You had me quite alarmed."

If Shelby guessed that the lady's alarm had caused her to summon the police, he was too tactful to mention it.

"I went up to Laura's place," he said. "I made a sentimental journey. This was to have been our wedding day, you know."

"Oh, I'd forgotten." Mrs. Treadwell caught his hand. He was sitting on the edge of the bed, comfortable and sure of himself.

"I couldn't sleep. And when that absurd phone call woke us, Auntie Sue, I was too upset to stay in my room. I felt such a longing for Laura, I wanted to be close to something she had loved. There was the garden. She'd cared for it herself, Mr. McPherson, with her own hands. It was lovely in the gray morning light."

"I don't know whether I quite believe you," Mrs. Treadwell said. "What's your opinion, Mr. McPherson?"

"You're embarrassing him, darling. Remember, he's a detective," Shelby said as if she had been talking about leprosy in front of a leper.

"Why couldn't you take that telephone call in the house?" asked Mrs. Treadwell. "Did you think I'd stoop so low as to listen on the extension?"

"If you hadn't been listening on the extension, you'd not have known that I had to go out to a phone booth," he said, laughing.

"Why were you afraid to have me hear?"

Shelby offered me a cigarette. He carried the pack in his pocket without a case.

"Was it a girl?" asked Mrs. Treadwell.

"I don't know. He . . . she . . . whoever it was . . . refused to leave a number. I called the Framingham three times, but they hadn't called back." He blew smoke rings toward the ceiling. Then, smiling at me like the King of England in a newsreel showing their majesties' visit to coal miners' huts, he said: "A yellow cab followed me all the way to the cottage and back. On these country roads at that hour your man couldn't very well hide himself. Don't be angry with the poor chap because I spotted him."

"He kept you covered. That was all he was told to do. Whether you knew or not makes no difference." I got up. "I'm going to be up at Miss Hunt's apartment at three o'clock. I want you to meet me there, Carpenter."

"Is it necessary? I rather dislike going up there today of all days. You know, we were to have been married . . . ."

"Consider it a sentimental journey," I said.

Mrs. Treadwell barely noticed when I left. She was busy with her face.

At the office I learned that Shelby's sentimental journey had added a five-hour taxi bill to the cost of the Laura Hunt case. Nothing had been discovered. Shelby had not even entered the house, but had stood in the garden in the rain and blown his nose vigorously. He might also, it was hinted, have been crying.

CHAPTER SIX

Mooney was waiting in my office with his report on Diane Red-fern.

She had not been seen since Friday. The landlady remembered because Diane had paid her room rent that day. She had come from work at five o'clock, stopped in the landlady's basement flat to hand her the money, gone to her room on the fourth floor, bathed, changed her clothes, and gone out again. The landlady had seen her hail a cab at the corner of Seventh Avenue and Christopher Street. She remembered because she considered taxis a sinful extravagance for girls like Diane.

The girl might have come in late on Friday night and gone out again on Saturday morning, but the landlady had not seen her. There were still boarders to be questioned, but the landlady had not known where they worked, and Mooney would have to go back at six o'clock to check with them.

"Did the landlady seem surprised that Diane hadn't been seen since Friday?"

"She says it doesn't matter to her whether the boarders use their rooms or not as long as they pay the rent. The girls that stay in places like that are often out all night."

"But it's five days," I said. "Was there nobody to bother about her disappearance?"

"You know how it is with those kind of girls, Mac. Here today, gone tomorrow. Who cares?"

"Hasn't she any friends? Didn't anyone come to see her or telephone?"

"There were some phone calls. Tuesday and Wednesday. I checked. Photographers calling her to come and work."

"Nothing personal?"

"There might have been a couple of other calls, but no messages. The landlady don't remember what she didn't write down on the pad."

I had known girls like that around New York. No home, no friends, not much money. Diane had been a beauty, but beauties are a dime a dozen on both sides of Fifth Avenue between Eighth Street and Ninety-Sixth. Mooney's report gave facts and figures, showed an estimate of Diane's earnings according to figures provided by the Models' Guild. She could have supported a husband and kids on the money she earned when she worked, but the work was unsteady. And according to Mooney's rough estimate, the clothes in her closet had cost plenty. Twenty pairs of shoes. There were no bills as there had been in Laura's desk, for Diane came from the lower classes, she paid cash. The sum of it all was a shabby and shiftless life. Fancy perfume bottles, Kewpie dolls, and toy animals were all she brought home from expensive dinners and suppers in night spots. The letters from her family, plain working people who lived in Paterson, New Jersey, were written in night-school English and told about lay-offs and money troubles.

Her name had been Jennie Swobodo.

Mooney had taken nothing from the room but the letters. He'd had a special lock put on the door and threatened the landlady with the clink if she opened her face.

He gave me a duplicate key. "You might want to look in yourself. I'll be back there at six to talk to the other tenants."

I had no time then to look into the life of Jennie Swobodo, alias Diane Redfern. But when I got up to Laura's apartment, I asked if there hadn't been any pocketbooks or clothes left there by the murdered model.

Laura said: "Yes, if Bessie had examined the clothes in the closet, she'd have found Diane's dress. And her purse was in my dresser drawer. She had put everything away neatly."

There was a dresser drawer filled with purses. Among them was the black silk bag that Diane had carried. There was eighteen dollars in it, the key to her room, lipstick, eyeshadow, powder, a little tin phial of perfume, and a straw cigarette case with a broken clasp.

Laura watched quietly while I examined Diane's belongings. When I went back to the living-room, she followed me like a child.

She had changed into a tan dress and brown high-heeled slippers that set off her wonderful ankles. Her earrings were little gold bells.

"I've sent for Bessie."

"How thoughtful you are!"

I felt like a hypocrite. My reason for sending for Bessie had been purely selfish. I wanted to observe her reaction to Laura's return.

When I explained, Laura said, "But you don't suspect poor old Bessie?"

"I just want to see how a non-suspect takes it."

"As a basis for comparison?"

"Maybe."

"Then there's someone you do suspect?"

I said, "There are several lies which will have to be explained."

When she moved, the gold bells tinkled. Her face was like a mask. "Mind a pipe?"

The bells tinkled again. I struck a match. It scraped like an emery wheel. I thought of Laura's lie and hated her because she was making a fool of herself for Shelby Carpenter. And trying to make a fool of me. I was glad when the doorbell rang. I told Laura to wait in the bedroom for my signal.

Bessie knew at once that something had happened. She looked around the room, she stared at the place where the body had fallen, she studied each ornament and every piece of furniture. I saw it with a housekeeper's eyes then, noticed that the newspaper had been folded carelessly and left on the big table, that Laura's lunch tray with an empty plate and coffee-cup remained on the coffee-table beside the couch, that a book lay open, that the fire burned behind the screen, and red-tipped cigarette stubs filled the ashtrays.

"Sit down," I told her. "Something's happened."

"What?"

"Sit down."

"I can take it standing."

"Someone has come to stay here," I said, and went to the bedroom door.

Laura came out.

I have heard women scream when their husbands beat them and mothers sobbing over dead and injured children, but I have never heard such eery shrieks as Bessie let out at the sight of Laura. She dropped her pocketbook. She crossed herself. Then, very slowly, she backed toward a chair and sat down.

"Do you see what I see, Mr. McPherson?"

"It's all right, Bessie. She's alive."

Bessie called upon God, Jesus, Mary, and her patron saint Elizabeth to witness the miracle.

"Bessie, calm yourself. I'm all right; I just went to the country. Someone else was murdered."

It was easier to believe in miracles. Bessie insisted upon telling Laura that she had herself found the body, that she had identified it as Laura Hunt's, that it had worn Laura's best negligee and silver mules. And she was just as positive about her uncle's sister-in-law's cousin who had met her dead sweetheart in an orchard in County Galway.

None of our arguments convinced her until Laura said, "Well, what are we going to have for dinner, Bessie?"

"Blessed Mary, I never thought I'd be hearing you ask that no more, Miss Laura."

"I'm asking, Bessie. How about a steak and French fried and apple pie, Bessie?"

Bessie brightened. "Would a ghost be asking for French fried and apple pie? Who was it got murdered, Miss Laura?"

"Miss Redfern, you remember . . . the girl who . . ."

"It's no more than she deserved," said Bessie, and went into the kitchen to change into her work clothes.

I told her to shop for dinner in stores where they did not know her as the servant of a murder victim, and warned her against mentioning the miracle of Laura's return.

"Evidently Bessie disapproved of Diane. Why?" I asked Laura when we were alone again.

"Bessie's opinionated," she said. "There was no particular reason."

"No?"

"No," said Laura firmly.

The doorbell rang again.

"Stay here this time," I whispered. "We'll try another kind of surprise."

She waited, sitting stiffly at the edge of the couch. I opened the door. I had expected to see Shelby, but it was Waldo Lydecker who walked in.

CHAPTER SEVEN

Self-centered people see only what they want to see. Astigmatism might have been his excuse for his failure to notice her at first, but I think it was covetousness. His gaze was so concentrated upon the antique glass vase that the rest of the room might have been sky or desert.

"Your office told me I'd find you here, McPherson. I've talked to my lawyer and he advises me to take my vase and let the bitch sue."

He had to pass the sofa on the way to the mantel. Laura turned her head, the gold bells tinkled. Waldo paused as if he had heard some ghostly warning. Then, like a man afraid of his imagination and determined to show himself above fear, he stretched his hands toward the shining globe. Laura turned to see how I was taking it. Her gold bells struck such a sharp note that Waldo whirled on his heels and faced her.

He was whiter than death. He did not stagger nor fall, but stood paralyzed, his arms raised toward the vase. He was like a caricature, pitiful and funny at the same time. The Van Dyke beard, the stick crooked over his arm, the well-cut suit, the flower in his buttonhole, were like decorations on the dead.

We were quiet. The clock ticked.

"Waldo," Laura said softly.

He seemed not to have heard.

She took hold of his rigid arms and led him to the couch. He moved like a mechanical doll. She urged him to a seat, gently pushed down his arms, handed me his hat and stick. "Waldo," she whispered in the voice of a mother to a hurt child. "Waldo, darling."

His neck turned like a mechanism on springs. His glazed eyes, empty of understanding, were fastened on her face.

"It's all right, Mr. Lydecker. She's alive and well. There's been a mistake."

My voice touched him, but not in the right place. He swayed backward on the couch, then jerked forward with a mechanical rather than willful reaction. He trembled so violently that some inner force seemed to be shaking his body. Sweat rose in crystals on his forehead and upper lip.

"There's brandy in the cabinet. Get some, Mark. Quickly," Laura said.

I fetched the brandy. She lifted the glass to his lips. Most of the liquor trickled down his chin. After a while he lifted his right hand, looked at it, dropped it, and lifted the left. He seemed to be testing himself to see if he was capable of willing his muscles to action.

Laura kneeled beside him, her hands on his knees. Her voice was gentle as she explained that it was Diane Redfern who had died and been buried while Laura was staying at her little house in the country. I could not tell whether he heard or whether it was her voice that soothed him, but when she suggested that he rest on the bed, he rose obediently. Laura took him into the bedroom, helped him lie down, spread her blue-and-white cover over his legs. He let himself be led around like a child.

When she came back she asked if I thought we ought to call a doctor.

"I don't know," I said. "He's not young and he's fat. But it doesn't look like any stroke I've ever seen."

"It's happened before."

"Like this?"

She nodded. "In the theatre one night. He got angry that we'd called a doctor. Maybe we'd better let him rest."

We sat like people in a hospital corridor.

"I'm sorry," I said. "If I'd known it was Waldo, I'd have warned him."

"You're still planning to do it to Shelby, aren't you?"

"Shelby's nerves are stronger. He'll take it better."

Her eyes were narrow with anger.

I said: "Look here, you know that Shelby's lied. I'm not saying that he's committed murder, but I know he's hiding something. There are several things he's got to explain."

"He can, I'm sure he can. Shelby can explain everything."

She went into the bedroom to see how Waldo was getting on.

"He seems to be sleeping. He's breathing regularly. Maybe we'd better just leave him."

We sat without speaking until the doorbell rang again. "You'll have to see him first and tell him," Laura said. "I'm not going to let anyone else go through that shock." She disappeared behind the swinging door that led to the kitchen.

The bell rang again. When I opened the door, Shelby pushed past. "Where is she?" he shouted.

"Oh, you know, then?"

I heard the back door open, and I knew that he had met Bessie on the stairs.

"God damn women," I said.

Then Laura came out of the kitchen. I saw at once that Bessie wasn't the woman who deserved my curses. The lovers' meeting was too perfect. They embraced, kissed, and clung. An actor after a dozen rehearsals would have groped for his handkerchief in that same dazed way. An actor would have held her at arm's length, staring at her with that choir-boy look on his face. There was something pre-arranged about the whole scene. His tenderness and her joy.

I turned my back.

Laura's voice was melted syrup. "Happy, darling?"

He answered in a whisper.

My pipe had gone out. If I turned and got a match from the table, they would think I was watching. I bit on the cold stem. The whispering and muttering went on. I watched the minute hand creep around the dial of my watch. I thought of the night I had waited for Pinky Moran to come out of his sweetheart's house. It had been four above at ten o'clock and by midnight it was below zero. I had waited in the snow and thought about the gangster lying warm in the arms of his fat slut. I turned and saw Shelby's hands feeling, touching, moving along the tan material of Laura's dress.

"How infinitely touching! What inexpressible tenderness! Juliet risen from the grave! Welcome, Romeo!"

It was, of course, Waldo. He had not only recovered his strength, but his bounce.

"Forgive me," he said, "for a wee touch of epilepsy. It's an old family custom." He jerked Laura away from Shelby, kissed both cheeks, whirled around with her as if they were waltzing. "Welcome, wench! Tell us how it feels to return from the grave."

"Be yourself, Waldo."

"More truly myself you have never seen me, you beautiful zombie. I, too, am resurrected. The news of your death had me at the brink of eternity. We are both reborn, we must celebrate the miracle of life, beloved. Let's have a drink."

She started toward the liquor cabinet, but Waldo barred her way. "No, darling, no whiskey tonight. We're drinking champagne." And he bustled to the kitchen, shouting that Bessie was to hurry over to Mosconi's and bring back some wine with a name that he had to write down on a piece of paper.

CHAPTER EIGHT

Laura sat with three men drinking champagne. It was a familiar scene to them, Old Home Week. Even Bessie took it like a veteran. They seemed ready to take up where they had left off last week, before someone rang the bell and blew a girl's face away with a charge of BB shot. That's why I was there, the third man.

When they drank a toast to Laura, I took a sip of the wine. The rest of it stayed in my glass until the bubbles died.

"Aren't you drinking?" Waldo asked me.

"I happen to be on a job," I said.

"He's a prig," said Waldo. "A proletarian snob with a Puritan conscience."

Because I was on a job and because Laura was there, I didn't use the only words I knew for describing him. They were short words and to the point.

"Don't be cross with us," Laura said. "These are my best friends in the whole world and naturally they want to celebrate my not being dead."

I reminded them that Diane Redfern's death was still a mystery.

"But I'm sure we know nothing about it," Shelby said.

"Ah-hah!" said Waldo. "The ghost at the feast. Shall we drink a respectful toast?"

Laura put down her glass and said, "Waldo, please."

"That's in questionable taste," said Shelby.

Waldo sighed. "How pious we've all grown! It's your influence, McPherson. As walking delegate for the Union of the Dead . . ."

"Please shut up!" said Laura.

She moved closer to Shelby. He took her hand. Waldo watched like a cat with a family of mice.

"Well, McPherson, since you insist upon casting the shadow of sobriety upon our sunny reunion, tell us how you're proceeding with the investigation. Have you cleared the confusion surrounding that bottle of Bourbon?"

Laura said quietly: "It was I who bought that bottle of Three Horses, Waldo. I know it's not as good as the stuff you taught me to buy, but one night I was in a hurry and brought it home. Don't you remember, Shelby?"

"I do indeed." Shelby pressed her hand.

They seemed to be getting closer together and shoving Waldo out into the cold. He poured himself another glass of champagne.

"Tell us, McPherson, were there any mysteries in the life of the little model? Have you discovered any evil companions? Do you know the secrets of her gay life in Greenwich Village?"

Waldo was using me as a weapon against Shelby. It was clear as water out of the old oaken bucket. Here he was, a man who had read practically all that was great in English literature, and a mug could have taught him the alphabet. I felt fine. He was shooting right up my alley.

"My assistant," I said with an official roll in my voice, "is on the trail of her enemies."

Waldo choked on his wine.

"Enemies," said Laura. "She?"

"There might have been things about her life that you didn't know," said Shelby.

"Pooh!"

"Most of those girls live very questionable lives," Shelby said firmly. "For all we know, the poor girl might have got herself mixed up with all sorts of people. Men she'd met in night clubs."

"How do you know so much about her?" Waldo asked.

"I don't know. I'm merely mentioning possibilities," Shelby said. He turned to me and asked, "These models, they're often friendly with underworld characters, aren't they?"

"Poor Diane," Laura said. "She wasn't the sort of person anyone could hate. I mean . . . she didn't have much . . . well, passion. Just beauty and vague dreams. I can't imagine anyone hating a kid like that. She was so . . . I mean . . . you wanted to help her."

"Was that Shelby's explanation?" Waldo asked. "His was a purely philanthropic interest, I take it."

Bright spots burned on Laura's cheeks. "Yes, it was!" she said hotly. "I'd asked him to be kind to her, hadn't I, Shelby?"

Shelby went to the cupboard for a log. He was glad for the excuse to move around. Laura's eyes followed his movements.

"Had you asked him to be particularly kind to her last Wednesday, darling?" Waldo pretended to ask the question innocently, but he was slanting curious glances at me.

"Wednesday?" she said with an effort to appear absent-minded.

"Last Wednesday. Or was it Tuesday? The night they did the Toccata and Fugue at the Stadium, wasn't that Wednesday?" He rolled his eyes toward the fireplace and Shelby. "When was your cocktail party, Laura?"

"Oh, that," she said. "On Wednesday."

"You should have been here, McPherson," Waldo said. "It was too, too jolly."

Laura said, "You're being silly, Waldo."

But Waldo wanted to put on a show and nothing could stop him. He got up with the champagne glass in his hand and gave an imitation of Laura as hostess to a lot of cocktail-drinkers. He did not merely speak in a falsetto voice and swing his hips the way most men do when they imitate women. He had a real talent for acting. He was the hostess, he moved from guest to guest, he introduced strangers, he saw that the glasses were filled, he carried a tray of sandwiches.

"Hello, darling, I'm so glad you could come . . . you must meet . . . I know you'll simply adore . . . Don't tell me you're not drinking . . . Not eating! . . . Come now, this tiny caviar sandwich wouldn't put weight on a sturgeon . . . You haven't met . . . but how incredible, everyone knows Waldo Lydecker, he's the heavyweight Noel Coward . . . Waldo darling, one of your most loyal admirers . . ."

It was a good show. You could see the stuffed shirts and the high-brow women, and all the time that he moved around the room, imitating Laura and carrying that imaginary tray, you knew she had been watching something that was going on at the bay window.

Now Waldo skipped to the bay window. He changed his movements and his gestures became manly. He was Shelby being gallant and cautious. And he was a girl, looking up at Shelby, blinking her eyes and tugging at his lapels. He caught Shelby's voice perfectly, and while I had never heard her voice, I'd known plenty of dolls who talked as he had Diane talking.

"Oh, but darling, you are the best-looking man in the room . . . Can't I even say so?" "You're drunk, baby, don't talk so loud." "What harm can there be, Shelby, if I just quietly worship you?" "Quietly, for

God's sakes, kid. Remember where we are." "Shelby, please, I'm not tight, I never get tight, I'm not talking loud." "Sh-sh, honey, everyone's looking at you." "Let 'em look, you think I care?" The doll-voice became shrill and angry. Drunken young girls in bars always scream like that.

Shelby had left the fire. His fists were clenched, his jaw pushed forward, his skin green.

Laura was trembling.

Waldo walked to the middle of the room, said in his own voice: "There was a terrible hush. Everyone looked at Laura. She was carrying that tray of hors d'oeuvres."

Everyone in the room must have felt sorry for Laura. Her wedding was to have taken place in a week and a day.

Waldo crossed toward the bay window with catlike, female steps. I watched as if Diane were there with Shelby.

"Diane had taken hold of his lapels . . ."

Laura, the real one, the girl on the couch in the tan dress, said: "I'm sorry. For God's sakes, how often do I have to say I'm sorry?"

Shelby raised his clenched fists and said: "Yes, Lydecker, we've had enough. Enough of your clowning."

Waldo looked at me. "What a shame, McPherson! You've missed the best part of the scene."

"What did she do?" I asked.

"May I tell him?" said Waldo.

"You'd better," said Shelby, "or he'll imagine something far worse."

Laura began to laugh. "I conked her with a tray of hors d'oeuvres. I conked her!"

We waited until her hysteria had died down. She was crying and laughing at the same time. Shelby tried to take her hand, but she pulled away. Then she looked at me with shame on her face and said: "I'd never done anything like that before. I didn't dream I could do such a thing. I wanted to die."

"Is that all?" I asked.

"All!" said Shelby.

"In my own house," Laura said.

"What happened afterward?"

"I went into my bedroom. I wouldn't let anyone come in and talk to me. I was so ashamed. Then after a while Shelby did come in and he told me Diane had left and that I'd simply have to come out and face my guests."

"After all," said Shelby.

"Everyone was tactful, but that made me feel worse. But Shelby was darling, he insisted that we go out and get a little tight so I wouldn't think about it and keep reproaching myself."

"How kind of him!" I couldn't help saying.

"Shelby's broad-minded, he forgives easily," added Waldo.

"Shelby couldn't help it if Diane fell in love with him." Laura ignored the other two; she was explaining it to me. "He'd been kind and polite and thoughtful as he always is. Diane was a poor kid who'd come from the sort of home where they beat up women. She'd never met a . . . a gentleman before."

"Oddzooks!" Waldo said.

"She wanted something better than she'd had at home. Her life had been terribly sordid. Even her name, silly as it sounded, showed that she wanted a better sort of life."

"You're breaking my heart," Waldo said.

Laura took a cigarette. Her hands were unsteady. "I'm not so different. I came to New York, too, a poor kid without friends or money. People were kind to me—" she pointed with the cigarette at Waldo "—and I felt almost an obligation toward kids like Diane. I was the only friend she had. And Shelby."

It sounded simple and human as she stood there, so close that I could smell her perfume. I backed away.

She said, "You believe me, don't you, Mark?"

"What was this lunch on Friday? An armistice?" I asked her.

She smiled. "Yes, yes, an armistice. I went around from Wednesday evening until Friday morning feeling like a heel. And I knew if I didn't see Diane and say I was sorry my whole vacation would be ruined. Do you think I'm very silly?"

"A soft-hearted slob," said Waldo.

Shelby picked up the poker, but it was only to stoke the fire. My nerves were on edge and I saw violence every time a cigarette was lighted. That was because I craved violence. My hands itched for a fat neck.

I took two steps forward and was close to Laura again. "Then it was at lunch that you smoked . . ."

I stopped right there. She was whiter than the white dress that Diane had been buried in.

"Smoked," she whispered the word.

"Smoked the pipe of peace," I said, "and offered her your apartment."

"Yes, the pipe of peace," Laura said. She had come to life again. Her eyes sparkled, her cheeks glowed with color. Her thin, strong fingers lay on my coat-sleeve. "You must believe me, Mark, you must believe that everything was all right when I offered her the apartment. Please, please believe me."

Shelby didn't say a word. But I think he was smiling. Waldo laughed aloud and said, "Careful, Laura, he's a detective."

Her hand slipped off my coat-sleeve.

CHAPTER NINE

I ate dinner again that night with Waldo. Ask me why. I asked myself as I looked at his fat face over a bowl of bird's-nest soup at the Golden Lizard. It was raining. I was lonely. I wanted to talk. I wanted to talk about Laura. She was eating steak and French fried with Shelby. I clung to Waldo. I was afraid of losing him. I despised the guy and he fascinated me. The deeper I got into this case, the less I seemed like myself and the more I felt like a green-horn in a new world.

My mind was foggy. I was going somewhere, but I'd lost the road. I remember asking myself about clues. What were clues, what had I looked for in other cases? A smile couldn't be brought into court as evidence. You couldn't arrest a man because he had trembled. Brown eyes had stolen a peep at gray eyes, so what? The tone of a voice was something that died with a word.

The Chinese waiter brought a platter of eggroll. Waldo reached for it like a man on the breadline.

"Well," he said, "what do you think of her now that you've met her?"

I helped myself to eggroll. "It's my job . . ."

He finished for me. ". . . to look at facts and hold no opinions. Where have I heard that before?"

The waiter brought a trayful of covered dishes. Waldo had to have his plate arranged just so, pork on this side, duck over there, noodles under the chicken-almond, sweet and pungent spareribs next to the lobster, Chinese ravioli on a separate plate because there might be a conflict in the sauces. Until he had tried each dish with and without beetle juice, there was no more talk at our table.

At last he stopped for breath, and said: "I remember something you said when you first came to see me on Sunday morning. Do you remember?"

"We said a lot of things on Sunday morning. Both of us."

"You said that it wasn't fingerprints you'd want to study in this case, but faces. That was very dull of you, I thought."

"Then why did you remember it?"

"Because I was moved by the sorry spectacle of a conventional young man thinking that he had become radically unconventional."

"So what?" I said.

He snapped his fingers. Two waiters came running. It seems they had forgotten the fried rice. There was more talk than necessary, and he had to rearrange his plate. Between giving orders to the Chinese and moaning because the ritual (his word) of his dinner was upset, he talked about Elwell and Dot King and Starr Faithful and several other well-known murder cases.

"And you think this is going to be the unsolved Diane Redfern case?" I asked.

"Not the Redfern case, my friend. In the public mind and in the newspapers, it will be the Laura Hunt case forevermore. Laura will go through life a marked woman, the living victim of unsolved murder."

He was trying to get me angry. There were no direct hits, only darts and pinpricks. I tried to avoid his face, but I could not escape that doughy smirk. If I turned around, he moved too, his fat head rolling like a ball-bearing in his starched collar.

"You'd die before you'd let that happen, my gallant Hawkshaw? You'd risk your precious hide before you'd let that poor innocent girl suffer such lifelong indignity, eh?" He laughed aloud. Two waiters poked their heads out of the kitchen.

"Your jokes aren't so funny," I said.

"Woof! Woof! How savage our bark is tonight. What's tormenting you? Is it fear of failure or the ominous competition with Apollo Belvedere?"

I could feel my face getting red. "Look here," I said.

Again he interrupted. "Look here, my dear lad, at the risk of losing your esteemed friendship . . . and the friendship of such an estimable character as yourself I do value, whether you believe me or not . . . at the risk, I say of losing . . ."

"Get to the point," I said.

"Advice to a young man: Don't lose your head. She's not for you."

"Mind your god-damned business," I said.

"Some day you will thank me for this. Unless you fail to heed my advice, of course. Didn't you hear her describing Diane's infatuation for Shelby? A gentleman, oddzooks! Do you think that Diane has died so completely that chivalry must die, too? If you were more astute, my friend, you would see that Laura is Diane and Diane was Laura . . ."

"Her real name was Jennie Swobodo. She used to work in a mill in Jersey."

"It's like a bad novel."

"But Laura's no dope. She must have known he was a heel."

"Long after the core of gentility is gone, the husks remain. The educated woman, no less than the poor mill girl, is bound by the shackles of romance. The aristocratic tradition, my dear good friend, with its faint sweet odor of corruption. Romantics are children, they never grow up." He helped himself to another round of chicken, pork, duck, and rice. "Didn't I tell you the day we met that Shelby was Laura's softer, less distinguished side? Do you see it now, the answer to that longing for perfection? Pass the soy sauce, please."

Romance was something for crooners, for the movies. The only person I ever heard use the word in common life was my kid sister, and she'd raised herself by romance, married the boss.

"I was hopeful once that Laura'd grow up, get over Shelby. She'd have been a great woman if she had, you know. But the dream still held her, the hero she could love forever immaturely, the mould of perfection whose flawlessness made no demands upon her sympathies or her intelligence."

I was tired of his talk. "Come on, let's get out of this dump," I said. He made me feel that everything was hopeless.

While we were waiting for change, I picked up his cane.

"What do you carry this for?" I said.

"Don't you like it?"

"It's an affectation."

"You're a prig," he said.

"Just the same," I said, "I think it's a phoney."

"Everyone in New York knows Waldo Lydecker's walking-stick. It gives me importance."

I was willing to let the subject drop, but he liked to brag about his possessions. "I picked it up in Dublin. The dealer told me that it had been carried by an Irish baronet whose lofty and furious temper became a legend in the country."

"Probably used it for beating up the poor devils who dug peat on his lands," I said, not being very sympathetic to hot-blooded noblemen, my grandmother's stories having given me the other side of the picture. The cane was one of the heaviest I have ever handled, weighing at least one pound, twelve ounces. Below the crook, the stick was encircled by two gold bands set about three inches apart.

He snatched it out of my hands. "Give it back to me."

"What's eating you? Nobody wants your damn cane."

The Chinese brought change. Waldo watched out of the corner of his eye, and I added a quarter to the tip, hating myself but too weak to give him a reason to sneer.

"Don't sulk," he said. "If you need a cane, I'll buy you one. With a rubber tip."

I felt like picking up that big hunk of blubber and bouncing him like a ball. But I couldn't take any chances of losing his friendship. Not now. He asked where I was going, and when I said downtown, asked me to drop him at the Lafayette.

"Don't be so ungracious," he said. "I should think you'd be glad for an extra quarter-hour of my admirable discourse."

While we were driving along Fourth Avenue, he grabbed my arm. The car almost skidded.

"What's the idea?" I said.

"You must stop! Please, you must. Be generous for once in your life."

I was curious to know the cause of his excitement, so I stopped the car. He hurried back along the block to Mr. Claudius' antique shop.

Mr. Claudius' last name was Cohen. He was more like a Yankee than a Jew. He was about five-foot eleven, weighed no more than a hundred and fifty, had light eyes and a bald head that rose to a point like a pear. I knew him because he had once had a partner who was a fence. Claudius was an innocent guy, absent-minded and so crazy about antiques that he had no idea of his partner's double-crossing. I had been able to keep him out of court, and in gratitude he had given me a set of the Encyclopaedia Britannica.

It was natural that he and Waldo should know each other. They could both go into a trance over an old teapot.

What Waldo had seen in Claudius' window was a duplicate of the vase he had given Laura. It was made like a globe set upon a pedestal. To me it looked like one of those silver balls that hang on Christmas trees, strictly Woolworth. And I understand that it is not so rare and costly as many of the pieces that cause collectors to swoon. Waldo valued it because he had started the craze for mercury glass among certain high-class antique snobs. In his piece, "Distortion and Refraction,"[1] he had written:

> Glass, blown bubble thin, is coated on the inner surface with a layer of quicksilver so that it shines like a mirror. And just as the mercury in a thermometer reveals the body's temperature, so do the refractions in that discerning globe discover the fevers of temperament in those unfortunate visitors who, upon entering my drawing-room, are first glimpsed in its globular surfaces as deformed dwarfs.

"Claudius, you dolt, why in the sacred name of Josiah Wedgwood have you been keeping this from me?"

Claudius took it out of the window. While Waldo made love to the vase, I looked at some old pistols. The conversation went on behind my back.

"Where did you get it?" Waldo asked.

"From a house in Beacon."

"How much are you going to soak me for it, you old horsethief?"

"It's not for sale."

"Not for sale! But my good man . . ."

"It's sold," Claudius said.

Waldo pounded his stick against the skinny legs of an old table. "What right have you to sell it without offering it to me first? You know my needs."

"I found it for a customer. He'd commissioned me to buy any mercury glass I found at any price I thought was right."

"You had it in your window. That means you're offering it for sale."

"It don't mean that at all. It means I like to show the public something nice. I got a right to put things in my window, Mr. Lydecker."

"Did you buy it for Philip Anthony?"

There was a silence. Then Waldo shouted: "You knew I'd be interested in anything he'd want. You had no right not to offer it to me."

His voice was like an old woman's. I turned around and saw that his face had grown beet-red.

Claudius said: "The piece belongs to Anthony, there's nothing I can do about it now. If you want it, submit an offer to him."

"You know he won't sell it to me."

The argument went on like that. I was looking at an old muzzle-loader that must have been a relic when Abe Lincoln was a boy. I heard a crash. I looked around. Silver splinters shone on the floor.

Claudius was pale. Something human might have been killed.

"It was an accident, I assure you," Waldo said. Claudius moaned.

"Your shop is badly lighted, the aisles are crowded, I tripped," Waldo said.

"Poor Mr. Anthony."

"Don't make such a fuss. I'll pay whatever you ask."

From where I stood, the shop looked like a dark cavern. The antique furniture, the old clocks, vases, dishes, drinking-glasses, China dogs, and tarnished candlesticks were like a scavenger's storehouse. The two men whispered. Waldo, with his thick body, his black hat and heavy stick, Claudius with his pear-shaped head, reminded me of old women like witches on Hallowe'en. I walked out.

Waldo joined me at the car. He had his wallet in his hand. But his mood had improved. He stood in the rain, looking back at Claudius' shop and smiling. Almost as if he'd got the vase anyway.

CHAPTER TEN

Mooney's report on the murdered model hadn't satisfied me. I wanted to investigate for myself.

By the time I got to Christopher Street he had already interviewed the other tenants. No one had seen Miss Redfern since Friday.

The house was one of a row of shabby old places that carried signs: VACANCY, PERSIAN CATS, DRESSMAKING, OCCULT SCIENCE, FRENCH HOME COOKING. As I stood in the drizzle, I understood why a girl would hesitate to spend a hot weekend here.

The landlady was like an old flour-sack, bleached white and tied in the middle. She said that she was tired of cops and that if you asked her opinion, Diane was staying with a man somewhere. There were so many girls in the city and they were such loose creatures that it didn't make any difference whether one of them got misplaced once in a while. She wouldn't be a bit surprised if Diane turned up in the morning.

I left her chattering in the vestibule and climbed three flights of mouldy stairs. I knew the smells: sleep, dried soap, and shoe leather. After I left home I'd lived in several of these houses. I felt sorry for the kid, being young and expecting something of her beauty, and coming home to this suicide staircase. And I thought of Laura, offering her apartment because she had probably lived in these dumps, too, and remembered the smells on a summer night.

Even the wallpaper, brown and mustard yellow, was familiar. There was a single bed, a second-hand dresser, a sagging armchair, and a wardrobe with an oval glass set in the door. Diane had made enough to live in a better place, but she had been sending money to the family. And the upkeep of her beauty had evidently cost plenty. She'd been crazy about clothes; there were hats and gloves and shoes of every color.

There were stacks of movie magazines in the room. Pages had been turned down and paragraphs marked. You could tell that Diane had dreamed of Hollywood. Less beautiful girls had become stars, married stars, and owned swimming pools. There were some of those confession magazines, too, the sort that told stories of girls who had sinned, suffered, and been reclaimed by the love of good men. Poor Jennie Swobodo.

Her consolation must have been the photographs which she had thumb-tacked upon the ugly wallpaper. They were proofs and glossy prints showing her at work; Diane Redfern in Fifth Avenue furs; Diane at the opera; Diane pouring coffee from a silver pot; Diane in a satin nightgown with a satin quilt falling off the chaise-lounge in a way that showed a pretty leg.

It was hard to think of those legs dead and gone forever.

I sat on the edge of her bed and thought about the poor kid's life. Perhaps those photographs represented a real world to the young girl. All day while she worked, she lived in their expensive settings. And at night she came home to this cell. She must have been hurt by the contrast between those sleek studio interiors and the second-hand furniture of the boarding-house; between the silky models who posed with her and the poor slobs she met on the mouldy staircase.

Laura's apartment must have seemed like a studio setting to Jennie Swobodo, who hadn't been so long away from Paterson and the silk mills. Laura's Upper East Side friends must have been posing all the time in her eyes, like models before a camera. And Shelby . . .

I saw it all then.

I knew why Shelby was so familiar.

I'd never met him while I was pursuing crooks. He'd never mixed with the gents I'd encountered in my professional life. I'd seen him in the advertisements.

Maybe it wasn't Shelby himself. There was no record of his ever actually having been a photographer's model. But the young men who drove Packards and wore Arrow shirts, smoked Chesterfields, and paid their insurance premiums and clipped coupons were Shelby. What had Waldo said? *The hero she could love forever immaturely, the mould of perfection whose flawlessness made no demands upon her sympathies or her intelligence.*

I was sore. First, at myself for having believed that I'd find a real clue in a man who wasn't real. I'd been thinking of Shelby as I had always thought of common killers, shysters, finks, goons, and hop-heads. The king of the artichoke racket had been real; the pinball gang had been flesh-and-blood men with hands that could pull triggers; even the Associated Dairymen had been living profiteers. But Shelby was a dream walking. He was God's gift to women. I hated him for it and I hated the women for falling for the romance racket. I didn't stop to think that men aren't much different, that I had wasted a lot of adult time on the strictly twelve-year-old dream of getting back to the old neighborhood with the world's championship and Hedy Lamarr beside me on the seat of a five-grand roadster.

But I had expected Laura to be above that sort of nonsense. I thought I had found a woman who would know a real man when she saw one; a woman whose bright eyes would go right through the mask and tell her that the man underneath was Lincoln and Columbus and Thomas A. Edison. And Tarzan, too.

I felt cheated.

There was still a job to be done. Sitting on a bed and figuring out the philosophy of love was not solving a murder. I had discovered the dream world of Jennie-Swobodo-Diane-Redfern, and so what? Not a shred of evidence that she might also have been playing around with the kind of pals who used sawed-off shotguns.

The trail led back to Laura's apartment and Shelby. I found evidence in Diane's green pocketbook.

Before I left the house, I checked with the landlady, who told me that Diane had carried the green pocketbook on Friday. But I knew without being told. She had respected her clothes; she had put her dresses on hangers and stuffed shoe-trees into twenty pairs of slippers. Even at Laura's, she had hung her dress away and put her hat on the shelf and her pocketbook in the drawer. So I knew she had dressed in a hurry for her date on Friday night. Green hat, gloves, and pocketbook had been left on the bed. Her shoes had been kicked under a chair. I had seen the same thing happen at home. When my sister used to get ready for a date with her boss, she always left stockings curled over the backs of chairs and pink step-ins on the bathroom floor.

I picked up the green pocketbook. It was heavy. I knew it should have been empty because Laura had showed me the black purse she had found in her drawer, the purse into which Diane had put her compact, her lipstick, her keys, her money, and a torn straw cigarette case.

There was a cigarette case in the green pocketbook. It was made of gold and it was initialed with the letters S. J. C.

CHAPTER ELEVEN

Twenty minutes later I was sitting in Laura's living room. The cigarette case was in my pocket.

Laura and Shelby were together on the couch. She had been crying. They had been together since Waldo and I left them at five o'clock. It was about ten. Bessie had gone home.

I wondered what they had been talking about for five hours.

I was business-like. I was crisp and efficient. I sounded like a detective in a detective story. "I am going to be direct," I said. "There are several facts in this case which need explaining. If you two will help me clear away these contradictions, I'll know you're as anxious as I am to solve this murder. Otherwise I'll be forced to believe you have some private reason for not wanting the murderer to be found."

Laura sat with her hands folded in her lap like a schoolgirl in the principal's office. I was the principal. She was afraid of me. Shelby wore a death mask. The clock ticked like a man's heart beating. I took out the gold cigarette case.

The muscles tightened around Shelby's eyes. Nobody spoke.

I held it toward Laura. "You knew where this was, didn't you? She had the green pocketbook with her at lunch Friday, didn't she? Tell me, Laura, did you invite her to use your apartment before or after you discovered the cigarette case?"

The tears began to roll down Laura's cheeks.

Shelby said: "Why don't you tell him what you just told me, Laura. It was *before!*"

She nodded like a Sunday School kid. "Yes, it was before."

They didn't look at each other, but I felt a swift interchange of some sort. Shelby had begun to whistle out of tune. Laura took off her gold earrings and rested her head against the back of the couch.

I said: "Laura was feeling bad because she had been rude to Diane on Wednesday. So she invited her to lunch, and then, because Diane complained about her uncomfortable room, Laura offered her the use of this apartment. Later, probably when they were having coffee, Diane pulled out this cigarette case. Forgetting who she was with, maybe . . ."

Laura said, "How did you know?"

"Isn't that what you want me to know?" I asked her. "Isn't that the easiest way to explain the situation?"

"But it's true," she said. "It's . . ."

Shelby interrupted. "See here, McPherson, I won't have you talking to her like that." He didn't wear the death mask any longer. The plaster had cracked. His eyes were narrow and mean, his mouth a tight line.

"Shelby," said Laura. "Please, Shelby."

He stood in front of her. His legs were apart, his fists clenched as if I had been threatening her. "I refuse to let this go on, McPherson. These insinuations . . ."

"Shelby, Shelby darling," Laura said. She pulled at his hands.

"I don't know what you assume that I'm insinuating, Carpenter," I said. "I asked Miss Hunt a question. Then I reconstructed a scene which she tells me is accurate. What's making you so nervous?"

The scene was unreal again. I was talking detective-story language. Shelby made it impossible for a person to be himself.

"You see, darling," Laura said. "You're only making it worse by getting so excited."

They sat down again, her hand resting on his coat-sleeve. You could see that he didn't want her to control him. He squirmed. He looked at her bitterly. Then he pulled his arm away and moved to the end of the couch.

He spoke like a man who wants to show authority. "Look here, if you insult Miss Hunt again, I'll have to lodge a complaint against you."

"Have I been insulting you, Miss Hunt?"

She started to speak, but he interrupted. "If she has anything to tell, her lawyer will make a statement."

Laura said: "You're making it worse, dear. There's no need to be so nervous."

It seemed to me that words were printed on a page or rolling off a sound-track. A gallant hero protecting a helpless female against a crude minion of the law. I lit my pipe, giving him time to recover from the attack of gallantry. Laura reached for a cigarette. He sprang to light it. She looked in the other direction.

"All I'm asking from you at this moment," I told him, "is the low-down on that bottle of Bourbon. Why have you told one story and Mosconi another?"

She slanted a look in his direction. Shelby gave no sign that he had noticed, but he could see her without moving his eyes. It struck me that these two were clinging together, not so much out of love as in desperation. But I couldn't trust my own judgment. Personal feelings were involved. I had got beyond the point where I cared to look at faces. Fact was all that I wanted now. It had to be black or white, direct question, simple answer. Yes or no, Mr. Carpenter, were you in the apartment with Diane Redfern on Wednesday night? Yes or no, Miss Hunt, did you know he was going to meet her in your house?

Laura began to speak. Shelby coughed. She glanced frankly in his direction, but she might have looked at a worm that way. "I'm going to tell the truth, Shelby."

He seized her hands. "Laura, you're crazy. Don't you see that he's trying to get a confession? Anything we say . . . will be . . . they'll misinterpret . . . don't talk unless you've consulted a lawyer . . . you can't hope . . ."

She said: "Don't be so frightened, Shelby. Since you didn't do it, you have nothing to fear." She looked up at me and said: "Shelby thinks I killed Diane. That's why he told those lies. He's been trying to protect me."

She might have been talking about the rain or a dress or a book she had read. Frankness was her rôle now. She put it on like a coat. "Mark," she said, in a gentle voice—"do you believe I killed her, Mark?"

There it lay in the lamplight, solid gold, fourteen-karat evidence of Shelby's treachery. Laura had bought it for him at Christmas, a gift she had to charge to her aunt's account. He had told her he lost it, and on Friday, when she was trying to make up for her rudeness to Diane, she had seen it in the green pocketbook.

She had got a sudden headache at lunch that day. She hadn't waited to take off her hat to telephone Waldo and tell him she couldn't keep her dinner date. She hadn't mentioned her change of plans because she hated having people ask her questions.

It was still Thursday. Thursday, ten-fourteen P.M. They were to have been married by this time and on their way to Nova Scotia. This was the bridal night.

The lamp shone on her face. Her voice was gentle. "Do you believe I killed her, Mark? Do you believe it, too?"

PART THREE

A stenographic report of the statement made by Shelby J. Carpenter to Lieutenant McPherson on Friday at 3.45 P.M., August 27, 1941.

Present: Shelby J. Carpenter, Lieutenant McPherson, N. T. Salsbury, Jr.

Mr. Carpenter: I, Shelby John Carpenter, do hereby swear that the following is a true statement of the facts known to me concerning the death of Diane Redfern. At times this will contradict certain statements I've made before, but . . .

Mr. Salsbury: You are to take into consideration, Lieutenant McPherson, that any conflict between this and previous statements made by my client is due to the fact that he felt it his moral duty to protect another person.

Lieutenant McPherson: We've promised your client immunity.

Mr. Salsbury: Go on, tell me what happened, Carpenter.

Mr. Carpenter: As you know, Miss Hunt wished a few days' rest before the wedding. She had worked exceedingly hard on a campaign for the Lady Lilith cosmetic account, and I did not blame her for requesting that we postpone the wedding until she had time to recover from the strain. I have often protested at her arduous and unflagging devotion to her career, since I believe that women are highly strung and delicate, so that the burden of her position, in addition to her social duties and personal obligations, had a definite effect upon her nerves. For this reason I have always tried to understand and sympathize with her temperamental vagaries.

On that Friday morning, just a week ago, I went into her office to consult her about a piece of copy which I had written the day before. Although I had come into the business several years after she was established as an important copy-writer, she had great respect for my judgment. More than anyone knew, we depended upon each other. It was as usual for her to come to me for help in planning and presenting a campaign or merchandising idea as it was for me to seek her advice about the wording of a piece of copy. Since I was to take over the Lady Lilith account, I naturally asked her criticism. She was enthusiastic about my headline, which read, as I remember, "Is yours just another face in a crowd? Or is it the radiant, magnetic countenance that men admire and women envy?" She suggested the word "magnetic."

Lieutenant McPherson: Let's get down to facts. You can explain the advertising business later.

Mr. Carpenter: I just wanted you to understand our relationship.

Lieutenant McPherson: Did she tell you she was going to have lunch with Diane?

Mr. Carpenter: That was a subject we had agreed not to discuss.

Lieutenant McPherson: Lunch?

Mr. Carpenter: Diane Redfern. As a matter of fact, I did ask her if she'd lunch with me, but she told me she had some errands. Naturally I asked no questions. I went out with some men in the office, and later our chief, Mr. Rose, joined us for coffee. At about two-fifteen, we went back to the office and I worked steadily until about three-thirty, when the telephone rang. It was Diane.

Lieutenant McPherson: Did she tell you she'd had lunch with Laura?

Mr. Carpenter: The poor child was quite distraught. You didn't know her, McPherson, but she was one of the most feminine creatures I have ever met. Like my own mother, although she was a girl of very different background and breeding. Yet she always felt the need of turning to a man when anything distressed her. It was unfortunate that I happened to be the man of her choice. Women—I hope you don't mind my saying this, McPherson, but I'm trying to be as frank as possible—have more than once attached themselves to me quite without encouragement. As Miss Hunt herself remarked, Diane had not been bred among gentlefolk. What we considered merely good manners she took as evidence of . . . shall we call it love? Her emotions were wild and undisciplined. Although she knew that I was engaged to marry Miss Hunt, she declared herself madly in love with me and, I must say, often embarrassed me with her declarations. Perhaps you've known young girls like this, McPherson, who love so violently that nothing exists for them except their passion and the man upon whom it is fixed.

Lieutenant McPherson: You didn't exactly discourage her, did you?

Mr. Salsbury: The question is irrelevant. You needn't answer it, Mr. Carpenter.

Mr. Carpenter: I tried not to be unkind. She was young and very sensitive.

Lieutenant McPherson: Did she say anything to you about having had lunch with Laura?

Mr. Carpenter: She told me she was desperate. At first I thought her fears were nothing more than hysteria. "Don't dramatize yourself," I told her, but there was something about her voice, a wild, frightened tone, that distressed me. I knew her to be both impulsive and courageous. I was afraid she might . . . you know what I mean, McPherson. So I said I'd take her to dinner, as a sort of farewell, you understand. I meant to talk some sense into her. We agreed to meet at Montagnino's.

Lieutenant McPherson: Montagnino's.

Mr. Carpenter: I felt that Diane's morale needed a stimulant. And since Miss Hunt had often mentioned Montagnino's as a favorite restaurant, Diane considered the place quite glamorous. You have no idea of the child's devotion to Miss Hunt.

Lieutenant McPherson: You didn't mention this to Laura, did you?

Mr. Carpenter: It would only have distressed her. She had been quite unhappy about having been so rude to Diane, you know. Although I did intend to tell her about it later. And besides she was dining with Waldo Lydecker . . . or at least that's what I thought.

Lieutenant McPherson: When you had cocktails with Miss Hunt at the Tropicale Bar, what did you talk about?

Mr. Carpenter: What did we talk about? Oh . . . well . . . our plans, of course. She seemed cold and rather listless, but I attributed this to her nervous condition. I begged her to have a good rest and not to worry. Miss Hunt, you know, is a very intelligent young woman, but sometimes her emotions get the better of her, and she becomes almost hysterical about world conditions. She suffers a sort of guilt complex, and sometimes declares that we, innocent people of our sort, share the responsibility for the horror and suffering that one reads about in the newspapers. This, added to a certain cynicism about the work she does, gives her an emotional instability which, I thought, I might help to correct. And so I begged her not to read newspapers or listen to news broadcasts during this week of rest, and she was rather charming about it, unusually submissive and quiet. When we parted, she allowed me to kiss her, but there was little warmth in her response. I gave the taxi-driver Waldo Lydecker's address, since she had said nothing to me of a change in her plans. Then I went back to the hotel, changed my clothes, and went on down to Montagnino's. I must tell you that I was disappointed in the place.

Lieutenant McPherson: You'd never been there before?

Mr. Carpenter: Mr. Lydecker had always taken Miss Hunt there. They were quite exclusive about it. We'd only known it by hearsay.

Lieutenant McPherson: Did Diane tell you about having had lunch with Laura and bringing out the cigarette case?

Mr. Carpenter: Yes, she did. And I was most unhappy.

Lieutenant McPherson: I suppose you and she tried to think of some excuse which you could give Laura.

Mr. Carpenter: I decided to tell my fiancé the truth.

Lieutenant McPherson: Before or after the wedding?

Mr. Salsbury: You needn't answer that, Mr. Carpenter.

Mr. Carpenter: You seem to think, McPherson, that there was something clandestine in my relationship with Diane.

Lieutenant McPherson: There were only two ways for her to have got hold of that cigarette case. Either she stole it or you gave it to her.

Mr. Carpenter: I admit that the incident looks very shabby, but if you knew the circumstances that brought about this . . . this . . . this gesture, I'm sure you'd understand.

Lieutenant McPherson: Diane was desperate, I suppose.

Mr. Carpenter: I don't like your tone, McPherson. What you imply was not the situation.

Lieutenant McPherson: I didn't imply anything except that you had to be a big shot for Diane. Bigger than Laura. But if you want me to imply anything else, I can think of a couple of reasons why you might have given her that gold cigarette case.

Mr. Salsbury: Personal and irrelevant detail, Lieutenant.

Mr. Carpenter: Thank you, Mr. Salsbury.

Lieutenant McPherson: Okay, go on.

Mr. Carpenter: At about ten o'clock we left the restaurant. I had expected her to have recovered by that time, but she was more nervous and upset than before. She seemed to be suffering some nameless terror, almost as if she were afraid of violence. Although she would not definitely name her fear, I could see that this hysteria was not entirely groundless. In the circumstances I couldn't leave her alone, and so I promised to come up with her for a little while.

Lieutenant McPherson: To Laura's apartment?

Mr. Carpenter: I confess that I didn't quite enjoy the prospect, but in the circumstances I couldn't talk to her in a public place. And since she obviously couldn't come to my room in a hotel for men, and male guests were not allowed upstairs in her boarding house, it seemed the only practical arrangement. So we drove uptown to the apartment . . .

Lieutenant McPherson: Where was she when you stopped in at Mosconi's to buy the Bourbon?

Mr. Carpenter: I ought to explain that, oughtn't I?

Lieutenant McPherson: It'd help.

Mr. Carpenter: Diane was distressed and needed a stimulant. We felt a little queer about taking Miss Hunt's liquor, and so I stopped at Mosconi's . . .

Lieutenant McPherson: Leaving Diane outside because Mosconi knew you as Laura's friend.

Mr. Carpenter: Not at all. Diane had to stop in the drugstore . . .

Mr. Salsbury: You went right on to Miss Hunt's apartment, didn't you?

Lieutenant McPherson: Where Diane took off her clothes and put on Laura's silk robe.

Mr. Carpenter: It was a very hot night, as you'll remember.

Lieutenant McPherson: There was a breeze in the bedroom, I suppose.

Mr. Carpenter: We talked for three hours. Then the doorbell rang and . . .

Lieutenant McPherson: Tell us exactly what happened. Don't skip anything.

Mr. Carpenter: We were both surprised, and Diane was frightened. But knowing Miss Hunt as I've known her, I've learned to be shocked at nothing. When her friends are upset about their marriages or love affairs or careers, they think nothing of disturbing her with their troubles. I told Diane to go to the door and explain that she was using the apartment while Laura was away.

Lieutenant McPherson: You stayed in the bedroom, huh?

Mr. Carpenter: Suppose one of Laura's friends had found me there? Better to avoid gossip, wasn't it?

Lieutenant McPherson: Go on.

Mr. Carpenter: The bell rang again. I heard Diane's mules clattering on the bare boards between the rugs. Then there was a moment of silence, and the shot. You can imagine how I felt. By the time I reached her, the door had closed and she lay there on the floor. The room was dark, I saw only a vague light shape, her silk robe. I asked if she had been hurt. There was no answer. Then I stooped down to feel her heart.

Lieutenant McPherson: Go on.

Mr. Carpenter: It's too hideous to talk about.

Lieutenant McPherson: And then what did you do?

Mr. Carpenter: My first instinct was to call the police.

Lieutenant McPherson: Why didn't you?

Mr. Carpenter: Just as I was about to lift the receiver, I was struck by a paralyzing thought. My hand fell at my side. I just stood there. You must remember, McPherson, that I loved Laura dearly.

Lieutenant McPherson: It wasn't Laura who was shot.

Mr. Carpenter: I owed her a certain loyalty. And in a way I felt some responsibility for this affair. I knew at once why Diane had been so terrified, after that display of bad manners Wednesday afternoon. As soon as I had put two and two together, I realized that I had one duty in regard to this tragedy. No matter how difficult it might be for me to control myself, I must keep out of it. My presence in this apartment would not only be extremely awkward, but would indubitably cast suspicion upon that one person whom I must protect. I can see now that it was extremely foolish for me to have acted upon this impulse, but there are times when a man is moved by something deeper than rational emotion.

Lieutenant McPherson: Did it occur to you that, by leaving the apartment and withholding the truth, you were obstructing the processes of law?

Mr. Carpenter: I had only one thought in mind: the safety of a person whose life was dearer to me than my own.

Lieutenant McPherson: On Saturday morning, when our men came to the Framingham to tell you that Laura was dead, you seemed sincerely shocked.

Mr. Carpenter: I must admit that I was not prepared for that interpretation.

Lieutenant McPherson: But you had your alibi ready, and no matter who was dead, you stuck to your story.

Mr. Carpenter: If I had become involved in the case, someone else would eventually have been suspected. This is what I hoped to avoid. But you must realize that my grief was real, both for Diane and the other person. I don't believe I've slept a full two hours since this thing happened. It's not like me to lie. I'm happiest when I can be completely frank with myself and the world.

Lieutenant McPherson: Although you knew Laura was not dead, you evidently made no effort to get in touch with her. Why not?

Mr. Carpenter: Wasn't it better to let her pursue her own course? I felt that if she wanted me, she'd call upon me, knowing that I'd stand by her to the bitter end.

Lieutenant McPherson: Why did you go and stay with Laura's aunt?

Mr. Carpenter: Since I was almost a member of the family, it was more or less my duty to attend to the unpleasant details. Mrs. Treadwell was very gracious, I must say, in suggesting that public curiosity made it uncomfortable for me at the hotel. After all, I was in mourning.

Lieutenant McPherson: And you allowed Diane to be buried—or cremated—as Laura Hunt.

Mr. Carpenter: I can't tell you what I suffered during those terrible four days.

Lieutenant McPherson: On the night that Laura came back, she phoned you at the Framingham, didn't she? And you'd given instructions that they weren't to give out your number . . .

Mr. Carpenter: The reporters were making me quite uncomfortable, McPherson. I thought it best anyway not to have her telephoning her aunt's house. When they phoned me on Wednesday night—or Thursday morning, it was—I knew at once. And although I don't wish to seem ungrateful to my hostess, I knew Mrs. Treadwell to be an inquisitive woman. And since it would have been a shock for her to hear the voice of a person whose funeral she had just attended, I went out to a pay booth to telephone Miss Hunt.

Lieutenant McPherson: Repeat that conversation as fully as you remember it.

Mr. Carpenter: She said, "Shelby?" and I said, "Hello, my darling," and she said, "Did you think I was dead, Shelby?" I asked her if she was all right.

Lieutenant McPherson: Did you say you thought she had died?

Mr. Carpenter: I asked if she was all right. She said that she felt terribly about poor Diane, and asked if I knew anyone who might have wished her to die. I knew then that Miss Hunt did not intend to give me her full confidence. Nor could I talk to her frankly on the telephone. But I knew there was one detail which might prove embarrassing—or downright dangerous—and I made up my mind to save her, if I could.

Lieutenant McPherson: What was that detail?

Mr. Carpenter: It's right there on your desk, McPherson.

Lieutenant McPherson: You knew she had the shotgun?

Mr. Carpenter: I had given it to her. She frequently stayed alone in her country house. Those initials are my mother's—Delilah Shelby Carpenter.

Lieutenant McPherson: And that's why you borrowed Mrs. Treadwell's car and drove up to Wilton?

Mr. Carpenter: Yes, that's right. But when your man followed me in the cab, I didn't dare go into the house. I stood in the garden for a while and I was considerably overcome because I couldn't help remembering what that little cottage and garden had meant to us. When I returned to town and found you with Mrs. Treadwell, I was not completely untruthful in saying that it had been a sentimental pilgrimage. Later in the day you asked me to come up to the apartment. I was to be surprised at finding Miss Hunt alive and as you were going to study my reactions, McPherson, I decided to give you the show that you expected, for I still believed that there was a chance to save the situation.

Lieutenant McPherson: But after I left, you talked it over with Laura. You told her exactly what you thought.

Mr. Carpenter: Miss Hunt has admitted nothing.

Mr. Salsbury: Lieutenant McPherson, my client has gone to considerable trouble and risked his personal safety in order to protect another person. He is not obliged to answer any question which might incriminate that person.

Lieutenant McPherson: Okay, I've got it straight. I'll get in touch with you if I need you, Carpenter. But don't leave the city.

Mr. Carpenter: Thank you so much for your understanding attitude, McPherson.

PART FOUR

CHAPTER ONE

Last week, when I thought I was to be married, I burned my girlhood behind me. And vowed never to keep another diary. The other night, when I came home and found Mark McPherson in my apartment, more intimate than my oldest friend, my first thought was gratitude for the destruction of those shameful pages. How inconsistent he would have thought me if he had read them! I can never keep a proper diary, simmer my life down to a line a day, nor make breakfast on the sixteenth of the month as important as falling in love on the seventeenth. It's always when I start on a long journey or meet an exciting man or take a new job that I must sit for hours in a frenzy of recapitulation. The idea that I am an intelligent woman is pure myth. I can never grasp an abstraction except through emotion, and before I can begin to think with my head about any fact, I must see it as a solid thing on paper.

At work, when I plan a campaign for Lady Lilith Face Powder or Jix Soap Flakes, my mind is orderly. I write dramatic headlines and follow them with sales arguments that have unity, coherence, and emphasis. But when I think about myself, my mind whirls like a merry-go-round. All the horses, the bright and the drab, dance around a shining, mirrored centre whose dazzling rays and frivolous music make concentration impossible. I am trying to think clearly of all that has happened in the last few days, to remember the facts and set them upon the horses and send them out in neat parade like sales arguments for Jix or Lady Lilith. They disobey, they whirl and dance to the music, and all I remember is that a man who had heard me accused of murder was concerned about my getting enough sleep.

"Sleep," he said to me, "get some sleep." As if sleep were something you could buy at the Five-and-Ten. After he'd been gone for a little while, he came back with a package from Schwartz's drugstore. They were pills to make me sleep, but he would only leave me two because he knew how sick I was with fear and worry.

"Do you believe I killed Diane?" I asked him again.

"It doesn't matter what I think." His voice grated. "It isn't my business to think; it's only facts I want, facts."

Shelby watched. He looked more than ever like a beautiful tomcat, ready to leap. Shelby said: "Be careful, Laura. Don't trust him."

"Yes," he said, "I'm a cop, you mustn't trust me. Anything you say might be used against you." His lips were drawn hard over his teeth; he spoke without opening his mouth.

"Are you going to arrest me?" I said.

Shelby became very man-of-the-house, protector of frail womanhood. It was all pretense, his courage was as thin as tissue paper, he trembled inwardly. Shelby used phrases like "false arrest" and "circumstantial evidence"; you could tell he was proud of displaying technical knowledge like when he could explain to people about the rules of fencing or backgammon. Auntie Sue once told me I'd grow tired of a six-foot child. Auntie Sue said that when a woman feels the need for a man that way, she ought to have a baby. I kept thinking of Auntie Sue's remarks while Shelby talked about circumstantial evidence and Mark walked around and around the room, looking at things, at my autographed baseball and my Mexican tray and the shelf where I keep my very favorite books.

"She'll get in touch with her lawyer," Shelby said. "That's what she'll do."

Mark came back to me. "You mustn't try to leave here, Laura."

"No, I won't leave."

"He's got a man outside. You couldn't leave anyway," Shelby said. "He's having you watched."

Mark left without another word, without telling me to sleep again or good-bye.

"I don't like that fellow. He's a sly one," Shelby said as soon as the door had closed.

"You said that before."

"You're gullible, Laura. You trust people too easily."

I stood with my back to Shelby, looking at the shelf with all my favorite books. "He's been very kind," I said—"considering. I think he's nice. You'd never think of a detective being like that."

I felt Shelby's hands stretching toward me and I moved away. He was quiet. I knew, without turning, how his face would look.

He picked up the two pills that Mark had left on the table. "Do you think you ought to take these, Laura?"

I whirled around. "Great God, you don't think he's trying to give me poison!"

"He ought to be hardboiled. You'd expect him to be tougher. I don't like his trying to act like a gentleman."

"Oh, pooh!" I said.

"You don't see it. The man's trying to make you like him so you'll break down and confess. That's what he's been working for all along, a confession. Damned caddish, I'd say."

I sat down on the sofa and pounded my fists against a pillow. "I hate that word. Caddish! I've begged you a million times to quit using it."

Shelby said, "It's a good English word."

"It's old-fashioned. It's out of date. People don't talk about cads any more. It's Victorian."

"A cad is a cad, whether the word is obsolete or not."

"Quit being so Southern. Quit being so righteous. You and your damn gallantry." I was crying. The tears ran down my cheeks and dripped off my jaws. My tan dress was all wet with tears.

"You're nervous, sweet," Shelby said. "That damned cad has been working on you subtly, he's been trying to wear you down."

"I told you," I screamed, "that I wish you'd stop using that word."

"It's a perfectly good English word," he said.

"You said that before. You've said it a million times."

"You'll find it in Webster," he said. "And in Funk and Wagnalls."

"I'm so tired," I said. I rubbed my eyes with my fists because I'm never able to find a handkerchief in a crisis.

"It's a perfectly good English word," Shelby said again.

I jumped up, the pillow in my arms like a shield against him. "A fine one you are to talk about cads, Shelby Carpenter."

"I've been trying to protect you!"

When he spoke like that, his voice deep with reproach, I felt as if I had hurt a helpless child. Shelby knew how his voice worked on me; he could color his voice with the precise shade of reproach so that I would hate that heartless bitch, Laura Hunt, and forgive his faults. He remembered as well as I the day we went duck hunting and he bragged and I said I despised him, and he won me again with the tones of his voice; he remembered the fight we had at the office party and the time he kept me waiting two hours in the Paramount lobby, and our terrible quarrel the night he gave me the gun. All of those quarrels rose in our minds now; there were almost two years of quarrels and reproach between us, and two years of love and forgiveness and the little jokes that neither could forget. I hated his voice for reminding me, and I was afraid because I had always been weak with a thirty-two-year-old baby.

"I've been trying to protect you," Shelby said.

"Great God, Shelby, we're right back where we started from. We've been saying the same thing over and over again since five o'clock this afternoon."

"You're getting bitter," he said, "terribly bitter, Laura. Of course, after what's happened, one can't completely blame you."

"Oh, go away," I said. "Go home and let me sleep."

I took the two white pills and went into the bedroom. I slammed the door hard. After a while I heard Shelby leave. I went to the window. There were two men on the steps. After Shelby had gone a little way, one followed him. The other lit a cigarette. I saw the match flame and die in the misty darkness. The houses opposite mine are rich people's private houses. Not one of my neighbors stays in town during the summer. There was only a cat, the thin yellow homeless cat that nuzzles against my legs when I come from work at night. The cat crossed the street daintily, pointing his feet like a ballet dancer, lifting them high as if his feet were too good for the pavement. On Friday night when Diane was killed, the street was quiet, too.

CHAPTER TWO

Sleep he had said, try to get some sleep. Two pills weren't enough. When I turned out the lights, the darkness whined around me. The old dead tenants came creeping up the stairs, their footsteps cautious on the tired boards. They sighed and whispered behind doors, they rattled the old latches, they plotted conspiracies. I saw Diane, too, in my aquamarine house coat; I saw her with dark hair flowing about her shoulders, running to answer the doorbell.

The doorbell had rung, Shelby told me, and he stayed in the bedroom while she ran to answer it. As soon as she had opened the front door, he heard the shot. Then the door snapped shut. After a time that might have been thirty seconds or thirty years, Shelby said, he had left the bedroom. He tried to speak to her, his lips framed her name, but his voice was dead. The room was dark, the light came in from the street lamp in stripes through the Venetian blinds. He saw the pale silk of my robe spread about her on the floor, but he could not see her face. It seemed gone. When his blood had thawed, Shelby said, he had stooped to feel for the place where her heart should have been. His hand was paralyzed, he felt nothing, he knew she was dead. He went to the telephone, meaning to call the police. When Shelby told me about that part of it, he stretched out his hand as he had stretched it toward the telephone, and then he pulled his hand back quickly just as he had done that night. If the police had known he was there in my apartment with Diane, they would have known, too, who had killed her, Shelby said.

"That was your guilty conscience," I told him. "Guilty because you were here. In my own house with her. You wanted to believe *that*, because you were ashamed."

"I was trying to protect you," Shelby said.

This was early in the evening, after Mark had gone off for dinner with Waldo, and before Mark came back with the cigarette case.

Auntie Sue told me I was a fool when I bought that cigarette case. I am so gullible that I trust a detective, but Auntie Sue didn't even trust Uncle Horace to make his will; she sat behind the curtains while he and the lawyer figured out the bequests. Auntie Sue said I'd always regret the cigarette case. I gave it to Shelby because he needed grandeur when he talked to prospective clients or had drinks with men he'd known at college. Shelby had his airs and graces, manner and a name that made him feel superior, but these were things that mattered in Covington, Kentucky, not in New York. Ten years in and out of precarious jobs hadn't taught him that gestures and phrases were of less importance in our world than aggressiveness and self-interest; and that the gentlemanly arts were not nearly so useful as proficiency in double-dealing, bootlicking, and pushing yourself ahead of the other fellow.

The tea was pale, pale green with one dark leaf curled in it, when I saw the cigarette case in Diane's hand. I saw Diane's pointed magenta nails curving over the edge of the gold case, but I could not look at her face. The tea had a delicate Chinese smell. I did not feel pain or anger, I felt giddy. I said to Diane, "Please, dear, I have a headache, do you mind if I leave now?" It was not like me to be calm. I tell the truth shrilly and then I am sorry. But this was deeper, so deep that I could only watch the leaf floating in the teacup.

Shelby had given her the cigarette case so that he might feel rich and generous, too. Like a gigolo seeking revenge against a fat old dowager with a jet band binding the wattles under her chin. It was all clear then, as if the tea leaf had been my fortune in the cup, for I knew why Shelby and I had quarreled so that we could go on pretending to love. He not sure of himself; he still needed the help I could give him; but he hated himself for clinging to me, and hated me because I let him cling.

They had been lovers since April eighteenth. I remember the date because it was Paul Revere's ride and Auntie Sue's birthday. The date smells of cleaning fluid. We were in a taxi on the way to the Coq d'Or where Auntie Sue was having her birthday party. I wore my sixteen-button fawn gloves; they had just come from the cleaner and the smell was stronger than the odor of taxi-leather and tobacco and the Tabu with which I had scented my handkerchief and my hair. That was when Shelby told me about losing the cigarette case. He used the hurt voice and his remorse was so real that I begged him not to feel it too deeply. Shelby said I was a wonderful woman, tolerant and for-giving. Damned patronizing bitch, he must have been thinking as we sat in the taxi, holding hands.

Lovers since April eighteenth. And this was almost the end of Au-gust. Diane and Shelby had been holding hands, too, and laughing behind my back.

When I walked through the office after lunch, I wondered if all the faces knew and were hiding themselves from my humiliation. My friends said they could understand my having fallen in love impul-sively with Shelby, but they did not see how I could go on caring. This would make me angry; I would say they judged unfairly because Shelby was too handsome. It was almost as if Shelby's looks were a handicap, a sort of deformity that had to be protected.

Usually I anger quickly. I flame and burn with shrill vehemence and suffer remorse at the spectacle of my petty female spleen. This time my fury had a new pattern. I can feel that frigid fury now as I remember how I counted the months, the weeks, the days since the eighteenth of April. I tried to remember when I had seen Diane alone and what she had said to me; and I thought of the three of us to-gether with Diane humbly acknowledging Shelby my lover; and I tried to count the evenings that I had spent alone or with other friends, giving Shelby to her on those evenings. How tolerant we were, how modern, how ridiculous and pitiful! But I had always told Shelby about dining with Waldo and he had never told me that he was seeing Diane.

Desperate, my mother used to say, I'm desperate, when she locked herself in her bedroom with a sick headache. I always envied her; I wanted to grow up and be desperate too. On Friday afternoon, as I walked up and down my office, I whispered it over and over. Desper-ate, desperate, at last I'm desperate, I said, as if the word were con-summation. I can see the office now, the desk and filing-case and a proof of a Lady Lilith color ad with Diane lying backward on a couch, head thrown back, breasts pointed upward like small hills. I feel, rather than smell, the arid, air-conditioned atmosphere, and I tense my right hand as if the letter-opener were still cutting a ridge across my palm. I was sick, I was desperate, I was afraid. I hid my face in my hands, my forehead against the wood of my desk.

I telephoned Waldo and told him I had a headache.

"Don't be difficult, wench," Waldo said. "Roberto has scoured the markets for our bachelor dinner."

"I'm desperate," I said.

Waldo laughed. "Put your headache off until tomorrow. The

country is a good place for headaches, that's all it's fit for; have your headache among the beetles. What time shall I expect you, angel?"

I knew that if I dined with Waldo, I should tell him about the cigarette case. He would have been glad to hear that I was done with Shelby, but he would have wrapped his satisfaction elegantly in sympathy. Waldo would never have said, I told you so, Laura, I told you at the start. Not Waldo. He would have opened his best champagne and, holding up his glass, would have said, "And now, Laura, you've grown up, let us drink to your coming of age."

No, thank you, no urbanity for me tonight, Waldo. I am drunk already.

When Shelby came to my office at five o'clock, I rode down in the elevator with him, I drank two dry Martinis with him, I let him put me into the cab and give Waldo's address to the driver just as if I had never seen the cigarette case.

CHAPTER THREE

On Saturday I thinned my sedum, transplanted primroses, and started a new iris bed near the brook. On Sunday I moved the peony plants. They were heavy, the roots so long that I had to dig deep holes in the ground. I had to keep myself occupied with hard physical work; the work soothed me and emptied my mind of Friday's terror.

When the gardener came on Monday, he said that I had moved the peonies too early, they would surely die now. Twenty times that day I went to look at them. I watered them gently with thin streams of tepid water, but they drooped, and I felt ashamed before the victims of my impatience.

Before the gardener left on Monday, I told him not to tell Shelby that I had killed the peony plants by moving them too early. Shelby would never have mourned the peonies, but he would have had cause to reproach me for doing a man's work in the garden instead of waiting until he came. It was curious that I should say this to the gardener because I knew that Shelby would never dig and mow and water my garden again. I was still defiant of Shelby; I was trying to irritate him by absent treatment, and provoke imaginary argument so that I could hurt him with sharp answers. Challenging Shelby, I worked in my house, washing and polishing and scrubbing on my hands and knees. He always said that I shouldn't do menial work, I could afford to hire servants; he could never know the fulfillment of working with your hands in your own house. My people were plain folk; the women went West with their men and none of them found gold. But Shelby came from "gentle" people; they had slaves to comb their hair and put on their shoes. A gentleman cannot see a lady work like a nigger;

a gentleman opens the door and pulls out a lady's chair and brings a whore into her bedroom.

I saw then, working on my knees, the pattern our marriage would have taken, shoddy and deceitful, taut emotion woven with slack threads of pretense.

The fault was mine more than Shelby's. I had used him as women use men to complete the design of a full life, playing at love for the gratification of my vanity, wearing him proudly as a successful prostitute wears her silver foxes to tell the world she owns a man. Going on thirty and unmarried, I had become alarmed. Pretending to love him and playing the mother game, I bought him an extravagant cigarette case, fourteen-karat gold, as a man might buy his wife an orchid or a diamond to expiate infidelity.

And now that tragedy has wiped away all the glib excuses, I see that our love was as bare of real passion as the mating of two choice vegetables which are to be combined for the purpose of producing a profitable new item for the markets. It was like love in the movies, contrived and opportune. And now it was over.

Two strangers sat at opposite ends of the couch. We tried to find words that had the same meaning for both of us. It was still Thursday evening, before dinner, after Mark and Waldo had left. We spoke softly because Bessie was in the kitchen.

"This will all blow over in a few days," Shelby said. "If we sit tight and match our stories properly. Who'll know? That detective is an ass."

"Why must you keep on calling him *that detective?* You know his name."

"Let's not be bitter," Shelby said. "It'll only make it more difficult for us to go on."

"What makes you think I want to go on? I don't hate you and I'm not bitter, but I couldn't go on. Not now."

"I tell you, Laura, I only came because she begged me so. She begged me to come and say good-bye to her. She was in love with me; I didn't care two hoots about her, honestly, but she threatened to do something desperate unless I came up here on Friday night."

I turned my head away.

"We've got to stick together now, Laura. We're in this thing too deeply to fight each other. And I know you love me. If you hadn't loved me, you couldn't have come back here on Friday night and . . ."

"Shut up! Shut up!" I said.

"If you weren't here on Friday night, if you are innocent, then how could you have known about the Bourbon bottle, how could you have responded so instinctively to the need to protect me?"

"Must we go over it all again, Shelby? Again and again and again?"

"You lied to protect me just as I lied to protect you."

It was all so dreary and so useless. Three Horses had been Shelby's brand of Bourbon, he had been buying it for himself when he started coming to my house, and then I began buying it so he'd always find a drink when he came. But one day Waldo laughed because I kept such cheap whiskey on my shelves and named a better brand, and I tried to please Shelby with expensive Bourbon. His buying the bottle of Three Horses that night, like his giving Diane the cigarette case, was defiance, Shelby's defiance of my patronage.

Bessie announced dinner. We washed our hands, we sat at the table, we spread napkins in our laps, we touched water to our lips, we held knives and forks in our hands for Bessie's sake. With her coming and going, we couldn't talk. We sat behind steak and French fried, we dipped our spoons ceremoniously into the rum pudding which Bessie had made, good soul, to celebrate my return from death. After she had brought the coffee to the table before the fire and we had the length of the room between us and the kitchen door, Shelby asked where I had hidden the gun.

"Gun!"

"Don't talk so loud!" He nodded toward the kitchen door. "My mother's gun; why do you suppose I drove up there last night?"

"Your mother's gun is in the walnut chest, just where you saw me put it, Shelby, after we had the fight."

The fight had started because I refused the gun. I was not nearly so afraid of staying alone in my little house as of having a gun there. But Shelby had called me a coward and insisted upon my keeping it for protection, had laughed me into learning to use it.

"The first fight or the second fight?" he asked.

The second fight had been about his shooting rabbits. I had complained about their eating the iris bulbs and the gladiolus corms, and Shelby had shot a couple of them.

"Why do you lie to me, darling? You know that I'll stick with you to the end."

I picked up a cigarette. He hurried to light it. "Don't do that," I said.

"Why not?"

"You can't call me a murderer and light my cigarette."

Now that I had said the word aloud, I felt freer. I stood up, stretched my legs, blew smoke at the ceiling. I felt that I belonged to myself and could fight my own battles.

"Don't be so childish," Shelby said. "Can't you see that you're in a tight spot and that I'm trying to help you? Don't you realize the chances I've taken, the lies I've told to protect you, and last night, driving up there? That makes me an accomplice; I'm in a rather bad spot myself, and for your sake."

"I wish I hadn't phoned you last night," I said.

"Don't be petty, Laura. Your instinct was sound. You knew as well as I that they'd go up and search your place as soon as they discovered that you were back."

"That's not why I called you."

Bessie came in to say good night and tell me again that she was happy that I had not died. Tears burned the edges of my eyes.

When the door had closed behind her, Shelby said: "I'd rest easier if I had that gun in my possession now. But how can we get it with detectives on our trail? I tried to shake the fellow, I took the back road, but the cab followed me all the way. If I'd as much as searched the place, I'd have given it away instantly. So I kept up the pretense of sorrow; I stood in the garden and wept for you; I called it a sentimental journey when that detective . . ."

"His name is McPherson," I said.

"You're so bitter," Shelby said. "You'll have to get over that bitterness, Laura, or you'll never be able to fight it out. Now, if we stand together, my sweet . . ."

Mark returned. I gave Shelby my hand and we sat on the couch, side by side, like lovers. Mark turned on the light; he looked into my face; he said he was going to speak the truth directly. That was when he brought out the cigarette case and Shelby lost his nerve and Mark's face became the face of a stranger. It's hard to deceive Mark; he looks at you as if he wants you to be honest. Shelby was afraid of honesty; he kept losing his temper like a schoolboy, and it was, in the end, Shelby's fear that told Mark that Shelby believed me guilty.

"Are you going to arrest me?" I asked Mark. But he went to Schwartz's and got me the sleeping pills, and when he left, although I did not say so to Shelby, I knew he was going to Wilton to search my house.

CHAPTER FOUR

S alsbury, Haskins, Warder, and Bone. Every little movement has a meaning all its own, Salsbury, Haskins, Warder, and Bone. A small black mustache parted in the middle, a voice, the smell of mint, and all of this an enigma, a rush of words and sense memories as I woke after a hard sleep and two small white pills. Salsbury, Haskins, Warder, and Bone . . . I attached the words to a melody . . . I heard music beyond my door and the words were Salsbury, Haskins, Warder, and Bone.

The music was the vacuum cleaner outside my bedroom door. Bessie brought coffee and orange juice. The glass was beaded with ice, and as my hand chilled, grasping it, I remembered a dewy silvered vessel, the smell of mint, and the small black mustache crowning a toothpaste smile. It was on the lawn of Auntie Sue's place at Sands Point; the black mustache had asked if I liked mint juleps and explained that he was young Salsbury of Salsbury, Haskins, Warder, and Bone.

Bessie breathed heavily, adjusted her jaw, asked if I would eat a nice poached egg.

"A lawyer," I said, aloud. "He told me that if I ever needed a lawyer, they're a very old firm."

Having worried enough over my failure to settle the poached egg question, Bessie sighed and departed while I, remembering Shelby's advice, heard myself telling it all to the black mustache.

"And your alibi, Laura? What is your alibi for Friday night, August twentieth?" young Salsbury would ask, tweaking the end, which might or might not be waxed. Then I should have to repeat for the mustache what I had told Mark about Friday night after I left Shelby waving after my taxi on Lexington Avenue.

Mark had asked me while we were having breakfast together—it seems a thousand breakfasts ago—to tell him precisely how I had spent every minute of that Friday night. He had known, of course, that I had let Shelby give the taxi-driver Waldo's address and that I had then instructed the man to take me to Grand Central.

"And after that?" Mark had said.

"I took the train."

"It was crowded?"

"Terribly."

"Did you see anyone you know? Or anyone who might be able to identify you?"

"Why do you ask me these questions?"

"Routine," he said, and handed me his empty cup. "You make excellent coffee, Laura."

"You ought to come up sometime when I bake a cake."

We laughed. The kitchen was cozy with the checked cloth and my blue Danish cups. I poured cream and put two lumps of sugar into his coffee.

"How did you know?" he said.

"I watched you before. Now when you come here, you will get so much cream and two lumps."

"I'll come often," he said.

He asked about my arrival in Wilton, and I told him about getting off the train at South Norwalk and of walking quickly alone down that deserted street to the garage back of Andrew Frost's house for my car. Mark wanted to know if there weren't any public garages near the station, and I said I saved two dollars a month this way. That made him laugh again. "So you do have some thrift in you." There was little of the detective in him and much of the admiring male, so that I laughed, throwing back my head and searching his eyes. He asked if Andrew Frost or any of his family had seen me, and when I told him that Mr. Frost is a misogynist of seventy-four who sees me only the first Saturday of the month when I give him two dollars, Mark laughed uproariously and said, "That's a hell of an alibi."

I told him about driving to Norwalk on Saturday for my groceries, and he asked if anyone there would remember. But I told him I had saved money again, going to the Super-Market and trundling a basket through aisles filled with the working people of Norwalk and the summer crowd from the surrounding countryside. I could not remember whether it had been the red-headed cashier who took my money or the man with the cast in his eye. After I left the market, I told him, I had driven home, worked in the garden again, cooked myself a light dinner, and read until bedtime.

He said, "Is that all, Laura?"

Safe and friendly in my warm kitchen, I shuddered. Mark's eyes were fixed on my face. I seized the coffee pot and ran with it to the stove, turning my back to him and chattering swiftly of irrelevant things, wanting to cleanse my mind. There, at the stove, the coffee pot in my hand, I felt his eyes burning through me, piercing flesh and bone, seeing me as he had seen Diane's face, with all the paint and prettiness gone and only blood and membrane and hideous shattered bone.

He said: "And you stayed alone for the rest of the time you were there, Laura? You didn't see anyone who might have heard the radio or read the newspaper and come to tell you that you were dead?"

I repeated what I had told him the night before, that my radio was broken, and that the only people I had seen were the gardener and the Polish farmer from whom I had bought some corn and lettuce and fresh eggs.

Mark shook his head.

"You don't believe me," I said.

"It doesn't sound like . . . like your sort of woman."

"What do you mean, my sort of woman?"

"You have so many friends, your life is so full, you're always surrounded by people."

"It's when you have friends that you can afford to be lonely. When you know a lot of people, loneliness becomes a luxury. It's only when you're forced to be lonely that it's bad," I said.

Thin fingers drummed the table. I set the coffee pot upon the blue tile and my hand ached to stretch out and touch the wrist that protruded bonily from his white cuff. Mark's loneliness had not been luxury. He did not say this aloud, for he was a strong man and would never be wistful.

As I thought about this, lying in bed with the breakfast tray balanced on my legs, I knew I could never speak so easily to the black mustache of young Salsbury. A hell of an alibi, he would say, too, but it would be without the humor or tolerance that were in Mark's eyes and his voice.

Bessie brought the poached egg. "He's a man," Bessie said abruptly. Bessie's attitudes are high Tenth Avenue; she is off the sidewalks of New York and as unrelenting as any snob that came out of Murray Hill's stone mansions. I had met her brothers, outspoken and opinionated workingmen whose black-and-white rules of virtue my intellectuals and advertising executives could never satisfy.

"A man," Bessie said. "Most of them that comes here are big babies or old women. For once, even if he's a dick, you've met a man." And then, completely in the groove of man-worship, added, "Guess I'll bake a chocolate cake."

I bathed and dressed slowly, and said to Bessie, "I'll wear my new suit on account of claustrophobia." In spite of the rain, I had decided to leave the house, looking so calmly adjusted to my own importance—like a model in *Vogue*—that the officer at the door would never dare question my leaving. I pulled on my best gloves and tucked my alligator bag under my arm. At the door, my courage failed. So long as I made no move that showed the desire to leave, this was my home; but it needed only a word from the man at the door to make it a prison.

This is a fear which has always lived in me. I leave my doors open because I am not so frightened of intruders as of being locked in. I thought of a movie I had once seen with Sylvia Sidney's pale, frightened face behind bars. "Bessie," I said, "I'd better stay home today. After all, the world still thinks I am dead."

My name was at that moment being shouted by hundreds of newsboys. When Bessie came from the market, she brought the papers. LAURA HUNT ALIVE! streamed across all the front pages. On one tabloid my face was blown up to page proportions and looked like a relief map of Asia Minor. What, I asked myself, would tomorrow's pages scream?

LAURA HUNT GUILTY?

I read that I was staying at an unnamed hotel. This was to fool the newspapermen and my friends and keep me safe from intrusion, Aunt Sue said when she came with red roses in her hands. She had not learned about me from the newspapers, but from Mark, who had awakened her that morning to bring the news.

"How thoughtful he is!" said Aunt Sue.

She had brought the roses to show that she was glad that I had not died, but she could do nothing except condemn me for having lent Diane my apartment. "I always said you'd get into trouble, being so easy with people."

Mark had not told her of the later developments. She knew nothing of the cigarette case nor of Shelby's suspicions. Shelby, who had been staying at her house, had not come home last night.

We talked about my funeral. "It was lovely," Aunt Sue said. "You couldn't expect a great attendance at this time of the year, too many people out of town, but most of them wired flowers. I was just about to write the thank-you notes. Now you can do it yourself."

"I wish I had seen the flowers," I said.

"You'll have to outlive them all. Nobody could take a second funeral seriously."

Bessie said there were people coming to the door in spite of the fact that I was supposed to be hidden in an unnamed hotel. But there were now two detectives on my doorstep and the bell did not ring. I kept looking at the clock, wondering why I had not heard from Mark.

"I'm sure he can't make more than eighteen hundred a year, two thousand at the most," Auntie Sue said suddenly.

I laughed. It was psychic, like Bessie's suddenly saying, "He's a man."

"Some men," said Auntie Sue, "are bigger than their incomes. It's not often that you find one like that."

"From you, Auntie Sue, that's heresy."

"Once I was crazy about a grip," she said. "Of course it was impossible. I had become a star and I was young. How would it have looked to the chorus girls? Natural selection is the bunk, darling, except in jungles."

Auntie Sue is always nicer when there are no men around. She is one of those women who must flirt with every taxi-driver and waiter. And then she is horrid because she must punish men for not desiring her. I love Auntie Sue, but when I am with her I am glad that I was never a famous beauty.

She said, "Are you in love with him, Laura?"

"Don't be silly," I said. "I've only known him . . ."

I couldn't count the hours.

She said: "You've been watching the clock and cocking your ear toward the door ever since I came. You don't hear half that I say . . ."

"There may be other things on my mind, Auntie Sue. Certain things about this murder," I said, knowing I should have asked about Salsbury, Haskins, Warder, and Bone.

"You're preoccupied, Laura. Your mind is filled with the man." She came across the room; she touched me with her soft, boneless hand. Through the varnish, I saw a young girl's face. "Don't fight yourself too hard, Laura. Not this time. I've seen you give yourself too easily to all the wrong people; don't hold out against the right one."

That was strange advice from Auntie Sue, but in it I saw the design of her discontent. After she had gone, I sat for a long time uncomfortably on the arm of a chair, thinking.

I thought of my mother and how she had talked of a girl's giving herself too easily. Never give yourself, Laura, she'd say, never give yourself to a man. I must have been very young when she first said it to me, for the phrase had become deeply part of my nature, like rhymes and songs I heard when I was too small to fasten my own buttons. That is why I have given so much of everything else; myself I have always withheld. A woman may yield without giving, as Auntie Sue had yielded to Uncle Horace when she had wanted to give herself to a grip in the theatre.

I was ashamed; I kept thinking of my own life that had seemed so honest; I hid my face from daylight; I thought of the way we proud moderns have twisted and perverted love, making arguments for this and that substitute, just as I make arguments for Jix and Lady Lilith when I write advertisements. Natural selection, Auntie Sue had said, was the bunk, except in jungles.

Someone had passed the detectives at the threshold. Feet ascended to my door. I hurried to open it.

And there was Waldo.

CHAPTER FIVE

M illions of people in the city and environs," Waldo said, with envy in his voice, "are talking about Laura Hunt. Your name, witch, is sizzling on all the wires in the country."

"Do stop being childish, Waldo. I need help. You're the only person in the world I can talk to. Will you be serious?"

His eyes were small islands beyond rippling light on thick lenses. "What of Shelby?" His voice rang richly with triumph. "Isn't it his place to be at your side in the hour of travail?"

"Waldo, darling, this is a terrible and serious moment. You mustn't torture me now with your jealousy."

"Jealousy!" He hurled the word like a weapon. "Oughtn't you to be more tolerant of jealousy, my sweet?"

We were strangers. A wall had risen between us. Waldo's jealousy had been there long before Shelby's time; Waldo had been clever and cruel at the expense of other attractive men. I had been wickedly amused and proud that my charms had roused passion in this curiously unimpassioned creature. What a siren I had thought myself, Laura Hunt, to have won the love of a man born without the capacity for loving! People used to remark, to tease, to raise questioning eyebrows when they spoke of Waldo's devotion, but I had smugly enjoyed my position as companion and protégée of a distinguished man. The solid quality of our friendship had been, from my side, founded on respect for his learning and joy in the gay acrobatics of his mind. He had always insisted on the gestures of courtship; wooing had gone on for seven years with flattery and flowers, expensive gifts and oaths of undying affection. The lover rôle had been too unwavering for honesty, but Waldo would never relax it, never for a moment let either of us forget that he wore trousers and I skirts. But there had been a certain delicacy in our avoiding any implication that the wooing might have purpose beyond its charm. Auntie Sue had often said that she would shiver if Waldo kissed her; he had kissed me often; it was his habit to kiss when we met and when we parted, and often affectionately over some compliment. I felt nothing, neither shivering repulsion nor answering flame. A kitten nuzzled against my legs, a dog licked my hands, a child's moist lips touched my cheeks: these were like Waldo's kisses.

He caught my two hands, sought my eyes, said: "I love your jealousy, Laura. You were magnificent when you assaulted her."

I jerked my hands free. "Waldo, what would you think if I were accused of the murder?"

"My dear child!"

"I have no alibi, Waldo, and there's a gun up at my place in the country. He went there last night, I'm sure. I'm frightened, Waldo."

The color had left his face. He was waxen.

"What are you trying to tell me, Laura?"

I told him about the cigarette case, the Bourbon bottle, about my lies and Shelby's lies, and of Shelby's saying before Mark that he had lied to protect me. "Shelby was here with Diane that night, you know. He says he knew when the gun was fired that I had come back."

Sweat shone on Waldo's upper lip and on his forehead. He had taken off his glasses and was staring at me through pale, naked eyes.

"There is one thing you haven't told me, Laura."

"But Waldo, you don't believe . . ."

"Did you, Laura?"

Newsboys filled the streets with gutturals whose syllable formed my name. The colors of the day were fading. A phosphorescent green streaked the sky. The rain was thin and chill like summer sleet.

"Laura!"

His naked eyes, conical in shape and gleaming with white light, were hard upon my face. I shrank from that strained scrutiny, but his eyes hypnotized me so that I could neither turn away nor lower my eyelids.

A far-off church clock struck five. This is the way one waits, I thought, for the doctor when he is coming to say that the sickness is fatal.

"You're thinking of that detective, you're waiting for him to come and arrest you! You want him to come, don't you?"

I was caught by his hands, pinioned by his eyes.

"You're in love with him, Laura. I saw it yesterday. You looked away from us, you shrank from your old friends, Shelby and I, we had ceased to matter. Your eyes were on him all the time; you fluttered like a moth; you rolled your eyes and smirked like a schoolgirl before a matinée idol."

His damp hands increased their cold pressure.

My voice, small and weak, denied his charges. He laughed.

"Don't lie, woman. I've got the eye of a fluoroscope. I perceive now the strange quiverings of the female heart. How romantic!" He shouted the word hideously. "The detective and the lady. Have you given yourself yet; has he won your confession?"

I pulled away. "Please don't talk like that, Waldo. We've only known each other since Wednesday night."

"He works fast."

"Do, do be serious, Waldo. I need help so badly."

"This, my pet, is the most serious and important help that I can give you. To put you on your guard against the most dangerous man you've ever known."

"That's ridiculous. Mark's done nothing."

"Nothing, darling, except seduce you. Nothing but win your heart, my girl. He's engaged your warm and ready affection for the honor and glory of the Detective Bureau."

"That's what Shelby said. He said that Mark was trying to make me confess."

"For once Shelby and I agree."

I went to the couch and sat on the edge, hugging a pillow. Rough linen scratched my cheek. Waldo came toward me gently and offered his scented handkerchief. Then I giggled and said, "When there's a crisis, I can never find my handkerchief."

"Depend upon me, child, I shan't desert you. Let them accuse you; we'll fight them." He stood above me, his legs spread apart, his head high, his hand thrust in his coat like Napoleon in the picture. "I've every weapon, money, connections, prestige, my column, Laura. From this day forth, every day, eighty syndicated essays will be devoted to the cause of Laura Hunt."

"Please, Waldo," I begged. "Please tell me. Do you believe me guilty, too?"

He held my hand between cold, perspiring palms. Softly, as if I were a sick, fractious child, Waldo said, "Why should I care whether you're guilty or not guilty as long as I love you, my dear?"

It was unreal; it was a scene from a Victorian novel. I sat with my hand locked in his hands, a frail creature, possessed, like a gentle, fading, troubled woman of long ago. And he, by contrast, had become strong and masterful, the protector.

"Do you think I'd condemn you for it, Laura? Or even blame you? On the contrary—" he pressed my hand "—on the contrary, I adore you as I've never adored you before. You shall be my heroine, Laura, my greatest creation; millions will read about you, will love you. I'll make you greater—" the words rolled on his tongue "—than Lizzie Borden."

He said it mischievously as if he had been asked in some parlor game, "What would you do if Laura were accused of murder?"

"Please," I begged him, "please be serious."

"Serious!" He caught my word and tossed it back, mocking me. "You've read enough of Waldo Lydecker to know how seriously I regard murder. It is," he said, "my favorite crime."

I leaped up, jerked my hand away; I put the room between us.

"Come back, my precious. You must rest. You're very nervous. And no wonder, darling, with those vultures feeding on you. Shelby, with his precious gallantry; the other one, that detective fellow scheming to raise himself to front-page glory; they would destroy your self-esteem and corrupt the courage of your passion."

"Then you do believe me guilty."

Phosphorescent light gave green tints to Waldo's skin. I felt that my face, too, must reflect the sickly tint of fear. With an almost surreptitious movement, I pulled the cord of the lamp. Out of shadows my room grew real. I saw familiar shapes and the solidity of furniture. On the table, red against the pale wall, were Auntie Sue's roses. I pulled one from the vase, touched the cool petal to my cheek.

"Say it, Waldo. You believe me guilty."

"I adore you for it. I see before me a great woman. We live in an unreal, a castrate world, you and I. Among us, there are few souls strong enough for violence. Violence—" he spoke it like a love-word, his voice was the voice of a lover on a pillow "—violence gives conviction to passion, my loveliest love. You are not dead, Laura; you are a violent, living, bloodthirsty woman."

Red petals lay scattered at my feet on the figured rug. My hands, cold and nervous, pulled the last petal from the rose.

CHAPTER SIX

This is no way to write the story. I should be simple and coherent, listing fact after fact, giving order to the chaos of my mind. When they ask me, "Did you return on Friday night to kill her, Laura?" I shall answer, "He hasn't the face of a man who would lie and flirt to get a confession"; and when they ask me about ringing the bell and waiting at the door for her to come and be killed, I shall tell them that I wish, more than anything in the world, that I had met him before this happened.

That's how my mind is now. For two hours I've been shivering in my slip, unable to go through the movements of undressing. Once, long ago, when I was twenty and my heart was broken, I used to sit like this at night on the edge of the bed in a room with stained walls. I'd think of the novel I was writing about a young girl and a man. The novel was bad; I never finished it; but the writing cleansed all my dusty emotional corners. But tonight writing thickens the dust. Now that Shelby has turned against me and Mark shown the nature of his trickery, I am afraid of facts in orderly sequence.

Shelby's treachery was served to us with dinner, accompanied by the raspings and groanings of rainy-weather static. I could not pretend to eat; my leaden hands refused to lift the fork; but Waldo ate as greedily as he listened to every morsel of news.

Shelby had gone to the police and sworn to the truth of his having been in the apartment with Diane on Friday night. He had told them, as he told me, how the doorbell rang and how Diane had clattered across the room in my silver mules, and how she had been shot when she opened my front door. Shelby said that Diane had summoned him to the apartment because she was afraid of violence. Diane had been threatened, Shelby said, and although he had not liked the idea of seeing her in Laura's house, she had begged so pitifully that he could not deny her.

Shelby's attorney was N. T. Salsbury, Jr. He explained that Shelby had not confessed earlier because he was shielding someone. The name of the suspect was not included in the broadcasts. Deputy Commissioner Preble had refused to tell reporters whether or not the police knew whom Shelby was shielding. Shelby's confession had turned him into a witness for the State.

In every broadcast Deputy Commissioner Preble's name was mentioned three times a minute. Mark's name was not used at all.

"Poor McPherson," Waldo said as he dropped two saccharine pills into his coffee cup; "between Shelby and the Deputy Commissioner, he's been crowded out of the limelight."

I left the table.

Waldo followed me to the couch again, the coffee cup in his hands.

"He's not that sort at all," I said. "Mark isn't like that, he'd never sacrifice anyone . . . anyone for the sake of notoriety and his own career."

"You poor dear child," Waldo said. The coffee cup rang against the wood of the table, and Waldo's free hands reached again for my hand.

"He's playing a game, Laura; the fellow's devilishly clever. Preble is enjoying his little victory now, but the plum in this pudding will be pulled out by our own little Jack Horner. Heed my warning, sweet, before you're lost. He's after you; he'll be here soon enough with some scheme to worm that confession out of you."

The shadow of hysteria returned. I pulled my hand away, stretched on the couch, closed my eyes and shivered.

"You're cold," Waldo said, and went into the bedroom to fetch my afghan. He spread it over my legs, smoothing out the wrinkled surface, tucking it under my feet, and then standing above the couch again, content and possessive.

"I must protect my sweet child."

"I can't believe he's only been trying to get a confession. Mark liked me. And he's sincere," I said.

"I know him better than you do, Laura."

"That's what you think," I said.

"I've dined with the fellow practically every night since this affair began, Laura. He's courted me strangely, why I cannot say, but I've had a rare chance to observe his nature and his methods."

"Then he must be interesting," I said. "In all the years I've known you, I've never seen you dine with a dull person."

"My dear babe, you must always justify your bad taste, mustn't you?" Waldo laughed. "I spend a few hours with the fellow; *ergo*, he becomes a man of wit and profundity."

"He's a lot more intelligent than a lot of people who go around calling themselves intellectuals."

"What a die-hard you are, once you're interested in a man! Very well, if it will please you I'll plead guilty to a certain shabby interest in the fellow. I must confess, though, that my curiosity was roused by observation of the blossoming of his love for you."

"For me!"

"Don't sing so high, sweet canary. You were dead. There was dignity in that frustrate passion. He could make no use of you, he could destroy you no further, you were unattainable and thus desirable beyond all desire."

"How you twist things, Waldo! You don't understand Mark. There's something about him," I insisted, "something that's alive. If he'd been wallowing in frustrated romance, he'd never have been so glad when I came back."

"Trickery."

"You and your words," I said. "You always have words, but they don't always tell meanings."

"The man's a Scot, child, as parsimonious with emotion as with shillings. Have you ever analyzed that particular form of romanticism which burgeons on the dead, the lost, the doomed? Mary of the Wild Moor and Sweet Alice With Hair So Brown, their heroines are always dead or tubercular, death is the leit-motif of all their love-songs. A most convenient rationale for the thriftiness of their passion toward living females. Mark's future unrolls as upon a screen." Waldo's plump hand unrolled the future. "I see him now, romanticizing frustration, asking poor cheated females to sigh with him over the dead love."

"But he was glad, glad when I came alive. There was a special quality about his gladness as if—" I flung the words bravely "—as if he'd been waiting for me."

"Ah!" said Waldo. "When you came alive!" His voice bubbled. "When Laura became reality within his grasp, the other side of sentiment was revealed. The basic parsimony, the need to make profit of the living Laura."

"You mean that all of his kindness and sincerity were tricks to get a confession? That's silly," I said.

"Had he merely been trying to get a confession, the thing would have been simple. But consider the contradiction in the case. Compensation as well as confession, Laura. You had become reality, you came within the man's reach, a woman of your sort, cultivated, fastidious, clearly his superior; he was seized with the need to possess you. Possess and revenge and destroy."

He had seated himself on the couch, balancing his fat buttocks on the edge, holding my hand for support!

"Do you know Mark's words for women? Dolls. Dames." His tongue clicked out the words like a telegraph instrument clattering out the dots and dashes of a code. "What further evidence do you need of a man's vulgarity and insolence? There's a doll in Washington Heights who got a fox fur out of him—got it out, my dear, his very words. And a dame in Long Island whom he boasted of deserting after she'd waited faithfully for years."

"I don't believe a word."

"Remember the catalogue of your suitors, darling. Consider the past," Waldo said. "Your defense is always so earnest, you blush in that same delightful way and rebuke me for intolerance."

I saw shadows on the carpet. A procession passed through my mind of those friends and lovers whose manliness had dwindled as Waldo's critical sense showed me their weaknesses. I remembered his laughter, fatherly and indulgent, the first time he had taken me to the theatre and I had admired a handsome actor's bad performance.

"I hope it's not too tactless of me to mention the name of Shelby Carpenter. How much abuse I've endured because I failed to discern the manliness, the integrity, the hidden strength of that gallant poop! I humored you, I allowed you to enjoy self-deceit because I knew you'd ultimately find out for yourself. And look, today." He spread his hands in a gesture that included the rueful present.

"Mark's a man," I said.

Waldo's pale eyes took color; on his forehead the veins rose fat and blue; the waxen color of the skin deepened to an umber flush. He tried to laugh. Each note was separate and painful. "Always the same pattern, isn't it? A lean, lithe body is the measure of masculinity. A chiseled profile indicates a delicate nature. Let a man be hard and spare and you clothe him in the garments of Romeo, Superman, and Jupiter disguised as a bull.

"To say nothing," he added after a moment's dreadful silence, "of the Marquis de Sade. That need is in your nature, too."

"You can't hurt me," I said. "No man's ever going to hurt me again."

"I'm not speaking of myself," Waldo said reproachfully. "We were discussing your frustrated friend."

"But you're mad," I said. "He's not frustrated. He's a strong man; he's not afraid."

Waldo smiled as if he were bestowing some rare confidence. "That incurable female optimism has, I dare say, blinded you to the fellow's most distinguishing defect. He guards it zealously, my dear, but watch the next time you see him. When you observe that wary, tortured gait, you'll remember Waldo's warnings."

"I don't understand you," I said. "You're making things up." I heard my voice as something outside of me, shrill and ugly, the voice of a sullen schoolgirl. Auntie Sue's red roses threw purple shadows on the green wall. There were calla lilies and water lilies in the design of the chintz curtains. I thought of colors and fabrics and names because I was trying to turn my mind from Waldo and his warnings.

"A man who distrusts his body, my love, seeks weakness and impotence in every other living creature. Beware, my dear. He'll find your weakness and there plant his seeds of destruction."

I felt sorry for myself; I had become disappointed in people and in living. I closed my eyes, I sought darkness; I felt my blood chill and my bones soften.

"You'll be hurt, Laura, because the need for pain is part of your nature. You'll be hurt because you're a woman who's attracted by a man's strength and held by his weakness."

Whether he knew it or not, this was the very history of our relationship, mine and Waldo's. In the beginning it had been the steely strength of his mind, but the ripeness of my affection had grown with my knowledge of his childlike, uncertain heart. It was not a lover that Waldo needed, but love itself. With this great fat man I had learned to be patient and careful as a woman is patient and careful with a sickly, sensitive child.

"The mother," Waldo said slowly, "the mother is always destroyed by her young."

I pulled my hand away quickly. I rose, I put the room between us; I retreated from lamplight and stood shivering in shadows.

Waldo spoke softly, a man speaking to shadows. "A clean blow," Waldo said, "a clean blow destroys quickly and without pain." His hands, it seems as I grope for clear recollection, were showing the precise shape of destruction.

He came toward me and I shrank deeper into the corner. This was strange. I had never felt anything but respect and tenderness for this brilliant, unhappy friend. And I made myself think of Waldo dutifully; I thought of the years we had known each other and of his kindness. I felt sick within myself, ashamed of hysteria and weak shrinking. I made myself stand firm; I did not pull away; I accepted the embrace as women accept the caresses of men they dare not hurt. I did not yield, I submitted. I did not soften, I endured.

"You are mine," he said. "My love and my own."

Dimly, beyond his murmuring, I heard footsteps. Waldo's lips were pressed against my hair, his voice buzzed in my ears. Then there were three raps at the door, the grating of the key in the lock, and his embrace relaxed.

Mark had climbed the stairs slowly, he was slow to open the door. I backed away from Waldo, I straightened my dress, pulled at my sleeves, and as I sat down, jerked my skirt over my knees.

"He enters with a latchkey," Waldo said.

"The doorbell was the murderer's signal," Mark said. "I don't like to remind her."

"The manners of the executioner are known to be excellent," Waldo said. "It was thoughtful of you to knock."

Waldo's warning had posted signals in my mind. Seeing Mark with his eyes, I became aware of the taut, vigilant erectness of his shoulders, the careful balance, the wary gait. It was not so much the quality of movement as the look on his face that told me Waldo had been right in saying that Mark guarded himself. He caught my curiosity and threw back a challenge as if he were saying that he could match scrutiny with scrutiny and, as mercilessly, expose my most cherished weakness.

Seating himself in the long chair, his thin hands gripping the arms, he seemed to relax watchfulness. Tired, I thought, and noticed the hint of purple in the shadows of the deep-set eyes, the tension of flesh across narrow cheek-bones. Then, quickly, hailing into my mind the scarlet caution signal, I banished quick and foolish tenderness. Dolls and dames, I said to myself; we're all dolls and dames to him.

He said, "I want to talk to you, Laura," and looked at Waldo as if to say that I must get rid of the intruder.

Waldo had grown roots in the couch. Mark settled himself in the long chair, took out his pipe, gave notice of endurance.

Bessie slammed the kitchen door and shouted good night. One of them in Washington Heights had got a fox fur out of him, I told myself, and I wondered how much it had cost him in pride and effort. Then I faced him boldly and asked, "Have you come to arrest me?"

Waldo swayed toward me. "Careful, Laura; anything you say to him can be used against you."

"How gallantly your friends protect you!" Mark said. "Didn't Shelby warn you of the same thing last night?"

I stiffened at the sound of Shelby's name. Mark might be laughing at me, too, for having trusted a weak man. I said boldly: "Well, what did you come here for? Have you been to Wilton? What did you find at my place?"

"Sh-sh," cautioned Waldo.

"I don't see how it can hurt if I ask where he's been."

"You told me that you knew nothing of the murder, that you bought no newspapers and that the radio at your cottage was out of order. Isn't that what you told me, Laura?"

"Yes," I said.

"The first thing I discovered is that your radio works perfectly."

My cheeks burned. "But it didn't work then. Honestly. They must have fixed it. I told the boys at the electric shop near the railroad station in Norwalk to go up there and fix it. Before I caught my train I stopped and told them. They've got my key, that will prove it."

I had become so nervous that I ached to tear, to break, to scream aloud. Mark's deliberate hesitancy was aimed, I felt, at torturing the scene to hysterical climax. He told of checking on my actions since my alleged (that was his word) arrival in Wilton on Friday night, and of finding nothing better than the flimsy alibi I had given.

I started to speak, but Waldo signaled with a finger on his lips.

"Nothing I discovered up there," Mark said, "mitigates the case against you."

Waldo said, "How pious! Quite as if he had gone to seek evidence of your innocence rather than proof of your guilt. Amazingly charitable for a member of the Detective Bureau, don't you think?"

"It's my job to uncover all evidence, whether it proves guilt or innocence," Mark said.

"Come, now, don't tell me that guilt isn't preferable. We're realists, McPherson. We know that notoriety will inevitably accompany your triumph in a case as startling as this. Don't tell me, my dear fellow, that you're going to let Preble take all the bows."

Mark's face darkened. His embarrassment pleased Waldo. "Why deny it, McPherson? Your career is nourished by notoriety. Laura and I were discussing it at dinner; quite interesting, wasn't it, pet?" He smiled toward me as if we shared opinions. "She's as well aware as you or I, McPherson, of the celebrity this case could give your name. Consider the mutations of this murder case, the fascinating facets of this contradictory crime. A murder victim arises from the grave and becomes the murderer! Every large daily will send its ace reporters, all the syndicates will fill the courtroom with lady novelists and psychic analysts. Radio networks will fight for the right to establish broadcast studios within the court building. War will be relegated to Page Two. Here, my little dears, is what the public wants, twopenny lust, Sunday supplement passion, sin in the Park Avenue sector. Hour by hour, minute by minute, a nation will wait for dollar-a-word coverage on the trial of the decade. And the murderess"—he rolled his eyes. "You, yourself, McPherson paid tribute to her ankles."

The muscles tightened on Mark's cheeks.

"Who emerges as the hero of this plushy crime?" Waldo went on, enjoying his eloquence. "The hero of it all, that dauntless fellow who uncovers the secrets of a modern Lucretia is none other—" Waldo rose, bowed low "—none other than our gallant McPherson, the limping Hawkshaw."

Mark's hand, curved around his pipe, showed white at the knuckles.

The quiet and the dignity irked Waldo. He had expected his victim to squirm. "All right, go ahead with it. Arrest her if you think you've got sufficient proof. Bring her to trial on your flimsy evidence; it will be a triumph, I assure you."

"Waldo," I said, "let's quit this. I'm quite prepared for anything that may happen."

"Our hero," Waldo said, with swelling pride and power. "But wait, Laura, until he hears a nation's laughter. Let him try to prove you guilty, my love, let him swagger on the witness stand with his few poor shreds of evidence. What a jackanapes he'll be after I get through with him! Millions of Lydecker fans will roll with mirth at the crude antics of the silver-shinned bumpkin."

Waldo had taken hold of my hand again, displaying possession triumphantly.

Mark said, "You speak, Lydecker, as if you wanted to see her tried for this murder."

"We are not afraid," Waldo said. "Laura knows that I will use all of my power to help her."

Mark became official. "Very well, then, since you're assuming responsibility for Miss Hunt's welfare, there's no reason why you shouldn't know that the gun has been discovered. It was in the chest under the window of her bedroom in her cottage. It's a lady's hunting gun marked with the initials D. S. C. and was once owned by Mrs. John Carpenter. It is still in good condition, has been cleaned, oiled, and discharged recently. Shelby has identified it as the gun he gave Miss Hunt . . ."

It had been like waiting for the doctor and being relieved when the final word killed all hope.

I pulled away from Waldo and stood before Mark. "All right," I said. "All right, I've been expecting it. My attorneys are Salsbury, Haskins, Warder, and Bone. Do I get in touch with them now, or do you arrest me first?"

"Careful, Laura."

That was Waldo. I paid no attention. Mark had risen, too; Mark stood with his hands on my shoulders, his eyes looking into mine. The air shivered between us. Mark looked sorry. I was glad, I wanted Mark to be sorry; I was less afraid because there was a sorry look in Mark's eyes. It is hard to be coherent, to set this all down in words; I can't always remember the right words. I know that I was crying and that Mark's coat-sleeve was rough.

Waldo watched us. I was looking at Mark's face, but I felt Waldo watching as if his eyes were shooting arrows into my back.

Waldo's voice said, "Is this an act, Laura?" Mark's arm tightened.

Waldo said: "A classic precedent, you know; you're not the first woman who's given herself to the jailer. But you'll never buy your freedom that way, Laura . . ."

Mark had deserted me, he stood beside Waldo, fists aimed at Waldo's waxen face. Waldo's eyes bulged behind his glasses, but he stood straight, his arms folded on his breast.

I ran to Mark, I pulled at his arms. I said: "Mark, please. It won't do any good to get angry. If you've got to arrest me, it's all right. I'm not afraid."

Waldo was laughing at us. "You see, my noble lad, she spurns your gallantry."

"I'm not afraid," I said to Waldo's laughter.

"You ought to have learned by now, my dear, that gallantry is the last refuge of a scoundrel."

I was looking at Mark's face. He had gone without sleep, he'd spent the night driving to Wilton, he was a tired man. But a man, as Bessie had said, and Auntie Sue, when she had contradicted her whole way of life to tell me that some men were bigger than their incomes. I had been gay enough, I'd had plenty of fun, enjoyed men's companionship, but there had been too many fussy old maids and grown-up babies. I took hold of Mark's arm again, I looked at him, I smiled to give myself courage. Mark wasn't listening to Waldo either, he was looking at my face and smiling delicately. I was tired, too, longing to cling and feel his strength, to rest my head against his shoulder.

"Tough, Hawkshaw, to have to pull in a doll? Before you've had the chance to make the grade with her, eh, Hawkshaw?"

Waldo's voice was shrill, his words crude and out of character. The voice and words came between Mark and me, our moment was gone, and I was holding air in my closed fingers.

Waldo had taken off his glasses. He looked at me with naked eyes. "Laura, I'm an old friend. What I'm saying may be distasteful, but I beg you to remember that you've known this man for only forty-eight hours . . ."

"I don't care," I said. "I don't care about time. Time doesn't mean anything."

"He's a detective."

"I don't care, Waldo. Maybe he could scheme and lay traps for crooks and racketeers, but he couldn't be anything but honest with me, could you, Mark?"

For all Mark saw of me, I might have lived in another world. He was staring at the mercury-glass vase on my mantel, the gift Waldo had given me at Christmas. I looked at Waldo, then; I saw the working of his thick, sensitive lips and the creeping mist that rose over his pale conical eyeballs.

Waldo's voice taunted and tore at me. "It's always the same, isn't it, Laura. The same pattern over and over, the same trap, the same eagerness and defeat. The lean, the lithe, the obvious and muscular, and you fail to sense the sickness and decay and corruption underneath. Do you remember a man named Shelby Carpenter? He used you, too . . ."

"Shut up! Shut up! Shut up!" I shouted at Waldo's swollen eyes. "You're right, Waldo, it's the same pattern, the same sickness and decay and corruption, only they're in you. You! You, Waldo. It's your malice; you've mocked and ridiculed and ruined every hope I've ever had, Waldo. You hate the men I like, you find their weak places, you make them weaker, you've teased and shamed them before my eyes until they've hated me!"

Bloodthirsty, Waldo had called me, and bloodthirsty I had become in the sudden fever of hating him. I had not seen it clearly with Shelby or the others, I had never smelled the malice until he tried to shame Mark before me. I shouted bravely; I spoke as if I had known before, but I had been too blind and obstinate to see how his sharp little knife-thrusts had hurt my friends and destroyed love for me. I saw it clearly now, as if I were a god upon a mountain, looking down at humans through a clear light. And I was glad for my anger; I exulted in hatred; I screamed for revenge; I was bloodthirsty.

"You're trying to destroy him, too. You hate him. You're jealous. He's a man. Mark's a man. That's why you've got to destroy him."

"Mark needs no help," Waldo said. "Mark seems quite capable of self-destruction."

Waldo could always do that to me, always diminish me in an argument, turning my just anger into a fish-wife's cheap frenzy. My face felt its ugliness and I turned so that Mark should not see me. But Mark was untouched, he held himself scornful. As I turned, Mark's arm caught me, pulled me close, and I stood beside Mark.

"So you've chosen?" Waldo said, his voice an echo of mockery. There was no more strength in the poison. Mark's hard, straight, unwavering gaze met Waldo's oblique, taunting glance and Waldo was left without defenses, except for the small shrill weapon of petulance.

"Blessings upon your self-destruction, my children," Waldo said, and settled his glasses on his nose.

He had lost the fight. He was trying to make a dignified retreat. I felt sorry. The anger was all drained out of me, and now that Mark had taken my fear, I had no wish to punish Waldo. We had quarreled, we had unclothed all the naked venom of our disappointments, we were finished with friendship; but I could not forget his kindness and generosity, the years behind us, the jokes and opinions we had shared. Christmas and birthdays, the intimacy of our little quarrels.

"Waldo," I said, and took a half-step toward him. Mark's arm tightened, he caught me, held me, and I forgot the old friend standing with his hat in his hand at my door. I forgot everything; I melted shamelessly, my mind clouded; I let go of all my taut fear; I lay back in his arms, a jade. I did not see Waldo leave nor hear the door close nor recollect the situation. What room was there in me for any sense of danger, any hint of trickery, any memory of warning? My mother had said, never give yourself, and I was giving myself with wayward delight, spending myself with such abandon that his lips must have known and his heart and muscles that he possessed me.

He let go so suddenly that I felt as if I'd been flung against a wall. He let go as if he had tried to conquer and had won, and were eager to be finished.

"Mark!" I cried. "Mark!"

He was gone.

That was three hours ago, three hours and eighteen minutes. I am still sitting on the edge of the bed, half-undressed. The night is damp and there is a dampness like dew on my flesh. I feel dull and dead; my hands are so cold that I can barely hold the pencil. But I must write; I have to keep on writing it down so I can clear my mind of confusion and think clearly. I have tried to remember every scene and incident and every word he said to me.

Waldo had warned me; and Shelby. He's a detective. But if he believed me guilty, why are there no more guards outside? Or had he grown fond of me and, believing me guilty, given me this chance to escape? Every excuse and every solace are crowded out of my mind by Waldo's warnings. I had tried to believe that these warnings were born of Waldo's jealousy; that Waldo had contrived with cruel cunning to equip Mark with a set of faults and sins that were Waldo's own disguised weaknesses.

The doorbell is ringing. Perhaps he has come back to arrest me. He will find me like a slut in a pink slip with a pink strap falling over my shoulder, my hair unfastened. Like a doll, like a dame, a woman to be used by a man and thrown aside.

The bell is still ringing. It's very late. The street has grown quiet. It must have been like this the night Diane opened the door for the murderer.

PART FIVE

CHAPTER ONE

In the files of the Department you will find full reports on the
Laura Hunt case. As officially recorded the case seems like hun-
dreds of other successful investigations: Report of Lieutenant
McPherson; Report of Sergeant Mooney; Report of Lieutenant
McPherson; case closed, August 28th.

The most interesting developments of the case never got into the
Department files. My report on that scene in Laura's living room, for
instance, read like this:

> At 8.15 found Lydecker in Hunt apartment with Laura. He
> was doing some fast talking to prove that I was plotting to get
> her to confess. Stayed until 9.40 (approx.), when he left; sent
> Behrens and Muzzio, who had been stationed at door, to trail
> him. I proceeded to Claudius Cohen's place . . ."

The story deserves more human treatment than police records allow.

I want to confess, before I write any more, that Waldo's unfinished story and Laura's manuscript were in my hands before I put a
word on paper. In writing that section which comes between his doc-
ument and Laura's, I have tried to tell what happened as it happened,
without too much of my own opinion or prejudice. But I am human. I
had seen what Waldo wrote about me and had read Laura's flattering
comments. My opinions were naturally influenced.

I can't help wondering what would have happened if the Deputy
Commissioner hadn't pulled the snide trick of assigning me to the
case when he knew I was counting on a Saturday afternoon at

Ebbetts Field. The murder might never have been uncovered. I say this without trying to take any bows for solving the mystery. I fell for a woman and she happened to like me. That circumstance furnished the key that unlocked the main door.

I knew from the start that Waldo was hiding something. I cannot honestly say that I suspected him of love or murder. That Sunday morning when he looked in the mirror and talked about his innocent face, I knew I was playing with a screwball. But it was not unpleasant; he was always good company. He had told me plainly that he had loved Laura, but I thought that he had become adjusted to the rôle of faithful friend.

I had to know what he was hiding, although I suspected the sort of game that would make an amateur feel superior to a professional detective. Waldo imagined himself a great authority on crime.

I played my own game. I flattered him, I sought his company, I laughed at his jokes; while I asked questions about Laura's habits, I studied his. What made a man collect old glassware and china? Why did he carry a stick and wear a beard? What caused him to scream when someone tried to drink out of his pet coffee cup? Clues to character are the only clues that add up to the solution of any but the crudest crime.

Before that night in Montagnino's back yard when he told me about the song, Waldo's talk had made his *love* for Laura sound like a paternal and unromantic relationship. It was then that I began to see his midnight walks as something besides the affectation of a man who considered himself an heir to the literary tradition. Perhaps he had not spent all of Friday night reading Gibbon in a tepid bath.

Then Laura returned. When I discovered that it was Diane Redfern who had been murdered, I went completely off the track. There were so many crossed wires; Shelby, three unexplained lies, a gold cigarette case. During that stage of the investigation, I couldn't help looking in the mirror and asking myself if I looked like the kind of sucker who trusts a woman.

Shelby honestly believed that his fatal beauty had led Laura to murder. To relieve his two-timing conscience, Shelby protected her. If I ever saw gallantry in the reverse, that was it.

But Shelby was no coward. He risked his neck that night he went up to her cottage to get the gun. He failed because a yellow taxi was on his trail, and even Shelby was smart enough to know the Department wasn't spending money just to give one of its men a joy ride. When Shelby saw that shotgun for the first time after the murder, it lay on my desk.

The gun was a clue to Shelby. It was marked with his mother's initials. C stood for Carpenter, S for Shelby, and D for Delilah. I could see him as a kid in knee-pants and a Buster Brown collar reciting pieces for a mother named Delilah.

He told me the gun had been used a month before. He had shot a rabbit.

I said: "Look here, Carpenter, you can relax. If you tell the truth now, we might be able to overlook a few dozen lies that make you an accessory after the fact. Tomorrow may be too late."

He looked at me as though I'd said out loud what I thought about Delilah. He would never turn State's evidence, no suh, not a descendant of the Shelbys of Kentucky. That was an underworld trick which no gentleman could sanction.

It took three hours for me to make him understand the difference between a gentleman and an ordinary heel. Then he broke down and asked if he might send for his lawyer.

I let Preble give out the news of Shelby's confession because I was playing a game with him, too. In world politics it's called appeasement. From Preble's point of view, the gun and Shelby's confession clinched the evidence against Laura. She looked as guilty as Ruth Snyder. We could have booked her then and there on suspicion of murder. A quick arrest, Preble thought, would bring a juicy confession. And orchids for the Department under the efficient administration of Deputy Commissioner Preble.

I could see his hand as clearly as though he'd shown me the cards. This was Friday, and on Monday the Commissioner would be back from his vacation. Preble had little time to garner his share of personal publicity. And this case, since Laura had come back alive, was strictly Front Page, and coast to coast on the networks. Preble's wife and kids were waiting at a summer hotel in the Thousand Islands to hear over the air waves that Papa had solved the murder mystery of the decade.

We had a knock-down and drag-out argument. I wanted time, he wanted action. I called him the worn-out wheelhorse of a political party that should have been buried years ago under a load of cow manure. He told the world that I was hanging on to the bandwagon of the party in power, a bunch of filthy Reds who'd sell the country short for thirty pieces of Moscow gold. I said he belonged back with the Indian chiefs who'd given their name to his stinking loyalties, and he said I'd send my old mother out on the Bowery if I thought it would further my career. I am not reporting our actual language because, as I mentioned before, I haven't had a college education and I keep my writing clean.

It ended in a draw.

"If you don't bring in the murderer, dead or alive, by tomorrow morning..."

"You're damned tooting," I said. "I'll have him stuffed and trussed and ready for your breakfast."

"Her," he said.

"Wait," I bluffed.

I hadn't a shred of evidence that wasn't against Laura. But even though my own hands had dragged that gun from the chest in her bedroom, I couldn't believe her guilty. She might conk a rival with a trayful of hors d'oeuvres, but she could no more plan a murder than I could go in for collecting antique glassware.

It was around eight o'clock. I had about twelve hours to clear Laura and prove that I wasn't one hundred per cent sucker.

I drove up to Sixty-Second Street. When I opened the door, I knew that I had burst in on a love-scene. It was the fat man's field day. Shelby had betrayed her and I seemed to be threatening her with arrest. He was the man in possession, and the deeper the spot she was in, the greater her need for him, the surer his hold. It would have been to his advantage in more ways than one to have her tried for murder.

My presence was poison to him. His face took on the color of cabbage and his fat flesh shook like cafeteria jello. He tried his best to make me look cheap, a cheap dick who'd try to make a woman fall for me so that I could advance myself. It was something like Preble's remark about my sending my mother out on the Bowery to help my career. Remarks like this are not so much accusations as revelations. Frightened people try to defend themselves by accusing others of their own motives. This was never so clear as when Waldo began to make cracks about my bad leg. When a man goes so far below the belt, you can be sure he's hiding his own weakness.

At that moment I quit thinking of Waldo as the faithful old friend. I understood why his manner toward me had changed after Laura came back. He had made a great romance of my interest in the dead girl; it gave him a companion in frustration. But with Laura alive, I had become a rival.

I sat back and listened while he called me names. The shabbier he tried to make me look, the more clearly I saw his motives. For eight years he had kept her for himself by the destruction of her suitors. Only Shelby had survived. Shelby might have been a weak man, but he was too stubborn to let himself be ousted. He had allowed Waldo to insult him again and again, but he had stuck, finding solace in playing big shot for Diane.

The pattern had straightened out, but evidence was lacking. I saw myself as the Deputy Commissioner might see me, a stubborn jackass working on instinct against known fact. Training and experience had taught me that instinct had no value in the courtroom. Your Honor, I know this man to have been bitterly jealous. Try that on the witness stand and see how far you get.

Under ordinary circumstances I do my love-making in private. But I had to turn the screws on Waldo's jealousy. When I took Laura in my arms, I was playing a scene. Her response almost ended my usefulness in the case. I knew she liked me, but I hadn't asked for heaven.

She believed that I was embracing her because she had been hurt and I, loving her, offered comfort and protection. That was the deeper truth. But I had Waldo on my mind, too. The love-scene was too strong for his sensitive nerves, and he slipped out.

I had no time to explain anything. It wasn't easy to break away, leaving Laura to think that Waldo had been right in accusing me of using her sincerity as a trap. But he was gone and I could take no chance of losing him.

I lost him.

Behrens and Muzzio let him pass. By my own instructions Waldo Lydecker had been allowed to come and go as he chose. The two cops had been lounging on the stoop, bragging about their kids probably, and not paying the slightest attention to his movements. It was my fault, not theirs.

There was no trace of his great bulk, his decorated chin, his thick cane, on Sixty-Second Street. Either he had turned the corner or he was hiding in some dark areaway. I sent Behrens toward Third Avenue and Muzzio to Lexington and ordered them to find and trail him. I jumped into my car.

It was just eighteen minutes of ten when I found Claudius putting up his shutters.

"Claudius," I said, "tell me something. Are people who collect antiques always screwy?"

He laughed.

"Claudius, when a man who's crazy about this old glassware finds a beautiful piece that he can't own, do you think he'd deliberately smash it so that no other man could ever enjoy it?"

Claudius licked his lips. "Guess I know what you're talking about, Mr. McPherson."

"Was it an accident last night?"

"I couldn't say yes and I couldn't say no. Mr. Lydecker was willing to pay and I took the money, but it could've been an accident. You see, I hadn't put any shot in . . ."

"Shot? What do you mean, shot?"

"Shot. We use it to weight down stuff when it's light and breakable."

"Not BB shot," I said.

"Yes," he said, "BB shot."

I had looked over Waldo's antiques once while I was waiting for him. There had been no BB shot weighing the old cups and vases down, but he was not such a cluck as to leave unmistakable evidence around for the first detective. I wanted to make a thorough examination this time, but I had no time to get a warrant. I entered the building through the basement and climbed eighteen flights to his apartment. This was to avoid the elevator man, who had begun to welcome me as Mr. Lydecker's best pal. If Waldo came home, he was not to have any suspicions that would cause him to leave hastily.

I let myself in with a passkey. The place was silent and dark.

There had been a murder. There had to be a gun. It wasn't a shotgun, whole or sawed-off. Waldo wasn't the type. If he owned a gun, it would look like another museum piece among the China dogs and shepherdesses and old bottles.

I made a search of cabinets and shelves in the living-room, then went into the bedroom and started on the dresser drawers. Everything he owned was special and rare. His favorite books had been bound in selected leathers, he kept his monogrammed handkerchiefs and shorts and pajamas in silk cases embroidered with his initials. Even his mouthwash and toothpaste had been made up from special prescriptions.

I heard the snap of the light switch in the next room. My hand went automatically to my hip pocket. But I had no gun. As I had once told Waldo, I carry weapons when I go out to look for trouble. I hadn't figured on violence as part of this evening's entertainment.

I turned quickly, put myself behind a chair, and saw Roberto in a black silk dressing-gown that looked as if he was paying the rent for this high-class apartment.

Before he had time to ask questions, I said: "What are you doing here? Don't you usually go home nights?"

"Mr. Lydecker need me tonight," he said.

"Why?"

"He not feel himself."

"Oh," I said, and took the cue. "That's why I'm here, Roberto. Mr. Lydecker didn't feel himself at dinner, so he gave me the key and asked me to come up and wait for him."

Roberto smiled.

"I was just going to the bathroom," I said. That seemed the simplest explanation of my being in the bedroom. I went to the bathroom. When I came out, Roberto was waiting in the parlor. He asked if I'd like a drink or a cup of coffee.

"No, thanks," I said. "You run along to bed. I'll see that Mr. Lydecker's okay." He started to leave, but I called him back. "What do you think's the matter with Mr. Lydecker, Roberto? He seems nervous, doesn't he?"

Roberto smiled.

I said, "It's this murder; it's been getting on his nerves, don't you think?"

His smile got me nervous. Even the Rhode Island clam was a big talker compared with this Filipino oyster.

I said, "Did you ever know Quentin Waco?"

That woke him up. There are only a few Filipinos in New York and they stick together like brothers. All the houseboys used to put their money on Quentin Waco, who was top lightweight until he got mixed up with the girls around the Sixty-Sixth Street dancehalls. He spent more than he made, and when young Kardansky knocked him out, they accused him of pulling the fight. One of Quentin's pals met him at the door of the Shamrock Ballroom one night and pulled a knife. For the honor of the Islands, he told the judge. A little later it came out that Quentin hadn't pulled the fight, and the boys made a martyr of him. The religious ones kept candles burning in a church on Ninth Avenue.

I happened to have been the man who got hold of the evidence that cleared Quentin's name and, without knowing it, restored the honor of the Islands. When I told this to Roberto, he stopped smiling and became human.

We talked about Mr. Lydecker's health. We talked about the murder and about Laura's return. Roberto's point of view was strictly out of the tabloids. Miss Hunt was a nice lady, always friendly to Roberto, but her treatment of Mr. Lydecker showed her to have been no better than a dance-hall hostess. According to Roberto all women were the same. They'd turn down a steady fellow every time for a big sport guy who knew all the latest steps.

I jerked the talk around to the dinner he had cooked on the night of the murder. It wasn't hard to get him going on that subject. He wanted to give me a mushroom by mushroom description of the menu. Every half-hour during the afternoon, Roberto said, Mr. Lydecker had quit his writing and come into the kitchen to taste, smell, and ask questions.

"We have champagne; six dollars a bottle," Roberto bragged.

"Oh, boy!" I said.

Roberto told me there had been more than food and wine prepared for that evening. Waldo had arranged the records on his automatic phonograph so that Laura should enjoy her favorite music with the meal.

"He certainly prepared. What a disappointment when Miss Hunt changed her mind!" I said. "What did he do, Roberto?"

"Not eat."

Waldo told us he had eaten a solitary meal and spent the evening reading Gibbon in the bathtub.

"He didn't eat, huh? Wouldn't go near the table?"

"He go table," Roberto said. "He have me bring food, he put on plate, not eat."

"I don't expect he played the phonograph either."

"No," said Roberto.

"He hasn't played it since, I suppose."

The phonograph was big and expensive. It played ten records, then turned them over and played the other side. I looked at them to see if any of the tunes checked with the music they had talked about. There was none of this Toccata and Fugue stuff, but a lot of old songs from shows. The last was "Smoke Gets in Your Eyes."

"Roberto," I said, "maybe I'll have a whiskey anyway."

I thought of that hot night in Montagnino's back yard. A storm had been rolling in and the lady at the next table sang with the music. Waldo had talked about hearing that song with Laura as if there had been a lot more to it than just listening to music with a woman.

"I think I'll have another, Roberto."

I needed Scotch less than I needed time to think it out. The pieces were beginning to fit together. The last dinner before her marriage. Champagne and her favorite songs. Memories of shows they had seen together, talk of the past. Old stories retold. And when the meal was over and they were drinking brandy, the last record would fall into place, the needle fit into the groove.

Roberto waited with a glass in his hand. I drank. I was cold and sweating.

Since that Sunday when I'd first walked into his apartment, I'd been reading the complete works of Waldo Lydecker. There is no better key to a man's character than his use of the written word. Read enough of any man's writing and you'll have his Number One Secret. There was a line that I remembered from one of his essays: "The high crisis of frustration."

He had planned so carefully that even the music was timed for it. And that night Laura had failed to show up.

I said: "Go to bed, Roberto. I'll wait up for Mr. Lydecker."

Roberto disappeared like a shadow.

I was alone in the room. Around me were his things, spindly overdecorated furniture, striped silks, books and music and antiques. There had to be a gun somewhere. When murder and suicide are planned like a seduction, a man must have his weapon handy.

CHAPTER TWO

While I waited in his parlor, Waldo was pounding his stick along the pavements. He dared not look backward. His pursuers might see him turn his head and know that he was frightened.

Muzzio caught sight of him almost a block ahead on Lexington. Waldo gave no sign that he observed Muzzio, but walked on quickly, turning east at Sixty-Fourth. At the end of the block, he saw Behrens, who had turned north on Third Avenue.

Waldo disappeared. The two men searched every areaway and vestibule on the block, but Waldo had evidently used the service tunnel of a big apartment house, gone through the basement to the rear of the building, and found another basement and service entrance on Seventy-Second.

He walked for three hours. He passed a lot of people on their way home from theatres and picture shows and bars. He met them in the light of arc lamps and under the lighted marquees of picture shows. We learned about it later the way we always do when an important case is finished and people phone in to make themselves important. Mary Lou Simmons, fifteen, of East Seventy-Sixth, had been frightened by a man who darted out of the vestibule as she came home from an evening at a girl chum's house. Gregory Finch and Enid Murphy thought it was Enid's father leaning over the banister in the dark hall where they were kissing. Mrs. Lea Kantor saw a giant ghost behind her newsstand. Several taxi-drivers had stopped in the hope of picking up a passenger. A couple of drivers had recognized Waldo Lydecker.

He walked until the streets were quiet. There were few taxis and hardly any pedestrians. He chose the darkest streets, hid in doorways, crouched on subway steps. It was almost two o'clock when he came back to Sixty-Second Street.

There was only one lighted window on the block. According to Shelby, that light had been burning on Friday night, too.

Her door was not guarded. Muzzio was still waiting on Sixty-Fourth Street and Behrens had gone off duty. I had given no instructions for a man to replace him, for I had no idea, when I left Laura alone and sent the men to follow him, that he was carrying his weapon.

He climbed the steps and rang her doorbell.

She thought I had come back to arrest her. That seemed more reasonable than a return of the murderer. For a moment she thought of Shelby's description of Diane's death. Then she wrapped herself in a white bathrobe and went to the door.

By that time I knew Waldo's secret. I found no gun in his apartment; he was carrying the gun concealed on his person, loaded with the rest of the BB shot. What I found was a pile of unfinished and unpublished manuscript. I read it because I was planning to wait in the apartment, confront him, make the accusation, and see what happened. I found the following sentence in a piece called "The Porches of Thy Father's Ear":

> In the cultivated individual, malice, a weapon darkly concealed, wears the garments of usefulness, flashes the disguise of wit or flaunts the ornaments of beauty.

The piece was about poisons hidden in antique rings, of swords in sticks, of firearms concealed in old prayer-books.

It took me about three minutes to realize that he was carrying a muzzle-loader. Last night, when we were leaving the Golden Lizard, I had tried to look at his stick. He had snatched it away with a crack about getting me a rubber-tipped cane. That crack was loaded. Resentment kept me from asking any more questions. Possessions were like people with Waldo. He wanted to protect his precious stick from my profane hands, so he brought out his malice without the garments of wit or beauty. I had thought that he was showing off another of his whims, like drinking his coffee from the Napoleon cup.

Now I knew why he had wanted to keep me from examining his cane. He carried it, he had told me, to give himself importance. There was the man's hidden power. He probably smiled as he stood before Laura's door, preparing to use his secret weapon. The second time was like the first. In his failing and disordered mind there was no original crime, no repetition.

When the doorknob turned, he aimed. He knew Laura's height and the place where her face would appear like an oval in the dark. As the door opened, he fired.

There was a shivering crash. Turning, Laura saw a thousand slivers of light. The shot, missing her by the fraction of an inch, had shattered the glass bowl. Its fragments shone on the dark carpet.

He had missed his aim because, as he fired, his legs were jerked out from under him. I had left his apartment as soon as I realized where the gun was hidden and remembered that I had deliberately put on a scene to stir up his jealousy. He was on the third-floor landing, his finger on the bell, when I opened the door downstairs.

The old-fashioned hall was dimly lighted. On the landings pale bulbs glowed. Waldo was struggling for his life with an enemy whose face he couldn't see. I am a younger man, in better condition, and know how to handle myself in a fight. But he had the strength of desperation. And a gun in his hand.

When I jerked his legs out from under him, he rolled over on top of me. Laura came out of her door, looked down at us, straining to see our dark struggle on the staircase. We rolled down the steps.

Under the bulb of the second-floor landing I saw his face. He had lost his glasses, but his pale eyes seemed to see into the distance. He said, "While a whole city pursued the killer, Waldo Lydecker, with his usual urbanity, pursued the law."

He laughed. My spine chilled. I was fighting a madman. His face contorted, his lips writhed, pointed eyeballs seemed to jerk out of their sockets. He wrenched his arm loose, raised the gun, waved it like a baton.

"Get back! Get out of the way!" I shouted up at Laura.

His flesh had seemed flabby, but there were over two hundred and fifty pounds of it, and when I jerked his arm back, he rolled over on me. The light flashed in his eyes, he recognized me, sanity returned, and with it, hatred. White streaks of foam soaped his lips. Laura called out, warning me, but his groans were closer to my ears. I managed to shove my knees up under his fat belly and push him back toward the post of the banister. He waved his gun, then shot wild, firing without aim. Laura screamed.

With the firing of that shot, his strength was gone. His eyes froze, his limbs became rigid. But I was taking no chances. I knocked his head against the banister post. On the third-floor landing, Laura heard bone crack against wood.

In the ambulance and at the hospital he kept on talking. Always about himself, always in the third person. Waldo Lydecker was someone far away from the dying fat man on the stretcher, he was like a hero a boy has always worshiped. It was the same thing over and over again, never straight and connected, but telling as much as a sworn confession.

Ever the connoisseur who cunningly mates flavor with occasion, Waldo Lydecker selected the vintage of the year '14 . . .

As might Cesare Borgia have diverted himself on an afternoon pregnant with the infant of new infamy, so Waldo Lydecker passed the nervous hours in civilized diversion, reading and writing . . .

A man might sit thus, erect as a tombstone, while composing his will; so sat Waldo Lydecker at his rosewood desk writing the essay that was to have been his legacy . . .

The woman had failed him. Secret and alone, Waldo Lydecker celebrated death's impotence. Bitter herbs mingled their savor with the mushrooms. The soup was rue-scented . . .

Habit led Waldo Lydecker that night past windows illumined by her treachery . . .

Calm and untroubled, Waldo Lydecker stood, pressing an imperious finger against her doorbell . . .

When he died, the doctor had to unclasp the fingers that gripped Laura's hand.

"Poor, poor Waldo," she said.

"He tried to kill you twice," I reminded her.

"He wanted so desperately to believe I loved him."

I looked at her face. She was honestly mourning the death of an old friend. The malice had died with him and Laura remembered that he had been kind. It is generosity, Waldo said, not evil, that flourishes like the green bay tree.

He is dead now. Let him have the last word. Among the papers on his desk I found the unfinished piece, that final legacy which he had written while the records were waiting on the phonograph, the wine being chilled in the icebox, Roberto cooking the mushrooms.

He had written:

Then, as the final contradiction, there remains the truth that she made a man of him as fully as man could be made of that stubborn clay. And when that frail manhood is threatened, when her own womanliness demands more than he can give, his malice seeks her destruction. But she is carved from Adam's rib, indestructible as legend, and no man will ever aim his malice with sufficient accuracy to destroy her.

THE END

REBECCA

CHAPTER ONE

Last night I dreamt I went to Manderley again. It seemed to me I stood by the iron gate leading to the drive, and for a while I could not enter for the way was barred to me. There was a padlock and a chain upon the gate. I called in my dream to the lodge-keeper, and had no answer, and peering closer through the rusted spokes of the gate I saw that the lodge was uninhabited.

No smoke came from the chimney, and the little lattice windows gaped forlorn. Then, like all dreamers, I was possessed of a sudden with supernatural powers and passed like a spirit through the barrier before me. The drive wound away in front of me, twisting and turning as it had always done, but as I advanced I was aware that a change had come upon it; it was narrow and unkept, not the drive that we had known. At first I was puzzled and did not understand, and it was only when I bent my head to avoid the low swinging branch of a tree that I realised what had happened. Nature had come into her own again and, little by little, in her stealthy, insidious way had encroached upon the drive with long, tenacious fingers. The woods, always a menace even in the past, had triumphed in the end. They crowded, dark and uncontrolled, to the borders of the drive. The beeches with white, naked limbs leant close to one another, their branches intermingled in a strange embrace, making a vault above my head like the archway of a church. And there were other trees as well, trees that I did not recognise, squat oaks and tortured elms that straggled cheek by jowl with the beeches, and had thrust themselves out of the quiet earth, along with monster shrubs and plants, none of which I remembered.

The drive was a ribbon now, a thread of its former self, with gravel surface gone, and choked with grass and moss. The trees had thrown out low branches, making an impediment to progress; the gnarled roots looked like skeleton claws. Scattered here and again amongst this jungle growth I would recognise shrubs that had been landmarks in our time, things of culture and of grace, hydrangeas whose blue heads had been famous. No hand had checked their progress, and they had gone native now, rearing to monster height without a bloom, black and ugly as the nameless parasites that grew beside them.

On and on, now east now west, wound the poor thread that once had been our drive. Sometimes I thought it lost, but it appeared again, beneath a fallen tree perhaps, or struggling on the other side of a muddied ditch created by the winter rains. I had not thought the way so long. Surely the miles had multiplied, even as the trees had done, and this path led but to a labyrinth, some choked wilderness, and not to the house at all. I came upon it suddenly; the approach masked by the unnatural growth of a vast shrub that spread in all directions, and I stood, my heart thumping in my breast, the strange prick of tears behind my eyes.

There was Manderley, our Manderley, secretive and silent as it had always been, the grey stone shining in the moonlight of my dream, the mullioned windows reflecting the green lawns and the terrace. Time could not wreck the perfect symmetry of those walls, nor the site itself, a jewel in the hollow of a hand.

The terrace sloped to the lawns, and the lawns stretched to the sea, and turning I could see the sheet of silver, placid under the moon, like a lake undisturbed by wind or storm. No waves would come to ruffle this dream water, and no bulk of cloud, wind-driven from the west, obscure the clarity of this pale sky. I turned again to the house, and though it stood inviolate, untouched, as though we ourselves had left but yesterday, I saw that the garden had obeyed the jungle law, even as the woods had done. The rhododendrons stood fifty feet high, twisted and entwined with bracken, and they had entered into alien marriage with a host of nameless shrubs, poor, bastard things that clung about their roots as though conscious of their spurious origin. A lilac had mated with a copper beech, and to bind them yet more closely to one another the malevolent ivy, always an enemy to grace, had thrown her tendrils about the pair and made them prisoners. Ivy held prior place in this lost garden, the long strands crept across the lawns, and soon would encroach upon the house itself. There was another plant too, some half-breed from the woods, whose seed had been scattered long ago beneath the trees and then forgotten, and now, marching in unison with the ivy, thrust its ugly form like a giant rhubarb towards the soft grass where the daffodils had blown.

Nettles were everywhere, the van-guard of the army. They choked the terrace, they sprawled about the paths, they leant, vulgar and lanky, against the very windows of the house. They made indifferent sentinels, for in many places their ranks had been broken by the rhubarb plant, and they lay with crumpled heads and listless stems, making a path-way for the rabbits. I left the drive and went on to the terrace, for the nettles were no barrier to me, a dreamer, I walked enchanted, and nothing held me back.

Moonlight can play odd tricks upon the fancy, even upon a dreamer's fancy. As I stood there, hushed and still, I could swear that the house was not an empty shell but lived and breathed as it had lived before.

Light came from the windows, the curtains blew softly in the night air, and there, in the library, the door would stand half open as we had left it, with my handkerchief on the table beside the bowl of autumn roses.

The room would bear witness to our presence. The little heap of library books marked ready to return, and the discarded copy of *The Times*. Ash-trays, with the stub of a cigarette; cushions, with the imprint of our heads upon them, lolling in the chairs; the charred embers of our log fire still smouldering against the morning. And Jasper, dear Jasper, with his soulful eyes and great, sagging jowl, would be stretched upon the floor, his tail a-thump when he heard his master's footsteps.

A cloud, hitherto unseen, came upon the moon, and hovered an instant like a dark hand before a face. The illusion went with it, and the lights in the windows were extinguished. I looked upon a desolate shell, soulless at last, unhaunted, with no whisper of the past about its staring walls.

The house was a sepulchre, our fear and suffering lay buried in the ruins. There would be no resurrection. When I thought of Manderley in my waking hours I would not be bitter. I should think of it as it might have been, could I have lived there without fear. I should remember the rose-garden in summer, and the birds that sang at dawn. Tea under the chestnut tree, and the murmur of the sea coming up to us from the lawns below.

I would think of the blown lilac, and the Happy Valley. These things were permanent, they could not be dissolved. They were memories that cannot hurt. All this I resolved in my dream, while the clouds lay across the face of the moon, for like most sleepers I knew that I dreamed. In reality I lay many hundred miles away in an alien land, and would wake, before many seconds had passed, in the bare little hotel bedroom, comforting in its very lack of atmosphere. I would sigh a moment, stretch myself and turn, and opening my eyes, be bewildered at that glittering sun, that hard, clean sky, so different from the soft moonlight of my dream. The day would lie before us both, long no doubt, and uneventful, but fraught with a certain stillness, a dear tranquillity we had not known before. We would not talk of Manderley, I would not tell my dream. For Manderley was ours no longer. Manderley was no more.

CHAPTER TWO

We can never go back again, that much is certain. The past is still too close to us. The things we have tried to forget and put behind us would stir again, and that sense of fear, of furtive unrest, struggling at length to blind unreasoning panic—now mercifully stilled, thank God—might in some manner unforeseen become a living companion, as it had been before.

He is wonderfully patient and never complains, not even when he remembers . . . which happens, I think, rather more often than he would have me know.

I can tell by the way he will look lost and puzzled suddenly, all expression dying away from his dear face as though swept clean by an unseen hand, and in its place a mask will form, a sculptured thing, formal and cold, beautiful still but lifeless. He will fall to smoking cigarette after cigarette, not bothering to extinguish them, and the glowing stubs will lie around on the ground like petals. He will talk quickly and eagerly about nothing at all, snatching at any subject as a panacea to pain. I believe there is a theory that men and women emerge finer and stronger after suffering, and that to advance in this or any world we must endure ordeal by fire. This we have done in full measure, ironic though it seems. We have both known fear, and loneliness, and very great distress. I suppose sooner or later in the life of everyone comes a moment of trial. We all of us have our particular devil who rides us and torments us, and we must give battle in the end. We have conquered ours, or so we believe.

The devil does not ride us any more. We have come through our crisis, not unscathed of course. His premonition of disaster was correct from the beginning; and like a ranting actress in an indifferent play, I might say that we have paid for freedom. But I have had enough melodrama in this life, and would willingly give my five senses if they could ensure us our present peace and security. Happiness is not a possession to be prized, it is a quality of thought, a state of mind. Of course we have our moments of depression; but there are other moments too, when time, unmeasured by the clock, runs on into eternity and, catching his smile, I know we are together, we march in unison, no clash of thought or of opinion makes a barrier between us.

We have no secrets now from one another. All things are shared. Granted that our little hotel is dull, and the food indifferent, and that day after day dawns very much the same, yet we would not have it otherwise. We should meet too many of the people he knows in any of the big hotels. We both appreciate simplicity, and if we are sometimes bored—well, boredom is a pleasing antidote to fear. We live very much by routine, and I—I have developed a genius for reading aloud. The only time I have known him show impatience is when the postman lags, for it means we must wait another day before the arrival of our English mail. We have tried wireless, but the noise is such an irritant, and we prefer to store up our excitement; the result of a cricket match played many days ago means much to us.

Oh, the Test matches that have saved us from ennui, the boxing bouts, even the billiard scores. Finals of schoolboy sports, dog racing, strange little competitions in the remoter counties, all these are grist to our hungry mill. Sometimes old copies of the *Field* come my way, and I am transported from this indifferent island to the realities of an English spring. I read of chalk streams, of the mayfly, of sorrel growing in green meadows, of rooks circling above the woods as they used to do at Manderley. The smell of wet earth comes to me from those thumbed and tattered pages, the sour tang of moorland peat, the feel of soggy moss spattered white in places by a heron's droppings.

Once there was an article on wood pigeons, and as I read it aloud it seemed to me that once again I was in the deep woods at Manderley, with pigeons fluttering above my head. I heard their soft, complacent call, so comfortable and cool on a hot summer's afternoon, and there would be no disturbing of their peace until Jasper came loping through the undergrowth to find me, his damp muzzle questing the ground. Like old ladies caught at their ablutions, the pigeons would flutter from their hiding-place, shocked into silly agitation, and, making a monstrous to-do with their wings, streak away from us above the tree-tops, and so out of sight and sound. When they were gone a new silence would come upon the place, and I—uneasy for no known reason—would realise that the sun no longer wove a pattern on the rustling leaves, that the branches had grown darker, the shadows longer; and back at the house there would be fresh raspberries for tea. I would rise from my bed of bracken then, shaking the feathery dust of last year's leaves from my skirt and whistling to Jasper, set off towards the house, despising myself even as I walked for my hurrying feet, my one swift glance behind.

How strange that an article on wood pigeons could so recall the past and make me falter as I read aloud. It was the grey look on his face that made me stop abruptly, and turn the pages until I found a paragraph on cricket, very practical and dull—Middlesex batting on a dry wicket at the Oval and piling up interminable dreary runs. How I blessed those stolid, flannelled figures, for in a few minutes his face had settled back into repose, the colour had returned, and he was deriding the Surrey bowling in healthy irritation.

We were saved a retreat into the past, and I had learnt my lesson. Read English news, yes, and English sport, politics and pomposity, but in future keep the things that hurt to myself alone. They can be my secret indulgence. Colour and scent and sound, rain and the lapping of water, even the mists of autumn and the smell of the flood tide, these are memories of Manderley that will not be denied. Some people have a vice of reading Bradshaws. They plan innumerable journeys across country for the fun of linking up impossible connections. My hobby is less tedious, if as strange. I am a mine of information on the English countryside. I know the name of every owner of every British moor, yes—and their tenants too. I know how many grouse are killed, how many partridge, how many head of deer. I know where trout are rising, and where the salmon leap. I attend all meets, I follow every run. Even the names of those who walk hound puppies are familiar to me. The state of the crops, the price of fat cattle, the mysterious ailments of swine, I relish them all. A poor pastime, perhaps, and not a very intellectual one, but I breathe the air of England as I read, and can face this glittering sky with greater courage.

The scrubby vineyards and the crumbling stones become things of no account, for if I wish I can give rein to my imagination, and pick foxgloves and pale campions from a wet, streaking hedge.

Poor whims of fancy, tender and un-harsh. They are the enemy to bitterness and regret, and sweeten this exile we have brought upon ourselves.

Because of them I can enjoy my afternoon, and return, smiling and refreshed, to face the little ritual of our tea. The order never varies. Two slices of bread-and-butter each, and China tea. What a hide-bound couple we must seem, clinging to custom because we did so in England. Here, on this clean balcony, white and impersonal with centuries of sun, I think of half-past four at Manderley, and the table drawn before the library fire. The door flung open, punctual to the minute, and the performance, never-varying, of the laying of the tea, the silver tray, the kettle, the snowy cloth. While Jasper, his spaniel ears a-droop, feigns indifference to the arrival of the cakes. That feast was laid before us always, and yet we ate so little.

Those dripping crumpets, I can see them now. Tiny crisp wedges of toast, and piping-hot, flaky scones. Sandwiches of unknown nature, mysteriously flavoured and quite delectable, and that very special gingerbread. Angel cake, that melted in the mouth, and his rather stodgier companion, bursting with peel and raisins. There was enough food there to keep a starving family for a week. I never knew what happened to it all, and the waste used to worry me sometimes.

But I never dared ask Mrs. Danvers what she did about it. She would have looked at me in scorn, smiling that freezing, superior smile of hers, and I can imagine her saying: "There were never any complaints when Mrs. de Winter was alive." Mrs. Danvers. I wonder what she is doing now. She and Favell. I think it was the expression on her face that gave me my first feeling of unrest. Instinctively I thought, "She is comparing me to Rebecca"; and sharp as a sword the shadow came between us. . . .

Well, it is over now, finished and done with. I ride no more tormented, and both of us are free. Even my faithful Jasper has gone to the happy hunting grounds, and Manderley is no more. It lies like an empty shell amidst the tangle of the deep woods, even as I saw it in my dream. A multitude of weeds, a colony of birds. Sometimes perhaps a tramp will wander there, seeking shelter from a sudden shower of rain and, if he is stout-hearted, he may walk there with impunity. But your timid fellow, your nervous poacher—the woods of Manderley are not for him. He might stumble upon the little cottage in the cove and he would not be happy beneath its tumbled roof, the thin rain beating a tattoo. There might linger there still a certain atmosphere of stress. . . . That corner in the drive, too, where the trees encroach upon the gravel is not a place in which to pause, not after the sun has set. When the leaves rustle, they sound very much like the stealthy movement of a woman in evening dress, and when they shiver suddenly, and fall, and scatter away along the ground, they might be the patter, patter, of a woman's hurrying footstep, and the mark in the gravel the imprint of a high-heeled satin shoe.

It is when I remember these things that I turn with relief to the prospect from our balcony. No shadows steal upon this hard glare, the stony vineyards shimmer in the sun and the bougainvillaea is white with dust. I may one day look upon it with affection. At the moment it inspires me, if not with love, at least with confidence. And confidence is a quality I prize, although it has come to me a little late in the day. I suppose it is his dependence upon me that has made me bold at last. At any rate I have lost my diffidence, my timidity, my shyness with strangers. I am very different from that self who drove to Manderley for the first time, hopeful and eager, handicapped by a rather desperate gaucherie and filled with an intense desire to please. It was my lack of poise of course that made such a bad impression on people like Mrs. Danvers. What must I have seemed like after Rebecca? I can see myself now, memory spanning the years like a bridge, with straight, bobbed hair and youthful, unpowdered face, dressed in an ill-fitting coat and skirt and a jumper of my own creation, trailing in the wake of Mrs. Van Hopper like a shy, uneasy colt. She would precede me in to lunch, her short body ill-balanced upon tottering, high heels, her fussy, frilly blouse a compliment to her large bosom and swinging hips, her new hat pierced with a monster quill aslant upon her head, exposing a wide expanse of forehead bare as a schoolboy's knee. One hand carried a gigantic bag, the kind that holds passports, engagement diaries, and bridge scores, while the other hand toyed with that inevitable lorgnette, the enemy to other people's privacy.

She would make for her usual table in the corner of the restaurant, close to the window, and lifting her lorgnette to her small pig's eyes survey the scene to the right and left of her, then she would let the lorgnette fall at length upon its black ribbon and utter a little exclamation of disgust: "Not a single well-known personality, I shall tell the management they must make a reduction on my bill. What do they think I come here for? To look at the page-boys?" And she would summon the waiter to her side, her voice sharp and staccato, cutting the air like a saw.

How different the little restaurant where we eat to-day to that vast dining-room, ornate and ostentatious, the hotel Côte d'Azur at Monte Carlo; and how different my present companion, his steady, well-shaped hands peeling a mandarin in quiet, methodical fashion, looking up now and again from his task to smile at me, compared to Mrs. Van Hopper, her fat, bejewelled fingers questing a plate heaped high with ravioli, her eyes darting suspiciously from her plate to mine for fear I should have made the better choice. She need not have disturbed herself, for the waiter, with the uncanny swiftness of his kind, had long sensed my position as inferior and subservient to hers, and had placed before me a plate of ham and tongue that somebody had sent back to the cold buffet half-an-hour before as badly carved. Odd, that resentment of servants, and their obvious impatience. I remember staying once with Mrs. Van Hopper in a country house, and the maid never answered my timid bell, or brought up my shoes, and early morning tea, stone cold, was dumped outside my bedroom door. It was the same at the Côte d'Azur, though to a lesser degree, and sometimes the studied indifference turned to familiarity, smirking and offensive, which made buying stamps from the reception clerk an ordeal I would avoid. How young and inexperienced I must have seemed, and how I felt it, too. One was too sensitive, too raw, there were thorns and pin-pricks in so many words that in reality fell lightly on the air.

I remember well that plate of ham and tongue. It was dry, unappetising, cut in a wedge from the outside, but I had not the courage to refuse it. We ate in silence, for Mrs. Van Hopper liked to concentrate on food, and I could tell by the way the sauce ran down her chin that her dish of ravioli pleased her.

It was not a sight that engendered into me great appetite for my own cold choice, and looking away from her I saw that the table next to ours, left vacant for three days, was to be occupied once more. The maître d'hôtel, with the particular bow reserved for his more special patrons, was ushering the new arrival to his place.

Mrs. Van Hopper put down her fork, and reached for her lorgnette. I blushed for her while she stared, and the new-comer, unconscious of her interest, cast a wondering eye over the menu. Then Mrs. Van Hopper folded her lorgnette with a snap, and leant across the table to me, her small eyes bright with excitement, her voice a shade too loud.

"It's Max de Winter," she said, "the man who owns Manderley. You've heard of it, of course. He looks ill, doesn't he? They say he can't get over his wife's death. . . ."

CHAPTER THREE

I wonder what my life would be to-day, if Mrs. Van Hopper had not been a snob.

Funny to think that the course of my existence hung like a thread upon that quality of hers. Her curiosity was a disease, almost a mania. At first I had been shocked, wretchedly embarrassed; I would feel like a whipping boy who must bear his master's pains when I watched people laugh behind her back, leave a room hurriedly upon her entrance, or even vanish behind a Service door on the corridor upstairs. For many years now she had come to the hotel Côte d'Azur, and, apart from bridge, her one pastime, which was notorious by now in Monte Carlo, was to claim visitors of distinction as her friends had she but seen them once at the other end of the post-office. Somehow she would manage to introduce herself, and before her victim had scented danger she had proffered an invitation to her suite. Her method of attack was so downright and sudden that there was seldom opportunity to escape. At the Côte d'Azur she staked a claim upon a certain sofa in the lounge, midway between the reception hall and the passage to the restaurant, and she would have her coffee there after luncheon and dinner, and all who came and went must pass her by. Sometimes she would employ me as a bait to draw her prey, and, hating my errand, I would be sent across the lounge with a verbal message, the loan of a book or paper, the address of some shop or other, the sudden discovery of a mutual friend. It seemed as though notables must be fed to her, much as invalids are spooned their jelly; and though titles were preferred by her, any face once seen in a social paper served as well. Names scattered in a gossip column, authors, artists, actors and their kind, even the mediocre ones, as long as she had learnt of them in print.

I can see her as though it were but yesterday, on that unforgettable afternoon—never mind how many years ago—when she sat at
her favourite sofa in the lounge, debating her method of attack. I
could tell by her abrupt manner, and the way she tapped her lorgnette
against her teeth, that she was questing possibilities. I knew, too,
when she had missed the sweet and rushed through dessert, that she
had wished to finish luncheon before the new arrival and so install
herself where he must pass. Suddenly she turned to me, her small
eyes alight.

"Go upstairs quickly and find that letter from my nephew. You remember, the one written on his honeymoon, with the snapshot. Bring
it down to me right away."

I saw then that her plans were formed, and the nephew was to be
the means of introduction. Not for the first time I resented the part
that I must play in her schemes. Like a juggler's assistant I produced
the props, then silent and attentive I waited on my cue. This new-
comer would not welcome intrusion, I felt certain of that. In the little
I had learnt of him at luncheon, a smattering of hearsay garnered by
her ten months ago from the daily papers and stored in her memory
for future use, I could imagine, in spite of my youth and inexperience
of the world, that he would resent this sudden bursting in upon his
solitude. Why he should have chosen to come to the Côte d'Azur at
Monte Carlo was not our concern, his problems were his own, and
anyone but Mrs. Van Hopper would have understood. Tact was a
quality unknown to her, discretion too, and because gossip was the
breath of life to her this stranger must be served for her dissection. I
found the letter in a pigeon-hole in her desk, and hesitated a moment
before going down again to the lounge. It seemed to me, rather sense-
lessly, that I was allowing him a few more moments of seclusion.

I wished I had the courage to go by the Service staircase and so
by roundabout way to the restaurant, and there warn him of the am-
bush. Convention was too strong for me though, nor did I know how
I should frame my sentence. There was nothing for it but to sit in my
usual place beside Mrs. Van Hopper while she, like a large, complacent spider, spun her wide net of tedium about the stranger's person.

I had been longer than I thought, for when I returned to the
lounge I saw he had already left the dining-room, and she, fearful of
losing him, had not waited for the letter, but had risked a bare-faced
introduction on her own. He was even now sitting beside her on the
sofa. I walked across to them, and gave her the letter without a word.
He rose to his feet at once, while Mrs. Van Hopper, flushed with her
success, waved a vague hand in my direction and mumbled my name.

"Mr. de Winter is having coffee with us, go and ask the waiter for another cup," she said, her tone just casual enough to warn him of my footing. It meant I was a youthful thing and unimportant, and that there was no need to include me in the conversation. She always spoke in that tone when she wished to be impressive, and her method of introduction was a form of self-protection, for once I had been taken for her daughter, an acute embarrassment for us both. This abruptness showed that I could safely be ignored, and women would give me a brief nod which served as a greeting and a dismissal in one, while men, with large relief, would realise they could sink back into a comfortable chair without offending courtesy.

It was a surprise, therefore, to find that this new-comer remained standing on his feet, and it was he who made a signal to the waiter.

"I'm afraid I must contradict you," he said to her, "you are both having coffee with me"; and before I knew what had happened he was sitting in my usual hard chair, and I was on the sofa beside Mrs. Van Hopper.

For a moment she looked annoyed, this was not what she had intended, but she soon composed her face, and thrusting her large self between me and the table she leant forward to his chair, talking eagerly and loudly, fluttering the letter in her hand.

"You know I recognised you just as soon as you walked into the restaurant," she said, "and I thought, 'Why, there's Mr. de Winter, Billy's friend, I simply must show him those snaps of Billy and his bride taken on their honeymoon,' and here they are. There's Dora. Isn't she just adorable? That little, slim waist, those great big eyes. Here they are sun-bathing at Palm Beach. Billy is crazy about her, you can imagine. He had not met her of course when he gave that party at Claridge's, and where I saw you first. But I dare say you don't remember an old woman like me?"

This with a provocative glance, and a gleam of teeth.

"On the contrary I remember you very well," he said, and before she could trap him into a resurrection of their first meeting he had handed her his cigarette case, and the business of lighting-up stalled her for the moment. "I don't think I should care for Palm Beach," he said, blowing the match, and glancing at him I thought how unreal he would look against a Florida background. He belonged to a walled city of the fifteenth century, a city of narrow, cobbled streets, and thin spires, where the inhabitants wore pointed shoes and worsted hose. His face was arresting, sensitive, medieval in some strange inexplicable way, and I was reminded of a portrait seen in a gallery I had forgotten where, of a certain Gentleman Unknown. Could one but rob him of his English tweeds, and put him in black, with lace at his throat and wrists, he would stare down at us in our new world from a long distant past—a past where men walked cloaked at night, and stood in the shadow of old doorways, a past of narrow stairways and dim dungeons, a past of whispers in the dark, of shimmering rapier blades, of silent, exquisite courtesy.

I wished I could remember the Old Master who had painted that portrait. It stood in a corner of the gallery, and the eyes followed one from the dusky frame. . . .

They were talking though, and I had lost the thread of conversation. "No, not even twenty years ago," he was saying. "That sort of thing has never amused me."

I heard Mrs. Van Hopper give her fat, complacent laugh. "If Billy had a home like Manderley he would not want to play around in Palm Beach," she said. "I'm told it's like fairy-land, there's no other word for it."

She paused, expecting him to smile, but he went on smoking his cigarette, and I noticed, faint as gossamer, the line between his brows.

"I've seen pictures of it, of course," she persisted, "and it looks perfectly enchanting. I remember Billy telling me it had all those big places beat for beauty. I wonder you can ever bear to leave it."

His silence now was painful, and would have been patent to anyone else, but she ran on like a clumsy goat, trampling and trespassing on land that was preserved, and I felt the colour flood my face, dragged with her as I was into humiliation.

"Of course you Englishmen are all the same about your homes," she said, her voice becoming louder and louder, "you depreciate them so as not to seem proud. Isn't there a minstrels' gallery at Manderley, and some very valuable portraits?" She turned to me by way of explanation. "Mr. de Winter is so modest he won't admit to it, but I believe that lovely home of his has been in the family's possession since the Conquest. They say that minstrels' gallery is a gem. I suppose your ancestors often entertained royalty at Manderley, Mr. de Winter?"

This was more than I had hitherto endured, even from her, but the swift lash of his reply was unexpected. "Not since Ethelred," he said, "the one who was called Unready. In fact, it was while staying with my family that the name was given him. He was invariably late for dinner."

She deserved it, of course, and I waited for her change of face, but incredible as it may seem his words were lost on her, and I was left to writhe in her stead, feeling like a child that had been smacked.

"Is that really so?" she blundered. "I'd no idea. My history is very shaky, and the kings of England always muddled me. How interesting though. I must write and tell my daughter, she's a great scholar."

There was a pause, and I felt the colour flood into my face. I was too young, that was the trouble. Had I been older I would have caught his eye and smiled, her unbelievable behaviour making a bond between us; but as it was I was stricken into shame, and endured one of the frequent agonies of youth.

I think he realised my distress, for he leant forward in his chair and spoke to me, his voice gentle, asking if I would have more coffee, and when I refused and shook my head I felt that his eyes were still upon me, puzzled, reflective. He was pondering my exact relationship to her, and wondering whether he must bracket us together in futility.

"What do you think of Monte Carlo, or don't you think of it at all?" he said. This including of me in the conversation found me at my worst, the raw ex-schoolgirl, red-elbowed and lanky-haired, and I said something obvious and idiotic about the place being artificial, but before I could finish my halting sentence Mrs. Van Hopper interrupted.

"She's spoilt, Mr. de Winter, that's her trouble. Most girls would give their eyes for the chance of seeing Monte."

"Wouldn't that rather defeat the purpose?" he said smiling.

She shrugged her shoulders, blowing a great cloud of cigarette into the air. I don't think she understood him for a moment. "I'm faithful to Monte," she told him; "the English winter gets me down, and my constitution just won't stand it. What brings you here? You're not one of the regulars. Are you going to play 'Chemy,' or have you brought your golf-clubs?"

"I have not made up my mind," he said, "I came away in rather a hurry."

His own words must have jolted a memory, for his face clouded again and he frowned very slightly. She babbled on, impervious. "Of course you miss the fogs at Manderley, it's quite another matter; the west country must be delightful in the spring." He reached for the ash-tray, squashing his cigarette, and I noticed the subtle change in his eyes, the indefinable something that lingered there, momentarily, and I felt I had looked upon something personal to himself with which I had no concern.

"Yes," he said shortly, "Manderley was looking its best."

A silence fell upon us, during a moment or two, a silence that brought something of discomfort in its train, and stealing a glance at him I was reminded more than ever of my Gentleman Unknown who, cloaked and secret, walked a corridor by night. Mrs. Van Hopper's voice pierced my dream like an electric bell.

"I suppose you know a crowd of people here, though I must say Monte is very dull this winter. One sees so few well-known faces. The Duke of Middlesex is here in his yacht, but I haven't been aboard yet." She never had, to my knowledge. "You know Nell Middlesex of course," she went on. "What a charmer she is. They always say that second child isn't his, but I don't believe it. People will say anything, won't they, when a woman is attractive? And she is so very lovely. Tell me, is it true the Caxton-Hyslop marriage is not a success?" She ran on, through a tangled fringe of gossip, never seeing that these names were alien to him, they meant nothing, and that as she prattled unaware he grew colder and more silent. Never for a moment did he interrupt or glance at his watch, it was as though he had set himself a standard of behaviour, since the original lapse when he had made a fool of her in front of me, and clung to it grimly rather than offend again. It was a page-boy in the end who released him, with the news that a dressmaker awaited Mrs. Van Hopper in the suite.

He got up at once, pushing back his chair. "Don't let me keep you," he said. "Fashions change so quickly nowadays they may even have altered by the time you get upstairs."

The sting did not touch her, she accepted it as a pleasantry. "It's so delightful to have run into you like this, Mr. de Winter," she said, as we went towards the lift; "now I've been brave enough to break the ice I hope I shall see something of you. You must come and have a drink some time in the suite. I may have one or two people coming in tomorrow evening. Why not join us?" I turned away so that I should not watch him search for an excuse.

"I'm so sorry," he said, "to-morrow I am probably driving to Sospel, I'm not sure when I shall get back."

Reluctantly she left it, but we still hovered at the entrance to the lift.

"I hope they've given you a good room, the place is half empty, so if you are uncomfortable mind you make a fuss. Your valet has unpacked for you I suppose?" This familiarity was excessive, even for her, and I caught a glimpse of his expression.

"I don't possess one," he said quietly, "perhaps you would like to do it for me?"

This time his shaft had found its mark, for she reddened, and laughed a little awkwardly.

"Why, I hardly think . . ." she began, and then suddenly, and unbelievably she turned upon me. "Perhaps you could make yourself useful to Mr. de Winter, if he wants anything done. You're a capable child in many ways."

There was a momentary pause, while I stood stricken, waiting for his answer. He looked down at us, mocking, faintly sardonic, a ghost of a smile on his lips.

"A charming suggestion," he said, "but I cling to the family motto. He travels the fastest who travels alone. Perhaps you have not heard of it."

And without waiting for her answer he turned and left us.

"What a funny thing," said Mrs. Van Hopper, as we went upstairs in the lift, "do you suppose that sudden departure was a form of humour? Men do such extraordinary things. I remember a well-known writer once who used to dart down the Service staircase whenever he saw me coming. I suppose he had a penchant for me and wasn't sure of himself. However, I was younger then."

The lift stopped with a jerk. We arrived at our floor. The page-boy flung open the gates. "By-the-way, dear," she said, as we walked along the corridor, "don't think I mean to be unkind, but you put yourself just a teeny bit forward this afternoon. Your efforts to monopolise the conversation quite embarrassed me, and I'm sure it did him. Men loathe that sort of thing."

I said nothing. There seemed no possible reply. "Oh, come, don't sulk," she laughed, and shrugged her shoulders; "after all, I am responsible for your behaviour here, and surely you can accept advice from a woman old enough to be your mother. Eh bien, Blaize, je viens . . ." and humming a tune she went into the bedroom where the dressmaker was waiting for her.

I knelt on the window seat and looked out upon the afternoon. The sun shone very brightly still, and there was a gay high wind. In half-an-hour we should be sitting to our bridge, the windows tightly closed, the central heating turned to the full. I thought of the ashtrays I would have to clear, and how the squashed stubs, stained with lipstick, would sprawl in company with discarded chocolate creams. Bridge does not come easily to a mind brought up on Snap and Happy Families; besides, it bored her friends to play with me.

I felt my youthful presence put a curb upon their conversation, much as a parlour-maid does until the arrival of dessert, and they could not fling themselves so easily into the melting-pot of scandal and insinuation. Her men-friends would assume a sort of forced heartiness, and ask me jocular questions about history or painting, guessing I had not long left school and that this would be my only form of conversation.

I sighed, and turned away from the window. The sun was so full of promise, and the sea was whipped white with a merry wind. I thought of that corner in Monaco which I had passed a day or two ago, and where a crooked house leant to a cobbled square. High up in the tumbled roof there was a window, narrow as a slit. It might have held a presence medieval; and, reaching to the desk for pencil and paper, I sketched in fancy with an absent mind a profile, pale and aquiline. A sombre eye, a high-bridged nose, a scornful upper lip. And I added a pointed beard and lace at the throat, as the painter had done, long ago in a different time.

Someone knocked at the door, and the lift-boy came in with a note in his hand. "Madame is in the bedroom," I told him, but he shook his head and said it was for me. I opened it, and found a single sheet of note-paper inside, with a few words written in an unfamiliar hand.

"Forgive me. I was very rude this afternoon." That was all. No signature, and no beginning. But my name was on the envelope, and spelt correctly, an unusual thing.

"Is there any answer?" asked the boy.

I looked up from the scrawled words. "No," I said. "No, there isn't any answer."

When he had gone I put the note away in my pocket, and turned once more to my pencil drawing, but for no known reason it did not please me any more, the face was stiff and lifeless, and the lace collar and the beard were like props in a charade.

CHAPTER FOUR

The morning after the bridge party Mrs. Van Hopper woke with a sore throat and a temperature of a hundred and two. I rang up her doctor, who came round at once and diagnosed the usual influenza. "You are to stay in bed until I allow you to get up," he told her; "I don't like the sound of that heart of yours, and it won't get better unless you keep perfectly quiet and still. I should prefer," he went on, turning to me, "that Mrs. Van Hopper had a trained nurse. You can't possibly lift her. It will only be for a fortnight or so."

I thought this rather absurd, and protested, but to my surprise she agreed with him. I think she enjoyed the fuss it would create, the sympathy of the people, the visits and messages from friends, and the arrival of flowers. Monte Carlo had begun to bore her, and this little illness would make a distraction.

The nurse would give her injections, and a light massage, and she would have a diet. I left her quite happy after the arrival of the nurse, propped up on pillows with a falling temperature, her best bed-jacket round her shoulders and be-ribboned boudoir cap upon her head. Rather ashamed of my light heart, I telephoned her friends, putting off the small party she had arranged for the evening, and went down to the restaurant for lunch, a good half hour before our usual time. I expected the room to be empty, nobody lunched generally before one o'clock. It was empty, except for the table next to ours. This was a contingency for which I was unprepared. I thought he had gone to Sospel. No doubt he was lunching early because he hoped to avoid us at one o'clock. I was already half-way across the room and could not go back. I had not seen him since we disappeared in the lift the day

before, for wisely he had avoided dinner in the restaurant, possibly
for the same reason that he lunched early now.

It was a situation for which I was ill-trained. I wished I was older,
different. I went to our table, looking straight before me, and immediately paid the penalty of gaucherie by knocking over the vase of stiff
anemones as I unfolded my napkin. The water soaked the cloth, and
ran down on to my lap. The waiter was at the other end of the room,
nor had he seen. In a second though my neighbour was by my side,
dry napkin in hand.

"You can't sit at a wet tablecloth," he said brusquely, "it will put
you off your food. Get out of the way."

He began to mop the cloth, while the waiter, seeing the distur-
bance, came swiftly to the rescue.

"I don't mind," I said, "it doesn't matter a bit. I'm all alone."

He said nothing, and then the waiter arrived and whipped away
the vase and the sprawling flowers.

"Leave that," he said suddenly, "and lay another place at my
table. Mademoiselle will have luncheon with me."

I looked up in confusion. "Oh, no," I said, "I couldn't possibly."

"Why not?" he said.

I tried to think of an excuse. I knew he did not want to lunch
with me. It was his form of courtesy. I should ruin his meal. I determined to be bold and speak the truth.

"Please," I begged, "don't be polite. It's very kind of you but I
shall be quite all right if the waiter just wipes the cloth."

"But I'm not being polite," he insisted, "I would like you to have
luncheon with me. Even if you had not knocked over that vase so
clumsily I should have asked you." I suppose my face told him my
doubt, for he smiled. "You don't believe me," he said, "never mind,
come and sit down. We needn't talk to each other unless we feel like
it."

We sat down, and he gave me the menu, leaving me to choose,
and went on with his *hors d'oeuvre* as though nothing had happened.

His quality of detachment was peculiar to himself, and I knew
that we might continue thus, without speaking, throughout the meal
and it would not matter. There would be no sense of strain. He would
not ask me questions on history.

"What's happened to your friend?" he said. I told him about the
influenza. "I'm so sorry," he said, and then, after pausing a moment,
"you got my note I suppose. I felt very much ashamed of myself. My
manners were atrocious. The only excuse I can make is that I've be-

come boorish through living alone. That's why it's so kind of you to lunch with me to-day."

"You weren't rude," I said, "at least, not the sort of rudeness she would understand. That curiosity of hers—she does not mean to be offensive, but she does it to everyone. That is, everyone of importance."

"I ought to be flattered then," he said, "why should she consider me of any importance?" I hesitated a moment before replying.

"I think because of Manderley," I said.

He did not answer, and I was aware again of that feeling of discomfort, as though I had trespassed on forbidden ground. I wondered why it was that this home of his, known to so many people by hearsay, even to me, should so inevitably silence him, making as it were a barrier between him and others.

We ate for a while without talking, and I thought of a picture post-card I had bought once at a village shop, when on holiday as a child in the west country. It was the painting of a house, crudely done of course and highly coloured, but even those faults could not destroy the symmetry of the building, the wide stone steps before the terrace, the green lawns stretching to the sea. I paid twopence for the painting—half my weekly pocket money—and then asked the wrinkled shop woman what it was meant to be. She looked astonished at my ignorance.

"That's Manderley," she said, and I remember coming out of the shop feeling rebuffed, yet hardly wiser than before.

Perhaps it was the memory of this post-card, lost long ago in some forgotten book, that made me sympathise with his defensive attitude. He resented Mrs. Van Hopper and her like with their intruding questions. Maybe there was something inviolate about Manderley that made it a place apart, it would not bear discussion. I could imagine her tramping through the rooms, perhaps paying sixpence for admission, ripping the quietude with her sharp, staccato laugh. Our minds must have run in the same channel for he began to talk about her.

"Your friend," he began, "she is very much older than you. Is she a relation? Have you known her long?" I saw he was still puzzled by us.

"She's not really a friend," I told him, "she's an employer. She's training me to be a thing called a companion, and she pays me ninety pounds a year."

"I did not know one could buy companionship," he said; "it sounds a primitive idea. Rather like the eastern slave market."

"I looked up the word companion once in the dictionary," I admitted, "and it said 'a companion is a friend of the bosom.' "

"You haven't much in common with her," he said.

He laughed, looking quite different, younger somehow and less detached. "What do you do it for?" he asked me.

"Ninety pounds is a lot of money to me," I said.

"Haven't you any family?"

"No—they're dead."

"You have a very lovely and unusual name."

"My father was a lovely and unusual person."

"Tell me about him," he said.

I looked at him over my glass of citronade. It was not easy to explain my father, and usually I never talked about him. He was my secret property. Preserved for me alone, much as Manderley was preserved for my neighbour. I had no wish to introduce him casually over a table in a Monte Carlo restaurant.

There was a strange air of unreality about that luncheon, and looking back upon it now it is invested for me with a curious glamour. There was I, so much of a schoolgirl still, who only the day before had sat with Mrs. Van Hopper, prim, silent and subdued, and twenty-four hours afterwards my family history was mine no longer, I shared it with a man I did not know. For some reason I felt impelled to speak, because his eyes followed me in sympathy like the Gentleman Unknown.

My shyness fell away from me, loosening as it did so my reluctant tongue, and out they all came, the little secrets of childhood, the pleasures and the pains. It seemed to me as though he understood, from my poor description, something of the vibrant personality that had been my father's, and something too of the love my mother had for him, making it a vital, living force, with a spark of divinity about it, so much that when he died that desperate winter, struck down by pneumonia, she lingered behind him for five short weeks and stayed no more. I remember pausing, a little breathless, a little dazed. The restaurant was filled now with people who chatted and laughed to an orchestral background and a clatter of plates, and glancing at the clock above the door I saw that it was two o'clock. We had been sitting there an hour and a half, and the conversation had been mine alone.

I tumbled down into reality, hot-handed and self-conscious, with my face aflame, and began to stammer my apologies. He would not listen to me.

"I told you at the beginning of lunch you had a lovely and unusual name," he said. "I shall go further, if you will forgive me, and say that it becomes you as well as it became your father. I've enjoyed this hour with you more than I have enjoyed anything for a very long time. You've taken me out of myself, out of despondency and intro-spection, both of which have been my devils for a year."

I looked at him, and believed he spoke the truth, he seemed less fettered than he had been before, more modern, more human, he was not hemmed in by shadows.

"You know," he said, "we've got a bond in common, you and I. We are both alone in the world. Oh, I've got a sister, though we don't see much of each other, and an ancient grandmother whom I pay duty visits to three times a year, but neither of them make for com-panionship. I shall have to congratulate Mrs. Van Hopper. You're cheap at ninety pounds a year."

"You forget," I said, "you have a home and I have none."

The moment I spoke I regretted my words, for the secret, in-scrutable look came back in his eyes again, and once again I suffered the intolerable discomfort that floods one after lack of tact. He bent his head to light a cigarette, and did not reply immediately.

"An empty house can be as lonely as a full hotel," he said at length. "The trouble is that it is less impersonal." He hesitated, and for a moment I thought he was going to talk of Manderley at last, but something held him back, some phobia that struggled to the surface of his mind and won supremacy, for he blew out his match and his flash of confidence at the same time.

"So the friend of the bosom has a holiday?" he said, on a level plane again, an easy camaraderie between us. "What does she pro-pose to do with it?"

I thought of the cobbled square in Monaco, and the house with the narrow window. I could be off there by three o'clock with my sketch-book and pencil, and I told him as much, a little shyly per-haps, like all untalented persons with a pet hobby.

"I'll drive you there in the car," he said, and would not listen to protests.

I remembered Mrs. Van Hopper's warning of the night before about putting myself forward, and was embarrassed that he might think my talk of Monaco was a subterfuge to win a lift. It was so bla-tantly the type of thing that she would do herself, and I did not want him to bracket us together. I had already risen in importance from my lunch with him, for as we got up from the table the little maître d'hô-tel rushed forward to pull away my chair. He bowed and smiled—a to-tal change from his usual attitude of indifference—picked up my handkerchief that had fallen on the floor, and hoped 'Mademoiselle had enjoyed her lunch.' Even the page-boy by the swing doors glanced at me with respect. My companion accepted it as natural, of course, he knew nothing of the ill-carved ham of yesterday. I found the change depressing, it made me despise myself. I remembered my father and his scorn of superficial snobbery.

"What are you thinking about?" We were walking along the corridor to the lounge, and looking up I saw his eyes fixed on me in curiosity.

"Has something annoyed you?" he said.

The attentions of the maître d'hôtel had opened up a train of thought, and as we drank our coffee I told him about Blaize, the dressmaker. She had been so pleased when Mrs. Van Hopper had bought three frocks, and I, taking her to the lift afterwards, had pictured her working upon them in her own small salon, behind the stuffy little shop, with a consumptive son wasting upon her sofa. I could see her, with tired eyes, threading needles, and the floor covered with snippets of material.

"Well?" he said smiling, "wasn't your picture true?"

"I don't know," I said, "I never found out." And I told him how I had rung the bell for the lift, and as I had done so she had fumbled in her bag and gave me a note for a hundred francs. "Here," she had whispered, her tone intimate and unpleasant, "I want you to accept this small commission in return for bringing your patron to my shop." When I had refused, scarlet with embarrassment, she had shrugged her shoulders disagreeably. "Just as you like," she had said, "but I assure you it's quite usual. Perhaps you would rather have a frock. Come along to the shop sometime without Madame and I will fix you up without charging you a sou." Somehow, I don't know why, I had been aware of that sick, unhealthy feeling I had experienced as a child when turning the pages of a forbidden book. The vision of the consumptive son faded, and in its stead arose the picture of myself had I been different, pocketing that greasy note with an understanding smile, and perhaps slipping round to Blaize's shop on this my free afternoon and coming away with a frock I had not paid for.

I expected him to laugh, it was a stupid story, I don't know why I told him, but he looked at me thoughtfully as he stirred his coffee.

"I think you've made a big mistake," he said, after a moment.

"In refusing that hundred francs?" I asked, revolted.

"No—good heavens, what do you take me for? I think you've made a mistake in coming here, in joining forces with Mrs. Van Hopper. You are not made for that sort of job. You're too young, for one thing, and too soft. Blaize and her commission, that's nothing. The first of many similar incidents from other Blaizes. You will either have to give in, and become a sort of Blaize yourself, or stay as you are and be broken. Who suggested you take on this thing in the first place?" It seemed natural for him to question me, nor did I mind. It was as though we had known one another for a long time, and had met again after a lapse of years.

"Have you ever thought about the future?" he asked me, "and what this sort of thing will lead to? Supposing Mrs. Van Hopper gets tired of her 'friend of the bosom,' what then?"

I smiled, and told him that I did not mind very much. There would be other Mrs. Van Hoppers, and I was young, and confident, and strong. But even as he spoke I remembered those advertisements seen often in good class magazines where a friendly society demands succour for young women in reduced circumstances; I thought of the type of boarding-house that answers the advertisement and gives temporary shelter, and then I saw myself, useless sketch-book in hand, without qualifications of any kind, stammering replies to stern employment agents. Perhaps I should have accepted Blaize's ten per cent.

"How old are you?" he said, and when I told him he laughed, and got up from his chair. "I know that age, it's a particularly obstinate one, and a thousand bogies won't make you fear the future. A pity we can't change over. Go upstairs and put your hat on, and I'll have the car brought round."

As he watched me into the lift I thought of yesterday, Mrs. Van Hopper's chattering tongue, and his cold courtesy. I had ill-judged him, he was neither hard nor sardonic, he was already my friend of many years, the brother I had never possessed. Mine was a happy mood that afternoon, and I remember it well. I can see the rippled sky, fluffy with cloud, and the white-whipped sea. I can feel again the wind on my face, and hear my laugh, and his that echoed it. It was not the Monte Carlo I had known, or perhaps the truth was that it pleased me better. There was a glamour about it that had not been there before. I must have looked upon it before with dull eyes. The harbour was a dancing thing, with fluttering paper boats, and the sailors on the quay were jovial, smiling fellows, merry as the wind. We passed the yacht, beloved of Mrs. Van Hopper because of its ducal owner, and snapped our fingers at the glistening brass, and looked at one another and laughed again. I can remember as though I wore it still my comfortable, ill-fitting flannel suit, and how the skirt was lighter than the coat through harder wear. My shabby hat, too broad about the brim, and my low-heeled shoes, fastened with a single strap. A pair of gauntlet gloves clutched in a grubby hand. I had never looked more youthful, I had never felt so old. Mrs. Van Hopper and her influenza did not exist for me. The bridge and the cocktail parties were forgotten, and with them my own humble status.

I was a person of importance, I was grown up at last. That girl, who, tortured by shyness, would stand outside the sitting-room door twisting a handkerchief in her hands, while from within came that babble of confused chatter so unnerving to the intruder—she had gone with the wind that afternoon. She was a poor creature, and I thought of her with scorn if I considered her at all.

The wind was too high for sketching, it tore in cheerful gusts around the corner of my cobbled square, and back to the car we went and drove I know not where. The long road climbed the hills, and the car climbed with it, and we circled in the heights like a bird in the air. How different his car to Mrs. Van Hopper's hireling for the season, a square old-fashioned Daimler that took us to Mentone on placid afternoons, when I, sitting on the little seat with my back to the driver, must crane my neck to see the view. This car had the wings of Mercury I thought, for higher yet we climbed, and dangerously fast, and the danger pleased me because it was new to me, because I was young.

I remember laughing aloud, and the laugh being carried by the wind away from me; and, looking at him, I realised he laughed no longer, he was once more silent and detached, the man of yesterday wrapped in his secret self.

I realised, too, that the car could climb no more, we had reached the summit, and below us stretched the way that we had come, precipitous and hollow. He stopped the car, and I could see that the edge of the road bordered a vertical slope that crumbled into vacancy, a fall of perhaps two thousand feet. We got out of the car and looked beneath us. This sobered me at last, I knew that but half the car's length had lain between us and the fall. The sea, like a crinkled chart, spread to the horizon, and lapped the sharp outline of the coast, while the houses were white shells in a rounded grotto, pricked here and there by a great orange sun. We knew another sunlight on our hill, and the silence made it harder, more austere. A change had come upon our afternoon, it was not the thing of gossamer it had been. The wind dropped, and it suddenly grew cold.

When I spoke my voice was far too casual, the silly, nervous voice of someone ill at ease. "Do you know this place?" I said. "Have you been here before?" He looked down at me without recognition, and I realised with a little stab of anxiety that he must have forgotten all about me, perhaps for some considerable time, and that he himself was so lost in the labyrinth of his own unquiet thoughts that I did not exist. He had the face of one who walks in his sleep, and for a wild moment the idea came to me that perhaps he was not normal, not altogether sane. There were people who had trances, I had surely heard of them, and they followed strange laws of which we could know nothing, they obeyed the tangled orders of their own sub-conscious minds. Perhaps he was one of them, and here we were within six foot of death.

"It's getting late, shall we go home?" I said, and my careless tone, my little ineffectual smile would scarcely have deceived a child.

I had misjudged him, of course, there was nothing wrong after all, for as soon as I spoke this second time he came clear of his dream and began to apologise. I had gone white, I suppose, and he had noticed it.

"That was an unforgivable thing for me to do," he said, and taking my arm he pushed me back towards the car, and we climbed in again, and he slammed the door. "Don't be frightened, the turn is far easier than it looks," he said, and while I, sick and giddy, clung to the seat with both hands, he manoeuvred the car gently, very gently, until it faced the sloping road once more.

"Then you have been here before?" I said to him, my sense of strain departing, as the car crept away down the twisting narrow road.

"Yes," he said, and then, after pausing a moment, "but not for many years. I wanted to see if it had changed."

"And has it?" I asked him.

"No," he said. "No, it has not changed."

I wondered what had driven him to this retreat into the past, with me an unconscious witness of his mood. What gulf of years stretched between him and that other time, what deed of thought and action, what difference in temperament? I did not want to know. I wished I had not come.

Down the twisting road we went without a check, without a word, a great ridge of clouds stretched above the setting sun, and the air was cold and clean. Suddenly he began to talk about Manderley. He said nothing of his life there, no word about himself, but he told me how the sun set there, on a spring afternoon, leaving a glow upon the headland. The sea would look like slate, cold still from the long winter, and from the terrace you could hear the ripple of the coming tide washing in the little bay. The daffodils were in bloom, stirring in the evening breeze, golden heads cupped upon lean stalks, and however many you might pick there would be no thinning of the ranks, they were massed like an army, shoulder to shoulder. On a bank below the lawns, crocuses were planted, golden, pink, and mauve, but by this time they would be past their best, dropping and fading, like the pallid snowdrops. The primrose was more vulgar, a homely pleasant creature who appeared in every cranny like a weed. Too early yet for bluebells, their heads were still hidden beneath last year's leaves, but when they came, dwarfing the more humble violet, they choked the very bracken in the woods, and with their colour made a challenge to the sky.

He never would have them in the house, he said. Thrust into vases they became dank and listless, and to see them at their best you must walk in the woods in the morning, about twelve o'clock, when the sun was overhead. They had a smoky, rather bitter smell, as though a wild sap ran in their stalks, pungent and juicy. People who plucked bluebells from the woods were vandals, he had forbidden it at Manderley. Sometimes, driving in the country, he had seen bicyclists with huge bunches strapped before them on the handles, the bloom already fading from the dying heads, the ravaged stalks straggling naked and unclean.

The primrose did not mind it quite so much, although a creature of the wilds it had a leaning towards civilisation, and preened and smiled in a jam-jar in some cottage window without resentment, living quite a week if given water. No wild flowers came in the house at Manderley. He had special cultivated flowers, grown for the house alone, in the walled garden. A rose was one of the few flowers, he said, that looked better picked than growing. A bowl of roses in a drawing-room had a depth of colour and scent they had not possessed in the open. There was something rather blowsy about roses in full bloom, something shallow and raucous, like women with untidy hair. In the house they became mysterious and subtle. He had roses in the house at Manderley for eight months in the year. Did I like syringa, he asked me? There was a tree on the edge of the lawn he could smell from his bedroom window. His sister, who was a hard, rather practical person, used to complain that there were too many scents at Manderley, they made her drunk. Perhaps she was right. He did not care. It was the only form of intoxication that appealed to him. His earliest recollection was of great branches of lilac, standing in white jars, and they filled the house with a wistful, poignant smell.

The little pathway down the valley to the bay had clumps of azalea and rhododendron planted to the left of it, and if you wandered down it on a May evening after dinner it was just as though the shrubs had sweated in the air. You could stoop down and pick a fallen petal, crush it between your fingers, and you had there, in the hollow of your hand, the essence of a thousand scents, unbearable and sweet. All from a curled and crumpled petal. And you came out of the valley, heady and rather dazed, to the hard white shingle of the beach and the still water. A curious, perhaps too sudden contrast....

As he spoke the car became one of many once again, dusk had fallen without my noticing it, and we were in the midst of light and sound in the streets of Monte Carlo. The clatter jagged on my nerves, and the lights were far too brilliant, far too yellow. It was a swift, unwelcome anti-climax.

Soon we would come to the hotel, and I felt for my gloves in the pocket of the car. I found them, and my fingers closed upon a book as well, whose slim covers told of poetry. I peered to read the title as the car slowed down before the door of the hotel. "You can take it and read it if you like," he said, his voice casual and indifferent now that the drive was over, and we were back again, and Manderley was many hundreds of miles distant.

I was glad, and held it tightly with my gloves. I felt I wanted some possession of his, now that the day was finished.

"Hop out," he said, "I must go and put the car away. I shan't see you in the restaurant this evening as I'm dining out. But thank you for to-day."

I went up the hotel steps alone, with all the despondency of a child whose treat is over. My afternoon had spoilt me for the hours that still remained, and I thought how long they would seem until my bed-time, how empty too my supper all alone. Somehow I could not face the bright enquiries of the nurse upstairs, or the possibilities of Mrs. Van Hopper's husky interrogation, so I sat down in the corner of the lounge behind a pillar and ordered tea.

The waiter appeared bored, seeing me alone there was no need for him to press, and anyway it was that dragging time of day, a few minutes after half-past five, when the normal tea is finished and the hour for drinks remote.

Rather forlorn, more than a little dissatisfied, I leant back in my chair and took up the book of poems. The volume was well-worn, well-thumbed, falling open automatically at what must be a much-frequented page.

"I fled Him, down the nights and down the days;
I fled Him, down the arches of the years;
I fled Him, down the labyrinthine ways
Of my own mind; and in the mist of tears
I hid from Him, and under running laughter.
    Up vistaed slopes I sped
    And shot, precipitated
Adown Titanic glooms of chasmed fears,
From those strong feet that followed, followed after."

I felt rather like someone peering through the keyhole of a locked door, and a little furtively I laid the book aside. What hound of heaven had driven him to the high hills this afternoon? I thought of his car, with half a length between it and that drop of two thousand feet, and the blank expression on his face. What footsteps echoed in his mind, what whispers, and what memories, and why, of all poems, must he keep this one in the pocket of his car? I wished he were less remote; and I anything but the creature that I was in my shabby coat and skirt, my broad-brimmed schoolgirl hat.

The sulky waiter brought my tea, and while I ate bread-and-butter dull as sawdust I thought of the pathway through the valley he had described to me this afternoon, the smell of the azaleas, and the white shingle of the bay. If he loved it all so much why did he seek the superficial froth of Monte Carlo? He had told Mrs. Van Hopper he had made no plans, he came away in rather a hurry. And I pictured him running down that pathway in the valley with his own hound of heaven at his heels.

I picked up the book again, and this time it opened at the title-page, and I read the dedication. "Max—from Rebecca. May 17th," written in a curious, slanting hand. A little blob of ink marred the white page opposite, as though the writer, in impatience, had shaken her pen to make the ink flow freely. And then, as it bubbled through the nib, it came a little thick, so that the name Rebecca stood out black and strong, the tall and sloping R dwarfing the other letters.

I shut the book with a snap, and put it away under my gloves; and stretching to a near-by chair, I took up an old copy of *L'Illustration* and turned the pages. There were some fine photographs of the châteaux of the Loire, and an article as well. I read it carefully, referring to the photographs, but when I finished I knew I had not understood a word. It was not Blois with its thin turrets and its spires that stared up at me from the printed page. It was the face of Mrs. Van Hopper in the restaurant the day before, her small pig's eyes darting to the neighbouring table, her fork, heaped high with ravioli, pausing in mid-air.

"An appalling tragedy," she was saying, "the papers were full of it of course. They say he never talks about it, never mentions her name. She was drowned you know, in a bay near Manderley. . . ."

CHAPTER FIVE

I am glad it cannot happen twice, the fever of first love. For it is a fever, and a burden, too, whatever the poets may say. They are not brave, the days when we are twenty-one. They are full of little cowardices, little fears without foundation, and one is so easily bruised, so swiftly wounded, one falls to the first barbed word. Today, wrapped in the complacent armour of approaching middle age, the infinitesimal pricks of day by day brush one but lightly and are soon forgotten, but then—how a careless word would linger, becoming a fiery stigma, and how a look, a glance over a shoulder, branded themselves as things eternal. A denial heralded the thrice crowing of a cock, and an insincerity was like the kiss of Judas. The adult mind can lie with untroubled conscience and a gay composure, but in those days even a small deception scoured the tongue, lashing one against the stake itself.

"What have you been doing this morning?" I can hear her now, propped against her pillows, with all the small irritability of the patient who is not really ill, who has lain in bed too long, and I, reaching to the bedside drawer for the pack of cards, would feel the guilty flush form patches on my neck.

"I've been playing tennis with the professional," I told her, the false words bringing me to panic, even as I spoke, for what if the professional himself should come up to the suite, then, that very afternoon, and bursting in upon her complain that I had missed my lesson now for many days?

"The trouble is with me laid up like this you haven't got enough to do," she said, mashing her cigarette in a jar of cleansing cream, and taking the cards in her hand she mixed them in the deft, irritating shuffle of the inveterate player, shaking them in threes, snapping the backs.

"I don't know what you find to do with yourself all day," she went on, "you never have any sketches to show me, and when I do ask you to do some shopping for me you forget to buy my Taxol. All I can say is that I hope your tennis will improve, it will be useful to you later on. A poor player is a great bore. Do you still serve underhand?" She flipped the Queen of Spades into the pool, and the dark face stared up at me like Jezebel.

"Yes," I said, stung by her question, thinking how just and appropriate her word. It described me well. I was underhand. I had not played tennis with the professional at all, I had not once played since she had lain in bed, and that was little over a fortnight now. I wondered why it was I clung to this reserve, and why it was I did not tell her that every morning I drove with de Winter in his car, and lunched with him too, at his table in the restaurant.

"You must come up to the net more, you will never play a good game until you do," she continued, and I agreed, flinching at my own hypocrisy, covering her Queen with the weak-chinned Knave of Hearts.

I have forgotten much of Monte Carlo, of those morning drives, of where we went, even our conversation; but I have not forgotten how my fingers trembled, cramming on my hat, and how I ran along the corridor and down the stairs, too impatient to wait for the slow whining of the lift, and so outside brushing the swing doors before the commissionaire could help me.

He would be there, in the driver's seat, reading a paper while he waited, and when he saw me he would smile, and toss it behind him in the back seat, and open the door, saying, "Well, how is the friend of the bosom this morning, and where does she want to go?" If he had driven round in circles it would not have mattered to me, for I was in that first flushed stage when to climb into the seat beside him, and lean forward to the wind-screen hugging my knees, was almost too much to bear. I was like a little scrubby schoolboy with a passion for a sixth-form prefect, and he kinder, and far more inaccessible.

"There's a cold wind this morning, you had better put on my coat."

I remember that, for I was young enough to win happiness in the wearing of his clothes, playing the schoolboy again who carries his hero's sweater and ties it about his throat choking with pride, and this borrowing of his coat, wearing it around my shoulders for even a few minutes at a time, was a triumph in itself, and made a glow about my morning.

Not for me the languor and the subtlety I had read about in books. The challenge and the chase. The sword-play, the swift glance, the stimulating smile. The art of provocation was unknown to me, and I would sit with his map upon my lap, the wind blowing my dull, lanky hair, happy in his silence yet eager for his words. Whether he talked or not made little difference to my mood. My only enemy was the clock on the dash-board, whose hands would move relentlessly to one o'clock. We drove east, we drove west, amidst the myriad villages that clung like limpets to the Mediterranean shore, and to-day I remember none of them.

All I remember is the feel of the leather seats, the texture of the map upon my knee, its frayed edges, its worn seams, and how one day, looking at the clock, I thought to myself, "This moment now, at twenty past eleven, this must never be lost," and I shut my eyes to make the experience more lasting. When I opened my eyes we were by a bend in the road, and a peasant girl in a black shawl waved to us; I can see her now, her dusty skirt, her gleaming, friendly smile, and in a second we had passed the bend and could see her no more. Already she belonged to the past, she was only a memory.

I wanted to go back again, to recapture the moment that had gone, and then it came to me that if we did it would not be the same, even the sun would be changed in the sky, casting another shadow, and the peasant girl would trudge past us along the road in a different way, not waving this time, perhaps not even seeing us. There was something chilling in the thought, something a little melancholy, and looking at the clock I saw that five more minutes had gone by. Soon we would have reached our time limit, and must return to the hotel.

"If only there could be an invention," I said impulsively, "that bottled up a memory, like scent. And it never faded, and it never got stale. And then, when one wanted it, the bottle could be uncorked, and it would be like living the moment all over again." I looked up at him, to see what he would say. He did not turn to me, he went on watching the road ahead.

"What particular moments in your young life do you wish uncorked?" he said. I could not tell from his voice whether he was teasing me or not. "I'm not sure," I began, and then blundered on, rather foolishly, not thinking of my words, "I'd like to keep this moment and never forget it."

"Is that meant to be a compliment to the day, or to my driving?" he said, and as he laughed, like a mocking brother, I became silent, overwhelmed suddenly by the great gulf between us, and how his very kindness to me widened it.

I knew then that I would never tell Mrs. Van Hopper about these morning expeditions, for her smile would hurt me as his laugh had done. She would not be angry, nor would she be shocked, she would raise her eyebrows very faintly, as though she did not altogether believe my story, and then with a tolerant shrug of the shoulder she would say, "My dear child, it's extremely sweet and kind of him to take you driving, the only thing is—are you sure it does not bore him dreadfully?" And then she would send me out to buy Taxol, patting me on the shoulder. What degradation lay in being young, I thought, and fell to tearing at my nails.

"I wish," I said savagely, still mindful of his laugh and throwing discretion to the wind, "I wish I was a woman of about thirty-six dressed in black satin with a string of pearls."

"You would not be in this car with me if you were," he said, "and stop biting those nails, they are ugly enough already."

"You'll think me impertinent and rude I dare say," I went on, "but I would like to know why you ask me to come out in the car, day after day. You are being kind, that's obvious, but why do you choose me for your charity?"

I sat up stiff and straight in my seat with all the poor pomposity of youth.

"I ask you," he said gravely, "because you are not dressed in black satin, with a string of pearls, nor are you thirty-six." His face was without expression, I could not tell whether he laughed inwardly or not.

"It's all very well," I said, "you know everything there is to know about me. There's not much, I admit, because I have not been alive for very long and nothing much has happened to me, except people dying, but you—I know nothing more about you than I did the first day we met."

"And what did you know then?" he asked.

"Why, that you lived at Manderley and—and that you had lost your wife." There, I had said it at last, the word that had hovered on my tongue for days. Your wife. It came out with ease, without reluctance, as though the mere mention of her must be the most casual thing in all the world. Your wife. The word lingered in the air once I had uttered it, dancing before me, and because he received it silently, making no comment, the word magnified itself into something heinous and appalling, a forbidden word, unnatural to the tongue. And I could not call it back, it could never be unsaid. Once again I saw the inscription on the fly-leaf of that book of poems, and the curious slanting R. I felt sick at heart and cold. He would never forgive me, and this would be the end of our friendship.

I remember staring straight in front of me at the wind-screen, seeing nothing of the flying road, my ears still tingling with that spoken word. The silence became minutes, and the minutes became miles, and everything is over now, I thought, I shall never drive with him again. To-morrow he will go away. And Mrs. Van Hopper will be up again. She and I will walk along the terrace as we did before. The porter will bring down his trunks, I shall catch a glimpse of them in the luggage lift, with new-plastered labels. The bustle and finality of departure. The sound of the car changing gear as it turned the corner, and then even that sound merging into the common traffic, and being lost, and so absorbed forever.

I was so deep in my picture, I even saw the porter pocketing his tip and going back through the swing-door of the hotel, saying something over his shoulder to the commissionaire, that I did not notice the slowing-down of the car, and it was only when we stopped, drawing up by the side of the road, that I brought myself back to the present once again. He sat motionless, looking without his hat and with his white scarf round his neck, more than ever like someone medieval who lived within a frame. He did not belong to the bright landscape, he should be standing on the steps of a gaunt cathedral, his cloak flung back, while a beggar at his feet scrambled for gold coins.

The friend had gone, with his kindliness and his easy camaraderie, and the brother too, who had mocked me for nibbling at my nails. This man was a stranger. I wondered why I was sitting beside him in the car.

Then he turned to me and spoke. "A little while ago you talked about an invention," he said, "some scheme for capturing a memory. You would like, you told me, at a chosen moment to live the past again. I'm afraid I think rather differently from you. All memories are bitter, and I prefer to ignore them. Something happened a year ago that altered my whole life, and I want to forget every phase in my existence up to that time. Those days are finished. They are blotted out. I must begin living all over again. The first day we met, your Mrs. Van Hopper asked me why I came to Monte Carlo. It put a stopper on those memories you would like to resurrect. It does not always work, of course, sometimes the scent is too strong for the bottle, and too strong for me. And then the devil in one, like a furtive peeping Tom, tries to draw the cork. I did that in the first drive we took together. When we climbed the hills and looked down over the precipice. I was there some years ago, with my wife. You asked me if it was still the same, if it had changed at all. It was just the same, but—I was thankful to realise—oddly impersonal. There was no suggestion of the other time. She and I had left no record. It may have been because you were with me. You have blotted out the past for me, you know, far more effectively than all the bright lights of Monte Carlo. But for you I should have left long ago, gone on to Italy, and Greece, and further still perhaps. You have spared me all those wanderings. Damn your puritanical little tight-lipped speech to me. Damn your idea of my kindness and my charity. I ask you to come with me because I want you and your company, and if you don't believe me you can leave the car now and find your own way home. Go on, open the door, and get out."

I sat still, my hands in my lap, not knowing whether he meant it or not.

"Well," he said, "what are you going to do about it?"

Had I been a year or two younger I think I should have cried. Children's tears are very near the surface, and come at the first crisis. As it was I felt them prick behind my eyes, felt the ready colour flood my face, and catching a sudden glimpse of myself in the glass above the wind-screen saw in full the sorry spectacle that I made, with troubled eyes and scarlet cheeks, lank hair flopping under broad felt hat.

"I want to go home," I said, my voice perilously near to trembling, and without a word he started up the engine, let in the clutch and turned the car round the way that we had come.

Swiftly we covered the ground, far too swiftly, I thought, far too easily, and the callous countryside watched us with indifference. We came to the bend in the road that I had wished to imprison as a memory, and the peasant girl was gone, and the colour was flat, and it was no more after all than any bend in any road passed by a hundred motorists. The glamour of it had gone with my happy mood, and at the thought of it my frozen face quivered into feeling, my adult pride was lost, and those despicable tears rejoicing at their conquest welled into my eyes and strayed upon my cheeks.

I could not check them, for they came unbidden, and had I reached in my pocket for a handkerchief he would have seen. I must let them fall untouched, and suffer the bitter salt upon my lips, plumbing the depths of humiliation. Whether he had turned his head to look at me I do not know, for I watched the road ahead with blurred and steady stare, but suddenly he put out his hand and took hold of mine, and kissed it, still saying nothing, and then he threw his handkerchief on my lap, which I was too ashamed to touch.

I thought of all those heroines of fiction who looked pretty when they cried, and what a contrast I must make with blotched and swollen face, and red rims to my eyes. It was a dismal finish to my morning, and the day that stretched ahead of me was long. I had to lunch with Mrs. Van Hopper in her room, because the nurse was going out, and afterwards she would make me play bezique with all the tireless energy of the convalescent. I knew I should stifle in that room. There was something sordid about the tumbled sheets, the sprawling blankets and the thumped pillows, and that bed-side table dusty with powder, split scent, and melting liquid rouge. Her bed would be littered with the separated sheets of the daily papers folded anyhow, while French novels with curling edges and the covers torn kept company with American magazines. The mashed stubs of cigarettes lay everywhere, in cleansing cream, in a dish of grapes, and on the floor beneath the bed. Visitors were lavish with their flowers, and the vases stood cheek-by-jowl in any fashion, hot-house exotics crammed beside mimosa, while a great be-ribboned casket crowned them all, with tier upon tier of crystallized fruit. Later her friends would come in for a drink, which I must mix for them, hating my task, shy and ill-at-ease in my corner hemmed in by their parrot chatter, and I would be a whipping boy again, blushing for her when, excited by her little crowd, she must sit up in bed and talk too loudly, laugh too long, reach to the portable gramophone and start a record, shrugging her large shoulders to the tune. I preferred her irritable and snappy, her hair done up in pins, scolding me for forgetting her Taxol. All this awaited me in the suite, while he, once he had left me at the hotel, would go away somewhere alone, towards the sea perhaps, feel the wind on his cheek, follow the sun; and it might happen that he would lose himself in those memories that I knew nothing of, that I could not share, he would wander down the years that were gone.

The gulf that lay between us was wider now than it had ever been, and he stood away from me, with his back turned, on the further shore. I felt young and small and very much alone, and now, in spite of my pride, I found his handkerchief and blew my nose, throwing my drab appearance to the winds. It could never matter.

"To hell with this," he said suddenly, as though angry, as though bored, and he pulled me beside him, and put his arm round my shoulder, still looking straight ahead of him, his right hand on the wheel. He drove, I remember, even faster than before. "I suppose you are young enough to be my daughter, and I don't know how to deal with you," he said. The road narrowed then to a corner, and he had to swerve to avoid a dog. I thought he would release me, but he went on holding me beside him, and when the corner was passed, and the road came straight again he did not let me go. "You can forget all I said to you this morning," he said, "that's all finished and done with. Don't let's ever think of it again. My family always call me Maxim, I'd like you to do the same. You've been formal with me long enough." He felt for the brim of my hat, and took hold of it, throwing it over his shoulder to the back seat, and then bent down and kissed the top of my head. "Promise me you will never wear black satin," he said. I smiled then, and he laughed back at me, and the morning was gay again, the morning was a shining thing. Mrs. Van Hopper and the afternoon did not matter a flip of the finger. It would pass so quickly, and there would be to-night, and another day to-morrow. I was cock-sure, jubilant, at that moment I almost had the courage to claim equality. I saw myself strolling into Mrs. Van Hopper's bedroom rather late for my bezique, and when questioned by her yawning carelessly, saying, "I forgot the time. I've been lunching with Maxim."

I was still child enough to consider a Christian name like a plume in the hat, though from the very first he had called me by mine. The morning, for all its shadowed moments, had promoted me to a new level of friendship, I did not lag so far behind as I had thought. He had kissed me too, a natural business, comforting and quiet. Not dramatic as in books. Not embarrassing. It seemed to bring about an ease in our relationship, it made everything more simple. The gulf between us had been bridged after all. I was to call him Maxim. And that afternoon playing bezique with Mrs. Van Hopper was not so tedious as it might have been, though my courage failed me and I said nothing of my morning. For when, gathering her cards together at the end, and reaching for the box, she said casually, "Tell me, is Max de Winter still in the hotel?" I hesitated a moment, like a diver on the brink, then lost my nerve and my tutored self-possession, saying, "Yes, I believe so—he comes into the restaurant for his meals."

Someone has told her, I thought, someone has seen us together, the tennis professional has complained, the manager has sent a note, and I waited for her attack. But she went on putting the cards back into the box, yawning a little, while I straightened the tumbled bed. I gave her the bowl of powder, the rouge compact, and the lip-stick, and she put away the cards and took up the hand glass from the table by her side. "Attractive creature," she said, "but queer-tempered I should think, difficult to know. I thought he might have made some gesture of asking one to Manderley that day in the lounge, but he was very close."

I said nothing. I watched her pick up the lip-stick and outline a bow upon her hard mouth. "I never saw her," she said, holding the glass away to see the effect, "but I believe she was very lovely. Exquisitely turned out, and brilliant in every way. They used to give tremendous parties at Manderley. It was all very sudden and tragic, and I believe he adored her. I need the darker shade of powder with this brilliant red, my dear, fetch it, will you, and put this box back in the drawer?"

And we were busy then with powder, scent, and rouge, until the bell rang and her visitors came in. I handed them their drinks, dully, saying little; I changed the records on the gramophone, I threw away the stubs of cigarettes.

"Been doing any sketching lately, little lady?" The forced heartiness of an old banker, his monocle dangling on a string, and my bright smile of insincerity: "No, not very lately; will you have another cigarette?"

It was not I that answered, I was not there at all. I was following a phantom in my mind, whose shadowy form had taken shape at last. Her features were blurred, her colouring indistinct, the setting of her eyes and the texture of her hair was still uncertain, still to be revealed.

She had beauty that endured, and a smile that was not forgotten. Somewhere her voice still lingered, and the memory of her words. There were places she had visited, and things that she had touched. Perhaps in cupboards there were clothes that she had worn, with the scent about them still. In my bedroom, under my pillow, I had a book that she had taken in her hands, and I could see her turning to that first white page, smiling as she wrote, and shaking the bent nib. Max from Rebecca. It must have been his birthday, and she had put it amongst her other presents on the breakfast table. And they had laughed together as he tore off the paper and the string. She leant, perhaps, over his shoulder, while he read. Max. She called him Max. It was familiar, gay, and easy on the tongue. The family could call him Maxim if they liked. Grandmothers and aunts. And people like myself, quiet and dull and youthful, who did not matter. Max was her choice, the word was her possession, she had written it with so great a confidence on the fly-leaf of that book. That bold, slanting hand, stabbing the white paper, the symbol of herself, so certain, so assured.

How many times she must have written to him thus, in how many varied moods.

Little notes, scrawled on half-sheets of paper, and letters, when he was away, page after page, intimate, *their* news. Her voice, echoing through the house, and down the garden, careless and familiar like the writing in the book.

And I had to call him Maxim.

CHAPTER SIX

Packing up. The nagging worry of departure. Lost keys, unwritten labels, tissue paper lying on the floor. I hate it all. Even now, when I have done so much of it, when I live, as the saying goes, in my boxes. Even to-day, when shutting drawers and flinging wide a hotel wardrobe, or the impersonal shelves of a furnished villa, is a methodical matter of routine, I am aware of sadness, of a sense of loss. Here, I say, we have lived, we have been happy. This has been ours, however brief the time. Though two nights only have been spent beneath a roof, yet we leave something of ourselves behind. Nothing material, not a hair-pin on a dressing-table, not an empty bottle of Aspirin tablets, not a handkerchief beneath a pillow, but something indefinable, a moment of our lives, a thought, a mood.

This house sheltered us, we spoke, we loved within those walls. That was yesterday. To-day we pass on, we see it no more, and we are different, changed in some infinitesimal way. We can never be quite the same again. Even stopping for luncheon at a wayside inn, and going to a dark, unfamiliar room to wash my hands, the handle of the door unknown to me, the wall-paper peeling in strips, a funny little cracked mirror above the basin, for this moment, it is mine, it belongs to me. We know one another. This is the present. There is no past and no future. Here I am washing my hands and the cracked mirror shows me to myself, suspended as it were, in time; this is me, this moment will not pass.

And then I open the door and go to the dining-room, where he is sitting waiting for me at a table, and I think how in that moment I have aged, and passed on, how I have advanced one step towards an unknown destiny.

We smile, we choose our lunch, we speak of this and that, but—I say to myself—I am not she who left him five minutes ago. She has stayed behind. I am another woman, older, more mature. . . .

I saw in a paper the other day that the hotel Côte d'Azur at Monte Carlo had gone to new management, and had a different name. The rooms had been re-decorated, and the whole interior changed. Perhaps Mrs. Van Hopper's suite on the first floor exists no more. Perhaps there is no trace of the small bedroom that was mine. I knew I should never go back, that day I knelt on the floor and fumbled with the awkward catch of her trunk.

The episode was finished, with the snapping of the lock. I glanced out the window, and it was like turning the page of a photograph album. Those roof tops and that sea were mine no more. They belonged to yesterday, to the past. The rooms already wore an empty air, stripped of our possessions, and there was something hungry about the suite, as though it wished us gone, and the new arrivals, who would come to-morrow, in our place. The heavy luggage stood ready strapped and locked in the corridor outside. The smaller stuff would be finished later. Waste-paper baskets groaned under litter. All her half-empty medicine bottles and discarded face-cream jars, with torn-up bills and letters. Drawers in tables gaped, the bureau was stripped bare.

She had flung a letter at me the morning before, as I poured out her coffee at breakfast. "Helen is sailing for New York on Saturday. Little Nancy has a threatened appendix, and they've cabled her to go home. That's decided me. We're going too. I'm tired to death of Europe, and we can come back in the early fall. How d'you like the idea of seeing New York?"

The thought was worse than prison. Something of my misery must have shown in my face, for at first she looked astonished, then annoyed.

"What an odd, unsatisfactory child you are. I can't make you out. Don't you realise that at home girls in your position without any money can have the grandest fun? Plenty of boys and excitement. All in your own class. You can have your own little set of friends, and needn't be at my beck and call as much as you are here. I thought you didn't care for Monte?"

"I've got used to it," I said lamely, wretchedly, my mind a conflict.

"Well, you'll just have to get used to New York, that's all. We're going to catch that boat of Helen's, and it means seeing about our passage at once. Go down to the reception office right away, and make that young clerk show some sign of efficiency. Your day will be so full that you won't have time to have any pangs about leaving Monte!" She laughed disagreeably, squashing her cigarette in the butter, and went to the telephone to ring up all her friends.

I could not face the office right away. I went into the bathroom and locked the door, and sat down on the cork mat, my head in my hands. It had happened at last, the business of going away. It was all over. To-morrow evening I should be in the train, holding her jewel case and her rug, like a maid, and she in that monstrous new hat with the single quill, dwarfed in her fur-coat, sitting opposite me in the wagon-lit. We would wash and clean our teeth in that stuffy little compartment with the rattling doors, the splashed basin, the damp towel, the soap with a single hair on it, the carafe half-filled with water, the inevitable notice on the wall *"Sous le lavabo se trouve une vase,"* while every rattle, every throb and jerk of the screaming train would tell me that the miles carried me away from him, sitting alone in the restaurant of the hotel, at the table I had known, reading a book, not minding, not thinking.

I should say good-bye to him in the lounge, perhaps, before we left. A furtive, scrambled farewell, because of her, and there would be a pause, and a smile, and words like "Yes, of course, do write," and "I've never thanked you properly for being so kind," and "You must forward those snapshots," "What about your address?" "Well, I'll have to let you know." And he would light a cigarette casually, asking a passing waiter for a light, while I thought, "Four and a half more minutes to go. I shall never see him again."

Because I was going, because it was over, there would suddenly be nothing more to say, we would be strangers, meeting for the last and only time, while my mind clamoured painfully, crying, "I love you so much. I'm terribly unhappy. This has never come to me before, and never will again." My face would be set in a prim, conventional smile, my voice would be saying, "Look at that funny old man over there, I wonder who he is, he must be new here." And we would waste the last moments laughing at a stranger, because we were already strangers to one another. "I hope the snapshots come out well," repeating oneself in desperation, and he "Yes, that one of the square ought to be good, the light was just right." Having both of us gone into all that at the time, having agreed upon it, and anyway I would not care if the result was fogged and black, because this was the last moment, the final good-bye had been attained.

"Well," my dreadful smile stretching across my face, "thanks most awfully once again, it's been so ripping ..." using words I had never used before. Ripping: what did it mean?—God knows, I did not care; it was the sort of word that schoolgirls had for hockey, wildly inappropriate to those past weeks of misery and exultation. Then the doors of the lift would open upon Mrs. Van Hopper and I would cross the lounge to meet her, and he would stroll back again to his corner and pick up a paper.

Sitting there, ridiculously, on the cork mat of the bathroom floor I lived it all, and our journey too, and our arrival in New York. The shrill voice of Helen, a narrower edition of her mother, and Nancy, her horrid little child. The college boys that Mrs. Van Hopper would have me know, and the young bank clerks, suitable to my station. "Let's make Wednesday night a date." "D'you like hot music?" Snub-nosed boys, with shiny faces. Having to be polite. And wanting to be alone with my own thoughts as I was now, locked behind the bathroom door. . . .

She came and rattled on the door. "What are you doing?"

"All right—I'm sorry, I'm coming now," and I made a pretence of turning on the tap, of bustling about and folding a towel on a rail.

She glanced at me curiously as I opened the door. "What a time you've been. You can't afford to dream this morning, you know, there's too much to be done."

He would go back to Manderley, of course, in a few weeks, I felt certain of that. There would be a great pile of letters waiting for him in the hall, and mine amongst them, scribbled on the boat. A forced letter, trying to amuse, describing my fellow passengers. It would lie about inside his blotter, and he would answer it weeks later, one Sunday morning in a hurry, before lunch, having come across it when he paid some bills. And then no more. Nothing until the final degradation of the Christmas card. Manderley itself perhaps, against a frosted background. The message printed, saying "A happy Christmas and a prosperous New Year from Maximilian de Winter." Gold lettering. But to be kind he would have run his pen through the printed name and written in ink underneath "from Maxim," as a sort of sop, and if there was space, a message, "I hope you are enjoying New York." A lick of the envelope, a stamp, and tossed in a pile of a hundred others.

"It's too bad you are leaving to-morrow," said the reception clerk, telephone in hand, "the Ballet starts next week you know. Does Mrs. Van Hopper know?" I dragged myself back from Christmas at Manderley to the realities of the wagon-lit.

Mrs. Van Hopper lunched in the restaurant for the first time since her influenza, and I had a pain in the pit of my stomach as I followed her into the room. He had gone to Cannes for the day, that much I knew, for he had warned me the day before, but I kept thinking the waiter might commit an indiscretion and say: "Will Mademoiselle be dining with Monsieur to-night as usual?" I felt a little sick whenever he came near the table, but he said nothing.

The day was spent in packing, and in the evening people came to say good-bye. We dined in the sitting-room, and she went to bed directly afterwards. Still I had not seen him. I went down to the lounge about half-past nine on the pretext of getting luggage labels and he was not there. The odious reception clerk smiled when he saw me. "If you are looking for Mr. de Winter we had a message from Cannes to say he would not be back before midnight."

"I want a packet of luggage labels," I said, but I saw by his eye that he was not deceived. So there would be no last evening after all. The hour I had looked forward to all day must be spent by myself alone, in my own bedroom, gazing at my Revelation suitcase and the stout hold-all. Perhaps it was just as well, for I should have made a poor companion, and he must have read my face.

I know I cried that night, bitter youthful tears that could not come from me to-day. That kind of crying, deep into a pillow, does not happen after we are twenty-one. The throbbing head, the swollen eyes, the tight, contracted throat. And the wild anxiety in the morning to hide all traces from the world, sponging with cold water, dabbing eau-de-Cologne, the furtive dash of powder that is significant in itself. The panic, too, that one might cry again, the tears swelling without control, and a fatal trembling of the mouth lead one to disaster. I remember opening wide my window and leaning out, hoping the fresh morning air would blow away the tell-tale pink under the powder, and the sun had never seemed so bright, nor the day so full of promise. Monte Carlo was suddenly full of kindliness and charm, the one place in the world that held sincerity. I loved it. Affection overwhelmed me. I wanted to live there all my life. And I was leaving it to-day. This is the last time I brush my hair before the looking-glass, the last time I shall clean my teeth into the basin. Never again sleep in that bed. Never more turn off the switch of that electric light. There I was, padding about in a dressing-gown, making a slough of sentiment out of a common-place hotel bedroom.

"You haven't started a cold, have you?" she said at breakfast.

"No," I told her, "I don't think so," clutching at a straw, for this might serve as an excuse later, if I was over-pink about the eyes.

"I hate hanging about once everything is packed," she grumbled; "we ought to have decided on the earlier train. We could get it if we made the effort, and then have longer in Paris. Wire Helen not to meet us, but arrange another *rendezvous*. I wonder"—she glanced at her watch—"I suppose they could change the reservations. Anyway it's worth trying. Go down to the office and see."

"Yes," I said, a dummy to her moods, going into my bedroom and flinging off my dressing-gown, fastening my inevitable flannel skirt and stretching my home-made jumper over my head. My indifference to her turned to hatred. This was the end then, even my morning must be taken from me. No last half-hour on the terrace, not even ten minutes perhaps to say good-bye. Because she had finished breakfast earlier than she expected, because she was bored. Well then, I would fling away restraint and modesty, I would not be proud any more. I slammed the door of the sitting-room and ran along the passage. I did not wait for the lift, I climbed the stairs, three at a time, up to the third floor. I knew the number of his room, 148, and I hammered at the door, very flushed in the face and breathless.

"Come in," he shouted, and I opened the door, repenting already, my nerve failing me, for perhaps he had only just woken up, having been late last night, and would be still in bed, tousled in the head and irritable.

He was shaving by the open window, a camel-hair jacket over his pyjamas, and I in my flannel suit and heavy shoes felt clumsy and overdressed. I was merely foolish, when I had felt myself dramatic.

"What do you want," he said, "is something the matter?"

"I've come to say good-bye," I said, "we're going this morning."

He stared at me, then put his razor down on the wash-stand. "Shut the door," he said.

I closed it behind me, and stood there, rather self-conscious, my hands hanging by my side. "What on earth are you talking about?" he asked.

"It's true, we're leaving to-day. We were going by the later train, and now she wants to catch the earlier one, and I was afraid I shouldn't see you again. I felt I must see you before I left, to thank you."

They tumbled out, the idiotic words, just as I had imagined them. I was stiff and awkward, in a moment I should say he had been ripping.

"Why didn't you tell me about this before?" he said.

"She only decided yesterday. It was all done in a hurry. Her daughter sails for New York on Saturday, and we are going with her. We're joining her in Paris, and going through to Cherbourg."

"She's taking you with her to New York?"

"Yes, and I don't want to go. I shall hate it; I shall be miserable."

"Why in heaven's name go with her then?"

"I have to, you know that. I work for a salary. I can't afford to leave her." He picked up his razor again, and took the soap off his face. "Sit down," he said. "I shan't be long. I'll dress in the bathroom, and be ready in five minutes."

He took his clothes off the chair and threw them on the bathroom floor, and went inside, slamming the door. I sat down on the bed and began biting my nails. The situation was unreal, and I felt like a lay-figure. I wondered what he was thinking, what he was going to do. I glanced round the room, and it was the room of any man, untidy and impersonal. Lots of shoes, more than were ever needed, and strings of ties. The dressing-table was bare, except for a large bottle of hair-wash and a pair of ivory hair-brushes. No photographs. No snapshots. Nothing like that. Instinctively I had looked for them, thinking there would be one photograph at least beside his bed, or in the middle of the mantelpiece. One large one, in a leather frame. There were only books though, and a box of cigarettes.

He was ready, as he had promised, in five minutes. "Come down to the terrace while I eat my breakfast," he said.

I looked at my watch. "I haven't time," I told him. "I ought to be in the office now, changing the reservations."

"Never mind about that, I've got to talk to you," he said.

We walked down the corridor and he rang for the lift. He can't re-alise, I thought, that the early train leaves in about an hour and a half. Mrs. Van Hopper will ring up the office, in a moment, and ask if I am there. We went down in the lift, not talking, and so out to the terrace, where the tables were laid for breakfast.

"What are you going to have?" he said.

"I've had mine already," I told him, "and I can only stay four minutes anyway."

"Bring me coffee, a boiled egg, toast, marmalade, and a tanger-ine," he said to the waiter. And he took an emery board out of his pocket and began filing his nails.

"So Mrs. Van Hopper has had enough of Monte Carlo," he said, "and now she wants to go home. So do I. She to New York and I to Manderley. Which would you prefer? You can take your choice."

"Don't make a joke about it, it's unfair," I said, "and I think I had better see about those tickets, and say good-bye now."

"If you think I'm one of the people who try to be funny at break-fast you're wrong," he said. "I'm invariably ill-tempered in the early morning. I repeat to you, the choice is open to you. Either you go to

America with Mrs. Van Hopper or you come home to Manderley with me."

"Do you mean you want a secretary or something?"

"No, I'm asking you to marry me, you little fool."

The waiter came with the breakfast, and I sat with my hands in my lap, watching while he put down the pot of coffee and the jug of milk.

"You don't understand," I said, when the waiter had gone, "I'm not the sort of person men marry."

"What the devil do you mean?" he said, staring at me, laying down his spoon.

I watched a fly settle on the marmalade, and he brushed it away impatiently.

"I'm not sure," I said slowly. "I don't think I know how to explain. I don't belong to your sort of world for one thing."

"What is my world?"

"Well—Manderley. You know what I mean."

He picked up his spoon again and helped himself to marmalade.

"You are almost as ignorant as Mrs. Van Hopper, and just as un-intelligent. What do you know of Manderley? I'm the person to judge that, whether you would belong there or not. You think I ask you this on the spur of the moment, don't you? Because you say you don't want to go to New York. You think I ask you to marry me for the same reason you believed I drove you about in the car, yes, and gave you dinner that first evening. To be kind. Don't you?"

"Yes," I said.

"One day," he went on, spreading his toast thick, "you may realise that philanthropy is not my strongest quality. At the moment I don't think you realise anything at all. You haven't answered my question. Are you going to marry me?"

I don't believe, even in my fiercest moments, I had considered this possibility. I had once, when driving with him and we had been silent for many miles, started a rambling story in my head about him being very ill, delirious I think, and sending for me and I having to nurse him. I had reached the point in my story where I was putting eau-de-Cologne on his head when we arrived at the hotel, and so it finished there. And another time I had imagined living in a lodge in the grounds of Manderley, and how he would visit me sometimes, and sit in front of the fire. This sudden talk of marriage bewildered me, even shocked me I think. It was as though the King asked one. It did not ring true. And he went on eating his marmalade as though everything were natural. In books men knelt to women, and it would be moonlight. Not at breakfast, not like this.

"My suggestion doesn't seem to have gone too well," he said. "I'm sorry. I rather thought you loved me. A fine blow to my conceit."

"I do love you," I said. "I love you dreadfully. You've made me very unhappy and I've been crying all night because I thought I should never see you again."

When I said this I remember he laughed, and stretched his hand to me across the breakfast table. "Bless you for that," he said; "one day, when you reach that exalted age of thirty-five which you told me was your ambition, I'll remind you of this moment. And you won't believe me. It's a pity you have to grow up."

I was ashamed already, and angry with him for laughing. So women did not make those confessions to men. I had a lot to learn.

"So that's settled, isn't it?" he said, going on with his toast and marmalade; "instead of being companion to Mrs. Van Hopper you become mine, and your duties will be almost exactly the same. I also like new library books, and flowers in the drawing-room, and bezique after dinner. And someone to pour out my tea. The only difference is that I don't take Taxol, I prefer Eno's, and you must never let me run out of my particular brand of tooth-paste."

I drummed with my fingers on the table, uncertain of myself and of him. Was he still laughing at me, was it all a joke? He looked up, and saw the anxiety on my face. "I'm being rather a brute to you, aren't I?" he said; "this isn't your idea of a proposal. We ought to be in a conservatory, you in a white frock with a rose in your hand, and a violin playing a waltz in the distance. And I should make violent love to you behind a palm tree. You would feel then you were getting your money's worth. Poor darling, what a shame. Never mind, I'll take you to Venice for our honeymoon and we'll hold hands in the gondola. But we won't stay too long, because I want to show you Manderley."

He wanted to show me Manderley. . . . And suddenly I realised that it would all happen, I would be his wife, we would walk in the garden together, we would stroll down that path in the valley to the shingle beach. I knew how I would stand on the steps after breakfast, looking at the day, throwing crumbs to the birds, and later wander out in a shady hat with long scissors in my hand, and cut flowers for the house. I knew now why I had bought that picture post-card as a child, it was a premonition, a blank step into the future.

He wanted to show me Manderley. . . . My mind ran riot then, figures came before me and picture after picture—and all the while he ate his tangerine, giving me a piece now and then, and watching me. We would be in a crowd of people, and he would say, "I don't think you have met my wife." Mrs. de Winter. I would be Mrs. de Winter. I considered my name, and the signature on cheques, to tradesmen, and in letters asking people to dinner. I heard myself talking on the telephone. "Why not come down to Manderley next weekend?" People, always a throng of people. "Oh, but she's simply charming, you must meet her–" This about me, a whisper on the fringe of a crowd, and I would turn away, pretending I had not heard.

Going down to the lodge with a basket on my arm, grapes and peaches for the old lady who was sick. Her hands stretched out to me, "The Lord bless you, Madam, for being so good," and my saying "Just send up to the house for anything you want." Mrs. de Winter. I would be Mrs. de Winter. I saw the polished table in the dining-room, and the long candles. Maxim sitting at the end. A party of twenty-four. I had a flower in my hair. Everyone looked towards me, holding up his glass. "We must drink the health of the bride," and Maxim saying afterwards, "I have never seen you look so lovely." Great cool rooms, filled with flowers. My bedroom, with a fire in the winter, someone knocking at the door. And a woman comes in, smiling, she is Maxim's sister, and she is saying, "It's really wonderful how happy you have made him, everyone is so pleased, you are such a success." Mrs. de Winter. I would be Mrs. de Winter.

"The rest of the tangerine is sour, I shouldn't eat it," he said, and I stared at him, the words going slowly to my head, then looked down at the fruit on my plate. The quarter was hard and pale. He was right. The tangerine was very sour. I had a sharp, bitter taste in my mouth, and I had only just noticed it.

"Am I going to break the news to Mrs. Van Hopper or are you?" he said.

He was folding up his napkin, pushing back his plate, and I wondered how it was he spoke so casually, as though the matter was of little consequence, a mere adjustment of plans. Whereas to me it was a bombshell, exploding in a thousand fragments.

"You tell her," I said, "she'll be so angry."

We got up from the table, I excited and flushed, trembling already in anticipation. I wondered if he would tell the waiter, take my arm smilingly and say, "You must congratulate us, Mademoiselle and I are going to be married." And all the other waiters would hear, would bow to us, would smile, and we would pass into the lounge, a wave of excitement following us, a flutter of expectation. But he said nothing. He left the terrace without a word, and I followed him to the lift. We passed the reception desk and no one even looked at us. The clerk was busy with a sheaf of papers, he was talking over his shoulder to his junior. He does not know, I thought, that I am going to be Mrs. de Winter. I am going to live at Manderley. Manderley will belong to me. We went up in the lift to the first floor, and so along the passage. He took my hand and swung it as we went along. "Does forty-two seem very old to you?" he said.

"Oh, no," I told him, quickly, too eagerly perhaps. "I don't like young men."

"You've never known any," he said.

We came to the door of the suite. "I think I had better deal with this alone," he said; "tell me something—do you mind how soon you marry me? You don't want a trousseau, do you, or any of that nonsense? Because the whole thing can be so easily arranged in a few days. Over a desk, with a licence, and then off in the car to Venice or anywhere you fancy."

"Not in a church?" I asked. "Not in white, with bridesmaids, and bells, and choir boys? What about your relations, and all your friends?"

"You forget," he said, "I had that sort of wedding before."

We went on standing in front of the door of the suite, and I noticed that the daily paper was still thrust through the letter-box. We had been too busy to read it at breakfast.

"Well?" he said, "what about it?"

"Of course," I answered, "I was thinking for the moment we would be married at home. Naturally I don't expect a church, or people, or anything like that."

And I smiled at him. I made a cheerful face. "Won't it be fun?" I said.

He had turned to the door though, and opened it, and we were inside the suite in the little entrance passage.

"Is that you?" called Mrs. Van Hopper from the sitting-room, "what in the name of Mike have you been doing? I've rang the office three times and they said they hadn't seen you."

I was seized with a sudden desire to laugh, to cry, to do both, and I had a pain, too, at the pit of my stomach. I wished, for one wild moment, that none of this had happened, that I was alone somewhere, going for a walk, and whistling.

"I'm afraid it's all my fault," he said, going into the sitting-room, shutting the door behind him, and I heard her exclamation of surprise.

Then I went into my bedroom and sat down by the open window.

It was like waiting in the ante-room at a doctor's. I ought to turn over the pages of a magazine, look at photographs that did not matter and read articles I should never remember, until the nurse came, bright and efficient, all humanity washed away by years of disinfectant: "It's all right, the operation was quite successful. There is no need to worry at all. I should go home and have some sleep."

The walls of the suite were thick, I could hear no hum of voices. I wondered what he was saying to her, how he phrased his words. Perhaps he said, "I fell in love with her, you know, the very first time we met. We've been seeing one another every day." And she in answer, "Why Mr. de Winter, it's quite the most romantic thing I've ever heard." Romantic, that was the word I had tried to remember coming up in the lift. Yes, of course. Romantic. That was what people would say. It was all very sudden and romantic. They suddenly decided to get married and there it was. Such an adventure. I smiled to myself as I hugged my knees on the window seat, thinking how wonderful it was, how happy I was going to be. I was to marry the man I loved. I was to be Mrs. de Winter. It was foolish to go on having that pain in the pit of my stomach when I was so happy. Nerves of course. Waiting like this; the doctor's ante-room. It would have been better, after all, more natural surely to have gone into the sitting-room hand in hand, laughing, smiling at one another and for him to say "We're going to be married, we're very much in love."

In love. He had not said anything yet about being in love. No time perhaps. It was all so hurried at the breakfast table. Marmalade, and coffee, and that tangerine. No time. The tangerine was very bitter. No, he had not said anything about being in love. Just that we would be married. Short and definite, very original. Original proposals were much better. More genuine. Not like other people. Not like younger men who talked nonsense probably, not meaning half they said. Not like younger men being very incoherent, very passionate, swearing impossibilities. Not like him the first time, asking Rebecca. . . . I must not think of that. Put it away. A thought forbidden, prompted by demons. Get thee behind me, Satan. I must never think about that, never, never, never. He loves me, he wants to show me Manderley. Would they ever have done with their talking, would they ever call me into the room?

There was the book of poems lying beside my bed. He had forgotten he had ever lent them to me. They could not mean much to him then. "Go on," whispered the demon, "open the title-page, that's what you want to do, isn't it? Open the title-page." Nonsense, I said, I'm only going to put the book with the rest of the things. I yawned, I

wandered to the table beside the bed. I picked up the book. I caught
my foot in the flex of the bedside lamp, and stumbled, the book
falling from my hands on to the floor. It fell open, at the title-page.
"Max from Rebecca." She was dead, and one must not have thoughts
about the dead. They slept in peace, the grass blew over their graves.
How alive was her writing though, how full of force. Those curious,
sloping letters. The blob of ink. Done yesterday. It was just as if it had
been written yesterday. I took my nail scissors from the dressing-case
and cut the page, looking over my shoulder like a criminal.

I cut the page right out of the book. I left no jagged edges, and
the book looked white and clean when the page was gone. A new
book, that had not been touched. I tore the page up in many little
fragments and threw them into the waste-paper basket. Then I went
and sat on the window seat again. But I kept thinking of the torn
scraps in the basket, and after a moment I had to get up and look in
the basket once more. Even now the ink stood up on the fragments
thick and black, the writing was not destroyed. I took a box of
matches and set fire to the fragments. The flame had a lovely light,
staining the paper, curling the edges, making the slanting writing impossible to distinguish. The fragments fluttered to grey ashes. The letter R was the last to go, it twisted in the flame, it curled outwards for
a moment, becoming larger than ever. Then it crumpled too; the
flame destroyed it. It was not ashes even, it was feathery dust. . . . I
went and washed my hands in the basin. I felt better, much better. I
had the clean, new feeling that one has when the calendar is hung on
the wall at the beginning of the year. January the 1st. I was aware of
the same freshness, the same gay confidence. The door opened and he
came into the room.

"All's well," he said; "shock made her speechless at first, but she's
beginning to recover, so I'm going downstairs to the office, to make
certain she will catch the first train. For a moment she wavered, I
think she had hopes of acting witness at the wedding, but I was very
firm. Go and talk to her."

He said nothing about being glad, about being happy. He did not
take my arm and go into the sitting-room with me. He smiled, and
waved his hand, and went off down the corridor alone. I went to Mrs.
Van Hopper, uncertain, rather self-conscious, like a maid who has
handed in her notice through a friend.

She was standing by the window, smoking a cigarette, an odd,
dumpy little figure I should not see again, her coat stretched tight
over her large breasts, her ridiculous hat perched sideways on her
head.

"Well," she said, her voice dry and hard, not the voice she would have used to him, "I suppose I've got to hand it to you for a double-time worker. Still waters certainly run deep in your case. How did you manage it?"

I did not know what to answer. I did not like her smile.

"It was a lucky thing for you I had the influenza," she said. "I realise now how you spent your days, and why you were so forgetful. Tennis lessons my eye. You might have told me, you know."

"I'm sorry," I said.

She looked at me curiously, she ran her eyes over my figure. "And he tells me he wants to marry you in a few days. Lucky again for you that you haven't a family to ask questions. Well, it's nothing to do with me any more, I wash my hands of the whole affair. I rather wonder what his friends will think, but I suppose that's up to him. You realise he's years older than you?"

"He's only forty-two," I said, "and I'm old for my age."

She laughed, she dropped cigarette ash on the floor. "You certainly are," she said. She went on looking at me in a way she had never done before. Appraising me, running her eyes over my points like a judge at a cattle show. There was something inquisitive about her eyes, something unpleasant.

"Tell me," she said, intimate, a friend to a friend, "have you been doing anything you shouldn't?"

She was like Blaize, the dressmaker, who had offered me that ten per cent.

"I don't know what you mean," I said.

She laughed, she shrugged her shoulders. "Oh, well . . . never mind. But I always said English girls were dark horses, for all their hockey-playing attitude. So I'm supposed to travel to Paris alone, and leave you here while your beau gets a marriage licence? I notice he doesn't ask me to the wedding."

"I don't think he wants anyone, and anyway you would have sailed," I said.

"H'm, h'm," she said. She took out her vanity case and began powdering her nose. "I suppose you really do know your own mind," she went on; "after all, the whole thing has been very hurried, hasn't it? A matter of a few weeks. I don't suppose he's too easy, and you'll have to adapt yourself to his ways. You've led an extremely sheltered life up to now, you know, and you can't say that I've run you off your feet. You will have your work cut out as mistress of Manderley. To be perfectly frank, my dear, I simply can't see you doing it."

Her words sounded like the echo of my own an hour before.

"You haven't the experience," she continued, "you don't know that milieu. You can scarcely string two sentences together at my bridge teas, what are you going to say to all his friends? The Manderley parties were famous when she was alive. Of course he's told you all about them?"

I hesitated, but she went on, thank heaven, not waiting for my answer.

"Naturally one wants you to be happy, and I grant you he's a very attractive creature but—well, I'm sorry; and personally I think you are making a big mistake—one you will bitterly regret."

She put down the box of powder, and looked at me over her shoulder. Perhaps she was being sincere at last, but I did not want that sort of honesty. I did not say anything. I looked sullen, perhaps, for she shrugged her shoulders and wandered to the looking-glass, straightening her little mushroom hat. I was glad she was going, glad I should not see her again. I grudged the months I had spent with her, employed by her, taking her money, trotting in her wake like a shadow, drab and dumb. Of course I was inexperienced, of course I was idiotic, shy and young. I knew all that. She did not have to tell me. I supposed her attitude was deliberate, and for some odd feminine reason she resented this marriage, her scale of values had received a shock.

Well, I would not care, I would forget her and her barbed words. A new confidence had been born in me when I burnt that page and scattered the fragments. The past would not exist for either of us, we were starting afresh, he and I. The past had blown away like the ashes in the waste-paper basket. I was going to be Mrs. de Winter. I was going to live at Manderley.

Soon she would be gone, rattling alone in the wagon-lit without me, and he and I would be together in the dining-room of the hotel, lunching at the same table, planning the future. The brink of a big adventure. Perhaps, once she had gone, he would talk to me at last, about loving me, about being happy. Up to now there had been no time, and anyway those things are not easily said, they must wait their moment. I looked up, and caught her reflection in the looking-glass. She was watching me, a little tolerant smile on her lips. I thought she was going to be generous after all, hold out her hand and wish me luck, give me encouragement and tell me that everything was going to be all right. But she went on smiling, twisting a stray hair into place beneath her hat.

"Of course," she said, "you know why he is marrying you, don't you? You haven't flattered yourself he's in love with you? The fact is that empty house got on his nerves to such an extent he nearly went off his head. He admitted as much before you came into the room. He just can't go on living there alone. . . ."

CHAPTER SEVEN

We came to Manderley in early May, arriving, so Maxim said, with the first swallows and the bluebells. It would be the best moment, before the full flush of summer, and in the valley the azaleas would be prodigal of scent, and the blood-red rhododendrons in bloom. We motored, I remember, leaving London in the morning in a heavy shower of rain, coming to Manderley about five o'clock, in time for tea. I can see myself now, unsuitably dressed as usual, although a bride of seven weeks, in a tan-coloured stockinette frock, a small fur known as a stone marten round my neck, and over all a shapeless mackintosh, far too big for me and dragging to my ankles. It was, I thought, a gesture to the weather, and the length added inches to my height. I clutched a pair of gauntlet gloves in my hands, and carried a large leather handbag.

"This is London rain," said Maxim when we left, "you wait, the sun will be shining for you when we come to Manderley"; and he was right, for the clouds left us at Exeter, they rolled away behind us, leaving a great blue sky above our heads and a white road in front of us.

I was glad to see the sun, for in superstitious fashion I looked upon rain as an omen of ill-will, and the leaden skies of London had made me silent.

"Feeling better?" said Maxim, and I smiled at him, taking his hand, thinking how easy it was for him, going to his own home, wandering into the hall, picking up letters, ringing a bell for tea, and I wondered how much he guessed of my nervousness, and whether his question "Feeling better?" meant that he understood. "Never mind, we'll soon be there. I expect you want your tea," he said, and he let go my hand because we had reached a bend in the road, and must slow down.

I knew then that he had mistaken my silence for fatigue, and it had not occurred to him I dreaded this arrival at Manderley as much as I had longed for it in theory. Now the moment was upon me I wished it delayed, I wanted to draw up at some wayside inn and stay there, in a coffee-room, by an impersonal fire. I wanted to be a traveller on the road, a bride in love with her husband. Not myself coming to Manderley for the first time, the wife of Maxim de Winter. We passed many friendly villages where the cottage windows had a kindly air. A woman, holding a baby in her arms, smiled at me from a doorway, while a man clanked across a road to a well, carrying a pail.

I wished we could have been one with them, perhaps their neighbours, and that Maxim could lean over a cottage gate in the evenings, smoking a pipe, proud of a very tall hollyhock he had grown himself, while I bustled in my kitchen, clean as a pin, laying the table for supper. There would be an alarm clock on the dresser ticking loudly, and a row of shining plates, while after supper Maxim would read his paper, boots on the fender, and I reach for a great pile of mending in the dresser drawer. Surely it would be peaceful and steady, that way of living, and easier, too, demanding no set standard?

"Only two miles further," said Maxim; "you see that great belt of trees on the brow of the hill there, sloping to the valley, with a scrap of sea beyond? That's Manderley, in there. Those are the woods."

I forced a smile, and did not answer him, aware now of a stab of panic, an uneasy sickness that could not be controlled. Gone was my glad excitement, vanished my happy pride. I was like a child brought to her first school, or a little untrained maid who has never left home before, seeking a situation. Any measure of self-possession I had gained hitherto, during the brief seven weeks of marriage, was like a rag now, fluttering before the wind; it seemed to me that even the most elementary knowledge of behaviour was unknown to me now, I should not know my right hand from my left, whether to stand or sit, what spoons and forks to use at dinner.

"I should shed that mackintosh," he said, glancing down at me, "it has not rained down here at all, and put your funny little fur straight. Poor lamb, I've bustled you down here like this, and you probably ought to have bought a lot of clothes in London."

"It doesn't matter to me, as long as you don't mind," I said.

"Most women think of nothing but clothes," he said absently, and turning a corner we came to a cross-road, and the beginning of a high wall.

"Here we are," he said, a new note of excitement in his voice, and I gripped the leather seat of the car with my two hands.

The road curved, and before us, on the left, were two high iron gates beside a lodge, open wide to the long drive beyond. As we drove through I saw faces peering through the dark window of the lodge, and a child ran round from the back, staring curiously. I shrank back against the seat, my heart beating quickly, knowing why the faces were at the window, and why the child stared.

They wanted to see what I was like. I could imagine them now, talking excitedly, laughing in the little kitchen. "Only caught sight of the top of her hat," they would say, "she wouldn't show her face. Oh, well, we'll know by to-morrow. Word will come from the house." Perhaps he guessed something of my shyness at last for he took my hand, and kissed it, and laughed a little, even as he spoke.

"You mustn't mind if there's a certain amount of curiosity," he said, "everyone will want to know what you are like. They have probably talked of nothing else for weeks. You've only got to be yourself and they will all adore you. And you don't have to worry about the house, Mrs. Danvers does everything. Just leave it all to her. She'll be stiff with you at first, I dare say, she's an extraordinary character, but you mustn't let it worry you. It's just her manner. See those shrubs? It's like a blue wall along here when the hydrangeas are in bloom."

I did not answer him, for I was thinking of that self who long ago bought a picture post-card in a village shop, and came out into the bright sunlight twisting it in her hands, pleased with her purchase, thinking "This will do for my album. 'Manderley,' what a lovely name." And now I belonged here, this was my home, I would write letters to people saying, "We shall be down at Manderley all the summer, you must come and see us," and I would walk along this drive, strange and unfamiliar to me now, with perfect knowledge, conscious of every twist and turn, marking and approving where the gardeners had worked, here a cutting back of the shrubs, there a lopping of a branch, calling at the lodge by the iron gates on some friendly errand, saying, "Well, how's the leg to-day?" while the old woman, curious no longer, bade me welcome to her kitchen. I envied Maxim, careless and at ease, and the little smile on his lips which meant he was happy to be coming home.

It seemed remote to me, and far too distant, the time when I too should smile and be at ease, and I wished it could come quickly, that I could be old even, with grey hair, and slow of step, having lived here many years, anything but the timid, foolish creature I felt myself to be.

The gates had shut to with a crash behind us, the dusty high-road was out of sight, and I became aware that this was not the drive I had imagined would be Manderley's, this was not a broad and spacious thing of gravel, flanked with neat turf at either side, kept smooth with rake and brush.

This drive twisted and turned as a serpent, scarce wider in places than a path, and above our heads was a great colonnade of trees, whose branches nodded and intermingled with one another, making an archway for us, like the roof of a church. Even the midday sun would not penetrate the interlacing of those green leaves, they were too thickly entwined, one with another, and only little flickering patches of warm light would come in intermittent waves to dapple the drive with gold. It was very silent, very still. On the high-road there had been a gay west wind blowing in my face, making the grass on the hedges dance in unison, but here there was no wind. Even the engine of the car had taken a new note, throbbing low, quieter than before. As the drive descended to the valley so the trees came in upon us, great beeches with lovely smooth white stems, lifting their myriad branches to one another, and other trees, trees I could not name, coming close, so close that I could touch them with my hands. On we went, over a little bridge that spanned a narrow stream, and still this drive that was no drive twisted and turned like an enchanted ribbon through the dark and silent woods, penetrating even deeper to the very heart surely of the forest itself, and still there was no clearing, no space to hold a house.

The length of it began to nag at my nerves, it must be this turn, I thought, or round that further bend, but as I leant forward in my seat I was forever disappointed, there was no house, no field, no broad and friendly garden, nothing but the silence and deep woods. The lodge gates were a memory, and the high-road something belonging to another time, another world.

Suddenly I saw a clearing in the dark drive ahead, and a patch of sky, and in a moment the dark trees had thinned, the nameless shrubs had disappeared, and on either side of us was a wall of colour, blood-red, reaching far above our heads. We were amongst the rhododendrons. There was something bewildering, even shocking, about the suddenness of their discovery. The woods had not prepared me for them. They startled me with their crimson faces, massed one upon the other in incredible profusion, showing no leaf, no twig, nothing but the slaughterous red, luscious and fantastic, unlike any rhododendron plant I had seen before.

I glanced at Maxim. He was smiling. "Like them?" he said.

I told him "Yes," a little breathlessly, uncertain whether I was speaking the truth or not, for to me a rhododendron was a homely, domestic thing, strictly conventional, mauve or pink in colour, standing one beside the other in a neat round bed. And these were monsters, rearing to the sky, massed like a battalion, too beautiful I thought, too powerful, they were not plants at all.

We were not far from the house now, I saw the drive broaden to the sweep I had expected, and with the blood-red wall still flanking us on either side, we turned the last corner, and so came to Manderley. Yes, there it was, the Manderley I had expected, the Manderley of my picture post-card long ago. A thing of grace and beauty, exquisite and faultless, lovelier even than I had ever dreamed, built in its hollow of smooth grass-land and mossy lawns, the terraces sloping to the gardens, and the gardens to the sea. As we drove up to the wide stone steps and stopped before the open door, I saw through one of the mullioned windows that the hall was full of people, and I heard Maxim swear under his breath. "Damn that woman," he said, "she knows perfectly well I did not want this sort of thing," and he put on the brakes with a jerk.

"What's the matter?" I said, "who are all those people?"

"I'm afraid you will have to face it now," he said, in irritation. "Mrs. Danvers has collected the whole damned staff in the house and on the estate to welcome us. It's all right, you won't have to say anything, I'll do it all."

I fumbled for the handle of the door, feeling slightly sick, and cold now too from the long drive, and as I fumbled with the catch the butler came down the steps, followed by a footman, and he opened the door for me.

He was old, he had a kind face, and I smiled up at him, holding out my hand, but I don't think he could have seen, for he took the rug instead, and my small dressing-case, and turned to Maxim, helping me from the car at the same time.

"Well, here we are, Frith," said Maxim, taking off his gloves, "it was raining when we left London. You don't seem to have had it here. Everyone well?"

"Yes, sir, thank you, sir. No, we have had a dry month on the whole. Glad to see you home, and hope you have been keeping well. And Madam too."

"Yes, we are both well, thank you, Frith. Rather tired from the drive, and wanting our tea. I didn't expect this business." He jerked his head to the hall.

"Mrs. Danvers' orders, sir," said the man, his face expressionless.

"I might have guessed it," said Maxim abruptly, "come on," he turned to me, "it won't take long, and then you shall have your tea."

We went together up the flight of steps, Frith and the footman following with the rug and my mackintosh, and I was aware of a little pain at the pit of my stomach, and a nervous contraction in my throat.

I can close my eyes now, and look back on it, and see myself as I must have been, standing on the threshold of the house, a slim, awkward figure in my stockinette dress, clutching in my sticky hands a pair of gauntlet gloves. I can see the great stone hall, the wide doors open to the library, the Peter Lelys and the Vandykes on the walls, the exquisite staircase leading to the minstrels' gallery, and there, ranged one behind the other in the hall, over-flowing to the stone passages beyond, and to the dining-room, a sea of faces, open-mouthed and curious, gazing at me as though they were the watching crowd about the block, and I the victim with my hands behind my back. Someone advanced from the sea of faces, someone tall and gaunt, dressed in deep black, whose prominent cheek-bones and great, hollow eyes gave her a skull's face, parchment-white, set on a skeleton's frame.

She came towards me, and I held out my hand, envying her for her dignity and her composure; but when she took my hand hers was limp and heavy, deathly cold, and it lay in mine like a lifeless thing.

"This is Mrs. Danvers," said Maxim, and she began to speak, still leaving that dead hand in mine, her hollow eyes never leaving my eyes, so that my own wavered and would not meet hers, and as they did so her hand moved in mine, the life returned to it, and I was aware of a sensation of discomfort and of shame.

I cannot remember her words now, but I know that she bade me welcome to Manderley, in the name of herself and the staff, a stiff, conventional speech rehearsed for the occasion, spoken in a voice as cold and lifeless as her hands had been. When she had finished she waited, as though for a reply, and I remember blushing scarlet, stammering some sort of thanks in return, and dropping both my gloves in my confusion. She stooped to pick them up, and as she handed them to me I saw a little smile of scorn upon her lips, and I guessed at once she considered me ill-bred. Something, in the expression of her face, gave me a feeling of unrest, and even when she had stepped back, and taken her place amongst the rest, I could see that black figure standing out alone, individual and apart, and for all her silence I knew her eye to be upon me. Maxim took my arm and made a little speech of thanks, perfectly easy and free from embarrassment, as though the making of it was no effort to him at all, and then he bore me off to the library to tea, closing the doors behind us, and we were alone again.

Two cocker spaniels came from the fireside to greet us. They pawed at Maxim, their long, silken ears strained back with affection, their noses questing his hands, and then they left him and came to me, sniffing at my heels, rather uncertain, rather suspicious. One was the mother, blind in one eye, and soon she had enough of me, and took herself with a grunt to the fire again, but Jasper, the younger, put his nose into my hand, and laid a chin upon my knee, his eyes deep with meaning, his tail a-thump when I stroked his silken ears.

I felt better when I had taken my hat off, and my wretched little fur, and thrown them both beside my gloves and my bag on to the window seat. It was a deep, comfortable room, with books lining the walls to the ceiling, the sort of room a man would move from never, did he live alone; solid chairs beside a great open fire-place, baskets for the two dogs in which I felt they never sat, for the hollows in the chairs had tell-tale marks. The long windows looked out upon the lawns, and beyond the lawns to the distant shimmer of the sea.

There was an old quiet smell about the room, as though the air in it was little changed, for all the sweet lilac scent and the roses brought to it throughout the early summer. Whatever air came to this room, whether from the garden or from the sea, would lose its first freshness, becoming part of the unchanging room itself, one with the books, musty and never read, one with the scrolled ceiling, the dark panelling, the heavy curtains.

It was an ancient mossy smell, the smell of a silent church where services are seldom held, where rusty lichen grows upon the stones and ivy tendrils creep to the very windows. A room for peace, a room for meditation.

Soon tea was brought to us, a stately little performance enacted by Frith and the young footman, in which I played no part until they had gone, and while Maxim glanced through his great pile of letters I played with two dripping crumpets, crumbled cake with my hands, and swallowed my scalding tea.

Now and again he looked up at me and smiled, and then returned to his letters, the accumulation of the last months I supposed, and I thought how little I knew of his life here at Manderley, of how it went, day by day, of the people he knew, of his friends, men and women, of what bills he paid, what orders he gave about his household. The last weeks had gone so swiftly, and I—driving by his side through France and Italy—thought only of how I loved him, seeing Venice with his eyes, echoing his words, asking no questions of the past and future, content with the little glory of the living present.

For he was gayer than I had thought, more tender than I had dreamed, youthful and ardent in a hundred happy ways, not the Maxim I had first met, not the stranger who sat alone at the table in the restaurant, staring before him, wrapped in his secret self. My Maxim laughed and sang, threw stones into the water, took my hand, wore no frown between his eyes, carried no burden on his shoulder. I knew him as a lover, as a friend, and during those weeks I had forgotten that he had a life, orderly, methodical, a life which must be taken up again, continued as before, making vanished weeks a brief discarded holiday.

I watched him read his letters, saw him frown at one, smile at another, dismiss the next with no expression, and but for the grace of God I thought, my letter would be lying there, written from New York, and he would read it in the same indifferent fashion, puzzled at first perhaps by the signature, and then tossing it with a yawn to the pile of others in the basket, reaching for his cup of tea. The knowledge of this chilled me, how narrow a chance had stood between me and what might-have-been, for he would have sat there to his tea, as he sat now, continuing his home life as he would in any case, and perhaps he would not have thought of me much, not with regret anyway, while I, in New York, playing bridge with Mrs. Van Hopper would wait day after day for a letter that never came.

I leant back in my chair, glancing about the room, trying to instill into myself some measure of confidence, some genuine realisation that I was here, at Manderley, the house of the picture post-card, the Manderley that was famous; I had to teach myself that all this was mine now, mine as much as his, the deep chair I was sitting in, that mass of books stretching to the ceiling, the pictures on the walls, the gardens, the woods, the Manderley I had read about, all of this was mine now because I was married to Maxim.

We should grow old here together, we should sit like this to our tea as old people, Maxim and I, with other dogs, the successors of these, and the library would wear the same ancient musty smell that it did now. It would know a period of glorious shabbiness and wear when the boys were young—our boys—for I saw them sprawling on the sofa with muddy boots, bringing with them always a litter of rods, and cricket bats, great clasp-knives, bows-and-arrows.

On the table there, polished now and plain, an ugly case would stand containing butterflies and moths, and another one with birds' eggs, wrapped in cotton wool. "Not all this junk in here," I would say, "take them to the schoolroom, darlings," and they would run off, shouting, calling to one another, but the little one staying behind, pottering on his own, quieter than the others.

My vision was disturbed by the opening of the door, and Frith came in with the footman to clear the tea. "Mrs. Danvers wondered, Madam, whether you would like to see your room," he said to me when the tea had been taken away.

Maxim glanced up from his letters. "What sort of job have they made of the east wing?" he said.

"Very nice indeed, sir, it seems to me; the men made a mess when they were working, of course, and for a time Mrs. Danvers was rather afraid it would not be finished by your return. But they cleared out last Monday. I should imagine you would be very comfortable there, sir, it's a lot lighter of course on that side of the house."

"Have you been making alterations?" I asked.

"Oh, nothing much," said Maxim briefly, "only redecorating and painting the suite in the east wing, which I thought we would use for ours. As Frith says, it's much more cheerful on that side of the house, and it has a lovely view of the rose-garden. It was the visitors' wing when my mother was alive. I'll just finish these letters and then I'll come up and join you. Run along and make friends with Mrs. Danvers, it's a good opportunity."

I got up slowly, my old nervousness returning, and went out into the hall. I wished I could have waited for him, and then, taking his arm, seen the rooms together. I did not want to go alone, with Mrs. Danvers. How vast the great hall looked now that it was empty. My feet rang on the flagged stones, echoing to the ceiling, and I felt guilty at the sound, as one does in church, self-conscious, aware of the same constraint. My feet made a stupid pitter-patter as I walked, and I thought that Frith, with his felt soles, must have thought me foolish.

"It's very big, isn't it?" I said, too brightly, too forced, a schoolgirl still, but he answered me in all solemnity. "Yes, Madam, Manderley is a big place. Not so big as some, of course, but big enough. This was the old banqueting hall, in old days. It is used still on great occasions, such as a big dinner, or a ball. And the public are admitted here, you know, once a week."

"Yes," I said, still aware of my loud footsteps, feeling, as I followed him, that he considered me as he would one of the public visitors, and I behaved like a visitor too, glancing politely to right and left, taking in the weapons on the wall, and the pictures, touching the carved staircase with my hands.

A black figure stood waiting for me at the head of the stairs, the hollow eyes watching me intently from the white skull's face. I looked round for the stolid Frith, but he had passed along the hall and into the further corridor.

I was alone now with Mrs. Danvers. I went up the great stairs towards her, and she waited motionless, her hands folded before her, her eyes never leaving my face. I summoned a smile, which was not returned, nor did I blame her, for there was no purpose to the smile, it was a silly thing, bright and artificial. "I hope I haven't kept you waiting," I said.

"It's for you to make your own time, Madam," she answered, "I'm here to carry out your orders," and then she turned, through the archway of the gallery, to the corridor beyond. We went along a broad, carpeted passage, and then turned left, through an oak door, and down a narrow flight of stairs and up a corresponding flight, and so to another door. This she flung open, standing aside to let me pass, and I came to a little ante-room, or boudoir, furnished with a sofa, chairs, and writing desk, which opened out to a large double bedroom with wide windows, and a bathroom beyond. I went at once to the window, and looked out. The rose-garden lay below, and the eastern part of the terrace, while beyond the rose-garden rose a smooth grass bank, stretching to the near woods.

"You can't see the sea from here then," I said, turning to Mrs. Danvers.

"No, not from this wing," she answered, "you can't even hear it, either. You would not know the sea was anywhere near, not from this wing."

She spoke in a peculiar way, as though something lay behind her words, and she laid an emphasis on the words, "this wing," as if suggesting that the suite where we stood now held some inferiority.

"I'm sorry about that, I like the sea," I said.

She did not answer, she just went on staring at me, her hands folded before her.

"However, it's a very charming room," I said, "and I'm sure I shall be comfortable. I understand that it's been done up for our return."

"Yes," she said.

"What was it like before?" I asked.

"It had a mauve paper, and different hangings; Mr. de Winter did not think it very cheerful. It was never much used, except for occa-

sional visitors. But Mr. de Winter gave special orders in his letter that
you would have this room."

"Then this was not his bedroom originally?" I said.

"No, Madam, he's never used the rooms in this wing before."

"Oh," I said, "he didn't tell me that," and I wandered to the dressing-table and began combing my hair. My things were already unpacked, my brushes and comb upon the tray. I was glad Maxim had
given me a set of brushes, and that they were laid out there, upon the
dressing-table for Mrs. Danvers to see. They were new, they had cost
money, I need not be ashamed of them.

"Alice has unpacked for you and will look after you until your
maid arrives," said Mrs. Danvers. I smiled at her again, I put down the
brush upon the dressing-table.

"I don't have a maid," I said awkwardly, "I'm sure Alice, if she is
the housemaid, will look after me all right."

She wore the same expression that she had done on our first
meeting, when I dropped my gloves so gauchely on the floor.

"I'm afraid that would not do for very long," she said. "It's usual,
you know, for ladies in your position, to have a personal maid."

I flushed, and reached for my brush again. There was a sting in
her words I understood too well. "If you think it necessary perhaps
you would see about it for me," I said, avoiding her eyes, "some
young girl perhaps, wanting to train."

"If you wish," she said. "It's for you to say."

There was silence between us, I wished she would go away. I
wondered why she must go on standing there, watching me, her
hands folded on her black dress.

"I suppose you have been at Manderley for many years," I said,
making a fresh effort, "longer than anyone else?"

"Not so long as Frith," she said, and I thought how lifeless her
voice was, and cold, like her hand when it had lain in mine; "Frith
was here when the old gentleman was living, when Mr. de Winter
was a boy."

"I see," I said, "so you did not come till after that?"

"No," she said, "not till after that."

Once more I glanced up at her, and once more I met her eyes,
dark and sombre, in that white face of hers, instilling into me, I knew
not why, a strange feeling of disquiet, of foreboding. I tried to smile,
and could not, I found myself held by those eyes, that had no light,
no flicker of sympathy towards me.

"I came here when the first Mrs. de Winter was a bride," she said,
and her voice, which had hitherto, as I said, been dull and toneless,

was harsh now with unexpected animation, with life and meaning, and there was a spot of colour on the gaunt cheek-bones.

The change was so sudden that I was shocked, and a little scared. I did not know what to do, or what to say. It was as though she had spoken words that were forbidden, words that she had hidden within herself for a long time and now would be repressed no longer. Still her eyes never left my face, they looked upon me with a curious mixture of pity and of scorn, until I felt myself to be even younger and more untutored to the ways of life than I had believed.

I could see she despised me, marking with all the snobbery of her class that I was no great lady, that I was humble, shy, and diffident. Yet there was something beside scorn in those eyes of hers, something surely of positive dislike, or actual malice?

I had to say something, I could not go on sitting there, playing with my hair-brush, letting her see how much I feared and mistrusted her.

"Mrs. Danvers," I heard myself saying, "I hope we shall be friends and come to understand one another. You must have patience with me, you know, because this sort of life is new to me, I've lived rather differently. And I do want to make a success of it, and above all to make Mr. de Winter happy. I know I can leave all household arrangements to you, Mr. de Winter said so, and you must just run things as they have always been run, I shan't want to make any changes."

I stopped, a little breathless, still uncertain of myself and whether I was saying the right thing, and when I looked up again I saw that she had moved, and was standing with her hand on the handle of the door.

"Very good," she said; "I hope I shall do everything to your satisfaction. The house has been in my charge now for more than a year, and Mr. de Winter has never complained. It was very different of course when the late Mrs. de Winter was alive, there was a lot of entertaining then, a lot of parties, and though I managed for her she liked to supervise things herself."

Once again I had the impression that she chose her words with care, that she was feeling her way, as it were, into my mind, and watching for the effect upon my face.

"I would rather leave it to you," I repeated, "much rather," and into her face came the same expression I had noticed before, when first I had shaken hands with her in the hall, a look surely of derision, of definite contempt. She knew that I would never withstand her, and that I feared her too.

"Can I do anything more for you?" she said, and I pretended to glance round the room. "No," I said. "No, I think I have everything. I shall be very comfortable here. You have made the room so charming,"—this last a final crawling sop to win her approval. She shrugged her shoulders, and still she did not smile. "I only followed out Mr. de Winter's instructions," she said.

She hesitated by the doorway, her hand on the handle of the open door. It was as though she still had something to say to me, and could not decide upon the words, yet waited there, for me to give her opportunity.

I wished she would go, she was like a shadow standing there, watching me, appraising me with her hollow eyes, set in that dead skull's face.

"If you find anything not to your liking you will tell me at once?" she asked.

"Yes," I said. "Yes, of course, Mrs. Danvers," but I knew this was not what she had meant to say, and silence fell between us once again.

"If Mr. de Winter asks for his big wardrobe," she said suddenly, "you must tell him it was impossible to move. We tried, but we could not get it through these narrow doorways. These are smaller rooms than those in the west wing. If he doesn't like the arrangement of this suite he must tell me. It was difficult to know how to furnish these rooms."

"Please don't worry, Mrs. Danvers," I said, "I'm sure he will be pleased with everything. But I'm sorry it's given you so much trouble. I had no idea he was having rooms redecorated and furnished, he shouldn't have bothered. I'm sure I should have been just as happy and comfortable in the west wing."

She looked at me curiously, and began twisting the handle of the door. "Mr. de Winter said you would prefer to be on this side," she said, "the rooms in the west wing are very old. The bedroom in the big suite is twice as large as this, a very beautiful room too, with a scrolled ceiling. The tapestry chairs are very valuable, and so is the carved mantelpiece. It's the most beautiful room in the house. And the windows look down across the lawns to the sea."

I felt uncomfortable, a little shy. I did not know why she must speak with such an undercurrent of resentment, implying as she did at the same time that this room, where I found myself to be installed, was something inferior, not up to Manderley standard, a second-rate room, as it were, for a second-rate person.

"I suppose Mr. de Winter keeps the most beautiful room to show to the public," I said. She went on twisting the handle of the door, and then looked up at me again, watching my eyes, hesitating before replying, and when she spoke her voice was quieter even, and more toneless, than it had been before.

"The bedrooms are never shown to the public," she said, "only the hall and the gallery, and the rooms below." She paused an instant, feeling me with her eyes. "They used to live in the west wing and use those rooms when Mrs. de Winter was alive. That big room, I was telling you about, that looked down to the sea, was Mrs. de Winter's bedroom."

Then I saw a shadow flit across her face, and she drew back against the wall, effacing herself, as a step sounded outside and Maxim came into the room.

"How is it?" he said to me, "all right? Do you think you'll like it?" He looked round with enthusiasm, pleased as a schoolboy. "I always thought this a most attractive room," he said. "It was wasted all those years as a guest-room, but I always thought it had possibilities. You've made a great success of it, Mrs. Danvers, I give you full marks."

"Thank you, sir," she said, her face expressionless, and then she turned, and went out of the room, closing the door softly behind her.

Maxim went and leant out of the window. "I love the rose-garden," he said; "one of the first things I remember is walking after my mother, on very small, unsteady legs, while she picked off the dead heads of the roses. There's something peaceful and happy about this room, and it's quiet too. You could never tell you were within five minutes of the sea, from this room."

"That's what Mrs. Danvers said," I told him.

He came away from the window, he prowled about the room, touching things, looking at the pictures, opening wardrobes, fingering my clothes, already unpacked.

"How did you get on with old Danvers?" he said abruptly.

I turned away, and began combing my hair again before the looking-glass. "She seems just a little bit stiff," I said, after a moment or two, "perhaps she thought I was going to interfere with the running of the house."

"I don't think she would mind your doing that," he said. I looked up and saw him watching my reflection in the looking-glass, and then he turned away and went over to the window again, whistling quietly, under his breath, rocking backwards and forwards on his heels.

"Don't mind her," he said, "she's an extraordinary character in many ways, and possibly not very easy for another woman to get on with. You mustn't worry about it. If she really makes herself a nuisance we'll get rid of her. But she's efficient, you know, and will take all housekeeping worries off your hands. I dare say she's a bit of a bully to the staff. She doesn't dare bully me though. I'd have given her the sack long ago if she had tried."

"I expect we shall get on very well when she knows me better," I said quickly, "after all, it's natural enough that she should resent me a bit at first."

"Resent you, why resent you? What the devil do you mean?" he said.

He turned from the window, frowning, an odd, half-angry expression on his face. I wondered why he should mind, and wished I had said something else.

"I mean, it must be much easier for a housekeeper to look after a man alone," I said. "I dare say she had got into the way of doing it, and perhaps she was afraid I should be very overbearing."

"Overbearing, my God . . ." he began, "if you think . . ." and then he stopped, and came across to me, and kissed me on the top of my head.

"Let's forget about Mrs. Danvers," he said; "she doesn't interest me very much I'm afraid. Come along, and let me show you something of Manderley."

I did not see Mrs. Danvers again that evening, and we did not talk about her any more. I felt happier, when I had dismissed her from my thoughts, less of an interloper, and as we wandered about the rooms downstairs, and looked at the pictures, and Maxim put his arm round my shoulder, I began to feel more like the self I wanted to become, the self I had pictured in my dreams, who made Manderley her home.

My footsteps no longer sounded foolish on the stone flags of the hall, for Maxim's nailed shoes made far more noise than mine, and the pattering feet of the two dogs was a comfortable, pleasing note.

I was glad, too, because it was the first evening, and we had only been back a little while, and the showing of the pictures had taken time, when Maxim, looking at the clock, said it was too late to change for dinner, so that I was spared the embarrassment of Alice, the maid, asking what I should wear, and of her helping me to dress, and myself walking down that long flight of stairs to the hall, cold, with bare shoulders, in a dress that Mrs. Van Hopper had given me because it did not suit her daughter. I had dreaded the formality of dinner in that austere dining-room, and now, because of the little fact that we had not changed, it was quite all right, quite easy, just the same as when we had dined together in restaurants. I was comfortable in my stockinette dress, I laughed and talked about things we had seen in Italy and France, we even had the snapshots on the table, and Frith and the footman were impersonal people, as the waiters had been, they did not stare at me as Mrs. Danvers had done.

We sat in the library after dinner, and presently the curtains were drawn, and more logs thrown on to the fire. It was cool for May; I was thankful for the warmth that came from the steady burning logs.

It was new for us to sit together like this, after dinner, for in Italy we had wandered about, walked or driven, gone into little cafés, leant over bridges. Maxim made instinctively now for the chair on the left of the open fireplace, and stretched out his hand for the papers. He settled one of the broad cushions behind his head, and lit a cigarette. "This is his routine," I thought, "this is what he always does, this has been his custom now for years."

He did not look at me, he went on reading his paper, contented, comfortable, having assumed his way of living, the master of his house. And as I sat there, brooding, my chin in my hands, fondling the soft ears of one of the spaniels, it came to me that I was not the first one to lounge there in possession of the chair, someone had been before me, had surely left an imprint of her person on the cushions, and on the arm where her hand had rested. Another one had poured the coffee from that same silver coffee pot, had placed the cup to her lips, had bent down to the dog, even as I was doing.

Unconsciously I shivered, as though someone had opened the door behind me, and let a draught into the room. I was sitting in Rebecca's chair, I was leaning against Rebecca's cushion, and the dog had come to me and laid his head upon my knee because that had been his custom, and he remembered, in the past, she had given sugar to him there.

CHAPTER EIGHT

I had never realised, of course, that life at Manderley would be so orderly and planned. I remember now, looking back, how on that first morning Maxim was up and dressed and writing letters, even before breakfast, and when I got downstairs, rather after nine o'clock, a little flurried by the booming summons of the gong, I found he had nearly finished, he was already peeling his fruit.

He looked up at me and smiled. "You mustn't mind," he said, "this is something you will have to get used to. I've no time to hang about at this hour of the day. Running a place like Manderley, you know, is a full-time job. The coffee and the hot dishes are on the sideboard. We always help ourselves at breakfast." I said something about my clock being slow, about having been too long in the bath, but he did not listen, he was looking down at a letter, frowning at something.

How impressed I was, I remember well; impressed and a little over-awed by the magnificence of the breakfast offered to us. There was tea, in a great silver urn, and coffee too, and on the heater, piping hot, dishes of scrambled eggs, of bacon, and another of fish. There was a little clutch of boiled eggs as well, in their own special heater, and porridge, in a silver porringer. On another side-board was a ham, and a great piece of cold bacon. There were scones too, on the table, and toast, and various pots of jam, marmalade, and honey, while dessert dishes, piled high with fruit, stood at either end. It seemed strange to me that Maxim, who in Italy and France had eaten a *croissant* and fruit only, and drunk a cup of coffee, should sit down to this breakfast at home, enough for a dozen people, day after day probably, year after year, seeing nothing ridiculous about it, nothing wasteful.

I noticed he had eaten a small piece of fish. I took a boiled egg. And I wondered what happened to the rest, all those scrambled eggs, that crisp bacon, the porridge, the remains of the fish. Were there menials, I wondered, whom I should never know, never see, waiting behind kitchen doors for the gift of our breakfast? Or was it all thrown away, shovelled into dustpans? I would never know, of course, I would never dare to ask.

"Thank the Lord I haven't a great crowd of relations to inflict upon you," said Maxim, "a sister I very rarely see, and a grandmother who is nearly blind. Beatrice, by-the-way, asks herself over to lunch. I half expected she would. I suppose she wants to have a look at you."

"To-day?" I said, my spirits sinking to zero.

"Yes, according to the letter I got this morning. She won't stay long. You'll like her, I think. She's very direct, believes in speaking her mind. No humbug at all. If she doesn't like you she'll tell you so, to your face."

I found this hardly comforting, and wondered if there was not some virtue in the quality of insincerity. Maxim got up from his chair, and lit a cigarette. "I've a mass of things to see to this morning, do you think you can amuse yourself?" he said. "I'd like to have taken you round the garden, but I must see Crawley, my agent. I've been away from things too long. He'll be in to lunch, too, by-the-way. You don't mind, do you, you will be all right?"

"Of course," I said, "I shall be quite happy."

Then he picked up his letters, and went out of the room, and I remember thinking this was not how I had imagined my first morning; I had seen us walking together, arms linked, to the sea, coming back rather late and tired and happy to a cold lunch, alone, and sitting afterwards under that chestnut tree I could see from the library window.

I lingered long over my first breakfast, spinning out the time, and it was not until I saw Frith come in and look at me, from behind the Service screen, that I realised it was after ten o'clock. I sprang to my feet at once, feeling guilty, and apologised for sitting there so late, and he bowed, saying nothing, very polite, very correct, but I caught a flicker of surprise in his eyes. I wondered if I had said the wrong thing. Perhaps it did not do to apologise. Perhaps it lowered me in his estimation. I wished I knew what to say, what to do. I wondered if he suspected, as Mrs. Danvers had done, that poise, and grace, and assurance were not qualities inbred in me, but were things to be acquired, painfully perhaps, and slowly, costing me many bitter moments.

As it was, leaving the room, I stumbled, not looking where I was going, catching my foot on the step by the door, and Frith came forward to help me, picking up my handkerchief, while Robert, the young footman, who was standing behind the screen, turned away to hide his smile.

I heard the murmur of their voices as I crossed the hall, and one of them laughed, Robert, I supposed. Perhaps they were laughing about me. I went upstairs again, to the privacy of my bedroom, but when I opened the door I found the housemaids in there doing the room, one was sweeping the floor, the other dusting the dressing-table. They looked at me in surprise. I quickly went out again. It could not be right then, for me to go to my room at that hour in the morning. It was not expected of me. It broke the household routine. I crept downstairs once more, silently, thankful of my slippers that made no sound on the stone flags, and so into the library which was chilly, the windows flung wide open, the fire laid but not lit.

I shut the windows, and looked round for a box of matches. I could not find one. I wondered what I should do. I did not like to ring. But the library, so snug and warm last night with the burning logs, was like an ice-house now, in the early morning. There were matches upstairs in the bedroom, but I did not like to go for them because it would mean disturbing the housemaids at their work. I could not bear their moon faces staring at me again. I decided that when Frith and Robert had left the dining-room I would fetch the matches from the side-board. I tiptoed out into the hall and listened. They were still clearing, I could hear the sound of voices, and the movement of trays. Presently all was silent, they must have gone through the Service doors into the kitchen quarters, so I went across the hall and into the dining-room once more. Yes, there was a box of matches on the side-board, as I expected. I crossed the room quickly, and picked them up, and as I did so Frith came back into the room. I tried to cram the box furtively into my pocket, but I saw him glance at my hand in surprise.

"Did you require anything, Madam?" he said.

"Oh, Frith," I said awkwardly, "I could not find any matches." He at once proffered me another box, handing me the cigarettes too, at the same time. This was another embarrassment, for I did not smoke.

"No, the fact is," I said, "I felt rather cool in the library, I suppose the weather seems chilly to me, after being abroad, and I thought perhaps I would just put a match to the fire."

"The fire in the library is not usually lit until the afternoon, Madam," he said. "Mrs. de Winter always used the morning-room.

There is a good fire in there. Of course if you should wish to have the fire in the library as well I will give orders for it to be lit."

"Oh, no," I said, "I would not dream of it. I will go into the morning-room. Thank you, Frith."

"You will find writing-paper, and pens, and ink, in there, Madam," he said. "Mrs. de Winter always did all her correspondence and telephoning in the morning-room, after breakfast. The house telephone is also there, should you wish to speak to Mrs. Danvers."

"Thank you, Frith," I said.

I turned away into the hall again, humming a little tune to give me an air of confidence. I could not tell him that I had never seen the morning-room, that Maxim had not shown it to me the night before. I knew he was standing in the entrance to the dining-room, watching me, as I went across the hall, and that I must make some show of knowing my way. There was a door to the left of the great staircase, and I went recklessly towards it, praying in my heart that it would take me to my goal, but when I came to it and opened it I saw that it was a garden-room, a place for odds and ends, there was a table where flowers were done, there were basket chairs stacked against the wall, and a couple of mackintoshes too, hanging on a peg. I came out, a little defiantly, glancing across the hall, and saw Frith still standing there. I had not deceived him though, not for a moment.

"You go through the drawing-room to the morning-room, Madam," he said, "through the door there, on your right, this side of the staircase. You go straight through the double drawing-room, and turn to your left."

"Thank you, Frith," I said humbly, pretending no longer.

I went through the long drawing-room, as he had directed, a lovely room this, beautifully proportioned, looking out upon the lawns down to the sea. The public would see this room, I supposed, and Frith, if he showed them round, would know the history of the pictures on the wall, and the period of the furniture. It was beautiful of course, I knew that, and those chairs and tables probably without price, but for all that I had no wish to linger there, I could not see myself sitting ever in those chairs, standing before that carved mantelpiece, throwing books down on to the tables. It had all the formality of a room in a museum, where alcoves were roped off, and a guardian, in cloak and hat like the guides in the French châteaux, sat in a chair beside the door. I went through then, and turned, to the left, and so on to the little morning-room I had not seen before.

I was glad to see the dogs there, sitting before the fire, and Jasper, the younger, came over to me at once, his tail wagging, and thrust his nose into my hand. The old one lifted her muzzle at my approach, and gazed in my direction with her blind eyes, but when she had sniffed the air a moment, and found I was not the one she sought, she turned her head away with a grunt, and looked steadily into the fire again. Then Jasper left me, too, and settled himself by the side of his companion, licking his side. This was their routine. They knew, even as Frith had known, that the library fire was not lit until the afternoon. They came to the morning-room from long custom. Somehow I guessed, before going to the window, that the room looked out upon the rhododendrons. Yes, there they were, blood-red and luscious, as I had seen them the evening before, great bushes of them, massed beneath the open window, encroaching on to the sweep of the drive itself. There was a little clearing too, between the bushes, like a miniature lawn, the grass a smooth carpet of moss, and in the centre of this, the tiny statue of a naked faun, his pipes to his lips.

The crimson rhododendrons made his background, and the clearing itself was like a little stage, where he would dance, and play his part. There was no musty smell about this room, as there had been in the library. There were no old well-worn chairs, no tables littered with magazines and papers, seldom if ever read, but left there from long custom, because Maxim's father, or even his grandfather perhaps, had wished it so.

This was a woman's room, graceful, fragile, the room of someone who had chosen every particle of furniture with great care, so that each chair, each vase, each small, infinitesimal thing should be in harmony with one another, and with her own personality. It was as though she who had arranged this room had said: "This I will have, and this, and this," taking piece by piece from the treasures in Manderley each object that pleased her best, ignoring the second-rate, the mediocre, laying her hand with sure and certain instinct only upon the best. There was no intermingling of style, no confusing of period, and the result was perfection in a strange and startling way, not coldly formal like the drawing-room shown to the public, but vividly alive, having something of the same glow and brilliance that the rhododendrons had, massed there, beneath the window. And I noticed then that the rhododendrons, not content with forming their theatre on the little lawn outside the window, had been permitted to the room itself. Their great warm faces looked down upon me from the mantelpiece, they floated in a bowl upon the table by the sofa, they stood, lean and graceful, on the writing-desk beside the golden candlesticks.

The room was filled with them, even the walls took colour from them, becoming rich and glowing in the morning sun. They were the only flowers in the room, and I wondered if there was some purpose in it, whether the room had been arranged originally with this one end in view, for nowhere else in the house did the rhododendrons obtrude. There were flowers in the dining-room, flowers in the library, but orderly and trim, rather in the background, not like this, not in profusion. I went and sat down at the writing-desk, and I thought how strange it was that this room, so lovely and so rich in colour, should be, at the same time, so business-like and purposeful. Somehow I should have expected that a room furnished as this was in such exquisite taste, for all the exaggeration of the flowers, would be a place of decoration only, languorous and intimate.

But this writing-table, beautiful as it was, was no pretty toy where a woman would scribble little notes, nibbling the end of a pen, leaving it, day after day, in carelessness, the blotter a little askew. The pigeon-holes were docketed, "letters-unanswered," "letters-to-keep," "household," "estate," "menus," "miscellaneous," "addresses"; each ticket written in that same scrawling pointed hand that I knew already. And it shocked me, even startled me, to recognise it again, for I had not seen it since I had destroyed the page from the book of poems, and I had not thought to see it again.

I opened a drawer at hazard, and there was the writing once more, this time in an open leather book, whose heading "Guests at Manderley" showed at once, divided into weeks and months, what visitors had come and gone, the rooms they had used, the food they had eaten. I turned over the pages, and saw that the book was a complete record of a year, so that the hostess, glancing back, would know to the day, almost to the hour, what guest had passed what night under her roof, and where he had slept, and what she had given him to eat. There was note-paper also in the drawer, thick white sheets, for rough writing, and the note-paper of the house, with the crest, and the address, and visiting cards, ivory-white, in little boxes.

I took one out and looked at it, unwrapped it from its thin tissue of paper. "Mrs. M. de Winter" it said, and in the corner "Manderley." I put it back in the box again, and shut the drawer, feeling guilty suddenly, and deceitful, as though I were staying in somebody else's house and my hostess had said to me, "Yes, of course, write letters at my desk," and I had unforgivably, in a stealthy manner, peeped at her correspondence. At any moment she might come back into the room, and she would see me there, sitting before her open drawer, which I had no right to touch.

And when the telephone rang, suddenly, alarmingly, on the desk in front of me, my heart leapt and I stared up in terror, thinking I had been discovered. I took the receiver off with trembling hands, and "Who is it?" I said, "who do you want?" There was a strange buzzing at the end of the line, and then a voice came, low and rather harsh, whether that of a woman or a man I could not tell, and "Mrs. de Winter?" it said, "Mrs. de Winter?"

"I'm afraid you have made a mistake," I said, "Mrs. de Winter has been dead for over a year." I sat there, waiting, staring stupidly into the mouthpiece, and it was not until the name was repeated again, the voice incredulous, slightly raised, that I became aware, with a rush of colour to my face, that I had blundered irretrievably, and could not take back my words. "It's Mrs. Danvers, Madam," said the voice, "I'm speaking to you on the house telephone." My faux-pas was so palpably obvious, so idiotic and unpardonable, that to ignore it would show me to be an even greater fool if possible, than I was already.

"I'm sorry, Mrs. Danvers," I said stammering, my words tumbling over one another, "the telephone startled me, I didn't know what I was saying, I didn't realise the call was for me, and I never noticed I was speaking on the house telephone."

"I'm sorry to have disturbed you, Madam," she said, and she knows, I thought, she guesses I have been looking through the desk, "I only wondered whether you wished to see me, and whether you approved of the menus for to-day."

"Oh," I said. "Oh, I'm sure I do, that is, I'm sure I approve of the menus, just order what you like, Mrs. Danvers, you needn't bother to ask me."

"It would be better I think if you read the list," continued the voice, "you will find the menu of the day on the blotter, beside you."

I searched feverishly about me on the desk, and found at last a sheet of paper I had not noticed before. I glanced hurriedly through it, curried prawns, roast veal, asparagus, cold chocolate mousse—was this lunch or dinner, I could not see, lunch I suppose.

"Yes, Mrs. Danvers," I said, "very suitable, very nice indeed."

"If you wish anything changed please say so," she answered, "and I will give orders at once. You will notice I have left a blank space beside the sauce, for you to mark your preference. I was not sure what sauce you are used to having served with the roast veal. Mrs. de Winter was most particular about her sauces, and I always had to refer to her."

"Oh," I said. "Oh, well . . . let me see, Mrs. Danvers, I hardly know; I think we had better have what you usually have, whatever you think Mrs. de Winter would have ordered."

"You have no preference, Madam?"

"No," I said. "No, really, Mrs. Danvers."

"I rather think Mrs. de Winter would have ordered a wine sauce, Madam."

"We will have the same then, of course," I said.

"I'm very sorry I disturbed you while you were writing, Madam."

"You didn't disturb me at all," I said, "please don't apologise."

"The post leaves at midday, and Robert will come for your letters, and stamp them himself," she said; "all you have to do is to ring through to him, on the telephone, if you have anything urgent to be sent, and he will give orders for them to be taken in to the post-office immediately."

"Thank you, Mrs. Danvers," I said. I listened for a moment, but she said no more, and then I heard a little click at the end of the telephone, which meant she had replaced the receiver. I did the same. Then I looked down again at the desk, and the note-paper, ready for use, upon the blotter. In front of me stared the ticketed pigeon-holes, and the words upon them "letters-unanswered," "estate," "miscellaneous," were like a reproach to me for my idleness. She who sat here before me had not wasted her time, as I was doing. She had reached out for the house telephone and given her orders for the day, swiftly, efficiently, and run her pencil through an item in the menu that had not pleased her. She had not said "Yes, Mrs. Danvers," and "Of course, Mrs. Danvers," as I had done. And then, when she had finished, she began her letters, five, six, seven perhaps to be answered, all written in that same curious, slanting hand I knew so well. She would tear off sheet after sheet of that smooth white paper, using it extravagantly, because of the long strokes she made when she wrote, and at the end of her personal letters she put her signature, "Rebecca," that tall sloping R dwarfing its fellows.

I drummed with my fingers on the desk. The pigeon-holes were empty now. There were no "letters-unanswered" waiting to be dealt with, no bills to pay that I knew anything about. If I had anything urgent, Mrs. Danvers said, I must telephone through to Robert and he would give orders for it to be taken to the post. I wondered how many urgent letters Rebecca used to write, and who they were written to. Dressmakers perhaps—"I must have the white satin on Tuesday, without fail," or to her hair-dresser—"I shall be coming up next Friday, and want an appointment at three o'clock with Monsieur Antoine himself. Shampoo, massage, set, and manicure." No letters of that type would be a waste of time. She would have a call put through to London, Frith would do it. Frith would say "I am speaking for Mrs. de

Winter." I went on drumming with my fingers on the desk. I could think of nobody to write to. Only Mrs. Van Hopper. And there was something foolish, rather ironical, in the realisation that here I was sitting at my own desk in my own home with nothing better to do than to write a letter to Mrs. Van Hopper, a woman I disliked, whom I should never see again. I pulled a sheet of note-paper towards me. I took up the narrow, slender pen, with the bright pointed nib. "Dear Mrs. Van Hopper," I began. And as I wrote, in halting, laboured fashion, saying I hoped the voyage had been good, that she had found her daughter better, that the weather in New York was fine and warm, I noticed for the first time how cramped and unformed was my own hand-writing, without individuality, without style, uneducated even, the writing of an indifferent pupil taught in a second-rate school.

CHAPTER NINE

When I heard the sound of the car in the drive I got up in sudden panic, glancing at the clock, for I knew that it meant Beatrice and her husband had arrived. It was only just gone twelve, they were much earlier than I expected. And Maxim was not yet back. I wondered if it would be possible to hide, to get out of the window into the garden, so that Frith, bringing them to the morning-room, would say "Madam must have gone out," and it would seem quite natural, they would take it as a matter of course. The dogs looked up enquiringly as I ran to the window, and Jasper followed me, wagging his tail.

The window opened out on to the terrace and the little grass clearing beyond, but as I prepared to brush past the rhododendrons the sound of voices came close, and I backed again into the room. They were coming to the house by way of the garden, Frith having told them doubtless that I was in the morning-room. I went quickly into the big drawing-room, and made for a door near me on the left. It led into a long stone passage, and I ran along it, fully aware of my stupidity, despising myself for this sudden attack of nerves, but I knew I could not face these people, not for a moment anyway. The passage seemed to be taking me to the back regions, and as I turned a corner, coming upon another staircase, I met a servant I had not seen before, a scullery-maid perhaps, she carried a mop and a pail in her hands. She stared at me in wonder, as though I were a vision, unexpected in this part of the house, and "Good-morning," I said, in great confusion, making for the stairway, and "Good-morning, Madam," she returned, her mouth open, her round eyes inquisitive as I climbed the stairs.

They would lead me, I supposed, to the bedrooms, and I could find my suite in the east wing, and sit up there a little while, until I judged it nearly time for lunch, when good manners would compel me to come down again.

I must have lost my bearings, for passing through a door at the head of the stairs I came to a long corridor that I had not seen before, similar in some ways to the one in the east wing, but broader and darker—dark owing to the panelling of the walls.

I hesitated, then turned left, coming upon a broad landing and another staircase. It was very quiet and dark. No one was about. If there had been housemaids here, during the morning, they had finished their work by now and gone downstairs. There was no trace of their presence, no lingering dust smell of carpets lately swept, and I thought, as I stood there, wondering which way to turn, that the silence was unusual, holding something of the same oppression as an empty house does, when the owners have gone away.

I opened a door at hazard, and found a room in total darkness, no chink of light coming through the closed shutters, while I could see dimly, in the centre of the room, the outline of furniture swathed in white dust-sheets. The room smelt close and stale, the smell of a room seldom if ever used, whose ornaments are herded together in the centre of a bed and left there, covered with a sheet. It might be too that the curtains had not been drawn from the window since some preceding summer, and if one crossed there now and pulled them aside, opening the creaking shutters, a dead moth who had been imprisoned behind them for many months would fall to the carpet and lie there, beside a forgotten pin, and dried leaf blown there before the windows were closed for the last time. I shut the door softly, and went uncertainly along the corridor, flanked on either side by doors, all of them closed, until I came to a little alcove, set in an outside wall, where a broad window gave me light at last. I looked out, and I saw below me the smooth grass lawns stretching to the sea, and the sea itself, bright green with white-topped crests, whipped by a westerly wind and scudding from the shore.

It was closer than I had thought, much closer; it ran surely, beneath that little knot of trees below the lawns, barely five minutes away, and if I listened now, my ear to the window, I could hear the surf breaking on the shores of some little bay I could not see. I knew then I had made the circuit of the house, and was standing in the corridor of the west wing. Yes, Mrs. Danvers was right. You could hear the sea from here. You might imagine, in the winter, it would creep up on to those green lawns and threaten the house itself, for even now, because of the high wind, there was a mist upon the window-glass, as though someone had breathed upon it. A mist salt-laden, borne upwards from the sea. A hurrying cloud hid the sun for a moment as I watched, and the sea changed colour instantly, becoming black, and the white crests with them very pitiless suddenly, and cruel, not the gay sparkling sea I had looked on first.

Somehow I was glad my rooms were in the east wing. I preferred the rose-garden, after all, to the sound of the sea. I went back to the landing then, at the head of the stairs, and as I prepared to go down, one hand upon the banister, I heard the door behind me open, and it was Mrs. Danvers. We stared at one another for a moment without speaking, and I could not be certain whether it was anger I read in her eyes or curiosity, for her face became a mask directly she saw me. Although she said nothing I felt guilty and ashamed, as though I had been caught trespassing, and I felt the tell-tale colour come up into my face.

"I lost my way," I said, "I was trying to find my room."

"You have come to the opposite side of the house," she said, "this is the west wing."

"Yes, I know," I said.

"Did you go into any of the rooms?" she asked me.

"No," I said. "No, I just opened a door, I did not go in. Everything was dark, covered up in dust-sheets. I'm sorry. I did not mean to disturb anything. I expect you like to keep all this shut up."

"If you wish to open up the rooms I will have it done," she said, "you have only to tell me. The rooms are all furnished, and can be used."

"Oh, no," I said. "No, I did not mean you to think that."

"Perhaps you would like me to show you all over the west wing?" she said.

I shook my head. "No, rather not," I said. "No, I must go downstairs." I began to walk down the stairs, and she came with me, by my side, as though she were a warder, and I in custody.

"Any time, when you have nothing to do, you have only to ask me, and I will show you the rooms in the west wing," she persisted, making me vaguely uncomfortable, I knew not why. Her insistence struck a chord in my memory, reminding me of a visit to a friend's house, as a child, when the daughter of the house, older than I, took my arm and whispered in my ear, "I know where there is a book, locked in a cupboard, in my mother's bedroom. Shall we go and look at it?" I remembered her white, excited face, and her small, beady eyes, and the way she kept pinching my arm.

"I will have the dust-sheets removed, and then you can see the rooms as they looked when they were used," said Mrs. Danvers. "I would have shown you this morning, but I believed you to be writing letters in the morning-room. You have only to telephone through to my room, you know, when you want me. It would only take a short while to have the rooms in readiness."

We had come down the short flight of stairs, and she opened another door, standing aside for me to pass through, her dark eyes questing my face.

"It's very kind of you, Mrs. Danvers," I said. "I will let you know some time."

We passed out together on to the landing beyond, and I saw we were at the head of the main staircase now, behind the minstrels' gallery.

"I wonder how you came to miss your way?" she said, "the door through to the west wing is very different to this."

"I did not come this way," I said.

"Then you must have come up the back way, from the stone passage?" she said.

"Yes," I said, not meeting her eyes. "Yes, I came through a stone passage."

She went on looking at me, as though she expected me to tell her why I left the morning-room in sudden panic, going through the back regions, and I felt suddenly that she knew, that she must have watched me, that she had seen me wandering perhaps in that west wing from the first, her eye to a crack in the door. "Mrs. Lacy, and Major Lacy, have been here some time," she said. "I heard their car drive up shortly after twelve."

"Oh!" I said. "I had not realised that."

"Frith will have taken them to the morning-room," she said, "it must be getting on for half-past twelve. You know your way now, don't you?"

"Yes, Mrs. Danvers," I said. And I went down the big stairway into the hall, knowing she was standing there above me, her eyes watching me.

I knew I must go back now, to the morning-room, and meet Maxim's sister and her husband. I could not hide in my bedroom now. As I went into the drawing-room I glanced back, over my shoulder, and I saw Mrs. Danvers still standing there at the head of the stairs, like a black sentinel.

I stood for a moment outside the morning-room, with my hand on the door, listening to the hum of voices. Maxim had returned then, while I had been upstairs, bringing his agent with him I supposed, for it sounded to me as if the room was full of people. I was aware of the same feeling of sick uncertainty I had experienced so often as a child, when summoned to shake hands with visitors, and turning the handle of the door I blundered in, to be met at once, it seemed, with a sea of faces and a general silence.

"Here she is at last," said Maxim. "Where have you been hiding? We were thinking of sending out a search party. Here is Beatrice, and this is Giles, and this is Frank Crawley. Look out, you nearly trod on the dog."

Beatrice was tall, broad-shouldered, very handsome, very much like Maxim about the eyes and jaw, but not as smart as I had expected, much tweedier; the sort of person who would nurse dogs through distemper, know about horses, shoot well. She did not kiss me. She shook hands very firmly, looking me straight in the eyes, and then she turned to Maxim, "Quite different from what I expected. Doesn't answer to your description at all."

Everyone laughed, and I joined in, not quite certain if the laugh was against me or not, wondering secretly what it was she had expected, and what had been Maxim's description.

And "This is Giles," said Maxim, prodding my arm, and Giles stretched out an enormous paw and wrung my hand, squeezing the fingers limp, genial eyes smiling from behind horn-rimmed glasses.

"Frank Crawley," said Maxim, and I turned to the agent, a colourless, rather thin man with a prominent Adam's apple, in whose eyes I read relief as he looked upon me. I wondered why, but I had no time to think of that, because Frith had come in, and was offering me sherry, and Beatrice was talking to me again. "Maxim tells me you only got back last night. I had not realised that, or of course we would never have thrust ourselves upon you so soon. Well, what do you think of Manderley?"

"I've scarcely seen anything of it yet," I answered, "it's beautiful, of course."

She was looking me up and down, as I had expected, but in a direct, straightforward fashion, not maliciously like Mrs. Danvers, not with unfriendliness. She had a right to judge me, she was Maxim's sister, and Maxim himself came to my side now, putting his arm through mine, giving me confidence.

"You're looking better, old man," she said to him, her head on one side, considering him, "you've lost that fine-drawn look, thank goodness. I suppose we've got you to thank for that?" nodding at me.

"I'm always very fit," said Maxim shortly, "never had anything wrong with me in my life. You imagine everyone ill who doesn't look as fat as Giles."

"Bosh," said Beatrice, "you know perfectly well you were a perfect wreck six months ago. Gave me the fright of my life when I came and saw you. I thought you were in for a breakdown. Giles, bear me out. Didn't Maxim look perfectly ghastly last time we came over, and didn't I say he was heading for a breakdown?"

"Well, I must say, old chap, you're looking a different person," said Giles. "Very good thing you went away. Doesn't he look well, Crawley?"

I could tell by the tightening of Maxim's muscles under my arm that he was trying to keep his temper. For some reason this talk about his health was not welcome to him, angered him even, and I thought it tactless of Beatrice to harp upon it in this way, making so big a point of it.

"Maxim's very sunburnt," I said shyly, "it hides a multitude of sins. You should have seen him in Venice, having breakfast on the balcony, trying to get brown on purpose. He thinks it makes him better-looking."

Everyone laughed, and Mr. Crawley said, "It must have been wonderful in Venice, Mrs. de Winter, this time of the year," and "Yes," I said, "we had really wonderful weather. Only one bad day, wasn't it, Maxim?" the conversation drawing away happily from his health, and so to Italy, safest of subjects, and the blessed topic of fine weather. Conversation was easy now, no longer an effort, Maxim and Giles and Beatrice were discussing the running of Maxim's car, and Mr. Crawley was asking if it was true there were no more gondolas in the canals now, only motor-boats. I don't think he would have cared at all had there been steamers at anchor in the Grand Canal, he was saying this to help me, it was his contribution to the little effort of steering the talk away from Maxim's health, and I was grateful to him, feeling him an ally, for all his dull appearance.

"Jasper wants exercise," said Beatrice, stirring the dog with her foot; "he's getting much too fat, and he's barely two years old. What do you feed him on, Maxim?"

"My dear Beatrice, he has exactly the same routine as your dogs," said Maxim. "Don't show off and make out you know more about animals than I do."

"Dear old boy, how can you pretend to know what Jasper has been fed on when you've been away for a couple of months? Don't tell me Frith walks to the lodge gates with him twice a day. This dog hasn't had a run for weeks, I can tell by the condition of his coat."

"I'd rather he looked colossal than half-starved like that half-wit dog of yours," said Maxim.

"Not a very intelligent remark when Lion won two firsts at Crufts' last February," said Beatrice.

The atmosphere was becoming rather strained again, I could tell by the narrow line of Maxim's mouth, and I wondered if brothers and sisters always sparred like this, making it uncomfortable for those who listened. I wished that Frith would come in and announce lunch. Or would we be summoned by a booming gong? I did not know what happened at Manderley.

"How far away from us are you?" I asked, sitting down by Beatrice, "did you have to make a very early start?"

"We're fifty miles away, my dear, in the next county, the other side of Trowchester. The hunting is so much better with us. You must come over and stay, when Maxim can spare you. Giles will mount you."

"I'm afraid I don't hunt," I confessed, "I learnt to ride, as a child, but very feebly, I don't remember much about it."

"You must take it up again," she said, "you can't possibly live in the country and not ride. You wouldn't know what to do with yourself. Maxim says you paint. That's very nice, of course, but there's no exercise in it, is there? All very well on a wet day when there's nothing better to do."

"My dear Beatrice, we are not all such fresh-air fiends as you," said Maxim.

"I wasn't talking to you, old boy. We all know you are perfectly happy slopping about the Manderley gardens and never breaking out of a slow walk."

"I'm very fond of walking too," I said swiftly, "I'm sure I shall never get tired of rambling about Manderley. And I can bathe too, when its warmer."

"My dear, you are an optimist," said Beatrice, "I can hardly ever remember bathing here. The water is far too cold, and the beach is shingle."

"I don't mind that," I said. "I love bathing. As long as the currents are not too strong. Is the bathing safe in the bay?"

Nobody answered, and I realised suddenly what I had said. My heart thumped, and I felt my cheeks go flaming red. I bent down to stroke Jasper's ear, in an agony of confusion. "Jasper could do with a swim, and get some of that fat off," said Beatrice, breaking the pause, "but he'd find it a bit too much for him in the bay, wouldn't you,

Jasper? Good old Jasper. Nice old man." We patted the dog together, not looking at one another.

"I say, I'm getting infernally hungry, what on earth is happening to lunch?" said Maxim.

"It's only just on one now," said Mr. Crawley, "according to the clock on the mantelpiece."

"That clock was always fast," said Beatrice.

"It's kept perfect time now for months," said Maxim.

At that moment the door opened and Frith announced that luncheon was served.

"I say, I must have a wash," said Giles, looking at his hands.

We all got up and wandered through the drawing-room to the hall in great relief, Beatrice and I a little ahead of the men, she taking my arm.

"Dear old Frith," she said, "he always looks exactly the same, and makes me feel like a girl again. You know, don't mind me saying so, but you are even younger than I expected. Maxim told me your age, but you're an absolute child. Tell me, are you very much in love with him?"

I was not prepared for this question, and she must have seen the surprise in my face for she laughed lightly, and squeezed my arm.

"Don't answer," she said, "I can see what you feel. I'm an interfering bore, aren't I? You mustn't mind me. I'm devoted to Maxim, you know, though we always bicker like cat and dog when we meet. I congratulate you again on his looks. We were all very worried about him this time last year, but of course you know the whole story." We had come to the dining-room by now, and she said no more, for the servants were there and the others had joined us, but as I sat down, and unfolded my napkin, I wondered what Beatrice would say did she realise that I knew nothing of that preceding year, no details of the tragedy that had happened down there, in the bay, that Maxim kept these things to himself, that I questioned him never.

Lunch passed off better than I had dared to hope. There were few arguments, or perhaps Beatrice was exercising tact at last, at any rate she and Maxim chatted about matters concerning Manderley, her horses, the garden, mutual friends, and Frank Crawley, on my left, kept up an easy patter with me for which I was grateful, as it required no effort. Giles was more concerned with food than with the conversation, though now and again he remembered my existence and flung me a remark at hazard.

"Same cook I suppose, Maxim?" he said, when Robert had offered him the cold soufflé for the second time. "I always tell Bee, Manderley's the only place left in England where one can get decent cooking. I remember this soufflé of old."

"I think we change cooks periodically," said Maxim, "but the standard of cooking remains the same. Mrs. Danvers has all the recipes, she tells them what to do."

"Amazing woman, that Mrs. Danvers," said Giles, turning to me, "don't you think so?"

"Oh, yes," I said, "Mrs. Danvers seems to be a wonderful person."

"She's no oil painting though, is she?" said Giles, and he roared with laughter. Frank Crawley said nothing, and looking up I saw Beatrice was watching me. She turned away then, and began talking to Maxim.

"Do you play golf at all, Mrs. de Winter?" said Mr. Crawley.

"No, I'm afraid I don't," I answered, glad that the subject had been changed again, that Mrs. Danvers was forgotten, and even though I was no player, knew nothing of the game, I was prepared to listen to him as long as he pleased; there was something solid and safe and dull about golf, it could not bring us into any difficulties. We had cheese, and coffee, and I wondered whether I was supposed to make a move. I kept looking at Maxim, but he gave no sign, and then Giles embarked upon a story, rather difficult to follow, about digging a car out of a snow-drift—what had started the train of thought I could not tell—and I listened to him politely, nodding my head now and again and smiling, aware of Maxim becoming restive at his end of the table. At last he paused, and I caught Maxim's eye. He frowned very slightly, and jerked his head towards the door.

I got up at once, shaking the table clumsily as I moved my chair, and upsetting Giles's glass of port. "Oh, dear," I said, hovering, wondering what to do, reaching ineffectively for my napkin, but "All right, Frith will deal with it," said Maxim, "don't add to the confusion. Beatrice, take her out in the garden, she's scarcely seen the place yet."

He looked tired, rather jaded. I began to wish none of them had come. They had spoilt our day anyway. It was too much of an effort, just as we returned. I felt tired too, tired and depressed. Maxim had seemed almost irritable when he suggested we should go into the garden. What a fool I had been, upsetting that glass of port.

We went out on to the terrace and walked down on to the smooth green lawns.

"I think it's a pity you came back to Manderley so soon," said Beatrice, "it would have been far better to potter about in Italy for three or four months, and then come back in the middle of the summer. Done Maxim a power of good too, besides being easier from your point of view. I can't help feeling it's all going to be rather a strain here for you at first."

"Oh, I don't think so," I said. "I know I shall come to love Manderley."

She did not answer, and we strolled backwards and forwards on the lawns.

"Tell me a bit about yourself," she said at last, "what was it you were doing in the south of France? Living with some appalling American woman, Maxim said."

I explained about Mrs. Van Hopper, and what had led to it, and she seemed sympathetic but a little vague, as though she was thinking of something else.

"Yes," she said, when I paused, "it all happened very suddenly, as you say. But of course we were all delighted, my dear, and I do hope you will be happy."

"Thank you, Beatrice," I said, "thank you very much."

I wondered why she said she hoped we would be happy, instead of saying she knew we would be so. She was kind, she was sincere, I liked her very much, but there was a tiny doubt in her voice that made me afraid.

"When Maxim wrote and told me," she went on, taking my arm, "and said he had discovered you in the south of France, and you were very young, very pretty, I must admit it gave me a bit of a shock. Of course we all expected a social butterfly, very modern and plastered with paint, the sort of girl you expect to meet in those sort of places. When you came into the morning-room before lunch you could have knocked me down with a feather."

She laughed, and I laughed with her. But she did not say whether or not she was disappointed in my appearance or relieved.

"Poor Maxim," she said, "he went through a ghastly time, and let's hope you have made him forget about it. Of course he adores Manderley."

Part of me wanted her to continue her train of thought, to tell me more of the past, naturally, and easily like this, and something else, way back in my mind, did not want to know, did not want to hear.

"We are not a bit alike, you know," she said, "our characters are poles apart. I show everything on my face, whether I like people or not, whether I am angry or pleased. There's no reserve about me. Maxim is entirely different. Very quiet, very reserved. You never know what's going on in that funny mind of his. I lose my temper on the slightest provocation, flare up, and then it's all over. Maxim loses his temper once or twice in a year, and when he does—my God—he *does* lose it. I don't suppose he ever will with you. I should think you are a placid little thing."

She smiled, and pinched my arm, and I thought about being placid, how quiet and comfortable it sounded, someone with knitting on her lap, with calm unruffled brow. Someone who was never anxious, never tortured by doubt and indecision, someone who never stood as I did, hopeful, eager, frightened, tearing at bitten nails, uncertain which way to go, what star to follow.

"You won't mind me saying so, will you?" she went on, "but I think you ought to do something to your hair. Why don't you have it waved? It's so very lanky, isn't it, like that? Must look awful under a hat. Why don't you sweep it back behind your ears?"

I did so obediently, and waited for her approval. She looked at me critically, her head on one side. "No," she said. "No, I think that's worse. It's too severe, and doesn't suit you. No, all you need is a wave, just to pinch it up. I never have cared for that Joan of Arc business or whatever they call it. What does Maxim say? Does he think it suits you?"

"I don't know," I said, "he's never mentioned it."

"Oh, well," she said, "perhaps he likes it. Don't go by me. Tell me, did you get any clothes in London or Paris?"

"No," I said, "we had no time. Maxim was anxious to get home. And I can always send for catalogues."

"I can tell by the way you dress that you don't care a hoot what you wear," she said. I glanced at my flannel skirt apologetically.

"I do," I said. "I'm very fond of nice things. I've never had much money to spend on clothes up to now."

"I wonder Maxim did not stay a week or so in London and get you something decent to wear," she said. "I must say, I think it's rather selfish of him. So unlike him too. He's generally so particular."

"Is he?" I said; "he's never seemed particular to me. I don't think he notices what I wear at all. I don't think he minds."

"Oh," she said. "Oh, well, he must have changed then."

She looked away from me, and whistled to Jasper, her hands in her pockets, and then stared up at the house above us.

"You're not using the west wing then," she said.

"No," I said. "No, we have the suite in the east wing. It's all been done up."

"Has it?" she said, "I didn't know that. I wonder why."

"It was Maxim's idea," I said, "he seems to prefer it."

She said nothing, she went on looking at the windows, and

whistling. "How do you get on with Mrs. Danvers?" she said suddenly.

I bent down, and began patting Jasper's head, and stroking his ears. "I have not seen very much of her," I said, "she scares me a little. I've never seen anyone quite like her before."

"I don't suppose you have," said Beatrice.

Jasper looked up at me with great eyes, humble, rather self-conscious. I kissed the top of his silken head, and put my hand over his black nose.

"There's no need to be frightened of her," said Beatrice, "and don't let her see it, whatever you do. Of course I've never had anything to do with her, and I don't think I ever want to either. However, she's always been very civil to me." I went on patting Jasper's head.

"Did she seem friendly?" said Beatrice.

"No," I said. "No, not very."

Beatrice began whistling again, and she rubbed Jasper's head with her foot. "I shouldn't have more to do with her than you can help," she said.

"No," I said. "She runs the house very efficiently, there's no need for me to interfere."

"Oh, I don't suppose she'd mind that," said Beatrice. That was what Maxim had said, the evening before, and I thought it odd that they should both have the same opinion. I should have imagined that interference was the one thing Mrs. Danvers did not want.

"I dare say she will get over it in time," said Beatrice, "but it may make things rather unpleasant for you at first. Of course she's insanely jealous. I was afraid she would be."

"Why?" I asked, looking up at her, "why should she be jealous? Maxim does not seem to be particularly fond of her."

"My dear child, it's not Maxim she's thinking of," said Beatrice, "I think she respects him and all that, but nothing more very much. No, you see"—she paused, frowning a little, looking at me uncertainly—"she resents your being here at all, that's the trouble."

"Why?" I said, "why should she resent me?"

"I thought you knew," said Beatrice; "I thought Maxim would have told you. She simply adored Rebecca."

"Oh," I said. "Oh, I see."

We both went on patting and stroking Jasper, who, unaccustomed to such attention, rolled over on his back in ecstasy.

"Here are the men," said Beatrice, "let's have some chairs out and sit under the chestnut. How fat Giles is getting, he looks quite repulsive beside Maxim. I suppose Frank will go back to the office. What a dull creature he is, never has anything interesting to say. Well, all of you. What have you been discussing? Pulling the world to bits I suppose." She laughed, and the others strolled towards us, and we all stood about. Giles threw a twig for Jasper to retrieve. We all looked at Jasper. Mr. Crawley looked at his watch. "I must be off," he said, "thank you very much for lunch, Mrs. de Winter."

"You must come often," I said, shaking hands.

I wondered if the others would go too. I was not sure whether they had just come over for lunch, or to spend the day. I hoped they would go. I wanted to be alone with Maxim again, and that it would be like when we were in Italy. We all went and sat down under the chestnut tree. Robert brought out chairs and rugs. Giles lay down on his back and tipped his hat over his eyes. After a while he began to snore, his mouth open.

"Shut up, Giles," said Beatrice. "I'm not asleep," he muttered, opening his eyes, and shutting them again. I thought him unattractive. I wondered why Beatrice had married him. She could never have been in love with him. Perhaps that was what she was thinking about me. I caught her eye upon me now and again, puzzled, reflective, as though she was saying to herself "What on earth does Maxim see in her?" but kind at the same time, not unfriendly. They were talking about their grandmother.

"We must go over and see the old lady," Maxim was saying, and "She's getting gaga," said Beatrice, "drops food all down her chin, poor darling."

I listened to them both, leaning against Maxim's arm, rubbing my chin on his sleeve. He stroked my hand absently, not thinking, talking to Beatrice.

"That's what I do to Jasper," I thought. "I'm being like Jasper now, leaning against him. He pats me now and again, when he remembers, and I'm pleased, I get closer to him for a moment. He likes me in the way I like Jasper."

The wind had dropped. The afternoon was drowsy, peaceful. The grass had been new-mown, it smelt sweet and rich, like summer. A bee droned above Giles's head, and he flicked at it with his hat. Jasper sloped in to join us, too warm in the sun, his tongue lolling from his mouth. He flopped beside me, and began licking his side, his large eyes apologetic. The sun shone on the mullioned windows of the house, and I could see the green lawns and the terrace reflected in them. Smoke curled thinly from one of the near chimneys, and I wondered if the library fire had been lit, according to routine.

A thrush flew across the lawn to the magnolia tree outside the dining-room window. I could smell the faint, soft magnolia scent as I sat here, on the lawn. Everything was quiet and still. Very distant now came the washing of the sea in the bay below. The tide must have gone out. The bee droned over us again, pausing to taste the chestnut blossom above our heads. "This is what I always imagined," I thought, "this is how I hoped it would be, living at Manderley."

I wanted to go on sitting here, not talking, not listening to the others, keeping the moment precious for all time, because we were peaceful all of us, we were content and drowsy even as the bee who droned above our heads. In a little while it would be different, there would come to-morrow, and the next day, and another year. And we would be changed perhaps, never sitting quite like this again. Some of us would go away, or suffer, or die, the future stretched away in front of us, unknown, unseen, not perhaps what we wanted, not what we planned. This moment was safe though, this could not be touched. Here we sat together, Maxim and I, hand-in-hand, and the past and the future mattered not at all. This was secure, this funny fragment of time he would never remember, never think about again. He would not hold it sacred, he was talking about cutting away some of the undergrowth in the drive, and Beatrice agreed, interrupting with some suggestion of her own, and throwing a piece of grass at Giles at the same time. For them it was just after lunch, quarter-past-three on a haphazard afternoon, like any hour, like any day. They did not want to hold it close, imprisoned and secure, as I did. They were not afraid.

"Well, I suppose we ought to be off," said Beatrice, brushing the grass from her skirt, "I don't want to be late, we've got the Cartrights dining."

"How is old Vera?" asked Maxim.

"Oh, same as ever, always talking about her health. He's getting very old. They're sure to ask all about you both."

"Give them my love," said Maxim.

We got up. Giles shook the dust off his hat. Maxim yawned and stretched. The sun went in. I looked up at the sky. It had changed already, a mackerel sky. Little clouds scurrying in formation, line upon line.

"Wind's backing," said Maxim.

"I hope we don't run into rain," said Giles.

"I'm afraid we've had the best of the day," said Beatrice.

We wandered slowly towards the drive and the waiting car.

"You haven't seen what's been done to the east wing," said Maxim.

"Come upstairs," I suggested, "it won't take a minute." We went into the hall, and up the big staircase, the men following behind.

It seemed strange that Beatrice had lived here for so many years. She had run down these same stairs as a little girl, with her nurse. She had been born here, bred here, she knew it all, she belonged here more than I should ever do. She must have many memories locked inside her heart. I wondered if she ever thought about the days that were gone, ever remembered the lanky pig-tailed child that she had been once, so different from the woman she had become, forty-five now, vigorous and settled in her ways, another person. . . .

We came to the rooms, and Giles, stooping under the low doorway, said, "How very jolly, this is a great improvement, isn't it, Bee?" and "I say, old boy, you have spread yourself," said Beatrice, "new curtains, new beds, new everything. You remember, Giles, we had this room that time you were laid up with your leg? It was very dingy then. Of course Mother never had much idea of comfort. And then, you never put people here, did you, Maxim? Except when there was an overflow. The bachelors were always dumped here. Well, it's charming, I must say. Looks over the rose-garden too, which was always an advantage. May I powder my nose?"

The men went downstairs, and Beatrice peered in the mirror.

"Did old Danvers do all this for you?" she said.

"Yes," I said. "I think she's done it very well."

"So she should, with her training," said Beatrice. "I wonder what on earth it cost. A pretty packet, I bet. Did you ask?"

"No, I'm afraid I did not," I said.

"I don't suppose it worried Mrs. Danvers," said Beatrice; "do you mind if I use your comb? These are nice brushes. Wedding present?"

"Maxim gave them to me."

"H'm. I like them. We must give you something of course. What do you want?"

"Oh, I don't really know. You mustn't bother," I said.

"My dear, don't be absurd. I'm not one to grudge you a present, even though we weren't asked to your wedding!"

"I hope you did not mind about that. Maxim wanted it to be abroad."

"Of course not. Very sensible of you both. After all, it wasn't as though . . ." she stopped in the middle of her sentence, and dropped her bag. "Damn, have I broken the catch? No, all is well. What was I saying? I can't remember. Oh, yes, wedding presents. We must think of something. You probably don't care for jewellery."

I did not answer. "It's so different from the ordinary young couple," she said. "The daughter of a friend of mine got married the other day, and of course they were started off in the usual way, with linen, and coffee sets, and dining-room chairs, and all that. I gave rather a nice standard lamp. Cost me a fiver at Harrod's. If you do go to London to buy clothes mind you go to my woman, Madame Carroux. She has damn good taste, and she doesn't rook you."

She got up from the dressing-table, and pulled at her skirt.

"Do you suppose you will have a lot of people down?" she said.

"I don't know. Maxim hasn't said."

"Funny old boy, one never quite knows with him. At one time one could not get a bed in the house, the place would be chock-a-block. I can't somehow see you . . ." she stopped abruptly, and patted my arm. "Oh, well," she said, "we'll see. It's a pity you don't ride or shoot, you must miss such a lot. You don't sail by any chance, do you?"

"No," I said.

"Thank God for that," she said.

She went to the door, and I followed her down the corridor.

"Come and see us if you feel like it," she said. "I always expect people to ask themselves. Life is too short to send out invitations."

"Thank you very much," I said.

We came to the head of the stairs looking down upon the hall. The men were standing on the steps outside. "Come on, Bee," shouted Giles, "I felt a spot of rain, so we've put on the cover. Maxim says the glass is falling."

Beatrice took my hand, and bending down gave me a swift peck on my cheek. "Good-bye," she said, "forgive me if I've asked you a lot of rude questions, my dear, and said all sort of things I shouldn't. Tact never was my strong point, as Maxim will tell you. And, as I told you before, you're not a bit what I expected." She looked at me direct, her lips pursed in a whistle, and then took a cigarette from her bag, and flashed her lighter.

"You see," she said, snapping the top, and walking down the stairs, "you are so very different from Rebecca."

And we came out on to the steps and found the sun had gone behind a bank of cloud, a little thin rain was falling, and Robert was hurrying across the lawn to bring in the chairs.

CHAPTER TEN

W e watched the car disappear round the sweep of the drive, and then Maxim took my arm and said, "Thank God that's that. Get a coat quickly, and come out. Damn the rain, I want a walk. I can't stand this sitting about." He looked white and strained, and I wondered why the entertaining of Beatrice and Giles, his own sister and brother-in-law, should have tired him so.

"Wait while I run upstairs for my coat," I said.

"There's a heap of mackintoshes in the flower-room, get one of them," he said impatiently, "women are always half-an-hour when they go to their bedrooms. Robert, fetch a coat from the flower-room, will you, for Mrs. de Winter? There must be half-a-dozen raincoats hanging there, left by people at one time or another." He was already standing in the drive, and calling to Jasper. "Come on, you lazy little beggar, and take some of that fat off." Jasper ran round in circles, barking hysterically at the prospect of his walk. "Shut up, you idiot," said Maxim, "what on earth is Robert doing?"

Robert came running out of the hall carrying a raincoat, and I struggled into it hurriedly, fumbling with the collar. It was too big, of course, and too long, but there was no time to change it, and we set off together across the lawn to the woods, Jasper running in front. "I find a little of my family goes a very long way," said Maxim. "Beatrice is one of the best people in the world, but she invariably puts her foot in it."

I was not sure where Beatrice had blundered, and thought it better not to ask. Perhaps he still resented the chat about his health before lunch.

"What did you think of her?" he went on.

"I liked her very much," I said, "she was very nice to me."

"What did she talk to you about out here, after lunch?"

"Oh, I don't know. I think I did most of the talking. I was telling her about Mrs. Van Hopper, and how you and I met, and all that. She said I was quite different to what she expected."

"What the devil did she expect?"

"Someone much smarter, more sophisticated, I imagine. A social butterfly, she said."

Maxim did not answer for a moment, he bent down, and threw a stick for Jasper. "Beatrice can sometimes be infernally unintelligent," he said.

We climbed the grass bank above the lawns, and plunged into the woods. The trees grew very close together, and it was dark. We trod upon broken twigs, and last year's leaves, and here and there the fresh green stubble of the young bracken, and the shoots of the bluebells soon to blossom. Jasper was silent now, his nose to the ground. I took Maxim's arm.

"Do you like my hair?" I said.

He stared down at me in astonishment. "Your hair?" he said, "why on earth do you ask? Of course I like it. What's the matter with it?"

"Oh, nothing," I said, "I just wondered."

"How funny you are," he said.

We came to a clearing in the woods, and there were two paths, going in opposite directions. Jasper took the right-hand path without hesitation.

"Not that way," called Maxim, "come on, old chap."

The dog looked back at us and stood there, wagging his tail, but did not return. "Why does he want to go that way?" I asked.

"I suppose he's used to it," said Maxim briefly, "it leads to a small cove, where we used to keep a boat. Come on, Jasper, old man."

We turned into the left-hand path, not saying anything, and presently I looked over my shoulder and saw that Jasper was following us.

"This brings us to the valley I told you about," said Maxim, "and you shall smell the azaleas. Never mind the rain, it will bring out the scent."

He seemed all right again now, happy and cheerful, the Maxim I knew and loved, and he began talking about Frank Crawley and what a good fellow he was, so thorough and reliable, and devoted to Manderley.

"This is better," I thought, "this is like it was in Italy," and I smiled up at him, squeezing his arm, relieved that the odd strained look on his face had passed away, and while I said "Yes," and "Really?" and "Fancy, darling," my thoughts wandered back to Beatrice, wondering why her presence should have disturbed him, what she had done; and I thought too of all she had said about his temper, how he lost it, she told me, about once or twice a year.

She must know him, of course; she was his sister. But it was not what I had thought; it was not my idea of Maxim. I could see him moody, difficult, irritable perhaps, but not angry as she had inferred, not passionate. Perhaps she had exaggerated; people very often were wrong about their relatives.

"There," said Maxim suddenly, "take a look at that."

We stood on a slope of a wooded hill, and the path wound away before us to a valley, by the side of a running stream. There were no dark trees here, no tangled undergrowth, but on either side of the narrow path stood azaleas and rhododendrons, not blood-coloured like the giants in the drive, but salmon, white, and gold, things of beauty and of grace, drooping their lovely, delicate heads in the soft summer rain.

The air was full of their scent, sweet and heady, and it seemed to me as though their very essence had mingled with the running waters of the stream, and become one with the falling rain and the tumbling of the little stream, and the quiet rain. When Maxim spoke, his voice was hushed too, gentle and low, as if he had no wish to break upon the silence.

"We call it the Happy Valley," he said.

We stood quite still, not speaking, looking down upon the clear white faces of the flowers closest to us, and Maxim stooped, and picked up a fallen petal and gave it to me. It was crushed and bruised, and turning brown at the curled edge, but as I rubbed it across my hand the scent rose to me, sweet and strong, vivid as the living tree from which it came.

Then the birds began. First a blackbird, his note clear and cool above the running stream, and after a moment he had answer, from his fellow hidden in the woods behind us, and soon the still air about us was made turbulent with song, pursuing us as we wandered down into the valley, and the fragrance of the white petals followed us too. It was disturbing, like an enchanted place. I had not thought it could be as beautiful as this.

The sky, now overcast and sullen, so changed from the early afternoon, and the steady, insistent rain could not disturb the soft quietude of the valley; the rain and the rivulet mingled with one another, and the liquid note of the blackbird fell upon the damp air in harmony with them both. I brushed the dripping heads of the azaleas as I passed, so close they grew together, bordering the path. Little drops of water fell on to my hands from the soaked petals. There were petals at my feet too, brown and sodden, bearing their scent upon them still, and a richer, older scent as well, the smell of deep moss and bitter earth, the stems of bracken, and the twisted buried roots of trees. I held Maxim's hand and I had not spoken. The spell of the Happy Valley was upon me. This at last was the core of Manderley, the Manderley I would know and learn to love. The first drive was forgotten, the black, herded woods, the glaring rhododendrons, luscious and overproud. And the vast house too, the silence of that echoing hall, the uneasy stillness of the west wing, wrapped in dust-sheets. There I was an interloper, wandering in rooms that did not know me, sitting at a desk and in a chair that was not mine. Here it was different. The Happy Valley knew no trespassers. We came to the end of the path, and the flowers formed an archway above our heads. We bent down, passing underneath, and when I stood straight again, brushing the raindrops from my hair, I saw that the valley was behind us, and the azaleas, and the trees, and, as Maxim had described to me that afternoon many weeks ago in Monte Carlo, we were standing in a little narrow cove, the shingle hard and white under our feet, and the sea was breaking on the shore beyond us.

Maxim smiled down at me, watching the bewilderment on my face.

"It's a shock, isn't it?" he said, "no one ever expects it. The contrast is too sudden, it almost hurts." He picked up a stone and flung it across the beach for Jasper. "Fetch it, good man," and Jasper streaked away in search of the stone, his long black ears flapping in the wind.

The enchantment was no more, the spell was broken. We were mortal again, two people playing on a beach. We threw more stones, went to the water's edge, flung ducks and drakes, and fished for driftwood. The tide had turned, and came lapping in the bay. The small rocks were covered, the seaweed washed on the stones. We rescued a big floating plank and carried it up the beach above high-water mark. Maxim turned to me, laughing, wiping the hair out of his eyes, and I unrolled the sleeves of my mackintosh caught by the sea spray. And then we looked round, and saw that Jasper had disappeared. We called and whistled, and he did not come. I looked anxiously towards the mouth of the cove where the waves were breaking upon the rocks.

"No," said Maxim, "we should have seen him, he can't have fallen. Jasper, you idiot, where are you? Jasper, Jasper?"

"Perhaps he's gone back to the Happy Valley?" I said.

"He was by that rock a minute ago, sniffing a dead sea-gull," said Maxim.

We walked up the beach towards the valley once again. "Jasper, Jasper?" called Maxim.

In the distance, beyond the rocks to the right of the beach, I heard a short, sharp bark. "Hear that?" I said. "He's climbed over this way." I began to scramble up the slippery rocks in the direction of the bark.

"Come back," said Maxim sharply, "we don't want to go that way. The fool of a dog must look after himself."

I hesitated, looking down from my rock. "Perhaps he's fallen," I said, "poor little chap. Let me fetch him." Jasper barked again, further away this time. "Oh, listen," I said, "I must get him. It's quite safe, isn't it? The tide won't have cut him off?"

"He's all right," said Maxim irritably, "why not leave him? He knows his own way back."

I pretended not to hear, and began scrambling over the rocks towards Jasper. Great jagged boulders screened the view, and I slipped and stumbled on the wet rocks, making my way as best I could in Jasper's direction. It was heartless of Maxim to leave Jasper, I thought, and I could not understand it. Besides, the tide was coming in. I came up beside the big boulder that had hidden the view, and looked beyond it. And I saw, to my surprise, that I was looking down into another cove, similar to the one I had left, but wider and more rounded. A small stone breakwater had been thrown out across the cove for shelter, and behind it the bay formed a tiny natural harbour. There was a buoy anchored there, but no boat. The beach in the cove was white shingle, like the one behind me, but steeper, shelving suddenly to the sea. The woods came right down to the tangle of seaweed marking high water, encroaching almost to the rocks themselves, and at the fringe of the woods was a long low building, half cottage, half boat-house, built of the same stone as the breakwater.

There was a man on the beach, a fisherman perhaps, in long boots and a sou'wester, and Jasper was barking at him, running round him in circles, darting at his boots. The man took no notice, he was bending down, and scraping in the shingle. "Jasper," I shouted, "Jasper, come here."

The dog looked up, wagging his tail, but he did not obey me. He went on baiting the solitary figure on the beach.

I looked over my shoulder. There was still no sign of Maxim. I climbed down over the rocks to the beach below. My feet made a crunching noise across the shingle, and the man looked up at the sound. I saw then that he had the small slit eyes of an idiot, and the red, wet mouth. He smiled at me, showing toothless gums.

"G'day," he said. "Dirty, ain't it?"

"Good afternoon," I said. "No, I'm afraid it's not very nice weather."

He watched me with interest, smiling all the while. "Diggin' for shell," he said. "No shell here. Been diggin' since forenoon."

"Oh," I said, "I'm sorry you can't find any."

"That's right," he said, "no shell here."

"Come on, Jasper," I said, "it's getting late. Come on, old boy."

But Jasper was in an infuriating mood. Perhaps the wind and sea had gone to his head, for he backed away from me, barking stupidly, and began racing round the beach after nothing at all. I saw he would never follow me, and I had no lead. I turned to the man, who had bent down again to his futile digging.

"Have you got any string?" I said.

"Eh?" he said.

"Have you got any string?" I repeated.

"No shell here," he said, shaking his head. "Been diggin' since forenoon." He nodded his head at me, and wiped his pale blue watery eyes.

"I want something to tie the dog," I said. "He won't follow me."

"Eh?" he said. And he smiled his poor idiot's smile.

"All right," I said, "it doesn't matter." He looked at me uncertainly, and then leant forward, and poked me in the chest.

"I know that dog," he said, "he comes fro' the house."

"Yes," I said. "I want him to come back with me now."

"He's not yourn," he said.

"He's Mr. de Winter's dog," I said gently. "I want to take him back to the house."

"Eh?" he said.

I called Jasper once more, but he was chasing a feather blown by the wind. I wondered if there was any string in the boat-house, and I walked up the beach towards it. There must have been a garden once, but now the grass was long and overgrown, crowded with nettles. The windows were boarded up. No doubt the door was locked, and I lifted the latch without much hope. To my surprise it opened after the first stiffness, and I went inside, bending my head because of the low door. I expected to find the usual boat store, dirty and dusty with disuse, ropes and blocks and oars upon the floor. The dust was there, and the dirt too in places, but there were no ropes or blocks. The room was furnished, and ran the whole length of the cottage. There was a desk in the corner, a table and chairs, and a bed-sofa pushed against the wall. There was a dresser too, with cups and plates. Bookshelves, the books inside them, and models of ships standing on the top of the shelves. For a moment I thought it must be inhabited—perhaps the poor man on the beach lived here—but I looked around me again, and saw no sign of recent occupation. That rusted grate knew no fire, this dusty floor no footsteps, and the china there on the dresser was blue-spotted with the damp. There was a queer musty smell about the place. Cobwebs spun threads upon the ship's models, making their own ghostly rigging. No one lived here. No one came here. The door had creaked on its hinges when I opened it. The rain pattered on the roof with a hollow sound, and tapped upon the boarded windows. The fabric of the sofa-bed had been nibbled by mice or rats. I could see the jagged holes, and the frayed edges. It was damp in the cottage, damp and chill. Dark, and oppressive. I did not like it. I had no wish to stay there. I hated the hollow sound of the rain pattering on the roof. It seemed to echo in the room itself, and I heard the water dripping too into the rusted grate.

I looked about me for some string. There was nothing that would serve my purpose, nothing at all. There was another door at the end of the room, and I went to it, and opened it, a little fearful now, a little afraid, for I had the odd, uneasy feeling that I might come upon something unawares, that I had no wish to see. Something that might harm me, that might be horrible.

It was nonsense of course, and I opened the door. It was only a boat store after all. Here were the ropes and blocks I had expected, two or three sails, fenders, a small punt, pots of paints, all the litter and junk that goes with the using of boats. A ball of twine lay on a shelf, a rusted clasp-knife beside it. This would be all I needed for Jasper. I opened the knife, and cut a length of twine, and came back into the room again. The rain still fell upon the roof, and into the grate. I came out of the cottage hurriedly, not looking behind me, trying not to see the torn sofa and the mildewed china, the spun cobwebs on the model ships, and so through the creaking gate and on to the white beach.

The man was not digging any more, he was watching me, Jasper at his side.

"Come along, Jasper," I said, "come on, good dog." I bent down, and this time he allowed me to touch him and pull hold of his collar. "I found some string in the cottage," I said to the man.

He did not answer, and I tied the string loosely round Jasper's collar.

"Good afternoon," I said, tugging at Jasper. The man nodded, staring at me with his narrow idiot's eyes. "I saw 'ee go in yonder," he said.

"Yes," I said, "it's all right. Mr. de Winter won't mind."

"She don't go in there now," he said.

"No," I said, "not now."

"She's gone in the sea, ain't she?" he said, "she won't come back no more?"

"No," I said, "she'll not come back."

"I never said nothing, did I?" he said.

"No, of course not, don't worry," I said.

He bent down again to his digging, muttering to himself. I went across the shingle and I saw Maxim waiting for me by the rocks, his hands in his pockets.

"I'm sorry," I said. "Jasper would not come. I had to get some string."

He turned abruptly on his heel, and made towards the woods.

"Aren't we going back over the rocks?" I said.

"What's the point, we're here now," he said briefly.

We went up past the cottage and struck into a path through the woods. "I'm sorry I was such a time, it was Jasper's fault," I said, "he kept barking at the man. Who was he?"

"Only Ben," said Maxim; "he's quite harmless, poor devil. His old father used to be one of the keepers, they live near the home farm. Where did you get that piece of twine?"

"I found it in the cottage on the beach," I said.

"Was the door open?" he asked.

"Yes, I pushed it open. I found the string in the other room, where the sails were, and a small boat."

"Oh," he said shortly. "Oh, I see," and then he added, after a moment or two: "That cottage is supposed to be locked, the door has no business to be open."

I said nothing, it was not my affair.

"Did Ben tell you the door was open?"

"No," I said, "he did not seem to understand anything I asked him."

"He makes out he's worse than he is," said Maxim. "He can talk quite intelligibly if he wants to. He's probably been in and out of the cottage dozens of times, and did not want you to know."

"I don't think so," I answered; "the place looked deserted, quite untouched. There was dust everywhere, and no footmarks. It was terribly damp. I'm afraid those books will be quite spoilt, and the chairs, and that sofa. There are rats there too, they have eaten away some of the covers."

Maxim did not reply. He walked at a tremendous pace, and the climb up from the beach was steep. It was very different from the Happy Valley. The trees were dark here and close together, there were no azaleas brushing the path. The rain dripped heavily from the thick branches. It splashed on my collar and trickled down my neck. I shivered, it was unpleasant, like a cold finger. My legs ached, after the unaccustomed scramble over the rocks. And Jasper lagged behind, weary from his wild scamper, his tongue hanging from his mouth.

"Come on, Jasper, for God's sake," said Maxim. "Make him walk up, pull at the twine or something, can't you? Beatrice was right. The dog is much too fat."

"It's your fault," I said, "you walk so fast. We can't keep up with you."

"If you had listened to me instead of rushing wildly over those rocks we would have been home by now," said Maxim, "Jasper knew his way back perfectly. I can't think what you wanted to go after him for."

"I thought he might have fallen, and I was afraid of the tide," I said.

"Is it likely I should have left the dog had there been any question of the tide?" said Maxim. "I told you not to go on those rocks, and now you are grumbling because you are tired."

"I'm not grumbling," I said. "Anyone, even if they had legs of iron, would be tired walking at this pace. I thought you would come with me when I went after Jasper anyway, instead of staying behind."

"Why should I exhaust myself careering after the damn dog?" he said.

"It was no more exhausting careering after Jasper on the rocks than it was careering after driftwood on the beach," I answered. "You just say that because you have not any other excuse."

"My good child, what am I supposed to excuse myself about?"

"Oh, I don't know," I said wearily, "let's stop this."

"Not at all, you began it. What do you mean by saying I was trying to find an excuse? Excuse for what?"

"Excuse for not having come with me over the rocks, I suppose," I said.

"Well, and why do you think I did not want to cross to the other beach?"

"Oh, Maxim, how should I know? I'm not a thought-reader. I know you did not want to, that's all. I could see it in your face."

"See what in my face?"

"I've already told you. I could see you did not want to go. Oh, do let's have an end to it. I'm sick to death of the subject."

"All women say that when they've lost an argument. All right, I did not want to go to the other beach. Will that please you? I never go near the bloody place, or that God-damned cottage. And if you had my memories you would not want to go there either, or talk about it, or even think about it. There. You can digest that if you like, and I hope it satisfies you."

His face was white, and his eyes strained and wretched with that dark lost look they had had when I first met him. I put out my hand to him, I took hold of his, holding it tight.

"Please, Maxim, please," I said.

"What's the matter?" he said roughly.

"I don't want you to look like that," I said. "It hurts too much. Please, Maxim. Let's forget all we said. A futile silly argument. I'm sorry, darling, I'm sorry. Please let everything be all right."

"We ought to have stayed in Italy," he said. "We ought never to have come back to Manderley. Oh, God, what a fool I was to come back."

He brushed through the trees impatiently, striding even faster than before, and I had to run to keep pace with him, catching at my breath, tears very near the surface, dragging poor Jasper after me on the end of his string.

At last we came to the top of the path, and I saw its fellow branching left to the Happy Valley. We had climbed the path then that Jasper had wished to take at the beginning of the afternoon. I knew now why Jasper had turned to it. It led to the beach he knew best, and the cottage. It was his old routine.

We came out on to the lawns, and went across them to the house without a word. Maxim's face was hard, with no expression. He went straight into the hall and on to the library without looking at me. Frith was in the hall.

"We want tea at once," said Maxim, and he shut the library door.

I fought to keep back my tears. Frith must not see them. He would think we had been quarrelling, and he would go to the servants' hall and say to them all, "Mrs. de Winter was crying in the hall just now. It looks as though things are not going very well." I turned away, so that Frith should not see my face. He came towards me though, he began to help me off with my mackintosh.

"I'll put your raincoat away for you in the flower-room, Madam," he said.

"Thank you, Frith," I replied, my face still away from him.

"Not a very pleasant afternoon for a walk I fear, Madam."

"No," I said. "No, it was not very nice."

"Your handkerchief, Madam?" he said, picking up something that had fallen on the floor. "Thank you," I said, putting it in my pocket.

I was wondering whether to go upstairs or whether to follow Maxim to the library. Frith took the coat to the flower-room. I stood there, hesitating, biting my nails. Frith came back again. He looked surprised to see me still there.

"There is a good fire in the library now, Madam."

"Thank you, Frith," I said.

I walked slowly across the hall to the library. I opened the door and went in. Maxim was sitting in his chair, Jasper at his feet, the old dog in her basket. Maxim was not reading the paper, though it lay on the arm of the chair beside him. I went and knelt down by his side and put my face close to his.

"Don't be angry with me any more," I whispered.

He took my face in his hands, and looked down at me with his tired, strained eyes. "I'm not angry with you," he said.

"Yes," I said. "I've made you unhappy. It's the same as making you angry. You're all wounded and hurt and torn inside. I can't bear to see you like this. I love you so much."

"Do you?" he said. "Do you?" He held me very tight, and his eyes questioned me, dark and uncertain, the eyes of a child in pain, a child in fear.

"What is it, darling?" I said. "Why do you look like that?"

I heard the door open before he could answer, and I sank back on my heels, pretending to reach for a log to throw on the fire, while Frith came into the room followed by Robert, and the ritual of our tea began.

The performance of the day before was repeated, the placing of the table, the laying of the snow-white cloth, the putting down of cakes and crumpets, the silver kettle of hot water placed on its little flame, while Jasper, wagging his tail, his ears stretched back in anticipation, watched my face. Five minutes must have passed before we were alone again, and when I looked at Maxim I saw the colour had come back into his face, the tired, lost look was gone, and he was reaching for a sandwich.

"Having all that crowd to lunch was the trouble," he said. "Poor old Beatrice always does rub me up the wrong way. We used to scrap like dogs as children. I'm so fond of her too, bless her. Such a relief though that they don't live too near. Which reminds me, we'll have to go over and see Granny some time. Pour out my tea, sweetheart, and forgive me for being a bear to you."

It was over then. The episode was finished. We must not speak of it again. He smiled at me over his cup of tea, and then reached for the newspaper on the arm of his chair. The smile was my reward. Like a pat on the head to Jasper. Good dog then, lie down, don't worry me any more. I was Jasper again. I was back where I had been before. I took a piece of crumpet and divided it between the two dogs. I did not want it myself, I was not hungry. I felt very weary now, very tired in a dull, spent way. I looked at Maxim but he was reading his paper, he had folded it over to another page. My fingers were messy with the butter from the crumpet, and I felt in my pocket for a handkerchief. I drew it out, a tiny scrap of a thing, lace-edged. I stared at it, frowning, for it was not mine. I remembered then that Frith had picked it up from the stone floor of the hall. It must have fallen out of the pocket in the mackintosh. I turned it over in my hand. It was grubby, little bits of fluff from the pocket clung to it. It must have been in the mackintosh pocket for a long time. There was a monogram in the corner. A tall sloping R, with the letters de W interlaced. The R dwarfed the other letters, the tail of it ran down into the cambric, away from the laced edge. It was only a small handkerchief, quite a scrap of a thing. It had been rolled in a ball and put away in the pocket and forgotten.

I must have been the first person to put on that mackintosh since the handkerchief was used. She who had worn the coat then was tall, slim, broader than I about the shoulders, for I had found it big and over-long, and the sleeves had come below my wrists. Some of the buttons were missing. She had not bothered then to do it up. She had thrown it over her shoulders like a cape, or worn it loose, hanging open, her hands deep in the pockets.

There was a pink mark upon the handkerchief. The mark of lipstick. She had rubbed her lips with the handkerchief, and then rolled it in a ball, and left it in the pocket. I wiped my fingers with the handkerchief, and as I did so I noticed that a dull scent clung about it still.

A scent I recognized, a scent I knew. I shut my eyes and tried to remember. It was something elusive, something faint and fragrant that I could not name. I had breathed it before, touched it surely, that very afternoon.

And then I knew that the vanished scent upon the handkerchief was the same as the crushed white petals of the azaleas in the Happy Valley.

CHAPTER ELEVEN

The weather was wet and cold for quite a week, as it often can be in the west country in early summer, and we did not go down to the beach again. I could see the sea from the terrace, and the lawns. It looked grey and uninviting, great rollers sweeping in to the bay past the beacon on the headland. I pictured them surging into the little cove and breaking with a roar upon the rocks, then running swift and strong to the shelving beach. If I stood on the terrace and listened I could hear the murmur of the sea below me, low and sullen. A dull, persistent sound that never ceased. And the gulls flew inland too, driven by the weather. They hovered above the house in circles, wheeling and crying, flapping their spread wings. I began to understand why some people could not bear the clamour of the sea. It has a mournful harping note sometimes, and the very persistence of it, that eternal roll and thunder and hiss, plays a jagged tune upon the nerves. I was glad our rooms were in the east wing and I could lean out of my window and look down upon the rose-garden. For sometimes I could not sleep, and getting softly out of bed in the quiet night I would wander to the window, and lean there, my arms upon the sill, and the air would be very peaceful, very still.

I could not hear the restless sea, and because I could not hear it my thoughts would be peaceful too. They would not carry me down that steep path through the woods to the grey cove and the deserted cottage. I did not want to think about the cottage. I remembered it too often in the day. The memory of it nagged at me whenever I saw the sea from the terrace. For I would see once more the blue spots on the china, the spun webs on the little masts of those model ships, and the rat holes on the sofa-bed. I would remember the pattering of the rain on the roof. And I thought of Ben, too, with his narrow watery blue eyes, his sly idiot's smile. These things disturbed me, I was not happy about them. I wanted to forget them but at the same time I wanted to know why they disturbed me, why they made me uneasy and unhappy. Somewhere, at the back of my mind, there was a frightened furtive seed of curiosity that grew slowly and stealthily, for all my denial of it, and I knew all the doubt and the anxiety of the child who has been told, "these things are not discussed, they are forbidden."

I could not forget the white, lost look in Maxim's eyes when we came up the path through the woods, and I could not forget his words, "Oh, God, what a fool I was to come back." It was all my fault, because I had gone down into the bay. I had opened up a road into the past again. And although Maxim had recovered, and was himself again, and we lived our lives together, sleeping, eating, walking, writing letters, driving to the village, working hour by hour through our day, I knew there was a barrier between us because of it.

He walked alone, on the other side, and I must not come to him. And I became nervous and fearful that some heedless word, some turn in a careless conversation should bring that expression back to his eyes again. I began to dread any mention of the sea, for the sea might lead to boats, to accidents, to drowning.... Even Frank Crawley, who came to lunch one day, put me in a little fever of fear when he said something about the sailing races in Kerrith harbour, three miles away. I looked steadily at my plate, a stab of sickness in my heart at once, but Maxim went on talking quite naturally, he did not seem to mind, while I sat in a sweat of uncertainty wondering what would happen and where the conversation would lead us.

It was during cheese, Frith had left the room, and I remember getting up and going to the side-board, and taking some more cheese, not wanting it, so as not to be at the table with them, listening; humming a little tune to myself so I could not hear. I was wrong of course, morbid, stupid, this was the hyper-sensitive behaviour of a neurotic, not the normal happy self I knew myself to be. But I could not help it. I did not know what to do. My shyness and gaucherie became worse, too, making me stolid and dumb when people came to the house. For we were called upon, I remember, during those first weeks, by people who lived near us in the county, and the receiving of them, and the shaking hands, and the spinning out of the formal half-hour became a worse ordeal than I first anticipated, because of this new fear of mine that they would talk about something that must not be discussed. The agony of those wheels on the drive, of that pealing bell, of my own first wild rush for flight to my own room.

The scrambled dab of powder on my nose, the hasty comb through my hair, and then the inevitable knock on the door and the entrance of the cards on a silver salver.

"All right. I'll be down immediately." The clap of my heels on the stairs and across the hall, the opening of the library door or, worse still, that long, cold, lifeless drawing-room, and the strange woman waiting there, or two of them perhaps, or a husband and a wife.

"How do you do? I'm so sorry, Maxim is in the garden somewhere, Frith has gone to find him."

"We felt we must come and pay our respects to the bride."

A little laughter, a little flurry of chat, a pause, a glance round the room.

"Manderley is looking as charming as ever. Don't you love it?"

"Oh, yes, rather..." And in my shyness and anxiety to please, those schoolgirl phrases would escape from me again, those words I never used except in moments like these, "Oh, ripping"; and "Oh, topping"; and "absolutely"; and "priceless"; even, I think, to one dowager who had carried a lorgnette "cheerio." My relief at Maxim's arrival would be tempered by the fear they might say something indiscreet, and I became dumb at once, a set smile on my lips, my hands in my lap. They would turn to Maxim then, talking of people and places I had not met or did not know, and now and again I would find their eyes upon me, doubtful, rather bewildered.

I could picture them saying to one another as they drove away, "My dear, what a dull girl. She scarcely opened her mouth"; and then the sentence I had first heard upon Beatrice's lips, haunting me ever since, a sentence I read in every eye, on every tongue—"She's so different to Rebecca."

Sometimes I would glean little snatches of information to add to my secret store. A word dropped here at random, a question, a passing phrase. And, if Maxim was not with me, the hearing of them would be a furtive, rather painful pleasure, guilty knowledge learnt in the dark.

I would return a call perhaps, for Maxim was punctilious in these matters and would not spare me, and if he did not come with me I must brave the formality alone, and there would be a pause in the conversation while I searched for something to say. "Will you be entertaining much at Manderley, Mrs. de Winter?" they would say and my answer would come, "I don't know, Maxim has not said much about it up to the present." "No, of course not, it's early yet. I believe the house was generally full of people in the old days." Another pause. "People from London, you know. There used to be tremendous parties." "Yes," I would say. "Yes, so I have heard." A further pause, and then the lowered voice that is always used about the dead or in a place of worship. "She was so tremendously popular, you know. Such a personality." "Yes," I would say. "Yes, of course." And after a moment or so I would glance at my watch under cover of my glove, and say "I'm afraid I ought to be going, it must be after four."

"Won't you stay for tea? We always have it quarter-past."

"No—no, really, thanks most awfully. I promised Maxim . . ." my sentence would go trailing off into nothing, but the meaning would be understood. We would both rise to our feet, both of us knowing I was not deceived about her offer to tea nor she in my mention of a promise to Maxim. I sometimes wondered what would happen if convention were denied, if, having got into the car and waved a hand to my hostess on the doorstep, I suddenly opened it again, and said "I don't think I'll go back after all. Let's go to your drawing-room again and sit down. I'll stay to dinner if you like or stop the night."

I used to wonder if convention and good county manners would brave the surprise, and whether a smile of welcome would be summoned to the frozen face. "But of course! How very delightful of you to suggest it." I used to wish I had the courage to try. But instead the door would slam, the car would go bowling away down the smooth gravel drive, and my late hostess would wander back to her room with a sigh of relief and become herself again. It was the wife of the bishop in the neighbouring cathedral town who said to me, "Will your husband revive the Manderley fancy dress ball, do you suppose? Such a lovely sight always, I shall never forget it."

I had to smile as though I knew all about it and say, "We have not decided. There have been so many things to do and to discuss."

"Yes, I suppose so. But I hope it won't be dropped. You must use your influence with him. There was not one last year of course. But I remember two years ago, the bishop and I went, and it was quite enchanting. Manderley so lends itself to anything like that. The hall looked wonderful. They danced there, and had the music in the gallery, it was all so in keeping. A tremendous thing to organise but everybody appreciated it so."

"Yes," I said. "Yes, I must ask Maxim about it."

I thought of the docketed pigeon-holes in the desk in the morning-room, I pictured the stack upon stack of invitation cards, the long list of names, the addresses, and I could see a woman sitting there at the desk and putting a V beside the names she wanted, and reaching for the invitation cards, dipping her pen in the ink, writing upon them swift and sure in that long, slanting hand.

"There was a garden party, too, we went to one summer," said the bishop's wife. "Everything always so beautifully done. The flowers at their best. A glorious day I remember. Tea was served at little tables in the rose-garden, such an attractive original idea. Of course, she was so clever . . ."

She stopped, turning a little pink, fearing a loss of tact, but I agreed with her at once to save embarrassment, and I heard myself saying boldly, brazenly, "Rebecca must have been a wonderful person."

I could not believe that I had said the name at last. I waited, wondering what would happen. I had said the name. I had said the word Rebecca aloud. It was a tremendous relief. It was as though I had taken a purge and rid myself of an intolerable pain. Rebecca. I had said it aloud.

I wondered if the bishop's wife saw the flush on my face, but she went on smoothly with the conversation, and I listened to her greedily, like an eavesdropper at a shuttered window.

"You never met her then?" she asked, and when I shook my head she hesitated a moment, a little uncertain of her ground. "We never knew her well personally, you know, the bishop was only inducted here four years ago, but of course she received us when we went to the ball and to the garden party. We dined there, too, one winter. Yes, she was a very lovely creature. So full of life."

"She seems to have been so good at everything too," I said, my voice just careless enough to show I did not mind, while I played with the fringe of my glove. "It's not often you get someone who is clever and beautiful and fond of sport."

"No, I suppose you don't," said the bishop's wife, "she was certainly very gifted. I can see her now, standing at the foot of the stairs on the night of the ball, shaking hands with everybody, that cloud of dark hair against the very white skin, and her costume suited her so. Yes, she was very beautiful."

"She ran the house herself, too," I said, smiling, as if to say, "I am quite at my ease, I often discuss her." "It must have taken a lot of time and thought. I'm afraid I leave it to the housekeeper."

"Oh, well, we can't all do everything. And you are very young, aren't you? No doubt in time, when you have settled down. Besides, you have your own hobby, haven't you? Someone told me you were fond of sketching."

"Oh, that," I said. "I don't know that I can count it for much."

"It's a nice little talent to have," said the bishop's wife; "it's not everyone that can sketch. You must not drop it. Manderley must be full of pretty spots to sketch."

"Yes," I said. "Yes, I suppose so," depressed by her words, having a sudden vision of myself wandering across the lawns with a camp-stool and a box of pencils under one arm, and my "little talent" as she described it, under the other. It sounded like a pet disease.

"Do you play any games, do you ride, or shoot?" she asked.

"No," I said, "I don't do anything like that. I'm fond of walking," I added, as a wretched anti-climax.

"The best exercise in the world," she said briskly, "the bishop and I walk a lot." I wondered if he went round and round the cathedral, in his shovel hat and his gaiters, with her on his arm. She began to talk about a walking holiday they had taken once, years ago, in the Pennines, how they had done an average of twenty miles a day, and I nodded my head, smiling politely, wondering about the Pennines, thinking they were something like the Andes, remembering afterwards, they were that chain of hills marked with a furry line in the middle of a pink England on my school atlas. And he all the time in his hat and gaiters.

The inevitable pause, the glance at the watch unnecessary, as her drawing-room clock chimed four in shrill tones, and my rise from the chair. "I'm so glad I found you in. I hope you will come and see us."

"We should love to. The bishop is always so busy, alas. Please remember me to your husband, and be sure and ask him to revive the ball."

"Yes, indeed I will." Lying, pretending I knew all about it; and in the car going home I sat in my corner, biting my thumb nail, seeing the great hall at Manderley thronged with people in fancy dress, the chatter, hum, and laughter of the moving crowd, the musicians in the gallery, supper in the drawing-room probably, long buffet tables against the wall, and I could see Maxim standing at the foot of the stairs, laughing, shaking hands, turning to someone who stood by his side, tall and slim, with dark hair, said the bishop's wife, dark hair against a white face, someone whose quick eyes saw to the comfort of her guests, who gave an order over her shoulder to a servant, someone who was never awkward, never without grace, who when she danced left a stab of perfume in the air like a white azalea.

"Will you be entertaining much at Manderley, Mrs. de Winter?" I heard the voice again, suggestive, rather inquisitive, in the voice of that woman I had called upon who lived the other side of Kerrith, and I saw her eye too, dubious, considering, taking in my clothes from top to toe, wondering, with that swift downward glance given to all brides, if I was going to have a baby.

I did not want to see her again. I did not want to see any of them again. They only came to call at Manderley because they were curious and prying. They liked to criticize my looks, my manners, my figure, they liked to watch how Maxim and I behaved to each other, whether we seemed fond of one another, so that they could go back afterwards and discuss us, saying, "Very different from the old days." They came because they wanted to compare me to Rebecca. . . . I would not return these calls any more, I decided, I should tell Maxim so. I did not mind if they thought me rude and ungracious. It would give them more to criticize, more to discuss. They could say I was ill-bred. "I'm not surprised," they would say, "after all, who was she?" And then a laugh and a shrug of the shoulder. "My dear, don't you know? He picked her up in Monte Carlo or somewhere, she hadn't a penny. She was a companion to some old woman." More laughter, more lifting of the eyebrows. "Nonsense, not really? How extraordinary men are. Maxim, of all people, who was so fastidious. How could he, after Rebecca?"

I did not mind. I did not care. They could say what they liked. As the car turned in at the lodge gates I leant forward in my seat to smile at the woman who lived there. She was bending down, picking flowers in the front garden. She straightened up as she heard the car, but she did not see me smile. I waved, and she stared at me blankly. I don't think she knew who I was. I leant back in my seat again. The car went on down the drive.

When we turned at one of the narrow bends I saw a man walking along the drive a little distance ahead. It was the agent, Frank Crawley. He stopped when he heard the car, and the chauffeur slowed down. Frank Crawley took off his hat and smiled when he saw me in the car. He seemed glad to see me. I smiled back at him. It was nice of him to be glad to see me. I liked Frank Crawley. I did not find him dull or uninteresting as Beatrice had done. Perhaps it was because I was dull myself. We were both dull. We neither of us had a word to say for ourselves. Like to like.

I tapped on the glass and told the chauffeur to stop.

"I think I'll get out and walk with Mr. Crawley," I said.

He opened the door for me. "Been paying calls, Mrs. de Winter?" he said.

"Yes, Frank," I said. I called him Frank because Maxim did, but he would always call me Mrs. de Winter. He was that sort of person. Even if we had been thrown on a desert island together, and lived there in intimacy for the rest of our lives, I should have been Mrs. de Winter.

"I've been calling on the bishop," I said, "and I found the bishop out but the bishop's lady was at home. She and the bishop are very fond of walking. Sometimes they do twenty miles a day, in the Pennines."

"I don't know that part of the world," said Frank Crawley, "they say the country round is very fine. An uncle of mine used to live there."

It was the sort of remark Frank Crawley always made. Safe, conventional, very correct.

"The bishop's wife wants to know when we are going to give a fancy dress ball at Manderley," I said, watching him out of the tail of my eye. "She came to the last one, she said, and enjoyed it very much. I did not know you have fancy dress dances here, Frank."

He hesitated a moment before replying. He looked a little troubled. "Oh, yes," he said after a moment, "the Manderley ball was generally an annual affair. Everyone in the county came. A lot of people from London too. Quite a big show."

"It must have taken a lot of organisation," I said.

"Yes," he said.

"I suppose," I said carelessly, "Rebecca did most of it?"

I looked straight ahead of me along the drive, but I could see his face was turned towards me, as though he wished to read my expression.

"We all of us worked pretty hard," he said quietly.

There was a funny reserve in his manner as he said this, a certain shyness that reminded me of my own. I wondered suddenly if he had been in love with Rebecca. His voice was the sort of voice I should have used in his circumstances, had this been so. The idea opened up a new field of possibilities. Frank Crawley being so shy, so dull. He would never have told anyone, least of all Rebecca.

"I'm afraid I should not be much use if we have a dance," I said, "I'm no earthly use at organising anything."

"There would be no need for you to do anything," he said, "you would just be your self and look decorative."

"That's very polite of you, Frank," I said, "but I'm afraid I should not be able to do that very well either."

"I think you would do it excellently," he said. Dear Frank Crawley, how tactful he was and considerate. I almost believed him. But he did not deceive me really.

"Will you ask Maxim about the ball?" I said.

"Why don't you ask him?" he answered.

"No," I said. "No, I don't like to."

We were silent then. We went on walking along the drive. Now that I had broken down my reluctance at saying Rebecca's name, first with the bishop's wife and now with Frank Crawley, the urge to continue was strong within me. It gave me a curious satisfaction, it acted upon me like a stimulant. I knew that in a moment or two I should have to say it again. "I was down on one of the beaches the other day," I said, "the one with the breakwater. Jasper was being infuriating, he kept barking at the poor man with the idiot's eyes."

"You must mean Ben," said Frank, his voice quite easy now, "he always potters about on the shore. He's quite a nice fellow, you need never be frightened of him. He would not hurt a fly."

"Oh, I wasn't frightened," I said. I waited a moment, humming a tune to give me confidence. "I'm afraid that cottage place is going to rack and ruin," I said lightly. "I had to go in, to find a piece of string or something to tie up Jasper. The china is mouldy and the books are being ruined. Why isn't something done about it? It seems such a pity."

I knew he would not answer at once. He bent down to tie up his shoe lace.

I pretended to examine a leaf on one of the shrubs. "I think if Maxim wanted anything done he would tell me," he said, still fumbling with his shoe.

"Are they all Rebecca's things?" I asked.

"Yes," he said.

I threw the leaf away and picked another, turning it over in my hands.

"What did she use the cottage for?" I asked, "it looked quite furnished. I thought from the outside it was just a boat-house."

"It was a boat-house originally," he said, his voice constrained again, difficult, the voice of someone who is uncomfortable about his subject. "Then—then she converted it like that, had furniture put, and china."

I thought it funny the way he called her "she." He did not say Rebecca or Mrs. de Winter, as I expected him to do.

"Did she use it a great deal?" I asked.

"Yes," he said. "Yes, she did. Moonlight picnics, and—and one thing and another."

We were walking again side by side, I still humming my little tune. "How jolly," I said brightly, "moonlight picnics must be great fun. Did you ever go to them?"

"Once or twice," he said. I pretended not to notice his manner, how quiet it had become, how reluctant to speak about these things.

"Why is the buoy there in the little harbour place?" I said.

"The boat used to be moored there," he said.

"What boat?" I asked.

"Her boat," he said.

A strange sort of excitement was upon me. I had to go on with my questions. He did not want to talk about it, I knew that, but although I was sorry for him and shocked at my own self I had to continue, I could not be silent.

"What happened to it?" I said, "was that the boat she was sailing when she was drowned?"

"Yes," he said quietly, "it capsized and sank. She was washed overboard."

"What sort of size boat was it?" I asked.

"About three tons. It had a little cabin."

"What made it capsize?" I said.

"It can be very squally in the bay," he said.

I thought of that green sea, foam-flecked, that ran down channel beyond the headland. Did the wind come suddenly, I wondered, in a funnel from the beacon on the hill, and did the little boat heel to it, shivering, the white sail flat against a breaking sea?

"Could not someone have got out to her?" I said.

"Nobody saw the accident, nobody knew she had gone," he said.

I was very careful not to look at him. He might have seen the surprise in my face. I had always thought it happened in a sailing race, that other boats were there, the boats from Kerrith, and that people were watching, from the cliffs. I did not know she had been alone. Quite alone, out there in the bay.

"They must have known up at the house?" I said.

"No," he said. "She often went out alone like that. She would come back any time of the night, and sleep at the cottage on the beach."

"Was not she nervous?"

"Nervous?" he said, "no, she was not nervous of anything."

"Did—did Maxim mind her going off alone like that?"

He waited a minute, and then "I don't know," he said shortly. I had the impression he was being loyal to someone. Either to Maxim or to Rebecca, or perhaps even to himself. He was odd. I did not know what to make of it.

"She must have been drowned then, trying to swim to shore, after the boat sank?" I said.

"Yes," he said.

I knew how the little boat would quiver and plunge, the water gushing into the steering well, and how the sails would press her down, suddenly, horribly, in that gust of wind. It must have been very dark out there in the bay. The shore must have seemed very far away to anyone swimming there, in the water.

"How long afterwards was it that they found her?" I said.

"About two months," he said.

Two months. I thought drowned people were found after two days. I thought they would be washed up close to the shore, when the tide came.

"Where did they find her?" I asked.

"Near Edgecoombe, about forty miles up channel," he said.

I had spent a holiday at Edgecoombe once, when I was seven. It was a big place, with a pier, and donkeys. I remembered riding a donkey along the sands.

"How did they know it was her, after two months, how could they tell?" I said. I wondered why he paused before each sentence, as though he weighed his words. Had he cared for her then, had he minded so much?

"Maxim went up to Edgecoombe to identify her," he said.

Suddenly I did not want to ask him any more. I felt sick at myself, sick and disgusted. I was like a curious sight-seer standing on the fringe of a crowd after someone had been knocked down. I was like a poor person in a tenement building, when someone has died, asking if I might see the body. I hated myself. My questions had been degrading, shameful. Frank Crawley must despise me.

"It was a terrible time for all of you," I said rapidly, "I don't suppose you like being reminded about it. I just wondered if there was anything one could do to the cottage, that's all. It seems such a pity, all the furniture being spoilt by the damp."

He did not say anything. I felt hot and uncomfortable. He must have sensed that it was not concern for the empty cottage that had prompted me to all these questions, and now he was silent because he was shocked at me. Ours had been a comfortable, steady sort of friendship. I had felt him an ally. Perhaps I had destroyed all this, and he would never feel the same about me again.

"What a long drive this is," I said, "it always reminds me of the path in the forest in a Grimm's fairy tale, where the prince gets lost, you know. It's always longer than one expects, and the trees are so dark, and close."

"Yes, it is rather exceptional," he said.

I could tell by his manner he was still on his guard, as though waiting for a further question from me. There was an awkwardness between us that could not be ignored. Something had to be done about it, even if it covered me with shame.

"Frank," I said desperately, "I know what you are thinking. You can't understand why I asked all those questions just now. You think I'm morbid, and curious, in a rather beastly way. It's not that, I promise you. It's only that—that sometimes I feel myself at such a disadvantage. It's all very strange to me, living here at Manderley. Not the sort of life I've been brought up to. When I go returning these calls, as I did this afternoon, I know people are looking me up and down, wondering what sort of success I'm going to make of it. I can imagine them saying, 'What on earth does Maxim see in her?' And then, Frank, I begin to wonder myself, and I begin to doubt, and I have a fearful haunting feeling that I should never have married Maxim, that we are not going to be happy. You see, I know that all the time, whenever I meet anyone new, they are all thinking the same thing— How different she is to Rebecca."

I stopped breathless, already a little ashamed of my outburst, feeling that now at any rate I had burnt my boats for all time. He turned to me looking very concerned and troubled.

"Mrs. de Winter, please don't think that," he said. "For my part I can't tell you how delighted I am that you have married Maxim. It will make all the difference to his life. I am positive that you will make a great success of it. From my point of view it's—it's very refreshing and charming to find someone like yourself who is not entirely—er—" he blushed, searching for a word, "not entirely *au fait*, shall we say, with the ways at Manderley. And if the people around here give you the impression that they are criticizing you, it's—well— it's most damnably offensive of them, that's all. I've never heard a word of criticism, and if I did I should take great care that it was never uttered again."

"That's very sweet of you, Frank," I said, "and what you say helps enormously. I dare say I've been very stupid. I'm not good at meeting people, I've never had to do it, and all the time I keep remembering how—how it must have been at Manderley before, when there was someone there who was born and bred to it, did it all naturally and without effort. And I realise, every day, that things I lack, confidence, grace, beauty, intelligence, wit—oh, all the qualities that mean most in a woman—she possessed. It doesn't help, Frank, it doesn't help."

He said nothing. He went on looking anxious, and distressed. He pulled out his handkerchief and blew his nose. "You must not say that," he said.

"Why not? It's true," I said.

"You have qualities that are just as important, far more so, in fact. It's perhaps cheek of me to say so, I don't know you very well. I'm a bachelor, I don't know very much about women, I lead a quiet sort of life down here at Manderley as you know, but I should say that kindliness, and sincerity, and if I may say so—modesty—are worth far more to a man, to a husband, than all the wit and beauty in the world."

He looked very agitated, and blew his nose again. I saw that I had upset him far more than I had upset myself, and the realisation of this calmed me and gave me a feeling of superiority. I wondered why he was making such a fuss. After all, I had not said so very much. I had only confessed my sense of insecurity, following as I did upon Rebecca. And she must have had these qualities that he presented to me as mine. She must have been kind and sincere, with all her friends, her boundless popularity. I was not sure what he meant by modesty. It was a word I had never understood. I always imagined it had something to do with minding meeting people in a passage on the way to a bathroom. . . . Poor Frank. And Beatrice had called him a dull man, with never a word to say for himself.

"Well," I said, rather embarrassed, "well, I don't know about all that. I don't think I'm very kind, or particularly sincere, and as for being modest, I don't think I've ever had much of a chance to be anything else. It was not very modest, of course, being married hurriedly like that, down in Monte Carlo, and being alone there in that hotel, beforehand, but perhaps you don't count that?"

"My dear Mrs. de Winter, you don't think I imagine for one moment that your meeting down there was not entirely above board?" he said in a low voice.

"No, of course not," I said gravely. Dear Frank. I think I had shocked him. What a Frank-ish expression, too, "above board." It made one think immediately of the sort of things that would happen below board.

"I'm sure," he began, and hesitated, his expression still troubled, "I'm sure that Maxim would be very worried, very distressed, if he knew how you felt. I don't think he can have any idea of it."

"You won't tell him?" I said hastily.

"No, naturally not, what do you take me for? But you see, Mrs. de Winter, I know Maxim pretty well, and I've seen him through many . . . moods. If he thought you were worrying about—well—about the past, it would distress him more than anything on earth I can promise you that. He's looking very well, very fit, but Mrs. Lacy was quite right the other day when she said he had been on the verge of a breakdown last year, that it was tactless of her to say so in front of him. That's why you are so good for him. You are fresh and young—and sensible, you have nothing to do with all that time that has gone. Forget it, Mrs. de Winter, forget it, as he has done, thank heaven, and the rest of us. We none of us want to bring back the past, Maxim least of all. And it's up to you, you know, to lead us away from it. Not to take us back there again."

He was right, of course he was right. Dear good Frank, my friend, my ally. I had been selfish and hyper-sensitive, a martyr to my own inferiority complex. "I ought to have told you all this before," I said.

"I wish you had," he said, "I might have spared you some worry."

"I feel happier," I said, "much happier. And I've got you for my friend whatever happens, haven't I, Frank?"

"Yes, indeed," he said.

We were out of the dark wooded drive into the light again. The rhododendrons were upon us. Their hour would soon be over. Already they looked a little over-blown, a little faded. Next month the petals would fall one by one from the great faces, and the gardeners would come and sweep them away. Theirs was a brief beauty. Not lasting very long.

"Frank," I said, "before we put an end to this conversation, for ever let's say, will you promise to answer me one thing, quite truthfully?"

He paused, looking at me a little suspiciously. "That's not quite fair," he said, "you might ask me something that I should not be able to answer, something quite impossible."

"No," I said, "it's not that sort of question. It's not intimate or personal, or anything like that."

"Very well, I'll do my best," he said.

We came round the sweep of the drive and Manderley was before us, serene and peaceful in the hollow of the lawns, surprising me as it always did, with its perfect symmetry and grace, its great simplicity.

The sunlight flickered on the mullioned windows, and there was a soft rusted glow about the stone walls where the lichen clung. A thin column of smoke curled from the library chimney. I bit my thumb nail, watching Frank out of the tail of my eye.

"Tell me," I said, my voice casual, not caring a bit, "tell me, was Rebecca very beautiful?"

Frank waited a moment. I could not see his face. He was looking away from me towards the house. "Yes," he said slowly, "yes, I suppose she was the most beautiful creature I ever saw in my life."

We went up the steps then to the hall, and I rang the bell for tea.

CHAPTER TWELVE

I did not see much of Mrs. Danvers. She kept very much to herself. She still rang the house telephone to the morning-room every day and submitted the menu to me as a matter of form, but that was the limit of our intercourse. She had engaged a maid for me, Clarice, the daughter of somebody on the estate, a nice quiet well-mannered girl, who, thank heaven, had never been in service before and had no alarming standards. I think she was the only person in the house who stood in awe of me. To her I was the mistress, I was Mrs. de Winter. The possible gossip of the others could not affect her. She had been away for some time, brought up by an aunt fifteen miles away, and in a sense she was as new to Manderley as I was. I felt at ease with her. I did not mind saying "Oh, Clarice, would you mend my stocking?"

The housemaid Alice had been so superior. I used to sneak my chemises and nightgowns out of my drawer and mend them myself rather than ask her to do them. I had seen her once, with one of my chemises over her arm, examining the plain material with its small edging of lace. I shall never forget her expression. She looked almost shocked, as though her own personal pride had received a blow. I had never thought about my underclothes before. As long as they were clean and neat I had not thought the material or the existence of lace mattered. Brides one read about had trousseaux, dozens of sets at a time, and I had never bothered. Alice's face taught me a lesson. I wrote quickly to a shop in London and asked for a catalogue of under-linen. By the time I had made my choice Alice was looking after me no longer and Clarice was installed instead. It seemed such a waste buying new underclothes for Clarice that I put the catalogue away in a drawer and never wrote to the shop after all.

I often wondered whether Alice told the others, and if my under-clothes became a topic of conversation in the servants' hall, something rather dreadful, to be discussed in low tones when the men were nowhere about. She was too superior for it to be made a joking question. Phrases like "Chemise to you" would never be bandied between her and Frith for instance.

No, my underclothes were more serious than that. More like a di-vorce case heard *in camera*. . . . At any rate I was glad when Alice surrendered me to Clarice. Clarice would never know real lace from false. It was considerate of Mrs. Danvers to have engaged her. She must have thought we would be fit company, one for the other. Now that I knew the reason for Mrs. Danvers' dislike and resentment it made things a little easier. I knew it was not just me personally she hated, but what I represented. She would have felt the same towards anyone who had taken Rebecca's place. At least that was what I un-derstood from Beatrice the day she came to lunch.

"Did not you know?" she had said, "she simply adored Rebecca."

The words had shocked me at the time. Somehow I had not ex-pected them. But when I thought it over I began to lose my first fear of Mrs. Danvers. I began to be sorry for her. I could imagine what she must feel. It must hurt her every time she heard me called "Mrs. de Winter." Every morning when she took up the house telephone and spoke to me, and I answered "Yes, Mrs. Danvers," she must be think-ing of another voice. When she passed through the rooms and saw traces of me about the place, a beret on a window seat, a bag of knit-ting on a chair, she must think of another one, who had done these things before. Even as I did. I, who had never known Rebecca. Mrs. Danvers knew how she walked and how she spoke. Mrs. Danvers knew the colour of her eyes, her smile, the texture of her hair. I knew none of these things, I had never asked about them, but sometimes I felt Rebecca was as real to me as she was to Mrs. Danvers.

Frank had told me to forget the past, and I wanted to forget it. But Frank did not have to sit in the morning-room as I did, every day, and touch the pen she had held between her fingers. He did not have to rest his hands on the blotter, and stare in front of him at her writ-ing on the pigeon-holes. He did not have to look at the candlesticks on the mantelpiece, the clock, the vase in which the flowers stood, the pictures on the walls and remember, every day, that they be-longed to her, she had chosen them, they were not mine at all. Frank did not have to sit at her place in the dining-room, hold the knife and fork that she had held, drink from her glass. He did not throw a coat over his shoulders which had been hers, nor find her handkerchief in the pocket. He did not notice, every day, as I did, the blind gaze of the old dog in its basket in the library, who lifted its head when it heard my footstep, the footstep of a woman, and sniffing the air drooped its head again, because I was not the one she sought.

Little things, meaningless and stupid in themselves, but they were there for me to see, for me to hear, for me to feel. Dear God, I did not want to think about Rebecca. I wanted to be happy, to make Maxim happy, and I wanted us to be together. There was no other wish in my heart but that. I could not help it if she came to me in thoughts, in dreams. I could not help it if I felt like a guest in Manderley, my home, walking where she had trodden, resting where she had lain. I was like a guest, biding my time, waiting for the return of the hostess. Little sentences, little reproofs reminding me every hour, every day.

"Frith," I said, coming into the library on a summer morning, my arms full of lilac, "Frith, where can I find a tall vase for these? They are all too small in the flower-room."

"The white alabaster vase in the drawing-room was always used for the lilac, Madam."

"Oh, wouldn't it be spoilt? It might get broken."

"Mrs. de Winter always used the alabaster vase, Madam."

"Oh, oh, I see."

Then the alabaster vase was brought for me, already filled with water, and as I put the sweet lilac in the vase and arranged the sprigs, one by one, the mauve warm scent filling the room, mingling with the smell of the new-mown lawn outside coming from the open window, I thought: "Rebecca did this. She took the lilac, as I am doing, and put the sprigs one by one in the white vase. I'm not the first to do it. This is Rebecca's vase, this is Rebecca's lilac." She must have wandered out into the garden as I did, in that floppy garden hat I had seen once at the back of a cupboard in the flower-room, hidden under some old cushions, and crossed the lawn to the lilac bushes, whistling perhaps, humming a tune, calling to the dogs to follow her, carrying in her hands the scissors that I carried now.

"Frith, could you move that book-stand from the table in the window, and I will put the lilac there?"

"Mrs. de Winter always had the alabaster vase on the table behind the sofa, Madam."

"Oh, well . . ." I hesitated, the vase in my hands, Frith's face impassive. He would obey me of course if I said I preferred to put the vase on the smaller table by the window. He would move the book-stand at once.

"All right," I said, "perhaps it would look better on the larger table." And the alabaster vase stood, as it had always done, on the table behind the sofa. . . .

Beatrice remembered her promise of a wedding present. A large parcel arrived one morning, almost too large for Robert to carry. I was sitting in the morning-room, having just read the menu for the day. I have always had a childish love of parcels. I snipped the string excitedly, and tore off the dark brown paper. It looked like books. I was right. It was books. Six big volumes. *A History of Painting.* And a sheet of notepaper in the first volume saying "I hope this is the sort of thing you like" and signed "Love from Beatrice." I could see her going into the shop in Wigmore Street and buying them. Looking about her in her abrupt, rather masculine way. "I want a set of books for someone who is keen on Art," she would say, and the attendant would answer, "Yes, Madam, will you come this way." She would finger the volumes a little suspiciously. "Yes, that's about the price. It's for a wedding present. I want them to look good. Are these all about Art?" "Yes, this is the standard work on the subject," the assistant would say. And then Beatrice must have written her note, and paid her cheque, and given the address "Mrs. de Winter, Manderley."

It was nice of Beatrice. There was something rather sincere and pathetic about her going off to a shop in London and buying me these books because she knew I was fond of painting. She imagined me, I expect, sitting down on a wet day and looking solemnly at the illustrations, and perhaps getting a sheet of drawing-paper and a paint-box and copying one of the pictures. Dear Beatrice. I had a sudden, stupid desire to cry. I gathered up the heavy volumes and looked round the morning-room for somewhere to put them. They were out of place in that fragile delicate room. Never mind, it was my room now, after all. I arranged them in a row on the top of the desk. They swayed dangerously, leaning one against the other. I stood back a bit, to watch the effect. Perhaps I moved too quickly, and it disturbed them. At any rate the foremost one fell, and the others slid after it. They upset a little china cupid who had hitherto stood alone on the desk except for the candlesticks. He fell to the ground, hitting the waste-paper basket as he did so, and broke into fragments. I glanced hurriedly at the door, like a guilty child. I knelt on the floor and swept up the pieces into my hand. I found an envelope to put them in. I hid the envelope at the back of one of the drawers in the desk. Then I took the books off to the library and found room for them on the shelves.

Maxim laughed when I showed them to him with pride.

"Dear old Bee," he said, "you must have had a success with her. She never opens a book if she can help it."

"Did she say anything about—well—what she thought of me?" I asked.

"The day she came to lunch? No, I don't think so."

"I thought she might have written or something."

"Beatrice and I don't correspond unless there's a major event in the family. Writing letters is a waste of time," said Maxim.

I supposed I was not a major event. Yet if I had been Beatrice, and had a brother, and the brother married, surely one would have said something, expressed an opinion, written two words? Unless of course one had taken a dislike to the wife, or thought her unsuitable. Then of course it would be different. Still, Beatrice had taken the trouble to go up to London and to buy the books for me. She would not have done that if she disliked me.

It was the following day I remember, when Frith, who had brought in the coffee after lunch to the library, waited a moment, hovering behind Maxim, and said,

"Could I speak to you, sir?" Maxim glanced up from his paper.

"Yes, Frith, what is it?" he said, rather surprised. Frith wore a stiff solemn expression, his lips pursed. I thought at once his wife had died.

"It's about Robert, sir. There has been a slight unpleasantness between him and Mrs. Danvers. Robert is very upset."

"Oh, Lord," said Maxim, making a face at me. I bent down to fondle Jasper, my unfailing habit in moments of embarrassment.

"Yes, sir. It appears Mrs. Danvers has accused Robert of secreting a valuable ornament from the morning-room. It is Robert's business to bring in the fresh flowers to the morning-room and place the vases. Mrs. Danvers went in this morning after the flowers had been done, and noticed one of the ornaments was missing. It was there yesterday, she said. She accused Robert of either taking the ornament or breaking it and concealing the breakage. Robert denied both accusations most emphatically, and came to me nearly in tears, sir. You may have noticed he was not himself at lunch."

"I wondered why he handed me the cutlets without giving me a plate," murmured Maxim. "I did not know Robert was so sensitive. Well, I suppose someone else did it. One of the maids."

"No, sir. Mrs. Danvers went into the room before the girl had done the room. Nobody had been there since Madam yesterday, and Robert first thing with the flowers. It makes it very unpleasant for Robert and myself, sir."

"Yes, of course it does. Well, you had better ask Mrs. Danvers to come here and we'll get to the bottom of it. What ornament was it, anyway?"

"The china cupid, sir, that stands on the writing-table."

"Oh! Oh, Lord. That's one of our treasures, isn't it? It will have to be found. Get hold of Mrs. Danvers at once."

"Very good, sir."

Frith left the room and we were alone again. "What a confounded nuisance," said Maxim, "that cupid is worth a hell of a lot. How I loathe servants' rows too. I wonder why they come to me about it. That's your job, sweetheart."

I looked up from Jasper, my face red as fire. "Darling," I said, "I meant to tell you before, but—but I forgot. The fact is I broke that cupid when I was in the morning-room yesterday."

"You broke it? Well, why the devil didn't you say so when Frith was here?"

"I don't know. I didn't like to. I was afraid he would think me a fool."

"He'll think you much more of a fool now. You'll have to explain to him and Mrs. Danvers."

"Oh, no, please, Maxim, you tell them. Let me go upstairs."

"Don't be a little idiot. Anyone would think you were afraid of them."

"I am afraid of them. At least, not afraid, but . . ."

The door opened, and Frith ushered Mrs. Danvers into the room. I looked nervously at Maxim. He shrugged his shoulders, half-amused, half-angry.

"It's all a mistake, Mrs. Danvers. Apparently Mrs. de Winter broke the cupid herself and forgot to say anything," said Maxim.

They all looked at me. It was like being a child again. I was still aware of my guilty flush. "I'm so sorry," I said, watching Mrs. Danvers, "I never thought Robert would get into trouble."

"Is it possible to repair the ornament, Madam?" said Mrs. Danvers. She did not seem to be surprised that I was the culprit. She looked at me with her white skull's face and her dark eyes. I felt she had known it was me all along and had accused Robert to see if I would have the courage to confess.

"I'm afraid not," I said, "it smashed in little pieces."

"What did you do with the pieces?" said Maxim.

It was like being a prisoner, giving evidence. How paltry and mean my actions sounded, even to myself. "I put them all into an envelope," I said.

"Well, what did you do with the envelope?" said Maxim lighting a cigarette, his tone a mixture of amusement and exasperation.

"I put it at the back of one of the drawers in the writing-desk," I said.

"It looks as though Mrs. de Winter thought you would put her in prison, doesn't it, Mrs. Danvers?" said Maxim; "perhaps you would find the envelope and send the pieces up to London. If they are too far gone to mend it can't be helped. All right, Frith. Tell Robert to dry his tears."

Mrs. Danvers lingered when Frith had gone. "I will apologise to Robert of course," she said, "but the evidence pointed so strongly to him. It did not occur to me that Mrs. de Winter had broken the ornament herself. Perhaps, if such a thing should happen again, Mrs. de Winter will tell me personally, and I will have the matter attended to? It would save everybody a lot of unpleasantness."

"Naturally," said Maxim impatiently, "I can't think why she didn't do so yesterday. I was just going to tell her when you came into the room."

"Perhaps Mrs. de Winter was not aware of the value of the ornament?" said Mrs. Danvers, turning her eyes upon me.

"Yes," I said wretchedly. "Yes, I was afraid it was valuable. That's why I swept the pieces up so carefully."

"And hid them at the back of a drawer where no one would find them, eh?" said Maxim, with a laugh, and a shrug of the shoulders. "Is not that the sort of thing the between-maid is supposed to do, Mrs. Danvers?"

"The between-maid at Manderley would never be allowed to touch the valuable things in the morning-room, sir," said Mrs. Danvers.

"No, I can't see you letting her," said Maxim.

"It's very unfortunate," said Mrs. Danvers, "I don't think we have ever had any breakages in the morning-room before. We were always so particular. I've done the dusting in there myself since—last year. There was no one I could trust. When Mrs. de Winter was alive we used to do the valuables together."

"Yes, well—it can't be helped," said Maxim. "All right, Mrs. Danvers."

She went out of the room, and I sat on the window seat, looking out of the window. Maxim picked up his paper again. Neither of us spoke.

"I'm awfully sorry, darling," I said, after a moment, "it was very careless of me. I can't think how it happened. I was just arranging those books on the desk, to see if they would stand, and the cupid slipped."

"My sweet child, forget it. What does it matter?"

"It does matter. I ought to have been more careful. Mrs. Danvers must be furious with me."

"What the devil has she got to be furious about? It's not her bit of china."

"No, but she takes such a pride in it all. It's so awful to think nothing in there has ever been broken before. It had to be me."

"Better you than the luckless Robert."

"I wish it had been Robert. Mrs. Danvers will never forgive me."

"Damn Mrs. Danvers," said Maxim, "she's not God Almighty, is she? I can't understand you. What do you mean by saying you are afraid of her?"

"I did not mean afraid exactly. I don't see much of her. It's not that. I can't really explain."

"You do such extraordinary things," said Maxim; "fancy not getting hold of her when you broke the thing and saying, 'Here, Mrs. Danvers, get this mended.' She'd understand that. Instead of which you scrape up the remains in an envelope and hide 'em at the back of a drawer. Just like a between-maid, as I said, and not the mistress of a house."

"I am like a between-maid," I said slowly, "I know I am, in lots of ways. That's why I have so much in common with Clarice. We are on the same sort of footing. And that's why she likes me. I went and saw her mother the other day. And do you know what she said? I asked her if she thought Clarice was happy with us, and she said, 'Oh, yes, Mrs. de Winter. Clarice seems quite happy. She says, "It's not like being with a lady, Mum, it's like being with one of ourselves." ' Do you suppose she meant it as a compliment or not?"

"God knows," said Maxim, "remembering Clarice's mother I should take it as a direct insult. Her cottage is generally a shambles and smells of boiled cabbage. At one time she had nine children under eleven, and she herself used to patter about in that patch of garden with no shoes and a stocking round her head. We nearly gave her notice to quit. Why Clarice looks as neat and clean as she does I can't imagine."

"She's been living with an aunt," I said, feeling rather subdued. "I know my flannel skirt has a dirty mark down the front, but I've never walked bare-foot with a stocking round my head." I knew now why Clarice did not disdain my underclothes as Alice had done. "Perhaps that's why I prefer calling on Clarice's mother to calling on people like the bishop's wife?" I went on, "the bishop's wife never said I was like one of themselves."

"If you wear that grubby skirt when you call on her I don't suppose she does," said Maxim.

"Of course I didn't call on her in my old skirt, I wore a frock," I said, "and anyway I don't think much of people who just judge one by one's clothes."

"I hardly think the bishop's wife cares twopence about clothes," said Maxim, "but she may have been rather surprised if you sat on the extreme edge of the chair and answered 'Yes' and 'No' like someone after a new job, which you did the only time we returned a call together."

"I can't help being shy."

"I know you can't, sweetheart. But you don't make an effort to conquer it."

"I think that's very unfair," I said. "I try every day, every time I go out or meet anyone new. I'm always making efforts. You don't understand. It's all very well for you, you're used to that sort of thing. I've not been brought up to it."

"Rot," said Maxim, "it's not a question of bringing up, as you put it. It's a matter of application. You don't think I like calling on people, do you? It bores me stiff. But it has to be done, in this part of the world."

"We're not talking about boredom," I said, "there's nothing to be afraid of in being bored. If I was just bored it would be different. I hate people looking me up and down as though I were a prize cow."

"Who looks you up and down?"

"All the people down here. Everybody."

"What does it matter if they do? It gives them some interest in life."

"Why must I be the one to supply the interest, and have all the criticism?"

"Because life at Manderley is the only thing that ever interests anybody down here."

"What a slap in the eye I must be to them then."

Maxim did not answer. He went on looking at his paper.

"What a slap in the eye I must be to them," I repeated. And then "I suppose that's why you married me," I said, "you knew I was dull and quiet and inexperienced, so that there would never be any gossip about me."

Maxim threw his paper on the ground and got up from his chair. "What do you mean?" he said.

His face was dark and queer, and his voice was rough, not his voice at all.

"I–I don't know," I said, leaning back against the window, "I don't mean anything. Why do you look like that?"

"What do you know about any gossip down here?" he said.

"I don't," I said, scared by the way he looked at me, "I only said it because–because of something to say. Don't look at me like that. Maxim, what have I said; what's the matter?"

"Who's been talking to you?" he said slowly.

"No one. No one at all."

"Why did you say what you did?"

"I tell you, I don't know. It just came to my head. I was angry, cross. I do hate calling on these people, I can't help it. And you criticised me for being shy. I didn't mean it. Really, Maxim, I didn't. Please believe me."

"It was not a particularly attractive thing to say, was it?" he said.

"No," I said. "No, it was rude, hateful."

He stared at me moodily, his hands in his pockets, rocking backwards and forwards on his heels. "I wonder if I did a very selfish thing in marrying you," he said. He spoke slowly, thoughtfully.

I felt very cold, rather sick. "How do you mean?" I said.

"I'm not much of a companion to you, am I?" he said. "There are too many years between us. You ought to have waited, and then married a boy of your own age. Not someone like myself, with half his life behind him."

"That's ridiculous," I said hurriedly, "you know age doesn't mean anything in marriage. Of course we are companions."

"Are we? I don't know," he said.

I knelt up on the window seat and put my arms round his shoulders. "Why do you say these things to me?" I said, "you know I love you more than anything in the world. There has never been anyone but you. You are my father and my brother and my son. All those things."

"It was my fault," he said, not listening. "I rushed you into it. I never gave you a chance to think it over."

"I did not want to think it over," I said, "there was no other choice. You don't understand, Maxim. When one loves a person . . ."

"Are you happy here?" he said, looking away from me, out of the window. "I wonder sometimes. You've got thinner. Lost your colour."

"Of course I'm happy," I said, "I love Manderley. I love the garden, I love everything. I don't mind calling on people. I just said that to be tiresome. I'll call on people every day, if you want me to. I don't mind what I do. I've never for one moment regretted marrying you, surely you must know that?"

He patted my cheek in his terrible absent way, and bent down, and kissed the top of my head. "Poor lamb, you don't have much fun, do you? I'm afraid I'm very difficult to live with."

"You're not difficult," I said eagerly, "you are easy, very easy. Much easier than I thought you would be. I used to think it would be dreadful to be married, that one's husband would drink, or use awful language, or grumble if the toast was soft at breakfast, and be rather unattractive altogether, smell possibly. You don't do any of those things."

"Good God, I hope not," said Maxim, and he smiled.

I seized advantage of his smile, I smiled too, and took his hands and kissed them. "How absurd to say we are not companions," I said, "why, look how we sit here every evening, you with a book or a paper, and me with my knitting. Just like cups of tea. Just like old people, married for years and years. Of course we are companions. Of course we are happy. You talk as though you thought we had made a mistake. You don't mean it like that, do you, Maxim? You know our marriage is a success, a wonderful success?"

"If you say so, then it's all right," he said.

"No, but you think it too, don't you, darling? It's not just me? We are happy, aren't we? Terribly happy?"

He did not answer. He went on staring out of the window while I held his hands. My throat felt dry and tight, and my eyes were burning. Oh, God, I thought, this is like two people in a play, in a moment the curtain will come down, we shall bow to the audience, and go off to our dressing-rooms. This can't be a real moment in the lives of Maxim and myself. I sat down on the window seat, and let go of his hands. I heard myself speaking in a hard cool voice. "If you don't think we are happy it would be much better if you would admit it. I don't want you to pretend anything. I'd much rather go away. Not live with you any more." It was not really happening of course. It was the girl in the play talking, not me to Maxim. I pictured the type of girl who would play the part. Tall and slim, rather nervy.

"Well, why don't you answer me?" I said.

He took my face in his hands and looked at me, just as he had before, when Frith had come into the room with tea, the day we went to the beach.

"How can I answer you?" he said. "I don't know the answer myself. If you say we are happy, let's leave it at that. It's something I know nothing about. I take your word for it. We are happy. All right then, that's agreed!" He kissed me again, and then walked away across the room. I went on sitting by the window, stiff and straight, my hands in my lap.

"You say all this because you are disappointed in me," I said. "I'm gauche and awkward, I dress badly, I'm shy with people. I warned you in Monte Carlo how it would be. You think I'm not right for Manderley."

"Don't talk nonsense," he said. "I've never said you dressed badly, or were gauche. It's your imagination. As for being shy, you'll get over that. I've told you so before."

"We've argued in a circle," I said, "we've come right back to where we started. This all began because I broke the cupid in the morning-room. If I hadn't broken the cupid none of this would have happened. We'd have drunk our coffee, and gone out into the garden."

"Oh, damn that infernal cupid," said Maxim wearily. "Do you really think I care whether it's in ten thousand pieces or not?"

"Was it very valuable?"

"Heaven knows. I suppose so. I've really forgotten."

"Are all those things in the morning-room valuable?"

"Yes, I believe so."

"Why were all the most valuable things put in the morning-room?"

"I don't know. I suppose they looked well there."

"Were they always there? When your mother was alive?"

"No. No, I don't think they were. They were scattered about the house. The chairs were in a lumber room I believe."

"When was the morning-room furnished as it is now?"

"When I was married."

"I suppose the cupid was put there then?"

"I suppose so."

"Was that found in a lumber room?"

"No. No, I don't think it was. As a matter of fact I believe it was a wedding present. Rebecca knew a lot about china."

I did not look at him. I began to polish my nails. He had said the word quite naturally, quite calmly. It had been no effort to him. After a minute I glanced at him swiftly. He was standing by the mantel-piece, his hands in his pockets. He was staring straight in front of him. He is thinking about Rebecca, I said to myself. He is thinking how strange it was that a wedding present to me should have been the cause of destroying a wedding present to Rebecca. He is thinking about the cupid. He is remembering who gave it to Rebecca. He is going over in his mind how the parcel came and how pleased she was. Rebecca knew a lot about china. Perhaps he came into the room, and she was kneeling on the floor, wrenching open the little crate in which the cupid was packed. She must have glanced up at him, and smiled. "Look, Max," she would have said, "look what we've been sent." And she then would have plunged her hand down into the shavings and brought out the cupid who stood on one foot, his bow in his hand. "We'll have it in the morning-room," she must have said, and he must have knelt down beside her, and they must have looked at the cupid together.

I went on polishing my nails. They were scrubby, like a schoolboy's nails. The cuticles grew up over the half moons. The thumb was bitten nearly to the quick. I looked at Maxim again. He was still standing in front of the fireplace.

"What are you thinking about?" I said.

My voice was steady and cool. Not like my heart, thumping inside me. Not like my mind, bitter and resentful. He lit a cigarette, surely the twenty-fifth that day, and we had only just finished lunch; he threw the match into the empty grate, he picked up the paper.

"Nothing very much, why?" he said.

"Oh, I don't know," I said, "you looked so serious, so far away."

He whistled a tune absently, the cigarette twisting in his fingers. "As a matter of fact I was wondering if they had chosen the Surrey side to play Middlesex at the Oval," he said.

He sat down in the chair again and folded the paper. I looked out of the window. Presently Jasper came to me and climbed on my lap.

CHAPTER THIRTEEN

Maxim had to go up to London at the end of June to some public dinner. A man's dinner. Something to do with the county. He was away for two days and I was left alone. I dreaded his going. When I saw the car disappear round the sweep in the drive I felt exactly as though it were to be a final parting and I should never see him again. There would be an accident of course and later on in the afternoon, when I came back from my walk, I should find Frith white and frightened waiting for me with a message. The doctor would have rung up from some cottage hospital. "You must be very brave," he would say, "I am afraid you must be prepared for a great shock."

And Frank would come, and we would go to the hospital together. Maxim would not recognise me. I went through the whole thing as I was sitting at lunch, I could see the crowd of local people clustering round the churchyard at the funeral, and myself leaning on Frank's arm. It was so real to me that I could scarcely eat any lunch, and I kept straining my ears to hear the telephone should it ring.

I sat out in the garden under the chestnut tree in the afternoon, with a book on my lap, but I scarcely read at all. When I saw Robert come across the lawn I knew it was the telephone and I felt physically sick. "A message from the club, Madam, to say Mr. de Winter arrived ten minutes ago."

I shut up my book. "Thank you, Robert. How quickly he got up."

"Yes, Madam. A very good run."

"Did he ask to speak to me, or leave any special message?"

"No, Madam. Just that he had arrived safely. It was the porter speaking."

"All right, Robert. Thanks very much."

The relief was tremendous. I did not feel sick any more. The pain had gone. It was like coming ashore after a channel crossing. I began to feel rather hungry, and when Robert had gone back into the house I crept into the dining-room through the long window and stole some biscuits from the side-board. I had six of them. Bath Olivers. And then an apple as well. I had no idea I was so empty. I went and ate them in the woods, in case one of the servants should see me on the lawn from the windows, and then go and tell the cook that they did not think Mrs. de Winter cared for the food prepared in the kitchen, as they had just seen her filling herself with fruit and biscuits. The cook would be offended, and perhaps go to Mrs. Danvers.

Now that Maxim was safe in London, and I had eaten my biscuits, I felt very well and curiously happy. I was aware of a sense of freedom, as though I had no responsibilities at all. It was rather like a Saturday when one was a child. No lessons, and no prep. One could do as one liked. One put on an old skirt and a pair of sand-shoes and played Hares and Hounds on the common with the children who lived next door.

I had just the same feeling. I had not felt like this all the time I had been at Manderley. It must be because Maxim had gone to London.

I was rather shocked at myself. I could not understand it at all. I had not wanted him to go. And now this lightness of heart, this spring in my step, this childish feeling that I wanted to run across the lawn, and roll down the bank. I wiped the biscuit crumbs from my mouth and called to Jasper. Perhaps I was just feeling like this because it was a lovely day. . . .

We went through the Happy Valley to the little cove. The azaleas were finished now, the petals lay brown and crinkled on the moss. The bluebells had not faded yet, they made a solid carpet in the woods above the valley, and the young bracken was shooting up, curling and green. The moss smelt rich and deep, and the bluebells were earthy, bitter. I lay down in the long grass beside the bluebells with my hands behind my head, and Jasper at my side. He looked down at me panting, his face foolish, the saliva dripping from his tongue and his heavy jowl. There were pigeons somewhere in the trees above. It was very peaceful and quiet. I wondered why it was that places are so much lovelier when one is alone. How commonplace and stupid it would be if I had a friend now, sitting beside me, someone I had known at school, who would say "By-the-way, I saw old Hilda the other day. You remember her, the one who was so good at tennis. She's married, with two children." And the bluebells beside us unnoticed, and the pigeons overhead unheard. I did not want anyone with me. Not even Maxim. If Maxim had been there I should not be lying as I was now, chewing a piece of grass, my eyes shut. I should have been watching him, watching his eyes, his expression. Wondering if he liked it, if he was bored. Wondering what he was thinking. Now I could relax, none of these things mattered. Maxim was in London. How lovely it was to be alone again. No, I did not mean that. It was disloyal, wicked. It was not what I meant. Maxim was my life and my world. I got up from the bluebells and called sharply to Jasper. We set off together down the valley to the beach. The tide was out, the sea very calm and remote. It looked like a great placid lake out there in the bay. I could not imagine it rough now, any more than I could imagine winter in summer. There was no wind, and the sun shone on the lapping water where it ran into the little pools in the rocks. Jasper scrambled up the rocks immediately, glancing back at me, one ear blown back against his head, giving him an odd rakish appearance.

"Not that way, Jasper," I said.

He cared nothing for me of course. He loped off, deliberately disobedient. "What a nuisance he is," I said aloud, and I scrambled up the rocks after him, pretending to myself I did not want to go to the other beach. "Oh, well," I thought, "it can't be helped. After all, Maxim is not with me. It's nothing to do with me."

I splashed through the pools on the rocks, humming a tune. The cove looked different when the tide was out. Less formidable. There was only about three foot of water in the tiny harbour. A boat would just float there comfortably I supposed, at dead low water. The buoy was still there. It was painted white and green, I had not noticed that before. Perhaps because it had been raining the colouring was indistinct. There was no one on the beach. I walked across the shingle to the other side of the cove, and climbed the low stone wall of the jetty-arm. Jasper ran on ahead as though it was his custom. There was a ring in the wall and an iron ladder descending to the water. That's where the dinghy would be tied, I supposed, and one would climb to it from the ladder. The buoy was just opposite, about thirty feet away. There was something written on it. I craned my neck sideways to read the lettering. "Je Reviens." What a funny name. Not like a boat. Perhaps it had been a French boat though, a fishing boat. Fishing boats sometimes had names like that. "Happy Return," "I'm Here," those sort of names. "Je Reviens"—"I come back." Yes, I supposed it was quite a good name for a boat. Only it had not been right for that particular boat which would never come back again.

It must be cold sailing out there in the bay, beyond the beacon away on the headland. The sea was calm in the bay, but even to-day, when it was so still, out there round the headland there was a ripple of white foam on the surface of the water where the tide was racing. A small boat would heel to the wind when she rounded the headland and came out of the land-locked bay. The sea would splash inboard perhaps, run down the deck. The person at the tiller would wipe the spray out of her eyes and hair, glance up at the straining mast. I wondered what colour the boat had been. Green and white perhaps, like the buoy. Not very big, Frank had said, with a little cabin.

Jasper was sniffing at the iron ladder. "Come away," I said. "I don't want to go in after you." I went back along the harbour wall to the beach. The cottage did not seem so remote and sinister at the edge of the wood as it had done before. The sun made such a difference. No rain to-day, pattering on the roof. I walked slowly up the beach towards it. After all, it was only a cottage, with nobody living in it. There was nothing to be frightened of. Nothing at all. Any place seemed damp and sinister when it had been uninhabited for a certain time. Even new bungalows and places. Beside, they had had moonlight picnics and things here. Week-end visitors probably used to come and bathe, and then go for a sail in the boat. I stood looking into the neglected garden choked with nettles. Someone ought to come and tidy it up. One of the gardeners. There was no need to leave it like this. I pushed the little gate and went to the door of the cottage. It was not entirely closed. I was certain I had closed it the last time. Jasper began growling, sniffing under the door.

"Don't, Jasper," I said. He went on sniffing deeply, his nose thrust to the lintel. I pushed the door open and looked inside. It was very dark. Like it had been before. Nothing was changed. The cobwebs still clung to the rigging of the model boats. The door into the boat-store at the end of the room was open though. Jasper growled again, and there was a sound of something falling. Jasper barked furiously, and darting between my legs into the room he tore to the open door of the store. I followed him, heart beating, and then stood uncertainly in the middle of the room. "Jasper, come back, don't be a fool," I said. He stood in the doorway, still barking furiously, an hysterical note in his voice. Something was there then, inside the store. Not a rat. He would have gone for a rat. "Jasper, Jasper. Come here," I said. He would not come. I went slowly to the door of the store.

"Is there anybody there?" I said.

No one answered. I bent down to Jasper, putting my hand on his collar, and looked round the edge of the door. Someone was sitting in the corner against the wall. Someone, who from his crouching position, was even more frightened than I. It was Ben. He was trying to hide behind one of the sails. "What is the matter, do you want something?" I said. He blinked at me stupidly, his mouth slightly open.

"I'm not doing nothing," he said.

"Quiet, Jasper," I scolded, putting my hand over his muzzle, and I took my belt off and ran it through his collar as a leash.

"What do you want, Ben?" I said, a little bolder this time.

He did not answer. He watched me with his sly idiot's eyes.

"I think you had better come out," I said. "Mr. de Winter doesn't like people walking in and out of here."

He shambled to his feet grinning furtively, wiping his nose with the back of his hand. The other hand he kept behind his back. "What have you got, Ben?" I said. He obeyed me like a child, showing me the other hand. There was a fishing line in it. "I'm not doing nothing," he repeated.

"Does that line belong here?" I asked.

"Eh?" he said.

"Listen, Ben," I said, "you can take that line if you want to, but you mustn't do it again. It's not honest, taking people's things."

He said nothing. He blinked at me and wriggled.

"Come along," I said firmly. I went into the main room and he followed me. Jasper had stopped barking, and was now sniffing at Ben's heels. I did not want to stop any longer in the cottage. I walked quickly out into the sunshine, Ben shuffling behind me. Then I shut the door.

"You had better go home," I said to Ben.

He held the fishing line clutched to his heart like a treasure. "You won't put me to the asylum, will you?" he said.

I saw then that he was trembling with fright. His hands were shaking, and his eyes were fixed on mine in supplication, like a dumb thing.

"Of course not," I said gently.

"I done nothing," he repeated, "I never told no one. I don't want to be put to the asylum." A tear rolled down his dirty face.

"That's all right, Ben," I said, "no one will put you away. But you must not go to the cottage again."

I turned away, and he came after me, pawing at my hand.

"Here," he said. "Here I got something for you."

He smiled foolishly, he beckoned with his finger, and turned towards the beach. I went with him, and he bent down and picked up a flat stone by a rock. There was a little heap of shells under the stone. He chose one, and presented it to me. "That's yourn," he said.

"Thank you, it's very pretty," I said.

He grinned again, rubbing his ear, his fright forgotten. "You've got angel's eyes," he said.

I glanced down at the shell, again, rather taken aback. I did not know what to say.

"You're not like the other one," he said.

"Who do you mean?" I said. "What other one?"

He shook his head. His eyes were sly again. He laid his finger against his nose. "Tall and dark she was," he said. "She gave you the feeling of a snake. I seen her here with me own eyes. By night she'd come. I seen her." He paused, watching me intently. I did not say anything. "I looked in on her once," he said, "and she turned on me, she did. 'You don't know me, do you?' she said. 'You've never seen me here, and you won't again. If I catch you looking at me through the windows here I'll have you put to the asylum,' she said. 'You wouldn't like that, would you? They're cruel to people in the asylum,' she said. 'I won't say nothing, Ma'am,' I said. And I touched me cap, like this here." He pulled at his sou'wester. "She's gone now, ain't she?" he said anxiously.

"I don't know who you mean," I said slowly, "no one is going to put you in the asylum. Good afternoon, Ben."

I turned away and walked up the beach to the path dragging Jasper by his belt. Poor wretch, he was potty of course. He did not know what he was talking about. It was hardly likely that anyone would threaten him with the asylum. Maxim had said he was quite harmless, and so had Frank. Perhaps he had heard himself discussed once, amongst his own people, and the memory of it lingered, like an ugly picture in the mind of a child. He would have a child's mentality too, regarding likes and dislikes. He would take a fancy to a person for no reason, and be friendly one day perhaps and sullen the next. He had been friendly with me because I had said he could keep the fishing line. To-morrow if I met him he might not know me. It was absurd to notice anything said by an idiot. I glanced back over my shoulder at the cove. The tide had begun to turn and was swirling slowly round the arm of the harbour wall. Ben had disappeared over the rocks. The beach was deserted again. I could just see the stone chimney of the cottage through a gap in the dark trees. I had a sudden unaccountable desire to run. I pulled at Jasper's leash and panted up the steep narrow path through the woods not looking back any more. Had I been offered all the treasures in the world I could not have turned and gone down to the cottage or the beach again. It was as though someone waited down there, in the little garden where the nettles grew. Someone who watched and listened.

Jasper barked as we ran together. He thought it was some new kind of game. He kept trying to bite the belt and worry it. I had not realised how closely the trees grew together here, their roots stretching across the path like tendrils ready to trip one. They ought to clear all this, I thought as I ran, catching my breath, Maxim should get the men on to it. There is no sense or beauty in this undergrowth. That tangle of shrubs there should be cut down to bring light to the path. It was dark, much too dark. That naked eucalyptus tree stifled by brambles looked like the white bleached limb of a skeleton, and there was a black earthy stream running beneath it, choked with the muddied rains of years, trickling silently to the beach below. The birds did not sing here as they did in the valley. It was quiet in a different way. And even as I ran and panted up the path I could hear the wash of the sea as the tide crept into the cove. I understood why Maxim disliked the path and the cove. I disliked it too. I had been a fool to come this way. I should have stayed on the other beach, on the white shingle, and come home by the Happy Valley.

I was glad to come out on to the lawn and see the house there in the hollow, solid and secure. The woods were behind me. I would ask Robert to bring me my tea under the chestnut tree. I glanced at my watch. It was earlier than I thought, not yet four. I would have to wait a bit. It was not the routine at Manderley to have tea before half-past. I was glad Frith was out. Robert would not make such a performance of bringing the tea out into the garden. As I wandered across the lawn to the terrace my eye was caught by a gleam of sunshine on something metal showing through the green of the rhododendron leaves at the turn in the drive. I shaded my eyes with my hand to see what it was. It looked like the radiator of a car. I wondered if someone had called. If they had though, they would have driven up to the house, not left their car concealed like that from the house, at the turn of the drive, by the shrubs. I went a little closer. Yes, it was a car all right. I could see the wings now and the hood. What a funny thing. Visitors never did that as a rule. And the tradesmen went round the back way by the old stables and the garage. It was not Frank's Morris. I knew that well. This was a long, low car, a sports car. I wondered what I had better do. If it was a caller Robert would have shown them into the library or the drawing-room. If the drawing-room they would be able to see me as I came across the lawn. I

did not want to face a caller dressed like this. I should have to ask
them to stay to tea. I hesitated, at the edge of the lawn. For no reason,
perhaps because the sunlight flickered a moment on the glass, I
looked up at the house, and as I did so I noticed with surprise that the
shutters of one of the windows in the west wing had been opened up.
Somebody stood by the window. A man. And then he must have
caught sight of me because he drew back abruptly, and a figure behind him put up an arm and closed the shutters.

The arm belonged to Mrs. Danvers. I recognised the black sleeve.
I wondered for a minute if it was a public day and she was showing
the rooms. It could not be so though because Frith always did that,
and Frith was out. Besides, the rooms in the west wing were not
shown to the public. I had not even been into them myself yet. No, I
knew it was not a public day. The public never came on a Tuesday.
Perhaps it was something to do with a repair in one of the rooms. It
was odd though the way the man had been looking out and directly
he saw me he whipped back into the room and the shutters were
closed. And the car too, drawn up behind the rhododendrons, so that
it could not be seen from the house. Still, that was up to Mrs. Danvers. It was nothing to do with me. If she had friends she took to the
west wing it was not exactly my affair. I had never known it happen
before though. Odd that it should occur on the only day Maxim was
from home.

I strolled rather self-consciously across the lawn to the house,
aware that they might be watching me still from a chink in the shutters.

I went up the steps and through the big front door to the hall.
There was no sign of a strange cap or stick, and no card on the salver.
Evidently this was not an official visitor. Well, it was not my affair. I
went into the flower-room and washed my hands in the basin to save
going upstairs. It would be awkward if I met them face to face on the
stairs or somewhere. I remembered I had left my knitting in the
morning-room before lunch, and I went along through the drawing-
room to fetch it, the faithful Jasper at my heels. The morning-room
door was open. And I noticed that my bag of knitting had been
moved. I had left it on the divan, and it had been picked up and
pushed behind a cushion. There was the imprint of a person on the
fabric of the divan where my knitting had been before. Someone had
sat down there recently, and picked up my knitting because it had
been in the way. The chair by the desk had also been moved. It looked
as though Mrs. Danvers entertained her visitors in the morning-room
when Maxim and I were out of the way. I felt rather uncomfortable. I

would rather not know. Jasper was sniffing round the divan and wagging his tail. He was not suspicious of the visitor anyway. I took my bag of knitting and went out. As I did so the door in the large drawing-room that led to the stone passage and the back premises opened, and I heard voices. I darted back into the morning-room again, just in time. I had not been seen. I waited behind the door frowning at Jasper who stood in the doorway looking at me, his tongue hanging out, wagging his tail. The little wretch would give me away. I stood very still, holding my breath.

Then I heard Mrs. Danvers speak. "I expect she has gone to the library," she said. "She's come home early for some reason. If she has gone to the library you will be able to go through the hall without her seeing you. Wait here while I go and see."

I knew they were talking about me. I began to feel more uncomfortable than ever. It was so furtive, the whole business. And I did not want to catch Mrs. Danvers in the wrong. Then Jasper turned his head sharply towards the drawing-room. He trotted out, wagging his tail.

"Hullo, you little tyke," I heard the man say. Jasper began to bark excitedly. I looked round desperately for somewhere to hide. Hopeless of course. And then I heard a footstep quite close to my ear, and the man came into the room. He did not see me at first because I was behind the door, but Jasper made a dive at me, still barking with delight.

The man wheeled round suddenly and saw me. I have never seen anyone look more astonished. I might have been the burglar and he the master of the house.

"I beg your pardon," he said, looking me up and down.

He was a big, hefty fellow, good-looking in a rather flashy, sunburnt way. He had the hot, blue eyes usually associated with heavy drinking and loose living. His hair was reddish like his skin. In a few years he would run to fat, his neck bulging over the back of his collar. His mouth gave him away, it was too soft, too pink. I could smell the whisky in his breath from where I stood. He began to smile. The sort of smile he would give to every woman.

"I hope I haven't startled you," he said.

I came out from behind the door looking no doubt as big a fool as I felt. "No, of course not," I said, "I heard voices, I was not quite sure who it was. I did not expect any callers this afternoon."

"What a shame," he said heartily, "it's too bad of me to butt in on you like this. I hope you'll forgive me. The fact is I just popped in to see old Danny, she's a very old friend of mine."

"Oh, of course, it's quite all right," I said.

"Dear old Danny," he said, "she's so anxious, bless her, not to disturb anyone. She didn't want to worry you."

"Oh, it does not matter at all," I said. I was watching Jasper, who was jumping up and pawing at the man in delight.

"This little beggar hasn't forgotten me, has he?" he said. "Grown into a jolly little beast. He was quite a youngster when I saw him last. He's too fat though. He needs more exercise."

"I've just taken him for a long walk," I said.

"Have you really? How sporting of you," he said. He went on patting Jasper and smiling at me in a familiar way. Then he pulled out his cigarette case. "Have one?" he said.

"I don't smoke," I told him.

"Don't you really?" He took one himself and lighted it.

I never minded those things, but it seemed odd to me, in somebody else's room. It was surely rather bad manners? Not polite to me.

"How's old Max?" he said.

I was surprised at his tone. It sounded as though he knew him well. It was queer, to hear Maxim talked of as Max. No one called him that.

"He's very well, thank you," I said, "he's gone up to London."

"And left the bride all alone? Why, that's too bad. Isn't he afraid someone will come and carry you off?"

He laughed, opening his mouth. I did not like his laugh. There was something offensive about it. I did not like him either. Just then Mrs. Danvers came into the room. She turned her eyes upon me and I felt quite cold. Oh, God, I thought, how she must hate me.

"Hullo, Danny, there you are," said the man, "all your precautions were in vain. The mistress of the house was hiding behind the door." And he laughed again. Mrs. Danvers did not say anything. She just went on looking at me. "Well, aren't you going to introduce me?" he said, "after all, it's the usual thing to do, isn't it, to pay one's respects to a bride?"

"This is Mr. Favell, Madam," said Mrs. Danvers. She spoke quietly, rather unwillingly. I don't think she wanted to introduce him to me.

"How do you do," I said, and then, with an effort to be polite, "Won't you stay to tea?"

He looked very amused. He turned to Mrs. Danvers.

"Now isn't that a charming invitation?" he said. "I've been asked to stay to tea. By heaven, Danny, I've a good mind to."

I saw her flash a look of warning at him. I felt very uneasy. It was all wrong, this situation. It ought not to be happening at all.

"Well, perhaps you're right," he said, "it would have been a lot of fun, all the same. I suppose I had better be going, hadn't I? Come and have a look at my car." He still spoke in a familiar rather offensive way. I did not want to go and look at his car. I felt very awkward and embarrassed. "Come on," he said, "it's a jolly good little car. Much faster than anything poor old Max ever has."

I could not think of an excuse. The whole business was so forced and stupid. I did not like it. And why did Mrs. Danvers have to stand there looking at me with that smouldering look in her eyes?

"Where is the car?" I said feebly.

"Round the bend in the drive. I didn't drive to the door. I was afraid of disturbing you. I had some idea you probably rested in the afternoon."

I said nothing. The lie was too obvious. We all walked out through the drawing-room and into the hall. I saw him glance over his shoulder and wink at Mrs. Danvers. She did not wink in return. I hardly expected she would. She looked very hard and grim. Jasper frolicked out on the drive. He seemed delighted with the sudden appearance of this visitor whom he appeared to know so well.

"I left my cap in the car I believe," said the man, pretending to glance round the hall. "As a matter of fact, I didn't come in this way. I slipped round and bearded Danny in her den. Coming out to see the car too?"

He looked enquiringly at Mrs. Danvers. She hesitated, watching me out of the tail of her eye.

"No," she said. "No, I don't think I'll come out now. Good-bye, Mr. Jack."

He seized her hand and shook it heartily. "Good-bye, Danny, take care of yourself. You know where to get in touch with me always. It's done me a power of good to see you again." He walked out on to the drive, Jasper dancing at his heels, and I followed him slowly, feeling very uncomfortable still.

"Dear old Manderley," he said, looking up at the windows, "the place hasn't changed much. I suppose Danny sees to that. What a wonderful woman she is, eh?"

"Yes, she's very efficient," I said.

"And what do you think of it all? Like being buried down here?"

"I'm very fond of Manderley," I said stiffly.

"Weren't you living somewhere down in the south of France when Max met you? Monte, wasn't it? I used to know Monte well."

"Yes, I was in Monte Carlo," I said.

We had come to his car now. A green sports thing, typical of its owner.

"What do you think of it?" he said.

"Very nice," I said politely.

"Come for a run to the lodge gates?" he said.

"No, I don't think I will," I said. "I'm rather tired."

"You don't think it would look too good for the mistress of Manderley to be seen driving with someone like me, is that it?" he said, and he laughed, shaking his head at me.

"Oh, no," I said, turning rather red. "No, really."

He went on looking me up and down in his amused way with those familiar, unpleasant blue eyes. I felt like a bar-maid.

"Oh, well," he said, "we mustn't lead the bride astray, must we, Jasper? It wouldn't do at all." He reached for his cap, and an enormous pair of motoring gloves. He threw his cigarette away on the drive.

"Good-bye," he said, holding out his hand, "it's been a lot of fun meeting you."

"Good-bye," I said.

"By-the-way," he said carelessly, "it would be very sporting and grand of you if you did not mention this little visit of mine to Max. He doesn't exactly approve of me, I'm afraid; I don't know why, and it might get poor old Danny into trouble."

"No," I said awkwardly. "No, all right."

"That's very sporting of you. Sure you won't change your mind and come for a run?"

"No, I don't think I will, if you don't mind."

"Bye-bye, then. Perhaps I'll come and look you up one day. Get down, Jasper, you devil, you'll scratch my paint. I say, I call it a damn shame Max going up to London and leaving you alone like this."

"I don't mind. I like being alone," I said.

"Do you, by Jove? What an extraordinary thing. It's all wrong, you know. Against nature. How long have you been married? Three months, isn't it?"

"About that," I said.

"I say, I wish I'd got a bride of three months waiting for me at home! I'm a poor lonesome bachelor." He laughed again, and pulled his cap down over his eyes. "Fare you well," he said, starting up the engine, and the car shot down the drive snorting, explosive fury from the exhaust, while Jasper stood looking after it, his ears drooping, his tail between his legs.

"Oh, come on, Jasper," I said, "don't be so idiotic." I walked slowly back to the house. Mrs. Danvers had disappeared. I stood in the hall and rang the bell. Nothing happened for about five minutes. I rang. Presently Alice appeared, her face rather aggrieved. "Yes, Madam?" she said.

"Oh, Alice," I said, "isn't Robert there? I rather fancied my tea out under the chestnut tree."

"Robert went to the post this afternoon, and isn't back yet, Madam," said Alice. "Mrs. Danvers gave him to understand you would be late for tea. Frith is out too of course. If you want your tea now I can get it for you. I don't think it's quite half-past four yet."

"Oh, it doesn't matter, Alice, I'll wait till Robert comes back," I said. I supposed when Maxim was away things automatically became slack. I had never known Frith and Robert to be out at the same time. It was Frith's day of course. And Mrs. Danvers had sent Robert to the post. And I myself was understood to have gone for a long walk. That man Favell had chosen his time well to pay his call on Mrs. Danvers. It was almost too well chosen. There was something not right about it, I was certain of that. And then he had asked me not to say anything to Maxim. It was all very awkward. I did not want to get Mrs. Danvers into trouble or make any sort of scene. More important still, I did not want to worry Maxim.

I wondered who he was, this man Favell. He had called Maxim "Max." No one ever called him Max. I had seen it written once, on the fly-leaf of a book, the letters thin and slanting, curiously pointed, the tail of the M very definite, very long. I thought there was only one person who had ever called him Max. . . .

As I stood there in the hall, undecided about my tea, wondering what to do, the thought suddenly came to me that perhaps Mrs. Danvers was dishonest, that all this time she was engaged in some business behind Maxim's back, and coming back early as I had to-day I had discovered her and this man, an accomplice, who had then bluffed his way out by pretending to be familiar with the house and with Maxim. I wondered what they had been doing in the west wing. Why had they closed the shutters when they saw me on the lawn? I was filled with vague disquiet. Frith and Robert had been away. The maids were generally in their bedrooms changing during the afternoon. Mrs. Danvers would have the run of the place. Supposing this man was a thief, and Mrs. Danvers was in his pay? There were valuable things in the west wing. I had a sudden rather terrifying impulse to creep upstairs now to the west wing and go into those rooms and see for myself.

Robert was not yet back. I would just have time before tea. I hesitated, glancing at the gallery. The house seemed very still and quiet. The servants were all in their own quarters beyond the kitchen. Jasper lapped noisily at his drinking bowl below the stairs, the sound echoing in the great stone hall. I began to walk upstairs. My heart was beating in a queer excited way.

CHAPTER FOURTEEN

I found myself in the corridor where I had stood that first morning. I had not been there since, nor had I wished to go. The sun streamed in from the window in the alcove and made gold patterns on the dark panelling.

There was no sound at all. I was aware of the same musty, unused smell that had been before. I was uncertain which way to go. The plan of the rooms was not familiar to me. I remembered then that last time Mrs. Danvers had come out of a door here, just behind me, and it seemed to me that the position of the room would make it the one I wanted, whose windows looked out upon the lawns to the sea. I turned the handle of the door and went inside. It was dark of course, because of the shutters. I felt for the electric light switch on the wall and turned it on. I was standing in a little ante-room, a dressing-room I judged, with big wardrobes round the wall, and at the end of this room was another door, open, leading to a larger room. I went through to this room, and turned on the light. My first impression was one of shock because the room was fully furnished, as though in use.

I had expected to see chairs and tables swathed in dust-sheets, and dust-sheets too over the great double bed against the wall. Nothing was covered up. There were brushes and combs on the dressing-table, scent, and powder. The bed was made up, I saw the gleam of white linen on the pillow-case, and the tip of a blanket beneath the quilted coverlet. There were flowers on the dressing-table and on the table beside the bed. Flowers too on the carved mantelpiece. A satin dressing-gown lay on a chair, and a pair of bedroom slippers beneath. For one desperate moment I thought that something had happened to my brain, that I was seeing back into Time, and looking upon the room as it used to be, before she died. . . . In a minute Rebecca herself would come back into the room, sit down before the looking-glass at her dressing-table, humming a tune, reach for her comb and run it through her hair. If she sat there I should see her reflection in the glass, and she would see me too, standing like this by the door. Nothing happened. I went on standing there, waiting for something to happen. It was the clock ticking on the wall that brought me to reality again. The hands stood at twenty-five past four. My watch said the same. There was something sane and comforting about the ticking of the clock. It reminded me of the present, and that tea would soon be ready for me on the lawn. I walked slowly into the middle of the room. No, it was not used. It was not lived in any more. Even the flowers could not destroy the musty smell. The curtains were drawn and the shutters were closed. Rebecca would never come back to the room again. Even if Mrs. Danvers did put the flowers on the mantelpiece and the sheets upon the bed, they would not bring her back. She was dead. She had been dead now for a year. She lay buried in the crypt of the church with all the other dead de Winters.

I could hear the sound of the sea very plainly. I went to the window and swung back the shutter. Yes, I was standing at the same window where Favell and Mrs. Danvers had stood, half an hour ago. The long shaft of daylight made the electric light look false and yellow. I opened the shutter a little more. The daylight cast a white beam upon the bed. It shone upon the nightdress case, lying on the pillow. It shone on the glass top of the dressing-table, on the brushes, and on the scent bottles.

The daylight gave an even greater air of reality to the room. When the shutter was closed and it had been lit by electricity the room had more the appearance of a setting on the stage. The scene set between performances. The curtain having fallen for the night, the evening over, and the first act set for to-morrow's matinée. But the daylight made the room vivid and alive. I forgot the musty smell and the drawn curtains of the other windows. I was a guest again. An uninvited guest. I had strolled into my hostess's bedroom by mistake. Those were her brushes on the dressing-table, that was her dressing-gown and slippers laid out upon the chair.

I realised for the first time since I had come into the room that my legs were trembling, weak as straw. I sat down on the stool by the dressing-table. My heart no longer beat in a strange excited way. It felt as heavy as lead. I looked about me in the room with a sort of dumb stupidity. Yes, it was a beautiful room. Mrs. Danvers had not exaggerated that first evening. It was the most beautiful room in the house. That exquisite mantelpiece, the ceiling, the carved bedstead and the curtain hangings, even the clock on the wall and the candle-sticks upon the dressing-table beside me, all were things I would have loved and almost worshipped had they been mine. They were not mine though. They belonged to somebody else. I put out my hand and touched the brushes. One was more worn than its fellow. I under-stood it well. There was always one brush that had the greater use. Often you forgot to use the other, and when they were taken to be washed there was one that was still quite clean and untouched. How white and thin my face looked in the glass, my hair hanging lank and straight. Did I always look like this? Surely I had more colour as a rule? The reflection stared back at me, sallow and plain.

I got up from the stool and went and touched the dressing-gown on the chair. I picked up the slippers and held them in my hand. I was aware of a growing sense of horror, of horror turning to despair. I touched the quilt on the bed, traced with my fingers the monogram on the nightdress case, R de W, interwoven and interlaced. The letters were corded and strong against the golden satin material. The night-dress was inside the case, thin as gossamer, apricot in colour. I touched it, drew it out from the case, put it against my face. It was cold, quite cold. But there was a dim mustiness about it still where the scent had been. The scent of the white azalea. I folded it, and put it back into the case, and as I did so I noticed with a sick dull aching in my heart that there were creases in the nightdress, the texture was ruffled, it had not been touched or laundered since it was last worn.

On a sudden impulse I moved away from the bed and went back to the little ante-room where I had seen the wardrobes. I opened one of them. It was as I thought. The wardrobe was full of clothes. There were evening dresses here, I caught the shimmer of silver over the top of the white bags that enfolded them. There was a piece of gold bro-cade. There, next to it, was velvet, wine-coloured, and soft. There was a train of white satin, dripping on the floor of the wardrobe. Peeping out from a piece of tissue paper on a shelf above was an ostrich feather fan.

The wardrobe smelt stuffy, queer. The azalea scent, so fragrant and delicate in the air, had turned stale inside the wardrobe, tarnish-ing the silver dresses and the brocade, and the breath of it wafted to-wards me now from the open doors, faded and old. I shut the doors. I went back into the bedroom once again. The gleam of light from the shutter still shone white and clear on the golden coverlet of the bed, picking out clearly and distinctly the tall sloping R of the monogram.

Then I heard a step behind me and turning round I saw Mrs. Danvers. I shall never forget the expression on her face. Triumphant, gloating, excited in a strange unhealthy way. I felt very frightened.

"Is anything the matter, Madam?" she said.

I tried to smile at her and could not. I tried to speak.

"Are you feeling unwell?" she said, coming nearer to me, speaking very softly. I backed away from her. I believe if she had come any closer to me I should have fainted. I felt her breath on my face.

"I'm all right, Mrs. Danvers," I said, after a moment, "I did not expect to see you. The fact is, I was looking up at the windows from the lawn. I noticed one of the shutters was not quite closed. I came up to see if I could fasten it."

"I will fasten it," she said, and she went silently across the room and clamped back the shutter. The daylight had gone. The room looked unreal again in the false yellow light. Unreal and ghastly.

Mrs. Danvers came back and stood beside me. She smiled, and her manner instead of being still and unbending as it usually was became startlingly familiar, fawning even.

"Why did you tell me the shutter was open?" she said. "I closed it before I left the room. You opened it yourself, didn't you, now? You wanted to see the room. Why have you never asked me to show it to you before? I was ready to show it to you every day. You had only to ask me."

I wanted to run away, but I could not move. I went on watching her eyes.

"Now you are here, let me show you everything," she said, her voice ingratiating and sweet as honey, horrible, false. "I know you want to see it all, you've wanted to for a long time, and you were too shy to ask. It's a lovely room, isn't it? The loveliest room you have ever seen."

She took hold of my arm, and walked me towards the bed. I could not resist her, I was like a dumb thing. The touch of her hand made me shudder. And her voice was low and intimate, a voice I hated and feared.

"That was her bed. It's a beautiful bed, isn't it? I keep the golden coverlet on it always, it was her favourite. Here is her nightdress inside the case. You've been touching it, haven't you? This was the nightdress she was wearing for the last time, before she died. Would you like to touch it again?" She took the nightdress from the case and held it before me. "Feel it, hold it," she said, "how soft and light it is, isn't it? I haven't washed it since she wore it for the last time. I put it out like this, and the dressing-gown and slippers, just as I put them out for her the night she never came back, the night she was drowned." She folded up the nightgown and put it back in the case. "I did everything for her, you know," she said, taking my arm again, leading me to the dressing-gown and slippers. "We tried maid after maid but not one of them suited. 'You maid me better than anyone, Danny,' she used to say, 'I won't have anyone but you.' Look, this is her dressing-gown. She was much taller than you, you can see by the length. Put it up against you. It comes down to your ankles. She had a beautiful figure. These are her slippers. 'Throw me my slips, Danny,' she used to say. She had little feet for her height. Put your hands inside the slippers. They are quite small and narrow, aren't they?"

She forced the slippers over my hands, smiling all the while, watching my eyes. "You never would have thought she was so tall, would you?" she said, "these slippers would fit a tiny foot. She was so slim too. You would forget her height, until she stood beside you. She was every bit as tall as me. But lying there in bed she looked quite a slip of a thing, with her mass of dark hair, standing out from her face like a halo."

She put the slippers back on the floor, and laid the dressing-gown on the chair. "You've seen her brushes, haven't you?" she said, taking me to the dressing-table, "there they are, just as she used them, unwashed and untouched. I used to brush her hair for her every evening. 'Come on, Danny, hair-drill,' she would say, and I'd stand behind her by the stool here, and brush away for twenty minutes at a time. She only wore it short the last few years, you know. It came down below the waist, when she was first married. Mr. de Winter used to brush it for her then. I've come into this room time and time again and seen him, in his shirt sleeves, with the two brushes in his hand. 'Harder, Max, harder,' she would say, laughing up at him, and he would do as she told him. They would be dressing for dinner, you see, and the house filled with guests. 'Here, I shall be late,' he would say, throwing the brushes to me, and laughing back at her. He was always laughing and gay then."

She paused, her hand still resting on my arm.

"Everyone was angry with her when she cut her hair," she said, "but she did not care. 'It's nothing to do with anyone but myself,' she would say. And of course short hair was much easier for riding and sailing. She was painted on horseback, you know. A famous artist did it. The picture hung in the Academy. Did you ever see it?"

I shook my head. "No," I said. "No."

"I understood it was the picture of the year," she went on, "but Mr. de Winter did not care for it, and would not have it at Manderley.

I don't think he considered it did her justice. You would like to see her clothes, wouldn't you?" She did not wait for my answer. She led me to the little ante-room and opened the wardrobes, one by one.

"I keep her furs in here," she said, "the moths have not got to them yet, and I doubt if they ever will. I'm too careful. Feel that sable wrap. That was a Christmas present from Mr. de Winter. She told me the cost once, but I've forgotten it now. This chinchilla she wore in the evenings mostly. Round her shoulders, very often, when the evenings were cold. This wardrobe here is full of her evening clothes. You opened it, didn't you? The latch is not quite closed. I believe Mr. de Winter liked her to wear silver mostly. But of course she could wear anything, stand any colour. She looked beautiful in this velvet. Put it against your face. It's soft, isn't it? You can feel it, can't you? The scent is still fresh, isn't it? You could almost imagine she had only just taken it off. I would always know when she had been before me in a room. There would be a little whiff of her scent in the room. These are her underclothes, in this drawer. This pink set here she had never worn. She was wearing slacks of course and a shirt when she died. They were torn from her body in the water though. There was nothing on the body when it was found, all those weeks afterwards."

Her fingers tightened on my arm. She bent down to me, her skull's face close, her dark eyes searching mine. "The rocks had battered her to bits, you know," she whispered, "her beautiful face unrecognisable, and both arms gone. Mr. de Winter identified her. He went up to Edgecoombe to do it. He went quite alone. He was very ill at the time but he would go. No one could stop him. Not even Mr. Crawley."

She paused, her eyes never leaving my face. "I shall always blame myself for the accident," she said, "it was my fault for being out that evening. I had gone into Kerrith for the afternoon and stayed there late, as Mrs. de Winter was up in London and not expected back until much later. That's why I did not hurry back. When I came in, about half-past nine, I heard she had returned just before seven, had her dinner, and then went out again. Down to the beach of course. I felt worried then. It was blowing up from the south-west. She would never have gone if I'd been in. She always listened to me. 'I wouldn't go out this evening, it's not fit,' I should have said, and she would have answered me 'All right, Danny, you old fusspot.' And we would have sat up here talking no doubt, she telling me all she had done up in London, like she always did."

My arm was bruised and numb from the pressure of her fingers. I could see how tightly the skin was stretched across her face, showing the cheek-bones. There were little patches of yellow beneath her ears.

"Mr. de Winter had been dining with Mr. Crawley down at his house," she went on. "I don't know what time he got back, I dare say it was after eleven. But it began to blow quite hard, just before midnight, and she had not come back. I went downstairs, but there were no lights under the library door. I came upstairs again and knocked on the dressing-room door. Mr. de Winter answered at once, 'Who is it, what do you want?' he said. I told him I was worried about Mrs. de Winter not being back. He waited a moment, and then he came and opened the door in his dressing-gown. 'She's spending the night down at the cottage I expect,' he said. 'I should go to bed if I were you. She won't come back here to sleep if it goes on like this.' He looked tired, and I did not like to disturb him. After all, she spent many nights at the cottage, and had sailed in every sort of weather. She might not even have gone for a sail, but just wanted the night at the cottage as a change after London. I said good night to Mr. de Winter and went back to my room. I did not sleep though. I kept wondering what she was doing."

She paused again. I did not want to hear any more. I wanted to get away from her, away from the room.

"I sat on my bed until half-past five," she said, "then I couldn't wait there any longer. I got up and put on my coat and went down through the woods to the beach. It was getting light, but there was still a misty sort of rain falling, although the wind had dropped. When I got to the beach I saw the buoy there in the water and the dinghy, but the boat had gone. . . ." It seemed to me that I could see the cove in the grey morning light, feel the thin drizzle on my face, and peering through the mist could make out, shadowy and indistinct, the low dark outline of the buoy.

Mrs. Danvers loosened the pressure on my arm. Her hand fell back again to her side. Her voice lost all expression, became the hard mechanical voice of every day.

"One of the life-buoys was washed up at Kerrith in the afternoon," she said, "and another was found the next day by some crabbers on the rocks below the headland. Bits and pieces of rigging too would come in with the tide." She turned away from me, and closed the chest of drawers. She straightened one of the pictures on the wall. She picked up a piece of fluff from the carpet. I stood watching her, not knowing what to do.

"You know now," she said, "why Mr. de Winter does not use these rooms any more. Listen to the sea."

Even with the windows closed and the shutters fastened I could hear it; a low sullen murmur as the waves broke on the white shingle in the cove. The tide would be coming in fast now and running up the beach nearly to the stone cottage.

"He has not used these rooms since the night she was drowned," she said. "He had his things moved out from the dressing-room. We made up one of the rooms at the end of the corridor. I don't think he slept much even there. He used to sit in the arm-chair. There would be cigarette-ash all round it in the morning. And in the daytime Frith would hear him in the library pacing up and down. Up and down, up and down."

I too could see the ash on the floor beside the chair. I too could hear his footsteps; one, two, one, two, backwards and forwards across the library. . . . Mrs. Danvers closed the door softly between the bedroom and the ante-room where we were standing, and put out the light. I could not see the bed any more, nor the nightdress case upon the pillow, nor the dressing-table, nor the slippers by the chair. She crossed the ante-room and put her hand on the knob of the door and stood waiting for me to follow her.

"I come to the rooms and dust them myself every day," she said. "If you want to come again you have only to tell me. Ring me on the house telephone. I shall understand. I don't allow the maids up here. No one ever comes but me."

Her manner was fawning again, intimate and unpleasant. The smile on her face was a false, unnatural thing. "Sometimes when Mr. de Winter is away, and you feel lonely, you might like to come up to these rooms and sit here. You have only to tell me. They are such beautiful rooms. You would not think she had been gone now for so long, would you, not by the way the rooms are kept? You would think she had just gone out for a little while and would be back in the evening."

I forced a smile. I could not speak. My throat felt dry and tight.

"It's not only this room," she said. "It's in many rooms in the house. In the morning-room, in the hall, even in the little flower-room. I feel her everywhere. You do too, don't you?"

She stared at me curiously. Her voice dropped to a whisper. "Sometimes, when I walk along the corridor here I fancy I hear her just behind me. That quick, light footstep. I could not mistake it anywhere. And in the minstrels' gallery above the hall. I've seen her leaning there, in the evenings in the old days, looking down at the hall below and calling to the dogs. I can fancy her there now from time to time. It's almost as though I catch the sound of her dress sweeping the stairs as she comes down to dinner." She paused. She went on looking at me, watching my eyes. "Do you think she can see us, talking to one another now?" she said slowly. "Do you think the dead come back and watch the living?"

I swallowed. I dug my nails into my hands.

"I don't know," I said. "I don't know." My voice sounded high-pitched and unnatural. Not my voice at all.

"Sometimes I wonder," she whispered. "Sometimes I wonder if she comes back here to Manderley and watches you and Mr. de Winter together."

We stood there by the door, staring at one another. I could not take my eyes away from hers. How dark and sombre they were in that white skull's face of hers, how malevolent, how full of hatred. Then she opened the door into the corridor. "Robert is back now," she said. "He came back a quarter of an hour ago. He has orders to take your tea out under the chestnut tree."

She stepped aside for me to pass. I stumbled out on to the corridor, not looking where I was going. I did not speak to her, I went down the stairs blindly, and turned the corner and pushed through the door that led to my own rooms in the east wing. I shut the door of my room and turned the key, and put the key in my pocket.

Then I lay down on my bed and closed my eyes. I felt deadly sick.

CHAPTER FIFTEEN

Maxim rang up the next morning to say he would be back about seven. Frith took the message. Maxim did not ask to speak to me himself. I heard the telephone ring while I was at breakfast and I thought perhaps Frith would come into the dining-room and say "Mr. de Winter on the telephone, Madam." I had put down my napkin and had risen to my feet. And then Frith came back into the dining-room and gave me the message.

He saw me push back my chair and go to the door. "Mr. de Winter has rung off, Madam," he said, "there was no message. Just that he would be back about seven."

I sat down in my chair again and picked up my napkin. Frith must have thought me eager and stupid rushing across the dining-room.

"All right, Frith. Thank you," I said.

I went on eating my eggs and bacon, Jasper at my feet, the old dog in her basket in the corner. I wondered what I should do with my day. I had slept badly; perhaps because I was alone in the room. I had been restless, waking up often, and when I glanced at my clock I saw the hands had scarcely moved. When I did fall asleep I had varied, wandering dreams. We were walking through woods, Maxim and I, and he was always just a little ahead of me. I could not keep up with him. Nor could I see his face. Just his figure, striding away in front of me all the time. I must have cried while I slept, for when I woke in the morning the pillow was damp. My eyes were heavy too, when I looked in the glass. I looked plain, unattractive. I rubbed a little rouge on my cheeks in a wretched attempt to give myself colour. But it made me worse. It gave me a false clown look. Perhaps I did not know the best way to put it on. I noticed Robert staring at me as I crossed the hall and went in to breakfast.

About ten o'clock as I was crumbling some pieces for the birds on the terrace the telephone rang again. This time it was for me. Frith came and said Mrs. Lacy wanted to speak to me.

"Good morning, Beatrice," I said.

"Well, my dear, how are you?" she said, her telephone voice typical of herself, brisk, rather masculine, standing no nonsense, and then not waiting for my answer, "I thought of motoring over this afternoon and looking up Gran. I'm lunching with people about twenty miles from you. Shall I come and pick you up and we'll go together? It's time you met the old lady, you know."

"I'd like to very much, Beatrice," I said.

"Splendid. Very well, then, I'll come along for you about half-past three. Giles saw Maxim at the dinner. Poor food, he said, but excellent wine. All right, my dear, see you later."

The click of the receiver, and she was gone. I wandered back into the garden. I was glad she had rung up and suggested the plan of going over to see the grandmother. It made something to look forward to, and broke the monotony of the day. The hours had seemed so long until seven o'clock. I did not feel in my holiday mood to-day, and I had no wish to go off with Jasper to the Happy Valley and come to the cove and throw stones in the water. The sense of freedom had departed, and the childish desire to run across the lawns in sand-shoes. I went and sat down with a book and *The Times* and my knitting in the rose-garden, domestic as a matron, yawning in the warm sun while the bees hummed amongst the flowers.

I tried to concentrate on the bald newspaper columns, and later to lose myself in the racy plot of the novel in my hands. I did not want to think of yesterday afternoon and Mrs. Danvers. I tried to forget that she was in the house at this moment, perhaps looking down on me from one of the windows. And now and again, when I looked up from my book or glanced across the garden, I had the feeling I was not alone.

There were so many windows in Manderley, so many rooms that were never used by Maxim and myself that were empty now, dust-sheeted, silent, rooms that had been occupied in the old days when his father and his grandfather had been alive, when there had been much entertaining, many servants. It would be easy for Mrs. Danvers to open those doors softly, and close them again, and then steal quietly across the shrouded room and look down upon me from behind the drawn curtains.

I should not know. Even if I turned in my chair and looked up to
the windows I would not see her. I remembered a game I had played
as a child that my friends next-door had called "Grandmother's
Steps" and myself "Old Witch." You had to stand at the end of the
garden with your back turned to the rest, and one by one they crept
nearer to you, advancing in short furtive fashion. Every few minutes
you turned to look at them, and if you saw one of them moving the
offender had to retire to the back line, and begin again. But there was
always one a little bolder than the rest, who came up very close,
whose movement was impossible to detect, and as you waited there,
your back turned, counting the regulation Ten, you knew, with a fatal
terrifying certainty, that before long, before even the Ten was
counted, this bold player would pounce upon you from behind, un-
heralded, unseen, with a scream of triumph. I felt as tense and expectant as I did then. I was playing "Old Witch" with Mrs. Danvers.

Lunch was a welcome break to the long morning. The calm efficiency of Frith, and Robert's rather foolish face, helped me more than
my book and my newspaper had done. And at half-past three, punctual to the moment, I heard the sound of Beatrice's car round the
sweep of the drive and pull up at the steps before the house. I ran out
to meet her, ready dressed, my gloves in my hand. "Well, my dear,
here I am, what a splendid day, isn't it?" She slammed the door of the
car and came up the steps to meet me. She gave me a hard swift kiss,
brushing me somewhere near the ear.

"You don't look well," she said immediately, looking me up and
down, "much too thin in the face, and no colour. What's wrong with
you?"

"Nothing," I said humbly, knowing the fault of my face too well,
"I'm not a person who ever has much colour."

"Oh, bosh," she replied, "you looked quite different when I saw
you before."

"I expect the brown of Italy has worn off," I said, getting into the
car.

"H'mph," she said shortly, "you're as bad as Maxim. Can't stand
any criticism about your health. Slam the door hard or it doesn't
shut." We started off down the drive, swerving at the corner, going
rather too fast. "You're not by any chance starting an infant, are
you?" she said, turning her hawk-brown eyes upon me.

"No," I said awkwardly. "No, I don't think so."

"No morning sickness or anything like that?"

"No."

"Oh, well—of course it doesn't always follow. I never turned a hair when Roger was born. Felt as fit as a fiddle the whole nine months. I played golf the day before he arrived. There's nothing to be embarrassed about in the facts of nature, you know. If you have any suspicions you had better tell me."

"No, really, Beatrice," I said, "there's nothing to tell."

"I must say I do hope you will produce a son and heir before long. It would be so terribly good for Maxim. I hope you are doing nothing to prevent it."

"Of course not," I said. What an extraordinary conversation.

"Oh, don't be shocked," she said, "you must never mind what I say. After all, brides of to-day are up to everything. It's a damn nuisance if you want to hunt and you land yourself with an infant your first season. Quite enough to break a marriage up if you are both keen. Wouldn't matter in your case. Babies needn't interfere with sketching. How is the sketching, by-the-way?"

"I'm afraid I don't seem to do much," I said.

"Oh, really? Nice weather too, for sitting out of doors. You only need a camp-stool and a box of pencils, don't you? Tell me, were you interested in those books I sent you?"

"Yes, of course," I said. "It was a lovely present, Beatrice."

She looked pleased. "Glad you liked them," she said.

The car sped along. She kept her foot permanently on the accelerator, and took every corner at an acute angle. Two motorists we passed looked out of their windows outraged as she swept by, and one pedestrian in a lane waved his stick at her. I felt rather hot for her. She did not seem to notice though. I crouched lower in my seat.

"Roger goes up to Oxford next term," she said, "heaven knows what he'll do with himself. Awful waste of time I think, and so does Giles, but we couldn't think what else to do with him. Of course he's just like Giles and myself. Thinks of nothing but horses. What on earth does this car in front think it's doing? Why don't you put out your hand, my good man? Really, some of these people on the road to-day ought to be shot."

We swerved into a main road, narrowly avoiding the car ahead of us. "Had any people down to stay?" she asked.

"No, we've been very quiet," I said.

"Much better, too," she said, "awful bore, I always think, those big parties. You won't find it alarming if you come to stay with us. Very nice lot of people all around, and we all know one another frightfully well. We dine in one another's houses, and have our bridge, and don't bother with outsiders. You do play bridge, don't you?"

"I'm not very good, Beatrice."

"Oh, we shan't mind that. As long as you can play. I've no patience with people who won't learn. What on earth can one do with them between tea and dinner in the winter, and after dinner? One can't just sit and talk."

I wondered why. However, it was simpler not to say anything.

"It's quite amusing now Roger is a reasonable age," she went on, "because he brings his friends to stay, and we have really good fun. You ought to have been with us last Christmas. We had charades. My dear, it was the greatest fun. Giles was in his element. He adores dressing-up, you know, and after a glass or two of champagne he's the funniest thing you've ever seen. We often say he's missed his vocation and ought to have been on the stage." I thought of Giles, and his large moon face, his horn spectacles. I felt the sight of him being funny after champagne would embarrass me. "He and another man, a great friend of ours, Dickie Marsh, dressed up as women and sang a duet. What exactly it had to do with the word in the charade nobody knew, but it did not matter. We all roared."

I smiled politely. "Fancy, how funny," I said.

I saw them all rocking from side to side in Beatrice's drawing-room. All these friends who knew one another so well. Roger would look like Giles. Beatrice was laughing again at the memory. "Poor Giles," she said. "I shall never forget his face when Dick squirted the soda syphon down his back. We were all in fits."

I had an uneasy feeling we might be asked to spend the approaching Christmas with Beatrice. Perhaps I could have influenza.

"Of course our acting was never very ambitious," she said. "It was just a lot of fun amongst ourselves. At Manderley now, there is scope for a really fine show. I remember a pageant they had there, some years ago. People from London came down to do it. Of course that type of thing needs terrific organisation."

"Yes," I said.

She was silent for a while, and drove without speaking.

"How is Maxim?" she said, after a moment.

"Very well, thanks," I said.

"Quite cheerful and happy?"

"Oh, yes. Yes, rather."

A narrow village street engaged her attention. I wondered whether I should tell her about Mrs. Danvers. About the man Favell. I did not want her to make a blunder though, and perhaps tell Maxim.

"Beatrice," I said, deciding upon it, "have you ever heard of someone called Favell? Jack Favell?"

"Jack Favell," she repeated. "Yes, I do know the name. Wait a minute. Jack Favell. Of course. An awful bounder. I met him once, ages ago."

"He came to Manderley yesterday to see Mrs. Danvers," I said.

"Really? Oh, well, perhaps he would...."

"Why?" I said.

"I rather think he was Rebecca's cousin," she said.

I was very surprised. That man her relation? It was not my idea of the sort of cousin Rebecca would have. Jack Favell her cousin. "Oh," I said. "Oh, I hadn't realised that."

"He probably used to go to Manderley a lot," said Beatrice. "I don't know. I couldn't tell you. I was very seldom there." Her manner was abrupt. It gave me the impression she did not want to pursue the subject.

"I did not take to him much," I said.

"No," said Beatrice. "I don't blame you."

I waited, but she did not say any more. I thought it wiser not to tell her how Favell had asked me to keep the visit a secret. It might lead to some complication. Besides, we were just coming to our destination. A pair of white gates and a smooth gravel drive.

"Don't forget the old lady is nearly blind," said Beatrice, "and she's not very bright these days. I telephoned to the nurse that we were coming so everything will be all right."

The house was large, red-bricked, and gabled. Late Victorian I supposed. Not an attractive house. I could tell in a glance it was the sort of house that was aggressively well-kept by a big staff. And all for one old lady who was nearly blind.

A trim parlour-maid opened the door.

"Good afternoon, Norah, how are you?" said Beatrice.

"Very well, thank you, Madam. I hope you are keeping well?"

"Oh, yes, we are all flourishing. How has the old lady been, Norah?"

"Rather mixed, Madam. She has one good day, and then a bad. She's not too bad in herself, you know. She will be pleased to see you I'm sure." She glanced curiously at me.

"This is Mrs. Maxim," said Beatrice.

"Yes, Madam. How do you do," said Norah.

We went through a narrow hall and a drawing-room crowded with furniture to a verandah facing a square clipped lawn. There were many bright geraniums in stone vases on the steps of the verandah. In the corner was a bath chair. Beatrice's grandmother was sitting there, propped up with pillows and surrounded by shawls. When we came close to her I saw that she had a strong, rather uncanny, resemblance to Maxim. That was what Maxim would look like, if he was very old, if he was blind. The nurse by her side got up from her chair and put a mark in the book she was reading aloud. She smiled at Beatrice.

"How are you, Mrs. Lacy?" she said.

Beatrice shook hands with her and introduced me. "The old lady looks all right," she said. "I don't know how she does it, at eighty-six. Here we are, Gran," she said, raising her voice, "arrived safe and sound."

The grandmother looked in our direction. "Dear Bee," she said, "how sweet of you to come and visit me. We're so dull here, nothing for you to do."

Beatrice leant over her and kissed her. "I've brought Maxim's wife over to see you," she said, "she wanted to come and see you before, but she and Maxim have been so busy."

Beatrice prodded me in the back. "Kiss her," she murmured. I too bent down and kissed her on the cheek.

The grandmother touched my face with her fingers. "You nice thing," she said, "so good of you to come. I'm very pleased to see you, dear. You ought to have brought Maxim with you."

"Maxim is in London," I said, "he's coming back to-night."

"You must bring him next time," she said. "Sit down, dear, in this chair, where I can see you. And Bee, come the other side. How is dear Roger? He's a naughty boy, he doesn't come and see me."

"He shall come during August," shouted Beatrice; "he's leaving Eton, you know, he's going up to Oxford."

"Oh, dear, he'll be quite a young man, I shan't know him."

"He's taller than Giles now," said Beatrice.

She went on, telling her about Giles, and Roger, and the horses, and the dogs. The nurse brought out some knitting, and clicked her needles sharply. She turned to me, very bright, very cheerful.

"How are you liking Manderley, Mrs. de Winter?"

"Very much, thank you," I said.

"It's a beautiful spot, isn't it?" she said, the needles jabbing one another. "Of course we don't get over there now, she's not up to it. I am so sorry, I used to love our days at Manderley."

"You must come over yourself sometime," I said.

"Thank you, I should love to. Mr. de Winter is well I suppose?"

"Yes, very well."

"You spent your honeymoon in Italy, didn't you? We were so pleased with the picture post-card Mr. de Winter sent."

I wondered whether she used "we" in the royal sense, or if she meant that Maxim's grandmother and herself were one.

"Did he send one? I don't remember."

"Oh, yes, it was quite an excitement. We love anything like that. We keep a scrapbook you know, and paste anything to do with the family inside it. Anything pleasant, that is."

"How nice," I said.

I caught snatches of Beatrice's conversation on the other side. "We had to put old Marksman down," she was saying. "You remember old Marksman? The best hunter I ever had."

"Oh, dear, not old Marksman?" said her grandmother.

"Yes, poor old man. Got blind in both eyes, you know."

"Poor Marksman," echoed the old lady.

I thought perhaps it was not very tactful to talk about blindness, and I glanced at the nurse. She was still busy clicking her needles.

"Do you hunt, Mrs. de Winter?" she said.

"No, I'm afraid I don't," I said.

"Perhaps you will come to it. We are all very fond of hunting in this part of the world."

"Yes."

"Mrs. de Winter is very keen on art," said Beatrice to the nurse. "I tell her there are heaps of spots in Manderley that would make very jolly pictures."

"Oh, rather," agreed the nurse, pausing a moment from the fury of knitting. "What a nice hobby. I had a friend who was a wonder with her pencil. We went to Provence together one Easter and she did such pretty sketches."

"How nice," I said.

"We're talking about sketching," shouted Beatrice to her grandmother, "you did not know we had an artist in the family, did you?"

"Who's an artist?" said the old lady. "I don't know any."

"Your new grand-daughter," said Beatrice; "you ask her what I gave her for a wedding present."

I smiled, waiting to be asked. The old lady turned her head in my direction. "What's Bee talking about?" she said. "I did not know you were an artist. We've never had any artists in the family."

"Beatrice was joking," I said; "of course I'm not an artist really. I like drawing as a hobby. I've never had any lessons. Beatrice gave me some lovely books as a present."

"Oh," she said, rather bewildered. "Beatrice gave you some books, did she? Rather like taking coals to Newcastle, wasn't it? There are so many books in the library at Manderley." She laughed heartily. We all joined in her joke. I hoped the subject would be left at that, but Beatrice had to harp on it. "You don't understand, Gran," she said. "They weren't ordinary books. They were volumes on art. Six of 'em."

The nurse leant forward to add her tribute. "Mrs. Lacy is trying to explain that Mrs. de Winter is very fond of sketching as a hobby. So she gave her six fine volumes all about painting as a wedding present."

"What a funny thing to do," said the grandmother. "I don't think much of books for a wedding present. Nobody ever gave me any books when I was married. I should never have read them if they had."

She laughed again. Beatrice looked rather offended. I smiled at her to show my sympathy. I don't think she saw. The nurse resumed her knitting.

"I want my tea," said the old lady querulously, "isn't it half-past four yet? Why doesn't Norah bring the tea?"

"What? Hungry again after our big lunch?" said the nurse, rising to her feet and smiling brightly at her charge.

I felt rather exhausted, and wondered, rather shocked at my callous thought, why old people were sometimes such a strain. Worse than young children or puppies because one had to be polite. I sat with my hands in my lap ready to agree with what anybody said. The nurse was thumping the pillows and arranging the shawls.

Maxim's grandmother suffered her in patience. She closed her eyes as though she too were tired. She looked more like Maxim than ever. I knew how she must have looked when she was young, tall and handsome, going round to the stables at Manderley with sugar in her pockets, holding her trailing skirt out of the mud. I pictured the nipped-in waist, the high collar, I heard her ordering the carriage for two o'clock. That was all finished now for her, all gone. Her husband had been dead for forty years, her son for fifteen. She had to live here in this bright, red-gabled house with the nurse until it was time for her to die. I thought how little we know about the feelings of old people. Children we understand, their fears and hopes and make-believe. I was a child yesterday. I had not forgotten. But Maxim's grandmother, sitting there in her shawl with her poor blind eyes, what did she feel, what was she thinking? Did she know that Beatrice was yawning and glancing at her watch? Did she guess that we had come to visit her because we felt it right, it was a duty, so that when she got home afterwards Beatrice would be able to say, "Well, that clears my conscience for three months?"

Did she ever think about Manderley? Did she remember sitting at the dining-room table, where I sat? Did she too have tea under the chestnut tree? Or was it all forgotten and laid aside, and was there nothing left behind that calm, pale face of hers but little aches and little strange discomforts, a blurred thankfulness when the sun shone, a tremor when the wind blew cold?

I wished that I could lay my hands upon her face and take the years away. I wished I could see her young, as she was once, with colour in her cheeks and chestnut hair, alert and active as Beatrice by her side, talking as she did about hunting, hounds, and horses. Not sitting there with her eyes closed while the nurse thumped the pillows behind her head.

"We've got a treat to-day, you know," said the nurse, "water-cress sandwiches for tea. We love water-cress, don't we?"

"Is it water-cress day?" said Maxim's grandmother, raising her head from the pillows, and looking towards the door. "You did not tell me that. Why does not Norah bring in the tea?"

"I wouldn't have your job, Sister, for a thousand a day," said Beatrice *sotto voce* to the nurse.

"Oh, I'm used to it, Mrs. Lacy," smiled the nurse; "it's very comfortable here, you know. Of course we have our bad days but they might be a great deal worse. She's very easy, not like some patients. The staff are obliging too, that's really the main thing. Here comes Norah."

The parlour-maid brought out a little gate-legged table and a snowy cloth.

"What a time you've been, Norah," grumbled the old lady.

"It's only just turned the half-hour, Madam," said Norah in a special voice, bright and cheerful like the nurse. I wondered if Maxim's grandmother realised that people spoke to her in this way. I wondered when they had done so for the first time, and if she had noticed then. Perhaps she had said to herself, "They think I'm getting old, how very ridiculous," and then little by little she had become accustomed to it, and now it was as though they had always done so, it was part of her background. But the young woman with the chestnut hair and the narrow waist who gave sugar to the horses, where was she?

We drew our chairs to the gate-legged table and began to eat the water-cress sandwiches. The nurse prepared special ones for the old lady.

"There, now, isn't that a treat?" she said.

I saw a slow smile pass over the calm, placid face. "I like water-cress day," she said.

The tea was scalding, much too hot to drink. The nurse drank hers in tiny sips.

"Boiling water to-day," she said, nodding at Beatrice. "I have such trouble about it. They will let the tea stew. I've told them time and time again about it. They will not listen."

"Oh, they're all the same," said Beatrice. "I've given it up as a bad job." The old lady stirred hers with a spoon, her eyes very far and distant. I wished I knew what she was thinking about.

"Did you have fine weather in Italy?" said the nurse.

"Yes, it was very warm," I said.

Beatrice turned to her grandmother. "They had lovely weather in Italy for their honeymoon, she says. Maxim got quite sunburnt."

"Why isn't Maxim here to-day?" said the old lady.

"We told you, darling, Maxim had to go to London," said Beatrice impatiently. "Some dinner you know. Giles went too."

"Oh, I see. Why did you say Maxim was in Italy?"

"He was in Italy, Gran. In April. They're back at Manderley now." She glanced at the nurse, shrugging her shoulders.

"Mr. and Mrs. de Winter are in Manderley now," repeated the nurse.

"It's been lovely there this month," I said, drawing nearer to Maxim's grandmother. "The roses are in bloom now. I wish I had brought you some."

"Yes, I like roses," she said vaguely, and then peering closer at me with her dim blue eyes, "Are you staying at Manderley too?"

I swallowed. There was a slight pause. Then Beatrice broke in with her loud, impatient voice, "Gran, darling, you know perfectly well she lives there now. She and Maxim are married."

I noticed the nurse put down her cup of tea and glance swiftly at the old lady. She had relaxed against the pillows, plucking at her shawl, and her mouth began to tremble. "You talk too much, all of you. I don't understand." Then she looked across at me, a frown on her face, and began shaking her head. "Who are you, my dear, I haven't seen you before? I don't know your face. I don't remember you at Manderley. Bee, who is this child? Why did not Maxim bring Rebecca? I'm so fond of Rebecca. Where is dear Rebecca?"

There was a long pause, a moment of agony. I felt my cheeks grow scarlet. The nurse got to her feet very quickly and went to the bath chair.

"I want Rebecca," repeated the old lady, "what have you done with Rebecca?" Beatrice rose clumsily from the table, shaking the cups and saucers. She too had turned very red, and her mouth twitched.

"I think you had better go, Mrs. Lacy," said the nurse, rather pink and flustered. "She's looking a little tired, and when she wanders like this it sometimes lasts a few hours. She does get excited like this from time to time. It's very unfortunate it should happen to-day. I'm sure you will understand, Mrs. de Winter?" She turned apologetically to me.

"Of course," I said quickly, "it's much better we should go."

Beatrice and I groped for our bags and gloves. The nurse had turned to her patient again. "Now, what's all this about? Don't you want your nice water-cress sandwich that I've cut for you?"

"Where is Rebecca? Why did not Maxim come and bring Rebecca?" replied the thin, tired, querulous voice.

We went through the drawing-room to the hall and let ourselves out of the front door. Beatrice started up the car without a word. We drove down the smooth gravel drive and out of the white gates.

I stared straight in front of me down the road. I did not mind for myself. I should not have cared if I had been alone. I minded for Beatrice.

The whole thing had been so wretched and awkward for Beatrice.

She spoke to me when we turned out of the village. "My dear," she began. "I'm so dreadfully sorry. I don't know what to say."

"Don't be absurd, Beatrice," I said hurriedly, "it doesn't matter a bit. It's absolutely all right."

"I had no idea she would do that," said Beatrice. "I would never have dreamt of taking you to see her. I'm so frightfully sorry."

"There's nothing to be sorry about. Please don't say any more."

"I can't make it out. She knew all about you. I wrote and told her, and so did Maxim. She was so interested in the wedding abroad."

"You forget how old she is," I said. "Why should she remember that? She doesn't connect me with Maxim. She only connects him with Rebecca." We went on driving in silence. It was a relief to be in the car again. I did not mind the jerky motion and the swaying corners.

"I'd forgotten she was so fond of Rebecca," said Beatrice slowly, "I was a fool not to expect something like this. I don't believe she ever took it in properly about the accident. Oh, Lord, what a ghastly afternoon. What on earth will you think of me?"

"Please, Beatrice, don't. I tell you I don't mind."

"Rebecca made a great fuss of her always. And she used to have the old lady over to Manderley. Poor darling Gran was much more alert then. She used to rock with laughter at whatever Rebecca said. Of course she was always very amusing, and the old lady loved that. She had an amazing gift, Rebecca I mean, of being attractive to people; men, women, children, dogs. I suppose the old lady has never forgotten her. My dear, you won't thank me for this afternoon."

"I don't mind, I don't mind," I repeated mechanically. If only Beatrice could leave the subject alone. It did not interest me. What did it matter after all? What did anything matter?

"Giles will be very upset," said Beatrice. "He will blame me for taking you over. 'What an idiotic thing to do, Bee.' I can hear him saying it. I shall get into a fine row."

"Don't say anything about it," I said. "I would much rather it was forgotten. The story will only get repeated and exaggerated."

"Giles will know something is wrong from my face. I never have been able to hide anything from him."

I was silent. I knew how the story would be tossed about in their immediate circle of friends. I could imagine the little crowd at Sunday lunch. The round eyes, the eager ears, and the gasps and exclamations—

"My Lord, how awful, what on earth did you do?" and then, "How did she take it? How terribly embarrassing for everyone!"

The only thing that mattered to me was that Maxim should never come to hear of it. One day I might tell Frank Crawley, but not yet, not for quite a while.

It was not long before we came to the high-road at the top of the hill. In the distance I could see the first grey roofs of Kerrith, while to the right, in a hollow, lay the deep woods of Manderley and the sea beyond.

"Are you in a frightful hurry to get home?" said Beatrice.

"No," I said. "I don't think so. Why?"

"Would you think me a perfect pig if I dropped you at the lodge gates? If I drive like hell now I shall just be in time to meet Giles by the London train, and it will save him taking the station taxi."

"Of course," I said. "I can walk down the drive."

"Thanks awfully," she said gratefully.

I felt the afternoon had been too much for her. She wanted to be alone again, and did not want to face another belated tea at Manderley.

I got out of the car at the lodge gates and we kissed good-bye.

"Put on some weight next time I see you," she said, "it doesn't suit you to be so thin. Give Maxim my love, and forgive me for today." She vanished in a cloud of dust and I turned in down the drive.

I wondered if it had altered much since Maxim's grandmother had driven down it in her carriage. She had ridden here as a young woman, she had smiled at the woman at the lodge as I did now. And in her day the lodge-keeper's wife had curtseyed, sweeping the path with her full wide skirt. This woman nodded to me briefly, and then called to her little boy who was grubbing with some kittens at the back. Maxim's grandmother had bowed her head to avoid the sweeping branches of the trees, and the horse had trotted down the twisting drive where I now walked. The drive had been wider then, and smoother too, better kept. The woods did not encroach upon it.

I did not think of her as she was now, lying against those pillows, with that shawl around her. I saw her when she was young, and when Manderley was her home. I saw her wandering in the gardens with a small boy, Maxim's father, clattering behind her on his hobby horse. He would wear a stiff Norfolk jacket and a round white collar. Picnics to the cove would be an expedition, a treat that was not indulged in very often. There would be a photograph somewhere, in an old album—all the family sitting very straight and rigid around a table-cloth set upon the beach, the servants in the background beside a huge lunch-basket. And I saw Maxim's grandmother when she was older too, a few years ago. Walking on the terrace at Manderley, leaning on a stick. And someone walked beside her, laughing, holding her arm. Someone tall and slim and very beautiful, who had a gift, Beatrice said, of being attractive to people. Easy to like, I supposed, easy to love.

When I came to the end of the long drive at last I saw that Maxim's car was standing in front of the house. My heart lifted, I ran quickly into the hall. His hat and gloves were lying on the table. I went towards the library, and as I came near I heard the sound of voices, one raised louder than the other, Maxim's voice. The door was shut. I hesitated a moment before going in.

"You can write and tell him from me to keep away from Manderley in future, do you hear? Never mind who told me, that's of no importance. I happen to know his car was seen here yesterday afternoon. If you want to meet him you can meet him outside Manderley. I won't have him inside the gates, do you understand? Remember, I'm warning you for the last time."

I slipped away from the door to the stairs. I heard the door of the library open. I ran swiftly up the stairs and hid in the gallery. Mrs. Danvers came out of the library, shutting the door behind her. I crouched against the wall of the gallery so that I should not be seen. I had caught one glimpse of her face. It was grey with anger, distorted, horrible.

She passed up the stairs swiftly and silently and disappeared through the door leading to the west wing.

I waited a moment. Then I went slowly downstairs to the library. I opened the door and went in. Maxim was standing by the window, some letters in his hand. His back was turned to me. For a moment I thought of creeping out again, and going upstairs to my room and sitting there. He must have heard me though, for he swung round impatiently.

"Who is it now?" he said.

I smiled, holding out my hands. "Hullo!" I said.

"Oh, it's you. . . ."

I could tell in a glance that something had made him very angry. His mouth was hard, his nostrils white and pinched. "What have you been doing with yourself?" he said. He kissed the top of my head and put his arm round my shoulder. I felt as if a very long time had passed since he had left me yesterday.

"I've been to see your grandmother," I said. "Beatrice drove me over this afternoon."

"How was the old lady?"

"All right."

"What's happened to Bee?"

"She had to get back to meet Giles."

We sat down together on the window seat. I took his hand in mine. "I hated you being away, I've missed you terribly," I said.

"Have you?" he said.

We did not say anything for a bit. I just held his hand.

"Was it hot up in London?" I said.

"Yes, pretty awful. I always hate the place."

I wondered if he would tell me what had happened just now in the library with Mrs. Danvers. I wondered who had told him about Favell.

"Are you worried about something?" I said.

"I've had a long day," he said, "that drive twice in twenty-four hours is too much for anyone."

He got up and wandered away, lighting a cigarette. I knew then that he was not going to tell me about Mrs. Danvers.

"I'm tired too," I said slowly, "it's been a funny sort of day."

CHAPTER SIXTEEN

It was one Sunday, I remember, when we had an invasion of visitors during the afternoon, that the subject of the fancy dress ball was first brought up. Frank Crawley had come over to lunch, and we were all three of us looking forward to a peaceful afternoon under the chestnut tree when we heard the fatal sound of a car rounding the sweep in the drive. It was too late to warn Frith, the car itself came upon us standing on the terrace with cushions and papers under our arms.

We had to come forward and welcome the unexpected guests. As it often happens in such cases, these were not to be the only visitors. Another car arrived about half-an-hour afterwards, followed by three local people who had walked from Kerrith, and we found ourselves, with the peace stripped from our day, entertaining group after group of dreary acquaintances, doing the regulation walk in the grounds, the tour of the rose-garden, the stroll across the lawns, and the formal inspection of the Happy Valley.

They stayed for tea of course, and instead of a lazy nibbling of cucumber sandwiches under the chestnut tree, we had the paraphernalia of a stiff tea in the drawing-room, which I always loathed. Frith in his element of course, directing Robert with a lift of his eyebrows, and myself rather hot and flustered with a monstrous silver tea-pot and kettle that I never knew how to manage. I found it very difficult to gauge the exact moment when it became imperative to dilute the tea with the boiling water, and more difficult still to concentrate on the small talk that was going on at my side.

Frank Crawley was invaluable at a moment like this. He took the cups from me and handed them to people, and when my answers seemed more than usually vague owing to my concentration on the silver tea-pot he quietly and unobtrusively put in his small wedge to the conversation, relieving me of responsibility. Maxim was always at the other end of the room, showing a book to a bore, or pointing out a picture, playing the perfect host in his own inimitable way, and the business of tea was a side-issue that did not matter to him. His own cup of tea grew cold, left on a side table behind some flowers, and I, steaming behind my kettle, and Frank, gallantly juggling with scones and angel cake, were left to minister to the common wants of the herd. It was Lady Crowan, a tiresome gushing woman who lived in Kerrith, who introduced the matter. There was one of those pauses in conversation that happen in every tea-party, and I saw Frank's lips about to form the inevitable and idiotic remark about an angel passing overhead, when Lady Crowan, balancing a piece of cake on the edge of her saucer, looked up at Maxim who happened to be beside her.

"Oh, Mr. de Winter," she said, "there is something I've been wanting to ask you for ages. Now tell me, is there any chance of you reviving the Manderley fancy dress ball?" She put her head on one side as she spoke, flashing her too prominent teeth in what she supposed was a smile. I lowered my head instantly, and became very busy with the emptying of my own tea-cup, screening myself behind the cosy.

It was a moment or two before Maxim replied, and when he did his voice was quite calm and matter-of-fact. "I haven't thought about it," he said, "and I don't think anyone else has."

"Oh, but I assure you we have all thought of it so much," continued Lady Crowan. "It used to make the summer for all of us in this part of the world. You have no idea of the pleasure it used to give. Can't I persuade you to think about it again?"

"Well, I don't know," said Maxim drily. "It was all rather a business to organise. You had better ask Frank Crawley, he'd have to do it."

"Oh, Mr. Crawley, do be on my side," she persisted, and one or two of the others joined in. "It would be a most popular move, you know, we all miss the Manderley gaiety."

I heard Frank's quiet voice beside me. "I don't mind organising the ball if Maxim has no objection to giving it. It's up to him and Mrs. de Winter. It's nothing to do with me."

Of course I was bombarded at once. Lady Crowan moved her chair so that the cosy no longer hid me from view. "Now, Mrs. de Winter, you get round your husband. You are the person he will listen to. He should give the ball in your honour as the bride."

"Yes, of course," said somebody else, a man. "We missed the fun of the wedding you know, it's a shame to deprive us of all excitement. Hands up for the Manderley fancy dress ball. There you see, de Winter? Carried unanimously." There was much laughter and clapping of hands.

Maxim lit a cigarette and his eyes met mine over the tea-pot.

"What do you think about it?" he said.

"I don't know," I said uncertainly. "I don't mind."

"Of course she longs to have a ball in her honour," gushed Lady Crowan. "What girl wouldn't? You'd look sweet, Mrs. de Winter, dressed as a little Dresden shepherdess, your hair tucked under a big three-cornered hat."

I thought of my clumsy hands and feet and the slope of my shoulders. A fine Dresden shepherdess I should make! What an idiot the woman was. I was not surprised when nobody agreed with her, and once more I was grateful to Frank for turning the conversation away from me.

"As a matter of fact, Maxim, someone was talking about it the other day. 'I suppose we shall be having some sort of celebration for the bride, shan't we, Mr. Crawley?' he said. 'I wish Mr. de Winter would give a ball again. It was rare fun for all of us.' It was Tucker, at the Home farm," he added, to Lady Crowan. "Of course they do adore a show of any kind. 'I don't know,' I told him. 'Mr. de Winter hasn't said anything to me.' "

"There you are," said Lady Crowan triumphantly to the drawing-room in general. "What did I say? Your own people are asking for a ball. If you don't care for us surely you care about them."

Maxim still watched me doubtfully over the tea-pot. It occurred to me that perhaps he thought I could not face it, that being shy, as he knew only too well, I should find myself unable to cope. I did not want him to think that. I did not want him to feel I should let him down.

"I think it would be rather fun," I said.

Maxim turned away, shrugging his shoulders. "That settles it of course," he said. "All right, Frank, you will have to go ahead with the arrangements. Better get Mrs. Danvers to help you. She will remember the form."

"That amazing Mrs. Danvers is still with you then?" said Lady Crowan.

"Yes," said Maxim shortly, "have some more cake, will you? Or have you finished? Then let's all go into the garden."

We wandered out on to the terrace, everyone discussing the prospect of the ball and suitable dates, and then, greatly to my relief, the car parties decided it was time to take their departure, and the walkers went too, on being offered a lift. I went back into the drawing-room and had another cup of tea which I thoroughly enjoyed now that the burden of entertaining had been taken from me, and Frank came too, and we crumbled up the remains of the scones and ate them, feeling like conspirators.

Maxim was throwing sticks for Jasper on the lawn. I wondered if it was the same in every home, this feeling of exuberance when visitors had gone. We did not say anything about the ball for a little while, and then, when I had finished my cup of tea and wiped my sticky fingers on a handkerchief, I said to Frank, "What do you truthfully think about this fancy dress business?"

Frank hesitated, half glancing out of the window at Maxim on the lawn. "I don't know," he said. "Maxim did not seem to object, did he? I thought he took the suggestion very well."

"It was difficult for him to do anything else," I said. "What a tiresome person Lady Crowan is. Do you really believe all the people round here are talking and dreaming of nothing but a fancy dress ball at Manderley?"

"I think they would all enjoy a show of some sort," said Frank. "We're very conventional down here, you know, about these things. I don't honestly think Lady Crowan was exaggerating when she said something should be done in your honour. After all, Mrs. de Winter, you are a bride."

How pompous and stupid it sounded. I wished Frank would not always be so terribly correct.

"I'm not a bride," I said. "I did not even have a proper wedding. No white dress or orange blossom or trailing bridesmaids. I don't want any silly dance given in my honour."

"It's a very fine sight, Manderley *en fête,*" said Frank. "You'll enjoy it, you see. You won't have to do anything alarming. You just receive the guests and there's nothing in that. Perhaps you'll give me a dance?"

Dear Frank. I loved his little solemn air of gallantry.

"You shall have as many dances as you like," I said. "I shan't dance with anyone except you and Maxim."

"Oh, but that would not look right at all," said Frank seriously. "People would be very offended. You must dance with the people who ask you."

I turned away to hide my smile. It was a joy to me the way he never knew when his leg had been pulled.

"Do you think Lady Crowan's suggestion about the Dresden shepherdess was a good one?" I said slyly.

He considered me solemnly without the trace of a smile. "Yes, I do," he said. "I think you'd look very well indeed."

I burst into laughter. "Oh, Frank, dear, I do love you," I said, and he turned rather pink, a little shocked I think at my impulsive words, and a little hurt too that I was laughing at him.

"I don't see that I've said anything funny," he said stiffly.

Maxim came in at the window, Jasper dancing at his heels. "What's all the excitement about?" he said.

"Frank is being so gallant," I said. "He thinks Lady Crowan's idea of my dressing up as a Dresden shepherdess is nothing to laugh at."

"Lady Crowan is a damned nuisance," said Maxim. "If she had to write out all the invitations and organise the affair she would not be so enthusiastic. It's always been the same though. The locals look upon Manderley as if it was a pavilion on the end of a pier, and expect us to put up a turn for their benefit. I suppose we shall have to ask the whole county."

"I've got the records in the office," said Frank. "It won't really entail much work. Licking the stamps is the longest job."

"We'll give that to you to do," said Maxim, smiling at me.

"Oh, we'll do that in the office," said Frank. "Mrs. de Winter need not bother her head about anything at all."

I wondered what they would say if I suddenly announced my intention of running the whole affair. Laugh, I supposed, and then begin talking of something else. I was glad, of course, to be relieved of responsibility, but it rather added to my sense of humility to feel that I was not even capable of licking stamps. I thought of the writing-desk in the morning-room, the docketed pigeon-holes all marked in ink by that slanting pointed hand.

"What will you wear?" I said to Maxim.

"I never dress up," said Maxim. "It's the one perquisite allowed to the host, isn't it, Frank?"

"I can't really go as a Dresden shepherdess," I said, "what on earth shall I do? I'm not much good at dressing-up."

"Put a ribbon round your hair and be Alice-in-Wonderland," said Maxim lightly; "you look like it now, with your finger in your mouth."

"Don't be so rude," I said. "I know my hair is straight, but it isn't as straight as that. I tell you what. I'll give you and Frank the surprise of your lives, and you won't know me."

"As long as you don't black your face and pretend to be a monkey I don't mind what you do," said Maxim.

"All right, that's a bargain," I said. "I'll keep my costume a secret to the last minute, and you won't know anything about it. Come on, Jasper, we don't care what they say, do we?" I heard Maxim laughing as I went out into the garden, and he said something to Frank which I did not catch.

I wished he would not always treat me as a child, rather spoilt, rather irresponsible, someone to be petted from time to time when the mood came upon him, but more often forgotten, more often patted on the shoulder and told to run away and play. I wished something would happen to make me look wiser, more mature. Was it always going to be like this? He away ahead of me, with his own moods that I did not share, his secret troubles that I did not know? Would we never be together, he a man and I a woman, standing shoulder to shoulder, hand in hand, with no gulf between us? I did not want to be a child. I wanted to be his wife, his mother. I wanted to be old.

I stood on the terrace, biting my nails, looking down towards the sea, and as I stood there I wondered for the twentieth time that day whether it was by Maxim's orders that those rooms in the west wing were kept furnished and untouched. I wondered if he went, as Mrs. Danvers did, and touched the brushes on the dressing-table, opened the wardrobe doors and put his hands amongst the clothes.

"Come on, Jasper," I shouted, "run, run with me, come on, can't you?" and I tore across the grass, savagely, angrily, the bitter tears behind my eyes, with Jasper leaping at my heels and barking hysterically.

The news soon spread about the fancy dress ball. My little maid Clarice, her eyes shining with excitement, talked of nothing else. I gathered from her that the servants in general were delighted. "Mr. Frith says it will be like old times," said Clarice eagerly. "I heard him saying so to Alice in the passage this morning. What will you wear, Madam?"

"I don't know, Clarice, I can't think," I said.

"Mother said I was to be sure and tell her," said Clarice. "She remembers the last ball they gave at Manderley, and she has never forgotten it. Will you be hiring a costume from London, do you think?"

"I haven't made up my mind, Clarice," I said. "But I tell you what. When I do decide, I shall tell you and nobody else. It will be a dead secret between us both."

"Oh, Madam, how exciting," breathed Clarice. "I don't know how I am going to wait for the day."

I was curious to know Mrs. Danvers' reaction to the news. Since that afternoon I dreaded even the sound of her voice down the house telephone, and by using Robert as mediator between us I was spared this last ordeal. I could not forget the expression on her face when she left the library after that interview with Maxim. I thanked God she had not seen me crouching in the gallery. And I wondered, too, if she thought that it was I who told Maxim about Favell's visit to the house. If so, she would hate me more than ever. I shuddered now when I remembered the touch of her hand on my arm, and that dreadful soft, intimate pitch of her voice close to my ear. I did not want to remember anything about that afternoon. That was why I did not speak to her, not even on the house telephone.

The preparations went on for the ball. Everything seemed to be done down at the estate office. Maxim and Frank were down there every morning. As Frank had said, I did not have to bother my head about anything. I don't think I licked one stamp. I began to get in a panic about my costume. It seemed so feeble not to be able to think of anything, and I kept remembering all the people who would come, from Kerrith and round about, the bishop's wife who had enjoyed herself so much the last time, Beatrice and Giles, that tiresome Lady Crowan, and many more people I did not know and who had never seen me, they would every one of them have some criticism to offer, some curiosity to know what sort of effort I should make. At last, in desperation, I remembered the books that Beatrice had given me for a wedding present, and I sat down in the library one morning turning over the pages as a last hope, passing from illustration to illustration in a sort of frenzy. Nothing seemed suitable, they were all so elaborate and pretentious, those gorgeous costumes of velvet and silk in the reproductions given of Rubens, Rembrandt and others. I got hold of a piece of paper and a pencil and copied one or two of them, but they did not please me, and I threw the sketches into the waste-paper basket in disgust, thinking no more about them.

In the evening, when I was changing for dinner, there was a knock at my bedroom door. I called "Come in," thinking it was Clarice. The door opened and it was not Clarice. It was Mrs. Danvers. She held a piece of paper in her hand. "I hope you will forgive me disturbing you," she said, "but I was not sure whether you meant to throw these drawings away. All the waste-paper baskets are always brought to me to check, at the end of the day, in case of mislaying anything of value. Robert told me this was thrown into the library basket."

I had turned quite cold all over at the sight of her, and at first I could not find my voice. She held out the paper for me to see. It was the rough drawing I had done during the morning.

"No, Mrs. Danvers," I said, after a moment, "it doesn't matter throwing that away. It was only a rough sketch. I don't want it."

"Very good," she said, "I thought it better to enquire from you personally to save any misunderstanding."

"Yes," I said. "Yes, of course." I thought she would turn and go, but she went on standing there by the door.

"So you have not decided yet what you will wear?" she said. There was a hint of derision in her voice, a trace of odd satisfaction. I supposed she had heard of my efforts through Clarice in some way.

"No," I said. "No, I haven't decided."

She continued watching me, her hand on the handle of the door.

"I wonder you don't copy one of the pictures in the gallery," she said.

I pretended to file my nails. They were too short and too brittle, but the action gave me something to do and I did not have to look at her.

"Yes, I might think about that," I said. I wondered privately why such an idea had never come to me before. It was an obvious and very good solution to my difficulty. I did not want her to know this though. I went on filing my nails.

"All the pictures in the gallery would make good costumes," said Mrs. Danvers, "especially that one of the young lady in white, with her hat in her hand. I wonder Mr. de Winter does not make it a period ball, everyone dressed more or less the same, to be in keeping. I never think it looks right to see a clown dancing with a lady in powder and patches."

"Some people enjoy the variety," I said. "They think it makes it all the more amusing."

"I don't like it myself," said Mrs. Danvers. Her voice was surprisingly normal and friendly, and I wondered why it was she had taken the trouble to come up with my discarded sketch herself. Did she want to be friends with me at last? Or did she realise that it had not been me at all who had told Maxim about Favell, and this was her way of thanking me for my silence?

"Has not Mr. de Winter suggested a costume for you?" she said.

"No," I said, after a moment's hesitation. "No, I want to surprise him and Mr. Crawley. I don't want them to know anything about it."

"It's not for me to make a suggestion, I know," she said, "but when you do decide, I should advise you to have your dress made in

London. There is no one down here can do that sort of thing well. Voce, in Bond Street, is a good place I know."

"I must remember that," I said.

"Yes," she said, and then, as she opened the door, "I should study the pictures in the gallery, Madam, if I were you, especially the one I mentioned. And you need not think I will give you away. I won't say a word to anyone."

"Thank you, Mrs. Danvers," I said. She shut the door very gently behind her. I went on with my dressing, puzzled at her attitude, so different from our last encounter, and wondering whether I had the unpleasant Favell to thank for it.

Rebecca's cousin. Why should Maxim dislike Rebecca's cousin? Why had he forbidden him to come to Manderley? Beatrice had called him a bounder. She had not said much about him. And the more I considered him the more I agreed with her. Those hot blue eyes, that loose mouth, and the careless familiar laugh. Some people would consider him attractive. Girls in sweet shops giggling behind the counter, and girls who gave one programmes in a cinema. I knew how he would look at them, smiling, and half whistling a tune under his breath. The sort of look and the type of whistle that would make one feel uncomfortable. I wondered how well he knew Manderley. He seemed quite at home, and Jasper certainly recognised him, but these two facts did not fit in with Maxim's words to Mrs. Danvers. And I could not connect him with my idea of Rebecca. Rebecca, with her beauty, her charm, her breeding, why did she have a cousin like Jack Favell? It was wrong, out of all proportion. I decided he must be the skeleton in the family cupboard, and Rebecca, with her generosity, had taken pity on him from time to time and invited him to Manderley, perhaps when Maxim was from home, knowing his dislike. There had been some argument about it probably, Rebecca defending him, and ever after this perhaps a slight awkwardness whenever his name was mentioned.

As I sat down to dinner in the dining-room in my accustomed place, with Maxim at the head of the table, I pictured Rebecca sitting where I sat now, picking up her fork for the fish, and then the telephone ringing and Frith coming into the room and saying "Mr. Favell on the 'phone, Madam, wishing to speak to you," and Rebecca would get up from her chair with a quick glance at Maxim, who would not say anything, who would go on eating his fish. And when she came back, having finished her conversation, and sat down in her place again, Rebecca would begin talking about something different, in a gay, careless way, to cover up the little cloud between them. At first

Maxim would be glum, answering in monosyllables, but little by little she would win his humour back again, telling him some story of her day, about someone she had seen in Kerrith, and when they had finished the next course he would be laughing again, looking at her and smiling, putting out his hand to her across the table.

"What the devil are you thinking about?" said Maxim.

I started, the colour flooding my face, for in that brief moment, sixty seconds in time perhaps, I had so identified myself with Rebecca that my own dull self did not exist, had never come to Manderley. I had gone back in thought and in person to the days that were gone.

"Do you know you were going through the most extraordinary antics instead of eating your fish?" said Maxim, "first you listened, as though you heard the telephone, and then your lips moved, and you threw half a glance at me. And you shook your head, and smiled, and shrugged your shoulders. All in about a second. Are you practising your appearance for the fancy dress ball?" He looked across at me, laughing, and I wondered what he would say if he really knew my thoughts, my heart, and my mind, and that for one second he had been the Maxim of another year, and I had been Rebecca. "You look like a little criminal," he said, "what is it?"

"Nothing," I said quickly, "I wasn't doing anything."

"Tell me what you were thinking?"

"Why should I? You never tell me what you are thinking about."

"I don't think you've ever asked me, have you?"

"Yes, I did once."

"I don't remember."

"We were in the library."

"Very probably. What did I say?"

"You told me you were wondering who had been chosen to play for Surrey against Middlesex."

Maxim laughed again. "What a disappointment to you. What did you hope I was thinking?"

"Something very different."

"What sort of thing?"

"Oh, I don't know."

"No, I don't suppose you do. If I told you I was thinking about Surrey and Middlesex I was thinking about Surrey and Middlesex. Men are simpler than you imagine, my sweet child. But what goes on in the twisted tortuous minds of women would baffle anyone. Do you know, you did not look a bit like yourself just now? You had quite a different expression on your face."

"I did? What sort of expression?"

"I don't know that I can explain. You looked older suddenly, deceitful. It was rather unpleasant."

"I did not mean to."

"No, I don't suppose you did."

I drank some water, watching him over the rim of my glass.

"Don't you want me to look older?" I said.

"No."

"Why not?"

"Because it would not suit you."

"One day I shall. It can't be helped. I shall have grey hair, and lines and things."

"I don't mind that."

"What do you mind then?"

"I don't want you to look like you did just now. You had a twist to your mouth and a flash of knowledge in your eyes. Not the right sort of knowledge."

I felt very curious, rather excited. "What do you mean, Maxim? What isn't the right sort of knowledge?"

He did not answer for a moment. Frith had come back into the room and was changing the plates. Maxim waited until Frith had gone behind the screen and through the Service door before speaking again.

"When I met you first you had a certain expression on your face," he said slowly, "and you have it still. I'm not going to define it, I don't know how to. But it was one of the reasons why I married you. A moment ago, when you were going through that curious little performance, the expression had gone. Something else had taken its place."

"What sort of thing? Explain to me, Maxim," I said eagerly.

He considered me a moment, his eyebrows raised, whistling softly. "Listen, my sweet. When you were a little girl, were you ever forbidden to read certain books, and did your father put those books under lock and key?"

"Yes," I said.

"Well, then. A husband is not so very different from a father after all. There is a certain type of knowledge I prefer you not to have. It's better kept under lock and key. So that's that. And now eat up your peaches, and don't ask me any more questions, or I shall put you in the corner."

"I wish you would not treat me as if I was six," I said.

"How do you want to be treated?"

"Like other men treat their wives."

"Knock you about, do you mean?"

"Don't be absurd. Why must you make a joke of everything?"

"I'm not joking. I'm very serious."

"No, you're not. I can tell by your eyes. You're playing with me all the time, just as if I was a silly little girl."

"Alice-in-Wonderland. That was a good idea of mine. Have you bought your sash and your hair-ribbon yet?"

"I warn you. You'll get the surprise of your life when you do see me in my fancy dress."

"I'm sure I shall. Get on with your peach and don't talk with your mouth full. I've got a lot of letters to write after dinner." He did not wait for me to finish. He got up and strolled about the room, and asked Frith to bring the coffee in the library. I sat still, sullenly, being as slow as I could, hoping to keep things back and irritate him, but Frith took no notice of me and my peach, he brought the coffee at once and Maxim went off to the library by himself.

When I had finished I went upstairs to the minstrels' gallery to have a look at the pictures. I knew them well of course by now, but had never studied them with a view to reproducing one of them as a fancy dress. Mrs. Danvers was right of course. What an idiot I had been not to think of it before. I always loved the girl in white, with a hat in her hand. It was a Raeburn, and the portrait was of Caroline de Winter, a sister of Maxim's great-great-grandfather. She married a great Whig politician, and was a famous London beauty for many years, but this portrait was painted before that, when she was still unmarried. The white dress should be easy to copy. Those puffed sleeves, the flounce, and the little bodice. The hat might be rather difficult, and I should have to wear a wig. My straight hair would never curl in that way. Perhaps that Voce place in London that Mrs. Danvers had told me about would do the whole thing. I would send them a sketch of the portrait and tell them to copy it faithfully, sending my measurements.

What a relief it was to have decided at last! Quite a weight off my mind. I began almost to look forward to the ball. Perhaps I should enjoy it after all, almost as much as little Clarice.

I wrote to the shop in the morning, enclosing a sketch of the portrait, and I had a very favourable reply, full of honour at my esteemed order, and saying the work would be put in hand right away, and they would manage the wig as well.

Clarice could hardly contain herself for excitement, and I, too, began to get party fever as the great day approached. Giles and Beatrice were coming for the night, but nobody else, thank heaven, although a lot of people were expected to dinner first. I had imagined we should have to hold a large house-party for the occasion but Maxim decided against it. "Having the dance alone is quite enough effort," he said; and I wondered whether he did it for my sake alone, or whether a large crowd of people really bored him as he said. I had heard so much of the Manderley parties in the old days, with people sleeping in bathrooms and on sofas because of the squash. And here we were alone in the vast house, with only Beatrice and Giles to count as guests.

The house began to wear a new, expectant air. Men came to lay the floor for dancing in the great hall, and in the drawing-room some of the furniture was moved so that the long buffet tables could be placed against the wall. Lights were put up on the terrace, and in the rose-garden too, wherever one walked there would be some sign of preparation for the ball. Workmen from the estate were everywhere, and Frank came to lunch nearly every day. The servants talked of nothing else, and Frith stalked about as though the whole of the evening would depend on him alone. Robert rather lost his head, and kept forgetting things, napkins at lunch, and handing vegetables. He wore a harassed expression, like someone who has got to catch a train. The dogs were miserable. Jasper trailed about the hall with his tail between his legs, and nipped every workman on sight. He used to stand on the terrace, barking idiotically, and then dash madly to one corner of the lawn and eat grass in a sort of frenzy. Mrs. Danvers never obtruded herself, but I was aware of her continually. It was her voice I heard in the drawing-room when they came to put the tables, it was she who gave directions for the laying of the floor in the hall. Whenever I came upon the scene she had always just disappeared; I would catch a glimpse of her skirt brushing the door, or hear the sound of her footsteps on the stairs. I was a lay-figure, no use to man or beast. I used to stand about doing nothing except get in the way. "Excuse me, Madam," I would hear a man say, just behind me, and he would pass, with a smile of apology, carrying two chairs on his back, his face dripping with perspiration.

"I'm awfully sorry," I would say, getting quickly to one side, and then as a cover to my idleness, "Can I help you? What about putting those chairs in the library?" The man would look bewildered. "Mrs. Danvers' orders, Madam, was that we were to take the chairs round to the back, to be out of the way."

"Oh," I said, "yes, of course. How silly of me. Take them round to the back, as she said." And I would walk quickly away murmuring something about finding a piece of paper and pencil, in a vain attempt to delude the man into thinking I was busy, while he went on across the hall, looking rather astonished, and I would feel I had not deceived him for a moment.

The great day dawned misty and over-cast, but the glass was high and we had no fears. The mist was a good sign. It cleared about eleven, as Maxim had foretold, and we had a glorious still summer's day without a cloud in the blue sky. All the morning the gardeners were bringing flowers into the house, the last of the white lilac, and great lupins and delphiniums, five foot high, roses in hundreds, and every sort of lily.

Mrs. Danvers showed herself at last; quietly, calmly, she told the gardeners where to put the flowers, and she herself arranged them, stacking the vases with quick, deft fingers. I watched her in fascination, the way she did vase after vase, carrying them herself through the flower-room to the drawing-room and the various corners of the house, massing them in just the right numbers and profusion, putting colour where colour was needed, leaving the walls bare where severity paid.

Maxim and I had lunch with Frank at his bachelor establishment next-door to the office to be out of the way. We were all three in the rather hearty, cheerful humour of people before a funeral. We made pointless jokes about nothing at all, our minds eternally on the thought of the next few hours. I felt very much the same as I did the morning I was married. The same stifled feeling that I had gone too far now to turn back.

The evening had got to be endured. Thank heaven Messrs. Voce had sent my dress in time. It looked perfect, in its folds of tissue paper. And the wig was a triumph. I had tried it on after breakfast, and was amazed at the transformation. I looked quite attractive, quite different altogether. Not me at all. Someone much more interesting, more vivid and alive. Maxim and Frank kept asking me about my costume.

"You won't know me," I told them, "you will both get the shock of your lives."

"You are not going to dress up as a clown, are you?" said Maxim gloomily. "No frightful attempt to be funny?"

"No, nothing like that," I said, full of importance.

"I wish you had kept to Alice-in-Wonderland," he said.

"Or Joan of Arc with your hair," said Frank shyly.

"I never thought of that," I said blankly, and Frank went rather pink. "I'm sure we shall all like whatever you wear," he said in his most pompous Frank-ish voice.

"Don't encourage her, Frank," said Maxim. "She's so full of her precious disguise already there's no holding her. Bee will put you in your place, that's one comfort. She'll soon tell you if she doesn't like your dress. Dear old Bee always looks just wrong on these occasions, bless her. I remember her once as Madame Pompadour and she tripped up going in to supper and her wig came adrift. 'I can't stand this damned thing,' she said, in that blunt voice of hers, and chucked it on a chair and went through the rest of the evening with her own cropped hair. You can imagine what it looked like, against a pale blue satin crinoline, or whatever the dress was. Poor old Giles did not cope that year. He came as a cook, and sat about in the bar all night looking perfectly miserable. I think he felt Bee had let him down."

"No, it wasn't that," said Frank, "he'd lost his front teeth trying out a new mare, don't you remember, and he was so shy about it he wouldn't open his mouth."

"Oh, was that it? Poor Giles. He generally enjoys dressing-up."

"Beatrice says he loves playing charades," I said. "She told me they always have charades at Christmas."

"I know," said Maxim, "that's why I've never spent Christmas with her."

"Have some more asparagus, Mrs. de Winter, and another potato?"

"No, really, Frank, I'm not hungry, thank you."

"Nerves," said Maxim, shaking his head. "Never mind, this time to-morrow it will all be over."

"I sincerely hope so," said Frank seriously. "I was going to give orders that all cars should stand by for five a.m."

I began to laugh weakly, the tears coming into my eyes. "Oh, dear," I said, "let's send wires to everybody not to come."

"Come on, be brave and face it," said Maxim. "We need not give another one for years. Frank, I have an uneasy feeling we ought to be going up to the house. What do you think?"

Frank agreed, and I followed them unwillingly, reluctant to leave the cramped, rather uncomfortable little dining-room that was so typical of Frank's bachelor establishment, and which seemed to me to-day the embodiment of peace and quietude. When we came to the house we found that the band had arrived, and were standing about in the hall rather pink in the face and self-conscious, while Frith, more important than ever, offered refreshments. The band were to be our guests for the night, and after we had welcomed them and exchanged a few slightly obvious jokes proper to the occasion, the band were borne off to their quarters, to be followed by a tour of the grounds.

The afternoon dragged, like the last hour before a journey when one is packed up and keyed to departure, and I wandered from room to room almost as lost as Jasper, who trailed reproachfully at my heels.

There was nothing I could do to help, and it would have been wiser on my part to have kept clear of the house altogether and taken the dog and myself for a long walk. By the time I decided upon this it was too late, Maxim and Frank were demanding tea, and when tea was over Beatrice and Giles arrived. The evening had come upon us all too soon.

"This is like old times," said Beatrice, kissing Maxim, and looking about her. "Congratulations to you for remembering every detail. The flowers are exquisite," she added, turning to me. "Did you do them?"

"No," I said, rather ashamed, "Mrs. Danvers is responsible for everything."

"Oh. Well, after all . . ." Beatrice did not finish her sentence, she accepted a light for her cigarette from Frank, and once it was lit she appeared to have forgotten what she was going to say.

"Have you got Mitchell's to do the catering as usual?" asked Giles.

"Yes," said Maxim. "I don't think anything has been altered, has it, Frank? We had all the records down at the office. Nothing has been forgotten, and I don't think we have left anyone out."

"What a relief to find only ourselves," said Beatrice. "I remember once arriving about this time, and there were about twenty-five people in the place already. All going to stop the night.

"What's everyone going to wear? I suppose Maxim, as always, refuses to play?"

"As always," said Maxim.

"Such a mistake I think. The whole thing would go with much more swing if you did."

"Have you ever known a ball at Manderley not to go with a swing?"

"No, my dear boy, the organisation is too good. But I do think the host ought to give the lead himself."

"I think it's quite enough if the hostess makes the effort," said Maxim. "Why should I make myself hot and uncomfortable and a damn fool into the bargain?"

"Oh, but that's absurd. There's no need to look a fool. With your appearance, my dear Maxim, you could get away with any costume. You don't have to worry about your figure like poor Giles."

"What is Giles going to wear to-night?" I asked, "or is it a dead secret?"

"No, rather not," beamed Giles, "as a matter of fact it's a pretty good effort. I got our local tailor to rig it up. I'm coming as an Arabian sheik."

"Good God," said Maxim.

"It's not at all bad," said Beatrice warmly. "He stains his face of course, and leaves off his glasses. The head-dress is authentic. We borrowed it off a friend who used to live in the East, and the rest the tailor copied from some paper. Giles looks very well in it."

"What are you going to be, Mrs. Lacy?" said Frank.

"Oh, I'm afraid I haven't coped much," said Beatrice. "I've got some sort of eastern get-up to go with Giles, but I don't pretend it's genuine. Strings of beads, you know, and a veil over my face."

"It sounds very nice," I said politely.

"Oh, it's not bad. Comfortable to wear, that's one blessing. I shall take off the veil if I get too hot. What are you wearing?"

"Don't ask her," said Maxim. "She won't tell any of us. There has never been such a secret. I believe she even wrote to London for it."

"My dear," said Beatrice, rather impressed, "don't say you have gone a bust and will put us all to shame? Mine is only home-made, you know."

"Don't worry," I said, laughing, "it's quite simple really. But Maxim would tease me, and I've promised to give him the surprise of his life."

"Quite right too," said Giles, "Maxim is too superior altogether. The fact is he's jealous, wishes he was dressing up like the rest of us, and doesn't like to say so."

"Heaven forbid," said Maxim.

"What are you doing, Crawley?" asked Giles.

Frank looked rather apologetic. "I've been so busy I'm afraid I've left things to the last moment. I hunted up an old pair of trousers last night, and a striped football jersey, and thought of putting a patch over one eye and coming as a pirate."

"Why on earth didn't you write to us and borrow a costume?" said Beatrice. "There's one of a Dutchman that Roger had last winter in Switzerland. It would have suited you excellently."

"I refuse to allow my agent to walk about as a Dutchman," said Maxim. "He'd never get rents out of anybody again. Let him stick to his pirate. It might frighten some of them."

"Anything less like a pirate," murmured Beatrice in my ear.

I pretended not to hear. Poor Frank, she was always rather down on him.

"How long will it take me to paint my face?" asked Giles.

"Two hours at least," said Beatrice. "I should begin thinking about it if I were you. How many shall we be at dinner?"

"Sixteen," said Maxim, "counting ourselves. No strangers. You know them all."

"I'm beginning to get dress fever already," said Beatrice. "What fun it all is. I'm so glad you decided to do this again, Maxim."

"You've got her to thank for it," said Maxim, nodding at me.

"Oh, it's not true," I said. "It was all the fault of Lady Crowan."

"Nonsense," said Maxim, smiling at me, "you know you're as excited as a child at its first party."

"I'm not."

"I'm longing to see your dress," said Beatrice.

"It's nothing out of the way. Really it's not," I insisted.

"Mrs. de Winter says we shan't know her," said Frank.

Everybody looked at me and smiled. I felt pleased and flushed and rather happy. People were being nice. They were all so friendly. It was suddenly fun, the thought of the dance, and that I was to be the hostess.

The dance was being given for me, in my honour, because I was the bride. I sat on the table in the library, swinging my legs, while the rest of them stood round, and I had a longing to go upstairs and put on my dress, try the wig in front of the looking-glass, turn this way and that before the long mirror on the wall. It was new, this sudden unexpected sensation of being important, of having Giles, and Beatrice, and Frank and Maxim all looking at me and talking about my dress. All wondering what I was going to wear. I thought of the soft white dress in its folds of tissue paper, and how it would hide my flat dull figure, my rather sloping shoulders. I thought of my own lank hair covered by the sleek and gleaming curls.

"What's the time?" I said carelessly, yawning a little, pretending I did not care. "I wonder if we ought to think about going upstairs . . . ?"

As we crossed the great hall on the way to our rooms I realised for the first time how the house lent itself to the occasion, and how beautiful the rooms were looking. Even the drawing-room, formal and cold to my consideration when we were alone, was a blaze of colour now, flowers in every corner, red roses in silver bowls on the white cloth of the supper table, the long windows open to the terrace, where, as soon as it was dusk, the fairy lights would shine. The band had stacked their instruments ready in the minstrels' gallery above the hall, and the hall itself wore a strange, waiting air; there was a warmth about it I had never known before, due to the night itself, so still and clear, to the flowers beneath the pictures, to our own laughter as we hovered on the wide stone stairs.

The old austerity had gone. Manderley had come alive in a fashion I would not have believed possible. It was not the still quiet Manderley I knew. There was a certain significance about it now that had not been before. A reckless air, rather triumphant, rather pleasing. It was as if the house remembered other days, long, long ago, when the hall was a banqueting hall indeed, with weapons and tapestry hanging upon the walls, and men sat at a long narrow table in the centre laughing louder than we laughed now, calling for wine, for song, throwing great pieces of meat upon the flags to the slumbering dogs. Later, in other years, it would still be gay, but with a certain grace and dignity, and Caroline de Winter, whom I should represent tonight, would walk down the wide stone stairs in her white dress to dance the minuet. I wished we could sweep away the years and see her. I wished we did not have to degrade the house with our modern jig-tunes, so out-of-place and unromantic. They would not suit Manderley. I found myself in sudden agreement with Mrs. Danvers. We should have made it a period ball, not the hotch-potch of humanity it was bound to be, with Giles, poor fellow, well-meaning and hearty in his guise of Arabian sheik. I found Clarice waiting for me in my bedroom, her round face scarlet with excitement. We giggled at one another like schoolgirls, and I bade her lock my door. There was much sound of tissue paper, rustling and mysterious. We spoke to one another softly like conspirators, we walked on tip-toe. I felt like a child again on the eve of Christmas. This padding to and fro in my room with bare feet, the little furtive bursts of laughter, the stifled exclamations, reminded me of hanging up my stocking long ago. Maxim was safe in his dressing-room, and the way through was barred against him. Clarice alone was my ally and favoured friend. The dress fitted perfectly. I stood still, hardly able to restrain my impatience while Clarice hooked me up with fumbling fingers.

"It's handsome, Madam," she kept saying, leaning back on her heels to look at me. "It's a dress fit for the Queen of England."

"What about under the left shoulder there?" I said, anxiously. "That strap of mine, is it going to show?"

"No, Madam, nothing shows."

"How is it? How do I look?" I did not wait for her answer, I twisted and turned in front of the mirror, I frowned, I smiled. I felt different already, no longer hampered by my appearance. My own dull personality was submerged at last. "Give me the wig," I said excitedly, "careful, don't crush it, the curls mustn't be flat. They are supposed to stand out from the face." Clarice stood behind my shoulder, I saw her round face beyond mine in the reflection of the looking-glass, her eyes shining, her mouth a little open. I brushed my own hair sleek behind my ears. I took hold of the soft gleaming curls with trembling fingers, laughing under my breath, looking up at Clarice.

"Oh, Clarice," I said, "what will Mr. de Winter say?"

I covered my own mousy hair with the curled wig trying to hide my triumph, trying to hide my smile. Somebody came and hammered on the door.

"Who's there?" I called in panic, "you can't come in."

"It's me, my dear, don't alarm yourself," said Beatrice, "how far have you got? I want to look at you."

"No, no," I said, "you can't come in, I'm not ready."

The flustered Clarice stood beside me, her hand full of hair-pins, while I took them from her one by one, controlling the curls that had become fluffed in the box.

"I'll come down when I am ready," I called. "Go on down, all of you. Don't wait for me. Tell Maxim he can't come in."

"Maxim's down," she said. "He came along to us. He said he hammered on your bathroom door and you never answered. Don't be too long, my dear, we are all so intrigued. Are you sure you don't want any help?"

"No," I shouted impatiently, losing my head, "go away, go on down."

Why did she have to come and bother just at this moment? It fussed me. I did not know what I was doing. I jabbed with a hairpin, flattening it against a curl. I heard no more from Beatrice, she must have gone along the passage. I wondered if she was happy in her eastern robes and if Giles had succeeded in painting his face. How absurd it was, the whole thing. Why did we do it, I wondered, why were we such children?

I did not recognise the face that stared at me in the glass. The eyes were larger surely, the mouth narrower, the skin white and clear? The curls stood away from the head in a little cloud. I watched this self that was not me at all and then smiled; a new, slow smile.

"Oh, Clarice!" I said. "Oh, Clarice!" I took the skirt of my dress in my hands and curtseyed to her, the flounces sweeping the ground. She giggled excitedly, rather embarrassed, flushed though, very pleased. I paraded up and down in front of my glass watching my reflection.

"Unlock the door," I said. "I'm going down. Run ahead and see if they are there." She obeyed me, still giggling, and I lifted my skirts off the ground and followed her along the corridor.

She looked back at me and beckoned. "They've gone down," she whispered, "Mr. de Winter, and Major and Mrs. Lacy. Mr. Crawley has just come. They are all standing in the hall." I peered through the archway at the head of the big staircase, and looked down on the hall below.

Yes, there they were. Giles, in his white Arab dress, laughing loudly, showing the knife at his side, Beatrice swathed in an extraordinary green garment and hung about the neck with trailing beads, poor Frank self-conscious and slightly foolish in his striped jersey and sea-boots, Maxim, the only normal one of the party, in his evening clothes.

"I don't know what she's doing," he said, "she's been up in her bedroom for hours. What's the time, Frank? The dinner crowd will be upon us before we know where we are."

The band were changed, and in the gallery already. One of the men was tuning his fiddle. He played a scale softly, and then plucked at a string. The light shone on the picture of Caroline de Winter.

Yes, the dress had been copied exactly from my sketch of the portrait. The puffed sleeve, the sash and the ribbon, the wide floppy hat I held in my hand. And my curls were her curls, they stood out from my face as hers did in the picture. I don't think I have ever felt so excited before, so happy and so proud. I waved my hand at the man with the fiddle, and then put my finger to my lips for silence. He smiled and bowed. He came across the gallery to the archway where I stood.

"Make the drummer announce me," I whispered, "make him beat the drum, you know how they do, and then call out Miss Caroline de Winter. I want to surprise them below." He nodded his head, he understood. My heart fluttered absurdly, and my cheeks were burning. What fun it was, what mad ridiculous childish fun! I smiled at Clarice still crouching in the corridor, I picked up my skirt in my hands. Then the sound of the drum echoed in the great hall, startling me for a moment, who had waited for it, who knew that it would come. I saw them look up surprised and bewildered from the hall below.

"Miss Caroline de Winter," shouted the drummer.

I came forward to the head of the stairs and stood there, smiling, my hat in my hand, like the girl in the picture. I waited for the clapping and the laughter that would follow as I walked slowly down the stairs. Nobody clapped, nobody moved.

They all stared at me like dumb things. Beatrice uttered a little cry and put her hand to her mouth. I went on smiling, I put one hand on the banister.

"How do you do, Mr. de Winter," I said.

Maxim had not moved. He stared up at me, his glass in his hand. There was no colour in his face. It was ashen white. I saw Frank go to him as though he would speak, but Maxim shook him off. I hesitated, one foot already on the stairs. Something was wrong, they had not understood. Why was Maxim looking like that? Why did they all stand like dummies, like people in a trance?

Then Maxim moved forward to the stairs, his eyes never leaving my face.

"What the hell do you think you are doing?" he said. His eyes blazed in anger. His face was still ashen white.

I could not move, I went on standing there, my hand on the banister.

"It's the picture," I said, terrified at his eyes, at his voice. "It's the picture, the one in the gallery."

There was a long silence. We went on staring at each other. Nobody moved in the hall. I swallowed, my hand moved to my throat. "What is it?" I said. "What have I done?"

If only they would not stare at me like that with dull blank faces. If only somebody would say something. When Maxim spoke again I did not recognise his voice. It was still and quiet, icy cold, not a voice I knew.

"Go and change," he said, "it does not matter what you put on. Find an ordinary evening frock, anything will do. Go now, before anybody comes."

I could not speak, I went on staring at him. His eyes were the only living things in the white mask of his face.

"What are you standing there for?" he said, his voice harsh and queer. "Didn't you hear what I said?"

I turned and ran blindly through the archway to the corridors beyond. I caught a glimpse of the astonished face of the drummer who had announced me. I brushed past him, stumbling, not looking where I went. Tears blinded my eyes. I did not know what was happening. Clarice had gone. The corridor was deserted. I looked about me stunned and stupid like a haunted thing. Then I saw that the door leading to the west wing was open wide, and that someone was standing there.

It was Mrs. Danvers. I shall never forget the expression on her face, loathsome, triumphant. The face of an exulting devil. She stood there, smiling at me.

And then I ran from her, down the long narrow passage to my own room, tripping, stumbling over the flounces of my dress.

CHAPTER SEVENTEEN

Clarice was waiting for me in my bedroom. She looked pale and scared. As soon as she saw me she burst into tears. I did not say anything. I began tearing at the hooks of my dress, ripping the stuff. I could not manage them properly, and Clarice came to help me, still crying noisily.

"It's all right, Clarice, it's not your fault," I said, and she shook her head, the tears running down her cheeks.

"Your lovely dress, Madam," she said, "your lovely white dress."

"It doesn't matter," I said. "Can't you find the hook? There it is, at the back. And another one somewhere, just below."

She fumbled with the hooks, her hands trembling, making worse trouble with it than I did myself, and all the time catching at her breath.

"What will you wear instead, Madam?" she said.

"I don't know," I said. "I don't know." She had managed to unfasten the hooks, and I struggled out of the dress. "I think I'd rather like to be alone, Clarice," I said, "would you be a dear and leave me? Don't worry, I shall manage all right. Forget what's happened. I want you to enjoy the party."

"Can't I press out a dress for you, Madam?" she said, looking up at me with swollen streaming eyes. "It won't take me a moment."

"No," I said, "don't bother, I'd rather you went, and Clarice . . ."

"Yes, Madam?"

"Don't—don't say anything about what's just happened."

"No, Madam." She burst into another torrent of weeping.

"Don't let the others see you like that," I said. "Go to your bedroom and do something to your face. There's nothing to cry about, nothing at all." Somebody knocked on the door. Clarice threw me a quick frightened glance.

"Who is it?" I said. The door opened and Beatrice came into the room. She came to me at once, a strange rather ludicrous figure in her eastern drapery, the bangles jangling on her wrists.

"My dear," she said, "my dear," and held out her hands to me.

Clarice slipped out of the room. I felt tired suddenly, and unable to cope. I went and sat down on the bed. I put my hand up to my head and took off the curled wig. Beatrice stood watching me.

"Are you all right?" she said. "You look very white."

"It's the light," I said. "It never gives one any colour."

"Sit down for a few minutes and you'll be all right," she said, "wait, I'll get you a glass of water."

She went into the bathroom, her bangles jangling with her every movement, and then she came back, the glass of water in her hands.

I drank some to please her, not wanting it a bit. It tasted warm from the tap; she had not let it run.

"Of course I knew at once it was just a terrible mistake," she said. "You could not possibly have known, why should you?"

"Known what?" I said.

"Why, the dress, you poor dear, the picture you copied of the girl in the gallery. It was what Rebecca did at the last fancy dress ball at Manderley. Identical. The same picture, the same dress. You stood there on the stairs, and for one ghastly moment I thought . . ."

She did not go on with her sentence, she patted me on the shoulder.

"You poor child, how wretchedly unfortunate, how were you to know?"

"I ought to have known," I said stupidly, staring at her, too stunned to understand. "I ought to have known."

"Nonsense, how could you know? It was not the sort of thing that could possibly enter any of our heads. Only it was such a shock, you see. We none of us expected it, and Maxim . . ."

"Yes, Maxim?" I said.

"He thinks, you see, it was deliberate on your part. You had some bet that you would startle him, didn't you? Some foolish joke. And of course, he doesn't understand. It was such a frightful shock for him. I told him at once you could not have done such a thing, and that it was sheer appalling luck that you had chosen that particular picture."

"I ought to have known," I repeated again. "It's all my fault, I ought to have seen. I ought to have known."

"No, no. Don't worry, you'll be able to explain the whole thing to him quietly. Everything will be quite all right. The first lot of people were arriving just as I came upstairs to you. They are having drinks. Everything's all right. I've told Frank and Giles to make up a story about your dress not fitting, and you are very disappointed."

I did not say anything. I went on sitting on the bed with my hands in my lap.

"What can you wear instead?" said Beatrice, going to my wardrobe and flinging open the doors. "Here, what's this blue? It looks charming. Put this on. Nobody will mind. Quick, I'll help you."

"No," I said. "No, I'm not coming down."

Beatrice stared at me in great distress, my blue frock over her arm.

"But, my dear, you must," she said in dismay. "You can't possibly not appear."

"No, Beatrice, I'm not coming down. I can't face them, not after what's happened."

"But nobody will know about the dress," she said. "Frank and Giles will never breathe a word. We've got the story all arranged. The shop sent the wrong dress, and it did not fit, so you are wearing an ordinary evening dress instead. Everyone will think it perfectly natural. It won't make any difference to the evening."

"You don't understand," I said. "I don't care about the dress. It's not that at all. It's what has happened, what I did. I can't come down now, Beatrice, I can't."

"But, my dear, Giles and Frank understand perfectly. They are full of sympathy. And Maxim too. It was just the first shock.... I'll try and get him alone a minute, I'll explain the whole thing."

"No!" I said. "No!"

She put my blue frock down beside me on the bed. "Everyone will be arriving," she said, very worried, very upset. "It will look so extraordinary if you don't come down. I can't say you've suddenly got a headache."

"Why not?" I said wearily. "What does it matter? Make anything up. Nobody will mind, they don't any of them know me."

"Come now, my dear," she said, patting my hand, "try and make the effort. Put on this charming blue. Think of Maxim. You must come down for his sake."

"I'm thinking about Maxim all the time," I said.

"Well then, surely ... ?"

"No," I said, tearing at my nails, rocking backwards and forwards on the bed. "I can't, I can't."

Somebody else knocked on the door. "Oh, dear, who on earth is that?" said Beatrice, walking to the door. "What is it?"

She opened the door. Giles was standing just outside.

"Everyone has turned up, Maxim sent me up to find out what's happening?" he said.

"She says she won't come down," said Beatrice. "What on earth are we going to say?"

I caught sight of Giles peering at me through the open door.

"Oh, Lord, what a frightful mix-up," he whispered. He turned away embarrassed when he noticed that I had seen him.

"What shall I say to Maxim?" he asked Beatrice. "It's five past eight now."

"Say she's feeling rather faint, but will try and come down later. Tell them not to wait dinner. I'll be down directly, I'll make it all right."

"Yes, right you are." He half glanced in my direction again, sympathetic but rather curious, wondering why I sat there on the bed, and his voice was low, as it might be after an accident, when people are waiting for the doctor.

"Is there anything else I can do?" he said.

"No," said Beatrice, "go down now, I'll follow in a minute."

He obeyed her, shuffling away in his Arabian robes. This is the sort of moment, I thought, that I shall laugh at years afterwards, that I shall say "Do you remember how Giles was dressed as an Arab, and Beatrice had a veil over her face, and jangling bangles on her wrist?" And time will mellow it, make it a moment for laughter. But now it was not funny, now I did not laugh. It was not the future, it was the present. It was too vivid and too real. I sat on the bed, plucking at the eiderdown, pulling a little feather out of a slit in one corner.

"Would you like some brandy?" said Beatrice, making a last effort. "I know it's only Dutch courage, but it sometimes works wonders."

"No," I said. "No, I don't want anything."

"I shall have to go down. Giles says they are waiting dinner. Are you sure it's all right for me to leave you?"

"Yes. And thank you, Beatrice."

"Oh, my dear, don't thank me. I wish I could do something." She stooped swiftly to my looking-glass and dabbed her face with powder. "God, what a sight I look," she said, "this damn veil is crooked I know. However it can't be helped." She rustled out of the room, closing the door behind her. I felt I had forfeited her sympathy by my refusal to go down. I had shown the white feather. She had not understood. She belonged to another breed of men and women, another race than I. They had guts, the women of her race. They were not like me. If it had been Beatrice who had done this thing instead of me she would have put on her other dress and gone down again to welcome her guests. She would have stood by Giles's side, and shaken hands with people, a smile on her face. I could not do that. I had not the pride, I had not the guts. I was badly bred.

I kept seeing Maxim's eyes blazing in his white face, and behind him Giles, and Beatrice and Frank standing like dummies, staring at me.

I got up from my bed and went and looked out of the window. The gardeners were going round to the lights in the rose-garden, testing them to see if they all worked. The sky was pale, with a few salmon clouds of evening streaking to the west. When it was dusk the lamps would all be lit. There were tables and chairs in the rose-garden for the couples who wanted to sit out. I could smell the roses from my window. The men were talking to one another and laughing. "There's one here gone," I heard a voice call out; "can you get me another small bulb? One of the blue ones, Bill." He fixed the light into position. He whistled a popular tune of the moment with easy confidence, and I thought how to-night perhaps the band would play the same tune in the minstrels' gallery above the hall. "That's got it," said the man, switching the light on and off, "they're all right here. No others gone. We'd better have a look at those on the terrace." They went off round the corner of the house, still whistling the song. I wished I could be the man. Later in the evening he would stand with his friend in the drive and watch the cars drive up to the house, his hands in his pockets, his cap on the back of his head. He would stand in a crowd with the other people from the estate, and then drink cider at the long table arranged for them in one corner of the terrace. "Like the old days, isn't it?" he would say. But his friend would shake his head, puffing at his pipe. "This new one's not like our Mrs. de Winter, she's different altogether." And a woman next them in the crowd would agree, other people too, all saying "That's right," and nodding their heads.

"Where is she to-night? She's not been on the terrace once."

"I can't say, I'm sure. I've not seen her."

"Mrs. de Winter used to be here, there, and everywhere."

"Aye, that's right."

And the woman would turn to her neighbours nodding mysteriously.

"They say she's not appearing to-night at all."

"Go on."

" 'Tis true. Ask Mary here."

"That's right. One of the servants from the house told me Mrs. de Winter hasn't come down from her room all the evening."

"What's wrong with the maid, is she bad?"

"No, sulky I reckon. They say her dress didn't please her."

A squeal of laughter and a murmur from the little crowd.

"Did you ever hear of such a thing? It's a shame for Mr. de Winter."

"I wouldn't stand for it, not from a chit like her."

"Maybe it's not true at all."

"It's true all right. They're full of it up at the house." One to the other. This one to the next. A smile, a wink, a shrug of the shoulder. One group, and then another group. And then spreading to the guests who walked on the terrace and strolled across the lawns. The couple who in three hours' time would sit in those chairs beneath me in the rose-garden.

"Do you suppose it's true what I heard?"

"What did you hear?"

"Why, that there's nothing wrong with her at all, they've had a colossal row, and she won't appear!"

"I say!" A lift of the eyebrows, a long whistle.

"I know. Well, it does look rather odd, don't you think? What I mean is, people don't suddenly for no reason have violent headaches. I call the whole thing jolly fishy."

"I thought he looked a bit grim."

"So did I."

"Of course I have heard before the marriage is not a wild success."

"Oh, really?"

"H'm. Several people have said so. They say he's beginning to realise he's made a big mistake. She's nothing to look at, you know."

"No, I've heard there's nothing much to her. Who was she?"

"Oh, no one at all. Some pick-up in the south of France, a nursery gov., or something."

"Good Lord!"

"I know. And when you think of Rebecca . . ."

I went on staring at the empty chairs. The salmon sky had turned to grey. Above my head was the evening star. In the woods beyond the rose-garden the birds were making their last little rustling noises before nightfall. A lone gull flew across the sky. I went away from the window, back to the bed again. I picked up the white dress I had left on the floor and put it back in the box with the tissue paper. I put the wig back in its box too. Then I looked in one of my cupboards for the little portable iron I used to have in Monte Carlo for Mrs. Van Hopper's dresses. It was lying at the back of a shelf with some woollen jumpers I had not worn for a long time. The iron was one of those universal kinds that go on any voltage and I fitted it to the plug in the wall. I began to iron the blue dress that Beatrice had taken from the wardrobe, slowly, methodically, as I used to iron Mrs. Van Hopper's dresses in Monte Carlo.

When I had finished I laid the dress ready on the bed. Then I cleaned the make-up off my face that I had put on for the fancy dress. I combed my hair, and washed my hands. I put on the blue dress and the shoes that went with it. I might have been my old self again, going down to the lounge of the hotel with Mrs. Van Hopper. I opened the door of my room and went along the corridor. Everything was still and silent. There might not have been a party at all. I tiptoed to the end of the passage and turned the corner. The door to the west wing was closed. There was no sound of anything at all. When I came to the archway by the gallery and the staircase I heard the murmur and hum of conversation coming from the dining-room. They were still having dinner. The great hall was deserted. There was nobody in the gallery either. The band must be having their dinner too. I did not know what arrangements had been made for them. Frank had done it—Frank or Mrs. Danvers.

From where I stood I could see the picture of Caroline de Winter facing me in the gallery. I could see the curls framing her face, and I could see the smile on her lips. I remembered the bishop's wife who had said to me that day I called, "I shall never forget her, dressed all in white, with that cloud of dark hair." I ought to have remembered that, I ought to have known. How queer the instruments looked in the gallery, the little stands for the music, the big drum. One of the men had left his handkerchief on a chair. I leant over the rail and looked down at the hall below. Soon it would be filled with people, like the bishop's wife had said, and Maxim would stand at the bottom of the stairs shaking hands with them, as they came into the hall. The sound of their voices would echo to the ceiling, and then the band would play from the gallery where I was leaning now, the man with the violin smiling, swaying to the music.

It would not be quiet like this any more. A board creaked in the gallery. I swung round, looking at the gallery behind me. There was nobody there. The gallery was empty, just as it had been before. A current of air blew in my face though, somebody must have left a window open in one of the passages. The hum of voices continued in the dining-room. I wondered why the board creaked when I had not moved at all. The warmth of the night perhaps, a swelling somewhere in the old wood. The draught still blew in my face though. A piece of music on one of the stands fluttered to the floor. I looked towards the archway above the stairs. The draught was coming from there. I went beneath the arch again, and when I came out on to the long corridor I saw that the door to the west wing had blown open and swung back against the wall. It was dark in the west passage, none of the lights had been turned on. I could feel the wind blowing on my face from an open window. I fumbled for a switch on the wall and could not find one. I could see the window in an angle of the passage, the curtain blowing softly, backwards and forwards. The grey evening light cast queer shadows on the floor. The sound of the sea came to me through the open window, the soft hissing sound of the ebb-tide leaving the shingle.

I did not go and shut the window. I stood there shivering a moment in my thin dress, listening to the sea as it sighed and left the shore. Then I turned quickly and shut the door of the west wing behind me, and came out again through the archway by the stairs.

The murmur of voices had swollen now and was louder than before. The door of the dining-room was open. They were coming out of dinner. I could see Robert standing by the open door, and there was a scraping of chairs, a babble of conversation, and of laughter.

I walked slowly down the stairs to meet them.

When I look back at my first party at Manderley, my first and my last, I can remember little isolated things standing alone out of the vast blank canvas of the evening. The background was hazy, a sea of dim faces none of whom I knew, and there was the slow drone of the band harping out a waltz that never finished, that went on and on. The same couples swung by in rotation, with the same fixed smiles, and to me, standing with Maxim at the bottom of the stairs to welcome the late-comers, these dancing couples seemed like marionettes twisting and turning on a piece of string, held by some invisible hand.

There was a woman, I never knew her name, never saw her again, but she wore a salmon-coloured gown hooped in crinoline form, a vague gesture to some past century but whether seventeenth, eighteenth, or nineteenth I could not tell, and every time she passed me it coincided with a sweeping bar of the waltz to which she dipped and swayed, smiling as she did so in my direction. It happened again and again until it became automatic, a matter of routine, like those promenades on board ship when we meet the same people bent on exercise like ourselves, and know with deadly certainty that we will pass them by the bridge.

I can see her now, the prominent teeth, the gay spot of rouge placed high upon her cheek-bones, and her smile, vacant, happy, enjoying her evening. Later I saw her by the supper table, her keen eyes searching the food, and she heaped a plate high with salmon and lobster mayonnaise and went off into a corner. There was Lady Crowan too, monstrous in purple, disguised as I know not what romantic figure of the past, it might have been Marie Antoinette or Nell Gwyn, for all I knew, or a strange erotic combination of the two, and she kept exclaiming in excited high-pitch tones, a little higher than usual because of the champagne she had consumed, "You all have me to thank for this, not the de Winters at all."

I remember Robert dropping a tray of ices, and the expression of Frith's face when he saw Robert was the culprit and not one of the minions hired for the occasion. I wanted to go to Robert and stand beside him and say "I know how you feel. I understand. I've done worse than you tonight." I can feel now the stiff, set smile on my face that did not match the misery in my eyes. I can see Beatrice, dear friendly tactless Beatrice, watching me from her partner's arms, nodding encouragement, the bangles jangling on her wrists, the veil slipping continually from her over-heated forehead. I can picture myself once more whirled round the room in a desperate dance with Giles, who with dog-like sympathy and kind warm heart would take no refusal, but must steer me through the stamping crowd as he would one of his own horses at a meet. "That's a jolly pretty dress you're wearing," I can hear him say, "it makes all these people look damn silly," and I blessed him for his pathetic simple gesture of understanding and sincerity, thinking, dear Giles, that I was disappointed in my dress, that I was worrying about my appearance, that I cared.

It was Frank who brought me a plate of chicken and ham that I could not eat, and Frank who stood by my elbow with a glass of champagne I would not drink.

"I wish you would," he said quietly, "I think you need it," and I took three sips of it to please him. The black patch over his eye gave him a pale odd appearance, it made him look older, different. There seemed to be lines on his face I had not seen before.

He moved amongst the guests like another host, seeing to their comfort, that they were supplied with drink, and food, and cigarettes, and he danced too in solemn painstaking fashion, walking his partners round the room with a set face. He did not wear his pirate costume with abandon, and there was something rather tragic about the side-whiskers he had fluffed under the scarlet handkerchief on his head. I thought of him standing before the looking-glass in his bare bachelor bedroom curling them round his fingers. Poor Frank. Dear Frank. I never asked, I never knew, how much he hated the last fancy dress ball ever given at Manderley.

The band played on, and the swaying couples twisted like bobbing marionettes, to and fro, to and fro, across the great hall and back again, and it was not I who watched them at all, not someone with feelings, made of flesh and blood, but a dummy-stick of a person in my stead, a prop who wore a smile screwed to its face. The figure who stood beside it was wooden too. His face was a mask, his smile was not his own. The eyes were not the eyes of the man I loved, the man I knew. They looked through me and beyond me, cold, expressionless, to some place of pain and torture I could not enter, to some private, inward hell I could not share.

He never spoke to me. He never touched me. We stood beside one another, the host and the hostess, and we were not together. I watched his courtesy to his guests. He flung a word to one, a jest to another, a smile to a third, a call over his shoulder to a fourth, and no one but myself could know that every utterance he made, every movement, was automatic and the work of a machine. We were like two performers in a play, but we were divided, we were not acting with one another. We had to endure it alone, we had to put up this show, this miserable, sham performance for the sake of all these people I did not know and did not want to see again.

"I hear your wife's frock never turned up in time," said someone with a mottled face and a sailor's pigtail, and he laughed, and dug Maxim in the ribs. "Damn shame, what? I should sue the shop for fraud. Same thing happened to my wife's cousin once."

"Yes, it was unfortunate," said Maxim.

"I tell you what," said the sailor, turning to me, "you ought to say you are a forget-me-not. They're blue, aren't they? Jolly little flowers, forget-me-nots. That's right, isn't it, de Winter? Tell your wife she must call herself a 'forget-me-not.'" He swept away, roaring with laughter, his partner in his arms. "Pretty good idea, what? A forget-me-not." Then Frank again hovering just behind me, another glass in his hand, lemonade this time. "No, Frank, I'm not thirsty."

"Why don't you dance? Or come and sit down a moment, there's a corner in the terrace."

"No, I'm better standing. I don't want to sit down."

"Can't I get you something, a sandwich, a peach?"

"No, I don't want anything."

There was the salmon lady again, she forgot to smile at me this time. She was flushed after her supper. She kept looking up into her partner's face. He was very tall, very thin, he had a chin like a fiddle.

The Destiny waltz, the Blue Danube, the Merry Widow, one-two-three, one-two-three, round-and-round, one-two-three, one-two-three, round-and-round. The salmon lady, a green lady, Beatrice again, her veil pushed back off her forehead, Giles, his face streaming with perspiration, and that sailor once more, with another partner, they stopped beside me, I did not know her, she was dressed as a Tudor woman, any Tudor woman, she wore a ruffle round her throat and a black velvet dress.

"When are you coming to see us?" she said, as though we were old friends, and I answered, "Soon of course, we were talking about it the other day," wondering why I found it so easy to lie suddenly, no effort at all. "Such a delightful party, I do congratulate you," she said, and "Thank you very much," I said. "It's fun, isn't it?"

"I hear they sent you the wrong dress?"

"Yes, absurd, wasn't it?"

"These shops are all the same. No depending on them. But you look delightfully fresh in that pretty blue. Much more comfortable than this hot velvet. Don't forget, you must both come and dine at the Palace soon."

"We should love to."

What did she mean, where, what palace? Were we entertaining royalty? She swept on to the Blue Danube in the arms of the sailor, her velvet frock brushing the ground like a carpet-sweeper, and it was not until long afterwards, in the middle of some night, when I could not sleep, that I remembered the Tudor woman was the bishop's wife who liked walking in the Pennines.

What was the time? I did not know. The evening dragged on, hour after hour, the same faces and the same tunes. Now and again the bridge people crept out of the library like hermits to watch the dancers, and then returned again. Beatrice, her draperies trailing behind her, whispered in my ear,

"Why don't you sit down? You look like death."

"I'm all right."

Giles, the make-up running on his face, poor fellow, and stifling in his Arab blanket, came up to me and said, "Come and watch the fireworks on the terrace."

I remember standing on the terrace and staring up at the sky as the foolish rockets burst and fell. There was little Clarice in a corner with some boy off the estate, she was smiling happily, squealing with delight as a squib spluttered at her feet. She had forgotten her tears.

"Hullo, this will be a big-un." Giles, his large face upturned, his mouth open. "Here she comes. Bravo, jolly fine show."

The slow hiss of the rocket as it sped into the air, the burst of the explosion, the stream of little emerald stars. A murmur of approval from the crowd, cries of delight, and a clapping of hands.

The salmon lady well to the front, her face eager with expectation, a remark for every star that fell. "Oh, what a beauty ... look at that one now, I say, how pretty.... Oh, that one didn't burst ... take care, it's coming our way ... what are those men doing over there?" ... Even the hermits left their lair and came to join the dancers on the terrace. The lawns were black with people. The bursting stars shone on their upturned faces.

Again and again the rockets sped into the air like arrows, and the sky became crimson and gold. Manderley stood out like an enchanted house, every window aflame, the grey walls coloured by the falling stars. A house bewitched, carved out of the dark woods. And when the last rocket burst and the cheering died away the night that had been fine before seemed dull and heavy in contrast, the sky became a pall. The little groups on the lawns and in the drive broke up and scattered. The guests crowded the long windows in the terrace back to the drawing-room again. It was anti-climax, the aftermath had come. We stood about with blank faces. Someone gave me a glass of champagne. I heard the sound of cars starting up in the drive.

"They're beginning to go," I thought. "Thank God, they're beginning to go." The salmon lady was having some more supper. It would take time yet to clear the hall. I saw Frank make a signal to the band. I stood in the doorway between the drawing-room and the hall beside a man I did not know.

"What a wonderful party it's been," he said.

"Yes," I said.

"I've enjoyed every minute of it," he said.

"I'm so glad," I said.

"Molly was wild with fury at missing it," he said.

"Was she?" I said.

The band began to play Auld Lang Syne. The man seized my hand and started swinging it up and down. "Here," he said, "come on, some of you." Somebody else swung my other hand, and more people joined us. We stood in a great circle singing at the top of our voices. The man who had enjoyed his evening and said Molly would be wild at missing it was dressed as a Chinese mandarin, and his false nails got caught up in his sleeve as we swung our hands up and down. He roared with laughter. We all laughed. "Should auld acquaintance be forgot," we sang.

The hilarious gaiety changed swiftly at the closing bars, and the drummer rattled his sticks in the inevitable prelude to God Save the King. The smiles left our faces as though wiped clean by a sponge. The mandarin sprung to attention, his hands stiff to his sides. I remember wondering vaguely if he was in the Army. How queer he looked with his long poker face, and his drooping mandarin moustache. I caught the salmon lady's eye. God Save the King had taken her unawares, she was still holding a plate heaped with chicken in aspic. She held it stiffly out in front of her like a church collection. All animation had gone from her face. As the last note of God Save the King died away she relaxed again, and attacked her chicken in a sort of frenzy, chattering over her shoulder to her partner. Somebody came and wrung me by the hand.

"Don't forget, you're dining with us on the fourteenth of next month."

"Oh, are we?" I stared at him blankly.

"Yes, we've got your sister-in-law to promise too."

"Oh. Oh, what fun."

"Eight-thirty, and black tie. So looking forward to seeing you."

"Yes. Yes rather."

People began to form up in queues to say good-bye. Maxim was at the other side of the room. I put on my smile again which had worn thin after Auld Lang Syne.

"The best evening I've spent for a long time."

"I'm so glad."

"Many thanks for a grand party."

"I'm so glad."

"Here we are, you see, staying to the bitter end."

"Yes, I'm so glad."

Was there no other sentence in the English language? I bowed and smiled like a dummy, my eyes searching for Maxim above their heads. He was caught up in a knot of people by the library. Beatrice too was surrounded, and Giles had led a team of stragglers to the buffet table in the drawing-room. Frank was out in the drive seeing that people got their cars. I was hemmed in by strangers.

"Good-bye, and thanks tremendously."

"I'm so glad."

The great hall began to empty. Already it wore that drab deserted air of a vanished evening and the dawn of a tired day. There was a grey light on the terrace, I could see the shapes of the blown firework stands taking form on the lawns.

"Good-bye, a wonderful party."

"I'm so glad."

Maxim had gone out to join Frank in the drive. Beatrice came up to me, pulling off her jangling bracelets. "I can't stand these things a moment longer. Heavens, I'm dead beat. I don't believe I've missed a dance. Anyway, it was a tremendous success."

"Was it?" I said.

"My dear, hadn't you better go to bed? You look worn out. You've been standing nearly all the evening. Where are the men?"

"Out on the drive."

"I shall have some coffee, and eggs and bacon. What about you?"

"No, Beatrice, I don't think I will."

"You looked very charming in your blue. Everyone said so. And nobody had an inkling about—about the other thing, so you mustn't worry."

"No."

"If I were you I should have a good long lie to-morrow morning. Don't attempt to get up. Have your breakfast in bed."

"Yes, perhaps."

"I'll tell Maxim you've gone up, shall I?"

"Please, Beatrice."

"All right, my dear. Sleep well." She kissed me swiftly, patting my shoulder at the same time, and then went off to find Giles in the supper-room. I walked slowly up the stairs, one step at a time. The band had turned the lights off in the gallery, and had gone down to have eggs and bacon too. Pieces of music lay about the floor. One chair had been upturned. There was an ash-tray full of the stubs of their cigarettes. The aftermath of the party. I went along the corridor to my room. It was getting lighter every moment, and the birds had started singing. I did not have to turn on the light to undress. A little chill wind blew in from the open window. It was rather cold. Many people must have used the rose-garden during the evening, for all the chairs were moved, and dragged from their places. There was a tray of empty glasses on one of the tables. Someone had left a bag behind on a chair. I pulled the curtains to darken the room, but the grey morning light found its way through the gaps at the sides.

I got into bed, my legs very weary, a niggling pain in the small of my back. I lay back and closed my eyes, thankful for the cool white comfort of clean sheets. I wished my mind would rest like my body, relax, and pass to sleep. Not hum round in the way it did, jigging to music, whirling in a sea of faces. I pressed my hands over my eyes but they would not go.

I wondered how long Maxim would be. The bed beside me looked stark and cold. Soon there would be no shadows in the room at all, the walls and the ceiling and the floor would be white with the morning. The birds would sing their songs, louder, gayer, less subdued. The sun would make a yellow pattern on the curtain. My little bed-side clock ticked out the minutes one by one. The hand moved round the dial. I lay on my side watching it. It came to the hour and passed it again. It started afresh on its journey. But Maxim did not come.

CHAPTER EIGHTEEN

I think I fell asleep a little after seven. It was broad daylight I remember, there was no longer any pretence that the drawn curtains hid the sun. The light streamed in at the open window and made patterns on the wall. I heard the men below in the rose-garden clearing away the tables and the chairs, and taking down the chain of fairy lights. Maxim's bed was still bare and empty. I lay across my bed, my arms over my eyes, a strange, mad position and the least likely to bring sleep, but I drifted to the border-line of the unconscious and slipped over it at last. When I awoke it was past eleven, and Clarice must have come in and brought me my tea without my hearing her, for there was a tray by my side, and a stone-cold tea-pot, and my clothes had been tidied, my blue frock put away in the wardrobe.

I drank my cold tea, still blurred and stupid from my short heavy sleep, and stared at the blank wall in front of me. Maxim's empty bed brought me to realisation with a queer shock to my heart, and the full anguish of the night before was upon me once again. He had not come to bed at all. His pyjamas lay folded on the turned-down sheet untouched. I wondered what Clarice had thought when she came into the room with my tea. Had she noticed? Would she have gone out and told the other servants, and would they all discuss it over their breakfast? I wondered why I minded that, and why the thought of the servants talking about it in the kitchen should cause me such distress. It must be that I had a small mean mind, a conventional, petty hatred of gossip.

That was why I had come down last night in my blue dress and had not stayed hidden in my room. There was nothing brave or fine about it, it was a wretched tribute to convention. I had not come down for Maxim's sake, for Beatrice's, for the sake of Manderley. I had come down because I did not want the people at the ball to think I had quarrelled with Maxim. I didn't want them to go home and say, "Of course you know they don't get on. I hear he's not at all happy." I had come for my own sake, my own poor personal pride. As I sipped my cold tea I thought with a tired bitter feeling of despair that I would be content to live in one corner of Manderley and Maxim in the other as long as the outside world should never know. If he had no more tenderness for me, never kissed me again, did not speak to me except on matters of necessity, I believed I could bear it if I were certain that nobody knew of this but our two selves. If we could bribe servants not to tell, play our part before relations, before Beatrice, and then when we were alone sit apart in our separate rooms, leading our separate lives.

It seemed to me, as I sat there in bed, staring at the wall, at the sunlight coming in at the window, at Maxim's empty bed, that there was nothing quite so shaming, so degrading, as a marriage that had failed. Failed after three months, as mine had done. For I had no illusions left now, I no longer made any effort to pretend. Last night had shown me too well. My marriage was a failure. All the things that people would say about it if they knew were true. We did not get on. We were not companions. We were not suited to one another. I was too young for Maxim, too inexperienced, and more important still, I was not of his world. The fact that I loved him in a sick, hurt, desperate way, like a child or a dog, did not matter. It was not the sort of love he needed. He wanted something else that I could not give him, something he had had before. I thought of the youthful almost hysterical excitement and conceit with which I had gone into this marriage, imagining I would bring happiness to Maxim who had known much greater happiness before. Even Mrs. Van Hopper, with her cheap views and common outlook, had known I was making a mistake. "I'm afraid you will regret it," she said. "I believe you are making a big mistake."

I would not listen to her, I thought her hard and cruel. But she was right. She was right in everything. That last mean thrust thrown at me before she said good-bye, "You don't flatter yourself he's in love with you, do you? He's lonely, he can't bear that great empty house," was the sanest, most truthful statement she had ever made in her life. Maxim was not in love with me, he had never loved me. Our honeymoon in Italy had meant nothing at all to him, nor our living here together. What I had thought was love for me, for myself as a person, was not love. It was just that he was a man, and I was his wife and was young, and he was lonely. He did not belong to me at all, he belonged to Rebecca. He still thought about Rebecca. He would never love me because of Rebecca. She was in the house still as Mrs. Danvers had said, she was in that room in the west wing, she was in the library, in the morning-room, in the gallery above the hall. Even in the little flower-room, where her mackintosh still hung. And in the garden, and in the woods, and down in the stone cottage on the beach. Her footsteps sounded in the corridors, her scent lingered on the stairs. The servants obeyed her orders still, the food we ate was the food she liked. Her favourite flowers filled the rooms. Her clothes were in the wardrobes in her room, her brushes were on the table, her shoes beneath the chair, her nightdress on her bed. Rebecca was still mistress of Manderley. Rebecca was still Mrs. de Winter. I had no business here at all. I had come blundering like a poor fool on ground that was preserved. "Where is Rebecca?" Maxim's grandmother had cried, "I want Rebecca. What have you done with Rebecca?" She did not know me, she did not care about me? Why should she? I was a stranger to her. I did not belong to Maxim or to Manderley. And Beatrice at our first meeting, looking me up and down, frank, direct, "You're so very different from Rebecca." Frank, reserved, embarrassed when I spoke of her, hating those questions I had poured upon him, even as I had hated them myself, and then answering that final one as we came towards the house, his voice grave and quiet, "Yes, she was the most beautiful creature I have ever seen."

Rebecca, always Rebecca. Wherever I walked in Manderley, wherever I sat, even in my thoughts and in my dreams, I met Rebecca. I knew her figure now, the long slim legs, the small and narrow feet. Her shoulders, broader than mine, the capable clever hands. Hands that could steer a boat, could hold a horse. Hands that arranged flowers, made the models of ships, and wrote "Max from Rebecca" on the fly-leaf of a book. I knew her face too, small and oval, the clear white skin, the cloud of dark hair. I knew the scent she wore, I could guess her laughter and her smile. If I heard it, even among a thousand others, I should recognise her voice. Rebecca, always Rebecca. I should never be rid of Rebecca.

Perhaps I haunted her as she haunted me; she looked down on me from the gallery as Mrs. Danvers had said, she sat beside me when I wrote my letters at her desk. That mackintosh I wore, that handkerchief I used. They were hers. Perhaps she knew and had seen me take them. Jasper had been her dog, and he ran at my heels now. The roses were hers and I cut them. Did she resent me and fear me as I resented her? Did she want Maxim alone in the house again? I could fight the living but I could not fight the dead. If there was some woman in London that Maxim loved, someone he wrote to, visited, dined with, slept with, I could fight with her. We would stand on common ground. I should not be afraid. Anger and jealousy were things that could be conquered. One day the woman would grow old or tired or different, and Maxim would not love her any more. But Rebecca would never grow old. Rebecca would always be the same. And her I could not fight. She was too strong for me.

I got out of bed and pulled the curtains. The sun streamed into the room. The men had cleared the mess away from the rose-garden. I wondered if people were talking about the ball in the way they do the day after a party.

"Did you think it quite up to their usual standard?"

"Oh, I think so."

"The band dragged a bit I thought."

"The supper was damn good."

"Fireworks weren't bad."

"Bee Lacy is beginning to look old."

"Who wouldn't in that get-up?"

"I thought he looked rather ill."

"He always does."

"What do you think of the bride?"

"Not much. Rather dull."

"I wonder if it's a success."

"Yes, I wonder . . ."

Then I noticed for the first time there was a note under my door. I went and picked it up. I recognised the square hand of Beatrice. She had scribbled it in pencil after breakfast. *"I knocked at your door but had no answer so gather you've taken my advice and are sleeping off last night. Giles is anxious to get back early as they have rung up from home to say he's wanted to take somebody's place in a cricket match, and it starts at two. How he is going to see the ball after all the champagne he put away last night heaven only knows! I'm feeling a bit weak in the legs, but slept like a top. Frith says Maxim was down to an early breakfast, and there's now no sign of him! So please give him our love, and many thanks to you both for our evening, which we thoroughly enjoyed. Don't think any more about the dress.* (This last was heavily underlined.) *Yours affectionately, Bee,"* and a postscript, *"You must both come over and see us soon."*

She had scribbled nine-thirty a.m. at the top of the paper, and it was now nearly half-past eleven. They had been gone about two hours. They would be home by now, Beatrice with her suit-case unpacked, going out into her garden and taking up her ordinary routine, and Giles preparing for his match, renewing the whipping on his bat.

In the afternoon Beatrice would change into a cool frock and a shady hat and watch Giles play cricket. They would have tea afterwards in a tent, Giles very hot and red in the face, Beatrice laughing and talking to her friends. "Yes, we went over for the dance at Manderley, it was great fun. I wonder Giles was able to run a yard." Smiling at Giles, patting him on the back. They were both middle-aged and unromantic. They had been married for twenty years and had a grown-up son who was going to Oxford. They were very happy. Their marriage was a success. It had not failed after three months as mine had done.

I could not go on sitting in my bedroom any longer. The maids would want to come and do the room. Perhaps Clarice would not have noticed about Maxim's bed after all. I rumpled it, to make it look as though he had slept there. I did not want the housemaids to know, if Clarice had not told them.

I had a bath and dressed, and went downstairs. The men had taken up the floor already in the hall and the flowers had been carried away. The music stands were gone from the gallery. The band must have caught an early train. The gardeners were sweeping the lawns and the drive clear of the spent fireworks. Soon there would be no trace left of the fancy dress ball at Manderley. How long the preparations had seemed, and how short and swift the clearance now.

I remembered the salmon lady standing by the drawing-room door with her plate of chicken, and it seemed to me a thing I must have fancied, or something that had happened very long ago. Robert was polishing the table in the dining-room. He was normal again, stolid, dull, not the fey excited creature of the past few weeks.

"Good morning, Robert," I said.

"Good morning, Madam."

"Have you seen Mr. de Winter anywhere?"

"He went out soon after breakfast, Madam, before Major and Mrs. Lacy were down. He has not been in since."

"You don't know where he went?"

"No, Madam, I could not say."

I wandered back again into the hall. I went through the drawing-room to the morning-room. Jasper rushed at me and licked my hands in a frenzy of delight as if I had been away for a long time. He had spent the evening on Clarice's bed and I had not seen him since tea-time yesterday. Perhaps the hours had been as long for him as they had for me.

I picked up the telephone and asked for the number of the estate office. Perhaps Maxim was with Frank. I felt I must speak to him, even if it was only for two minutes. I must explain to him that I had not meant to do what I had done last night. Even if I never spoke to him again. I must tell him that. The clerk answered the telephone, and told me that Maxim was not there.

"Mr. Crawley is here, Mrs. de Winter," said the clerk, "would you speak to him?" I would have refused, but he gave me no chance, and before I could put down the receiver I heard Frank's voice.

"Is anything the matter?" It was a funny way to begin a conversation. The thought flashed through my mind. He did not say good morning, or did you sleep well? Why did he ask if something was the matter?

"Frank, it's me," I said, "where's Maxim?"

"I don't know, I haven't seen him. He's not been in this morning."

"Not been to the office?"

"No."

"Oh! Oh, well, it doesn't matter."

"Did you see him at breakfast?" said Frank.

"No, I did not get up."

"How did he sleep?"

I hesitated, Frank was the only person I did not mind knowing. "He did not come to bed last night."

There was silence at the other end of the line, as though Frank was thinking hard for an answer.

"Oh," he said at last, very slowly. "Oh, I see," and then, after a minute, "I was afraid something like that would happen."

"Frank," I said desperately, "what did he say last night when everyone had gone? What did you all do?"

"I had a sandwich with Giles and Mrs. Lacy," said Frank. "Maxim did not come. He made some excuse and went into the library. I came back home almost at once. Perhaps Mrs. Lacy can tell you."

"She's gone," I said, "they went after breakfast. She sent up a note. She had not seen Maxim, she said."

"Oh," said Frank. I did not like it. I did not like the way he said it. It was sharp, ominous.

"Where do you think he's gone?" I said.

"I don't know," said Frank, "perhaps he's gone for a walk." It was the sort of voice doctors used to relatives at a nursing-home when they came to enquire.

"Frank, I must see him," I said. "I've got to explain about last night."

Frank did not answer. I could picture his anxious face, the lines on his forehead.

"Maxim thinks I did it on purpose," I said, my voice breaking in spite of myself, and the tears that had blinded me last night and I had not shed came coursing down my cheeks sixteen hours too late. "Maxim thinks I did it as a joke, a beastly damnable joke!"

"No," said Frank. "No."

"He does, I tell you. You didn't see his eyes, as I did. You didn't stand beside him all the evening, watching him, as I did. He didn't speak to me, Frank. He never looked at me again. We stood there together the whole evening and we never spoke to one another."

"There was no chance," said Frank. "All those people. Of course I saw, don't you think I know Maxim well enough for that? Look here . . ."

"I don't blame him," I interrupted. "If he believes I played that vile hideous joke he has a right to think what he likes of me, and never talk to me again, never see me again."

"You mustn't talk like that," said Frank. "You don't know what you're saying. Let me come up and see you. I think I can explain."

What was the use of Frank coming to see me, and us sitting in the morning-room together, Frank smoothing me down, Frank being tactful, Frank being kind? I did not want kindness from anybody now. It was too late.

"No," I said. "No, I don't want to go over it and over it again. It's happened, it can't be altered now. Perhaps it's a good thing, it's made me realise something I ought to have known before, that I ought to have suspected when I married Maxim."

"What do you mean?" said Frank.

His voice was sharp, queer. I wondered why it should matter to him about Maxim not loving me. Why did he not want me to know?

"About him and Rebecca," I said, and as I said her name it sounded strange and sour like a forbidden word, a relief to me no longer, not a pleasure, but hot and shaming as a sin confessed.

Frank did not answer for a moment. I heard him draw in his breath at the other end of the wire.

"What do you mean?" he said again, shorter and sharper than before. "What do you mean?"

"He doesn't love me, he loves Rebecca," I said. "He's never forgotten her, he thinks about her still, night and day. He's never loved me, Frank. It's always Rebecca, Rebecca, Rebecca."

I heard Frank give a startled cry but I did not care how much I shocked him now. "Now you know how I feel," I said, "now you understand."

"Look here," he said, "I've got to come and see you, I've got to, do you hear? It's vitally important, I can't talk to you down the telephone. Mrs. de Winter? Mrs. de Winter?"

I slammed down the receiver, and got up from the writing-desk. I did not want to see Frank. He could not help me over this. No one could help me but myself. My face was red and blotchy from crying. I walked about the room biting the corner of my handkerchief, tearing at the edge.

The feeling was strong within me that I should never see Maxim again. It was certainty, born of some strange instinct. He had gone away and would not come back. I knew in my heart that Frank believed this too and would not admit it to me on the telephone. He did not want to frighten me. If I rang him up again at the office now I should find that he had gone. The clerk would say "Mr. Crawley has just gone out, Mrs. de Winter," and I could see Frank, hatless, climbing into his small, shabby Morris, driving off in search of Maxim.

I went and stared out of the window at the little clearing where the satyr played his pipes. The rhododendrons were all over now. They would not bloom again for another year. The tall shrubs looked dark and drab now that the colour had gone. A fog was rolling up from the sea, and I could not see the woods beyond the bank. It was very hot, very oppressive. I could imagine our guests of last night saying to one another, "What a good thing this fog kept off for yesterday, we should never have seen the fireworks." I went out of the morning-room and through the drawing-room to the terrace. The sun had gone in now behind a wall of mist. It was as though a blight had fallen upon Manderley taking the sky away and the light of the day. One of the gardeners passed me with a barrow full of bits of paper, and litter, and the skins of fruit left on the lawns by the people last night.

"Good morning," I said.

"Good morning, Madam."

"I'm afraid the ball last night has made a lot of work for you," I said.

"That's all right, Madam," he said. "I think everyone enjoyed themselves good and hearty, and that's the main thing, isn't it?"

"Yes, I suppose so," I said.

He looked across the lawns to the clearing in the woods where the valley sloped to the sea. The dark trees loomed thin and indistinct.

"It's coming up very thick," he said.

"Yes," I said.

"A good thing it wasn't like this last night," he said.

"Yes," I said.

He waited a moment, and then he touched his cap and went off trundling his barrow. I went across the lawns to the edge of the woods. The mist in the trees had turned to moisture and dripped upon my bare head like a thin rain. Jasper stood by my feet dejected, his tail downcast, his pink tongue hanging from his mouth. The clammy oppression of the day made him listless and heavy. I could hear the sea from where I stood, sullen and slow, as it broke in the coves below the woods. The white fog rolled on past me towards the house smelling of damp salt and sea-weed. I put my hand on Jasper's coat. It was wringing wet. When I looked back at the house I could not see the chimneys or the contour of the walls, I could only see the vague substance of the house, the windows in the west wing, and the flower tubs on the terrace. The shutter had been pulled aside from the window of the large bedroom in the west wing, and someone was standing there, looking down upon the lawns. The figure was shadowy and indistinct and for one moment of shock and fear I believed it to be Maxim. Then the figure moved, I saw the arm reach up to fold the shutter, and I knew it was Mrs. Danvers. She had been watching me then as I stood at the edge of the woods bathed in that white wall of fog. She had seen me walk slowly from the terrace to the lawns. She may have listened to my conversation with Frank on the telephone from the connecting line in her own room. She would know that Maxim had not been with me last night. She would have heard my voice, known about my tears. She knew the part I had played through the long hours, standing by Maxim's side in my blue dress at the bottom of the stairs, and that he had not looked at me nor spoken to me. She knew because she had meant it to happen. This was her triumph, hers and Rebecca's.

I thought of her as I had seen her last night watching me through the open door to the west wing, and that diabolical smile on her white skull's face, and I remembered that she was a living breathing woman like myself, she was made of flesh and blood. She was not dead, like Rebecca. I could speak to her, but I could not speak to Rebecca.

I walked back across the lawns on sudden impulse to the house. I went through the hall and up the great stairs, I turned in under the archway by the gallery, I passed through the door to the west wing, and so along the dark silent corridor to Rebecca's room. I turned the handle of the door and went inside.

Mrs. Danvers was still standing by the window, and the shutter was folded back.

"Mrs. Danvers," I said. "Mrs. Danvers." She turned to look at me, and I saw her eyes were red and swollen with crying, even as mine were, and there were dark shadows in her white face.

"What is it?" she said, and her voice was thick and muffled from the tears she had shed, even as mine had been.

I had not expected to find her so. I had pictured her smiling as she had smiled last night, cruel and evil. Now she was none of these things, she was an old woman who was ill and tired.

I hesitated, my hand still on the knob of the open door, and I did not know what to say to her now or what to do.

She went on staring at me with those red, swollen eyes and I could not answer her. "I left the menu on the desk as usual," she said. "Do you want something changed?" Her words gave me courage and I left the door and came to the middle of the room.

"Mrs. Danvers," I said, "I have not come to talk about the menu. You know that, don't you?"

She did not answer me. Her left hand opened and shut.

"You've done what you wanted, haven't you?" I said, "you meant this to happen, didn't you? Are you pleased now, are you happy?"

She turned her head away, and looked out of the window as she had done when I first came into the room. "Why did you ever come here?" she said. "Nobody wanted you at Manderley. We were all right until you came. Why did not you stay where you were out in France?"

"You seem to forget I love Mr. de Winter," I said.

"If you loved him you would never have married him," she said.

I did not know what to say. The situation was mad, unreal. She kept talking in that choked muffled way with her head turned from me.

"I thought I hated you but I don't now," she said, "it seems to have spent itself, all the feeling I had."

"Why should you hate me?" I asked, "what have I ever done to you that you should hate me?"

"You tried to take Mrs. de Winter's place," she said.

Still she would not look at me. She stood there sullen, her head turned from me. "I had nothing changed," I said. "Manderley went on as it had always been. I gave no orders, I left everything to you. I would have been friends with you, if you had let me, but you set yourself against me from the first. I saw it in your face, the moment I shook hands with you."

She did not answer, and her hand kept opening and shutting against her dress. "Many people marry twice, men and women," I said. "There are thousands of second marriages taking place every day. You talk as though my marrying Mr. de Winter was a crime, a sacrilege against the dead. Haven't we as much right to be happy as anyone else?"

"Mr. de Winter is not happy," she said, turning to look at me at last, "any fool can see that. You have only to look at his eyes. He's still in hell, and he's looked like that ever since she died."

"It's not true," I said. "It's not true. He was happy when we were in France together, he was younger, much younger, and laughing and gay."

"Well, he's a man isn't he?" she said. "No man denies himself on a honeymoon does he? Mr. de Winter's not forty-six yet."

She laughed contemptuously, and shrugged her shoulders.

"How dare you speak to me like that, how dare you?" I said.

I was not afraid of her any more. I went up to her, shook her by the arm. "You made me wear that dress last night," I said, "I should never have thought of it but for you. You did it because you wanted to hurt Mr. de Winter, you wanted to make him suffer. Hasn't he suffered enough without your playing that vile hideous joke upon him? Do you think his agony and pain will bring Mrs. de Winter back again?"

She shook herself clear of me, the angry colour flooded her dead white face. "What do I care for his suffering?" she said, "he's never cared about mine. How do you think I've liked it, watching you sit in her place, walk in her footsteps, touch the things that were hers? What do you think it's meant to me all these months knowing that you wrote at her desk in the morning-room, using the very pen that she used, speaking down the house telephone where she used to speak, every morning of her life to me, ever since she first came to Manderley. What do you think it meant to me to hear Frith and Robert and the rest of the servants talking about you as 'Mrs. de Winter?' 'Mrs. de Winter has gone out for a walk.' 'Mrs. de Winter wants the car this afternoon at three o'clock.' 'Mrs. de Winter won't be in to tea till five o'clock.' And all the while my Mrs. de Winter, my lady with her smile and her lovely face and brave ways, the real Mrs. de Winter, lying dead and cold and forgotten in the church crypt. If he suffers then he deserves to suffer, marrying a young girl like you not ten months afterwards. Well, he's paying for it now, isn't he? I've seen his face, I've seen his eyes. He's made his own hell and there's no one but himself to thank for it. He knows she sees him, he knows she comes by night and watches him. And she doesn't come kindly, not she, not my lady. She was never one to stand mute and still and be wronged. 'I'll see them in hell, Danny,' she'd say, 'I'll see them in hell first.' 'That's right, my dear,' I'd tell her, 'no one will put upon you. You were born into this world to take what you could out of it,' and she did, she didn't care, she wasn't afraid. She had all the courage and the spirit of a boy, had my Mrs. de Winter. She ought to have been a boy, I often told her that. I had the care of her as a child. You knew that, didn't you?"

"No!" I said, "no. Mrs. Danvers, what's the use of all this? I don't want to hear any more, I don't want to know. Haven't I got feelings as well as you? Can't you understand what it means to me, to hear her mentioned, to stand here and listen while you tell me about her?"

She did not hear me, she went on raving like a madwoman, a fanatic, her long fingers twisting and tearing the black stuff of her dress.

"She was lovely then," she said. "Lovely as a picture, men turning to stare at her when she passed, and she not twelve years old. She knew then, she used to wink at me like the little devil she was. 'I'm going to be a beauty, aren't I, Danny?' she said, and 'We'll see about that, my love, we'll see about that,' I told her. She had all the knowledge then of a grown person, she'd enter into conversation with men and women as clever and full of tricks as someone of eighteen. She twisted her father round her little finger, and she'd have done the same with her mother, had she lived. Spirit, you couldn't beat my lady for spirit. She drove a four-in-hand on her fourteenth birthday, and her cousin, Mr. Jack, got up on the box beside her and tried to take the reins from her hands. They fought it out there together, for three minutes, like a couple of wild cats, and the horses galloping to glory. She won though, my lady won. She cracked her whip over his head and down he came, head-over-heels, cursing and laughing. They were a pair, I tell you, she and Mr. Jack. They sent him in the Navy, but he wouldn't stand the discipline, and I don't blame him. He had too much spirit to obey orders, like my lady."

I watched her, fascinated, horrified; a queer ecstatic smile was on her lips making her older than ever, making her skull's face vivid and real. "No one got the better of her, never, never," she said. "She did what she liked, she lived as she liked. She had the strength of a little lion too. I remember her at sixteen getting up on one of her father's horses, a big brute of an animal too, that the groom said was too hot for her to ride. She stuck to him, all right. I can see her now, with her hair flying out behind her, slashing at him, drawing blood, digging the spurs into his side, and when she got off his back he was trembling all over, full of froth and blood. 'That will teach him, won't it, Danny?' she said, and walked off to wash her hands as cool as you please. And that's how she went at life, when she grew up. I saw her, I was with her. She cared for nothing and for no one. And then she was beaten in the end. But it wasn't a man, it wasn't a woman. The sea got her. The sea was too strong for her. The sea got her in the end."

She broke off, her mouth working strangely, and dragging at the corners. She began to cry noisily, harshly, her mouth open and her eyes dry.

"Mrs. Danvers," I said. "Mrs. Danvers." I stood before her helplessly, not knowing what to do. I mistrusted her no longer, I was afraid of her no more, but the sight of her sobbing there, dry-eyed, made me shudder, made me ill. "Mrs. Danvers," I said, "you're not well, you ought to be in bed. Why don't you go to your room and rest? Why don't you go to bed?"

She turned on me fiercely. "Leave me alone, can't you?" she said. "What's it to do with you if I show my grief? I'm not ashamed of it, I don't shut myself up in my room to cry. I don't walk up and down, up and down, in my room like Mr. de Winter, with the door locked on me."

"What do you mean?" I said. "Mr. de Winter does not do that."

"He did," she said, "after she died. Up and down, up and down, in the library. I heard him. I watched him too, through the key-hole, more than once. Backwards and forwards, like an animal in a cage."

"I don't want to hear," I said. "I don't want to know."

"And then you say you made him happy on his honeymoon," she said, "made him happy, you, a young ignorant girl, young enough to be his daughter. What do you know about life, what do you know about men? You come here and think you can take Mrs. de Winter's place. You. You take my lady's place. Why, even the servants laughed at you when you came to Manderley. Even the little scullery-maid you met in the back passage there on your first morning. I wonder what Mr. de Winter thought when he got you back here at Manderley, after his precious honeymoon was over. I wonder what he thought when he saw you sitting at the dining-room table for the first time."

"You'd better stop this, Mrs. Danvers," I said; "you'd better go to your room."

"Go to my room," she mimicked, "go to my room. The mistress of the house thinks I had better go to my room. And after that, what then? You'll go running to Mr. de Winter and saying, 'Mrs. Danvers has been unkind to me. Mrs. Danvers has been rude.' You'll go running to him like you did before when Mr. Jack came to see me."

"I never told him," I said.

"That's a lie," she said, "who else told him, if you didn't? No one else was here. Frith and Robert were out, and none of the other servants knew. I made up my mind then I'd teach you a lesson, and him too. Let him suffer, I say. What do I care? What's his suffering to me? Why shouldn't I see Mr. Jack here at Manderley? He's the only link I have left now with Mrs. de Winter. 'I'll not have him here,' he said, 'I'm warning you, it's the last time.' He's not forgotten to be jealous, has he?"

I remembered crouching in the gallery when the library door was open. I remembered Maxim's voice raised in anger, using the words that Mrs. Danvers had just repeated. Jealous. Maxim jealous. . . .

"He was jealous while she lived, and now he's jealous when she's dead," said Mrs. Danvers. "He forbids Mr. Jack the house now like he did then. That shows you he's not forgotten her, doesn't it? Of course he was jealous. So was I. So was everyone who knew her. She didn't care. She only laughed. 'I shall live as I please, Danny,' she told me, 'and the whole world won't stop me.' A man had only to look at her once and be mad about her. I've seen them here, staying in the house, men she'd meet up in London and bring for weekends. She would take them bathing from the boat, she would have a picnic supper at her cottage in the cove. They made love to her of course, who would not? She laughed, she would come back and tell me what they had said, and what they'd done. She did not mind, it was like a game to her. Like a game. Who wouldn't be jealous? They were all jealous, all mad for her. Mr. de Winter, Mr. Jack, Mr. Crawley, everyone who knew her, everyone who came to Manderley."

"I don't want to know," I said. "I don't want to know."

Mrs. Danvers came close to me, she put her face near to mine. "It's no use, is it?" she said. "You'll never get the better of her. She's still mistress here, even if she is dead. She's the real Mrs. de Winter, not you. It's you that's the shadow and the ghost. It's you that's forgotten and not wanted and pushed aside. Well, why don't you leave Manderley to her? Why don't you go?"

I backed away from her towards the window, my old fear and horror rising up in me again. She took my arm and held it like a vice.

"Why don't you go?" she said. "We none of us want you. He doesn't want you, he never did. He can't forget her. He wants to be alone in the house again, with her. It's you that ought to be lying there in the church crypt, not her. It's you who ought to be dead, not Mrs. de Winter."

She pushed me towards the open window. I could see the terrace below me grey and indistinct in the white wall of fog. "Look down there," she said. "It's easy, isn't it? Why don't you jump? It wouldn't hurt, not to break your neck. It's a quick, kind way. It's not like drowning. Why don't you try it? Why don't you go?"

The fog filled the open window, damp and clammy, it stung my eyes, it clung to my nostrils. I held on to the window-sill with my hands.

"Don't be afraid," said Mrs. Danvers. "I won't push you. I won't stand by you. You can jump of your own accord. What's the use of your staying here at Manderley? You're not happy. Mr. de Winter doesn't love you. There's not much for you to live for, is there? Why don't you jump now and have done with it? Then you won't be unhappy any more."

I could see the flower tubs on the terrace and the blue of the hydrangeas clumped and solid. The paved stones were smooth and grey. They were not jagged and uneven. It was the fog that made them look so far away. They were not far really, the window was not so very high.

"Why don't you jump?" whispered Mrs. Danvers. "Why don't you try?"

The fog came thicker than before and the terrace was hidden from me. I could not see the flower tubs any more, nor the smooth paved stones. There was nothing but the white mist about me, smelling of seaweed dank and chill. The only reality was the window-sill beneath my hands and the grip of Mrs. Danvers on my left arm. If I jumped I should not see the stones rise up to meet me, the fog would hide them from me. The pain would be sharp and sudden as she said. The fall would break my neck. It would not be slow, like drowning. It would soon be over. And Maxim did not love me. Maxim wanted to be alone again, with Rebecca.

"Go on," whispered Mrs. Danvers. "Go on, don't be afraid."

I shut my eyes. I was giddy from staring down at the terrace, and my fingers ached from holding to the ledge. The mist entered my nostrils and lay upon my lips rank and sour. It was stifling, like a blanket, like an anaesthetic. I was beginning to forget about being unhappy, and about loving Maxim. I was beginning to forget Rebecca. Soon I would not have to think about Rebecca any more. . . .

As I relaxed my hands and sighed, the white mist and the silence that was part of it was shattered suddenly, was rent in two by an explosion that shook the window where we stood. The glass shivered in its frame. I opened my eyes. I stared at Mrs. Danvers. The burst was followed by another, and yet a third and fourth. The sound of the explosions stung the air and the birds rose unseen from the woods around the house and made an echo with their clamour.

"What is it?" I said stupidly. "What has happened?"

Mrs. Danvers relaxed her grip upon my arm. She stared out of the window into the fog. "It's the rockets," she said; "there must be a ship gone ashore there in the bay."

We listened, staring into the white fog together. And then we heard the sound of footsteps running on the terrace beneath us.

CHAPTER NINETEEN

It was Maxim. I could not see him but I could hear his voice. He was shouting for Frith as he ran. I heard Frith answer from the hall and come out on to the terrace. Their figures loomed out of the mist beneath us.

"She's ashore all right," said Maxim. "I was watching her from the headland and I saw her come right into the bay, and head for the reef. They'll never shift her, not with these tides. She must have mistaken the bay for Kerrith harbour. It's like a wall out there, in the bay. Tell them in the house to stand by with food and drink in case these fellows want anything, and ring through to the office to Mr. Crawley and tell him what's happened. I'm going back to the cove to see if I can do anything. Get me some cigarettes, will you?"

Mrs. Danvers drew back from the window. Her face was expressionless once more, the cold white mask that I knew.

"We had better go down," she said, "Frith will be looking for me to make arrangements. Mr. de Winter may bring the men back to the house as he said. Be careful of your hands, I'm going to shut the window." I stepped back into the room still dazed and stupid, not sure of myself or of her. I watched her close the window and fasten the shutters, and draw the curtains in their place.

"It's a good thing there is no sea running," she said, "there wouldn't have been much chance for them then. But on a day like this there's no danger. The owners will lose their ship though if she's run on the reef as Mr. de Winter said."

She glanced round the room to make certain that nothing was disarranged or out of place. She straightened the cover on the double bed. Then she went to the door and held it open for me. "I will tell them in the kitchen to serve cold lunch in the dining-room after all," she said, "and then it won't matter what time you come for it. Mr. de Winter may not want to rush back at one o'clock if he's busy down there in the cove."

I stared at her blankly and then passed out of the open door, stiff and wooden like a dummy.

"When you see Mr. de Winter, Madam, will you tell him it will be quite all right if he wants to bring the men back from the ship. There will be a hot meal ready for them any time."

"Yes," I said. "Yes, Mrs. Danvers."

She turned her back on me and went along the corridor to the Service staircase, a weird gaunt figure in her black dress, the skirt just sweeping the ground like the full, wide skirts of thirty years ago. Then she turned the corner of the corridor and disappeared.

I walked slowly along the passage to the door by the archway, my mind still blunt and slow as though I had just woken from a long sleep. I pushed through the door and went down the stairs with no set purpose before me. Frith was crossing the hall towards the dining-room. When he saw me he stopped, and waited until I came down into the hall.

"Mr. de Winter was in a few moments ago, Madam," he said. "He took some cigarettes, and then went back again to the beach. It appears there is a ship gone ashore."

"Yes," I said.

"Did you hear the rockets, Madam?" said Frith.

"Yes, I heard the rockets," I said.

"I was in the pantry with Robert and we both thought at first that one of the gardeners had let off a firework left over from last night," said Frith, "and I said to Robert, 'What do they want to do that for in this weather? Why don't they keep them for the kiddies on Saturday night?' And then the next one came, and then the third. 'That's not fireworks,' says Robert, 'that's a ship in distress.' 'I believe you're right,' I said, and I went out to the hall and there was Mr. de Winter calling me from the terrace."

"Yes," I said.

"Well, it's hardly to be wondered at in this fog, Madam. That's what I said to Robert just now. It's difficult to find your way on the road, let alone on the water."

"Yes," I said.

"If you want to catch Mr. de Winter he went straight across the lawn only two minutes ago," said Frith.

"Thank you, Frith," I said.

I went out on to the terrace. I could see the trees taking shape beyond the lawns. The fog was lifting, it was rising in little clouds to the sky above. It whirled above my head in wreaths of smoke. I looked up at the windows above my head. They were tightly closed, and the shutters were fastened. They looked as though they would never open, never be thrown wide.

It was by the large window in the centre that I had stood five minutes before. How high it seemed above my head, how lofty and remote. The stones were hard and solid under my feet. I looked down at my feet and then up again to the shuttered window, and as I did so I became aware suddenly that my head was swimming and I felt hot. A little trickle of perspiration ran down the back of my neck. Black dots jumped about in the air in front of me. I went into the hall again and sat down on a chair. My hands were quite wet. I sat very still, holding my knees.

"Frith," I called, "Frith, are you in the dining-room?"

"Yes, Madam?" He came out at once, and crossed the hall towards me.

"Don't think me very odd, Frith, but I rather think I'd like a small glass of brandy."

"Certainly, Madam."

I went on holding my knees and sitting very still. He came back with a liqueur glass on a silver salver.

"Do you feel a trifle unwell, Madam?" said Frith. "Would you like me to call Clarice?"

"No, I'll be all right, Frith," I said. "I felt a bit hot, that's all."

"It's a very warm morning, Madam. Very warm indeed. Oppressive, one might almost say."

"Yes, Frith. Very oppressive."

I drank the brandy and put the glass back on the silver salver.

"Perhaps the sound of those rockets alarmed you," said Frith, "they went off so very sudden."

"Yes, they did," I said.

"And what with the hot morning and standing about all last night you are not perhaps feeling quite like yourself, Madam," said Frith.

"No, perhaps not," I said.

"Will you lie down for half-an-hour? It's quite cool in the library."

"No. No, I think I'll go out in a moment or two. Don't bother, Frith."

"No. Very good, Madam."

He went away and left me alone in the hall. It was quiet sitting there, quiet and cool. All trace of the party had been cleared away. It might never have happened. The hall was as it had always been, grey and silent and austere, with the portraits and the weapons on the wall. I could scarcely believe that last night I had stood there in my blue dress at the bottom of the stairs, shaking hands with five hundred people. I could not believe that there had been music stands in the minstrels' gallery, and a band playing there, a man with a fiddle, a man with a drum. I got up and went out on to the terrace again.

The fog was rising, lifting to the tops of the trees. I could see the woods at the end of the lawns. Above my head a pale sun tried to penetrate the heavy sky. It was hotter than ever. Oppressive, as Frith had said. A bee hummed by me in search of scent, bumbling, noisy, and then creeping inside a flower was suddenly silent. On the grass banks above the lawns the gardener started his mowing machine. A startled linnet fled from the whirring blades towards the rose-garden. The gardener bent to the handles of the machine and walked slowly along the bank scattering the short-tipped grass and the pin-point daisy heads. The smell of the sweet warm grass came towards me on the air, and the sun shone down upon me full and strong from out of the white mist. I whistled for Jasper but he did not come. Perhaps he had followed Maxim when he went down to the beach. I glanced at my watch. It was after half-past twelve, nearly twenty to one. This time yesterday Maxim and I were standing with Frank in the little garden in front of his house, waiting for his housekeeper to serve lunch.

Twenty-four hours ago. They were teasing me, baiting me about my dress. "You'll both get the surprise of your lives," I had said.

I felt sick with shame at the memory of my words. And then I realised for the first time that Maxim had not gone away as I had feared. The voice I had heard on the terrace was calm and practical. The voice I knew. Not the voice of last night when I stood at the head of the stairs. Maxim had not gone away. He was down there in the cove somewhere. He was himself, normal and sane. He had just been for a walk as Frank had said. He had been on the headland, he had seen the ship closing in towards the shore. All my fears were without foundation. Maxim was safe. Maxim was all right. I had just experienced something that was degrading and horrible and mad, something that I did not fully understand even now, that I had no wish to remember, that I wanted to bury forever more deep in the shadows of my mind with the old forgotten terrors of childhood; but even this did not matter as long as Maxim was all right.

Then I, too, went down the steep twisting path through the dark woods to the beach below.

The fog had almost gone and when I came to the cove I could see the ship at once, lying about two miles off-shore with her bows pointed towards the cliffs. I went along the breakwater and stood at the end of it, leaning against the rounded wall. There was a crowd of people on the cliffs already who must have walked along the coast-guard path from Kerrith. The cliffs and the headland were part of Manderley but the public had always used the right-of-way along the cliffs. Some of them were scrambling down the cliff face to get a closer view of the stranded ship. She lay at an awkward angle, her stern tilted, and there were a number of rowing-boats already pulling round her. The life-boat was standing off. I saw someone stand up in her and shout through a megaphone. I could not hear what he was saying. It was still misty out in the bay, and I could not see the horizon. Another motor-boat chugged into the light with some men aboard. The motor-boat was dark grey. I could see someone in uniform. That would be the harbour-master from Kerrith, and the Lloyd's agent with him. Another motor-boat followed, a party of holiday-makers from Kerrith aboard. They circled round and round the stranded steamer chatting excitedly. I could hear their voices echoing across the still water.

I left the breakwater and the cove and climbed up the path over the cliffs towards the rest of the people. I did not see Maxim anywhere. Frank was there, talking to one of the coast-guards. I hung back when I saw him, momentarily embarrassed. Barely an hour ago I had been crying to him, down the telephone. I was not sure what I ought to do. He saw me at once and waved his hand. I went over to him and the coast-guard. The coast-guard knew me.

"Come to see the fun, Mrs. de Winter?" he said smiling. "I'm afraid it will be a hard job. The tugs may shift her but I doubt it. She's hard and fast where she is on that ledge."

"What will they do?" I said.

"They'll send a diver down directly to see if she's broken her back," he replied. "There's the fellow there in the red stocking cap. Like to see through these glasses?"

I took his glasses and looked at the ship. I could see a group of men staring over her stern. One of them was pointing at something. The man in the life-boat was still shouting through the megaphone.

The harbour-master from Kerrith had joined the group of men in the stern of the stranded ship. The diver in his stocking cap was sitting in the grey motor-boat belonging to the harbour-master.

The pleasure-boat was still circling round the ship. A woman was standing up taking a snapshot. A group of gulls had settled on the water and were crying foolishly, hoping for scraps.

I gave the glasses back to the coast-guard.

"Nothing seems to be happening," I said.

"They'll send him down directly," said the coast-guard. "They'll argue a bit first no doubt like all foreigners. Here come the tugs."

"They'll never do it," said Frank. "Look at the angle she's lying at. It's much shallower there than I thought."

"That reef runs out quite a way," said the coast-guard, "you don't notice it in the ordinary way, going over that piece of water in a small boat. But a ship with her depth would touch all right."

"I was down in the first cove by the valley when they fired the rockets," said Frank. "I could scarcely see three yards in front of me where I was. And then the things went off out of the blue."

I thought how alike people were in a moment of common interest. Frank was Frith all over again, giving his version of the story, as though it mattered, as though we cared. I knew that he had gone down to the beach to look for Maxim. I knew that he had been frightened, as I had been. And now all this was forgotten and put aside, our conversation down the telephone, our mutual anxiety, his insistence that he must see me. All because a ship had gone ashore in the fog.

A small boy came running up to us. "Will the sailors be drowned?" he asked.

"Not them. They're all right, sonny," said the coast-guard. "The sea's as flat as the back of my hand. No one's going to be hurt this time."

"If it had happened last night we should never have heard them," said Frank. "We must have let off more than fifty rockets at our show, besides all the smaller things."

"We'd have heard all right," said the coast-guard. "We'd have seen the flash and known the direction. There's the diver, Mrs. de Winter. See him putting on his helmet?"

"I want to see the diver," said the small boy.

"There he is," said Frank, bending and pointing, "that chap there putting on the helmet. They're going to lower him into the water."

"Won't he be drowned?" said the child.

"Divers don't drown," said the coast-guard. "They have air pumped into them all the time. Watch him disappear. There he goes."

The surface of the water was disturbed a minute and then was clear again. "He's gone," said the small boy.

"Where's Maxim?" I said.

"He's taken one of the crew into Kerrith," said Frank, "the fellow lost his head and jumped for it apparently when the ship struck. We found him clinging on to one of the rocks here under the cliff. He was soaked to the skin of course and shaking like a jelly. Couldn't speak a word of English of course. Maxim went down to him, and found him bleeding like a pig from a scratch on the rocks. He spoke to him in German. Then he hailed one of the motor-boats from Kerrith that was hanging around like a hungry shark, and he's gone off with him to get him bandaged by a doctor. If he's lucky he'll just catch old Phillips sitting down to lunch."

"When did he go?" I said.

"He went just before you turned up," said Frank, "about five minutes ago. I wonder you didn't see the boat. He was sitting in the stern with this German fellow."

"He must have gone while I was climbing up the cliff," I said.

"Maxim is splendid at anything like this," said Frank. "He always gives a hand if he can. You'll find he will invite the whole crew back to Manderley, and feed them, and give them beds into the bargain."

"That's right," said the coast-guard. "He'd give the coat off his back for any of his own people, I know that. I wish there was more like him in the county."

"Yes, we could do with them," said Frank.

We went on staring at the ship. The tugs were standing off still, but the life-boat had turned and gone back towards Kerrith.

"It's not their turn to-day," said the coast-guard.

"No," said Frank, "and I don't think it's a job for the tugs either. It's the ship-breaker who's going to make money this time."

The gulls wheeled overhead, mewing like hungry cats; some of them settled on the ledges of the cliff, while others, bolder, rode the surface of the water beside the ship.

The coast-guard took off his cap and mopped his forehead.

"Seems kind of airless, doesn't it?" he said.

"Yes," I said.

The pleasure-boat with the camera people went chugging off towards Kerrith. "They've got fed up," said the coast-guard.

"I don't blame them," said Frank. "I don't suppose anything will happen for hours. The diver will have to make his report before they try and shift her."

"That's right," said the coast-guard.

"I don't think there's much sense in hanging about here," said Frank, "we can't do anything. I want my lunch."

I did not say anything. He hesitated. I felt his eyes upon me.

"What are you going to do?" he said.

"I think I shall stay here a bit," I said. "I can have lunch any time. It's cold. It doesn't matter. I want to see what the diver's going to do." Somehow I could not face Frank just at the moment. I wanted to be alone, or with someone I did not know, like the coast-guard.

"You won't see anything," said Frank; "there won't be anything to see. Why not come back and have some lunch with me?"

"No," I said. "No, really . . ."

"Oh, well," said Frank, "you know where to find me if you do want me. I shall be at the office all the afternoon."

"All right," I said.

He nodded to the coast-guard and went off down the cliff towards the cove. I wondered if I had offended him. I could not help it. All these things would be settled some day, one day. So much seemed to have happened since I spoke to him on the telephone and I did not want to think about anything any more. I just wanted to sit there on the cliff and stare at the ship.

"He's a good sort, Mr. Crawley," said the coast-guard.

"Yes," I said.

"He'd give his right hand for Mr. de Winter too," he said.

"Yes, I think he would," I said.

The small boy was still hopping round on the grass in front of us.

"When's the diver coming up again?" he said.

"Not yet, sonny," said the coast-guard.

A woman in a pink striped frock and a hair-net came across the grass towards us. "Charlie? Charlie? Where are you?" she called.

"Here's your mother coming to give you what-for," said the coast-guard.

"I've seen the diver, Mum," shouted the boy.

The woman nodded to us and smiled. She did not know me. She was a holiday-maker from Kerrith. "The excitement all seems to be over, doesn't it?" she said; "they are saying down on the cliff there the ship will be there for days."

"They're waiting for the diver's report," said the coast-guard.

"I don't know how they get them to go down under the water like that," said the woman, "they ought to pay them well."

"They do that," said the coast-guard.

"I want to be a diver, Mum," said the small boy.

"You must ask your Daddy, dear," said the woman, laughing at us. "It's a lovely spot up here, isn't it?" she said to me. "We brought a picnic lunch never thinking it would turn foggy and we'd have a wreck into the bargain. We were just thinking of going back to Kerrith when the rockets went off under our noses it seemed. I nearly jumped out of my skin. 'Why, whatever's that?' I said to my husband. 'That's a distress signal,' he said, 'let's stop and see the fun.' There's no dragging him away, he's as bad as my little boy. I don't see anything in it myself."

"No, there's not much to see now," said the coast-guard.

"Those are nice-looking woods over there, I suppose they're private," said the woman.

The coast-guard coughed awkwardly, and glanced at me. I began eating a piece of grass and looked away.

"Yes, that's all private in there," he said.

"My husband says all these big estates will be chopped up in time and bungalows built," said the woman. "I wouldn't mind a nice little bungalow up here facing the sea. I don't know that I'd care for this part of the world in the winter though."

"No, it's very quiet here winter times," said the coast-guard.

I went on chewing my piece of grass. The little boy kept running round in circles. The coast-guard looked at his watch. "Well, I must be getting on," he said, "Good afternoon!" He saluted me, and turned back along the path towards Kerrith. "Come on, Charlie, come and find Daddy," said the woman.

She nodded to me in friendly fashion, and sauntered off to the edge of the cliff, the little boy running at her heels. A thin man in khaki shorts and a striped blazer waved to her. They sat down by a clump of gorse bushes, and the woman began to undo paper packages.

I wished I could lose my own identity and join them. Eat hard-boiled eggs and potted meat sandwiches, laugh rather loudly, enter their conversation, and then wander back with them during the afternoon to Kerrith and paddle on the beach, run races across the stretch of sand, and so to their lodgings and have shrimps for tea. Instead of which I must go back alone through the woods to Manderley and wait for Maxim. And I did not know what we should say to one another, how he would look at me, what would be his voice. I went on sitting there on the cliff. I was not hungry, I did not think about lunch.

More people came and wandered over the cliffs to look at the ship. It made an excitement for the afternoon. There was nobody I knew. They were all holiday-makers from Kerrith. The sea was glassy calm. The gulls no longer wheeled overhead, they had settled on the water a little distance from the ship. More pleasure-boats appeared during the afternoon. It must be a field day for Kerrith boat-men. The diver came up and then went down again. One of the tugs steamed away while the other still stood by. The harbour-master went back in his grey motor-boat, taking some men with him, and the diver who had come to the surface for the second time. The crew of the ship leant against the side throwing scraps to the gulls, while visitors in pleasure-boats rowed slowly round the ship. Nothing happened at all. It was dead low water now, and the ship was heeled at an angle, the propeller showing clean. Little ridges of white cloud formed in the western sky and the sun became pallid. It was still very hot. The woman in the pink striped frock with the little boy got up and wandered off along the path towards Kerrith, the man in the shorts following with the picnic basket.

I glanced at my watch. It was after three o'clock. I got up and went down the hill to the cove. It was quiet and deserted as always. The shingle was dark and grey. The water in the little harbour was glassy like a mirror. My feet made a queer crunching noise as I crossed the shingle. The ridges of white cloud now covered all the sky above my head, and the sun was hidden. When I came to the further side of the cove I saw Ben crouching by a little pool between two rocks scraping winkles into his hand. My shadow fell upon the water as I passed, and he looked up and saw me.

"G'day," he said, his mouth opening in a grin.

"Good afternoon," I said.

He scrambled to his feet and opened a dirty handkerchief he had filled with winkles.

"You eat winkles?" he said.

I did not want to hurt his feelings. "Thank you," I said.

He emptied about a dozen winkles into my hand, and I put them in the two pockets of my skirt. "They'm all right with bread-an'-butter," he said, "you must boil 'em first."

"Yes, all right," I said.

He stood there grinning at me. "Seen the steamer?" he said.

"Yes," I said, "she's gone ashore, hasn't she?"

"Eh?" he said.

"She's run aground," I repeated. "I expect she's got a hole in her bottom."

His face went blank and foolish. "Aye," he said, "she's down there all right. She'll not come back again."

"Perhaps the tugs will get her off when the tide makes," I said.

He did not answer. He was staring out towards the stranded ship. I could see her broadside on from here, the red under-water section showing against the black of the top-sides, and the single funnel

leaning rakishly towards the cliffs beyond. The crew were still leaning over her side feeding the gulls and staring into the water. The
rowing boats were pulling back to Kerrith.

"She's a Dutchman, ain't she?" said Ben.

"I don't know," I said. "German or Dutch."

"She'll break up there where she's to," he said.

"I'm afraid so," I said.

He grinned again, and wiped his nose with the back of his hand.

"She'll break up bit by bit," he said, "she'll not sink like a stone
like the little 'un." He chuckled to himself, picking his nose. I did not
say anything. "The fishes have eaten her up by now, haven't they?"
he said.

"Who?" I said.

He jerked his thumb towards the sea. "Her," he said, "the other
one."

"Fishes don't eat steamers, Ben," I said.

"Eh?" he said. He stared at me, foolish and blank once more.

"I must go home now," I said; "good afternoon."

I left him and walked towards the path through the woods. I did
not look at the cottage. I was aware of it on my right hand, grey and
quiet. I went straight to the path and up through the trees. I paused to
rest halfway and looking through the trees I could still see the
stranded ship leaning towards the shore. The pleasure-boats had all
gone. Even the crew had disappeared below. The ridges of cloud covered the whole sky. A little wind sprang from nowhere and blew into
my face. A leaf fell on to my hand from the tree above. I shivered for
no reason. Then the wind went again, it was hot and sultry as before.
The ship looked desolate there upon her side, with no one on her
decks, and her thin black funnel pointing to the shore. The sea was so
calm that when it broke upon the shingle in the cove it was like a
whisper, hushed and still. I turned once more to the steep path
through the woods, my legs reluctant, my head heavy, a strange sense
of foreboding in my heart.

The house looked very peaceful as I came upon it from the woods
and crossed the lawns. It seemed sheltered and protected, more beautiful than I had ever seen it. Standing there, looking down upon it
from the banks, I realised, perhaps for the first time, with a funny
feeling of bewilderment and pride that it was my home, I belonged
there, and Manderley belonged to me. The trees and the grass and the
flower tubs on the terrace were reflected in the mullioned windows. A
thin column of smoke rose in the air from one of the chimneys. The
new-cut grass on the lawn smelt sweet as hay. A blackbird was sing-

ing on the chestnut tree. A yellow butterfly winged his foolish way before me to the terrace.

I went into the hall and through to the dining-room. My place was still laid, but Maxim's had been cleared away. The cold meat and salad awaited me on the side-board. I hesitated, and then rang the dining-room bell. Robert came in from behind the screen.

"Has Mr. de Winter been in?" I said.

"Yes, Madam," said Robert; "he came in just after two, and had a quick lunch, and then went out again. He asked for you and Frith said he thought you must have gone down to see the ship."

"Did he say when he would be back again?" I asked.

"No, Madam."

"Perhaps he went to the beach by another way," I said; "I may have missed him."

"Yes, Madam," said Robert.

I looked at the cold meat and the salad. I felt empty but not hungry. I did not want cold meat now. "Will you be taking lunch?" said Robert.

"No," I said. "No, you might bring me some tea, Robert, in the library. Nothing like cakes or scones. Just tea and bread-and-butter."

"Yes, Madam."

I went and sat on the window seat in the library. It seemed funny without Jasper. He must have gone with Maxim. The old dog lay asleep in her basket. I picked up *The Times* and turned the pages without reading it. It was queer this feeling of marking time, like sitting in a waiting-room at a dentist's. I knew I should never settle to my knitting or to a book. I was waiting for something to happen, something unforeseen. The horror of my morning and the stranded ship and not having any lunch had all combined to give birth to a latent sense of excitement at the back of my mind that I did not understand. It was as though I had entered into a new phase of my life and nothing would be quite the same again. The girl who had dressed for the fancy dress ball the night before had been left behind. It had all happened a very long time ago. This self who sat on the window seat was new, was different.... Robert brought in my tea, and I ate my bread-and-butter hungrily. He had brought scones as well, and some sandwiches, and an angel cake. He must have thought it derogatory to bring bread-and-butter alone, nor was it Manderley routine. I was glad of the scones and the angel cake. I remembered I had only had cold tea at half-past eleven, and no breakfast. Just after I had drunk my third cup Robert came in again.

"Mr. de Winter is not back yet, is he, Madam?" he said.

"No," I said. "Why? Does someone want him?"

"Yes, Madam," said Robert, "it's Captain Searle, the harbour-master of Kerrith, on the telephone. He wants to know if he can come up and see Mr. de Winter personally."

"I don't know what to say," I said. "He may not be back for ages."

"No, Madam."

"You'd better tell him to ring again at five o'clock," I said. Robert went out of the room and came back again in a few minutes.

"Captain Searle would like to see you, if it would be convenient, Madam," said Robert. "He says the matter is rather urgent. He tried to get Mr. Crawley, but there was no reply."

"Yes, of course I must see him if it's urgent," I said. "Tell him to come along at once if he likes. Has he got a car?"

"Yes, I believe so, Madam."

Robert went out of the room. I wondered what I should say to Captain Searle. His business must be something to do with the stranded ship. I could not understand what concern it was of Maxim's. It would have been different if the ship had gone ashore in the cove. That was Manderley property. They might have to ask Maxim's permission to blast away rocks or whatever it was that was done to move a ship. But the open bay and the ledge of rock under the water did not belong to Maxim. Captain Searle would waste his time talking to me about it all.

He must have got into his car right away after talking to Robert because in less than quarter-of-an-hour he was shown into the room.

He was still in his uniform as I had seen him through the glasses in the early afternoon. I got up from the window seat and shook hands with him. "I'm sorry my husband isn't back yet, Captain Searle," I said; "he must have gone down to the cliffs again, and he went into Kerrith before that. I haven't seen him all day."

"Yes, I heard he'd been to Kerrith but I missed him there," said the harbour-master. "He must have walked back across the cliffs when I was in my boat. And I can't get hold of Mr. Crawley either."

"I'm afraid the ship has disorganised everybody," I said. "I was out on the cliffs and went without my lunch, and I know Mr. Crawley was there earlier on. What will happen to her? Will tugs get her off do you think?"

Captain Searle made a great circle with his hands. "There's a hole that deep in her bottom," he said, "she'll not see Hamburg again. Never mind the ship. Her owner and Lloyd's agent will settle that between them. No, Mrs. de Winter, it's not the ship that's brought me here. Indirectly of course she's the cause of my coming. The fact is,

I've got some news for Mr. de Winter, and I hardly know how to break it to him." He looked at me very straight with his bright blue eyes.

"What sort of news, Captain Searle?"

He brought a large white handkerchief out of his pocket and blew his nose. "Well, Mrs. de Winter, it's not very pleasant for me to tell you either. The last thing I want to do is to cause distress or pain to you and your husband. We're all very fond of Mr. de Winter in Kerrith, you know, and the family has always done a lot of good. It's hard on him and hard on you that we can't let the past lie quiet. But I don't see how we can under the circumstances." He paused, and put his handkerchief back in his pocket. He lowered his voice, although we were alone in the room.

"We sent the diver down to inspect the ship's bottom," he said, "and while he was down there he made a discovery. It appears he found the hole in the ship's bottom and was working round to the other side to see what further damage there was when he came across the hull of a little sailing boat, lying on her side, quite intact and not broken up at all. He's a local man, of course, and he recognised the boat at once. It was the little boat belonging to the late Mrs. de Winter."

My first feeling was one of thankfulness that Maxim was not there to hear. This fresh blow coming swiftly upon my masquerade of the night before was ironic, and rather horrible.

"I'm so sorry," I said slowly, "it's not the sort of thing one expected would happen, is it necessary to tell Mr. de Winter? Couldn't the boat be left there, as it is, it's not doing any harm, is it?"

"It would be left, Mrs. de Winter, in the ordinary way. I'm the last man in the world to want to disturb it. And I'd give anything, as I said before, to spare Mr. de Winter's feelings. But that wasn't all, Mrs. de Winter. My man poked round the little boat and he made another, more important discovery. The cabin door was tightly closed, it was not stove in, and the portlights were closed too. He broke one of the ports with a stone from the sea bed, and looked into the cabin. It was full of water, the sea must have come through some hole in the bottom, there seemed no damage elsewhere. And then he got the fright of his life, Mrs. de Winter."

Captain Searle paused, he looked over his shoulder as though one of the servants might hear him. "There was a body in there, lying on the cabin floor," he said quietly. "It was dissolved of course, there was no flesh on it. But it was a body all right. He saw the head and the limbs. He came up to the surface then and reported it direct to me.

And now you understand, Mrs. de Winter, why I've got to see your husband."

I stared at him, bewildered at first, then shocked, then rather sick.

"She was supposed to be sailing alone," I whispered, "there must have been someone with her then, all the time, and no one ever knew?"

"It looks like it," said the harbour-master.

"Who could it have been?" I said. "Surely relatives would know if anyone had been missing? There was so much about it at the time, it was all in the papers. Why should one of them be in the cabin and Mrs. de Winter herself be picked up many miles away, months afterwards?"

Captain Searle shook his head. "I can't tell any more than you," he said. "All we know is that the body is there, and it has got to be reported. There'll be publicity, I'm afraid, Mrs. de Winter. I don't know how we're going to avoid it. It's very hard on you and Mr. de Winter. Here you are, settled down quietly, wanting to be happy, and this has to happen."

I knew now the reason for my sense of foreboding. It was not the stranded ship that was sinister, nor the crying gulls, nor the thin black funnel pointing to the shore. It was the stillness of the black water, and the unknown things that lay beneath. It was the diver going down into those cool quiet depths and stumbling upon Rebecca's boat, and Rebecca's dead companion. He had touched the boat, and looked into the cabin, and all the while I sat on the cliffs and had not known.

"If only we did not have to tell him," I said. "If only we could keep the whole thing from him."

"You know I would if it were possible, Mrs. de Winter," said the harbour-master, "but my personal feelings have to go, in a matter like this. I've got to do my duty. I've got to report that body." He broke off short as the door opened, and Maxim came into the room.

"Hullo," he said, "what's happening? I didn't know you were here, Captain Searle. Is anything the matter?"

I could not stand it any longer. I went out of the room like the coward I was and shut the door behind me. I had not even glanced at Maxim's face. I had the vague impression that he looked tired, untidy, hatless.

I went and stood in the hall by the front door. Jasper was drinking noisily from his bowl. He wagged his tail when he saw me and went on drinking. Then he loped towards me, and stood up, pawing at my dress. I kissed the top of his head and went and sat on the terrace. The moment of crisis had come, and I must face it. My old fears, my diffidence, my shyness, my hopeless sense of inferiority, must be conquered now and thrust aside. If I failed now I should fail forever. There would never be another chance. I prayed for courage in a blind despairing way, and dug my nails into my hands. I sat there for five minutes staring at the green lawns and the flower tubs on the terrace. I heard the sound of a car starting up in the drive. It must be Captain Searle. He had broken his news to Maxim and had gone. I got up from the terrace and went slowly through the hall to the library. I kept turning over in my pockets the winkles that Ben had given me. I clutched them tight in my hands.

Maxim was standing by the window. His back was turned to me. I waited by the door. Still he did not turn round. I took my hands out of my pockets and went and stood beside him. I reached out for his hand and laid it against my cheek. He did not say anything. He went on standing there.

"I'm so sorry," I whispered, "so terribly, terribly sorry." He did not answer. His hand was icy cold. I kissed the back of it, and then the fingers, one by one. "I don't want you to bear this alone," I said. "I want to share it with you. I've grown up, Maxim, in twenty-four hours. I'll never be a child again."

He put his arm round me and pulled me to him very close. My reserve was broken, and my shyness too. I stood there with my face against his shoulder. "You've forgiven me, haven't you?" I said.

He spoke to me at last. "Forgiven you?" he said. "What have I got to forgive you for?"

"Last night," I said; "you thought I did it on purpose."

"Ah, that," he said, "I'd forgotten. I was angry with you, wasn't I?"

"Yes," I said.

He did not say any more. He went on holding me close to his shoulder. "Maxim," I said, "can't we start all over again? Can't we begin from to-day, and face things together? I don't want you to love me, I won't ask impossible things. I'll be your friend and your companion, a sort of boy. I don't ever want more than that."

He took my face between his hands and looked at me. For the first time I saw how thin his face was, how lined and drawn. And there were great shadows beneath his eyes.

"How much do you love me?" he said.

I could not answer. I could only stare back at him, at his dark tortured eyes, and his pale drawn face.

"It's too late, my darling, too late," he said. "We've lost our little chance of happiness."

"No, Maxim. No," I said.

"Yes," he said. "It's all over now. The thing has happened."

"What thing?" I said.

"The thing I've always foreseen. The thing I've dreamt about, day after day, night after night. We're not meant for happiness, you and I." He sat down on the window seat, and I knelt in front of him, my hands on his shoulders.

"What are you trying to tell me?" I said.

He put his hands over mine and looked into my face. "Rebecca has won," he said.

I stared at him, my heart beating strangely, my hands suddenly cold beneath his hands.

"Her shadow between us all the time," he said. "Her damned shadow keeping us from one another. How could I hold you like this, my darling, my little love, with the fear always in my heart that this would happen? I remembered her eyes as she looked at me before she died. I remembered that slow treacherous smile. She knew this would happen even then. She knew she would win in the end."

"Maxim," I whispered, "what are you saying, what are you trying to tell me?"

"Her boat," he said, "they've found it. The diver found it this afternoon."

"Yes," I said. "I know. Captain Searle came to tell me. You are thinking about the body, aren't you, the body the diver found in the cabin?"

"Yes," he said.

"It means she was not alone," I said. "It means there was somebody sailing with Rebecca at the time. And you have to find out who it was. That's it, isn't it, Maxim?"

"No," he said. "No, you don't understand."

"I want to share this with you, darling," I said. "I want to help you."

"There was no one with Rebecca, she was alone," he said.

I knelt there watching his face, watching his eyes.

"It's Rebecca's body lying there on the cabin floor," he said.

"No," I said. "No."

"The woman buried in the crypt is not Rebecca," he said. "It's the body of some unknown woman, unclaimed, belonging nowhere. There never was an accident. Rebecca was not drowned at all. I killed her. I shot Rebecca in the cottage in the cove. I carried her body to the cabin, and took the boat out that night and sunk it there, where they found it to-day. It's Rebecca who's lying dead there on the cabin floor. Will you look into my eyes and tell me that you love me now?"

CHAPTER TWENTY

It was very quiet in the library. The only sound was that of Jasper licking his foot. He must have caught a thorn in his pads, for he kept biting and sucking at the skin. Then I heard the watch on Maxim's wrist ticking close to my ear. The little normal sounds of every day. And for no reason the stupid proverb of my school-days ran through my mind, "Time and Tide wait for no man." The words repeated themselves over and over again. "Time and Tide wait for no man." These were the only sounds then, the ticking of Maxim's watch and Jasper licking his foot on the floor beside me.

When people suffer a great shock, like death, or the loss of a limb, I believe they don't feel it just at first. If your hand is taken from you you don't know, for a few minutes, that your hand is gone. You go on feeling the fingers. You stretch and beat them on the air, one by one, and all the time there is nothing there, no hand, no fingers. I knelt there by Maxim's side, my body against his body, my hands upon his shoulders, and I was aware of no feeling at all, no pain and no fear, there was no horror in my heart. I thought how I must take the thorn out of Jasper's foot and I wondered if Robert would come in and clear the tea-things. It seemed strange to me that I should think of these things, Jasper's foot, Maxim's watch, Robert and the tea-things. I was shocked at my lack of emotion and this queer cold absence of distress. Little by little the feeling will come back to me, I said to myself, little by little I shall understand. What he has told me and all that has happened will tumble into place like pieces of a jig-saw puzzle. They will fit themselves into a pattern. At the moment I am nothing, I have no heart, and no mind, and no senses, I am just a wooden thing in

Maxim's arms. Then he began to kiss me. He had not kissed me like this before. I put my hands behind his head and shut my eyes.

"I love you so much," he whispered. "So much."

This is what I have wanted him to say every day and every night, I thought, and now he is saying it at last. This is what I imagined in Monte Carlo, in Italy, here in Manderley. He is saying it now. I opened my eyes and looked at a little patch of curtain above his head. He went on kissing me, hungry, desperate, murmuring my name. I kept on looking at the patch of curtain, and saw where the sun had faded it, making it lighter than the piece above. How calm I am, I thought. How cool. Here I am looking at the piece of curtain, and Maxim is kissing me. For the first time he is telling me he loves me.

Then he stopped suddenly, he pushed me away from him, and got up from the window seat. "You see, I was right," he said. "It's too late. You don't love me now. Why should you?" He went and stood over by the mantelpiece. "We'll forget that," he said, "it won't happen again."

Realisation flooded me at once, and my heart jumped in quick and sudden panic. "It's not too late," I said swiftly, getting up from the floor and going to him, putting my arms about him; "you're not to say that, you don't understand. I love you more than anything in the world. But when you kissed me just now I felt stunned and shaken, I could not feel anything. I could not grasp anything. It was just as though I had no more feeling left in me at all."

"You don't love me," he said, "that's why you did not feel anything. I know. I understand. It's come too late for you, hasn't it?"

"No," I said.

"This ought to have happened four months ago," he said. "I should have known. Women are not like men."

"I want you to kiss me again," I said, "please, Maxim."

"No," he said, "it's no use now."

"We can't lose each other now," I said. "We've got to be together always, with no secrets, no shadows. Please, darling, please."

"There's no time," he said. "We may only have a few hours, a few days. How can we be together now that this has happened? I've told you they've found the boat. They've found Rebecca."

I stared at him stupidly, not understanding. "What will they do?" I said.

"They'll identify her body," he said, "there's everything to tell them, there in the cabin. The clothes she had, the shoes, the rings on her fingers. They'll identify her body; and then they will remember the other one, the woman buried up there, in the crypt."

"What are you going to do?" I whispered.

"I don't know," he said. "I don't know."

The feeling was coming back to me, little by little, as I knew it would. My hands were cold no longer. They were clammy, warm. I felt a wave of colour come into my face, my throat. My cheeks were burning hot. I thought of Captain Searle, the diver, the Lloyd's agent, all those men on the stranded ship leaning against the side, staring down into the water. I thought of the shopkeepers in Kerrith, of errand boys whistling in the street, of the vicar walking out of church, of Lady Crowan cutting roses in her garden, of the woman in the pink dress and her little boy on the cliffs. Soon they would know. In a few hours. By breakfast-time tomorrow. "They've found Mrs. de Winter's boat, and they say there is a body in the cabin." A body in the cabin. Rebecca was lying there on the cabin floor. She was not in the crypt at all. Some other woman was lying in the crypt. Maxim had killed Rebecca. Rebecca had not been drowned at all. Maxim had killed her. He had shot her in the cottage in the woods. He had carried her body to the boat, and sunk the boat there in the bay. That grey, silent cottage, with the rain pattering on the roof. The jig-saw pieces came tumbling thick and fast upon me. Disjointed pictures flashed one by one through my bewildered mind. Maxim sitting in the car beside me in the south of France. "Something happened nearly a year ago that altered my whole life. I had to begin living all over again. . . ." Maxim's silence, Maxim's moods. The way he never talked about Rebecca. The way he never mentioned her name. Maxim's dislike of the cove, of the stone cottage. "If you had my memories you would not go there either." The way he climbed the path through the woods not looking behind him. Maxim pacing up and down the library after Rebecca died. Up and down. Up and down. "I came away in rather a hurry," he said to Mrs. Van Hopper, a line, thin as gossamer, between his brows. "They say he can't get over his wife's death." The fancy dress dance last night, and I coming down to the head of the stairs, in Rebecca's dress. "I killed Rebecca," Maxim had said. "I shot Rebecca in the cottage in the woods." And the diver had found her lying there, on the cabin floor. . . .

"What are we going to do?" I said. "What are we going to say?"

Maxim did not answer. He stood there by the mantelpiece, his eyes wide and staring, looking in front of him, not seeing anything.

"Does anyone know?" I said, "anyone at all?"

He shook his head. "No," he said.

"No one but you and me?" I asked.

"No one but you and me," he said.

"Frank," I said suddenly, "are you sure Frank does not know?"

"How could he?" said Maxim, "there was nobody there but myself. It was dark..." He stopped. He sat down on a chair, he put his hand up to his forehead. I went and knelt beside him. He sat very still a moment. I took his hands away from his face and looked into his eyes. "I love you," I whispered, "I love you. Will you believe me now?" He kissed my face and my hands. He held my hands very tightly like a child who would gain confidence.

"I thought I should go mad," he said, "sitting here, day after day, waiting for something to happen. Sitting down at the desk there, answering those terrible letters of sympathy. The notices in the papers, the interviews, all the little aftermath of death. Eating and drinking, trying to be normal, trying to be sane. Frith, the servants, Mrs. Danvers. Mrs. Danvers, who I had not the courage to turn away, because with her knowledge of Rebecca she might have suspected, she might have guessed.... Frank, always by my side, discreet, sympathetic. 'Why don't you get away?' he used to say, 'I can manage here. You ought to get away.' And Giles, and Bee, poor dear tactless Bee. 'You're looking frightfully ill, can't you go and see a doctor?' I had to face them, all these people, knowing every word I uttered was a lie."

I went on holding his hands very tight. I leant close to him, quite close. "I nearly told you, once," he said, "that day Jasper ran to the cove, and you went to the cottage for some string. We were sitting here, like this, and then Frith and Robert came in with the tea."

"Yes," I said. "I remember. Why didn't you tell me? The time we've wasted when we might have been together. All these weeks and days."

"You were so aloof," he said, "always wandering into the garden with Jasper, going off on your own. You never came to me like this."

"Why didn't you tell me?" I whispered. "Why didn't you tell me?"

"I thought you were unhappy, bored," he said. "I'm so much older than you. You seemed to have more to say to Frank than you ever had to me. You were funny with me, awkward, shy."

"How could I come to you when I knew you were thinking about Rebecca?" I said. "How could I ask you to love me when I knew you loved Rebecca still?"

He pulled me close to him and searched my eyes.

"What are you talking about, what do you mean?" he said.

I knelt up straight beside him. "Whenever you touched me I thought you were comparing me to Rebecca," I said. "Whenever you spoke to me or looked at me, walked with me in the garden, sat down to dinner, I felt you were saying to yourself, 'This I did with Rebecca, and this, and this.' " He stared at me bewildered as though he did not understand.

"It was true, wasn't it?" I said.

"Oh, my God," he said. He pushed me away, he got up and began walking up and down the room, clasping his hands.

"What is it? What's the matter?" I said.

He whipped round and looked at me as I sat there huddled on the floor. "You thought I loved Rebecca?" he said. "You thought I killed her, loving her? I hated her, I tell you, our marriage was a farce from the very first. She was vicious, damnable, rotten through and through. We never loved each other, never had one moment of happiness together. Rebecca was incapable of love, of tenderness, of decency. She was not even normal."

I sat on the floor, clasping my knees, staring at him.

"She was clever of course," he said. "Damnably clever. No one would guess meeting her that she was not the kindest, most generous, most gifted person in the world. She knew exactly what to say to different people, how to match her mood to theirs. Had she met you, she would have walked off into the garden with you, arm-in-arm, calling to Jasper, chatting about flowers, music, painting, whatever she knew to be your particular hobby; and you would have been taken in, like the rest. You would have sat at her feet and worshipped her."

Up and down he walked, up and down across the library floor.

"When I married her I was told I was the luckiest man in the world," he said. "She was so lovely, so accomplished, so amusing. Even Gran, the most difficult person to please in those days, adored her from the first. 'She's got the three things that matter in a wife,' she told me; 'breeding, brains, and beauty.' And I believed her, or forced myself to believe her. But all the time I had a seed of doubt at the back of my mind. There was something about her eyes. . . ."

The jig-saw pieces came together piece by piece, and the real Rebecca took shape and form before me, stepping from her shadow world like a living figure from a picture frame. Rebecca slashing at her horse; Rebecca seizing life with her two hands; Rebecca, triumphant, leaning down from the minstrels' gallery with a smile on her lips.

Once more I saw myself standing on the beach beside poor startled Ben. "You're kind," he said, "not like the other one. You won't put me to the asylum, will you?" There was someone who walked through the woods by night, someone tall and slim. She gave you the feeling of a snake. . . .

Maxim was talking though. Maxim was walking up and down the

library floor. "I found her out at once," he was saying, "five days after we were married. You remember that time I drove you in the car, to the hills above Monte Carlo? I wanted to stand there again, to remember. She sat there, laughing, her black hair blowing in the wind; she told me about herself, told me things I shall never repeat to a living soul. I knew then what I had done, what I had married. Beauty, brains, and breeding. Oh, my God."

He broke off abruptly. He went and stood by the window, looking out upon the lawns. He began to laugh. He stood there laughing. I could not bear it, it made me frightened, ill. I could not stand it. "Maxim!" I cried. "Maxim."

He lit a cigarette, and stood there smoking, not saying anything. Then he turned away again, and paced up and down the room once more. "I nearly killed her then," he said. "It would have been so easy. One false step, one slip. You remember the precipice. I frightened you, didn't I? You thought I was mad. Perhaps I was. Perhaps I am. It doesn't make for sanity, does it, living with the devil."

I sat there watching him, up and down, up and down.

"She made a bargain with me up there, on the side of the precipice," he said. " 'I'll run your house for you,' she told me, 'I'll look after your precious Manderley for you, make it the most famous show-place in all the country, if you like. And people will visit us, and envy us, and talk about us; they'll say we are the luckiest, happiest, handsomest couple in all England. What a leg-pull, Max,' she said, 'what a God-damn triumph!' She sat there on the hillside, laughing, tearing a flower to bits in her hands."

Maxim threw his cigarette away, a quarter smoked, into the empty grate.

"I did not kill her," he said, "I watched her, I said nothing, I let her laugh. We got into the car together and drove away. And she knew I would do as she suggested, come here to Manderley, throw the place open, entertain, have our marriage spoken of as the success of the century. She knew I would sacrifice pride, honour, personal feeling, every damned quality on earth, rather than stand before our little world after a week of marriage and have them know the things about her that she had told me then. She knew I would never stand in a divorce court and give her away, have fingers pointing at us, mud flung at us in the newspapers, all the people who belong down here whispering when my name was mentioned, all the trippers from Kerrith trooping to the lodge gates, peering into the grounds and saying, 'That's where he lives, in there. That's Manderley. That's the place that belongs to the chap who had that divorce case we read about. Do you remember what the judge said about his wife . . . ?' "

He came and stood before me. He held out his hands. "You despise me, don't you?" he said. "You can't understand my shame, and loathing, and disgust."

I did not say anything. I held his hands against my heart. I did not care about his shame. None of the things that he had told me mattered to me at all. I clung to one thing only, and repeated it to myself, over and over again. Maxim did not love Rebecca. He had never loved her, never, never. They had never known one moment's happiness together. Maxim was talking, and I listened to him, but his words meant nothing to me. I did not really care.

"I thought about Manderley too much," he said. "I put Manderley first, before anything else. And it does not prosper, that sort of love. They don't preach about it in the churches. Christ said nothing about stones, and bricks, and walls, the love that a man can bear for his plot of earth, his soil, his little kingdom. It does not come into the Christian creed."

"My darling," I said, "my Maxim, my love." I laid his hands against my face, I put my lips against them.

"Do you understand?" he said, "do you, do you?"

"Yes," I said, "my sweet, my love." But I looked away from him so he should not see my face. What did it matter whether I understood him or not? My heart was light like a feather floating in the air. He had never loved Rebecca.

"I don't want to look back on those years," he said slowly. "I don't want ever to tell you about them. The shame and the degradation. The lie we lived, she and I. The shabby, sordid farce we played together. Before friends, before relations, even before the servants, before faithful, trusting creatures like old Frith. They all believed in her down here, they all admired her, they never knew how she laughed at them behind their backs, jeered at them, mimicked them. I can remember days when the place was full for some show or other, a garden party, a pageant, and she walked about with a smile like an angel on her face, her arm through mine, giving prizes afterwards to a little troop of children; and then the day afterwards she would be up at dawn driving to London, streaking to that flat of hers by the river like an animal to its hole in the ditch, coming back here at the end of the week, after five unspeakable days. Oh, I kept to my side of the bargain all right. I never gave her away. Her blasted taste made Manderley the thing it is to-day. The gardens, the shrubs, even the azaleas in the Happy Valley, do you think they existed when my father was alive? God, the place was a wilderness, lovely yes, wild and lonely with a beauty of its own, yes, but crying out for skill and care and the money that he would never give to it, that I would not have thought of giving to it—but for Rebecca. Half the stuff you see here in the rooms was never here originally. The drawing-room as it is to-day, the morning-room—that's all Rebecca. Those chairs that Frith points out so proudly to the visitors on the public day, and that panel of tapestry—Rebecca again. Oh, some of the things were here admittedly, stored away in back rooms, my father knew nothing about furniture or pictures, but the majority was bought by Rebecca. The beauty of Manderley that you see to-day, the Manderley that people talk about and photograph and paint, it's all due to her, to Rebecca."

I did not say anything. I held him close. I wanted him to go on talking like this, that his bitterness might loosen and come away, carrying with it all the pent-up hatred and disgust and muck of the lost years.

"And so we lived," he said, "month after month, year after year. I accepted everything—because of Manderley. What she did in London did not touch me—because it did not hurt Manderley. And she was careful those first years, there was never a murmur about her, never a whisper. Then little by little she began to grow careless. You know how a man starts drinking? He goes easy at first, just a little at a time, a bad bout perhaps every five months or so. And then the period between grows less and less. Soon it's every month, every fortnight, every few days. There's no margin of safety left and all his secret cunning goes. It was like that with Rebecca. She began to ask her friends down here. She would have one or two of them and mix them up at a week-end party so that at first I was not quite sure, not quite certain. She would have picnics down at her cottage in the cove. I came back once, having been away shooting in Scotland, and found her there, with half-a-dozen of them, people I had never seen before. I warned her, and she shrugged her shoulders. 'What the hell's it got to do with you?' she said. I told her she could see her friends in London, but Manderley was mine. She must stick to that part of the bargain. She smiled, she did not say anything. Then she started on Frank, poor shy faithful Frank. He came to me one day and said he wanted to leave Manderley and take another job. We argued for two hours, here in the library, and then I understood. He broke down and told me. She never left him alone, he said, she was always going down to his house, trying to get him to the cottage. Dear, wretched Frank, who had not understood, who had always thought we were the normal happy married couple we pretended to be.

"I accused Rebecca of this, and she flared up at once, cursing me, using every filthy word in her particular vocabulary. We had a sickening, loathsome scene. She went up to London after that and stayed there for a month. When she came back again she was quiet at first, I thought she had learnt her lesson. Bee and Giles came for a week-end. And I realised then what I had sometimes suspected before, that Bee did not like Rebecca. I believe, in her funny, abrupt, downright way, she saw through her, guessed something was wrong. It was a tricky, nervy sort of week-end. Giles went out sailing with Rebecca. Bee and I lazed on the lawn. And when they came back I could tell by Giles's rather hearty jovial manner and by a look in Rebecca's eye that she had started on him, as she had done on Frank. I saw Bee watching Giles at dinner, who laughed louder than usual, talked a little too much. And all the while Rebecca sitting there at the head of the table, looking like an angel."

They were all fitting into place, the jig-saw pieces. The odd strained shapes that I had tried to piece together with my fumbling fingers and they had never fitted. Frank's odd manner when I spoke about Rebecca. Beatrice, and her rather diffident negative attitude. The silence that I had always taken for sympathy and regret was a silence born of shame and embarrassment. It seemed incredible to me now that I had never understood. I wondered how many people there were in the world who suffered, and continued to suffer, because they could not break out from their own web of shyness and reserve, and to their blindness and folly built up a great distorted wall in front of them that hid the truth. This was what I had done. I had built up false pictures in my mind and sat before them. I had never had the courage to demand the truth. Had I made one step forward out of my own shyness Maxim would have told me these things four months, five months ago.

"That was the last week-end Bee and Giles ever spent at Manderley," said Maxim. "I never asked them alone again. They came officially, to garden-parties, and dances. Bee never said a word to me or I to her. But I think she guessed my life, I think she knew. Even as Frank did. Rebecca grew cunning again. Her behaviour was faultless, outwardly. But if I happened to be away when she was here at Manderley I could never be certain what might happen. There had been Frank, and Giles. She might get hold of one of the workmen on the estate, someone from Kerrith, anyone. . . . And then the bomb would have to fall. The gossip, the publicity I dreaded."

It seemed to me I stood again by the cottage in the woods, and I heard the drip-drip of the rain upon the roof. I saw the dust on the model ships, the rat holes on the divan. I saw Ben with his poor staring idiot's eyes. "You'll not put me to the asylum, will you?" And I thought of the dark steep path through the woods, and how, if a woman stood there behind the trees, her evening dress would rustle in the thin night breeze.

"She had a cousin," said Maxim slowly, "a fellow who had been abroad, and was living in England again. He took to coming here, if ever I was away. Frank used to see him. A fellow called Jack Favell."

"I know him," I said, "he came here the day you went to London."

"You saw him too?" said Maxim, "why didn't you tell me? I heard it from Frank, who saw his car turn in at the lodge gates."

"I did not like to," I said, "I thought it would remind you of Rebecca."

"Remind me?" whispered Maxim. "Oh, God, as if I needed reminding."

He stared in front of him, breaking off from his story, and I wondered if he was thinking, as I was, of that flooded cabin beneath the waters in the bay.

"She used to have this fellow Favell down to the cottage," said Maxim, "she would tell the servants she was going to sail, and would not be back before the morning. Then she would spend the night down there with him. Once again I warned her. I said if I found him here, anywhere on the estate, I'd shoot him. He had a black, filthy record. . . . The very thought of him walking about the woods in Manderley, in places like the Happy Valley, made me mad. I told her I would not stand for it. She shrugged her shoulders. She forgot to blaspheme. And I noticed she was looking paler than usual, nervy, rather haggard. I wondered then what the hell would happen to her when she began to look old, feel old. Things drifted on. Nothing very much happened. Then one day she went up to London, and came back again the same day, which she did not do as a rule. I did not expect her. I dined that night with Frank at his house, we had a lot of work on at the time."

He was speaking now in short, jerky sentences. I had his hands very tightly between my two hands.

"I came back after dinner, about half-past ten, and I saw her scarf and gloves lying on a chair in the hall. I wondered what the devil she had come back for. I went into the morning-room but she was not there. I guessed she had gone off there then, down to the cove. And I knew then I could not stand this life of lies and filth and deceit any longer. The thing had got to be settled, one way or the other. I thought I'd take a gun and frighten the fellow, frighten them both. I went down right away to the cottage. The servants never knew I had come back to the house at all. I slipped out into the garden and through the woods. I saw the light in the cottage window, and I went straight in. To my surprise Rebecca was alone. She was lying on the divan with an ash-tray full of cigarette stubs beside her. She looked ill, queer.

"I began at once about Favell and she listened to me without a word. 'We've lived this life of degradation long enough, you and I,' I said. 'This is the end, do you understand? What you do in London does not concern me. You can live with Favell there, or with anyone you like. But not here. Not at Manderley.'

"She said nothing for a moment. She stared at me, and then she smiled. 'Suppose it suits me better to live here, what then?' she said.

" 'You know the conditions,' I said, 'I've kept my part of our dirty, damnable bargain, haven't I? But you've cheated. You think you can treat my house and my home like your own sink in London. I've stood enough, but my God, Rebecca, this is your last chance.'

"I remember she squashed out her cigarette in the tub by the divan, and then she got up, and stretched herself, her arms above her head.

" 'You're right, Max,' she said. 'It's time I turned over a new leaf.'

"She looked very pale, very thin. She began walking up and down the room, her hands in the pockets of her trousers. She looked like a boy in her sailing kit, a boy with a face like a Botticelli angel.

" 'Have you ever thought,' she said, 'how damned hard it would be for you to make a case against me? In a court of law, I mean. If you wanted to divorce me. Do you realise that you've never had one shred of proof against me, from the very first? All your friends, even the servants, believe our marriage to be a success.'

" 'What about Frank?' I said. 'What about Beatrice?'

"She threw back her head and laughed. 'What sort of a story could Frank tell against mine?' she said. 'Don't you know me well enough for that? As for Beatrice, wouldn't it be the easiest thing in the world for her to stand in a witness box as the ordinary jealous woman whose husband once lost his head and made a fool of himself? Oh, no, Max, you'd have a hell of a time trying to prove anything against me.'

"She stood watching me, rocking on her heels, her hands in her pockets and a smile on her face. 'Do you realise that I could get Danny, as my personal maid, to swear anything I asked her to swear, in a court of law? And that the rest of the servants, in blind ignorance, would follow her example and swear too? They think we live together at Manderley as husband and wife, don't they? And so does everyone, your friends, all our little world. Well, how are you going to prove that we don't?'

"She sat down on the edge of the table, swinging her legs, watching me.

" 'Haven't we acted the parts of a loving husband and wife rather too well?' she said. I remember watching that foot of hers in its striped sandal swinging backwards and forwards, and my eyes and my brain began to burn in a strange quick way.

" 'We could make you look very foolish, Danny and I,' she said softly. 'We could make you look so foolish that no one would believe you, Max, nobody at all.' Still that foot of hers, swinging to and fro, that damned foot in its blue and white striped sandal.

"Suddenly she slipped off the table and stood in front of me, smiling still, her hands in her pockets.

" 'If I had a child, Max,' she said, 'neither you, nor anyone in the world, would ever prove that it was not yours. It would grow up here in Manderley, bearing your name. There would be nothing you could do. And when you died Manderley would be his. You could not prevent it. The property's entailed. You would like an heir, wouldn't you, for your beloved Manderley? You would enjoy it, wouldn't you, seeing my son lying in his pram under the chestnut tree, playing leapfrog on the lawn, catching butterflies in the Happy Valley? It would give you the biggest thrill of your life, wouldn't it, Max, to watch my son grow bigger day by day, and to know that when you died, all this would be his?'

"She waited a minute, rocking on her heels, and then she lit a cigarette and went and stood by the window. She began to laugh. She went on laughing. I thought she would never stop. 'God, how funny,' she said, 'how supremely, wonderfully funny. Well, you heard me say I was going to turn over a new leaf, didn't you? Now you know the reason. They'll be happy, won't they, all these smug locals, all your blasted tenants? "It's what we've always hoped for, Mrs. de Winter," they will say. I'll be the perfect mother, Max, like I've been the perfect wife. And none of them will ever guess, none of them will ever know.'

"She turned round and faced me, smiling, one hand in her pocket, the other holding her cigarette. When I killed her she was smiling still. I fired at her heart. The bullet passed right through. She did not fall at once. She stood there, looking at me, that slow smile on her face, her eyes wide open . . ."

Maxim's voice had sunk low, so low, that it was like a whisper. The hand that I held between my own was cold. I did not look at him.

I watched Jasper's sleeping body on the carpet beside me, the little thump of his tail, now and then, upon the floor.

"I'd forgotten," said Maxim, and his voice was slow now, tired, without expression, "that when you shot a person there was so much blood."

There was a hole there on the carpet beneath Jasper's tail. The burnt hole from a cigarette. I wondered how long it had been there. Some people said ash was good for the carpets.

"I had to get water from the cove," said Maxim. "I had to keep going backwards and forwards to the cove for water. Even by the fireplace, where she had not been, there was a stain. It was all round her where she lay on the floor. It began to blow too. There was no catch on the window. The window kept banging backwards and forwards, while I knelt there on the floor, with that dishcloth, and the bucket beside me."

And the rain on the roof, I thought, he does not remember the rain on the roof. It pattered thin and light and very fast.

"I carried her out to the boat," he said, "it must have been halfpast eleven by then, nearly twelve. It was quite dark. There was no moon. The wind was squally, from the west. I carried her down to the cabin and left her there. Then I had to get under way, with the dinghy astern, and beat out of the little harbour against the tide. The wind was with me but it came in puffs, and I was in the lee there, under cover of the headland. I remember I got the mainsail jammed halfway up the mast. I had not done it, you see, for a long time. I never went out with Rebecca.

"And I thought of the tide, how swift it ran and strong into the little cove. The wind blew down from the headland like a funnel. I got the boat out into the bay. I got her out there, beyond the beacon, and I tried to go about, to clear the ridge of rocks. The little jib fluttered. I could not sheet it in. A puff of wind came and the sheet tore out of my hands, went twisting round the mast. The sail thundered and shook. It cracked like a whip above my head. I could not remember what one had to do. I could not remember. I tried to reach that sheet and it blew above me in the air. Another blast of wind came straight ahead. We began to drift sideways, closer to the ridge. It was dark, so damned dark I couldn't see anything on the black, slippery deck. Somehow I blundered down into the cabin. I had a spike with me. If I didn't do it now it would be too late. We were getting so near to the ridge, and in six or seven minutes, drifting like this, we should be out of deep water. I opened the sea-cocks. The water began to come in. I drove the spike into the bottom boards. One of the planks split right across. I took the spike out and began to drive in another plank. The water came up over my feet. I left Rebecca lying there, on the floor. I fastened both the scuttles. I bolted the door. When I came up on deck I saw we were within twenty yards of the ridge. I threw some of the loose stuff on the deck into the water. There was a life-buoy, a pair of sweeps, a coil of rope. I climbed into the dinghy. I pulled away, and lay back on the paddles, and watched. The boat was drifting still. She was sinking too. Sinking by the head. The jib was still shaking and cracking like a whip. I thought someone must hear it, someone walking the cliffs late at night, some fisherman from Kerrith away beyond me in the bay, whose boat I could not see. The boat was smaller, like a black shadow on the water. The mast began to shiver, began to crack. Suddenly she heeled right over and as she went the mast broke in two, split right down the centre. The life-buoy and the sweeps floated away from me on the water. The boat was not there any more. I remember staring at the place where she had been. Then I pulled back to the cove. It started raining."

Maxim waited. He stared in front of him still. Then he looked at me, sitting beside him on the floor.

"That's all," he said, "there's no more to tell. I left the dinghy on the buoy, as she would have done. I went back and looked at the cottage. The floor was wet with the salt water. She might have done it herself. I walked up the path through the woods. I went into the house. Up the stairs to the dressing-room. I remember undressing. It began to blow and rain very hard. I was sitting there, on the bed, when Mrs. Danvers knocked on the door. I went and opened it, in my dressing-gown, and spoke to her. She was worried about Rebecca. I told her to go back to bed. I shut the door again. I went back and sat by the window in my dressing-gown, watching the rain, listening to the sea as it broke there, in the cove."

We sat there together without saying anything. I went on holding his cold hands. I wondered why Robert did not come to clear the tea.

"She sank too close in," said Maxim. "I meant to take her right out in the bay. They would never have found her there. She was too close in."

"It was the ship," I said; "it would not have happened but for the ship. No one would have known."

"She was too close in," said Maxim. We were silent again. I began to feel very tired.

"I knew it would happen one day," said Maxim, "even when I went up to Edgecoombe and identified that body as hers, I knew it meant nothing, nothing at all. It was only a question of waiting, of marking time. Rebecca would win in the end. Finding you has not made any difference has it? Loving you does not alter things at all. Rebecca knew she would win in the end. I saw her smile, when she died."

"Rebecca is dead," I said. "That's what we've got to remember. Rebecca is dead. She can't speak, she can't bear witness. She can't harm you any more."

"There's her body," he said, "the diver has seen it. It's lying there, on the cabin floor."

"We've got to explain it," I said. "We've got to think out a way to explain it. It's got to be the body of someone you don't know. Someone you've never seen before."

"Her things will be there still," he said. "The rings on her fingers. Even if her clothes have rotted in the water there will be something there to tell them. It's not like a body lost at sea, battered against rocks. The cabin is untouched. She must be lying there on the floor as I left her. The boat has been there, all these months. No one has moved anything. There is the boat, lying on the sea-bed where she sank."

"A body rots in water, doesn't it?" I whispered; "even if it's lying there, undisturbed, the water rots it, doesn't it?"

"I don't know," he said. "I don't know."

"How will you find out, how will you know?" I said.

"The diver is going down again at five-thirty to-morrow morning," said Maxim. "Searle has made all the arrangements. They are going to try to raise the boat. No one will be about. I'm going with them. He's sending his boat to pick me up in the cove. Five-thirty to-morrow morning."

"And then?" I said, "if they get it up, what then?"

"Searle's going to have his big lighter anchored there, just out in the deep water. If the boat's wood has not rotted, if it still holds together, his crane will be able to lift it on to the lighter. They'll go back to Kerrith then. Searle says he will moor the lighter at the head of that disused creek half-way up Kerrith harbour. It drives out very easily. It's mud there at low water and the trippers can't row up there. We shall have the place to ourselves. He says we'll have to let the water drain out of the boat, leaving the cabin bare. He's going to get hold of a doctor."

"What will he do?" I said. "What will the doctor do?"

"I don't know," he said.

"If they find out it's Rebecca you must say the other body was a mistake," I said. "You must say that body in the crypt was a mistake, a ghastly mistake. You must say that when you went to Edgecoombe you were ill, you did not know what you were doing. You were not sure, even then. You could not tell. It was a mistake, just a mistake. You will say that, won't you?"

"Yes," he said. "Yes."

"They can't prove anything against you," I said. "Nobody saw you that night. You had gone to bed. They can't prove anything. No one knows but you and I. No one at all. Not even Frank. We are the only two people in the world to know, Maxim. You and I."

"Yes," he said, "yes."

"They will think the boat capsized and sank when she was in the cabin," I said, "they will think she went below for a rope, for something, and while she was there the wind came from the headland, and the boat heeled over, and Rebecca was trapped. They'll think that, won't they?"

"I don't know," he said. "I don't know."

Suddenly the telephone began ringing in the little room behind the library.

CHAPTER TWENTY-ONE

Maxim went into the little room and shut the door. Robert came in a few minutes afterwards to clear away the tea. I stood up, my back turned to him so that he should not see my face. I wondered when they would begin to know, on the estate, in the servants' hall, in Kerrith itself. I wondered how long it took for news to trickle through.

I could hear the murmur of Maxim's voice in the little room beyond. I had a sick expectant feeling at the pit of my stomach. The sound of the telephone ringing seemed to have woken every nerve in my body. I had sat there on the floor beside Maxim in a sort of dream, his hand in mine, my face against his shoulder. I had listened to his story and part of me went with him like a shadow in his tracks. I too had killed Rebecca, I too had sunk the boat there in the bay. I had listened beside him to the wind and water. I had waited for Mrs. Danvers' knocking on the door. All this I had suffered with him, all this and more beside. But the rest of me sat there on the carpet, unmoved and detached, thinking and caring for one thing only, repeating a phrase over and over again, "He did not love Rebecca, he did not love Rebecca." Now, at the ringing of the telephone, these two selves merged and became one again. I was the self that I had always been, I was not changed. But something new had come upon me that had not been before. My heart, for all its anxiety and doubt, was light and free. I knew then that I was no longer afraid of Rebecca. I did not hate her any more. Now that I knew her to have been evil and vicious and rotten I did not hate her any more. She could not hurt me. I could go to the morning-room and sit down at her desk and touch her pen and look at her writing on the pigeon-holes, and I should not mind. I could go to her room in the west wing, stand by the window even as I had done this morning, and I should not be afraid. Rebecca's power had dissolved into the air, like the mist had done. She would never haunt me again. She would never stand behind me on the stairs, sit beside me in the dining-room, lean down from the gallery and watch me standing in the hall. Maxim had never loved her. I did not hate her any more. Her body had come back, her boat had been found with its queer prophetic name, Je Reviens, but I was free of her forever.

I was free now to be with Maxim, to touch him, and hold him, and love him. I would never be a child again. It would not be I, I, I any longer, it would be we, it would be us. We would be together. We would face this trouble together, he and I. Captain Searle, and the diver, and Frank, and Mrs. Danvers, and Beatrice, and the men and women of Kerrith reading their newspapers, could not break us now. Our happiness had not come too late. I was not young any more. I was not shy. I was not afraid. I would fight for Maxim. I would lie and perjure and swear, I would blaspheme and pray. Rebecca had not won. Rebecca had lost.

Robert had taken away the tea and Maxim came back into the room.

"It was Colonel Julyan," he said, "he's just been talking to Searle. He's coming out with us to the boat to-morrow. Searle has told him."

"Why Colonel Julyan, why?" I said.

"He's the magistrate for Kerrith. He has to be present."

"What did he say?"

"He asked me if I had any idea whose body it could be."

"What did you say?"

"I said I did not know. I said we believed Rebecca to be alone. I said I did not know of any friend."

"Did he say anything after that?"

"Yes."

"What did he say?"

"He asked me if I thought it possible that I made a mistake when I went up to Edgecoombe."

"He said that? He said that already?"

"Yes."

"And you?"

"I said it might be possible. I did not know."

"He'll be with you then to-morrow when you look at the boat? He, and Captain Searle, and a doctor."

"Inspector Welch too."

"Inspector Welch?"

"Yes."

"Why? Why Inspector Welch?"

"It's the custom, when a body has been found."

I did not say anything. We stared at one another. I felt the little pain come again at the pit of my stomach.

"They may not be able to raise the boat," I said.

"No," he said.

"They couldn't do anything then about the body, could they?" I said.

"I don't know," he said.

"He glanced out of the window. The sky was white and overcast as it had been when I came away from the cliffs. There was no wind though. It was still and quiet.

"I thought it might blow from the south-west about an hour ago but the wind has died away again," he said.

"Yes," I said.

"It will be a flat calm to-morrow for the diver," he said.

The telephone began ringing again from the little room. There was something sickening about the shrill urgent summons of the bell. Maxim and I looked at one another. Then he went into the room to answer it, shutting the door behind him as he had done before. The queer nagging pain had not left me yet. It returned again in greater force with the ringing of the bell. The feel of it took me back across the years to my childhood. This was the pain I had known when I was very small and the maroons had sounded in the streets of London, and I had sat, shivering, not understanding, under a little cupboard beneath the stairs. It was the same feeling, the same pain.

Maxim came back into the library. "It's begun," he said slowly.

"What do you mean, what's happened?" I said, grown suddenly cold.

"It was a reporter," he said, "the fellow from the *County Chronicle*. Was it true, he said, that the boat belonging to the late Mrs. de Winter had been found?"

"What did you say?"

"I said, Yes, a boat had been found, but that was all we know. It might not be her boat at all."

"Was that all he said?"

"No. He asked if I could confirm the rumour that a body had been found in the cabin."

"No!"

"Yes. Someone must have been talking. Not Searle, I know that.

The diver, one of his friends. You can't stop these people. The whole
story will be all over Kerrith by breakfast time to-morrow."

"What did you say, about the body?"

"I said I did not know. I had no statement to make. And I should
be obliged if he did not ring me up again."

"You will irritate them. You will have them against you."

"I can't help that. I don't make statements to newspapers. I won't
have those fellows ringing up and asking questions."

"We might want them on our side," I said.

"If it comes to fighting, I'll fight alone," he said. "I don't want a
newspaper behind me."

"The reporter will ring up someone else," I said. "He will get on to
Colonel Julyan or Captain Searle."

"He won't get much change out of them," said Maxim.

"If only we could do something," I said, "all these hours ahead of
us, and we sit here, idle, waiting for to-morrow morning."

"There's nothing we can do," said Maxim.

We went on sitting in the library. Maxim picked up a book but I
know he did not read. Now and again I saw him lift his head and listen, as though he heard the telephone again. But it did not ring again.
No one disturbed us. We dressed for dinner as usual. It seemed incredible to me that this time last night I had been putting on my
white dress, sitting before the mirror at my dressing-table, arranging
the curled wig. It was like an old forgotten nightmare, something remembered months afterwards with doubt and disbelief. We had dinner. Frith served us, returned from his afternoon. His face was
solemn, expressionless. I wondered if he had been in Kerrith, if he
had heard anything.

After dinner we went back again to the library. We did not talk
much. I sat on the floor at Maxim's feet, my head against his knees.
He ran his fingers through my hair. Different from his old abstracted
way. It was not like stroking Jasper any more. I felt his finger tips on
the scalp of my head. Sometimes he kissed me. Sometimes he said
things to me. There were no shadows between us any more, and when
we were silent it was because the silence came to us of our own asking. I wondered how it was I could be so happy when our little world
about us was so black. It was a strange sort of happiness. Not what I
had dreamt about or expected. It was not the sort of happiness I had
imagined in the lonely hours. There was nothing feverish or urgent
about this. It was a quiet, still happiness. The library windows were
open wide, and when we did not talk or touch one another we looked
out at the dark dull sky.

* * *

It must have rained in the night for when I woke the next morning, just after seven, and got up, and looked out the window, I saw the roses in the garden below were folded and drooping, and the grass banks leading to the woods were wet and silver. There was a little smell in the air of mist and damp, the smell that comes with the first fall of the leaf. I wondered if autumn would come upon us two months before her time. Maxim had not woken me when he got up at five. He must have crept from his bed and gone through the bathroom to his dressing-room without a sound. He would be down there now, in the bay, with Colonel Julyan, and Captain Searle, and the men from the lighter. The lighter would be there, the crane and the chain, and Rebecca's boat coming to the surface. I thought about it calmly, coolly, without feeling. I pictured them all down there in the bay, and the little dark hull of the boat rising slowly to the surface, sodden, dripping, the grass-green seaweed and the shells clinging to her sides. When they lifted her on to the lighter the water would stream from her sides, back into the sea again. The wood of the little boat would look soft and grey, pulpy in places. She would smell of mud and rust, and that dark black weed that grows deep beneath the sea beside rocks that are never uncovered. Perhaps the name-board still hung upon her stern. Je Reviens. The lettering green and faded. The nails rusted through. And Rebecca herself was there, lying on the cabin floor.

I got up and had my bath and dressed, and went down to breakfast at nine o'clock as usual. There were a lot of letters on my plate. Letters from people thanking us for the dance. I skimmed through them, I did not read them all. Frith wanted to know whether to keep the breakfast hot for Maxim. I told him I did not know when he would be back. He had to go out very early, I said. Frith did not say anything. He looked very solemn, very grave. I wondered again if he knew.

After breakfast I took my letters along to the morning-room. The room smelt fusty, the windows had not been opened. I flung them wide, letting in the cool fresh air. The flowers on the mantelpiece were drooping, many of them dead. The petals lay on the floor. I rang the bell, and Maud, the under-housemaid, came into the room.

"This room has not been touched this morning," I said, "even the windows were shut. And the flowers are dead. Will you please take them away."

She looked nervous and apologetic. "I'm very sorry, Madam," she said. She went to the mantelpiece and took the vases.

"Don't let it happen again," I said.

"No, Madam," she said. She went out of the room, taking the flowers with her. I had not thought it would be so easy to be severe. I wondered why it had seemed hard for me before. The menu for the day lay on the writing-desk. Cold salmon and mayonnaise, cutlets in aspic, galantine of chicken, soufflé. I recognised them all from the buffet-supper of the night of the ball. We were evidently still living on the remains. This must be the cold lunch that was put out in the dining-room yesterday and I had not eaten. The staff were taking things easily it seemed. I put a pencil through the list and rang for Robert. "Tell Mrs. Danvers to order something hot," I said. "If there's still a lot of cold stuff to finish we don't want it in the dining-room."

"Very good, Madam," he said.

I followed him out of the room and went to the little flower-room for my scissors. Then I went into the rose-garden and cut some young buds. The chill had worn away from the air. It was going to be as hot and airless as yesterday had been. I wondered if they were still down in the bay or whether they had gone back to the creek in Kerrith harbour. Presently I should hear. Presently Maxim would come back and tell me. Whatever happened I must be calm and quiet. Whatever happened I must not be afraid. I cut my roses and took them back into the morning-room. The carpet had been dusted, and the fallen petals removed. I began to arrange the flowers in the vases that Robert had filled with water. When I had nearly finished there was a knock on the door.

"Come in," I said.

It was Mrs. Danvers. She had the menu list in her hand. She looked pale and tired. There were great rings round her eyes.

"Good morning, Mrs. Danvers," I said.

"I don't understand," she began, "why you sent the menu out and the message by Robert. Why did you do it?"

I looked across at her, a rose in my hand.

"Those cutlets and that salmon were sent in yesterday," I said. "I saw them on the side-board. I should prefer something hot today. If they won't eat the cold in the kitchen you had better throw the stuff away. So much waste goes on in this house anyway that a little more won't make any difference."

She stared at me. She did not say anything. I put the rose in the vase with the others.

"Don't tell me you can't think of anything to give us, Mrs. Danvers," I said. "You must have menus for all occasions in your room."

"I'm not used to having messages sent to me by Robert," she said.

"If Mrs. de Winter wanted anything changed she would ring me personally on the house telephone."

"I'm afraid it does not concern me very much what Mrs. de Winter used to do," I said. "I am Mrs. de Winter now, you know. And if I choose to send a message by Robert I shall do so."

Just then Robert came into the room. "The *County Chronicle* on the telephone, Madam," he said.

"Tell the *County Chronicle* I'm not at home," I said.

"Yes, Madam," he said. He went out of the room.

"Well, Mrs. Danvers, is there anything else?" I said.

She went on staring at me. Still she did not say anything. "If you have nothing else to say you had better go and tell the cook about the hot lunch," I said. "I'm rather busy."

"Why did the *County Chronicle* want to speak to you?" she said.

"I haven't the slightest idea, Mrs. Danvers," I said.

"Is it true," she said slowly, "the story Frith brought back with him from Kerrith last night, that Mrs. de Winter's boat has been found?"

"Is there such a story?" I said. "I'm afraid I don't know anything about it."

"Captain Searle, the Kerrith harbour-master, called here yesterday, didn't he?" she said. "Robert told me, Robert showed him in. Frith says the story in Kerrith is that the diver who went down about the ship there in the bay found Mrs. de Winter's boat."

"Perhaps so," I said. "You had better wait until Mr. de Winter himself comes in and ask him about it."

"Why was Mr. de Winter up so early?" she asked.

"That was Mr. de Winter's business," I said.

She went on staring at me. "Frith said the story goes that there was a body in the cabin of the little boat," she said. "Why should there be a body there? Mrs. de Winter always sailed alone."

"It's no use asking me, Mrs. Danvers," I said. "I don't know any more than you do."

"Don't you?" she said slowly. She kept on looking at me. I turned away, I put the vase back on the table by the window.

"I will give the orders about the lunch," she said. She waited a moment. I did not say anything. Then she went out of the room. She can't frighten me any more, I thought. She has lost her power with Rebecca. Whatever she said or did now it could not matter to me or hurt me. I knew she was my enemy and I did not mind. But if she should learn the truth about the body in the boat and become Maxim's enemy too—what then? I sat down in the chair. I put the scissors on the table. I did not feel like doing any more roses. I kept wondering what Maxim was doing. I wondered why the reporter from the *County Chronicle* had rung us up again. The old sick feeling came back inside me. I went and leant out of the window. It was very hot. There was thunder in the air. The gardeners began to mow the grass again. I could see one of the men with his machine walk backwards and forwards on the top of the bank. I could not go on sitting in the morning-room. I left my scissors and my roses and went out on to the terrace. I began to walk up and down. Jasper padded after me, wondering why I did not take him for a walk. I went on walking up and down the terrace. About half-past eleven Frith came out to me from the hall.

"Mr. de Winter on the telephone, Madam," he said.

I went through the library to the little room beyond. My hands were shaking as I lifted the receiver.

"Is that you?" he said, "it's Maxim. I'm speaking from the office. I'm with Frank."

"Yes?" I said.

There was a pause. "I shall be bringing Frank and Colonel Julyan back to lunch at one o'clock," he said.

"Yes," I said.

I waited. I waited for him to go on. "They were able to raise the boat," he said. "I've just got back from the creek."

"Yes," I said.

"Searle was there, and Colonel Julyan, and Frank, and the others," he said. I wondered if Frank was standing beside him at the telephone, and if that was the reason he was so cool, so distant.

"All right then," he said, "expect us about one o'clock."

I put back the receiver. He had not told me anything. I still did not know what had happened. I went back again to the terrace, telling Frith first that we should be four to lunch instead of two.

An hour dragged past, slow, interminable. I went upstairs and changed into a thinner frock. I came down again. I went and sat in the drawing-room and waited. At five minutes to one I heard the sound of a car in the drive, and then voices in the hall. I patted my hair in front of the looking-glass. My face was very white. I pinched some colour into my cheeks and stood up waiting for them to come into the room. Maxim came in, and Frank, and Colonel Julyan. I remembered seeing Colonel Julyan at the ball dressed as Cromwell. He looked shrunken now, different. A smaller man altogether.

"How do you do?" he said. He spoke quietly, gravely, like a doctor.

"Ask Frith to bring the sherry," said Maxim. "I'm going to wash."

"I'll have a wash too," said Frank. Before I rang the bell Frith appeared with the sherry. Colonel Julyan did not have any. I took some to give me something to hold. Colonel Julyan came and stood beside me by the window.

"This is a most distressing thing, Mrs. de Winter," he said gently. "I do feel for you and your husband most acutely."

"Thank you," I said. I began to sip my sherry. Then I put the glass back again on the table. I was afraid he would notice that my hand was shaking.

"What makes it so difficult was the fact of your husband identifying that first body, over a year ago," he said.

"I don't quite understand," I said.

"You did not hear then, what we found this morning?" he said.

"I knew there was a body. The diver found a body," I said.

"Yes," he said. And then, half glancing over his shoulder towards the hall: "I'm afraid it was her, without a doubt," he said, lowering his voice. "I can't go into details with you, but the evidence was sufficient for your husband and Doctor Phillips to identify."

He stopped suddenly, and moved away from me. Maxim and Frank had come back into the room.

"Lunch is ready, shall we go in," said Maxim.

I led the way into the hall, my heart like a stone, heavy, numb. Colonel Julyan sat on my right, Frank on my left. I did not look at Maxim. Frith and Robert began to hand the first course. We all talked about the weather. "I see in *The Times* they had it well over eighty in London yesterday," said Colonel Julyan.

"Really?" I said.

"Yes. Must be frightful for the poor devils who can't get away."

"Yes, frightful," I said.

"Paris can be hotter than London," said Frank. "I remember staying a week-end in Paris in the middle of August, and it was quite impossible to sleep. There was not a breath of air in the whole city. The temperature was over ninety."

"Of course the French always sleep with their windows shut, don't they?" said Colonel Julyan.

"I don't know," said Frank. "I was staying in a hotel. The people were mostly Americans."

"You know France of course, Mrs. de Winter?" said Colonel Julyan.

"Not so very well," I said.

"Oh, I had the idea you had lived many years out there."

"No," I said.

"She was staying in Monte Carlo when I met her," said Maxim. "You don't call that France, do you?"

"No, I suppose not," said Colonel Julyan, "it must be very cosmopolitan. The coast is pretty though, isn't it?"

"Very pretty," I said.

"Not so rugged as this, eh? Still, I know which I'd rather have. Give me England every time, when it comes to settling down. You know where you are over here."

"I dare say the French feel that about France," said Maxim.

"Oh, no doubt," said Colonel Julyan.

We went on eating awhile in silence. Frith stood behind my chair. We were all thinking of one thing, but because of Frith we had to keep up our little performance. I supposed Frith was thinking about it too, and I thought how much easier it would be if we cast aside convention and let him join in with us, if he had anything to say. Robert came with the drinks. Our plates were changed. The second course was handed. Mrs. Danvers had not forgotten my wish for hot food. I took something out of a casserole covered in mushroom sauce.

"I think everyone enjoyed your wonderful party the other night," said Colonel Julyan.

"I'm so glad," I said.

"Does an immense amount of good locally, that sort of thing," he said.

"Yes, I suppose it does," I said.

"It's a universal instinct of the human species, isn't it, that desire to dress up in some sort of disguise?" said Frank.

"I must be very inhuman then," said Maxim.

"It's natural I suppose," said Colonel Julyan, "for all of us to wish to look different. We are all children in some ways."

I wondered how much pleasure it had given him to disguise himself as Cromwell. I had not seen much of him at the ball. He had spent most of the evening in the morning-room, playing bridge.

"You don't play golf, do you, Mrs. de Winter?" said Colonel Julyan.

"No, I'm afraid I don't," I said.

"You ought to take it up," he said. "My eldest girl is very keen, and she can't find many young people to play with her. I gave her a small car for her birthday and she drives herself over to the north coast nearly every day. It gives her something to do."

"How nice," I said.

"She ought to have been the boy," he said. "My lad is different altogether. No earthly use at games. Always writing poetry. I suppose he'll grow out of it."

"Oh, rather," said Frank. "I used to write poetry myself when I was his age. Awful nonsense too. I never write any now."

"Good heavens, I should hope not," said Maxim.

"I don't know where my boy gets it from," said Colonel Julyan, "certainly not from his mother or from me."

There was another long silence. Colonel Julyan had a second dip into the casserole. "Mrs. Lacy looked very well the other night," he said.

"Yes," I said.

"Her dress came adrift as usual," said Maxim.

"Those eastern garments must be the devil to manage," said Colonel Julyan, "and yet they say, you know, they are far more comfortable and far cooler than anything you ladies wear in England."

"Really?" I said.

"Yes, so they say. It seems all that loose drapery throws off the hot rays of the sun."

"How curious," said Frank, "you'd think it would have just the opposite effect."

"No, apparently not," said Colonel Julyan.

"Do you know the East, sir?" said Frank.

"I know the far East," said Colonel Julyan. "I was in China for five years. Then Singapore."

"Isn't that where they make the curry?" I said.

"Yes, they gave us very good curry in Singapore," he said.

"I'm fond of curry," said Frank.

"Ah, it's not curry at all in England, it's hash," said Colonel Julyan.

The plates were cleared away. A soufflé was handed, and a bowl of fruit salad. "I suppose you are coming to the end of your raspberries," said Colonel Julyan. "It's been a wonderful summer for them, hasn't it? We've put down pots and pots of jam."

"I never think raspberry jam is a great success," said Frank, "there are always so many pips."

"You must come and try some of ours," said Colonel Julyan. "I don't think we have a great lot of pips."

"We're going to have a mass of apples this year at Manderley," said Frank. "I was saying to Maxim a few days ago we ought to have a record season. We shall be able to send a lot up to London."

"Do you really find it pays?" said Colonel Julyan, "by the time you've paid your men for the extra labour, and then the packing, and carting, do you make any sort of profit worth while?"

"Oh, Lord yes," said Frank.

"How interesting. I must tell my wife," said Colonel Julyan.

The soufflé and the fruit salad did not take long to finish. Robert appeared with cheese and biscuits, and a few minutes later Frith came with the coffee and cigarettes. Then they both went out of the room and shut the door. We drank our coffee in silence. I gazed steadily at my plate.

"I was saying to your wife before luncheon, de Winter," began Colonel Julyan, resuming his first quiet confidential tone, "that the awkward part of this whole distressing business is the fact that you identified that original body."

"Yes, quite," said Maxim.

"I think the mistake was very natural under the circumstances," said Frank quickly. "The authorities wrote to Maxim, asking him to go up to Edgecoombe, presupposing before he arrived there that the body was hers. And Maxim was not well at the time. I wanted to go with him, but he insisted on going alone. He was not in a fit state to undertake anything of the sort."

"That's nonsense," said Maxim. "I was perfectly well."

"Well, it's no use going into all that now," said Colonel Julyan. "You made that first identification, and now the only thing to do is to admit the error. There seems to be no doubt about it this time."

"No," said Maxim.

"I wish you could be spared the formality and the publicity of an inquest," said Colonel Julyan, "but I'm afraid that's quite impossible."

"Naturally," said Maxim.

"I don't think it need take very long," said Colonel Julyan. "It's just a case of you reaffirming identification, and then getting Tabb, who you say converted the boat when your wife brought her from France, just to give his piece of evidence that the boat was seaworthy and in good order when he last had her in his yard. It's just red-tape you know. But it has to be done. No, what bothers me is the wretched publicity of the affair. So sad and unpleasant for you and your wife."

"That's quite all right," said Maxim. "We understand."

"So unfortunate that wretched ship going ashore there," said Colonel Julyan, "but for that the whole matter would have rested in peace."

"Yes," said Maxim.

"The only consolation is that now we know poor Mrs. de Winter's death must have been swift and sudden, not the dreadful slow lingering affair we all believed it to be. There can have been no question of trying to swim."

"None," said Maxim.

"She must have gone down for something, and then the door jammed, and a squall caught the boat without anyone at the helm," said Colonel Julyan. "A dreadful thing."

"Yes," said Maxim.

"That seems to be the solution, don't you think, Crawley?" said Colonel Julyan, turning to Frank.

"Oh, yes, undoubtedly," said Frank.

I glanced up and I saw Frank looking at Maxim. He looked away again immediately but not before I had seen and understood the expression in his eyes. Frank knew. And Maxim did not know that he knew. I went on stirring my coffee. My hand was hot, damp.

"I suppose sooner or later we all make a mistake in judgement," said Colonel Julyan, "and then we are for it. Mrs. de Winter must have known how the wind comes down like a funnel in that bay, and that it was not safe to leave the helm of a small boat like that. She must have sailed alone over that spot scores of times. And then the moment came, she took a chance—and the chance killed her. It's a lesson to all of us."

"Accidents happen so easily," said Frank, "even to the most experienced people. Think of the number killed out hunting every season."

"Oh, I know. But then it's the horse falling generally that lets you down. If Mrs. de Winter had not left the helm of her boat the accident would never have happened. An extraordinary thing to do. I must have watched her many times in the handicap race on Saturdays from Kerrith, and I never saw her make an elementary mistake. It's the sort of thing a novice would do. In that particular place too, just by the ridge."

"It was very squally that night," said Frank, "something may have happened to the gear. Something may have jammed. And then she slipped down for a knife."

"Of course. Of course. Well, we shall never know. And I don't suppose we should be any the better for it if we did. As I said before, I wish I could stop this inquest but I can't. I'm trying to arrange it for Tuesday morning, and it will be as short as possible. Just a formal matter. But I'm afraid we shan't be able to keep the reporters out of it."

There was another silence. I judged the time had come to push back my chair.

"Shall we go into the garden?" I said.

We all stood up, and then I led the way to the terrace. Colonel Julyan patted Jasper.

"He's grown into a nice-looking dog," he said.

"Yes," I said.

"They make nice pets," he said.

"Yes," I said.

We stood about for a minute. Then he glanced at his watch.

"Thank you for your most excellent lunch," he said. "I have rather a busy afternoon in front of me, and I hope you will excuse me dashing away."

"Of course," I said.

"I'm so very sorry this should have happened. You have all my sympathy. I consider it's almost harder for you than for your husband. However, once the inquest is over you must both forget all about it."

"Yes," I said, "yes, we must try."

"My car is here in the drive. I wonder whether Crawley would like a lift. Crawley? I can drop you at your office if it's any use."

"Thank you, sir," said Frank.

He came and took my hand. "I shall be seeing you again," he said.

"Yes," I said.

I did not look at him. I was afraid he would understand my eyes. I did not want him to know that I knew. Maxim walked with them to the car. When they had gone he came back to me on the terrace. He took my arm. We stood looking down at the green lawns towards the sea and the beacon on the headland.

"It's going to be all right," he said. "I'm quite calm, quite confident. You saw how Julyan was at lunch, and Frank. There won't be any difficulty at the inquest. It's going to be all right."

I did not say anything. I held his arm tightly.

"There was never any question of the body being someone unknown," he said. "What we saw was enough for Doctor Phillips even to make the identification alone without me. It was straightforward, simple. There was no trace of what I'd done. The bullet had not touched the bone."

A butterfly sped past us on the terrace, silly and inconsequent.

"You heard what they said," he went on, "they think she was trapped there, in the cabin. The jury will believe that at the inquest too. Phillips will tell them so." He paused. Still I did not speak.

"I only mind for you," he said, "I don't regret anything else. If it had to come all over again I should not do anything different. I'm glad I killed Rebecca, I shall never have any remorse for that, never, never. But you. I can't forget what it has done to you. I was looking at you, thinking of nothing else all through lunch. It's gone forever, that funny, young, lost look that I loved. It won't come back again. I killed that too, when I told you about Rebecca. It's gone, in twenty-four hours. You are so much older. . . ."

CHAPTER TWENTY-TWO

That evening, when Frith brought in the local paper, there were great headlines right across the top of the page. He brought the paper and laid it down on the table. Maxim was not there, he had gone up early to change for dinner. Frith stood a moment, waiting for me to say something, and it seemed to me stupid and insulting to ignore a matter that must mean so much to everyone in the house.

"This is a very dreadful thing, Frith," I said.

"Yes, Madam, we are all most distressed outside," he said.

"It's so sad for Mr. de Winter," I said, "having to go through it all again."

"Yes, Madam. Very sad. Such a shocking experience, Madam, having to identify the second body having seen the first. I suppose there is no doubt then, that the remains in the boat are genuinely those of the late Mrs. de Winter?"

"I'm afraid not, Frith. No doubt at all."

"It seems so odd to us, Madam, that she should have let herself be trapped like that in the cabin. She was so experienced in a boat."

"Yes, Frith. That's what we all feel. But accidents will happen. And how it happened I don't suppose any of us will ever know."

"I suppose not, Madam. But it's a great shock, all the same. We are most distressed about it outside. And coming suddenly, just after the party. It doesn't seem right somehow, does it?"

"No, Frith."

"It seems there is to be an inquest, Madam?"

"Yes. A formality, you know."

"Of course, Madam. I wonder if any of us will be required to give evidence?"

"I don't think so."

"I shall be only too pleased to do anything that might help the family, Mr. de Winter knows that."

"Yes, Frith. I'm sure he does."

"I've told them outside not to discuss the matter, but it's very difficult to keep an eye on them, especially the girls. I can deal with Robert of course. I'm afraid the news has been a great shock to Mrs. Danvers."

"Yes, Frith. I rather expected it would."

"She went up to her room straight after lunch, and has not come down again. Alice took her a cup of tea and the paper a few minutes ago. She said Mrs. Danvers looked very ill indeed."

"It would be better really if she stayed where she is," I said. "It's no use her getting up and seeing to things if she is ill. Perhaps Alice would tell her that. I can very well manage the ordering. The cook and I between us."

"Yes, Madam. I don't think she is physically ill, Madam, it's just the shock of Mrs. de Winter being found. She was very devoted to Mrs. de Winter."

"Yes," I said. "Yes, I know."

Frith went out of the room after that, and I glanced quickly at the paper before Maxim came down. There was a great column, all down the front page, and an awful blurred photograph of Maxim that must have been taken at least fifteen years ago. It was dreadful, seeing it there on the front page staring at me. And the little line about myself at the bottom, saying who Maxim had married as his second wife, and how he had just given the fancy dress ball at Manderley. It sounded so crude and callous, in the dark print of the newspaper. Rebecca, whom they described as beautiful, talented, and loved by all who knew her, having been drowned a year ago, and then Maxim marrying again the following spring, bringing his bride straight to Manderley (so it said) and giving the big fancy dress ball in her honour. And then the following morning the body of his first wife being found, trapped in the cabin of her sailing boat, at the bottom of the bay.

It was true of course, though sprinkled with little inaccuracies that added to the story, making it strong meat for the hundreds of readers who wanted value for their pennies. Maxim sounded vile in it, a sort of satyr. Bringing back his "young bride," as it described me, to Manderley, and giving the dance, as though we wanted to display ourselves before the world.

I hid the paper under the cushion of the chair so that Maxim should not see it. But I could not keep the morning editions from him. The story was in our London papers too. There was a picture of Manderley, and the story underneath. Manderley was news, and so was Maxim. They talked about him as Max de Winter. It sounded racy, horrible. Each paper made great play of the fact that Rebecca's body had been found the day after the fancy dress ball, as though there was something deliberate about it. Both papers used the same word, "ironic." Yes, I supposed it was ironic. It made a good story. I watched Maxim at the breakfast table getting whiter and whiter as he read the papers, one after the other, and then the local one as well. He did not say anything. He just looked across at me, and I stretched out my hand to him. "Damn them," he whispered, "damn them, damn them."

I thought of all the things they could say, if they knew the truth. Not one column, but five or six. Placards in London. Newsboys shouting in the streets, outside the underground stations. That frightful word of six letters, in the middle of the placard, large and black.

Frank came up after breakfast. He looked pale and tired, as though he had not slept. "I've told the exchange to put all calls for Manderley through to the office," he said to Maxim. "It doesn't matter who it is. If reporters ring up I can deal with them. And anyone else too. I don't want either of you to be worried at all. We've had several calls already from locals. I gave the same answer to each. Mr. and Mrs. de Winter were grateful for all sympathetic enquiries, and they hoped their friends would understand that they were not receiving calls during the next few days. Mrs. Lacy rang up about eight-thirty. Wanted to come over at once."

"Oh, my God . . ." began Maxim.

"It's all right, I prevented her. I told her quite truthfully that I did not think she would do any good by coming over. That you did not want to see anyone but Mrs. de Winter. She wanted to know when they were holding the inquest but I told her it had not been settled. I don't know that we can stop her from coming to that, if she finds it in the papers."

"Those blasted reporters," said Maxim.

"I know," said Frank, "we all want to wring their necks, but you've got to see their point of view. It's their bread-and-butter, they've got to do the job for their paper. If they don't get a story the editor probably sacks them. If the editor does not produce a saleable edition the proprietor sacks him. And if the paper doesn't sell, the proprietor loses all his money. You won't have to see them or speak to

them, Maxim. I'm going to do all that for you. All you have to concentrate on is your statement at the inquest."

"I know what to say," said Maxim.

"Of course you do, but don't forget old Horridge is the coroner.
He's a sticky sort of chap, goes into details that are quite irrelevant
just to show the jury how thorough he is at his job. You must not let
him rattle you."

"Why the devil should I be rattled? I have nothing to be rattled
about."

"Of course not. But I've attended these coroner's inquests before,
and it's so easy to get nervy and irritable. You don't want to put the
fellow's back up."

"Frank's right," I said. "I know just what he means. The swifter
and smoother the whole thing goes the easier it will be for everyone.
Then, once the wretched thing is over we shall forget all about it, and
so will everyone else, won't they, Frank?"

"Yes, of course," said Frank.

I still avoided his eye, but I was more convinced than ever that he
knew the truth. He had always known it. From the very first. I remembered the first time I met him, that first day of mine at Manderley, when he, and Beatrice, and Giles had all been at lunch, and Beatrice had been tactless about Maxim's health. I remembered Frank, his
quiet turning of the subject, the way he had come to Maxim's aid in
his quite unobtrusive manner if there was ever any question of difficulty. That strange reluctance of his to talk about Rebecca, his stiff,
funny, pompous way of making conversation whenever we had approached anything like intimacy. I understood it all. Frank knew, but
Maxim did not know that he knew. And Frank did not want Maxim
to know that he knew. And we all stood there, looking at one another,
keeping up these little barriers between us.

We were not bothered with the telephone again. All the calls were
put through to the office. It was just a question of waiting now. Waiting until the Tuesday.

I saw nothing of Mrs. Danvers. The menu was sent through as
usual, and I did not change it. I asked little Clarice about her. She said
she was going about her work as usual but she was not speaking to
anybody. She had all her meals alone in her sitting-room.

Clarice was wide-eyed, evidently curious, but she did not ask me
any questions, and I was not going to discuss it with her. No doubt
they talked of nothing else, out in the kitchen, and on the estate too,
in the lodge, on the farms. I supposed all Kerrith was full of it. We

stayed in Manderley, in the gardens close to the house. We did not even walk in the woods. The weather had not broken yet. It was still hot, oppressive. The air was full of thunder, and there was rain behind the white dull sky, but it did not fall. I could feel it, and smell it, pent up there, behind the clouds. The inquest was to be on the Tuesday afternoon at two o'clock.

We had lunch at a quarter-to-one. Frank came. Thank heaven Beatrice had telephoned that she could not get over. The boy Roger had arrived home with measles; they were all in quarantine. I could not help blessing the measles. I don't think Maxim could have borne it, with Beatrice sitting here, staying in the house, sincere, anxious, and affectionate, but asking questions all the time. Forever asking questions.

Lunch was a hurried, nervous meal. We none of us talked very much. I had that nagging pain again. I did not want anything to eat. I could not swallow. It was a relief when the farce of the meal was over, and I heard Maxim go out on to the drive and start up the car. The sound of the engine steadied me. It meant we had to go, we had to be doing something. Not just sitting at Manderley. Frank followed us in his own car. I had my hand on Maxim's knee all the way as he drove. He seemed quite calm. Not nervous in any way. It was like going with someone to a nursing-home, someone who was to have an operation. And not knowing what would happen. Whether the operation would be successful. My hands were very cold. My heart was beating in a funny, jerky way. And all the time that little nagging pain beneath my heart. The inquest was to be held at Lanyon, the market town six miles the other side of Kerrith. We had to park the cars in the big cobbled square by the market-place. Doctor Phillips' car was there already, and also Colonel Julyan's. Other cars too. I saw a passerby stare curiously at Maxim, and then nudge her companion's arm.

"I think I shall stay here," I said. "I don't think I'll come in with you after all."

"I did not want you to come," said Maxim. "I was against it from the first. You'd much better have stayed at Manderley."

"No," I said. "No, I'll be all right here, sitting in the car."

Frank came and looked in at the window. "Isn't Mrs. de Winter coming?" he said.

"No," said Maxim. "She wants to stay in the car."

"I think she's right," said Frank, "there's no earthly reason why she should be present at all. We shan't be long."

"It's all right," I said.

"I'll keep a seat for you," said Frank, "in case you should change your mind."

They went off together and left me sitting there. It was early-closing day. The shops looked drab and dull. There were not many people about. Lanyon was not much of a holiday centre anyway, it was too far inland. I sat looking at the silent shops. The minutes went by. I wondered what they were doing, the coroner, Frank, Maxim, Colonel Julyan. I got out of the car and began walking up and down the market square. I went and looked in a shop window. Then I walked up and down again. I saw a policeman watching me curiously. I turned up a side-street to avoid him.

Somehow, in spite of myself, I found I was coming to the building where the inquest was being held. There had been little publicity about the actual time, and because of this there was no crowd waiting, as I had feared and expected. The place seemed deserted. I went up the steps and stood just inside the door.

A policeman appeared from nowhere. "Do you want anything?" he said.

"No," I said. "No."

"You can't wait here," he said.

"I'm sorry," I said. I went back towards the steps into the street.

"Excuse me, Madam," he said, "aren't you Mrs. de Winter?"

"Yes," I said.

"Of course that's different," he said, "you can wait here if you like. Would you like to take a seat just inside this room?"

"Thank you," I said.

He showed me into a little bare room with a desk in it. It was like a waiting-room at a station. I sat there, with my hands on my lap. Five minutes passed. Nothing happened. It was worse than being outside, than sitting in the car. I got up and went into the passage. The policeman was still standing there.

"How long will they be?" I said.

"I'll go and enquire if you like," he said.

He disappeared along the passage. In a moment he came back again. "I don't think they will be very much longer," he said. "Mr. de Winter has just given his evidence. Captain Searle, and the diver, and Doctor Phillips have already given theirs. There's only one more to speak. Mr. Tabb, the boat-builder from Kerrith."

"Then it's nearly over," I said.

"I expect so, Madam," he said. Then he said, on a sudden thought,

"Would you like to hear the remaining evidence? There is a seat there, just inside the door. If you slip in now nobody will notice you."

"Yes," I said. "Yes, I think I will."

It was nearly over. Maxim had finished giving his evidence. I did not mind hearing the rest. It was Maxim I had not wanted to hear. I had been nervous of listening to his evidence. That was why I had not gone with him and Frank in the first place. Now it did not matter. His part of it was over.

I followed the policeman, and he opened a door at the end of the passage. I slipped in, I sat down just by the door. I kept my head low so that I did not have to look at anybody. The room was smaller than I had imagined. Rather hot and stuffy. I had pictured a great bare room with benches, like a church. Maxim and Frank were sitting down at the other end. The coroner was a thin, elderly man in pince-nez. There were people there I did not know. I glanced at them out of the tail of my eye. My heart gave a jump suddenly as I recognised Mrs. Danvers. She was sitting right at the back. And Favell was beside her. Jack Favell, Rebecca's cousin. He was leaning forward, his chin in his hands, his eyes fixed on the coroner, Mr. Horridge. I had not expected him to be there. I wondered if Maxim had seen him. James Tabb, the boat-builder, was standing up now and the coroner was asking him a question.

"Yes, sir," answered Tabb, "I converted Mrs. de Winter's little boat. She was a French fishing boat originally, and Mrs. de Winter bought her for next to nothing over in Brittany, and had her shipped over. She gave me the job of converting her and doing her up like a little yacht."

"Was the boat in a fit state to put to sea?" said the coroner.

"She was when I fitted her out in April of last year," said Tabb. "Mrs. de Winter laid her up as usual at my yard in October, and then in March I had word from her to fit her up as usual, which I did. That would be Mrs. de Winter's fourth season with the boat since I did the conversion job for her."

"Had the boat ever been known to capsize before?" asked the coroner.

"No, sir. I should soon have heard of it from Mrs. de Winter had there been any question of it. She was delighted with the boat in every way, according to what she said to me."

"I suppose great care was needed to handle the boat?" said the coroner.

"Well, sir, everyone has to have their wits about them, when they go sailing boats, I won't deny it. But Mrs. de Winter's boat wasn't one of those cranky little crafts that you can't leave for a moment, like some of the boats you see in Kerrith. She was a stout sea-worthy boat, and could stand a lot of wind. Mrs. de Winter had sailed her in worse weather than she ever found that night. Why, it was only blowing in fits and starts at the time. That's what I've said all along. I couldn't understand Mrs. de Winter's boat being lost on a night like that."

"But surely, if Mrs. de Winter went below for a coat, as is supposed, and a sudden puff of wind was to come down from that headland, it would be enough to capsize the boat?" asked the coroner.

James Tabb shook his head. "No," he said stubbornly, "I don't see that it would."

"Well, I'm afraid that is what must have happened," said the coroner. "I don't think Mr. de Winter or any of us suggest that your workmanship was to blame for the accident at all. You fitted the boat out at the beginning of the season, you reported her sound and seaworthy, and that's all I want to know. Unfortunately the late Mrs. de Winter relaxed her watchfulness for a moment and she lost her life, the boat sinking with her aboard. Such accidents have happened before. I repeat again we are not blaming you."

"Excuse me, sir," said the boat-builder, "but there is a little bit more to it than that. And if you would allow me I should like to make a further statement."

"Very well, go on," said the coroner.

"It's like this, sir. After the accident last year a lot of people in Kerrith made unpleasantness about my work. Some said I had let Mrs. de Winter start the season in a leaky, rotten boat. I lost two or three orders because of it. It was very unfair, but the boat had sunk, and there was nothing I could say to clear myself. Then that steamer went ashore, as we all know, and Mrs. de Winter's little boat was found, and brought to the surface. Captain Searle himself gave me permission yesterday to go and look at her, and I did. I wanted to satisfy myself that the work I had put into her was sound, in spite of the fact that she had been waterlogged for twelve months or more."

"Well, that was very natural," said the coroner, "and I hope you were satisfied."

"Yes, sir, I was. There was nothing wrong with that boat as regards the work I did to her. I examined every corner of her there on the lighter up the pill where Captain Searle had put her. She had sunk on sandy bottom, I asked the diver about that, and he told me so. She had not touched the ridge at all. The ridge was a clear five feet away. She was lying on sand, and there wasn't the mark of a rock on her."

He paused. The coroner looked at him expectantly.

"Well?" he said, "is that all you want to say?"

"No, sir," said Tabb emphatically, "It's not. What I want to know is this. Who drove the holes in her planking? Rocks didn't do it. The nearest rock was five feet away. Besides, they weren't the sort of marks made by a rock. They were holes. Done with a spike."

I did not look at him. I was looking at the floor. There was oil-cloth laid on the boards. Green oil-cloth. I looked at it.

I wondered why the coroner did not say something. Why did the pause last so long? When he spoke at last his voice sounded rather far away.

"What do you mean?" he said, "what sort of holes?"

"There were three of them altogether," said the boat-builder, "one right for'ard, by her chain locker, on her starboard planking, below the water-line. The other two close together amidships, underneath her floor-boards, in the bottom. The ballast had been shifted too. It was lying loose. And that's not all. The sea-cocks had been turned on."

"The sea-cocks? What are they?" asked the coroner.

"The fitting that plugs the pipes leading from a wash-basin or lavatory, sir. Mrs. de Winter had a little place fitted up right aft. And there was a sink for'ard, where the washing-up was done. There was a sea-cock there, and another in the lavatory. These are always kept tight closed when you're under way, otherwise the water would flow in. When I examined the boat yesterday both sea-cocks were turned full on."

It was hot, much too hot. Why didn't they open a window? We should be suffocated if we sat here with the air like this, and there were so many people, all breathing the same air, so many people.

"With those holes in her planking, sir, and the sea-cocks not closed, it wouldn't take long for a small boat like her to sink. Not much more than ten minutes, I should say. Those holes weren't there when the boat left my yard. I was proud of my work, and so was Mrs. de Winter. It's my opinion, sir, that the boat never capsized at all. She was deliberately scuttled."

I must try and get out of the door. I must try and go back to the waiting-room again. There was no air left in this place, and the person next to me was pressing close, close. . . . Someone in front of me was standing up, and they were talking, too, they were all talking. I did not know what was happening. I could not see anything. It was hot, so very hot. The coroner was asking everybody to be silent. And he said something about "Mr. de Winter." I could not see. That woman's hat was in front of me. Maxim was standing up now. I could not look at him. I must not look at him. I felt like this once before. When was it? I don't know. I don't remember. Oh, yes, with Mrs. Danvers. The time Mrs. Danvers stood with me by the window. Mrs. Danvers was in this place now, listening to the coroner. Maxim was standing up over there. The heat was coming up at me from the floor, rising in slow waves. It reached my hands, wet and slippery, it touched my neck, my chin, my face.

"Mr. de Winter, you heard the statement from James Tabb, who had the care of Mrs. de Winter's boat? Do you know anything of these holes driven in the planking?"

"Nothing whatever."

"Can you think of any reason why they should be there?"

"No, of course not."

"It's the first time you have heard them mentioned?"

"Yes."

"It's a shock to you, of course?"

"It was shock enough to learn that I made a mistake in identification over twelve months ago, and now I learn that my late wife was not only drowned in the cabin of her boat, but that holes were bored in the boat with the deliberate intent of letting in the water so that the boat should sink. Does it surprise you that I should be shocked?"

No, Maxim, no. You will put his back up. You heard what Frank said. You must not put his back up. Not that voice. Not that angry voice, Maxim. He won't understand. Please, darling, please. Oh, God, don't let Maxim lose his temper. Don't let him lose his temper.

"Mr. de Winter, I want you to believe that we all feel very deeply for you in this matter. No doubt you have suffered a shock, a very severe shock, in learning that your late wife was drowned in her own cabin, and not at sea as you supposed. And I am enquiring into the matter for you. I want, for your sake, to find out exactly how and why she died. I don't conduct this enquiry for my own amusement."

"That's rather obvious, isn't it?"

"I hope that it is. James Tabb has just told us that the boat which contained the remains of the late Mrs. de Winter had three holes hammered through her bottom. And that the sea-cocks were open. Do you doubt his statement?"

"Of course not. He's a boat-builder, he knows what he is talking about."

"Who looked after Mrs. de Winter's boat?"

"She looked after it herself."

"She employed no hand?"

"No, nobody at all."

"The boat was moored in the private harbour belonging to Manderley?"

"Yes."

"Any stranger who tried to tamper with the boat would be seen? There is no access to the harbour by public foot-path?"

"No, none at all."

"The harbour is quiet, is it not, and surrounded by trees?"

"Yes."

"A trespasser might not be noticed?"

"Possibly not."

"Yet James Tabb has told us, and we have no reason to disbelieve him, that a boat with those holes drilled in her bottom and the sea-cocks open could not float for more than ten or fifteen minutes."

"Quite."

"Therefore we can put aside the idea that the boat was tampered with maliciously before Mrs. de Winter went for her evening sail. Had that been the case the boat would have sunk at her moorings."

"No doubt."

"Therefore we must assume that whoever took the boat out that night drove in the planking and opened the sea-cocks."

"I suppose so."

"You have told us already that the door of the cabin was shut, the port-holes closed, and your wife's remains were on the floor. This was in your statement, and Doctor Phillips', and in Captain Searle's?"

"Yes."

"And now added to this is the information that a spike was driven through the bottom, and the sea-cocks were open. Does not this strike you, Mr. de Winter, as being very strange?"

"Certainly."

"You have no suggestion to make?"

"No, none at all."

"Mr. de Winter, painful as it may be, it is my duty to ask you a very personal question."

"Yes."

"Were relations between you and the late Mrs. de Winter perfectly happy?"

They had to come of course, those black spots in front of my eyes, dancing, flickering, stabbing the hazy air, and it was hot, so hot with all those people, all those faces, and no open window; the door, from being near to me, was farther away than I had thought, and all the time the ground coming up to meet me.

And then, out of the queer mist around me, Maxim's voice, clear and strong, "Will someone take my wife outside? She is going to faint."

CHAPTER TWENTY-THREE

I was sitting in the little room again. The room like a waiting-room at the station. The policeman was there, bending over me, giving me a glass of water, and someone's hand was on my arm, Frank's hand. I sat quite still, the floor, the walls, the figures of Frank and the policeman taking solid shape before me.

"I'm so sorry," I said, "such a stupid thing to do. It was so hot in that room, so very hot."

"It gets very airless in there," said the policeman, "there's been complaints about it often, but nothing's ever done. We've had ladies fainting in there before."

"Are you feeling better, Mrs. de Winter?" said Frank.

"Yes. Yes, much better. I shall be all right again. Don't wait with me."

"I'm going to take you back to Manderley."

"No."

"Yes. Maxim has asked me to."

"No. You ought to stay with him."

"Maxim told me to take you back to Manderley."

He put his arm through mine and helped me to get up. "Can you walk as far as the car or shall I bring it round?"

"I can walk. But I'd much rather stay. I want to wait for Maxim."

"Maxim may be a long time."

Why did he say that? What did he mean? Why didn't he look at me? He took my arm and walked with me along the passage to the door, and so down the steps into the street. Maxim may be a long time. . . .

We did not speak. We came to the little Morris car belonging to

Frank. He opened the door, and helped me in. Then he got in himself and started up the engine. We drove away from the cobbled market-place, through the empty town, and out on to the road to Kerrith.

"Why will they be a long time? What are they going to do?"

"They may have to go over the evidence again." Frank looked straight in front of him along the hard white road.

"They've had all the evidence," I said. "There's nothing more anyone can say."

"You never know," said Frank, "the coroner may put his questions in a different way. Tabb has altered the whole business. The coroner will have to approach it now from another angle."

"What angle? How do you mean?"

"You heard the evidence? You heard what Tabb said about the boat? They won't believe in an accident any more."

"It's absurd, Frank, it's ridiculous. They should not listen to Tabb. How can he tell, after all these months, how holes came to be in a boat? What are they trying to prove?"

"I don't know."

"That coroner will go on and on harping at Maxim, making him lose his temper, making him say things he doesn't mean. He will ask question after question, Frank, and Maxim won't stand it, I know he won't stand it."

Frank did not answer. He was driving very fast. For the first time since I had known him he was at a loss for the usual conventional phrase. That meant he was worried, very worried. And usually he was such a slow careful driver, stopping dead at every cross-roads, peering to right and left, blowing his horn at every bend in the road.

"That man was there," I said, "that man who came once to Manderley to see Mrs. Danvers."

"You mean Favell?" said Frank. "Yes, I saw him."

"He was sitting there, with Mrs. Danvers."

"Yes, I know."

"Why was he there? What right had he to go to the inquest?"

"He was her cousin."

"It's not right that he and Mrs. Danvers should sit there, listening to that evidence. I don't trust them, Frank."

"No."

"They might do something; they might make mischief."

Again Frank did not answer. I realised that his loyalty to Maxim was such that he would not let himself be drawn into a discussion, even with me. He did not know how much I knew. Nor could I tell for certainty how much he knew. We were allies, we travelled the same

road, but we could not look at one another. We neither of us dared
risk a confession. We were turning in now at the lodge gates, and
down the long twisting narrow drive to the house. I noticed for the
first time how the hydrangeas were coming into bloom, their blue
heads thrusting themselves from the green foliage behind. For all
their beauty there was something sombre about them, funereal; they
were like the wreaths, stiff and artificial, that you see beneath glass
cases in a foreign churchyard. There they were, all the way along the
drive, on either side of us, blue, monotonous, like spectators lined up
in a street to watch us pass.

We came to the house at last and rounded the great sweep before
the steps. "Will you be all right now?" said Frank. "You can lie down,
can't you?"

"Yes," I said, "yes, perhaps."

"I shall go back to Lanyon," he said, "Maxim may want me."

He did not say anything more. He got quickly back into the car
again and drove away. Maxim might want him. Why did he say
Maxim might want him? Perhaps the coroner was going to question
Frank as well. Ask him about that evening, over twelve months ago,
when Maxim had dined with Frank. He would want to know the exact time that Maxim left his house. He would want to know if anybody saw Maxim when he returned to the house. Whether the servants knew that he was there. Whether anybody could prove that
Maxim went straight up to bed and undressed. Mrs. Danvers might be
questioned. They might ask Mrs. Danvers to give evidence. And
Maxim beginning to lose his temper, beginning to go white. . . .

I went into the hall. I went upstairs to my room, and lay down
upon my bed, even as Frank had suggested. I put my hands over my
eyes. I kept seeing that room and all the faces. The lined, painstaking,
aggravating face of the coroner, the gold pince-nez on his nose.

"I don't conduct this enquiry for my own amusement." His slow
careful mind, easily offended. What were they all saying now? What
was happening? Suppose in a little while Frank came back to Manderley, alone?

I did not know what happened. I did not know what people did. I
remembered pictures of men in the papers, leaving places like that,
and being taken away. Suppose Maxim was taken away? They would
not let me go to him. They would not let me see him. I should have to
stay here at Manderley day after day, night after night, waiting, as I
was waiting now. People like Colonel Julyan being kind. People saying "You must not be alone. You must come to us." The telephone,
the newspapers, the telephone again. "No, Mrs. de Winter can't see

anyone. Mrs. de Winter has no story to give the *County Chronicle*." And another day. And another day. Weeks that would be blurred and non-existent. Frank at last taking me to see Maxim. He would look thin, queer, like people in hospital. . . .

Other women had been through this. Women I had read about in papers. They sent letters to the Home Secretary and it was not any good. The Home Secretary always said that justice must take its course. Friends sent petitions too, everybody signed them, but the Home Secretary could never do anything. And the ordinary people who read about it in the papers said why should the fellow get off, he murdered his wife, didn't he? What about the poor, murdered wife? This sentimental business about abolishing the death penalty simply encourages crime. This fellow ought to have thought about that before he killed his wife. It's too late now. He will have to hang for it, like any other murderer. And serve him right too. Let it be a warning to others.

I remember seeing a picture on the back of a paper once, of a little crowd collected outside a prison gate, and just after nine o'clock a policeman came and pinned a notice on the gate for the people to read. The notice said something about the sentence being carried out. "Sentence of death was carried out this morning at nine o'clock. The governor, the prison doctor, and the sheriff of the county were present." Hanging was quick. Hanging did not hurt. It broke your neck at once. No, it did not. Someone said once it did not always work. Someone who had known the governor of a prison. They put that bag over your head, and you stand on the little platform, and then the floor gives way beneath you. It takes exactly three minutes to go from the cell to the moment you are hanged. No, fifty seconds, someone said. No, that's absurd. It could not be fifty seconds. There's a little flight of steps down the side of the shed, down to the pit. The doctor goes down there to look. They die instantly. No, they don't. The body moves for some time, the neck is not always broken. Yes, but even so they don't feel anything. Someone said they did. Someone who had a brother who was a prison doctor said it was not generally known, because it would be such a scandal, but they did not always die at once. Their eyes are open, they stay open for quite a long time.

God, don't let me go on thinking about this. Let me think about something else. About other things. About Mrs. Van Hopper in America. She must be staying with her daughter now. They had that house on Long Island in the summer. I expect they played a lot of bridge. They went to the races. Mrs. Van Hopper was fond of the races. I wonder if she still wears that little yellow hat. It was too small for her. Much too small on that big face. Mrs. Van Hopper sitting about in the garden of that house on Long Island, with novels, and magazines, and papers on her lap. Mrs. Van Hopper putting up her lorgnette and calling to her daughter, "Look at this, Helen. They say Max de Winter murdered his first wife. I always did think there was something peculiar about him. I warned that fool of a girl she was making a mistake, but she wouldn't listen to me. Well, she's cooked her goose now all right. I suppose they'll make her a big offer to go on the pictures."

Something was touching my hand. It was Jasper. It was Jasper, thrusting his cold damp nose in my hands. He had followed me up from the hall. Why did dogs make one want to cry? There was something so quiet and hopeless about their sympathy. Jasper, knowing something was wrong, as dogs always do. Trunks being packed. Cars being brought to the door. Dogs standing with drooping tails, dejected eyes. Wandering back to their baskets in the hall when the sound of the car dies away. . . .

I must have fallen asleep because I woke suddenly with a start, and heard that first crack of thunder in the air. I sat up. The clock said five. I got up and went to the window. There was not a breath of wind. The leaves hung listless on the trees, waiting. The sky was slatey grey. The jagged lightning split the sky. Another rumble in the distance. No rain fell. I went out into the corridor and listened. I could not hear anything. I went to the head of the stairs. There was no sign of anybody. The hall was dark because of the menace of thunder overhead. I went down and stood on the terrace. There was another burst of thunder. One spot of rain fell on my hand. One spot. No more. It was very dark. I could see the sea beyond the dip in the valley like a black lake. Another spot fell on my hand, and another crack of thunder came. One of the housemaids began shutting the windows in the rooms upstairs. Robert appeared and shut the windows of the drawing-room behind me.

"The gentlemen are not back yet, are they, Robert?" I asked.

"No, Madam, not yet. I thought you were with them, Madam."

"No. No, I've been back some time."

"Will you have tea, Madam?"

"No, no, I'll wait."

"It looks as though the weather was going to break at last, Madam."

"Yes."

No rain fell. Nothing since those two drops on my hand. I went back and sat in the library. At half-past five Robert came into the room.

"The car has just driven up to the door now, Madam," he said.

"Which car?" I said.

"Mr. de Winter's car, Madam," he said.

"Is Mr. de Winter driving it himself?"

"Yes, Madam."

I tried to get up but my legs were things of straw, they would not bear me. I stood leaning against the sofa. My throat was very dry. After a minute Maxim came into the room. He stood just inside the door.

He looked very tired, old. There were lines at the corner of his mouth I had never noticed before.

"It's all over," he said.

I waited. Still I could not speak or move towards him.

"Suicide," he said, "without sufficient evidence to show the state of mind of the deceased. They were all at sea of course, they did not know what they were doing."

I sat down on the sofa. "Suicide," I said, "but the motive? Where was the motive?"

"God knows," he said. "They did not seem to think a motive was necessary. Old Horridge, peering at me, wanting to know if Rebecca had any money troubles. Money troubles, God in heaven."

He went and stood by the window, looking out at the green lawns. "It's going to rain," he said. "Thank God it's going to rain at last."

"What happened?" I said, "what did the coroner say? Why have you been there all this time?"

"He went over and over the same ground again," said Maxim. "Little details about the boat that no one cared about a damn. Were the sea-cocks hard to turn on? Where exactly was the first hole in relation to the second? What was ballast? What effect upon the stability of the boat would the shifting of the ballast have? Could a woman do this unaided? Did the cabin door shut firmly? What pressure of water was necessary to burst open the door? I thought I should go mad. I kept my temper though. Seeing you there, by the door, made me remember what I had to do. If you had not fainted like that, I should never have done it. It brought me up with a jerk. I knew exactly what I was going to say. I faced Horridge all the time, I never took my eyes off his thin, pernickety, little face and those gold-rimmed pince-nez. I shall remember that face of his to my dying day. I'm tired, darling; so tired I can't see, or hear, or feel anything."

He sat down on the window seat. He leant forward, his head in his hands. I went and sat beside him. In a few minutes Frith came in, followed by Robert carrying the table for tea. The solemn ritual went forward as it always did, day after day, the leaves of the table pulled out, the legs adjusted, the laying of the snowy cloth, the putting down of the silver tea-pot and the kettle with the little flame beneath. Scones, sandwiches, three different sorts of cake. Jasper sat close to the table, his tail thumping now and again upon the floor, his eyes fixed expectantly on me. It's funny, I thought, how the routine of life goes on, whatever happens, we do the same things, go through the little performances of eating, sleeping, washing. No crisis can break through the crust of habit. I poured out Maxim's tea, I took it to him on the window seat, gave him his scone, and buttered one for myself.

"Where's Frank?" I asked.

"He had to go and see the vicar. I would have gone too but I wanted to come straight back to you. I kept thinking of you, waiting here, all by yourself, not knowing what was going to happen."

"Why the vicar?" I said.

"Something has to happen this evening," he said. "Something at the church."

I stared at him blankly. Then I understood. They were going to bury Rebecca. They were going to bring Rebecca back from the mortuary.

"It's fixed for six-thirty," he said. "No one knows but Frank, and Colonel Julyan, and the vicar, and myself. There won't be anyone hanging about. This was arranged yesterday. The verdict doesn't make any difference."

"What time must you go?"

"I'm meeting them there at the church at twenty-five past six."

I did not say anything. I went on drinking my tea. Maxim put his sandwich down untasted. "It's still very hot, isn't it?" he said.

"It's the storm," I said. "It won't break. Only little spots at a time. It's there in the air. It won't break."

"It was thundering when I left Lanyon," he said, "the sky was like ink over my head. Why in the name of God doesn't it rain?"

The birds were hushed in the trees. It was still very dark.

"I wish you did not have to go out again," I said.

He did not answer. He looked tired, so deathly tired.

"We'll talk over things this evening when I get back," he said presently. "We've got so much to do together, haven't we? We've got to begin all over again. I've been the worst sort of husband for you."

"No!" I said. "No!"

"We'll start again, once this thing is behind us. We can do it, you and I. It's not like being alone. The past can't hurt us if we are together. You'll have children too." After a while he glanced at his watch. "It's ten past six," he said, "I shall have to be going. It won't take long, not more than half-an-hour. We've got to go down to the crypt."

I held his hand. "I'll come with you. I shan't mind. Let me come with you."

"No," he said. "No, I don't want you to come."

Then he went out of the room. I heard the sound of the car starting up in the drive. Presently the sound died away, and I knew he had gone.

Robert came to clear away the tea. It was like any other day. The routine was unchanged. I wondered if it would have been so had Maxim not come back from Lanyon. I wondered if Robert would have stood there, that wooden expression on his young sheep's face, brushing the crumbs from the snow-white cloth, picking up the table, carrying it from the room.

It seemed very quiet in the library when he had gone. I began to think of them down at the church, going through that door and down the flight of stairs to the crypt. I had never been there. I had only seen the door. I wondered what a crypt was like, if there were coffins standing there. Maxim's father and mother. I wondered what would happen to the coffin of that other woman who had been put there by mistake. I wondered who she was, poor unclaimed soul, washed up by the wind and tide. Now another coffin would stand there. Rebecca would lie there in the crypt as well. Was the vicar reading the burial service there, with Maxim, and Frank, and Colonel Julyan standing by his side? Ashes to ashes. Dust to dust. It seemed to me that Rebecca had no reality any more. She had crumbled away when they had found her on the cabin floor. It was not Rebecca who was lying in that coffin in the crypt, it was dust. Only dust.

Just after seven the rain began to fall. Gently at first, a light pattering in the trees, and so thin I could not see it. Then louder and faster, a driving torrent falling slantways from the slate sky, like water from a sluice. I left the windows open wide. I stood in front of them and breathed the cold clean air. The rain splashed into my face and on my hands. I could not see beyond the lawns, the falling rain came thick and fast. I heard it sputtering in the gutter-pipes above the window, and splashing on the stones of the terrace. There was no more thunder. The rain smelt of moss and earth and of the black bark of trees.

I did not hear Frith come in at the door. I was standing by the window, watching the rain. I did not see him until he was beside me.

"Excuse me, Madam," he said, "do you know if Mr. de Winter will be long?"

"No," I said, "not very long."

"There's a gentleman to see him, Madam," said Frith, after a moment's hesitation. "I'm not quite sure what I ought to say. He's so very insistent about seeing Mr. de Winter."

"Who is it?" I said. "Is it anyone you know?"

Frith looked uncomfortable. "Yes, Madam," he said, "it's a gentleman who used to come here frequently at one time, when Mrs. de Winter was alive. A gentleman called Mr. Favell."

I knelt on the window seat and shut the window. The rain was coming in on to the cushions. Then I turned round and looked at Frith.

"I think perhaps I had better see Mr. Favell," I said.

"Very good, Madam."

I went and stood over on the rug beside the empty fireplace. It was just possible that I should be able to get rid of Favell before Maxim came back. I did not know what I was going to say to him, but I was not frightened.

In a few moments Frith returned and showed Favell into the library. He looked much the same as before but a little rougher if possible, a little more untidy. He was the sort of man who invariably went hatless, his hair was bleached from the sun of the last days and his skin was deeply tanned. His eyes were rather bloodshot. I wondered if he had been drinking.

"I'm afraid Maxim is not here," I said. "I don't know when he will be back. Wouldn't it be better if you made an appointment to see him at the office in the morning?"

"Waiting doesn't worry me," said Favell, "and I don't think I shall have to wait very long, you know. I had a look in the dining-room as I came along, and I see Max's place is laid for dinner all right."

"Our plans have been changed," I said. "It's quite possible Maxim won't be home at all this evening."

"He's run off has he?" said Favell, with a half-smile I did not like. "I wonder if you really mean it. Of course under the circumstances it's the wisest thing he can do. Gossip is an unpleasant thing to some people. It's more pleasant to avoid it, isn't it?"

"I don't know what you mean," I said.

"Don't you?" he said. "Oh, come, you don't expect me to believe that, do you? Tell me, are you feeling better? Too bad fainting like that at the inquest this afternoon. I would have come and helped you out but I saw you had one knight-errant already. I bet Frank Crawley enjoyed himself. Did you let him drive you home? You wouldn't let me drive you five yards when I offered to."

"What did you want to see Maxim about?" I asked.

Favell leant forward to the table and helped himself to a cigarette. "You don't mind my smoking, I suppose?" he said, "it won't make you sick, will it? One never knows with brides."

He watched me over his lighter. "You've grown up a bit since I saw you last, haven't you?" he said. "I wonder what you have been doing. Leading Frank Crawley up the garden-path?" He blew a cloud of smoke in the air. "I say, do you mind asking old Frith to get me a whisky-and-soda?"

I did not say anything. I went and rang the bell. He sat down on the edge of the sofa, swinging his legs, that half-smile on his lips. Robert answered the bell. "A whisky-and-soda for Mr. Favell," I said.

"Well, Robert?" said Favell, "I haven't seen you for a very long time. Still breaking the hearts of the girls in Kerrith?"

Robert flushed. He glanced at me, horribly embarrassed.

"All right, old chap, I won't give you away. Run along and get me a double whisky, and jump on it."

Robert disappeared. Favell laughed, dropping ash all over the floor.

"I took Robert out once on his half-day," he said. "Rebecca bet me a fiver I wouldn't ask him. I won my fiver all right. Spent one of the funniest evenings of my life. Did I laugh? Oh, boy! Robert on the razzle takes a lot of beating, I tell you. I must say he's got a good eye for a girl. He picked the prettiest of the bunch we saw that night."

Robert came back again with the whisky-and-soda on a tray. He still looked very red, very uncomfortable. Favell watched him with a smile as he poured out his drink, and then he began to laugh, leaning back on the arm of the sofa. He whistled the bar of a song, watching Robert all the while.

"That was the one, wasn't it?" he said, "that was the tune. Do you still like ginger hair, Robert?"

Robert gave him a flat weak smile. He looked miserable. Favell laughed louder still. Robert turned and went out of the room.

"Poor kid," said Favell. "I don't suppose he's been on the loose since. That old ass Frith keeps him on a leading string."

He began drinking his whisky-and-soda, glancing round the room, looking at me every now and again, and smiling.

"I don't think I shall mind very much if Max doesn't get back to dinner," he said. "What say you?"

I did not answer. I stood by the fireplace, my hands behind my back. "You wouldn't waste that place at the dining-room table would you?" he said. He looked at me, smiling still, his head on one side.

"Mr. Favell," I said, "I don't want to be rude, but as a matter of fact I'm very tired. I've had a long and fairly exhausting day. If you can't tell me what you want to see Maxim about it's not much good your sitting here. You had far better do as I suggest, and go round to the estate office in the morning."

He slid off the arm of the sofa and came towards me, his glass in his hand. "No, no," he said. "No, no, don't be a brute. I've had an exhausting day too. Don't run away and leave me. I'm quite harmless, really I am. I suppose Max has been telling tales about me to you?"

I did not answer. "You think I'm the big, bad wolf, don't you?" he said, "but I'm not, you know. I'm a perfectly ordinary, harmless bloke. And I think you are behaving splendidly over all this, perfectly splendidly. I take off my hat to you, I really do." This last speech of his was very slurred and thick. I wished I had never told Frith I would see him.

"You come down here to Manderley," he said, waving his arm vaguely, "you take on all this place, meet hundreds of people you've never seen before, you put up with old Max and his moods, you don't give a fig for anyone, you just go your own way, I call it a damn good effort, and I don't care who hears me say so. A damn good effort." He swayed a little as he stood. He steadied himself, and put the empty glass down on the table. "This business has been a shock to me, you know," he said. "A bloody awful shock. Rebecca was my cousin. I was damn fond of her."

"Yes," I said. "I'm very sorry for you."

"We were brought up together," he went on. "Always tremendous pals. Liked the same things, the same people. Laughed at the same jokes. I suppose I was fonder of Rebecca than anyone else in the world. And she was fond of me. All this has been a bloody shock."

"Yes," I said. "Yes, of course."

"And what is Max going to do about it, that's what I want to know? Does he think he can sit back quietly now that sham inquest is over? Tell me that?" He was not smiling any more. He bent towards me.

"I'm going to see justice is done to Rebecca," he said, his voice growing louder. "Suicide. . . . God Almighty, that doddering old fool of a coroner got the jury to say suicide. You and I know it wasn't suicide, don't we?" He leant closer to me still. "Don't we?" he said slowly.

The door opened and Maxim came into the room, with Frank just behind him. Maxim stood quite still, with the door open, staring at Favell. "What the hell are you doing here?" he said.

Favell turned round, his hands in his pockets. He waited a moment, and then he began to smile. "As a matter of fact, Max, old chap, I came to congratulate you on the inquest this afternoon."

"Do you mind leaving the house?" said Max, "or do you want Crawley and me to chuck you out?"

"Steady a moment, steady a moment," said Favell. He lit another cigarette, and sat down once more on the arm of the sofa.

"You don't want Frith to hear what I'm going to say, do you?" he said. "Well, he will, if you don't shut that door."

Maxim did not move. I saw Frank close the door very quietly.

"Now, listen here, Max," said Favell, "you've come very well out of this affair, haven't you? Better than you ever expected. Oh, yes, I was in the court this afternoon, and I dare say you saw me. I was there from start to finish. I saw your wife faint, at a rather critical moment, and I don't blame her. It was touch and go, then, wasn't it, Max, what way the enquiry would go? And luckily for you it went the way it did. You hadn't squared those thick-headed fellows who were acting jury, had you? It looked damn like it to me."

Maxim made a move towards Favell, but Favell held up his hand.

"Wait a bit, can't you?" he said. "I haven't finished yet. You realise, don't you, Max, old man, that I can make things damned unpleasant for you if I choose? Not only unpleasant, but shall I say dangerous?"

I sat down on the chair beside the fireplace. I held the arms of the chair very tight. Frank came over and stood behind the chair. Still Maxim did not move. He never took his eyes off Favell.

"Oh, yes?" he said, "in what way can you make things dangerous?"

"Look here, Max," said Favell, "I suppose there are no secrets between you and your wife, and from the look of things Crawley there just makes the happy trio. I can speak plainly then, and I will. You all know about Rebecca and me. We were lovers, weren't we? I've never denied it, and I never will. Very well then. Up to the present I believed, like every other fool, that Rebecca was drowned sailing in the bay, and that her body was picked up at Edgecoombe weeks afterwards. It was a shock to me then, a bloody shock. But I said to myself, 'That's the sort of death Rebecca would choose, she'd go out like she lived, fighting.' " He paused, he sat there on the edge of the sofa, looking at all of us in turn. "Then I pick up the evening paper a few days ago and I read that Rebecca's boat had been stumbled on by the local diver and that there was a body in the cabin. I couldn't understand it. Who the hell would Rebecca have as a sailing companion? It didn't make sense. I came down here, and put up at a pub just outside Kerrith. I got in touch with Mrs. Danvers. She told me then that the body in the cabin was Rebecca's. Even so I thought like everyone else that the first body was a mistake and Rebecca had somehow got shut in the cabin when she went to fetch a coat. Well, I attended that inquest to-day, as you know. And everything went smoothly, didn't it, until Tabb gave his evidence? But after that? Well, Max, old man, what have you got to say about those holes in the floor-boards, and those sea-cocks turned full on?"

"Do you think," said Maxim slowly, "that after those hours of talk this afternoon I am going into it again—with you? You heard the evidence, and you heard the verdict. It satisfied the coroner, and it must satisfy you."

"Suicide, eh?" said Favell. "Rebecca committing suicide. The sort of thing she would do, wasn't it? Listen, you never knew I had this note, did you? I kept it, because it was the last thing she ever wrote to me. I'll read it to you. I think it will interest you."

He took a piece of paper out of his pocket. I recognised that thin, pointed, slanting hand. *"I tried to ring you from the flat, but could get no answer,"* he read. *"I'm going down to Manderley right away. I shall be at the cottage this evening, and if you get this in time will you get the car and follow me. I'll spend the night at the cottage, and leave the door open for you. I've got something to tell you and I want to see you as soon as possible. Rebecca."*

He put the note back in his pocket. "That's not the sort of note you write when you're going to commit suicide, is it?" he said. "It was waiting for me at my flat when I got back about four in the morning. I had no idea Rebecca was to be in London that day or I should have got in touch with her. It happened, by a vile stroke of fortune, I was on a party that night. When I read the note at four in the morning I decided it was too late to go crashing down on a six-hour run to Manderley. I went to bed, determined to put a call through later in the day. I did. About twelve o'clock. And I heard Rebecca had been drowned!"

He sat there, staring at Maxim. None of us spoke.

"Supposing the coroner this afternoon had read that note, it would have made it a little bit more tricky for you, wouldn't it, Max, old man?" said Favell.

"Well," said Maxim. "Why didn't you get up and give it to him?"

"Steady, old boy, steady. No need to get rattled. I don't want to smash you, Max. God knows you've never been a friend to me, but I don't bear malice about it. All married men with lovely wives are jealous, aren't they? And some of 'em just can't help playing Othello. They're made that way. I don't blame them. I'm sorry for them. I'm a bit of a Socialist in my way, you know, and I can't think why fellows can't share their women instead of killing them. What difference does it make? You can get your fun just the same. A lovely woman isn't like a motor tyre, she doesn't wear out. The more you use her the better she goes. Now, Max. I've laid all my cards on the table. Why can't we come to some agreement? I'm not a rich man. I'm too fond of gambling for that. But what gets me down is never having any capital to fall back upon. Now if I had a settlement of two or three thousand a year for life I could jog along quite comfortably. And I'd never trouble you again. I swear before God I would not."

"I've asked you before to leave the house," said Maxim. "I'm not going to ask you again. There's the door behind me. You can open it yourself."

"Half a minute, Maxim," said Frank, "it's not quite so easy as all that." He turned to Favell. "I see what you're driving at. It happens, very unfortunately, that you could, as you say, twist things round and make it difficult for Maxim. I don't think he sees it as clearly as I do. What is the exact amount you propose Maxim should settle on you?"

I saw Maxim go very white, and a little pulse began to show on his forehead. "Don't interfere with this, Frank," he said, "this is my affair entirely. I'm not going to give way to blackmail."

"I don't suppose your wife wants to be pointed out as Mrs. de Winter, the widow of a murderer, of a fellow who was hanged," said Favell. He laughed, and glanced towards me.

"You think you can frighten me, don't you, Favell?" said Maxim. "Well, you are wrong. I'm not afraid of anything you can do. There is the telephone, in the next room. Shall I ring up Colonel Julyan and ask him to come over? He's the magistrate. He'll be interested in your story." Favell stared at him, and laughed.

"Good bluff," he said, "but it won't work. You wouldn't dare ring up old Julyan. I've got enough evidence to hang you, Max, old man." Maxim walked slowly across the room and passed through to the little room beyond. I heard the click of the telephone.

"Stop him!" I said to Frank. "Stop him, for God's sake."

Frank glanced at my face, he went swiftly towards the door.

I heard Maxim's voice, very cool, very calm. "I want Kerrith 17," he said. Favell was watching the door, his face curiously intense.

"Leave me alone," I heard Maxim say to Frank. And then, two minutes afterwards: "Is that Colonel Julyan speaking? It's de Winter here. Yes. Yes, I know. I wonder if you could possibly come over here at once. Yes, to Manderley. It's rather urgent. I can't explain why on the telephone, but you shall hear everything directly you come. I'm very sorry to have to drag you out. Yes. Thank you very much. Goodbye."

He came back again into the room. "Julyan is coming right away," he said. He crossed over and threw open the windows. It was still raining very hard. He stood there, with his back to us, breathing the cold air.

"Maxim," said Frank quietly. "Maxim."

He did not answer. Favell laughed, and helped himself to another cigarette. "If you want to hang yourself, old fellow, it's all the same to me," he said. He picked up a paper from the table and flung himself down on the sofa, crossed his legs, and began to turn over the pages. Frank hesitated, glancing from me to Maxim. Then he came beside me.

"Can't you do something?" I whispered. "Go out and meet Colonel Julyan, prevent him from coming, say it was all a mistake?" Maxim spoke from the window without turning round.

"Frank is not to leave this room," he said. "I'm going to manage this thing alone. Colonel Julyan will be here in exactly ten minutes."

We none of us said anything. Favell went on reading his paper. There was no sound but the steady falling rain. It fell without a break, steady, straight, and monotonous. I felt helpless, without strength. There was nothing I could do. Nothing that Frank could do. In a book or in a play I would have found a revolver, and we should have shot Favell, hidden his body in a cupboard. There was no revolver. There was no cupboard. We were ordinary people. These things did not happen. I could not go to Maxim now and beg him on my knees to give Favell the money. I had to sit there, with my hands in my lap, watching the rain, watching Maxim with his back turned to me, standing by the window.

It was raining too hard to hear the car. The sound of the rain covered all other sounds. We did not know Colonel Julyan had arrived until the door opened, and Frith showed him into the room.

Maxim swung round from the window. "Good evening," he said. "We meet again. You've made very good time."

"Yes," said Colonel Julyan, "you said it was urgent, so I came at once. Luckily, my man had left the car handy. What an evening."

He glanced at Favell uncertainly, and then came over and shook hands with me, nodding to Frank. "A good thing the rain has come," he said. "It's been hanging about too long. I hope you're feeling better."

I murmured something, I don't know what, and he stood there looking from one to the other of us, rubbing his hands.

"I think you realise," Maxim said, "that I haven't brought you out on an evening like this for a social half-hour before dinner. This is Jack Favell, my late wife's first cousin. I don't know if you have ever met."

Colonel Julyan nodded. "Your face seems familiar. I've probably met you here in the old days."

"Quite," said Maxim. "Go ahead, Favell."

Favell got up from the sofa and chucked the paper back on the table. The ten minutes seemed to have sobered him. He walked quite steadily. He was not smiling any longer. I had the impression that he was not entirely pleased with the turn in the events, and he was ill-prepared for the encounter with Colonel Julyan. He began speaking in a loud, rather domineering voice. "Look here, Colonel Julyan," he said, "there's no sense in beating about the bush. The reason why I'm here is that I'm not satisfied with the verdict given at the inquest this afternoon."

"Oh?" said Colonel Julyan, "isn't that for de Winter to say, not you?"

"No, I don't think it is," said Favell. "I have a right to speak, not only as Rebecca's cousin, but as her prospective husband, had she lived."

Colonel Julyan looked rather taken aback. "Oh," he said. "Oh, I see. That's rather different. Is this true, de Winter?"

Maxim shrugged his shoulders. "It's the first I've heard of it," he said.

Colonel Julyan looked from one to the other doubtfully. "Look here, Favell," he said, "what exactly is your trouble?"

Favell stared at him a moment. I could see he was planning something in his mind, and he was still not sober enough to carry it through. He put his hand slowly in his waistcoat pocket and brought out Rebecca's note. "This was written a few hours before Rebecca was supposed to have set out on that suicidal sail. Here it is. I want you to read it, and say whether you think a woman who wrote that note had made up her mind to kill herself."

Colonel Julyan took a pair of spectacles from a case in his pocket and read the note. Then he handed it back to Favell. "No," he said, "on the face of it, no. But I don't know what the note refers to. Perhaps you do. Or perhaps de Winter does?"

Maxim did not say anything. Favell twisted the piece of paper in his fingers, considering Colonel Julyan all the while. "My cousin made a definite appointment in that note, didn't she?" he said. "She deliberately asked me to drive down to Manderley that night because she had something to tell me. What it actually was I don't suppose we shall ever know, but that's beside the point. She made the appointment, and she was to spend the night in the cottage on purpose to see me alone. The mere fact of her going for a sail never surprised me. It was the sort of thing she did, for an hour or so, after a long day in London. But to plug holes in the cabin and deliberately drown herself, the hysterical, impulsive freak of a neurotic girl—oh, no, Colonel Julyan, by Christ, no!" The colour had flooded into his face, and the last words were shouted. His manner was not helpful to him, and I could see by the thin line of Colonel Julyan's mouth that he had not taken to Favell.

"My dear fellow," he said, "it's not the slightest use your losing your temper with me. I'm not the coroner who conducted the enquiry this afternoon, nor am I a member of the jury who gave the verdict. I'm merely the magistrate of the district. Naturally I want to help you all I can, and de Winter, too. You say you refuse to believe your cousin committed suicide. On the other hand you heard, as we all did, the evidence of the boat-builder. The sea-cocks were open, the holes were there. Very well. Suppose we get to the point. What do you suggest really happened?"

Favell turned his head and looked slowly towards Maxim. He was still twisting the note between his fingers. "Rebecca never opened those sea-cocks, nor split the holes in the planking. Rebecca never committed suicide. You've asked for my opinion, and by God you shall have it. Rebecca was murdered. And if you want to know who the murderer is, why there he stands, by the window there, with that God-damned superior smile on his face. He couldn't even wait, could he, until the year was out, before marrying the first girl he set eyes on? There he is, there's your murderer for you, Mr. Maximilian de Winter. Take a good long look at him. He'd look well hanging, wouldn't he?"

And Favell began to laugh, the laugh of a drunkard, high-pitched, forced and foolish, and all the while twisting Rebecca's note between his fingers.

CHAPTER TWENTY-FOUR

Thank God for Favell's laugh. Thank God for his pointing finger, his flushed face, his staring blood-shot eyes. Thank God for the way he stood there swaying on his two feet. Because it made Colonel Julyan antagonistic, it put him on our side. I saw the disgust on his face, the quick movement of his lips. Colonel Julyan did not believe him. Colonel Julyan was on our side.

"The man's drunk," he said quietly. "He doesn't know what he's saying."

"Drunk, am I?" shouted Favell. "Oh, no, my fine friend. You may be a magistrate and a colonel into the bargain, but it won't cut any ice with me. I've got the law on my side for a change, and I'm going to use it. There are other magistrates in this bloody county besides you. Fellows with brains in their heads, who understand the meaning of justice. Not soldiers who got the sack years ago for incompetence and walk about with a string of putty medals on their chest. Max de Winter murdered Rebecca and I'm going to prove it."

"Wait a minute, Mr. Favell," said Colonel Julyan quietly, "you were present at the enquiry this afternoon, weren't you? I remember you now. I saw you sitting there. If you felt so deeply about the injustice of the verdict why didn't you say so then, to the jury, to the coroner himself? Why didn't you produce that letter in court?"

Favell stared at him, and laughed. "Why?" he said, "because I did not choose to, that's why. I preferred to come and tackle de Winter personally."

"That's why I rang you up," said Maxim, coming forward from the window; "we've already heard Favell's accusations. I asked him the same question. Why didn't he tell his suspicions to the coroner?

He said he was not a rich man, and that if I cared to settle two or three thousand on him for life he would never worry me again. Frank was here, and my wife. They both heard him. Ask them."

"It's perfectly true, sir," said Frank. "It's blackmail pure and simple."

"Yes, of course," said Colonel Julyan, "the trouble is that blackmail is not very pure, nor is it particularly simple. It can make a lot of unpleasantness for a great many people, even if the blackmailer finds himself in gaol at the end of it. Sometimes innocent people find themselves in gaol as well. We want to avoid that, in this case. I don't know whether you are sufficiently sober, Favell, to answer my questions, and if you keep off irrelevant personalities we may get through with the business quicker. You have just made a serious accusation against de Winter. Have you any proof to back that accusation?"

"Proof?" said Favell. "What the hell do you want with proof? Aren't those holes in the boat proof enough?"

"Certainly not," said Colonel Julyan, "unless you can bring a witness who saw him do it. Where's your witness?"

"Witness be damned," said Favell. "Of course de Winter did it. Who else would kill Rebecca?"

"Kerrith has a large population," said Colonel Julyan. "Why not go from door to door making enquiries? I might have done it myself. You appear to have no more proof against de Winter there than you would have against me."

"Oh, I see," said Favell, "you're going to hold his hand through this. You're going to back de Winter. You won't let him down because you've dined with him, and he's dined with you. He's a big name down here. He's the owner of Manderley. You poor bloody little snob."

"Take care, Favell, take care."

"You think you can get the better of me, don't you? You think I've got no case to bring to a court of law. I'll get my proof for you all right. I tell you de Winter killed Rebecca because of me. He knew I was her lover, he was jealous, madly jealous. He knew she was waiting for me at the cottage on the beach, and he went down that night and killed her. Then he put her body in the boat and sank her."

"Quite a clever story, Favell, in its way, but I repeat again you have no proof. Produce your witness who saw it happen and I might begin to take you seriously. I know that cottage on the beach. A sort of picnic place, isn't it? Mrs. de Winter used to keep the gear there for the boat. It would help your story if you could turn it into a bungalow with fifty replicas alongside of it. There would be a chance then that one of the inhabitants might have seen the whole affair."

"Hold on," said Favell slowly, "hold on. . . . There is a chance de Winter might have been seen that night. Quite a good chance too. It's worth finding out. What would you say if I did produce a witness?"

Colonel Julyan shrugged his shoulders. I saw Frank glance enquiringly at Maxim. Maxim did not say anything. He was watching Favell. I suddenly knew what Favell meant. I knew who he was talking about. And in a flash of fear and horror I knew that he was right. There had been a witness that night. Little sentences came back to me. Words I had not understood, phrases I believed to be the fragments of a poor idiot's mind. "She's down there, isn't she? She won't come back again." "I didn't tell no one." "They'll find her there, won't they? The fishes have eaten her, haven't they?" "She'll not come back no more." Ben knew. Ben had seen. Ben, with his queer crazed brain, had been a witness all the time. He had been hiding in the woods that night. He had seen Maxim take the boat from the moorings, and pull back in the dinghy, alone. I knew all the colour was draining away from my face. I leant back against the cushion of the chair.

"There's a local half-wit who spends his time on the beach," said Favell. "He was always hanging about, when I used to come down and meet Rebecca. I've often seen him. He used to sleep in the woods, or on the beach, when the nights were hot. The fellow's cracked, he would never have come forward on his own. But I could make him talk, if he did see anything that night. And there's a bloody big chance he did."

"Who is this? What's he talking about?" said Colonel Julyan.

"He must mean Ben," said Frank, with another glance at Maxim. "He's the son of one of our tenants. But the man's not responsible for what he says or does. He's been an idiot since birth."

"What the hell does that matter?" said Favell. "He's got eyes, hasn't he? He knows what he sees. He's only got to answer yes or no. You're getting windy now, aren't you? Not so mighty confident?"

"Can we get hold of this fellow and question him?" asked Colonel Julyan.

"Of course," said Maxim. "Tell Robert to cut down to his mother's cottage, Frank, and bring him back."

Frank hesitated. I saw him glance at me out of the tail of his eye.

"Go on, for God's sake," said Maxim. "We want to end this thing, don't we?" Frank went out of the room. I began to feel the old nagging pain beneath my heart.

In a few minutes Frank came back again into the room.

"Robert's taken my car," he said. "If Ben is at home he won't be more than ten minutes."

"The rain will keep him at home all right," said Favell, "he'll be there. And I think you will find I shall be able to make him talk." He laughed, and looked at Maxim. His face was still very flushed. Excitement had made him sweat; there were beads of perspiration on his forehead. I noticed how his neck bulged over the back of his collar, and how low his ears were set on his head. Those florid good looks would not last him very long. Already he was out of condition, puffy. He helped himself to another cigarette. "You're like a little trades union here at Manderley, aren't you?" he said; "no one going to give anyone else away. Even the local magistrate is on the same racket. We must exempt the bride of course. A wife doesn't give evidence against her husband. Crawley of course has been squared. He knows he would lose his job if he told the truth. And if I guess rightly there's a spice of malice in his soul towards me too. You didn't have much success with Rebecca, did you, Crawley? That garden-path wasn't quite long enough, eh? It's a bit easier this time, isn't it? The bride will be grateful for your fraternal arm every time she faints. When she hears the judge sentence her husband to death that arm of yours will come in very handy."

It happened very quickly. Too quick for me to see how Maxim did it. But I saw Favell stagger and fall against the arm of the sofa, and down on to the floor. And Maxim was standing just beside him. I felt rather sick. There was something degrading in the fact that Maxim had hit Favell. I wished I had not known. I wished I had not been there to see. Colonel Julyan did not say anything. He looked very grim. He turned his back on them and came and stood beside me.

"I think you had better go upstairs," he said quietly.

I shook my head. "No," I whispered. "No."

"That fellow is in a state capable of saying anything," he said. "What you have just seen was not very attractive, was it? Your husband was right of course, but it's a pity you saw it."

I did not answer. I was watching Favell who was getting slowly to his feet. He sat down heavily on the sofa and put his handkerchief to his face.

"Get me a drink," he said, "get me a drink."

Maxim looked at Frank. Frank went out of the room. None of us spoke. In a moment Frank came back with the whisky-and-soda on a tray. He mixed some in a glass and gave it to Favell. Favell drank it greedily, like an animal. There was something sensual and horrible the way he put his mouth to the glass. His lips folded upon the glass in a peculiar way. There was a dark red patch on his jaw where Maxim had hit him. Maxim had turned his back on him again and had returned to the window. I glanced at Colonel Julyan and saw that he was looking at Maxim. His gaze was curious, intent. My heart began beating very quickly. Why did Colonel Julyan look at Maxim in that way?

Did it mean that he was beginning to wonder, to suspect?

Maxim did not see. He was watching the rain. It fell straight and steady as before. The sound filled the room. Favell finished his whisky-and-soda and put the glass back on the table beside the sofa. He was breathing heavily. He did not look at any of us. He was staring straight in front of him at the floor.

The telephone began ringing in the little room. It struck a shrill, discordant note. Frank went to answer it.

He came back at once and looked at Colonel Julyan. "It's your daughter," he said; "they want to know if they are to keep dinner back."

Colonel Julyan waved his hand impatiently. "Tell them to start," he said, "tell them I don't know when I shall be back." He glanced at his watch. "Fancy ringing up," he muttered, "what a moment to choose."

Frank went back into the little room to give the message. I thought of the daughter at the other end of the telephone. It would be the one who played golf. I could imagine her calling to her sister, "Dad says we're to start. What on earth can he be doing? The steak will be like leather." Their little household disorganised because of us. Their evening routine upset. All these foolish inconsequent threads hanging upon one another, because Maxim had killed Rebecca. I looked at Frank. His face was pale and set.

"I heard Robert coming back with the car," he said to Colonel Julyan. "The window in there looks on to the drive."

He went out of the library to the hall. Favell had lifted his head when he spoke. Then he got to his feet once more and stood looking towards the door. There was a queer, ugly smile on his face.

The door opened, and Frank came in. He turned and spoke to someone in the hall outside.

"All right, Ben," he said quietly, "Mr. de Winter wants to give you some cigarettes. There's nothing to be frightened of."

Ben stepped awkwardly into the room. He had his sou'wester in his hands. He looked odd and naked without his hat. I realised for the first time that his head was shaved all over, and he had no hair. He looked different, dreadful.

The light seemed to daze him. He glanced foolishly round the room, blinking his small eyes. He caught sight of me, and I gave him a weak, rather tremulous smile. I don't know if he recognised me or not. He just blinked his eyes. Then Favell walked slowly towards him and stood in front of him.

"Hullo," he said, "how's life treated you since we last met?"

Ben stared at him. There was no recognition on his face. He did not answer.

"Well?" said Favell, "you know who I am, don't you?"

Ben went on twisting his sou'wester, "Eh?" he said.

"Have a cigarette," said Favell, handing him the box. Ben glanced at Maxim and Frank.

"All right," said Maxim, "take as many as you like."

Ben took four and stuck two behind each ear. Then he stood twisting his cap again.

"You know who I am, don't you?" repeated Favell.

Still Ben did not answer. Colonel Julyan walked across to him. "You shall go home in a few moments, Ben," he said. "No one is going to hurt you. We just want you to answer one or two questions. You know Mr. Favell, don't you?"

This time Ben shook his head. "I never seen 'un," he said.

"Don't be a bloody fool," said Favell roughly; "you know you've seen me. You've seen me go to the cottage on the beach, Mrs. de Winter's cottage. You've seen me there, haven't you?"

"No," said Ben. "I never seen no one."

"You damned half-witted liar," said Favell, "are you going to stand there and say you never saw me, last year, walk through those woods with Mrs. de Winter, and go into the cottage? Didn't we catch you once, peering at us from the window?"

"Eh?" said Ben.

"A convincing witness," said Colonel Julyan sarcastically.

Favell swung round on him. "It's a put-up job," he said. "Someone has got at this idiot and bribed him too. I tell you he's seen me scores of times. Here. Will this make you remember?" He fumbled in his hip-pocket and brought out a note-case. He flourished a pound note in front of Ben. "Now do you remember me?" he said.

Ben shook his head. "I never seen 'un," he said, and then he took hold of Frank's arm. "Has he come here to take me to the asylum?" he said.

"No," said Frank. "No, of course not, Ben."

"I don't want to go to the asylum," said Ben. "They'm cruel to folk in there. I want to stay home. I done nothing."

"That's all right, Ben," said Colonel Julyan. "No one's going to put you in the asylum. Are you quite sure you've never seen this man before?"

"No," said Ben, "I've never seen 'un."

"You remember Mrs. de Winter, don't you?" said Colonel Julyan.

Ben glanced doubtfully towards me.

"No," said Colonel Julyan gently, "not this lady. The other lady, who used to go to the cottage."

"Eh?" said Ben.

"You remember the lady who had the boat?"

Ben blinked his eyes. "She's gone," he said.

"Yes, we know that," said Colonel Julyan. "She used to sail the boat, didn't she? Were you on the beach when she sailed the boat the last time? One evening, over twelve months ago. When she didn't come back again?"

Ben twisted his sou'wester. He glanced at Frank, and then at Maxim.

"Eh?" he said.

"You were there, weren't you?" said Favell, leaning forward. "You saw Mrs. de Winter come down to the cottage, and presently you saw Mr. de Winter too. He went into the cottage after her. What happened then? Go on. What happened?"

Ben shrank back against the wall. "I seen nothing," he said. "I want to stay home. I'm not going to the asylum. I never seen you. Never before. I never seen you and she in the woods." He began to blubber like a child.

"You crazy little rat," said Favell slowly, "you bloody crazy little rat."

Ben was wiping his eyes with the sleeve of his coat.

"Your witness does not seem to have helped you," said Colonel Julyan. "The performance has been rather a waste of time, hasn't it? Do you want to ask him anything else?"

"It's a plot," shouted Favell. "A plot against me. You're all in it, every one of you. Someone's paid this half-wit, I tell you. Paid him to tell his string of dirty lies."

"I think Ben might be allowed to go home," said Colonel Julyan.

"All right, Ben," said Maxim. "Robert shall take you back. And no one will put you in the asylum, don't be afraid. Tell Robert to find him something in the kitchen," he added to Frank. "Some cold meat, whatever he fancies."

"Payment for services rendered, eh?" said Favell. "He's done a good day's work for you, Max, hasn't he?"

Frank took Ben out of the room. Colonel Julyan glanced at Maxim. "The fellow appeared to be scared stiff," he said, "he was shaking like a leaf. I was watching him. He's never been ill-treated, has he?"

"No," said Maxim, "he's perfectly harmless, and I've always let him have the run of the place."

"He's been frightened at some time," said Colonel Julyan. "He was showing the whites of his eyes, just like a dog does, when you're going to whip him."

"Well, why didn't you?" said Favell, "he'd have remembered me all right if you'd whipped him. Oh, no, he's going to be given a good supper for his work to-night. Ben's not going to be whipped."

"He has not helped your case, has he?" said Colonel Julyan quietly, "we're still where we are. You can't produce one shred of evidence against de Winter and you know it. The very motive you gave won't stand the test. In a court of law, Favell, you wouldn't have a leg to stand on. You say you were Mrs. de Winter's prospective husband, and that you held clandestine meetings with her in that cottage on the beach. Even the poor idiot we have just had in this room swears he never saw you. You can't even prove your own story, can you?"

"Can't I?" said Favell. I saw him smile. He came across to the fireplace and rang the bell.

"What are you doing?" said Colonel Julyan.

"Wait a moment and you'll see," said Favell.

I guessed already what was going to happen. Frith answered the bell.

"Ask Mrs. Danvers to come here," said Favell.

Frith glanced at Maxim. Maxim nodded shortly.

Frith went out of the room. "Isn't Mrs. Danvers the housekeeper?" said Colonel Julyan.

"She was also Rebecca's personal friend," said Favell. "She was with her for years before she married, and practically brought her up. You are going to find Danny a very different sort of witness to Ben."

Frank came back into the room. "Packed Ben off to bed?" said Favell. "Given him his supper and told him he was a good boy? This time it won't be quite so easy for the trades union."

"Mrs. Danvers is coming down," said Colonel Julyan. "Favell seems to think he will get something out of her."

Frank glanced quickly at Maxim. Colonel Julyan saw the glance. I saw his lips tighten. I did not like it. No, I did not like it. I began biting my nails.

We all waited, watching the door. And Mrs. Danvers came into the room. Perhaps it was because I had generally seen her alone, and beside me she had seemed tall and gaunt, but she looked shrunken now in size, more wizened, and I noticed she had to look up to Favell and to Frank and Maxim. She stood by the door, her hands folded in front of her, looking from one to the other of us.

"Good evening, Mrs. Danvers," said Colonel Julyan.

"Good evening, sir," she said.

Her voice was that old, dead, mechanical one I had heard so often.

"First of all, Mrs. Danvers, I want to ask you a question," said Colonel Julyan, "and the question is this. Were you aware of the relationship between the late Mrs. de Winter and Mr. Favell here?"

"They were first cousins," said Mrs. Danvers.

"I was not referring to blood-relationship, Mrs. Danvers," said Colonel Julyan. "I mean something closer than that."

"I'm afraid I don't understand, sir," said Mrs. Danvers.

"Oh, come off it, Danny," said Favell, "you know damn well what he's driving at. I've told Colonel Julyan already, but he doesn't seem to believe me. Rebecca and I had lived together off and on for years, hadn't we? She was in love with me, wasn't she?"

To my surprise Mrs. Danvers considered him a moment without speaking, and there was something of scorn in the glance she gave him.

"She was not," she said.

"Listen here, you old fool . . ." began Favell, but Mrs. Danvers cut him short.

"She was not in love with you, or with Mr. de Winter. She was not in love with anyone. She despised all men. She was above all that."

Favell flushed angrily. "Listen here. Didn't she come down the path through the woods to meet me, night after night? Didn't you wait up for her? Didn't she spend the week-ends with me in London?"

"Well," said Mrs. Danvers, with sudden passion, "and what if she did? She had a right to amuse herself, didn't she? Love-making was a game with her, only a game. She told me so. She did it because it made her laugh. It made her laugh, I tell you. She laughed at you like she did at the rest. I've known her come back and sit upstairs on her bed and rock with laughter at the lot of you."

There was something horrible in the sudden torrent of words, something horrible and unexpected. It revolted me, even though I knew. Maxim had gone very white. Favell stared at her blankly, as though he had not understood. Colonel Julyan tugged at his small moustache. No one said anything for a few minutes. And there was no sound but that inevitable falling rain. Then Mrs. Danvers began to cry. She cried like she had done that morning in the bedroom. I could not look at her. I had to turn away. No one said anything. There were just the two sounds in the room, the falling rain and Mrs. Danvers crying. It made me want to scream. I wanted to run out of the room and scream and scream.

No one moved towards her, to say anything, or to help her. She went on crying. Then at last, it seemed eternity, she began to control herself. Little by little the crying ceased. She stood quite still, her face working, her hands clutching the black stuff of her frock. At last she was silent again. Then Colonel Julyan spoke, quietly, slowly.

"Mrs. Danvers," he said, "can you think of any reason, however remote, why Mrs. de Winter should have taken her own life?"

Mrs. Danvers swallowed. She went on clutching at her frock. She shook her head. "No," she said. "No."

"There you see?" Favell said swiftly. "It's impossible. She knows that as well as I do. I've told you already."

"Be quiet, will you?" said Colonel Julyan. "Give Mrs. Danvers time to think. We all of us agree that on the face of it the thing's absurd, out of the question. I'm not disputing the truth or veracity of that note of yours. It's plain for us to see. She wrote you that note sometime during those hours she spent in London. There was something she wanted to tell you. It's just possible that if we knew what that something was we might have an answer to the whole appalling problem. Let Mrs. Danvers read the note. She may be able to throw light on it." Favell shrugged his shoulders. He felt in his pocket for the note and threw it on the floor at Mrs. Danvers' feet. She stooped and picked it up. We watched her lips move as she read the words. She read it twice. Then she shook her head. "It's no use," she said, "I don't know what she meant. If there was something important she had to tell Mr. Jack she would have told me first."

"You never saw her that night?"

"No, I was out. I was spending the afternoon and evening in Kerrith. I shall never forgive myself for that. Never till my dying day."

"Then you know of nothing on her mind, you can't suggest a solution, Mrs. Danvers? Those words 'I have something to tell you,' do not convey anything to you at all?"

"No," she answered. "No, sir, nothing at all."

"Does anybody know how she spent that day in London?"

Nobody answered. Maxim shook his head. Favell swore under his breath. "Look here, she left that note at my flat at three in the afternoon," he said. "The porter saw her. She must have driven down here straight after that, and gone like the wind too."

"Mrs. de Winter had a hair appointment from twelve until one-thirty," said Mrs. Danvers. "I remember that, because I had to telephone through to London from here earlier in the week and book it for her. I remember doing it. Twelve to one-thirty. She always lunched at her club after a hair appointment so that she could leave the pins in her hair. It's almost certain she lunched there that day."

"Say it took her half-an-hour to have lunch, what was she doing from two until three? We ought to verify that," said Colonel Julyan.

"Oh, Christ Jesus, who the hell cares what she was doing?" shouted Favell. "She didn't kill herself, that's the only bloody thing that matters, isn't it?"

"I've got her engagement diary locked in my room," said Mrs. Danvers slowly. "I kept all those things. Mr. de Winter never asked me for them. It's just possible she may have noted down her appointments for that day. She was methodical in that way. She used to put everything down and then tick the items off with a cross. If you think it would be helpful I'll go and fetch the diary."

"Well, de Winter?" said Colonel Julyan, "what do you say? Do you mind us seeing this diary?"

"Of course not," said Maxim. "Why on earth should I?"

Once again I saw Colonel Julyan give him that swift, curious glance. And this time Frank noticed it. I saw Frank look at Maxim too. And then back again to me. This time it was I who got up and went towards the window. It seemed to me that it was no longer raining quite so hard. The fury was spent. The rain that was falling now had a quieter, softer note. The grey light of evening had come into the sky. The lawns were dark and drenched with the heavy rain, and the trees had a shrouded humped appearance. I could hear the housemaid overhead drawing the curtains for the night, shutting down the windows that had not been closed already. The little routine of the day going on inevitably as it had always done. The curtains drawn, shoes taken down to be cleaned, the towel laid out on the chair in the bathroom and the water run for my bath. Beds turned down, slippers put beneath a chair. And here were we in the library, none of us speaking, knowing in our hearts that Maxim was standing trial here for his life.

I turned round when I heard the soft closing of the door. It was Mrs. Danvers. She had come back again with the diary in her hand.

"I was right," she said quietly. "She had marked down the engagements as I said she would. Here they are on the date she died."

She opened the diary, a small, red leather book. She gave it to Colonel Julyan. Once more he brought his spectacles from his case. There was a long pause while he glanced down the page. It seemed to me then that there was something about that particular moment, while he looked at the page of the diary, and we stood waiting, that frightened me more than anything that had happened that evening.

I dug my nails in my hands. I could not look at Maxim. Surely Colonel Julyan must hear my heart beating and thumping in my breast?

"Ah!" he said. His finger was in the middle of the page. Something is going to happen, I thought, something terrible is going to happen. "Yes," he said, "yes, here it is. Hair at twelve, as Mrs. Danvers said. And a cross beside it. She kept her appointment then. Lunch at the club, and a cross beside that. What have we here, though? Baker, two o'clock. Who was Baker?" He looked at Maxim. Maxim shook his head. Then at Mrs. Danvers.

"Baker?" repeated Mrs. Danvers. "She knew no one called Baker. I've never heard the name before."

"Well here it is," said Colonel Julyan, handing her the diary. "You can see for yourself. Baker. And she's put a great cross beside it as though she wanted to break the pencil. She evidently saw this Baker whoever he may have been."

Mrs. Danvers was staring at the name written in the diary, and the black cross beside it. "Baker," she said. "Baker."

"I believe if we knew who Baker was we'd be getting to the bottom of the whole business," said Colonel Julyan. "She wasn't in the hands of money-lenders, was she?"

Mrs. Danvers looked at him with scorn. "Mrs. de Winter?" she said.

"Well, blackmailers perhaps?" said Colonel Julyan, with a glance at Favell.

Mrs. Danvers shook her head. "Baker," she repeated. "Baker."

"She had no enemy, no one who had ever threatened her, no one she was afraid of?"

"Mrs. de Winter afraid?" said Mrs. Danvers. "She was afraid of nothing and no one. There was only one thing ever worried her, and that was the idea of getting old, of illness, of dying in her bed. She has said to me a score of times, 'When I go, Danny, I want to go quickly, like the snuffing out of a candle.' That used to be the only thing that consoled me, after she died. They say drowning is painless, don't they?"

She looked searchingly at Colonel Julyan. He did not answer. He hesitated, tugging at his moustache. I saw him throw another glance at Maxim.

"What the hell's the use of all this?" said Favell, coming forward. "We're streaking away from the point the whole bloody time. Who cares about this Baker fellow? What's he got to do with it? It was probably some damn merchant who sold stockings, or face-cream. If he had been anyone important Danny here would know him. Rebecca had no secrets from Danny."

But I was watching Mrs. Danvers. She had the book in her hands and was turning the leaves. Suddenly she gave an exclamation.

"There's something here," she said, "right at the back among the telephone numbers. Baker. And there's a number beside it: 0488. But there is no exchange."

"Brilliant Danny," said Favell, "becoming quite a sleuth in your old age, aren't you? But you're just twelve months too late. If you'd done this a year ago there might have been some use in it."

"That's his number all right," said Colonel Julyan, "0488, and the name Baker beside it. Why didn't she put the exchange?"

"Try every exchange in London," jeered Favell. "It will take you through the night but we don't mind. Max doesn't care if his telephone bill is a hundred pounds, do you, Max? You want to play for time and so should I, if I were in your shoes."

"There is a mark beside the number but it might mean anything," said Colonel Julyan, "take a look at it, Mrs. Danvers. Could it possibly be an M?"

Mrs. Danvers took the diary in her hands again. "It might be," she said doubtfully. "It's not like her usual M, but she may have scribbled it in a hurry. Yes, it might be M."

"Mayfair 0488," said Favell, "what a genius, what a brain!"

"Well?" said Maxim, lighting his first cigarette, "something had better be done about it. Frank? Go through and ask the exchange for Mayfair 0488."

The nagging pain was strong beneath my heart. I stood quite still, my hands by my side. Maxim did not look at me.

"Go on, Frank," he said. "What are you waiting for?"

Frank went through to the little room beyond. We waited while he called the exchange. In a moment he was back again. "They're going to ring me," he said quietly. Colonel Julyan clasped his hands behind his back and began walking up and down the room. No one said anything. After about four minutes the telephone rang shrill and insistent, that irritating, monotonous note of a long-distance call. Frank went through to answer it. "Is that Mayfair 0488?" he said. "Can you tell me if anyone of the name of Baker lives there? Oh, I see. I'm so sorry. Yes, I must have got the wrong number. Thank you very much."

The little click as he replaced the receiver. Then he came back into the room. "Someone called Lady Eastleigh lives at Mayfair 0488. It's an address in Grosvenor Street. They've never heard of Baker."

Favell gave a great cackle of laughter. "The butcher, the baker, the candlestick-maker, They all jumped out of a rotten potato," he said. "Carry on, detective Number One, what's the next exchange on the list?"

"Try Museum," said Mrs. Danvers.

Frank glanced at Maxim. "Go ahead," said Maxim.

The farce was repeated all over again. Colonel Julyan repeated his walk up and down the room. Another five minutes went by, and the telephone rang again. Frank went to answer it. He left the door wide open, I could see him lean down to the table where the telephone stood, and bend to the mouth-piece.

"Hullo? Is that Museum 0488? Can you tell me if anyone of the name of Baker lives there? Oh; who is that speaking? A night porter. Yes. Yes, I understand. Not offices. No, no of course. Can you give me the address? Yes, it's rather important." He paused. He called to us over his shoulder. "I think we've got him," he said.

Oh, God, don't let it be true. Don't let Baker be found. Please, God, make Baker be dead. I knew who Baker was. I had known all along. I watched Frank through the door, I watched him lean forward suddenly, reach for a pencil and a piece of paper. "Hullo? Yes, I'm still here. Could you spell it? Thank you. Thank you very much. Good night." He came back into the room, the piece of paper in his hands. Frank who loved Maxim, who did not know that the piece of paper he held was the one shred of evidence that was worth a damn in the whole nightmare of our evening, and that by producing it he could destroy Maxim as well and truly as though he had a dagger in his hand and stabbed him in the back.

"It was the night porter from an address in Bloomsbury," he said. "There are no residents there at all. The place is used during the day as a doctor's consulting rooms. Apparently Baker's given up practice, and left six months ago. But we can get hold of him all right. The night porter gave me his address. I wrote it down on this piece of paper."

CHAPTER TWENTY-FIVE

It was then that Maxim looked at me. He looked at me for the first time that evening. And in his eyes I read a message of farewell. It was as though he leant against the side of a ship, and I stood below him on the quay. There would be other people touching his shoulder, and touching mine, but we would not see them. Nor would we speak or call to one another, for the wind and the distance would carry away the sound of our voices. But I should see his eyes and he would see mine before the ship drew away from the side of the quay. Favell, Mrs. Danvers, Colonel Julyan, Frank with the slip of paper in his hands, they were all forgotten at this moment. It was ours, inviolate, a fraction of time suspended between two seconds. And then he turned away and held out his hand to Frank.

"Well done," he said. "What's the address?"

"Somewhere near Barnet, north of London," said Frank, giving him the paper. "But it's not on the telephone. We can't ring him up."

"Satisfactory work, Crawley," said Colonel Julyan, "and from you too, Mrs. Danvers. Can you throw any light on the matter now?"

Mrs. Danvers shook her head. "Mrs. de Winter never needed a doctor. Like all strong people she despised them. We only had Doctor Phillips from Kerrith here once, that time she sprained her wrist. I've never heard her speak of this Doctor Baker, she never mentioned his name to me."

"I tell you the fellow was a face-cream mixer," said Favell. "What the hell does it matter who he was? If there was anything to it Danny would know. I tell you it's some fool fellow who had discovered a new way of bleaching her hair or whitening the skin, and Rebecca had probably got the address from her hair-dresser that morning and went along after lunch out of curiosity."

"No," said Frank. "I think you're wrong there. Baker wasn't a quack. The night porter at Museum 0488 told me he was a very well-known woman's specialist."

"H'm," said Colonel Julyan, pulling at his moustache, "there must have been something wrong with her after all. It seems very curious that she did not say a word to anybody, not even to you, Mrs. Danvers."

"She was too thin," said Favell, "I told her about it, but she only laughed. Said it suited her. Banting I suppose, like all these women. Perhaps she went to this chap Baker for a diet sheet."

"Do you think that's possible, Mrs. Danvers?" asked Colonel Julyan.

Mrs. Danvers shook her head slowly. She seemed dazed, bewildered by this sudden news about Baker. "I can't understand it," she said. "I don't know what it means. Baker. A Doctor Baker. Why didn't she tell me? Why did she keep it from me? She told me everything."

"Perhaps she didn't want to worry you," said Colonel Julyan. "No doubt she made an appointment with him, and saw him, and then when she came down that night she was going to have told you all about it."

"And the note to Mr. Jack," said Mrs. Danvers suddenly. "That note to Mr. Jack, 'I have something to tell you. I must see you.' She was going to tell him too?"

"That's true," said Favell slowly. "We were forgetting the note." Once more he pulled it out of his pocket and read it to us aloud. " 'I've got something to tell you and I want to see you as soon as possible. Rebecca.' "

"Of course, there's no doubt about it," said Colonel Julyan, turning to Maxim. "I wouldn't mind betting a thousand pounds on it. She was going to tell Favell the result of that interview with this Doctor Baker."

"I believe you're right after all," said Favell. "The note and that appointment seem to hang together. But what the hell was it all about, that's what I want to know? What was the matter with her?"

The truth screamed in their faces and they did not see. They all stood there, staring at one another, and they did not understand. I dared not look at them. I dared not move lest I betray my knowledge. Maxim said nothing. He had gone back to the window and was looking out into the garden that was hushed and dark and still. The rain had ceased at last, but the spots fell from the dripping leaves and from the gutter above the window.

"It ought to be quite easy to verify," said Frank. "Here is the doctor's present address. I can write him a letter and ask him if he remembers an appointment last year with Mrs. de Winter."

"I don't know if he would take any notice of it," said Colonel Julyan, "there is so much of this etiquette in the medical profession. Every case is confidential you know. The only way to get anything out of him would be to get de Winter to see him privately and explain the circumstances. What do you say, de Winter?"

Maxim turned round from the window. "I'm ready to do whatever you care to suggest," he said quietly.

"Anything for time, eh?" said Favell, "a lot can be done in twenty-four hours, can't it? Trains can be caught, ships can sail, aeroplanes can fly?"

I saw Mrs. Danvers look sharply from Favell to Maxim, and I realised then, for the first time, that Mrs. Danvers had not known about Favell's accusation. At last she was beginning to understand. I could tell from the expression on her face. There was doubt written on it, then wonder and hatred mixed, and then conviction. Once again those lean, long hands of hers clutched convulsively at her dress, and she passed her tongue over her lips. She went on staring at Maxim. She never took her eyes away from Maxim. It's too late, I thought, she can't do anything to us now, the harm is done. It does not matter what she says to us now, or what she does. The harm is done. She can't hurt us any more. Maxim did not notice her, or if he did he gave no sign. He was talking to Colonel Julyan.

"What do you suggest?" he said. "Shall I go up in the morning, drive to this address at Barnet? I can wire Baker to expect me."

"He's not going alone," said Favell, with a short laugh. "I have a right to insist on that, haven't I? Send him up with Inspector Welch and I won't object."

If only Mrs. Danvers would take her eyes away from Maxim. Frank had seen her now. He was watching her, puzzled, anxious. I saw him glance once more at the slip of paper in his hands, on which he had written Doctor Baker's address. Then he too glanced at Maxim. I believe then that some faint idea of the truth began to force itself to his conscience, for he went very white and put the paper down on the table.

"I don't think there is any necessity to bring Inspector Welch into the affair—yet," said Colonel Julyan. His voice was different, harsher. I did not like the way he used the word "yet." Why must he use it at all? I did not like it. "If I go with de Winter, and stay with him the whole time, and bring him back, will that satisfy you?" he said.

Favell looked at Maxim, and then at Colonel Julyan. The expression on his face was ugly, calculating, and there was something of triumph too in his light blue eyes. "Yes," he said slowly, "yes, I suppose so. But for safety's sake do you mind if I come with you too?"

"No," said Colonel Julyan, "unfortunately I think you have the right to ask that. But if you do come, I have the right to insist on your being sober."

"You needn't worry about that," said Favell, beginning to smile, "I'll be sober all right. Sober as the judge will be when he sentences Max in three months' time. I rather think this Doctor Baker is going to prove my case, after all."

He looked around at each one of us and began to laugh. I think he too had understood at last the significance of that visit to the doctor.

"Well?" he said, "what time are we going to start in the morning?"

Colonel Julyan looked at Maxim. "How early can you be ready?"

"Any time you say," said Maxim.

"Nine o'clock?"

"Nine o'clock," said Maxim.

"How do we know he won't do a bolt in the night?" said Favell. "He's only got to cut round to the garage and get his car."

"Is my word enough for you?" said Maxim, turning to Colonel Julyan. And for the first time Colonel Julyan hesitated. I saw him glance at Frank. And a flush came over Maxim's face. I saw the little pulse beating on his forehead. "Mrs. Danvers," he said slowly, "when Mrs. de Winter and I go to bed to-night will you come up yourself and lock the door on the outside? And call us yourself, at seven in the morning."

"Yes, sir," said Mrs. Danvers. Still she kept her eyes on him, still her hands clutched at her dress.

"Very well then," said Colonel Julyan brusquely. "I don't think there is anything else we need discuss, to-night. I shall be here sharp at nine in the morning. You will have room for me in your car, de Winter?"

"Yes," said Maxim.

"And Favell will follow us in his?"

"Right on your tail, my dear fellow, right on your tail," said Favell.

Colonel Julyan came up to me and took my hand. "Good night," he said. "You know how I feel for you in all this, there's no need for me to tell you. Get your husband to bed early, if you can. It's going to be a long day." He held my hand a minute, and then he turned away. It was curious how he avoided my eye. He looked at my chin. Frank held the door for him as he went out. Favell leant forward and filled his case with cigarettes from the box on the table.

"I suppose I'm not going to be asked to stop to dinner?" he said.

Nobody answered. He lit one of the cigarettes, and blew a cloud of smoke into the air. "It means a quiet evening at the pub on the highroad then," he said, "and the barmaid has a squint. What a hell of a night I'm going to spend! Never mind, I'm looking forward to tomorrow. Good night, Danny, old lady, don't forget to turn the key on Mr. de Winter, will you?"

He came over to me and held out his hand.

Like a foolish child I put my hands behind my back. He laughed and bowed.

"It's just too bad, isn't it?" he said. "A nasty man like me coming and spoiling all your fun. Don't worry, it will be a great thrill for you when the yellow Press gets going with your life story, and you see the headlines 'From Monte Carlo to Manderley. Experiences of murderer's girl-bride,' written across the top. Better luck next time."

He strolled across the room to the door, waving his hand to Maxim by the window. "So long, old man," he said, "pleasant dreams. Make the most of your night behind that locked door." He turned and laughed at me, and then he went out of the room. Mrs. Danvers followed him. Maxim and I were alone. He went on standing by the window. He did not come to me. Jasper came trotting in from the hall. He had been shut outside all the evening. He came fussing up to me, biting the edge of my skirt.

"I'm coming with you in the morning," I said to Maxim. "I'm coming up to London with you in the car."

He did not answer for a moment. He went on looking out of the window. Then "Yes," he said, his voice without expression. "Yes, we must go on being together."

Frank came back into the room. He stood in the entrance, his hand on the door. "They've gone," he said, "Favell and Colonel Julyan. I watched them go."

"All right, Frank," said Maxim.

"Is there anything I can do?" said Frank, "anything at all? Wire to anyone, arrange anything? I'll stay up all night if only there's anything I can do. I'll get that wire off to Baker of course."

"Don't worry," said Maxim, "there's nothing for you to do—yet.

There may be plenty—after to-morrow. We can go into all that when the time comes. To-night we want to be together. You understand, don't you?"

"Yes," said Frank. "Yes, of course."

He waited a moment, his hand on the door. "Good night," he said.

"Good night," said Maxim.

When he had gone, and shut the door behind him, Maxim came over to me where I was standing by the fireplace. I held out my arms to him and he came to me like a child. I put my arms round him and held him. We did not say anything for a long time. I held him and comforted him as though he were Jasper. As though Jasper had hurt himself in some way and had come to me to take his pain away.

"We can sit together," he said, "driving up in the car."

"Yes," I said.

"Julyan won't mind," he said.

"No," I said.

"We shall have to-morrow night too," he said. "They won't do anything at once, not for twenty-four hours perhaps."

"No," I said.

"They aren't so strict now," he said. "They let one see people. And it all takes such a long time. If I can I shall try and get hold of Hastings. He's the best. Hastings or Birkett. Hastings used to know my father."

"Yes," I said.

"I shall have to tell him the truth," he said. "It makes it easier for them. They know where they are."

"Yes," I said.

The door opened and Frith came into the room. I pushed Maxim away, I stood up straight and conventional, patting my hair into place.

"Will you be changing, Madam, or shall I serve dinner at once?"

"No, Frith, we won't be changing, not to-night," I said.

"Very good, Madam," he said.

He left the door open. Robert came in and began drawing the curtains. He arranged the cushions, straightened the sofa, tidied the books and papers on the table. He took away the whisky-and-soda and the dirty ash-trays. I had seen him do these things as a ritual every evening I had spent at Manderley, but to-night they seemed to take on a special significance, as though the memory of them would last forever and I should say, long after, in some other time, "I remember this moment."

Then Frith came in and told us that dinner was served.

I remember every detail of that evening. I remember the ice-cold consommé in the cups, and the filets of sole, and the hot shoulder of lamb.

I remember the burnt-sugar sweet, the sharp savoury that followed.

We had new candles in the silver candlesticks, they looked white and slim and very tall. The curtains had been drawn here too against the dull grey evening. It seemed strange to be sitting in the dining-room and not look out on to the lawns. It was like the beginning of autumn.

It was while we were drinking our coffee in the library that the telephone rang. This time it was I who answered it. I heard Beatrice speaking at the other end. "Is that you?" she said, "I've been trying to get through all the evening. Twice it was engaged."

"I'm so sorry," I said, "so very sorry."

"We had the evening papers about two hours ago," she said, "and the verdict was a frightful shock to both Giles and myself. What does Maxim say about it?"

"I think it was a shock to everybody," I said.

"But, my dear, the thing is preposterous. Why on earth should Rebecca have committed suicide? The most unlikely person in the world. There must have been a blunder somewhere."

"I don't know," I said.

"What does Maxim say, where is he?" she said.

"People have been here," I said, "Colonel Julyan, and others. Maxim is very tired. We're going up to London to-morrow."

"What on earth for?"

"Something to do with the verdict. I can't very well explain."

"You ought to get it squashed," she said. "It's ridiculous, quite ridiculous. And so bad for Maxim, all this frightful publicity. It's going to reflect on him."

"Yes," I said.

"Surely Colonel Julyan can do something?" she said. "He's a magistrate. What are magistrates for? Old Horridge from Lanyon must have been off his head. What was her motive supposed to be? It's the most idiotic thing I've ever heard in my life. Someone ought to get hold of Tabb. How can he tell whether those holes in the boat were made deliberately or not? Giles said of course it must have been the rocks."

"They seemed to think not," I said.

"If only I could have been there," she said. "I should have insisted on speaking. No one seems to have made any effort. Is Maxim very upset?"

"He's tired," I said, "more tired than anything else."

"I wish I could come up to London and join you," she said, "but I don't see how I can. Roger has a temperature of 103, poor old boy, and the nurse we've got in is a perfect idiot, he loathes her. I can't possibly leave him."

"Of course not," I said. "You mustn't attempt it."

"Whereabouts in London will you be?"

"I don't know," I said. "It's all rather vague."

"Tell Maxim he must try and do something to get that verdict altered. It's so bad for the family. I'm telling everybody here it's absolutely wicked. Rebecca would never have killed herself, she wasn't the type. I've a good mind to write to the coroner myself."

"It's too late," I said. "Much better leave it. It won't do any good."

"The stupidity of it gets my goat," she said. "Giles and I think it much more likely that if those holes weren't done by the rocks they were done deliberately, by some tramp or other. A Communist perhaps. There are heaps of them about. Just the sort of thing a Communist would do."

Maxim called to me from the library. "Can't you get rid of her? What on earth is she talking about?"

"Beatrice," I said desperately, "I'll try and ring you up from London."

"Is it any good my tackling Dick Godolphin?" she said. "He's your M.P. I know him very well, much better than Maxim does. He was at Oxford with Giles. Ask Maxim whether he would like me to telephone Dick and see if he can do anything to squash the verdict. Ask Maxim what he thinks of this Communist idea."

"It's no use," I said. "It can't do any good. Please, Beatrice, don't try and do anything. It will make it worse, much worse. Rebecca may have had some motive we don't know anything about. And I don't think Communists go ramming holes in boats, what would be the use? Please, Beatrice, leave it alone."

Oh, thank God she had not been with us to-day. Thank God for that at least. Something was buzzing in the telephone. I heard Beatrice shouting, "Hullo, hullo, don't cut us off, exchange," and then there was a click, and silence.

I went back into the library, limp and exhausted. In a few minutes the telephone began ringing again. I did not do anything. I let it ring. I went and sat down at Maxim's feet. It went on ringing. I did not move. Presently it stopped, as though cut suddenly in exasperation. The clock on the mantelpiece struck ten o'clock. Maxim put his arms round me and lifted me against him. We began to kiss one another, feverishly, desperately, like guilty lovers who have not kissed before.

CHAPTER TWENTY-SIX

When I awoke the next morning, just after six o'clock, and got up and went to the window there was a foggy dew upon the grass like frost, and the trees were shrouded in a white mist. There was a chill in the air and a little, fresh wind, and the cold, quiet smell of autumn.

As I knelt by the window looking down on to the rose-garden where the flowers themselves drooped upon their stalks, the petals brown and dragging after last night's rain, the happenings of the day before seemed remote and unreal. Here at Manderley a new day was starting, the things of the garden were not concerned with our troubles. A blackbird ran across the rose-garden to the lawns in swift, short rushes, stopping now and again to stab at the earth with his yellow beak. A thrush, too, went about his business, and two stout, little wagtails, following one another, and a little cluster of twittering sparrows. A gull poised himself high in the air, silent and alone, and then spread his wings wide and swooped beyond the lawns to the woods and the Happy Valley. These things continued, our worries and anxieties had no power to alter them. Soon the gardeners would be astir, brushing the first leaves from the lawns and the paths, raking the gravel in the drive. Pails would clank in the courtyard behind the house, the hose would be turned on the car, the little scullery maid would begin to chatter through the open door to the men in the yard. There would be the crisp, hot smell of bacon. The housemaids would open up the house, throw wide the windows, draw back the curtains.

The dogs would crawl from their baskets, yawn and stretch themselves, wander out on to the terrace and blink at the first struggles of the pale sun coming through the mist. Robert would lay the table for breakfast, bring in those piping scones, the clutch of eggs, the glass dishes of honey, jam, and marmalade, the bowl of peaches, the cluster of purple grapes with the bloom upon them still, hot from the green-houses.

Maids sweeping in the morning-room, the drawing-room, the fresh clean air pouring into the long open windows. Smoke curling from the chimneys, and little by little the autumn mist fading away and the trees and the banks and the woods taking shape, the glimmer of the sea showing with the sun upon it below the valley, the beacon standing tall and straight upon the headland.

The peace of Manderley. The quietude and the grace. Whoever lived within its walls, whatever trouble there was and strife, however much uneasiness and pain, no matter what tears were shed, what sorrows borne, the peace of Manderley could not be broken or the love-liness destroyed. The flowers that died would bloom again another year, the same birds build their nests, the same trees blossom. That old quiet moss smell would linger in the air, and bees would come, and crickets, the herons build their nests in the deep dark woods. The butterflies would dance their merry jig across the lawns, and spiders spin foggy webs, and small startled rabbits who had no business to come trespassing poke their faces through the crowded shrubs. There would be lilac, and honeysuckle still, and the white magnolia buds unfolding slow and tight beneath the dining-room window. No one would ever hurt Manderley. It would lie always in its hollow like an enchanted thing, guarded by the woods, safe, secure, while the sea broke and ran and came again in the little shingle bays below.

Maxim slept on and I did not wake him. The day ahead of us would be a weary thing and long. High-roads, and telegraph poles, and the monotony of passing traffic, the slow crawl into London. We did not know what we should find at the end of our journey. The future was unknown. Somewhere to the north of London lived a man called Baker who had never heard of us, but he held our future in the hollow of his hand. Soon he too would be waking, stretching, yawn-ing, going about the business of his day. I got up, and went into the bathroom, and began to run my bath. These actions held for me the same significance as Robert and his clearing of the library had the night before. I had done these things before mechanically, but now I was aware as I dropped my sponge into the water, as I spread my towel on the chair from the hot rail, as I lay back and let the water run over my body. Every moment was a precious thing, having in it the essence of finality. When I went back to the bedroom and began to dress I heard a soft footstep come and pause outside the door, and the key turn quietly in the lock. There was silence a moment, and then the footsteps went away. It was Mrs. Danvers.

She had not forgotten. I had heard the same sound the night before, after we had come up from the library. She had not knocked upon the door, she had not made herself known; there was just the sound of footsteps and the turning of the key in the lock. It brought me to reality, and the facing of the immediate future.

I finished dressing, and went and turned on Maxim's bath. Presently Clarice came with our tea. I woke Maxim. He stared at me at first like a puzzled child, and then he held out his arms. We drank our tea. He got up and went to his bath and I began putting things methodically in my suit-case. It might be that we should have to stay in London.

I packed the brushes Maxim had given me, a nightdress, my dressing-gown and slippers, and another dress too and a pair of shoes. My dressing-case looked unfamiliar as I dragged it from the back of a wardrobe. It seemed so long since I had used it, and yet it was only four months ago. It still had the Customs mark upon it they had chalked at Calais. In one of the pockets was a concert ticket from the casino in Monte Carlo. I crumpled it and threw it into the waste-paper basket. It might have belonged to another age, another world. My bedroom began to take on the appearance of all rooms when the owner goes away. The dressing-table was bare without my brushes. There was tissue-paper lying on the floor, and an old label. The beds where we had slept had a terrible emptiness about them. The towels lay crumpled on the bathroom floor. The wardrobe doors gaped open. I put on my hat so that I should not have to come up again, and I took my bag and my gloves and my suit-case. I glanced round the room to see if there was anything I had forgotten. The mist was breaking, the sun was forcing its way through and throwing patterns on the carpet. When I was half-way down the passage I had a curious, inexplicable feeling that I must go back and look in my room again. I went without reason, and stood a moment looking at the gaping wardrobe and the empty bed, and the tray of tea upon the table. I stared at them, impressing them forever on my mind, wondering why they had the power to touch me, to sadden me, as though they were children that did not want me to go away.

Then I turned and went downstairs to breakfast. It was cold in the dining-room, the sun not yet on the windows, and I was grateful for the scalding bitter coffee and heartening bacon. Maxim and I ate in silence. Now and again he glanced at the clock. I heard Robert put the

suit-cases in the hall with the rug, and presently there was the sound
of the car being brought to the door.

I went out and stood on the terrace. The rain had cleared the air,
and the grass smelt fresh and sweet. When the sun was higher it
would be a lovely day. I thought how we might have wandered in the
valley before lunch, and then sat out afterwards under the chestnut
tree with books and papers. I closed my eyes a minute and felt the
warmth of the sun on my face and on my hands.

I heard Maxim calling to me from the house. I went back, and
Frith helped me into my coat. I heard the sound of another car. It was
Frank.

"Colonel Julyan is waiting at the lodge gates," he said. "He did
not think it worth while to drive right up to the house."

"No," said Maxim.

"I'll stand by in the office all day and wait for you to telephone,"
said Frank. "After you've seen Baker you may find you want me, up
in London."

"Yes," said Maxim. "Yes, perhaps."

"It's just nine now," said Frank. "You're up to time. It's going to
be fine too. You should have a good run."

"Yes."

"I hope you won't get over-tired, Mrs. de Winter," he said to me.
"It's going to be a long day for you."

"I shall be all right," I said. I looked at Jasper who was standing
by my feet with ears drooping and sad reproachful eyes.

"Take Jasper back with you to the office," I said. "He looks so
miserable."

"Yes," he said. "Yes, I will."

"We'd better be off," said Maxim. "Old Julyan will be getting impatient. All right, Frank."

I climbed in the car beside Maxim. Frank slammed the door.

"You will telephone, won't you?" he said.

"Yes, of course," said Maxim.

I looked back at the house. Frith was standing at the top of the
steps, and Robert just behind. My eyes filled with tears for no reason.
I turned away and groped with my bag on the floor of the car so that
nobody should see. Then Maxim started up the car and we swept
round and into the drive and the house was hidden.

We stopped at the lodge gates and picked up Colonel Julyan. He
got in at the back. He looked doubtful when he saw me.

"It's going to be a long day," he said. "I don't think you should have attempted it. I would have taken care of your husband you know."

"I wanted to come," I said.

He did not say any more about it. He settled himself in the corner. "It's fine, that's one thing," he said.

"Yes," said Maxim.

"That fellow Favell said he would pick us up at the cross-roads. If he's not there don't attempt to wait, we'd do much better without him. I hope the damned fellow has over-slept himself."

When we came to the cross-roads though I saw the long green body of his car, and my heart sank. I had thought he might not be on time. Favell was sitting at the wheel, hatless, a cigarette in his mouth. He grinned when he saw us, and waved us on. I settled down in my seat for the journey ahead, one hand on Maxim's knee. The hours passed, and the miles were covered. I watched the road ahead in a kind of stupor. Colonel Julyan slept at the back from time to time, I turned occasionally and saw his head loll against the cushions, and his mouth open. The green car kept close beside us. Sometimes it shot ahead, sometimes it dropped behind. But we never lost it. At one we stopped for lunch at one of those inevitable old-fashioned hotels in the main street of a county town. Colonel Julyan waded through the whole set lunch, starting with soup and fish, and going on to roast beef and Yorkshire pudding. Maxim and I had cold ham and coffee.

I half expected Favell to wander into the dining-room and join us, but when we came out to the car again I saw his car had been drawn up outside a café on the opposite side of the road. He must have seen us from the window, for three minutes after we had started he was on our tail again.

We came to the suburbs of London about three o'clock. It was then that I began to feel tired, the noise and the traffic blocks started a humming in my head. It was warm in London too. The streets had that worn dusty look of August, and the leaves hung listless on dull trees. Our storm must have been local, there had been no rain here.

People were walking about in cotton frocks and the men were hatless. There was a smell of waste-paper, and orange-peel, and feet, and burnt dried grass. Buses lumbered slowly, and taxis crawled. I felt as though my coat and skirt were sticking to me, and my stockings pricked my skin.

Colonel Julyan sat up and looked out through his window. "They've had no rain here," he said.

"No," said Maxim.

"Looks as though the place needed it, too."

"Yes."

"We haven't succeeded in shaking Favell off. He's still on our tail."

"Yes."

Shopping centres on the outskirts seemed congested. Tired women with crying babies in prams stared into windows, hawkers shouted, small boys hung on to the back of lorries. There were too many people, too much noise. The very air was irritable and exhausted and spent.

The drive through London seemed endless, and by the time we had drawn clear again and were out beyond Hampstead there was a sound in my head like the beating of a drum, and my eyes were burning.

I wondered how tired Maxim was. He was pale, and there were shadows under his eyes, but he did not say anything. Colonel Julyan kept yawning at the back. He opened his mouth very wide and yawned aloud, sighing heavily afterwards. He would do this every few minutes. I felt a senseless stupid irritation come over me, and I did not know how to prevent myself from turning round and screaming to him to stop.

Once we had passed Hampstead he drew out a large-scale map from his coat-pocket and began directing Maxim to Barnet. The way was clear and there were sign-posts to tell us, but he kept pointing out every turn and twist in the road, and if there was any hesitation on Maxim's part Colonel Julyan would turn down the window and call for information from a passerby.

When we came to Barnet itself he made Maxim stop every few minutes. "Can you tell us where a house called Roselands is? It belongs to a Doctor Baker, who's retired, and come to live there lately," and the passerby would stand frowning a moment, obviously at sea, ignorance written plain upon his face.

"Doctor Baker? I don't know a Doctor Baker. There used to be a house called Rose Cottage near the church, but a Mrs. Wilson lives there."

"No, it's Roselands we want, Doctor Baker's house," said Colonel Julyan, and then we would go on and stop again in front of a nurse and a pram. "Can you tell us where Roselands is?"

"I'm sorry. I'm afraid I've only just come to live here."

"You don't know a Doctor Baker?"

"Doctor Davidson. I know Doctor Davidson."

"No, it's Doctor Baker we want."

I glanced up at Maxim. He was looking very tired. His mouth was set hard. Behind us crawled Favell, his green car covered in dust.

It was a postman who pointed out the house in the end. A square house, ivy-covered, with no name on the gate, which we had already passed twice. Mechanically I reached for my bag and dabbed my face with the end of the powder puff. Maxim drew up outside at the side of the road. He did not take the car into the short drive. We sat silently for a few minutes.

"Well, here we are," said Colonel Julyan, "and it's exactly twelve minutes past five. We shall catch them in the middle of their tea. Better wait for a bit."

Maxim lit a cigarette, and then stretched out his hand to me. He did not speak. I heard Colonel Julyan crinkling his map.

"We could have come right across without touching London," he said, "saved us forty minutes I dare say. We made good time the first two hundred miles. It was from Chiswick on we took the time."

An errand-boy passed us whistling on his bicycle. A motor-coach stopped at the corner and two women got out. Somewhere a church clock chimed the quarter. I could see Favell leaning back in his car behind us and smoking a cigarette. I seemed to have no feeling in me at all. I just sat and watched the little things that did not matter. The two women from the bus walk along the road. The errand-boy disappear round the corner. A sparrow hop about in the middle of the road pecking at dirt.

"This fellow Baker can't be much of a gardener," said Colonel Julyan. "Look at those shrubs tumbling over his wall. They ought to have been pruned right back." He folded up the map and put it back in his pocket. "Funny sort of place to choose to retire in," he said. "Close to the main road and overlooked by other houses. Shouldn't care about it myself. I dare say it was quite pretty once before they started building. No doubt there's a good golf-course somewhere handy."

He was silent for a while, then he opened the door and stood out on the road. "Well, de Winter," he said, "what do you think about it?"

"I'm ready," said Maxim.

We got out of the car. Favell strolled up to meet us.

"What were you all waiting for, cold feet?" he said.

Nobody answered him. We walked up the drive to the front door, a strange incongruous little party. I caught sight of a tennis lawn beyond the house, and I heard the thud of balls. A boy's voice shouted "Forty-fifteen, not thirty all. Don't you remember hitting it out, you silly ass?"

"They must have finished tea," said Colonel Julyan.

He hesitated a moment, glancing at Maxim. Then he rang the bell.

It tinkled somewhere in the back premises. There was a long pause. A very young maid opened the door to us. She looked startled at the sight of so many of us.

"Doctor Baker?" said Colonel Julyan.

"Yes, sir, will you come in?"

She opened a door on the left of the hall as we went in. It would be the drawing-room, not used much in the summer. There was a portrait of a very plain dark woman on the wall. I wondered if it was Mrs. Baker. The chintz covers on the chairs and on the sofa were new and shiny. On the mantelpiece were photographs of two schoolboys with round, smiling faces. There was a very large wireless in the corner of the room by the window. Cords trailed from it, and bits of aerial. Favell examined the portrait on the wall. Colonel Julyan went and stood by the empty fireplace. Maxim and I looked out of the window. I could see a deck-chair under a tree, and the back of a woman's head. The tennis court must be round the corner. I could hear the boys shouting to each other. A very old Scotch terrier was scratching himself in the middle of a path. We waited there for about five minutes. It was as though I was living the life of some other person and had come to this house to call for a subscription to a charity. It was unlike anything I had ever known. I had no feeling, no pain.

Then the door opened and a man came into the room. He was medium height, rather long in the face, with a keen chin. His hair was sandy, turning grey. He wore flannels, and a dark blue blazer.

"Forgive me for keeping you waiting," he said, looking a little surprised, as the maid had done, to see so many of us. "I had to run up and wash. I was playing tennis when the bell rang. Won't you sit down?" He turned to me. I sat down in the nearest chair and waited.

"You must think this a very unorthodox invasion, Doctor Baker," said Colonel Julyan, "and I apologise very humbly for disturbing you like this. My name is Julyan. This is Mr. de Winter, Mrs. de Winter, and Mr. Favell. You may have seen Mr. de Winter's name in the papers recently."

"Oh," said Doctor Baker, "yes, yes I suppose I have. Some inquest or other wasn't there? My wife was reading all about it."

"The jury brought in a verdict of suicide," said Favell coming forward, "which I say is absolutely out of the question. Mrs. de Winter was my cousin, I knew her intimately. She would never have done such a thing, and what's more she had no motive. What we want to know is what the devil she came to see you about on the very day she died."

"You had better leave this to Julyan and myself," said Maxim quietly. "Doctor Baker has not the faintest idea what you are driving at."

He turned to the doctor who was standing between them with a line between his brows, and his first polite smile frozen on his lips. "My late wife's cousin is not satisfied with the verdict," said Maxim, "and we've driven up to see you to-day because we found your name, and the telephone number of your old consulting rooms, in my wife's engagement diary. She seems to have made an appointment with you, and kept it, at two o'clock on the last day she ever spent in London. Could you possibly verify this for us?"

Doctor Baker was listening with great interest, but when Maxim had finished he shook his head. "I'm most awfully sorry," he said, "but I think you've made a mistake. I should have remembered the name de Winter. I've never attended a Mrs. de Winter in my life."

Colonel Julyan brought out his note-case and gave him the page he had torn from the engagement diary. "Here it is, written down," he said, "Baker, two o'clock. And a big cross beside it, to show that the appointment was kept. And here is the telephone address. Museum 0488."

Doctor Baker stared at the piece of paper. "That's very odd, very odd indeed. Yes, the number is quite correct as you say."

"Could she have come to see you and given a false name?" said Colonel Julyan.

"Why, yes, that's possible. She may have done that. It's rather un-usual of course. I've never encouraged that sort of thing. It doesn't do us any good in the profession if people think they can treat us like that."

"Would you have any record of the visit in your files?" said Colonel Julyan. "I know it's not etiquette to ask, but the circumstances are very unusual. We do feel her appointment with you must have some bearing on the case and her subsequent—suicide."

"Murder," said Favell.

Doctor Baker raised his eyebrows, and looked enquiringly at Maxim. "I'd no idea there was any question of that," he said quietly. "Of course I understand, and I'll do anything in my power to help you. If you will excuse me a few minutes I will go and look up my files. There should be a record of every appointment booked through-out the year, and a description of the case. Please help yourself to cigarettes. It's too early to offer you sherry, I suppose?"

Colonel Julyan and Maxim shook their heads. I thought Favell was going to say something but Doctor Baker had left the room before he had a chance.

"Seems a decent sort of fellow," said Colonel Julyan.

"Why didn't he offer us whisky-and-soda?" said Favell. "Keeps it locked up I suppose. I didn't think much of him. I don't believe he's going to help us now."

Maxim did not say anything. I could hear the sound of the tennis balls from the court. The Scotch terrier was barking. A woman's voice shouted to him to be quiet. The summer holidays. Baker playing with his boys. We had interrupted their routine. A high-pitched, gold clock in a glass case ticked very fast on the mantelpiece. There was a postcard of the Lake of Geneva leaning against it. The Bakers had friends in Switzerland.

Doctor Baker came back into the room with a large book and a file-case in his hands. He carried them over to the table. "I've brought the collection for last year," he said. "I haven't been through them yet since we moved. I only gave up practice six months ago you know." He opened the book and began turning the pages. I watched him fascinated. He would find it of course. It was only a question of moments now, of seconds. "The seventh, eighth, tenth," he murmured, "nothing here. The twelfth did you say? At two o'clock? Ah!"

We none of us moved. We all watched his face.

"I saw a Mrs. Danvers on the twelfth at two o'clock," he said.

"Danny? What on earth . . ." began Favell, but Maxim cut him short.

"She gave a wrong name of course," he said. "That was obvious from the first. Do you remember the visit now, Doctor Baker?"

But Doctor Baker was already searching his files. I saw his fingers delve into the pocket marked with D. He found it almost at once. He glanced down rapidly at his own hand-writing. "Yes," he said slowly. "Yes, Mrs. Danvers. I remember now."

"Tall, slim, dark, very handsome?" said Colonel Julyan quietly.

"Yes," said Doctor Baker. "Yes."

He read through the files, and then replaced them in the case. "Of course," he said, glancing at Maxim, "this is unprofessional you know? We treat patients as though they were in the confessional. But your wife is dead, and I quite understand the circumstances are exceptional. You want to know if I can suggest any motive why your wife should have taken her life? I think I can. The woman who called herself Mrs. Danvers was very seriously ill."

He paused. He looked at every one of us in turn.

"I remember her perfectly well," he said, and he turned back to the files again. "She came to me for the first time a week previously to the date you mentioned. She complained of certain symptoms, and I took some X-rays of her. The second visit was to find out the result of those X-rays. The photographs are not here, but I have the details written down. I remember her standing in my consulting room and holding out her hand for the photographs. 'I want to know the truth,' she said, 'I don't want soft words and a bedside manner. If I'm in for it you can tell me right away.'" He paused, he glanced down at the files once again.

I waited, waited. Why couldn't he get done with it and finish and let us go? Why must we sit there, waiting, our eyes upon his face?

"Well," he said, "she asked for the truth, and I let her have it. Some patients are better for it. Shirking the point does them no good. This Mrs. Danvers, or Mrs. de Winter rather, was not the type to accept a lie. You must have known that. She stood it very well. She did not flinch. She said she had suspected it for some time. Then she paid my fee and went out. I never saw her again."

He shut up the box with a snap, and closed the book. "The pain was slight as yet but the growth was deep-rooted," he said, "and in three or four months' time she would have been under morphia. An operation would have been no earthly use at all. I told her that. The thing had got too firm a hold. There is nothing anyone can do in a case like that, except give morphia, and wait."

No one said a word. The little clock ticked on the mantelpiece, and the boys played tennis in the garden. An aeroplane hummed overhead.

"Outwardly of course she was a perfectly healthy woman," he said, "rather too thin I remember, rather pale, but then that's the fashion nowadays, pity though it is. It's nothing to go upon with a patient. No, the pain would increase week by week, and as I told you, in four or five months' time she would have had to be kept under morphia. The X-rays showed a certain malformation of the uterus, I remember, which meant she could never have had a child, but that was quite apart, it had nothing to do with the disease."

I remember hearing Colonel Julyan speak, saying something about Doctor Baker being very kind to have taken so much trouble. "You have told us all we want to know," he said, "and if we could possibly have a copy of the memoranda in your file it might be very useful."

"Of course," said Doctor Baker. "Of course."

Everyone was standing up. I got up from my chair too. I shook hands with Doctor Baker. We all shook hands with him. We followed him out into the hall. A woman looked out of the room on the other side of the hall and darted back when she saw us. Someone was running a bath upstairs, the water ran loudly. The Scotch terrier came in from the garden and began sniffing at my heels.

"Shall I send the report to you or to Mr. de Winter?" said Doctor Baker.

"We may not need it at all," said Colonel Julyan. "I rather think it won't be necessary. Either de Winter or I will write. Here is my card."

"I'm so glad to have been of use," said Doctor Baker; "it never entered my head for a moment that Mrs. de Winter and Mrs. Danvers could be the same person."

"No, naturally," said Colonel Julyan.

"You'll be returning to London I suppose?"

"Yes. Yes, I imagine so."

"Your best way then is to turn sharp left by that pillar-box, and then right by the church. After that it's a straight road."

"Thank you. Thank you very much."

We came out on to the drive and went towards the cars. Doctor Baker pulled the Scotch terrier inside the house. I heard the door shut. A man with one leg and a barrel-organ began playing Roses in Picardy, at the end of the road.

CHAPTER TWENTY-SEVEN

We went and stood by the car. No one said anything for a few minutes. Colonel Julyan handed round his cigarette case. Favell looked grey, rather shaken. I noticed his hands were trembling as he held the match. The man with the barrel-organ ceased playing for a moment and hobbled towards us, his cap in his hand. Maxim gave him two shillings. Then he went back to the barrel-organ and started another tune. The church clock struck six o'clock. Favell began to speak. His voice was diffident, careless, but his face was still grey. He did not look at any of us, he kept glancing down at his cigarette and turning it over in his fingers. "This cancer business," he said, "does anybody know if it's contagious?"

No one answered him. Colonel Julyan shrugged his shoulders.

"I never had the remotest idea," said Favell jerkily. "She kept it a secret from everyone, even Danny. What a God-damned appalling thing, eh? Not the sort of thing one would ever connect with Rebecca. Do you fellows feel like a drink? I'm all out over this, and I don't mind admitting it. Cancer! Oh, my God!"

He leant up against the side of the car and shaded his eyes with his hands. "Tell that bloody fellow with the barrel-organ to clear out," he said. "I can't stand that God-damned row."

"Wouldn't it be simpler if we went ourselves?" said Maxim. "Can you manage your own car or do you want Julyan to drive it for you?"

"Give me a minute," muttered Favell. "I'll be all right. You don't understand. This thing has been a damned unholy shock to me."

"Pull yourself together, man, for heaven's sake," said Colonel Julyan. "If you want a drink go back to the house and ask Baker. He knows how to treat for shock I dare say. Don't make an exhibition of yourself in the street."

"Oh, you're all right, you're fine," said Favell, standing straight and looking at Colonel Julyan and Maxim. "You've got nothing to worry about any more. Max is on a good wicket now, isn't he? You've got your motive, and Baker will supply it in black and white free of cost, whenever you send the word. You can dine at Manderley once a week on the strength of it and feel proud of yourself. No doubt Max will ask you to be god-father to his first child."

"Shall we get into the car and go?" said Colonel Julyan to Maxim. "We can make our plans going along."

Maxim held open the door of the car, and Colonel Julyan climbed in. I sat down in my seat in the front. Favell still leant against the car and did not move. "I should advise you to get straight back to your flat and go to bed," said Colonel Julyan shortly, "and drive slowly, or you will find yourself in gaol for manslaughter. I may as well warn you now, as I shall not be seeing you again, that as a magistrate I have certain powers that will prove effective if you ever turn up in Kerrith or the district. Blackmail is not much of a profession, Mr. Favell. And we know how to deal with it in our part of the world, strange though it may seem to you."

Favell was watching Maxim. He had lost the grey colour now, and the old unpleasant smile was forming on his lips. "Yes, it's been a stroke of luck for you, Max, hasn't it?" he said slowly; "you think you've won, don't you? The law can get you yet, and so can I, in a different way. . . ."

Maxim switched on the engine. "Have you anything else you want to say?" he said. "Because if you have you had better say it now."

"No," said Favell. "No, I won't keep you. You can go." He stepped back on to the pavement, the smile still on his lips. The car slid forward. As we turned the corner I looked back and saw him standing there, watching us, and he waved his hand and he was laughing.

We drove on for a while in silence. Then Colonel Julyan spoke. "He can't do anything," he said. "That smile and that wave was part of his bluff. They're all alike, those fellows. He hasn't a thread of a case to bring now. Baker's evidence would squash it."

Maxim did not answer. I glanced sideways at his face but it told me nothing. "I always felt the solution would lie in Baker," said Colonel Julyan, "the furtive business of that appointment, and the way she never even told Mrs. Danvers. She had her suspicions you see. She knew something was wrong. A dreadful thing, of course. Very dreadful. Enough to send a young and lovely woman right off her head."

We drove on along the straight main road. Telegraph poles, motor-coaches, open sports cars, little semi-detached villas with new gardens, they flashed past making patterns in my mind I should always remember.

"I suppose you never had any idea of this, de Winter?" said Colonel Julyan.

"No," said Maxim. "No."

"Of course some people have a morbid dread of it," said Colonel Julyan. "Women especially. That must have been the case with your wife. She had courage for every other thing but that. She could not face pain. Well, she was spared that at any rate."

"Yes," said Maxim.

"I don't think it would do any harm if I quietly let it be known down in Kerrith and in the county that a London doctor has supplied us with a motive," said Colonel Julyan. "Just in case there should be any gossip. You never can tell, you know. People are odd, sometimes. If they knew about Mrs. de Winter it might make it a lot easier for you."

"Yes," said Maxim, "yes, I understand."

"It's curious and very irritating," said Colonel Julyan slowly, "how long stories spread in country districts. I never know why they should but unfortunately they do. Not that I anticipate any trouble over this but it's as well to be prepared. People are inclined to say the wildest things if they are given half a chance."

"Yes," said Maxim.

"You and Crawley of course can squash any nonsense in Manderley or the estate, and I can deal with it effectively in Kerrith. I shall say a word to my girl too. She sees a lot of the younger people, who very often are the worst offenders in story-telling. I don't suppose the newspapers will worry you any more, that's one good thing. You'll find they will drop the whole affair in a day or two."

"Yes," said Maxim.

We drove on through the northern suburbs and came once more to Finchley and Hampstead.

"Half-past six," said Colonel Julyan, "what do you propose doing? I've got a sister living in St. John's Wood, and feel inclined to take her unawares and ask for dinner, and then catch the last train from Paddington. I know she doesn't go away for another week. I'm sure she would be delighted to see you both as well."

Maxim hesitated, and glanced at me. "It's very kind of you," he said, "but I think we had better be independent. I must ring up Frank, and one thing and another. I dare say we shall have a quiet meal somewhere and start off again afterwards, spending the night at a pub, on the way. I rather think that's what we shall do."

"Of course," said Colonel Julyan, "I quite understand. Could you throw me out at my sister's? It's one of those turnings off the Avenue Road."

When we came to the house Maxim drew up a little way ahead of the gate. "It's impossible to thank you," he said, "for all you've done to-day. You know what I feel about it without my telling you."

"My dear fellow," said Colonel Julyan, "I've been only too glad. If only we'd known what Baker knew of course there would have been none of this at all. However, never mind about that now. You must put the whole thing behind you as a very unpleasant and unfortunate episode. I'm pretty sure you won't have any more trouble from Favell. If you do, I count on you to tell me at once. I shall know how to deal with him." He climbed out of the car, collecting his coat and his map. "I should feel inclined," he said, not looking directly at us, "to get away for a bit. Take a short holiday. Go abroad perhaps."

We did not say anything. Colonel Julyan was fumbling with his map. "Switzerland is very nice this time of the year," he said. "I remember we went once for the girl's holidays, and thoroughly enjoyed ourselves. The walks are delightful." He hesitated, cleared his throat. "It is just faintly possible certain little difficulties might arise," he said, "not from Favell, but from one or two people in the district. One never knows quite what Tabb has been saying, and repeating, and so on. Absurd of course. But you know the old saying? Out of sight, out of mind. If people aren't there to be talked about the talk dies. It's the way of the world."

He stood a moment, counting his belongings. "I've got everything I think. Map, glasses, stick, coat. Everything complete. Well, good-bye, both of you. Don't get over-tired. It's been a long day."

He turned in at the gate and went up the steps. I saw a woman come to the window and smile and wave her hand. We drove away down the road and turned the corner. I leant back in my seat and closed my eyes. Now that we were alone again and the strain was over, the sensation was one of almost unbearable relief. It was like the bursting of an abscess. Maxim did not speak. I felt his hand cover mine. We drove on through the traffic and I saw none of it. I heard the rumble of the buses, the hooting of taxis, that inevitable, tireless London roar, but I was not part of it. I rested in some other place that was cool and quiet and still. Nothing could touch us any more. We had come through our crisis.

When Maxim stopped the car I opened my eyes and sat up. We were opposite one of those numerous little restaurants in a narrow street in Soho. I looked about me, dazed and stupid.

"You're tired," said Maxim briefly. "Empty and tired and fit for nothing. You'll be better when you've had something to eat. So shall I. We'll go in here and order dinner right away. I can telephone to Frank, too."

We got out of the car. There was no one in the restaurant but the maître d'hôtel and a waiter and a girl behind a desk. It was dark and cool. We went to a table right in the corner. Maxim began ordering the food. "Favell was right about wanting a drink," he said. "I want one too and so do you. You're going to have some brandy."

The maître d'hôtel was fat and smiling. He produced long thin rolls in paper envelopes. They were very hard, very crisp. I began to eat one ravenously. My brandy-and-soda was soft, warming, curiously comforting.

"When we've had dinner we'll drive slowly, very quietly," said Maxim. "It will be cool, too, in the evening. We'll find somewhere on the road we can put up for the night. Then we can get along to Manderley in the morning."

"Yes," I said.

"You didn't want to dine with Julyan's sister and go down by the late train?"

"No."

Maxim finished his drink. His eyes looked large and they were ringed with shadows. They seemed very dark against the pallor of his face.

"How much of the truth," he said, "do you think Julyan guessed?"

I watched him over the rim of my glass. I did not say anything.

"He knew," said Maxim slowly, "of course he knew."

"If he did," I said, "he will never say anything. Never, never."

"No," said Maxim. "No."

He ordered another drink from the maître d'hôtel. We sat silent and peaceful in our dark corner.

"I believe," said Maxim, "that Rebecca lied to me on purpose. The last supreme bluff. She wanted me to kill her. She foresaw the whole thing. That's why she laughed. That's why she stood there laughing when she died."

I did not say anything. I went on drinking my brandy-and-soda.

It was all over. It was all settled. It did not matter any more. There was no need for Maxim to look white and troubled.

"It was her last practical joke," said Maxim, "the best of them all. And I'm not sure if she hasn't won, even now."

"What do you mean? How can she have won?" I said.

"I don't know," he said. "I don't know." He swallowed his second drink. Then he got up from the table. "I'm going to ring up Frank," he said.

I sat there in my corner, and presently the waiter brought me my fish. It was lobster. Very hot and good. I had another brandy-and-soda, too. It was pleasant and comfortable sitting there and nothing mattered very much. I smiled at the waiter. I asked for some more bread in French for no reason. It was quiet and happy and friendly in the restaurant. Maxim and I were together. Everything was over. Everything was settled. Rebecca was dead. Rebecca could not hurt us. She had played her last joke as Maxim had said. She could do no more to us now. In ten minutes Maxim came back again.

"Well," I said, my own voice sounding far away, "how was Frank?"

"Frank was all right," said Maxim. "He was at the office, been waiting there for me to telephone him ever since four o'clock. I told him what had happened. He sounded glad, relieved."

"Yes," I said.

"Something rather odd though," said Maxim slowly, a line between his brows. "He thinks Mrs. Danvers has cleared out. She's gone, disappeared. She said nothing to anyone but apparently she'd been packing up all day, stripping her room of things, and the fellow from the station came for her boxes at about four o'clock. Frith telephoned down to Frank about it, and Frank told Frith to ask Mrs. Danvers to come down to him at the office. He waited, and she never came. About ten minutes before I rang up, Frith telephoned to Frank again and said there had been a long-distance call for Mrs. Danvers which he had switched through to her room, and she had answered. This must have been about ten past six. At a quarter-to-seven he knocked on the door and found her room empty. Her bedroom too. They looked for her and could not find her. They think she's gone. She must have gone straight out of the house and through the woods. She never passed the lodge gates."

"Isn't it a good thing?" I said. "It saves us a lot of trouble. We should have had to send her away, anyway. I believe she guessed, too. There was an expression on her face last night. I kept thinking of it, coming up in the car."

"I don't like it," said Maxim. "I don't like it."

"She can't do anything," I argued. "If she's gone, so much the better. It was Favell who telephoned of course. He must have told her about Baker. He would tell her what Colonel Julyan said. Colonel Julyan said if there was any attempt at blackmail we were to tell him. They won't dare do it. They can't. It's too dangerous."

"I'm not thinking of blackmail," said Maxim.

"What else can they do?" I said. "We've got to do what Colonel Julyan said. We've got to forget it. We must not think about it any more. It's all over, darling, it's finished. We ought to go down on our knees and thank God that it's finished."

Maxim did not answer. He was staring in front of him at nothing.

"Your lobster will be cold," I said; "eat it, darling. It will do you good, you want something inside you. You're tired." I was using the words he had used to me. I felt better and stronger. It was I now who was taking care of him. He was tired, pale. I had got over my weakness and fatigue and now he was the one to suffer from reaction. It was just because he was empty, because he was tired. There was nothing to worry about at all. Mrs. Danvers had gone. We should praise God for that, too. Everything had been made so easy for us, so very easy. "Eat up your fish," I said.

It was going to be very different in the future. I was not going to be nervous and shy of the servants any more. With Mrs. Danvers gone I should learn bit by bit to control the house. I would go and interview the cook in the kitchen. They would like me, respect me. Soon it would be as though Mrs. Danvers had never had command. I would learn more about the estate, too. I should ask Frank to explain things to me. I was sure Frank liked me. I liked him, too. I would go into things, and learn how they were managed. What they did at the farm. How the work in the grounds was planned. I might take to gardening myself, and in time have one or two things altered. That little square lawn outside the morning-room window with the statue of the satyr. I did not like it. We would give the satyr away. There were heaps of things that I could do, little by little. People would come and stay and I should not mind. There would be the interest of seeing to their rooms, having flowers and books put, arranging the food. We would have children. Surely we would have children.

"Have you finished?" said Maxim suddenly. "I don't think I want any more. Only coffee. Black, very strong, please, and the bill," he added to the maître d'hôtel.

I wondered why we must go so soon. It was comfortable in the restaurant, and there was nothing to take us away. I liked sitting there, with my head against the sofa back, planning the future idly in a hazy pleasant way. I could have gone on sitting there for a long while.

I followed Maxim out of the restaurant, stumbling a little, and yawning. "Listen," he said, when we were on the pavement, "do you think you could sleep in the car if I wrapped you up with the rug, and tucked you down in the back? There's the cushion there, and my coat as well."

"I thought we were going to put up somewhere for the night?" I said blankly. "One of those hotels one passes on the road."

"I know," he said, "but I have this feeling I must get down tonight. Can't you possibly sleep in the back of the car?"

"Yes," I said doubtfully. "Yes, I suppose so."

"If we start now, it's a quarter-to-eight, we ought to be there by half-past two," he said. "There won't be much traffic on the road."

"You'll be so tired," I said. "So terribly tired."

"No," he shook his head. "I shall be all right. I want to get home. Something's wrong. I know it is. I want to get home."

His face was anxious, strange. He pulled open the door and began arranging the rugs and the cushion at the back of the car.

"What can be wrong?" I said. "It seems so odd to worry now, when everything's over. I can't understand you."

He did not answer. I climbed into the back of the car and lay down with my legs tucked under me. He covered me with the rug. It was very comfortable. Much better than I imagined. I settled the pillow under my head.

"Are you all right?" he said. "Are you sure you don't mind?"

"No," I said smiling. "I'm all right. I shall sleep. I don't want to stay anywhere on the road. It's much better to do this and get home. We'll be at Manderley long before sunrise."

He got in front and switched on the engine. I shut my eyes. The car drew away and I felt the slight jolting of the springs under my body. I pressed my face against the cushion. The motion of the car was rhythmic, steady, and the pulse of my mind beat with it. A hundred images came to me when I closed my eyes, things seen, things known, and things forgotten. They were jumbled together in a senseless pattern. The quill of Mrs. Van Hopper's hat, the hard straight-backed chairs in Frank's dining-room, the wide window in the west wing at Manderley, the salmon-coloured frock of the smiling lady at the fancy dress ball, a peasant-girl in a road near Monte Carlo.

Sometimes I saw Jasper chasing butterflies across the lawns; sometimes I saw Doctor Baker's Scotch terrier scratching his ear beside a deck-chair. There was the postman who had pointed out the house to us to-day, and there was Clarice's mother wiping a chair for me in the back parlour. Ben smiled at me, holding winkles in his hands, and the bishop's wife asked me if I would stay to tea. I could feel the cold comfort of my sheets in my own bed, and the gritty shingle in the cove. I could smell the bracken in the woods, the wet moss, and the dead azalea petals. I fell into a strange broken sleep, waking now and again to the reality of my narrow cramped position and the sight of Maxim's back in front of me. The dusk had turned to darkness. There were the lights of passing cars upon the road. There were villages with drawn curtains and little lights behind them. And I would move, and turn upon my back, and sleep again.

I saw the staircase at Manderley, and Mrs. Danvers standing at the top in her black dress, waiting for me to go to her. As I climbed the stairs she backed under the archway and disappeared. I looked for her and I could not find her. Then her face looked at me through a hollow door and I cried out and she had gone again.

"What's the time?" I called. "What's the time?"

Maxim turned round to me, his face pale and ghostly in the darkness of the car. "It's half-past eleven," he said. "We're over half-way already. Try and sleep again."

"I'm thirsty," I said.

He stopped at the next town. The man at the garage said his wife had not gone to bed and she would make us some tea. We got out of the car and stood inside the garage. I stamped up and down to bring the blood back to my hands and feet. Maxim smoked a cigarette. It was cold. A bitter wind blew in through the open garage door, and rattled the corrugated roof. I shivered, and buttoned up my coat.

"Yes, it's nippy to-night," said the garage man, as he wound the petrol pump. "The weather seemed to break this afternoon. It's the last of the heat-waves for this summer. We shall be thinking of fires soon."

"It was hot in London," I said.

"Was it?" he said. "Well, they always have the extremes up there, don't they? We get the first of the bad weather down here. It will blow hard on the coast before morning."

His wife brought us the tea. It tasted of bitter wood, but it was hot. I drank it greedily, thankfully. Already Maxim was glancing at his watch.

"We ought to be going," he said. "It's ten minutes to twelve." I left the shelter of the garage reluctantly. The cold wind blew in my face. The stars raced across the sky. There were threads of cloud too. "Yes," said the garage man, "summer's over for this year."

We climbed back into the car. I settled myself once more under the rug. The car went on. I shut my eyes. There was the man with the wooden leg winding his barrel-organ, and the tune of Roses in Picardy hummed in my head against the jolting of the car. Frith and Robert carried the tea into the library. The woman at the lodge nodded to me abruptly, and called her child into the house. I saw the model boats in the cottage in the cove, and the feathery dust. I saw the cobwebs stretching from the little mass. I heard the rain upon the roof and the sound of the sea. I wanted to get to the Happy Valley and it was not there. There were woods about me, there was no Happy Valley. Only the dark trees and the young braken. The owls hooted. The moon was shining in the windows of Manderley. There were nettles in the garden, ten foot, twenty foot high.

"Maxim!" I cried. "Maxim!"

"Yes," he said. "It's all right. I'm here."

"I had a dream," I said. "A dream."

"What was it?" he said.

"I don't know. I don't know."

Back again into the moving unquiet depths. I was writing letters in the morning-room. I was sending out invitations. I wrote them all myself with a thick black pen. But when I looked down to see what I had written it was not my small square hand-writing at all, it was long, and slanting, with curious pointed strokes. I pushed the cards away from the blotter and hid them. I got up and went to the looking-glass. A face stared back at me that was not my own. It was very pale, very lovely, framed in a cloud of dark hair. The eyes narrowed and smiled. The lips parted. The face in the glass stared back at me and laughed. And I saw then that she was sitting on a chair before the dressing-table in her bedroom, and Maxim was brushing her hair. He held her hair in his hands, and as he brushed it he wound it slowly into a thick long rope. It twisted like a snake, and he took hold of it with both hands and smiled at Rebecca and put it round his neck.

"No," I screamed. "No, no. We must go to Switzerland. Colonel Julyan said we must go to Switzerland."

I felt Maxim's hand upon my face. "What is it?" he said. "What's the matter?"

I sat up and pushed my hair away from my face.

"I can't sleep," I said. "It's no use."

"You've been sleeping," he said. "You've slept for two hours. It's quarter-past two. We're four miles the other side of Lanyon."

It was even colder than before. I shuddered in the darkness of the car.

"I'll come beside you," I said. "We shall be back by three."

I climbed over and sat beside him, staring in front of me through the wind-screen. I put my hand on his knee. My teeth were chattering.

"You're cold," he said.

"Yes," I said.

The hills rose in front of us, and dipped, and rose again. It was quite dark. The stars had gone.

"What time did you say it was?" I asked.

"Twenty past two," he said.

"It's funny," I said. "It looks almost as though the dawn was breaking over there, beyond those hills. It can't be though, it's too early."

"It's the wrong direction," he said, "you're looking west."

"I know," I said. "It's funny, isn't it?"

He did not answer and I went on watching the sky. It seemed to get lighter even as I stared. Like the first red streaks of sunrise. Little by little it spread across the sky.

"It's in winter you see the northern lights, isn't it?" I said. "Not in summer?"

"That's not the northern lights," he said, "that's Manderley."

I glanced at him and saw his face. I saw his eyes.

"Maxim," I said. "Maxim, what is it?"

He drove faster, much faster. We topped the hill before us and saw Lanyon lying in a hollow at our feet. There to the left of us was the silver streak of the river, widening to the estuary at Kerrith six miles away. The road to Manderley lay ahead. There was no moon. The sky above our heads was inky black. But the sky on the horizon was not dark at all. It was shot with crimson, like a splash of blood. And the ashes blew towards us with the salt wind from the sea.